"Au-Set Of Kemet"

(The story of Isis)

By Sharon M. Desruisseaux

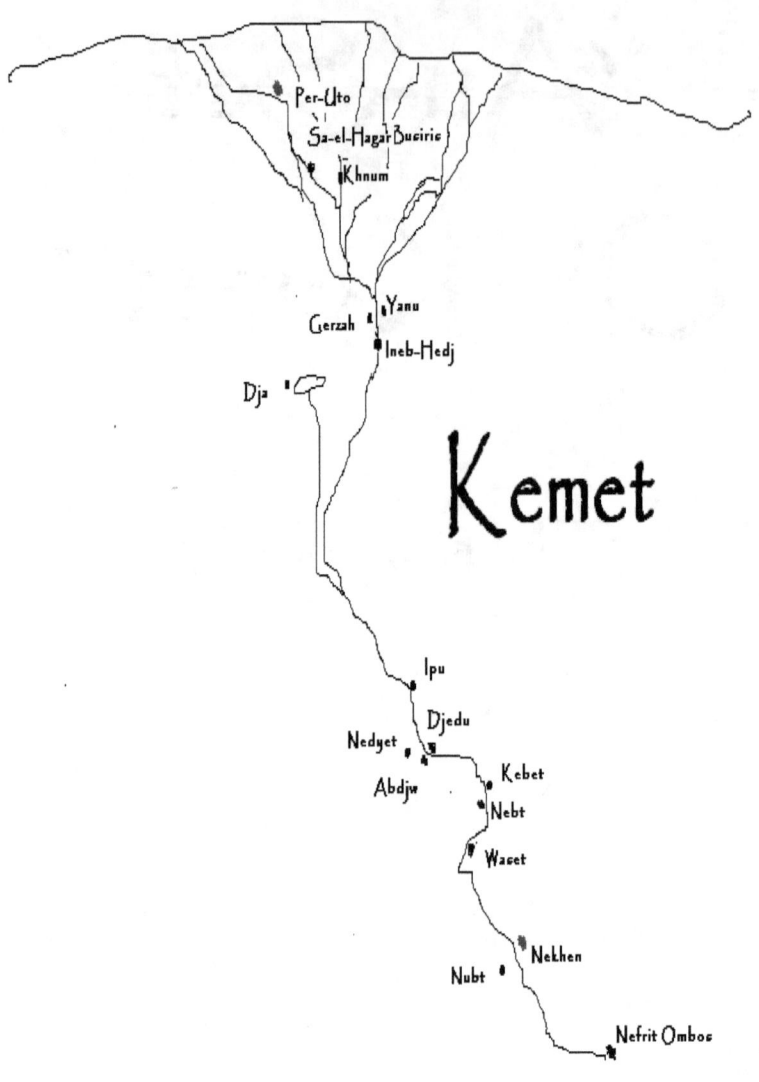

Kemet

(Drawing by Lucille Hemphill Jewett)

This is the third edition of the tale of Au-Set. The first edition was in the form of a book published through Publish America under the name of "Au-Set the Woman." Since then the author has changed and modified the original novel to the one before you today. The author values dearly her readers opinions and would love to hear from you on your ideas and input. You may reach her at her email at smbrooksie@myfairpoint.net . Please feel free to contact her as well on Amazon, Goodreads or through her home site at www.sharondnovels.com .

Dedications

"This novel is dedicated to my amazing friends and family who have always believed in me and never once dissuaded me from my dreams. I cherish each moment with you all. You kept my thoughts on track and never once faltered in your faith. Thank you!" - Sharon

**Note to readers: please let me know what you think. I am always open to feed back and would love to hear from you. As you can see, my novels are constantly being revised as I listen to you and all you have to offer ☺ You can contact me at the official author site at www.sharondnovels.com
On Facebook: Sharondnovels.com or Sharon Desruisseaux
On Twitter: smbrooksi
Or on Amazon amazon.com/author/sharondnovels

*Edited by Sharon Goding, you can find her at smbrooksie@myfairpoint.net

Book cover design and illustrations by Lucille Hemphill Jewett lucillehemhillljewett@yahoo.com

Prologue...

My name is known to the modern world as Isis. It has been a long journey to arrive at this name from all of my life's travails. It has made me what I am today and forevermore. I am considered a Goddess to this land of Kemet. Kemet is a land that my family had adopted, to carry on their traditions in a completely new light. I was deified in the later part of my rule to this untouched and pure land of the mighty backwards river and the vibrant black soil of a land that is now called Egypt in the modern tongue.

I have had many names. The one most famous is the name of Isis, "the Great Mother of Egypt and the keeper of the throne for the pharaohs." It interesting to note, that most of those pharaohs since my lifetime were male. This name "Isis" was given out of love and admiration by the Greek culture, which eventually conquered my newfound land under the rule of a very young Emperor, named Alexander from Macedonia. The dynasty that followed this great man lasted over four hundred years and was later led by the family of his favored general Ptolemy.

From the time that I initially arrived to that great black, abundant and unscathed land as a young girl to the present time; the tale of my family has become a legend and a myth of which I have witnessed blossoms pour forth from the most foreign of seeds sown initially so many millennia's ago. I whisper into the ear of one who still keeps my teachings true; that I have witnessed so many great and horrid things that have happened to that once untouched land that I first arrived at five thousand and five hundred years from the date of this actual writing. I have seen it conquered repeatedly, cherished for times and then to sadly fall into decay. I have cried in glory as Kemet arose from ashes carefully revived by rulers who were inspired through the great color that once covered all of its marvelous gilded halls. The very same colorful paintings that my own people added to the original bland mud-colored villages that I had first stepped foot into as a young girl those many millennia's ago.

What most people recall about the magnificent culture that had flourished upon the arrival of my family with their influence was the glory and justice. Kemet had been tainted by the Aryan and male dominated cultures that bruised over most of the good that was originally wrought there in just and equality from my original inspired teachings during my actual lifetime. It has been changed into a culture that now dominates your history books of the men who ruled and the women who sat silently behind them on the throne. That was not the real story. Most of the evidence of this truth I now whisper is lost under the stormy sands of millennia's that have since passed over in a timely eloquence or have been blatantly painted over and even chiseled out all that bore witness to such claims.

The name I had been born with was Au-Set. I have been called "As-ti" for through me in much later generations, which have been called the Old Kingdom, the Middle Kingdom and the New Kingdom; have the male pharaohs been able to sit on the throne. The name literally means "successor. Upon the time of my own rule, I sat on the throne in equality in rule with my brother-husband known to you as Osiris. Osiris was a later Greek name given to him. However, during my lifetime we knew him as Au-Sar, my other-half. I came from a land where women ruled from seemingly endless generations prior. A time in which men served as consorts and attained any rule allowed through the women they were born from and had consorted with.

Upon the time of our arrival to Kemet, we saw that the old ways were waning and needed more of a balance to survive the change we saw unfolding all around us. There was a large conflicting movement occurring that opposed significantly the rule of women in Goddess cults. This opposition was primarily in force to dominate the women by God cults as instigated by the newly arrived tribes of the far north that I have referred to as "Aryans". The Aryans were the same people from the northern

tribes who instituted a male dominated hierarchy that
fast spread through all of the known lands of the world at
that time. This dominance was causing the world to
change in such a rapid pace of popularity that many were
killed trying to defend the old ways. The landscapes
were swept barren from war and fires that were never to
be regained. It marked the end of an era. Our family saw
this and we sought to be there at the beginning of the
next era with all we have learned and stood witness to.
We, my family and I, felt that an equality of rule with the
equal rendering of a male and female cooperation would
balance the world to a better and much sought after
peace that was fervently prayed for in multitudes. It is
believed that when a man and a woman work beside one
another it can only enhance the known strengths and
weaknesses of each other to create a perfect balance and
an unconquerable rule.

Many names have touched the memory of my life and
rule. I have been called "Ast", as "the wife of Osiris (Au-
Sar) and the mother of Horus" or Heru as he was called
by me at his actual birth before the Greeks changed his
name as well. Moreover, "Ast urt mut neter" which means
"Isis the Great and mother of the god (Horus)" is another
one of my known names. Finally, there is the last of
numerous subsequent names of which would make
another novel in just the listing of them "Ast netrit em
renus nebu," which means "Isis in all names".

I have seen many things in my life and therefore write
this for the real story behind the legend. A legend, which
prevails even now so late in the memory of what, I have
become. I have started a ripple which turned into the tidal
wave of history and thus blossomed before me like the
morning whisperings of the white lotus blossom of which
the delta is shaped. It is amazing how one small action,
deed or suggestion could create such chaos or balance of
the situation of the time that we are allotted to in this
reality called life on the material plane of existence. It is
amazing how a whisper could prevent battles, or start
them! When one is born to extreme power one must learn

to yield it with a patient hand or the blows that follow could devastate all in the way on ones path and create others to weep over the scale tipping the wrong way.

I was born to a very powerful and ancient family that gained the rule of the city of Erech of the lands of Eshnunna, later known in classical history as Sumer and then even later in time as Babylon, and finally to the modern day name of Iraq. Eshnunna was a cold land to the north of Kemet. It was the fragrant and rich land where I was born. How I even arrived to be born there is a tale in itself of preservation and creativity, both of which thankfully, I inherited in multitudes. Unfortunately it is something that I cannot always say of my fellow siblings of whom I shared my cradle days at the side of my mother.

My mother was the High Priestess of the temple of Innana in the City of Erech. She was born in the city of Eridu. Eridu was the cultural center of their land of Eshnunna. She was born the princess of Eridu with the name of Ninnuit. Ninnuit was born of the highest lineage of her land, therefore it was her duty from birth to be raised for her role upon entering the sacred form of womanhood to serve as the High Priestess in the holiest of temples.

She was the oldest daughter of the high priestess of the temple of Eridu in Eshnunna, named Tefnut. Ninnuit was born of her mother's consort named Shu of a land far to the south of which I later became a part of in history and of which I ruled over in life called Kemet. Tefnut had two younger daughters named Ishurti and Nemothi who later became known as Ua-Zit and Nekhebt who would grace in rule over Kemet as well. They would grow up to rule over the "upper "and "lower "parts of that barbaric land Kemet. Ua- Zit ruled over the northern part of the land in the delta that was known to the people as Lower Kemet since the Great River flowed in that direction from regions unknown deep in the jungles. She ruled from her city of Per-Uto.

That strange land was backwards from the rest of the world since they based their known land around the currents of the Great River, which flowed in the opposite direction of all of the other known rivers of the world. In further accord to ancient tradition, Ua-Zit's oldest born daughter Astarte was sent to rule over the temple of Syria at a city called Gubla, later known as Byblos. I cannot recall the names of their fathers, though they bravely served the Goddess as her official consorts and then met their fate, as did Shu the consort from Kemet.

Ua-Zit and Ninnuit's sister Nemothi or Nekhebt ruled from the city of Nekhen in the upper part of Kemet. She ruled in turn over Upper Kemet and the lower part of that black and fertile land at the stem end of the lotus shaped Great River. Upper Kemet was the imagined source of that mysterious river which flowed all the way out to the blossom of the delta to the Great Sea. The land of my birth was across the desert between the two lands of Kemet and Eshnunna.

My mother, Ninnuit (High Priestess for the Goddess Innana) was raised in a long and ancient line of high priestesses that passed down their knowledge and power to their daughters. Their lives were never lax or dull in any form with constant pressures facing them on a daily basis. The priestesses presided over their lands and the surrounding areas with their wisdom and fairness in the rule to which they were born unquestioned. They never took a husband for long, most often it was for only one year and a day. Their consorts would live under them in the most lavish way, while they performed their duty in making the high priestess pregnant. When this service was done, they met their fate to their great dismay. This was in accordance with traditions that had been in existence from time's primordial wakening.

All of the priestess consorts chosen went willingly to perform the ancient and sacred rite. The chosen consorts knew that by their impregnating the high priestess, they were also saving the land to which they served with their own fertility in providing for the future of the land. Many men lined up and strutted about before the high priestess at the choosing ceremony, though only the most handsome and virile were chosen.

My mother, as did hers, had a long line of men who served her and provided life in her womb. Their lower priestesses raised their sons in the temple while the daughters born were educated alongside the sons for future power and greatness.

All of the men chosen to work in the temple near my mother and the other priestesses were eunuchs, none were allowed to enter besides the consort who was fertile and only he was saved for the high priestess. The consort was kept in the most luxurious surroundings and utterly spoiled, as it was his duty to keep his high priestess happy in all of her appetites. Should he fail, he was "removed" or made into a temple eunuch.

The priestesses also performed their own ancient duties for the temple. All priestesses were of the most noble of families around the great two rivers of the northern lands from which all life began. Most temples had waiting lists for their daughters to serve in the temples. It was a great honor to serve the Goddess. The priestesses were chaste for the most part and kept busy with the many duties in maintaining the temple and in feeding and healing the poor. They were also busy with raising the holy children born to the select priestesses who served the Goddess who were born in the temple of sacred rites. All of the children born to the temple were raised in full equality under the generous and loving arms of the Goddess and her daughters.

The priestesses would serve willingly the Goddess on special feast nights for those holy suppliants who would petition for this honor. Any children born from these holy unions did not belong to the priestesses who bore them but to the temple and to the Goddess herself. The children thus born were sent off, weaned to live very important and productive lives with their birth-earned status, and thus worked in the highest of positions in the land with the greatest of honors heaped upon them and all transactions that they made.

It was also the law of the land prior to a woman's union or alliance with a mate that she must serve the Goddess for at least one evening before the sacred alliance took place. A woman's virginity was the most valuable gift that she could give to the Goddess and thus was cherished and saved for her to be able to grant willingly to the temple in service, prior to her chosen consort's knowledge of her body. A child born to this union was given for the priestesses to raise and would often be granted a higher status than the mothers who bore them. It was quite common of that era for some women to return to the temple whenever they wanted to serve the Goddess, of their own free will, with the full consent of their husbands.

Women in my homeland were the sacred and most powerful forces of life; they were revered and cherished for the power they had to bring forth new life from their bodies. Only a daughter could inherit land and title. The authority was given to her over the family from her mother. When a woman took a consort or mate, he moved into the home of his wife under the main rule of her mother. It is obvious that no woman could ever fake what was born of her womb and paternity could easily stand an error or maliciously lied about. Thus, it was the way of our people from the time before time that women had full authority over their lives and of the life that was conceived and birthed from their wombs.

My mother, Ninnuit had many consorts and then children from them. Due to all of the life that was born from her womb, she had served the Goddess well. She was called by her Goddess name of Innana, only her own mother and her children could ever think of calling her by her birth name of Ninnuit.

My mother was beautiful, even from my earliest memories of her that will never fade from my memory. She was tall and graceful and slight of waist despite her several pregnancies and births. She had long flowing hair of the evening's darkest shadows. In later years, it was carefully speckled with the brightest of white strands that my mother would teasingly tell us were the stars of the heavens as they streaked from their perches above to the earth. Her birth name of Ninnuit meant "night flower" and it fit her gloriously with her legendary perfection. She loved to be surrounded by stars both real and painted. The murals of painted stars that she commissioned in the temple displayed rather eloquently her role for the people of her land as "Queen of Heaven."

Innana had many consorts as fit her position, though none were as loved and cherished as my own father, a farmer from the south of Erech named Geb. My father was a child of the earth and smelled of it, even during his time while he was doted upon in the temple during the service of my mother. He was her first and most holy of all consorts that she was obligated to union with for the Great Rite symbolizing the fertility of our future. She fought to preserve him from that fateful execution. She had even hidden him away, so great was her love for him. My father was tall and beautiful, I was told, and had great wisdom despite his humble origins. His wisdom came from the earth in which he tilled lovingly and took such great care to cultivate. They secretly hid a rare form of love forbidden to the high priestess in her important tasks and Goddess given duties.

My mother was warned many times not to become involved with her consorts for they would always die in the end when their duty was performed. All came to the Goddess willingly to be chosen for the Great Rite and all knew what was in store for them. They had complete knowledge of the splendors of the temples and of the riches that would be heaped upon them until the fertility of the Goddess Representative was revealed in her pregnancy. They had all lined up by the thousands to be chosen for this honor from many faraway places. The families of the chosen consorts of the Goddess would also be given riches beyond their wildest dreams. Some of the consorts chosen were even married and had proved their fertility with the wives that they left behind, some to the worst state of poverty. The wives that sacrificed their husbands to the Great Rite were richly compensated for their sacrifice and duty to the Goddess.

My mother did the inevitable and fell in love with her first consort. From this holy union when Geb, the simple farmer, took my mother's maidenhead in duty and *thus twins were born. Born to them were my identical twin sister, Neb-Het and myself. My own name of Au-Set was given to me since I was the first-born daughter of the holiest of unions to the representative of the Goddess herself. I was born to inherit the throne and the power of the Great Goddess and the name of Innana.*

My mother hid her beloved for two whole months and was almost executed herself, until my grandmother had conducted a powerful psychic search of my mother while she lay asleep and found the answers in my mother's dreams.

I had heard about this glorious death from temple whispers. My mother as Innana was supposed to perform the Great Death and Sacrifice by donning the golden mask of a cow, which was the Goddess mask of the beast who tamed the fields for planting by towing the blades which cut through the ready and waiting earth. So young and heartbroken was my mother that my own grandmother had to don the priestly robes that she had once worn before her first-born daughter had proved fruitful and wielded the robes of the Goddess herself. In the cycle of life and in the temple my grandmother was delegated to the grander role of the Crone-Goddess of Innana in her wiser role.

The Goddess had three roles performed by her high priestess. The first of which was the Maiden, upon attaining her first moon-blood cycle. The second role was the Mother, upon naturally reaching her mother-hood status. The last role of the Goddess was that of the Crone-Goddess. This was reached when her first-born daughter had become a mother of the next generation female to inherit. The older mother then would take over the last role of the Great Goddess, and when the moon-blood ceased that role was solidified. At the time of my birth, there were two women as the Goddess on earth, which were my mother and her mother, Shub-Ad. Those who were close to her and adored her also called Shub-Ad by the loving name of "Tefnut".

However, it was the duty of the Mother-Goddess to sacrifice her consort to the Great Goddess in completion of the holiest of rites in the land. Any deviation of this rite was blasphemy, in which the Mother-Goddess who did not perform this rite in its ancient entirety would have to submit herself to be killed in a bloody ritual to compensate for the lack she brought forth with her inaction. This new ritual involved all of the priestesses in the temple armed with small golden knives lashing out to cause the death of the priestess who brought about this lack in the continuity of the temple cycle of life. Examples must be set and followed to each detail etched in their memory since time began. This insured that the disobeying priestesses would suffer the longest and one of the most horrifying and painful deaths their law allowed. This ritual was very important to the people of Eshnunna and the surrounding lands. It was so important that it explained why the punishment for disobeying it was so intense and painful. In fact, there was only one time in the history of their land when it had been disobeyed and the priestess' name long forgotten.

My grandmother, out of the great love that she had for her daughter, donned the robes and the golden mask herself to perform her daughter's duty in the name of the Mother Innana. So great was the acting skills of my grandmother, that no one ever knew. Her family only suspected, though no proof was ever attained of this alleged suspicion.

Thus were the deaths of my father and the first of Ninnuit's consorts in her role as Mother-Goddess.

Next, there arrived a man from Kemet as the consort of my mother. He was from a land far to the south in Kemet, and his name was Re. Re was from a village of Kemet called Ineb-Hedj. He was statuesque and dark-skinned with long, thick black curly hair of which he laboriously braided with golden beads that tipped each of them off at ends and sparkled whenever he turned, much to the amusement of my mother. He gave her my brother, Tehuti, who was sent to the temple to learn the arts of writing in cuneiform. Cuneiform was the writing language of our people and though simple in appearance was quite laborious in concept. Tehuti showed a promising aptitude for it since his earliest days and even before he could walk, his tiny fingers were tracing the symbols placed before him or on the walls of the temple that where he was raised. He was left-handed, which was another sign that the Gods blessed him.

Re had performed his duty and before the great sacrifice to the Goddess was planned, he had managed to escape the temple and fled the land of Eshnunna to his homeland of Kemet. Thus, he had escaped his fate. The temple and the lands were in a great uproar and considered this a great and evil omen.

It did turn out to be a bad omen in some ways. The events that would follow would set the tide of time viciously against what they believed in so violently that all of their faith was tested.

The next of my mother's consorts was named En of the city of Erech and home place of my own mother. His father was a man of great status named Lugal Banda, and his mother was of a mysterious northern tribe, which was furiously stomping down on the lands of the Goddess. So great was his mother's influence on En, in later times known as Gilgamesh and still later as Noah; that it affected Ninnuit deeply. En was handsome of face and vain of soul. My mother called him her "eye sweet", since that was all she said he was good at in being handsome. He was constantly trying to preach to her of the ways of his mother of the far northern lands where the Goddess ways had long disappeared to the ways of the Gods. En was charming, though none of his words struck fertile ground, as his seed did to her womb.

Ninnuit tried to ignore him and laugh off his frivolous views in life. Nevertheless, my mother was at the same time wise enough to be warned of a possible threat to all that she had ever known. She heard whispers of this dominating philosophy, which threatened the very life of the Goddess in which she served. She pretended ignorance while in truth she planned for a possible battle that lay ahead of her.

She knew that the ancient Goddess representatives could kill him for his attitude and lack of submission to her. Cautiously, she calmed her hand, since she felt that new days were dawning and that with the tide of events lately, it would not be a wise move politically.

For Innana-Ninnuit was the daughter of a long line of daughters that were of the people later called the Catal-Huyuk. The peoples of this philosophy conducted their lives based on the laws of the Great Goddess in her three forms of Maiden, Mother, and Crone. Primarily they were from the Upper reaches of the great Tigris River above the lands of Gubla or Byblos in a land called Anatolia and still later called Turkey. The priestesses and holy women of that land were called the Tawawannas. All of the women born to my line were the most famous of Tawawannas.

They were the people that had created the wheeled vehicles and brought the talents of forging metal into great works of art for war and beauty. They were the people who bought to the lands of Eshnunna the wonders in architecture of the arches, columns, and arcades of which later cultures took the credit for, such as the Greeks.

Around the time and controversy of which En brought to the temple priestesses, it was the time for the earthly Shub-Ad or Tefnut to end, to the great dismay of my own mother at her passing. Since the last great act that she had performed in her daughter's name, she had fallen ill and had lost her normal lively hold on this earthly plane. Tefnut had readied herself to join the Goddess in time eternal as she slowly faded on this material plane with each breath that she took until her last.

Ninnuit held her head up high and performed the last great funeral for her mother in keeping with the oldest and most sacred of traditions of the priestesses in the Crone-form of the Goddess.

The day stretched out its roaring head with a fruitful letting loose of the heavens in a torrential downpour, which seemed to fill the whole valley between the Tigris and Euphrates Rivers.

However, sometimes in anger, Mother Goddess would pour her vengeance on her people. There was only one other storm that was worse than on the day of Tefnut's funeral. This past storm occurred only a year after Re had escaped. It was the greatest storm Eshnunna had seen in many generations. In this last storm, thousands of people were lost in the flooding that followed; it was ten times worse than any normal flooding of the valley. Due to the events that transpired because of that storm, En gained his fame and became a consort for the fertile Goddess representative. En had saved many people and animals in a large boat that he had built, while the smaller low-lying villages were destroyed. His town just outside of Erech was lost except for his whole family that he had rescued along with the animals from the surrounding farms. He was a merchant prior to this catastrophic event and imported goods along the rivers to earn a decent living. En had the foresight to sense the coming of this great flood and prepared carefully for it. He was a local hero and his village sent him to the temple for further glory and deification.

However, on this day of the funeral of Shub-Ad Tefnut, the rain roared its anger at the old ways dissolving with the entrance of En and his ways that were fast enveloping the peoples of Eshnunna. That was how the rains were justified in the eyes of the Mother-Goddess on this day of the funeral of her mother and of the Crone-Goddess. Ninnuit had En follow her to watch and to sit dutifully by her side, while the rite of the funeral was performed. She was in her full glory of the pregnancy of my brother Au-Sar at that time, later to be known by the Greeks as Osiris.

En kept silent vigil and sat humbly by the side of Innana while she invoked the Goddess in the full glory and wrath over the form of her mother, the Crone-Innana. En was mute for he knew that as soon as the child was born he would follow this woman in death as a part of the sacred and ancient sacrifice, as was his duty. However, he also knew that his time was not now as it should have been after he impregnated Ninnuit.

Now, all normal activities were placed on hold as it was the time of the sacrifice of all connected with the woman who was dead in earthly form before all of them on this raised dais of pink granite. The body of Tefnut or Crone-Innana was sung over and praised in ceremony that lasted from sunrise to sunset. At the rise of the moon, her earthly sacrifices were lined up to join her.

The form of Tefnut was carefully placed on a wagon gilded in gold and pulled by the finest of temple donkeys at the lead of a procession, which would carry her to her final tomb and resting place beneath the temple confines in the lowest portion.

It was the custom of ancient Eshnunna for the living to bury their dead beneath the dwelling place where they resided. This allowed the living the practical access of the dutiful daily worship of their ancestors beneath them literally. That is, in most common houses until the decaying stench could no longer be endured when the numbers of the deceased below them, even in their houses made of stone, outgrew the living above them. In this way, there were whole sections of the city of houses abandoned to the dead, of which the numbers fast outnumbered the living as time progressed.

However, the tombs for the high priestesses were carved deep into the earth under the high temple-palace above so that the stench would never reach those living above.

Thus, Tefnut or Shub-Ad was wheeled around the city with her daughter crying in grief over her body until they reached the temple confines where the procession began. The sacrifices humbly followed in their wake, each knowing their destiny. In life, they passed on that thought in the grandeur in which they lived serving the Goddess in human form. They blocked out the knowledge, as most humans do, which had become apparent to the servants, as fate had soon caught up with their humanity and service under the Goddess Innana.

The suite where Shub-Ad reigned from in her life was replicated in her tomb, so that she would recognize her surroundings. In the great bedroom of her tomb, my mother placed a finely made replica of the sacred cow mask on her head that was gilded in gold and then nodded officially for the sacrifices to commence. All of her mother's finest musicians were there, along with her cooks, seamstresses, toilers, and handmaidens. There were also her finest clothes meticulously placed so that in her afterlife she might be adorned in them for the ceremonies in the sky. Every person who exclusively served Shub-Ad in life was there to honor the Goddess in human form. Those servants of the next reign under her daughter dutifully watched this important ceremony.

Ninnuit's long black hair gleamed in the torchlight and sparkled with the brilliance of her "becoming". We witnessed her almost all-encompassing crone strands of wisdom shine as if stars had actually been allotted to her birth-name. Her brilliant mane vividly glowed to those that surrounded her in her trance. So great was her own mother's beauty, even in her crone form, that all around her bowed to the loss of Tefnut's earthly presence. All in the presence of her human form mourned her passing and awaited their fate.

The last consort was the first to join his mistress. He was spared the fate of the usual consort of the Great-Sacrifice after the traditional "year and a day", unless he got her pregnant, since her moon-blood had stopped during his reign. This allowed him to finish his life beside her side as her companion to her actual death. His name was Mes-Anni-Padda and he was graciously called the King of Erech for his throne was gained from his marriage to his beloved Shub-Ad, a name who all of us who where close to her called her. It meant "breath of starlight."

A woman has many names in her life to those who love them and to the services that she performs. An average woman is first a daughter and sometimes a sister, and then a wife, mother and even grandmother. My grandmother was Tefnut to her mother; Maiden, Mother, and Crone Innana; Shub-Ad as "breath of starlight'. In later times the name of my mother as Ninnuit was kept for her for the later Parthenon of Kemet and she was turned into the Goddess of the stars and evening sky. While the name Tefnut was kept for my grandmother and she was made the Goddess of Air for Kemet. Such interpretations of my life held sway in the telling of my tale in legend so long after my earthy death.

Mes-Anni-Padda, in a land so far away from his birth, shed his tears of faithful duty and gladly gave his neck for the ceremonial blade to end his last thought over the form of his beloved friend and wife. My own mother shed great tears at the love they had for each other and in each time, that she told this tale.

My mother, as was her duty in her full pregnancy of her son Au-Sar, nodded her head for the rest of her mother's servants to join her and her last consort. A vast bloodbath then ensued. The temple eunuchs performed their duty and went over to kill the handmaidens, then the cooks, and the other attendants of the life of the late Queen of Erech. My mother stayed as witness until the last drop of blood had fallen. Next, the priestesses who had not yet received their moon-blood came in to throw flowers all over the chambers to cover the scent, so as Shub-Ad would not be offended by the stench. Oil lamps were burned with Frankincense, Myrrh, and other precious scents to appease the Goddess. When the ritual was completed, my mother then returned to the land of the living and to her duties as Supreme Goddess of the temple and the land surrounding.

All children of the Earthly Goddess form were spared this fate, since they belonged to the Goddess and not to the woman who shared their body with her in life. The sisters of my mother Ishurti and Nemothi were already ruling in temples as Ua-Zit and Nekhebt, of their own from the land of Shu called Kemet. The blood of the consorts chosen to be their father's was of the same family and thus by blood, they inherited their new positions in life. Even the oldest daughter of Ua-Zit had just taken her position in the main temple of Gubla to the south of this temple in and along the shores of this Great Sea. Astarte's new home was mostly a land of deserts and shepherds. This land would someday become known as Israel.

Astarte had already taken her first consort by the name of Baal, the first of her consorts of that name to perform that duty for the Goddess called in that land "Anat".

Nemothi and Ishurti were by the side of my mother. All were equally grand in their demeanor and strength in this ceremony.

In conference later that evening, the sisters of my mother warned her about her new consort En and of the trouble that he was stirring even with their own men and attendants. His word was fast spreading and reaching fertile ground in the hearts of men. The sisters planned what to do, should their fate be threatened in any way. Astarte was the least worried but was fast outranked by her mother and aunts that stood in full splendor of their ages and rankings above her.

As the women argued and planned, it was then that En took his lead and escaped the temple. Therefore, there was another great omen for the religion of the Goddess. The Goddess Inanna's future was threatened. The escape of En was not enough to cause a stir, he had also recruited around a thousand men from the temple confines to his cause in vengeance and was amassing quite an army spouting venom towards all women and the ways of the Goddess.

In council word had reached them that En was fast teaching the people that his God Enkil was the Greatest and most powerful of all of the other Gods and Goddesses of their region. He claimed that his God had raped the Goddess Innana and had forced her to sit submissively by his side in servitude!

So great was the horror of the women in my family that they realized that despite it all, life and normalcy must go on for the sake of the people. It must be enforced to prove to the people that the tales told by En were false and that the Goddess was as powerful as ever before and was never swayed by a lesser and foreign God.

Thus, Astarte, Ua-Zit, and Nekhebt had returned to their rule well warned of the turning point of the world around them.

En was joined by the people of his own mother from the land of the far north. These people were taller than most of the people in this area with fair hair of gold and sometimes the bright red of a sunset. They slowly joined in with the local populace, intermarried with the women of the land, dominating them, suppressing them with their powerful God, and mocking the ways of the Goddess. En's followers called her priestesses unholy and unclean. They enforced harsh rules on the women over whom they were ruling by taking them in their weakest form. Most women were impregnated and thus, made vulnerable by the wiles of these tall god-like men who were at first considered beautiful and charming to the women and even to the priestesses of the land, until they were enslaved and forced to fight for the rights of their own selves and their own children. With such clever and violent force had En taken his vengeance that the torrential rainstorm that fell down upon them and ruined most of their harvests not long after the evening of the funeral of the Crone-Innana; that it was later viewed in retrospect as the final bleak omen that foretold their destruction.

Not missing a step despite all that was being destroyed around her, my mother took her next consort by the name of Enkidu of which she was impregnated with her son Heru. A year after the sacrifice of Enkidu, a grievous battle led by the men of En overtook the temple in which the priestesses were raped and taken against their will, including my own mother. The leader of the men, which invaded her very own secret chambers, was named Enlil of the brightest red hair and temper to match the fire. This man named Enlil was of the fierce barbaric tribes of the north and had hair the color of fire and wrath, and some would later say of blood similar to the numerous amounts shed in their name. Nine months later, she took back her thoughts of the red hair of Enlil, when the child that she bore from his rape of her was born with an even brighter shade than thought possible. Ninnuit proudly named her son with the fierce temper Suti.

After the attack on the most secret confines of the temple, all of the men were captured and executed into the fiery pit of oblivion, deep inside the temple. This fierce fire pit was reserved for the worst offenders since it would totally consume the body of the punished making it unfit for the honor of burial reserved for the good citizens of Eshnunna. From this doomed way of death, the body was forced to walk eternity searching for a body that it would never be able to find. Enlil had met the worst of fates to be doled out by the Goddess even in her merciful and forgiving ways. It was well known that to defile a priestess was blasphemy and the worst of crimes. To take any woman against her will especially her own earthly representative was considered the most horrific of crimes.

Even though the aggressors were captured and all were executed, the threat remained. My mother took her last and final consort who was again a simple man. He was named Dimuzi and he was a shepherd, though divinely handsome. He looked more like her son in his all too apparent youth.

About the time that I was nearing my first moon-blood, my mother's was ending and thus, Dimuzi was granted the honor of being her life-end consort and friend. His sigh of relief could almost be heard throughout all of Eshnunna! Yet, he still doted all upon my mother and her children who were always by her side.

Dimuzi was only four years older than I was though deemed the property of the Goddess and could be with no other woman but the woman that he was chosen for as consort. Any woman touching him, even a priestess would be put to death for anything as slight as a small friendly kiss.

So the two of them sat side by side and watched over us as we grew. Neb-Het and I looked so much alike that few could tell us apart. We often would switch places as twins often do, fooling everyone around us. We were doubly blessed and the land finally had hope again due to our birth. Two healthy first-born daughters had sprung from her maiden-hood with only the first union. We were glorified around the lands in poetry and song. Our beauty was evident from conception, or so they sang.

Dimuzi had grown fond of all of us children, even of Suti with his fiery red hair and matching temper. Suti and Au-Sar were very close. Au-Sar was constantly protecting every step of the baby Suti as well as the infant Heru. Tehuti played devoted attendant upon his two oldest and most revered sisters whenever he was not with the temple scribes learning his letters and prose.

My mother had often told us of how our family came to be in the land of Eshnunna. She had told us that the present dynasty, which had its primary seat of power in the city of Erech of my childhood, was founded by her family and only were here due to their own conquering of the people now in the lower class. She told us that the dynasty from which we were born was new to this land long ago.

She stated that her family had come from the mountains to the northwest of the present boundaries, from the steep mountains and lands of Anatolia. Her people were of the culture of the Goddess people of Catal-Huyuk and had their own vast legacy. They found this land and a people willing to learn from them. According to my mother, there was not one drop of blood shed when our people came, only willing supplicants to the wise culture that had come to save and educate them. The conquered people lived in small villages made of huts that were constantly destroyed by the flooding of the valley between the Tigris and the Euphrates Rivers. The people of the Catal-Huyuk knew how to build in stone and even made false mountains in the shape of mounds to place their dwellings on, thus, saving them from the constant flooding of the valley of the two rivers.

All of the inhabitants of this land prior were living in separate small villages that constantly warred with one another and had no localized government. Each village had their own deity that it worshipped and none would conform to the other, each bleating their own supremacy over the others nearby. Much blood was shed before my family came to this area with their just and knowledgeable reign. Our people brought with us knowledge of the arts and a culture never seen before in the great valley they sought as their new home. Before the Goddess people came into the valley, the inhabitants were primarily shepherds, farmers, and fishermen and their Gods grew numerous and untidy in their vastly conflicting rules of etiquette.

All of the people who dwelled here prior to our family and rule, the northern lands of the two rivers were inhabited by a people called the Martu of Semitic origin and had dark skin and hair. Most were small of stature and were very strong to make up for their lack of height. The Martu lived in the north of the valley above the Euphrates River, were primarily nomadic, and were experienced shepherds. Therefore, they were not city dwellers and hated to be walled in. The Martu populated only two cities and they were small. The cities were called Sippar and Opis and they were barely more than humble villages upon the arrival of my family according to the secret tablets of our history. We also brought to them a form a writing that helped to unify the lands that our family conquered. These villages were on the neck of the land where the two rivers called the Tigris and the Euphrates met.

The Martu and the Hill peoples that surrounded them had many patron deities of their numerous and scattered villages and centers. The deities left of the ancient times before my family was allowed to continue their guard in my own lifetime. Ninsikil was the patron Goddess of Dilmun or the Paradise of Eshnunna. Nanshe of Lagash was known as the mother who loves orphans and the sick and she who seeks justice for the poor and shelter for the weak. This Goddess judged over all the peoples on the first of the New Year. Then there was Nammu, who was known as the Goddess who gave birth to the heavens and earth and had temples throughout the land.

Then there was the patron Goddess of Eridu,
where my mother was born. Ninnuit would have been
known as this Goddess, had she not been sent to Erech
to serve as the Goddess Innana. Her mother, Tefnut
followed her daughter until her younger sister was well
enough to lead Eridu. Tefnut's younger sister Emesha
had fallen ill while serving in the temple of Eridu and
Tefnut had come to assist her. That was why Ninnuit
was born in Eridu and not in Erech.

To the north and east of these nomadic peoples
were a fair-haired people who lived in the Zagros Hills
across the plain of the Tigris River. They were called the
Hill Peoples as mentioned above. Our family was mostly
from this country, in its paternal origins. That is why the
ruling class, in the words of my mother, was taller so that
they could have a better reach to speak with the heavens.
They were fair of hair and face for the most part.
However, the people of the Martu thwarted them in their
progress into the valley of the River Tigris.

The mothers of our family came from the Goddess
herself, I was told for they were always tall and graceful
with long flowing black hair and the fairest of winter
white skin that would bronze under the kiss of the sun
that blessed them. We came from a long line of ethereal
and Goddess possessed women in our family and have
held the ranks of priestess Tawawannas since time was
first written down many generations ago.

Our family gave this land the name of Eshnunna
along with its present success in the grand scheme of the
world around us. We brought to these people of the Martu
and of the hills; skill and knowledge in which they
willingly embraced while we held them under our wings
and protected them from the insurgence of the tribes who
were always trying to take all that we had worked for in
our peaceful union of blended tribes.

The ruling classes were those in the direct service
of the Goddess. These powerful women were called the
Naditu. All of the priestesses from time unwritten were of
the Naditu class. We were the untouchables of our society
and to defile us or harm us in any way would
automatically result in death, no matter how small the

infraction against us. Naditu were women of royal birth who threw down their life in service for the Goddess and some were even chosen to keep the temple accounts and histories.

The city of Erech housed our family for the most part, except for when my grandmother was in the service of the Goddess of Eridu where my own mother was born. Erech was the sister city of Uruk. Erech later became known as Ur and the future birthplace of Abraham of the Old Testament.

My great and many more times great grandmother was of the tribe of the Hatti peoples of the Catal-Huyuk. The Goddess name of her mother was Arinna and she was known as the Sun Goddess, who took on a consort who ruled as a thunder God. Nowhere is it written their true names only that they all became Arinna while in the Goddess' earthly form as her representative. The eldest daughter would take over where her mother left off in her service for the Goddess. Daughters in our line were sent away to fill in vacancies of where the matriarchal lines died off and there were no daughters.

Before Innana was the Goddess' Mother named Nikkal, which meant "Great Mother" in the land of Eshnunna. She was known as the wife of Nannar, the Moon God and sometimes the priestesses added to it the name of Arinna, which was probably the doings of my mother's line who had originally served under that Goddess in the lands of the Hatti and the Catal-Huyuk. The people also knew her from the smaller villages as Nina.

Arinna's consort was the king of that land, who gained power by marrying into the line of my mother. The women in my family were very powerful and war-like women who were known for protecting their men and children. The men would feed the women and children and the women would fight wars for their protection. All of the children born were raised by the whole village and only the priestesses cared about who the actual mothers or even fathers of the children that were born to the people for the records of the tribes. This was the earliest history of my family when life was very simple, before the great cities of stone that in later generations came to be.

Our mother told us of a time when the whole village would raise all of the children together. Each person owned the material goods equally. It was a time when no one starved or was left alone or neglected at all. Our culture was a very Utopian society that many generations and millenniums later only dreamed about and never thought possible or ever to have actually existed. Nevertheless, it did exist, way before time and history was ever recorded.

The last Arinna came to this land to become Innana for the city of Erech more than six generations before my own birth. Several generations of daughters led to the birth of my great grandmother Tiamut who had taken Tmu and Amun as consorts at the same time. The daughter that was born to her was my grandmother, Tefnut or Shub-Ad, as her family lovingly called her.

From Tefnut and Shu was born my mother, Ninnuit and from her other consorts were born Ishurti and Nemothi. This was the complicated web woven by the mothers of my family. Intricately connected was the sum of the blood in our veins that one could say that all of the rulers of the known world were in some form related to one another.

The land in which I was born was along the bottom near the delta of the Great Euphrates River as it was later called in generations not yet even thought of. There were no large tributaries of this great river only the land in between the two great rivers. This was where civilization began according to the legends. With the advent of our family, plans of irrigation were created and implemented throughout the large valley making it wealthy and fertile as a result. All life had depended on the flow of the rivers when it was high and when it was low. The marshes were drained and vast farmlands were set up creating even larger cities and towns with their new prosperity. Deities took over in the newly created cities that were more powerful than those they conquered from ancient times long past event then. Steep and treacherous mountains protected us from most invaders.

Yet, now that was not even true anymore. Some invaders were slowly entering this land as I had mentioned before. The latest ones in their clever determination were rapidly winning our most valuable assets, the women of this land with their charm and promises of protection. With the chariots that were pulled by donkeys that our family brought down with us, we tilled this valley and made it thrive. Horses were unheard of in this region and none knew yet of their value when seen in travels in the northlands.

As a child my mother would often bring my sister and I to watch this miracle of the valley, of the people who nurtured us and coaxed the Goddess to bring forth her riches to sustain us. The long lines of cultivation would seem to stretch far beyond our eyes could possibly fathom as we clung to the revered skirts of our mother.

At those visits, Ninnuit as the Goddess Inanna would stand in full Goddess splendor in her own chariot surveying all around us. She would wear the ceremonial garb of the high priestess of Eshnunna with its flowing and long finely woven linen plaits of her ominous skirt of many colors that would catch and play with the winds in the fields. Our mother, tall and proud stood regally with her breasts naked to the elements as was proper for a high priestess, for they nourished life. Her raven hair pulled up in her long black tresses and ringlets and held intricately in place with tiny complicated braids and feathers. She often took with her two trained snakes that guarded her at all times who were named Eshur and Elapi.

The snakes were a powerful totem to the people of her wisdom and bravery. They were large and born poisonous. As a priestess, we were taught early to tame the snakes after developing immunity to their toxins. A priestess was rarely seen without her trained snakes much to the delight of her devoted followers and they cherished snakes often slept with her, much to the fear and dismay of her consorts!

My mother made a powerful and regal sight in her full priestly costume as she patrolled the lands and explained them to my sister and I when very young."

"Ninnuit"

The mists rolled foppishly across the tranquil waters trying to catch some sort of prayer or whisper of hope. On the banks of this pool of water, the Sycamore trees reached out to stop it in its path, desperately. Ninnuit tried to fathom where this dream sequence was in her life and reached helplessly in the vortex of the moment of what was playing out for her. She was the Goddess in human form and she knew from her first step into this dream-state, that it was a message for her and her own children's future. She watched and waited for the message to become clear to her. The evening before, sensing the change in the land that she ruled over she had taken a draught of the Goddess potion, becoming the ceremony of destiny that she was the major participant in.

Ninnuit found herself in the vision on a branch of the sacred Sycamore fig tree that was a symbol of the Goddess. She was sitting there watching, helpless as events unfurled below her. On the banks of this body of water was a large city that was slowly coming into view, as the format of a dreamscape is prone to do. It slowly peeked out of the mists that rolled across the land, and though dream-like in appearance, she knew instantly that it was a reality. The reality of what was yet to come in time. Rays of sun peered out hesitantly through the clouds that obscured the message initially. Her focus of that city was becoming clearer as she slipped deeper into the vision as it slowly let her in.

The buildings of the city had almost touched the clouds that were parting way for them to spring through. There were huge walls that surrounded it allowing only the tallest of buildings to reach above them. The rays of the sun tickled seductively across the tallest of those walls, turning them a bright crimson to match the rays coming forth. The walls must have been of the purest white from some imported stone that she could not recognize to have absorbed the rays so brilliantly before her.

Still she sat on the branch on a shore that overlooked this city as it dazzled before her. Her vision was then directed into the city itself as she was whisked away on a cloud and into the home of a merchant and his wife. Ninnuit as the Goddess Innana would have assumed the woman was the merchant and the husband her consort according to the ways of her own culture. Nevertheless, something told her that it was the man who was the merchant and not the woman. They were dressed in clothes of brilliant colors, unlike any that she had seen before.

Ninnuit knew from her surroundings that she was seeing her own city of Erech in a time far in the future.

She observed the people inside this dwelling and noticed that the woman of the house covered her breasts and hair as if in shame. Ninnuit felt the shame emanating from this woman who was brought to her attention. She felt the shame at the domination of this man in the room from the woman. Ninnuit felt this demeanor rather odd, but still she kept her silence and observed as she was sent to do.

The man spoke, "Woman, I cast you out from this house to take your punishment for your sins against our God Marduk, the king of Gods. You are no longer my wife, my property. You will be cast out to face the punishment for your evil ways. That abomination in your belly is the seed of the harlot Ishtar! This Ishtar is same harlot who was killed rightfully by her lover Tammuz! All women who defile their shame to flaunt it into the faces of their husbands as this great harlot did to her protector and master Marduk, shall face the laws of this land. No woman of my house shall play the whore to that weak Goddess Ishtar! No woman shall weaken my name! You whore are no longer welcome in this house! With this act against me, our sacrifice of our first-born and only son to Baal has been made null and void for your shame! Woman, you must adhere to the laws of this house and then to the laws of Babylon, as I am your master and I no longer deem you worthy to clean my feet!"

The woman prostrated before him and trembled in fear at the wrath of his words, yet still she found the strength deep inside to speak out in her defense. She slowly stood up before him. Perhaps this was the famous last surge of adrenalin that people were famous for before their death was known to them as imminent and soon? Ninnuit could feel the power of the Goddess in this woman who was covered from head to toe in a garment that covered her beauty. The beauty of this woman shone through at that moment with the power of the Goddess strong in her veins and gender.

"Husband, I now leave you to your evil ways and the ways of this land that have held in bondage all women who birthed them. Where your God makes a woman simply a vessel to carry life and no more as compared to common livestock, as your God preaches.....No, in my heart and soul, I believe and know that all women, men and children are from the bodies of women who carry us all and nurture us in the ways of the Goddess. Ishtar protects us and holds value to love and all that it entails. How you defile an act that brought you into being angers her! You are wrong, I know in my heart and from my own mother that I am good. For centuries, women have been held in bondage obeying the ways and whims of men. However, this was not always so. There was a time when all people worked together and the children belonged to all not as property of the men forgetting who gave birth to them. Women were holy, being the very force of life! "

She continued breathlessly, not knowing which word would be her last, "We are slowly losing our rights and no longer own the life from our own wombs. Yes, you may be physically stronger and had stolen an education that was meant for all, but you are weak! The men of this city have not evolved and the women that you hold in bondage cry out in pity for your silly and weak toys of war. You have denied the Goddess and her power, yet she has not forgotten you and all that the men of Ur in Babylon have done, she is waiting patiently!

"You have also forgotten all that I have done for your name! I have borne our five children and have cleaned your house and prepared your meals. I have nursed your wounds and your ego, yet, because I had served in the temple in the name of the Goddess, which is not forbidden.... You cast me out! You do not own my body and never will! Only I do and the Goddess!"

"Yes, I cast you out woman, for you are nothing but a whore who speaks empty words! The Goddess of yours is weak and was already punished for her evil ways. The women who serve her at her temple are nothing but evil harlots. Enlil and Marduk will punish them for their filthy ways for their days are numbered. We have tolerated their ways for long enough! Out damned whore!"

With those last words, his fist sprang out and caught his obedient wife on the chin, knocking her off balance and crashing her out of the door onto the cold street outside. Awaiting her were the men of the city council who were brandishing sticks and large rocks that were suddenly hurled at the nod of her husband who had filled the door. He had notified them prior to returning home of her shame and they had waited outside while he confronted her. One by one, the rocks struck the woman causing her to lie immobile and bloodied on the ground on the neatly paved streets of her home in Babylon.

As the last breaths of the doomed woman were broken out of her, a man stood over her, his light brown hair captured the sprinkling rays fighting to break free in the morning mists that surrounded them and spoke to the crowd that participated in this bloody act. His loud voice bounced off the buildings around them, "This woman is wretched and has followed the ways of the Goddess Ishtar, the seed of the evil Goddess Innana of the old ways. Ishtar is weak and only a small essence of her mother who was punished for her destruction for the horrid ways of their women and the suppression of the men of this very land we are born.

"Let all of you men heed this lesson, of why the Goddess and her ways must be destroyed! Women are crafty and turn our sons against us! They are filled with lust and destruction; they must be molded to the ways of the righteous and just Marduk, protector of us all!"

The men around the shattered soul of the dying woman broke out in a chorus of agreement of those words and listened for more.

"Hear me now, Babylon will no longer tolerate these rabid women who are bent on killing our sons, and taking our heritage away from us, they must be stopped and brought under submission from their ways! Follow me and let us find each of the women, who work the rancid ways of Ishtar, let us bring them to Marduk for judgment....."

The men then ran off to different parts of the city returning with their mothers, wives, and daughters who were known to have served in the temple in the name of the new Goddess Innana called Ishtar. Most of the women were bound in the ways of the ancients by ropes poked through their ankles as they were then flung bleeding over their husbands or fathers, and sometimes their own brother's shoulders. Some of the women and girls brought forth in such a state were too numb to speak, actually trusting the men who brought them to the temple of Marduk, even in their pain and confusion.

The temple of Marduk was a huge and daunting Ziggurat. It was chosen in the fervor during the large panic that swept through the streets of the city as the central place to bring the women that they owned to atone for their evil ways. They were brought before this huge ziggurat by the men of the city who they raised from their own wombs and even bore children for, and by the men who dangled them on their laps when little girls. The same men who vowed to protect them as a father should protect his little girls. Each woman was stunned as each found the very men they loved drag them from their sleep so brutally.

The walls of the ziggurat loomed ominously in front of them and at the top stood a garishly garmented man in full fury, his voice amplified down on all of the people below, waiting their judgment.

"I Marduk have come to answer your demands, let the fires of doom await them for the abominations committed in their Goddesses name. Let their blood pour down upon you all for their evil ways against me! I am angry! After this day, seek out new women to warm your beds, as these have gone bad and have rotted. Keep only those daughters who have not been touched by men, even you from this day forth. We will destroy all of "Her" evil ways and start fresh!

"Hear me now! The so-called priestess of Ishtar is dead! I have killed her after having my power over her lies and seductions!" He held up the priestess' bloody head as a gruesome confirmation and trophy. Her blonde hair turned red from the coagulated blood of her recent demise. Her face frozen in twisted fear with tormented eyes glazed over at her violent fate.

Innana and Ninnuit was horrified at this grotesque man, who spoke with his own words to the people of his own corrupt mind and demented visions, as he held aloft for all to see the head of the high priestess.

One by one, the mothers, daughters and wives of the men of this city were brought forth up the steps of the daunting temple. Innana awoke inside Ninnuit at this moment showing with pride to her daughter Ninnuit, the power, "her power" in each of these seemingly defeated women.

As each of the women were brought up to the top of this ziggurat and was in turn brutalized by the six priests and even the high priest who pretended to speak as their God Marduk-they were protected by the Goddess Ishtar as she took them out of their earthly bodies to meet their fate from a distance. The women, no matter how young or old, had a faraway look in her eyes. It was a knowing look. The look of extreme power and boldness that spoke to the observant Ninnuit of their bravery and powerful protection of the Goddess in which they were dying for, glowed internally from within each woman brought forth. The eyes told her that though it might look as defeat for the ways of the Goddess, they would never die in heart. No matter how beaten and suppressed the women of the world of the future may be, they would never lose the love and power of the Goddess within.

Ninnuit knew that Ishtar, the daughter of Innana had protected her daughters by blanketing their minds from the horror of their fate, that Ishtar took each rape into herself for it was not the fault of her daughters, but her own for being a weaker version of her mother. After the rape of each woman, their bodies were tossed into the waiting and powerful stone arms of Baal, the servant of Marduk. They were taken into his fiery wrath where he burned their bodies so that they would not have the proper burial that they would have earned in the course of their normal lives, had not this riot ensued changing their destiny radically. They were treated as common criminals for they were not even granted the ceremony of a sacrifice. There was no ceremony or holy words spoken, only the wrath of a man who called himself a God and the men held in his spell. Their souls would wander forever in search of the tombs that they would never have and of their bodies turned to ash and ripped apart by the winds.

Many girls and women perished that dreadful morning, breaking a new dawn into the folds of history with a fiery and bloody start. Yet, each of the females had a look before they were taken of pity for those who defiled them, so bravely had they faced their deaths. The men were stunned for they had not expected the power of the women. The women they thought they had known and had thought broken to their power. The power they thought had disappeared that very day as the last of the ashes had blown away in the wind. Forever stamped in their memory glowed the incredible courage they had witnessed and the pity that the women that they had killed beamed into their faces before they had died.

Innana had sent this dream and future vision to Ninnuit for a reason. Ninnuit in response immediately commenced plans that would protect her children and the ways of the Goddess.

For that very morning, she had called an emergency council and even requested the presence of her sisters Ua-Zit and Nekhebt as they now were called, to her council for familial advice.

Chapter 1

After the brutal rape of she and her priestesses two years prior, Ninnuit's council worked at a feverish pitch through most hours of the daylight working on some way to save her people for the ancient ways of the Goddess.

The new people to her land were stealthily taking control over the land by the most innate means possible and were vastly overwhelming all she knew.

Ninnuit and her council tried to find the cause of this and even narrowed it down to the mastermind of the foreign tribal leader named Enlil. In vain, she tried to block out that dreaded evening when Enlil had snuck into the compounds prior to his capture to commit the most blasphemous of acts possible. It was the most horrific defilement of her sacred priestesses that pressed painfully against her heart. It was an act of aggression and violent suppression over the women of the temple. The very thought was unknown in their history to defile a priestess in this way that it sent tremors throughout the whole land. A priestess was sacred and the very human vessel of the Goddess herself.

Since that moment, the acts against women and their domination had been occurring more frequently at an almost maniacal pace. The warrior women of the area had all been called to help. Suddenly they were disappearing, their bodies found mutilated and each one bore the pains of multiple rapes that they had endured before their deaths. Some were found in groups dismembered with an angry male God representative looking menacingly upon them with atrocious and slanderous words uttered forth in anger, denouncing the women warriors an abomination and ordering the people to join with this cause against the priestesses and all of her women attendants.

The week prior to the fortuitous event that led rise to this meeting, one hundred women were found on the banks of the delta with their eyes cut out, their hands all in a pile nearby. Sticks were forced into their ears and sacred parts screaming out to all to who had found them that they were not worthy to see, hear, feel, or to work for the Goddess. A plaque was found over the mangled bodies upon which horrid words were written in a strange language. When deciphered, the words translated to "Whores of the harlot must be killed for their sins!"

Groups of redheaded women from the foreign countries were taking to the streets of Erech, Dilmun, Lagash, Eridu, and other surrounding cities preaching the abomination of the Goddess and the acts performed in her name. They were preaching the "so-called" goodness of the men who were committing those atrocious acts! It was hard to stop these demented women once under the laws of the Goddess of justice. To their advantage, it was well known that any woman who stood on the central dais near the community wells must be heard in peace. It was the core speaking ground of the community and anyone who stood on it and pleaded their case to the populace must be heard and gained instant access to the Goddess and her priestesses if she chose to voice her words to a greater audience.

These women of foreign birth knew this and pleaded their cases against the Goddess in this very fashion. They were growing in numbers and wailing to all hours of the days and evenings with their very articulate reasoning and soft lamentations of the alleged sins of the very women that they were pleading with!

Some had been ordered to attend for this very reason a private council with high priestess to reason with them on their plight. Posts of great import were offered to these women in the temple in hopes of seeing the error of what they sought to suppress. Yet, the stubborn women who insisted their cry be heard and taken seriously denied all posts. Still the women came in increasing numbers to beseech the women of the land to stop their evil ways and to follow the "just" ways of their great God Enlil.

The strange foreign women claimed that the man who was the leader and the defiler of the priestesses was their God in human form and that it was "he" who was

placed on earth to dole out the punishment of the
temple whores and harlots, as they called them, for their
horrid ways against men. The women cried that in
killing Enlil, the human representation of their God; he
became more powerful and would wipe out and destroy
any wood or metal representation that stood for the
Goddess Innana in revenge. They demanded the
destruction of all personal fertility Goddess icons and for
the women stay away from the temples for Goddess
rites. The strange new women and men of the northern
tribes made the most sacred act of all, the act creating
life, seem crude and shameful.

The foreigners stated that the men of this new
land were holy as they stated of themselves and that the
women must submit to them for protection. They cried
out that the men were strong and just and would
protect them from the harm that their God Enlil would
throw in the path if the women would not adhere to
their rule.

The strange women with their fiery hair would
wail out for the children born to the temple and told of
how these holy children were minions of the false
Goddess and were not the sons and daughters of men,
but something evil.

Ninnuit's despair was increasing with each day,
since the persistence of these women was beginning to
take hold on the people of her city of Erech. She had
seen less men partitioning for a position in the temple to
serve as priests and eunuchs than ever before.
Thankfully, there was no cause for the choosing "a year
and a day" king since her moon-blood had stopped. This
she had secretly hoped would help for the moment due
to the hostilities of the people. Even less girls were
arriving from the surrounding areas to serve as
priestesses and attendants than ever noted before in the
history of the temple. For some unknown reason the
pleas of these poor women were grasping hold over her
people and the ways of the Goddess might be actually
nearing its sunset.

There had even been accounts of rape and of
women stolen and taken in captivity to serve the strange

men and their ways. The women taken in this way were allegedly forced into marriages against their will. This was an unheard of situation in the lands surrounding Eshnunna, in its being unprecedented in all of their known history. These women were brutally taken from their homes and from the protection of their parents. Their ankles were pierced with a rope forced painfully through so the unfortunate women literally could not flee their captors. Their heads were shorn and their jewels taken away from them as they were forced to wear rags with the yellow armbands of servitude for this new God called *Enlil*. Ninnuit had seen the blank look in those poor women's eyes as she passed them while touring nearby cities. They were the sad stares of women who had lost the power to fight along with all hope in the ability of the Goddess to save them.

Ninnuit as the Goddess Inanna had even asked one of the women one day, why she did not appeal to the justice of the Goddess, "For what reason?" The decrepit creature had replied to Ninnuit. "They would only kill me if I disobeyed and my mother and my daughters would die as well. They told me that the Goddess is dead and that a good woman should serve her man and be thankful for his protection and for the food that he places on the table. We are told that we must bow down to them for the ways of the world are changing and we are lost. We must even wash their feet." The women's eyes misted as if they had lost the power to cry, that all hope had been drained out of her. It had appeared to Ninnuit that all of the woman's emotions had long ago been torn away and left only the shell of the woman who stood before her.

Ninnuit replied in turn to the poor woman, "No the Goddess is not dead, come to the temple and sit by her side and she will save you."

"No priestess that I cannot do. Can you not see divine woman that our cause is lost; all of the women are coming into the power of this strange new way and their God Enlil. This new God demands our obedience and has taken away all of our power. Women are being denied an education upon the deaths of their fiercest weakness, their own children. Any child born of an act from the temple faces death. They sneak into our homes and kill the women who carry them! Where is the Goddess in all of this? Men come into our houses and take control of all inside. They kill our fathers and brothers beside us and force us to bend and honor their ways through our hearts and souls. They have stolen our pride.

"Now, please priestess let me be on my way, if I do not return from the market, I will come home to the deaths of my mother and three daughters that allegedly belong to this man who owns me." The woman trudged on, while Ninnuit stood there mute from what she had heard.

She had left the temple that day in normal priestess garb to investigate the true feelings of the village and city women on her own. No one had suspected that she was the Goddess representative in her simple garb and thus it made it easier to approach the average woman.

Being secluded in the temple for most of her time had kept all of this from her ears or attention, she had no idea how strong their movement had become. The strange new men who came from afar were raging a much, more violent war. Rather than coming into the cities and wiping them out in bloodshed, they attracted more people to their cause by sparing them and by capturing the most valued of citizens in bondage through their hearts and with their own weaknesses. Though little blood had been shed in this new war, she sensed that more was soon to follow, since this new movement was rapidly increasing by the day.

Ninnuit was amazed at the clever determination of the northern men in their tactics. It is well known that women who were born in power and the freedom of independence break more violently in their souls when all is taken away from them. This eats away at their soul and destroys any thought of hope they had left in such a shattering way that it seemed quite cruel to Ninnuit and thus the more deadly effective as it was proving too accurate a weapon in its all-encompassing reach.

After the discussion with this woman, Ninnuit became the Goddess in all of her glory and stood in her chariot in full splendor. The Goddess Inanna's mind taking control of her servant Ninnuit to speak her words upon the people who gathered in this place on this particular morning held all in its powerful demeanor.

"Hear me now people, for the Goddess speaks! A strange new way is infiltrating the hearts of our most valued people by trying to close our mouths! This foreign people of the red hair seek to destroy all the love we have built up in the name of the Goddess. Since time unremembered, I have protected and valued you all. Each man, woman and child has been taken in and nourished by me. Each person has been valued and the children born in my name deemed sacred.

"Our land has long been fertile under my name as have the women and the men. This new race seeks to destroy and muddy a function that is natural and a part of life, making the women feel as if she has done something wrong! Yet, you are human and you love in my name! I nourish and protect you for all being my children. This land thanks you for all you have done in my name. Women are the vessels that bring forth life and are to be valued and even revered for such, not brought down. A woman's greatest strength is her children, especially those born in her name from service in my temple. Men are valued under my name for their ability to place life in the wombs of women.

"Yet, these new red-haired men are here to destroy the women and take them under their power and control. Such men are truly weak and must be brought down to my feet.

"Any red-haired man or woman that you see must be stopped for their horrid ways and silent destruction of our people and our ways. Bring them to me and I will stop this! Send them out of our land and if they do not leave, make them listen! If it takes a raised sword for them to listen, so let it be! I have spoken, obey me or this land will die!"

Above the clouds rolled in, as if in response to the fury of the Goddess. Then in rapid succession to those powerful words uttered forth by the Goddess a storm crushed down in waves upon the people that surrounded the high priestess Innana who stood before them as if a statue. Her long soft black hair had fallen from its confines to greet the wind as if in prayer. The same wind seemed to fill her very essence on the chariot. Her long flowing skirts reached out to the wind as if beckoning to it and to the heavens above. The pleats of her skirt rippled in power almost making it seem as if the high priestess were trembling with rage. The sleeves that were attached in the back of her gown were golden and glowed with the rage of the Goddess that clung to the high priestess in desperation of her rank. Inanna's breasts were bared as if unafraid of the elements that she brought forth to make her mission's import strike the people. Her snakes writhed as if screaming out to the people to obey their Goddess who stood before them, their fangs barred to them as if in menacing and daring prayer.

The people who stood in her presence ignored the increasing danger of the elements and stood mute and stupefied in the power and the full glory of their Goddess. They then bowed down to kiss the ground to her in supplication. One by one, they stood up and ran back to their homes to obey the command of their Goddess. Still Innana stood silently in the square until each of them had left to carry out the will of her words. Her attendants slowly brought the beasts to attention as they left to return to the temple. Even though she was dressed as a normal priestess of the Nugig, all by then knew that Ninnuit was the high priestess herself and as Innana, she spoke to them all in a voice that only the most powerful of priestesses could ever possess.

The mortal Ninnuit was stunned when she heard about the words that she uttered in the name of the Goddess. She usually went into a trance when the Goddess came into her form to speak. She was completely thrown off guard when she heard that the Goddess had commanded the actual spread of blood in her name. Never before in history had this occurred. The Goddess was always the peacekeeper and the nurturer.

This movement must be very destructive indeed for such a violent command!

Chapter 2

One evening as the young children of the Mother
Goddess were sitting in the temple nursery by the light
of the fading sun, their mother had arrived in the
chamber before them. This was a very special occasion,
for rarely had she time to enter into the nursery at this
hour. Normally Ninnuit would only enter her children's
nursery at this time for official occasions in her Goddess
personae. Her children symbolized her power in fertility.

There they sat amongst the pillows strewn about
in the softest hues of the sunrise in stark contrast to the
vivid crimson sunset that rapidly filled the room with its
splendor. Attendants silently went about the room
lighting the copper oil lamps that hung from the marble
vaulted ceilings. The room gradually grew brighter
almost making the presence of their mother's approach
more unusual and almost ethereal.

Au-Set and Neb-Het bent their heads together
over their lessons, their soft black curls blending into
one mass of solitude. They perked up at the approach of
their mother, as did the eyes of their brothers Tehuti,
and Au-Sar who was holding in his arms the youngest
and barely walking Suti, as he had just placed the
toddler down on the clay-tiled floor. Suti was whining
over a toy that he claimed was taken by his older
brother Heru. An impossible feat for the docile Heru but
vehemently believed by the older brother. Au-Sar
protectively scooped up the hurt and crying younger
brother Heru from the wrath of Suti. They in turn
stopped in their tracks, so powerful was the force of
their mother that she would always gain control from
any room that she had entered. Au-Sar protected the
little Suti, but more often than not, protected others
from Suti's temper.

Ninnuit was not dressed in her usual impeccable
Goddess attire had it been a normal day. This evening
she was exhausted after endless secret meetings that
lasted throughout the day. By her side were her sisters.
It seemed another anomaly in their normal palace and
temple life. These aunts were rarely seen, especially

their legendary cousin from Gubla from the north. Their lives up until that moment had been a carefully orchestrated order of planned events. Nothing, not even a hair on any of their heads was ever out of place. However, before the children appeared exhausted and stressed out women, as they had never been seen in this way before this evening.

Everything seemed wrong on this day. Everything seemed out of balance in their world and all that they ever knew in their lives. They knew something grand was about to occur and waited in silence for the voice of their mother, who always spoke first...always.

"Children, now I am appearing to you as your mother, only as Ninnuit not as the Goddess; so heed my words as the one who carried you in her womb. The Goddess has given me a vision, which I chose to take fast action on and have come to tell you of my decision."

The great aunts and cousin stood silently by Ninnuit in support, as it was obvious that they had met prior on this matter. Ua-Zit held the hand of her sister Nekhebt, while Astarte leaned closer and found the very little angry red-haired Suti to place on her lap as she joined the sides of her young cousins to take a part in this great news about to enter the room and their very lives.

Ninnuit continued, "My loves and future of our family, we are about to change history in order that we may preserve the destiny of this family and all that we have fought hard for. The land that we preserve for the Goddess is in the process of being destroyed and all of us with her to a new race of people. The people with the red hair..." The mother was silent for a minute because she knew that all in the room had thought of the toddler Suti with his flaming red hair and politely passed to hear the rest of this momentous news.

She continued. "We need to gather forces to protect the ways of this family and the ways of the Goddess, especially in light of our last attack. I have decided to send you all away for your protection in fosterage with your aunts. Our family must be broken asunder in order to protect it." The eyes of her children welled up in tears that fought desperately to break free of the confines of propriety. Nevertheless, Ninnuit pressed on to continue.

"Au-Set and Au-Sar, you will be sent to your aunt Ua-Zit to carry on her rule of the lower black land of Kemet, while Neb-Het and Suti will be sent with your aunt Nekhebt in the upper part of that land to rule. Au-Set and Au-Sar, you will be joined in sacred union and live as husband and wife in co-ruler-ship over the land after the death of your aunt Ua-Zit, for her oldest daughter was sent to rule over her kingdom in Gubla. In turn, Neb-Het and Suti will be in another sacred union and rule as well. Tehuti, you will go with your brother and sister with your Aunt Ua-Zit, while Heru will go with Nekhebt. Do not worry, Neb-Het, Suti will grow up someday, and you will have a few more years yet of being a little girl.

"I expect you all to remember your stations in life and we will all meet in the days ahead in order to make all of the necessary plans for this to work for the preservation and further greatness of this family. I must remain behind to protect all that is here and make it safe for your return. You must remember your vow to the Goddess and to union as I have deemed to keep the line pure for the strong future of this family.

"Tehuti, the reason why you cannot create a sacred union with Au-Set is that you have great talents in writing and you are more valued there. We need someone to write all of this down for the future generations to come. The art you create will be the beginning of something much grander that we all could possibly realize on this day in this room, and I need your attention devoted to that rather than by being distracted in the day-to-day affairs of rule. For you see, we all have our places in life and it is best that we find out what purpose we each have and to utilize it to the best potential. To put someone in a place, in which he or she was not destined to fulfill, will only bring forth disaster. You are also brave and very protective of your sisters and this position for you will serve her for the best, rather than as her consort. Do you agree Tehuti?"

He nodded solemnly and let it all sink in.

She continued and addressed the young Heru, reached over and placed him in her lap. "And you my brave one, you will be the binding force of all of your brothers and sisters together. You are always on the outside and have never taken sides. They all love you and never have any of them fought against you, just each other, except occasionally little Suti!" She looked at each of the others and smiled; Heru giggled and knew his mother was correct even in his youth.

"Heru, my love have that special gift of being the peacemaker, which along with Tehuti's role, is the most important to this family. If any of them shall fight against each other, all that I have fought hard against for the preservation of this family will attack stronger than ever before and this family will be doomed." She hugged him close hoping her words had sunk in to him and to all of the rest in the room. Since they were all very young, they had to act much older than their years and to take on the burdens of adults.

Ninnuit also had a sinking feeling that she kept from all of them, the portent that she might not survive the whole ordeal that loomed large before them on this calm evening. That is why she felt it crucial how important they all were and of the roles, they would have for the rest of their lives. She knew that they were at the dawn of something huge...life and destiny altering and that her family and children would be playing a great part in all of this. She dreamed of this often, yet now those dreams were taking on a life of its own and the reality of the daylight no longer washed them out but made it even more vivid and bold that she could no longer deny it.

"Neb-Het, you are not the shadow of your sister as you think, you are just as grand as she. Both of you will create legends I just feel it! You have a bond that is rare and magical, use it, and grow with it!"

"And darling Suti," She reached over and placed Suti on her lap next to Heru. Both of her youngest snuggled into each other and in the warmth of their mother happily mesmerized, absorbing each soft word into their hearts.

"Suti, you have great energy and it is needed to lead vast armies in defense of your family with Neb-Het by your side! I have faith in you for your passions are strong; though do not let them get the best of you! Au-Sar, you already have proven your devotion to Au-Set and the others. You also are a fast learner and it will serve your family well. Create more projects and inventions in the name of our family, as I know they will be great indeed! In addition Au-Set, as you are my first-born daughter, you know well by now what responsibilities come with that position. Serve me well daughter!" Ninnuit struggled to gain control of her emotions; for she knew that, she was placing a huge burden on all of them. Yet, she knew that she had no choice.

"My little ones, I know that this is a monstrous burden that is placed upon you all; nevertheless, it is your destiny in the great scheme of things. I have seen it in dreams. You will save all we have fought for and create a wonderful new culture in the process! This might be a new culture of gorgeous colors and incredible brightness that might even dull the memory of Eshnunna! Therefore, you all must stand together! If there is any anger among any of you, your greatness will be diminished. It will still be grand, but not as it could be! Your lives will change drastically, and I ask each of you in the name of the Goddess, to be brave!

"Promise me also, that if one of you ever falls when I am not around, all of the rest must pick them up for the life of our family. For it to survive, you all must remember that you all were nourished in the same womb and are one. All of you are me and the Goddess herself!"

The children sat there stunned and silent. They were too hurt to cry or to react to this life altering news. Before they knew it, their mother had exited the room leaving only the aunts who silently remained behind to console the cries and pleas of the children at the fate of their family and of the destruction of the security, they had always known until this very moment.

Chapter 3

The next evening Ninnuit sat in the dining hall with her most valued advisors Ma-At and Neferet along with her sisters and niece.

The large chamber was vaulted in the technical precision taught long ago to the people of Eshnunna by her family. The stone imported generations before were revealed in the intricately carved spines around the richly painted indigo paneling. In each panel that reached high up to the vaults, many elaborate peaks were painted large and garish stars that were tenderly inlaid with countless layers of gold leaf. The gold stars glittered in the subdued lights of the oil lamps placed strategically around the room to create the affect of the stars, almost as if whispering in unison their power over the people below them. The vanity of the stars sparkled in delight over the attention they created. The heavens in evening representation with the golden stars were a favorite motif of Ninnuit and it covered her own sleeping chambers as well.

However, the evening motif seemed all too ominous to the woman Ninnuit for it seemed to emanate the reality of the symbolic evening of her known way of life in servitude of the Goddess Innana. She knew that the day was setting on her family traditions and ancient ways of her land Eshnunna.

Ninnuit spoke to them, "Most glorious women of my earthly family and temple of Innana, we must do something about this crisis that has befallen our land." The women nodded assent as they gathered around the long table made of imported cedar from Lebann.

They were all weary and eagerly waited for their mistress to speak for they knew that she had finally arrived at a plan to save them all, for her wisdom was well noted in past matters of import.

"We must protect our daughters and our sons from this new way that is vastly taking a hold on us and all that we have ever known. I have had a vision of the future of this land and it does look good for us at all. The ways of Innana will be lost and a weaker daughter will be weaned to take her place. Men will grab a foothold on our women and daughters, suppressing our powers and us. The women of this new Goddess will be kept from education and her children stolen and owned by men. No longer will the life born from our wombs belong to us. We must prevent this by any means possible for Innana has blessed me with her creativity in this crisis that will destroy our very ways of life. Soon the blood will start to flow from our sisters and our children will be ripped from our wombs and our words taken from our mouths and made dirty by this new God who seeks our submission!"

"I have seen atrocities committed in the name of this new God and laws made which render our gender invalid in the new land of men. In our world, the life from our wombs is valued and all are raised no matter who the woman was who cast forth life from her very essence. Each child is raised and nourished with love. No man is bound to our side, even those in sacred union; we do not forbid them the use of the temple services from our most valued and noble of women of the land who love them in the ways of the Goddess. We do not seek to control men or to hold them hostage to our rule and ways. We revel in our beauty and display it for all, never hiding the glory of the Goddess within us all.

"This new world dominated by the strangers with red hair, seeks to dirty the natural tendencies of humanity and call it a horrible thing that is shared between them. In their language, they claim the need of each other base and a dirty word in their language- "lust." They call that feeling the fault of the woman and it is blamed on us. They make it her fault and call her a whore. Another word that they created and made a normal tendency- is "evil." These new men to our land seek to destroy the loving ways of the Mother, to take possession of the women in their name and power for their connivance, and in order to serve them. These new men seek to take any child not knowingly born from their seed and to destroy them and the women who made them.

"Women of this land used to be warriors before they were priestesses. They fought to protect their men and them and the whole village raised all children, none were treated different but given the love of the whole village as equals. No son or man was cast aside in favor of his or her daughters or women. They were nourished and protected by all. Even to this day, we cherish our men and encourage all natural instincts and attractions of the body for each other in the loving name of the Goddess. We have fought beside our men in battle for many generations. Yet, in the most recent generations, the women have grown soft, seemingly content in all that we have gained.

"Yet, these new men from the north have brought new words to our people. The new words are "whore" and "harlot." Such harsh words used in anger for the natural acts of women. Making it appear wrong and dirty. They seek to change the laws of nature to bend it to their will and power, creating new words to help it along." She paused to gather new strength to continue.

"In this clever way, the men of our land have been given the power to listen to the new ways and have forgotten all that we have done for them. They are using our weaknesses to destroy the power that we still yield. They had fought a war unlike any that has ever been known in the history of human kind. The weapons used are not made of copper or flint, but of words, reason, and cunning manipulation. Those are their most valued weapons, far more than blood is lost here our very souls and will to live and to protect ourselves!

"We all know that a women's strength is her forgiveness and ability to nurture...however, it is also our greatest weakness. Such is the duality of a woman's very being! The men have figured this out! They have learned that by capturing us and forcing us to their physical will against our wishes breaks our spirit, our fire. By keeping us locked up and filling us with only their own selfish seed, it grows within us and is born to us with our full senses endowed since the turn of time to love and nurture that very same child.

"Yet, that same child born to us from them is being held against us for our submission, using our natural instincts against us. The men to bend us to their will and power over the threat of its death use that child! We need to grab our children, no matter who put their lives in our wombs and flee this land while they are still young enough not to be broken and used against us!"

The chamber fell silent at these words, yet Astarte spoke up, "Beloved aunt, I do not think the threat is as dark as you present it to us, I hardly see it in Gubla."

Ua-Zit then spoke up, "In my land the beginnings are there, we do need strength to unite both of the broken lands of Kemet for I hear that our women weep at night."

"As do I sister, I will take your children and raise them, but how will we protect them from the same?" cried out Nekhebt.

"Sisters, your land is still young and nothing of stone is built there to proclaim the power of the Gods. Build in stone and awe the people there, create a new order and religion to culture your people, become Gods for them and give them just laws to unite them. There needs to be order in that land so that they are not made vulnerable to the ways of the northern men who are busy here for the present moment. You still have centuries of time ahead of you to prepare the way. Please be careful with the words of the Goddess so they may stand up to the tests of time and to future battles on the horizon. You must make the women of your land strong to defend themselves."

Ua-Zit spoke up, "Sister, your children are more than welcome in my kingdom. My own daughter has found her new home in Gubla and is more than happy there." Astarte nodded in assent to the truth uttered by her mother. She had long given up the dreams of returning to her birthplace of Per-Uto in Kemet to take over her mother's place. She had grown to love her new land and fought with her mother for many years so that she was able to stay in Gubla.

"And I am more than happy to take your children as my own since my womb-children have all perished from the marsh sickness. In my dreams, my daughters had voices as sweet as the river winds. They cried out for their cousins and gave permission for them to lead the land in their stead. My daughters accept your children, their cousins! Now I know the reason for those dreams. I thought them rather odd before this moment. Your children hold the blood of Shu, the greatest of Kemet in nobility, as our own fathers. They are welcome in Kemet dear sister!"

Ninnuit spoke again, "I am sending down healer priestesses who will ensure that this marsh sickness will end. As of now, it is still an issue. We must be stronger than this for our family's future!" All in the room nodded.

"I need your help to raise Au-Sar and Au-Set as king and queen of equal ranking upon the people of Kemet when it is their time to rule. This would be the same for their siblings, Neb-Het and Suti. The equality will appeal to the people. It is something that has been lost for generations here. Possibly this is the reason for the rebellion. Possibly that is also where our strength lay- in the equal division of the sexes, as in the time before in the very beginning. May they rule side by side, each needing the other to sustain life. Never in each other's power over the other in suppression shall they ever be if they heed our words this night.

"Perhaps our women have grown too bold and the men silently felt cheated so they were made vulnerable to the new men who have reached this land. Their contented ways made them vulnerable. I hope that by bringing the balance back it will enable this new land to have a better base for which to fight off this need for suppression of any kind."

Ma-At and Neferet nodded to the wisdom of the Goddess Innana in the form of their familiar Ninnuit and were joined with the other women of the room bowing supplication to her beautiful wisdom and judgment.

For the children's protection were Ma-At and Neferet who were the cherished women of the Naditu and were called the *Nugig*. They were the women of the class most cherished in the land for their royal birth and were the highest in rank under the high priestess. These women were valued for their beauty, intelligence, and strength. They were also the personal bodyguards of the Goddess in human form besides her attendant eunuchs who normally surrounded her during all of her waking hours. Ma-At and Neferet were of the royal houses of Eshnunna and were related to the three queens in this chamber. Their bodies belonged to the Goddess and only kings could possess them in ceremony and only with their permission. They were the oldest daughters of their family and were deemed from before their birth to serve the Goddess Innana.

Chapter 4

Ma-At and Neferet at the nodding of their mistress, returned to the scribes that they were in charge of and proceeded to write down a history that was to be brought with the children of the high priestess to their new land. They also set about ordering food, works of art, and valuable commodities of marble and granite to be shipped down before them for the building of the new temples. They set about composing a new language that would appease to the simple people there, which would be loaded with legends and mythology. It was their duty and honor to do this for their high priestess that had chosen them to serve the Goddess on her behalf for this matter. They were the Hands of Innana and of her earthly representative.

Neferet had found all that was required and set into motion the plans of Innana. Ma-At used her judgment in finding the most creative way to rebirth this new land in the most lasting image.

Ma-At learned all that she could about this faraway land to the south of them and questioned Ua-Zit and Nekhebt way into the wee hours of the night when not in session with their sister.

She had learned that the people of Kemet were mostly fisher folk who sailed on boats made from the mighty grasses called papyrus that grew numerous along its banks. The land was only fertile along the banks of the "Great River"; it had no other name. The people relied heavily on the moods of the river and could not predict it. However, when happy, this great river provided an abundance of food for the people, which led to the creation of great villages made of mud and grasses. The houses were made mostly of poles and palm matting with mud-plaster on some of the more elaborate houses. They were bleached white from the sun and were often swept away with the flooding that occurred each year, which quenched the appetites of the minions of Sobek. Sobek was the God of the crocodile, which constantly took the children away in sacrifice. Such tales were whispered among the many villagers of

Kemet. This Sobek and its numerous minions was a fierce beast that showed no mercy on any age. It was a large lizard with powerful jaws that would attack when unprovoked. It never ate live meat, but preferred to drag away unsuspecting victims in the night and to drown them to feed on when cold and dead. This was a strong problem to the vulnerable people.

The flooding of the river tested the people and their faith and due to this never bothered to move their houses to higher and more permanent grounds.

There were also the dangers of the mighty and large Hippopotami. They were almost peaceful looking as they slowly ambled their way in marshlands eating the vegetation. The fear was from provoking them in any way. They were known to charge and any hit from them meant instant death due to their great size.

Moreover, there was also the threat of the jackals in the evening and the wild boars that would enter villages to forage. She pondered this greatly.

Ua-Zit stated very eloquently, "...and do not forget the cobra of the land, a fierce snake that prefers to sneak into the dwellings and huts at night to suck the life out of us and our children while we sleep! If you are lucky enough to be asleep when this occurs that is... If alive when confronted by a cobra, it is a frightful sight to witness, the hood flares up and the stare is enough to kill you alone, along with the agility in which it strikes having no mercy and enough power to kill six grown men in one fell swoop."

Ma-At smiled, "Oh lady, I could definitely work with this. Kemet was a land where small creatures could be feared over the larger ones... Are there more?"

Nekhebt spoke up after nodding at the thoughts of her sister next to her, "There is also the dreaded scorpion. It is an insect that has six legs and a large tail that comes up from behind in a curl with enough venom to rival that of the cobra or *iaret*, and that is from the smallest of them! The larger scorpions only look more formidable, but only make you sick!"

All of the women shone at the sudden knowledge that had passed before them. They each knew how this knowledge could be wielded to protect them in this strange new hostile land. The weeks they had left on this plan passed quickly by in creating a new destiny for their future.

Chapter 5

The time had finally arrived. Ninnuit looked down upon her sleeping children as their mother, not as the Goddess that she represented. Silently she wept, and prayed for their safety. She felt in her soul that she would never see her children or family again. She knew that they would not be here to honor her after she was sacrificed in the name of the Goddess that she lived for.

Yet as their mother, she looked down at each one of them. How Au-Set clung to her brother Au-Sar, showing how much they were made for each other. However, she worried about Suti and Neb-Het, and of how even in sleep, she pushed her half-brother away as if offended by his bright red curls so different from the rest of the siblings. She raptured over her oldest son Tehuti and how he had always chosen to sleep by the foot of the bed as if protection of them all. Tears struggled to escape her calm façade as she felt the warmth of her second youngest and darling Heru, still in slumber from her own bed and on her hip, as he clung feverishly as if afraid that she would let him go. She placed in the bed little Heru beside the others. Heru then snuggled up in the very middle of all of the siblings as if playing the peacemaker even in their sleep. How could a mother fail to be proud at children who defined their roles in life even before they knew it themselves?

Why did they all have to be torn away from her nurturing embrace when they were still so young and needed it? She feared for their safety and knew that all of them would be in great danger if she did not carry out her plans. As a mother, she knew that she was going to die for their very survival. In remembrance of her for their journey, she had small silver necklaces made for each of them that represented her name in birth. So she could look over them in slumber and be allowed entrance into their dreams for guidance. The stars were made from a stone that shone as brilliantly and as stunningly as the rays of the moon. She was called Queen of the Heavens and she wanted her children to make sure that they would never forget her love or her sacrifice for them.

Ninnuit knew that they would be safe in the hands of her sisters, and even her chosen Nugig, her Ma-At and Neferet would accompany her children to their new land and future rule. In Kemet, they would aid her children and help them create a path in their own destiny, and never let them forget their homeland nor the ways of the Goddess.

That evening, she had carefully reviewed all Ma-At and Neferet had planned for action that was to commence at the birth of the moon this evening. She felt that they had to move now in this plan, before it grew too late.

She noticed the first rays of the moon flow nimbly across the arched windowsill of the nursery chambers and climb across the tiled floors to reach the toes of her oldest son Tehuti.

Tehuti, with a deep connection to his mother, awoke at her silent command, felt the rays of the moon upon him, and knew what he could do for his mother.

He looked up at her and nodded, silently getting up to wake his siblings while his mother looked on and watched him with pride. Suti was about to stir, when Ninnuit tenderly hushed her smallest child laying in a tumble of blankets and placed a delicate kiss on his tiny rosy cheeks.

Au-Set and her very image and younger sister woke up and ran to the skirt of their mother who stood there with tears in her eyes.

"Mama, please let us stay here with you!" cried Neb-Het. Au-Set nodded her head in affirmation.

"Hush darlings, you know that you must do this most valued duty for your mother and for the greatest mother of all- Goddess Innana!"

"But, Mama, I no wanna go!" uttered Suti, "I will protect you from bad men! Mamma!"

"Shhhh dear, I more than anyone know how brave you are and strong, but you must grow older and even more strong so that you may fight my battles and your own on another day! You will never get that chance if you stay behind!"

Her faithful oldest son Tehuti in all of his glorious nine years, acted more bold than any man that she had known and whispered, "Mother do not worry, I will make sure they obey you and never forget where we came from. I will make sure that they all have your courage and strength."

He bowed to his mother and carefully took the tiny boy Heru from her trembling arms, since he had woken and ran to her immediately. Tehuti gathered his other siblings and left her alone in the chamber to follow them all to the secret docks of the temple to the underground river that would carry them out to the larger river under the weight of the stars and away from her tears that she knew would fall soon after their departure. Ninnuit knew that they would have to cross a dangerous desert to reach their destination. She trembled in her heart at this, though felt in her heart that it would be all right in the end.

Their departure would take them to a river grander than any that she had known in her lifetime contained the banks of the cities that her children would grow up along, without her. Ninnuit hoped in her heart that this mighty river would protect her children better than the two rivers that they were born near ever have.

The core of her followed her son and tucked them all into their shelter on the barge for this journey. The barge would cradle the shores until they reached the great desert. They would cross it in a large caravan under the light of the moon and then arrive at the delta region of the great river of the black lands of Kemet.

This same barge would take her babies away from her, but at the same time would protect them from the bloodshed that she knew would occur very soon. She could still hear the faint drums of the enemies surrounding the temple and city of Erech in the wee hours of the night. Thumping the heartbeat of the violence that was soon to be, growing louder to mark the end of times, the drums called out in warning. She knew her own soul echoed it in resolution of what she had to do at the sunset of the Goddess Innana as her representative on earth.

"My loves, know that I will always watch over you and love you as long as there are stars in the sky above us. Know that in the moon I am with you and will hear your prayers. Listen to my songs for you in the whispering winds of the moon and feel my undying love for you all. Feel my laughter and love for you tickle your feet with the precious rays of the sun. Know that this has to be done and that there is no other way. I love you my precious ones, may you create large and powerful dynasties in your name and in the name of the Great Mother!"

Chapter 6

Only when the long line of barges was safely out of sight deep in the tunnels underground, did the woman, Ninnuit feel safe to cry. All of her most valued priestesses journeyed with her children leaving her alone in the temple, with only her warrior priestesses to stand by her side.

The warrior priestesses were trained in the temple and were more fervently in training over the past few months than ever before. Ninnuit ordered a resurrection of the most ancient ways of her people for the warrior priestesses to learn. Ninnuit trained along with them in preparation for what was soon to occur and felt that she was at her full power to fight with every bit of strength that she would ever possess. She even made sure that her own children had the rudimentary and basic skills of battle before sending them out into the world.

Only now, without her children, the woman that she was, no longer existed. No comfort from anyone, not even her cherished companion and last consort was able to console her after her babies had left her that evening. Ninnuit took those few moments to grieve the woman that she once was and thus felt herself draining as if readying herself for the Goddess to gain the complete entry of her form for the time ahead of her.

She walked back to the temple and climbed the seemingly ominous steps to the great throne room to sit by the side of her last consort and death mate. All of the tears shed had taken the essence of her soul with it. Numbly she sat behind him calling to her side all of her priestess warriors to await their fate.

Chapter 7

There sat Innana and Dimuzi in the throne room on the great dais with their last remaining eunuchs, warriors and attendants. Those chosen to stay behind knew that they might never survive this day that had at last arrived. All of the people left behind felt as if most of their lives all they ever learned were in training and preparation for this very moment that was bearing heavily upon them.

The Goddess representative Innana gave them all a special ceremony, blessing each one of them with the love of the Goddess as any sacrifice was so deeply honored in temple life. She told each person present in that room that they were to become the most sacred of sacrifices to the Goddess; for they were fighting for the very essence of the Goddess herself, not only in the survival of their city and her human representative but for the future of their very faith.

She also ceremoniously blessed those priestesses who would leave with her children to the raw new land of Kemet. Before the last boats were sent out to Kemet, Ninnuit as Inanna spoke to each one personally and told them that they had her permission to leave and they would still have her respect and love and even more as they were performing their own mission for the Goddess and their very faith as well as those left behind. Yet each one of them that she had chosen for this last great sacrifice to Innana had chosen without hesitation to stay behind and to fight beside her and for their cherished way of life.

Chapter 8

The warriors were trained in the ways of the most ancient warfare of their land. They looked regal in their full glory of the twilight of their lives. The women warriors were dressed in the most ancient of battle-gear whose design was taken from paintings from the oldest of temples of the land. Ninnuit made sure they resembled the temple paintings as accurately as possible. She wanted Innana to look down on them and for her to be proud.

The women warriors had their hair braided in small intricate paths down their heads that were topped off with small copper beads. Only the most natural of copper was chosen, not any that was smelted by her metal smiths. The natural deposits were the most sacred as they came directly from the Goddess herself.

Their breastplates were made of hammered copper and then carved intricately with the ancient writings from the most archaic and magical of protection texts found deep within the temple. Their outer-skirts were made of copper plates to bend and move when they did. Underneath their armor, they wore a heavy padded undergarment made of wool, taken from the darkest of sheep in the temple flocks. On their heads, they wore a helmet, again made of hammered copper that had the coiled body of a snake worked around the part that covered their heads with tall pointy horns similar to a cow local to their area, the symbol of Innana. Their sandals were made of leather that was strapped up to their knees. On their arms, they wore bracelets that resembled the sacred snakes of the Goddess that wound its way up each arm.

Innana looked over at her beloved, last and most cherished of consorts and spoke softly to him, "It is time for us to be together in the name of the Goddess one last time."

He nodded and whispered, "May this last time be for us?" His full head of sandy blonde hair caught a stray beam of the sun as it came unrepentantly through the point of the arched windows of the throne room in the highest part of the temple and made the his speckled sun-bleached youthful mane of hair almost glow. This looked incredibly handsome to the human and all too aware mortal Ninnuit.

Ninnuit stood up from her throne that was gilded in the finest of gold found in the deepest and most prosperous mines of their own land. Their goldsmiths were the most talented in any of the civilized lands and were sought from many lands.

On the head of Ninnuit was the elaborate carved crown worked in the finest filigree of intricate carvings in the purest and pinkest of gold molded to imitate the horns of the great cow form of Innana. The horns crept up menacingly from the side of the headdress and curved towards the top of her head and the outward towards the heavens from which she symbolically sprang to protect all of her people. The band around her head was inlaid in beads of every stone found in her own land.

The crown was heavy and stiff, in fact it was the same one last used at the funeral of her mother that seemed an eternity ago. Ninnuit wished that she had the guidance of her mother now, for in the few moments when the Goddess did not possess her she felt as if she were still a frail and helpless little girl. This she successfully hid from everyone around. It was a part of her station to bear this burden of the Goddess in royal state and she did it with grace.

Her gown of ceremony was dyed a rich purple taken from the snails pink stomachs carefully siphoned to form the rich color of the Gods. This color was sought all around the world and was from the city of Tyre, near Gubla where her cousin Astarte ruled. The cloth was the finest and most ethereally woven garments in its rich hue, all of one splendid color without adornment as it was all on her headdress of gold and sparkling gems from the known world.

Ninnuit stood and Dimuzi followed her, she looked only like the Goddess in that moment and lost any hint of her humanity as she floated from the room with her consort following her lost in the spell that she wove with her beauty and flowing grace. Her feet were small and highly arched from many years of dance and supplication to her Goddess and were adorned with the tiniest of bells, which surrounded her ankles and played the most seductive of tunes. Her feet swayed in movement as she glided to the soft music of the Goddess that only she could hear. In her dance, she was followed by Dimuzi who became lost in the spell with each note that emanated from her tiny feet, as she led the way to her most secret of chambers.

This most sacred of chambers that was her final destination was even higher than the throne room and looked openly over the whole city of Erech. This chamber was the most holy of rooms of the Goddess. This chamber that looked over all in its being the highest point in her land that she knew of, a chamber where she gave birth to each of her children, a room where she honored the Goddess in which her children were conceived in as well. This was the room where it was her destiny to die.

All those left behind in the room below bowed down as the two lovers left to complete one final ritual for the Goddess, her most sacred. Though no new life would come of this, since her time of the moon had ceased, it was still the greatest act a Goddess could perform for the dying fertility of the land that she cared for and nurtured. They would join in love one last time in symbolic and ancient prayer for their deaths.

Only in the most heated moment when their souls united, a woman in her human form would become one with the Goddess and could in that brief moment, experience the closest thing on earth to immortality. When a woman climaxed, she experienced what the Eshnunnaians called "the little death". In the moment after this instance, she was reborn and revitalized with the essence left behind from her partner while he was left depleted. The woman from that act carried not only the strength of her partner, but of the God as well. The power of the Gods dwelt in every man. This made each woman close to the Goddess and most secretly blessed in this most magical of moments. That is why any child born of this, especially in the temple was considered born of the Goddess. Those not conceived from this magical state were not considered holy.

Woe to the man who did not have the power to achieve this rite in the woman with whom he lay! Since that act would have only to be called normal and mundane. When a boy reaches his time of manhood, he would learn this art from the temple priestess, so that he would be better able to serve the Goddess and his future union mate. In ceremony at the temple, after he was trained, he had to make sure that the priestess, with whom he lay, would reach this state, or his gift to the temple would not be deemed valid and accepted by the Goddess. Any child that was conceived by his union mate or wife in this state was considered holy as well, though ranked second to the temple conceived from the actual priestesses.

Innana left the throne room and led her consort Dimuzi to that sacred chamber. He followed the Goddess and was lost with each note left behind in every step that she seductively took. The woman Ninnuit was lost behind the flowing garments as they swayed in the breeze of the open stone staircase that spiraled up to the uppermost part of the temple. The air caught each pleat and fold and rippled it while he followed mutely behind her, awaiting her next command. Her golden crown sparkled in the bright sunlight at the highest hour of the sun. Dimuzi followed the dance of the steps of the Goddess as he was led to the highest part of the temple above the throne room.

They arrived at the chamber that was used only on special occasions. A room was open to the city and was topped with a roof inlaid with gold that overlooked all of Erech at the highest point of the city. The room was open to the eyes of the Gods and Goddesses as witness to the sacred rites performed therein. In each corner standing sentinel were large and elaborate columns around which were carved in meticulous detail the depictions of serpents who wove their way to the roof along the columns. The floor was edged in mosaics of flowers and in the center of the chamber, which took up most of the space, was the most holy of sacred spaces. It was the very place where all of the children from the consorts of the Goddess were created and born. It was the place where each representative of the Goddess used also as her deathbed from the time that the temple was built six generations ago. Life and death mingled in one unknown by the restraints of time itself and made this room holy in its ritual of life.

In the throne room below, the musicians took up their cue. In the chamber where they lay, it was almost as if the Gods above were praying for them, so otherworldly was the music that wafted from below to their entranced souls in echoing form. It made this moment even more glorious than any before for both of the two lovers became lost in their last embrace on this earthly realm.

Each kiss was glorious and savored to last an eternity. Each touch was holy and captured their souls in delight. They made love to what seemed to them an incredible and blissful infinity. Their passion was not of an earthly nature, so all consuming that it was, it reached the most glorious heights from whence it originated. Innana and Dimuzi embraced their rapture of the Gods and knew that they were made immortal in this instant, even though Ninnuit inside of Innana and Dimuzi were mortal down deep in the recesses of their flesh.

Below them, they heard voices and then all too mortal screams. Suddenly the music ceased and was wrenched asunder punctuating fiercely the dying cries of the musicians. They knew that blood flowed below them and that it would soon be their own bloodshed that would end an era.

The cries were swiftly terminated as the smoke from below in the city had finally drifted softly to their holy place on earth mingled with the cries and smells of the dying and burning people below them. Only then did they experience a glimmer of their mortality for only the briefest of moments. The tortured screams permeated the air, almost bringing Ninnuit back to her form from the bliss of the Goddess who possessed her.

Innana fought to keep her high priestess in steady control and under her power to save her from what was about to occur. She would preserve her most precious representative with her own pride and power, so that this moment would be immortal and not destroyed with human weakness.

Suddenly footsteps drunkenly climbed up the steps, armor clinking against the narrow walls of the inside of the open staircase as they spiraled upwards to kill the lovers.

Innana felt pity for those poor misguided men who were following in the guise of their new deified leader Enlil. She knew they were ignorant and would eventually be avenged for their actions this evening and for many generations prior to this pinnacle of power.

Yet, still they came, forever upward in time that seemed to last an eternity. Although there were only three times seven steps carved out that led to this chamber, it seemed to them as if they had climbed a thousand steps or more.

They were drunk with the power of bloodshed. They wielded the power of life and death that was given by their swords and bare hands to those who pleaded below at their mercy. They stopped for no one, almost showing more hatred on the women and children of the city than for the fathers, sons, and husbands that pleaded for that same mercy denied them. There was much bloodshed in the height of the brightest and sunniest of days that year and this was its zenith.

The men arrived at the top, covered in dried blood. The sweat from their exertions below and from climbing the steps which had led to the chamber, stood out in the falling umber droplets of sweat from their foreheads. The stench of death permeated their leather armor that was woven with scales of metal that glowed in the light at the top of the city of Erech at its highest point.

Four men had arrived to the holy chamber. The last to arrive was waited for upon orders of the first.

They stood there and addressed the Goddess Innana and her consort Dimuzi. The first to arrive was the age of Ninnuit herself, whom she would actually have recognized had she been in her earthly form. He was the son of the scribe of her father Shu, the most valued of her mother Tefnut's servants who had left them six years prior. His name was Ishut and he had escaped the temple before his execution was to occur. Ninnuit did not know much of the matter that is, until now.

They must have looked odd to the men who had reached the top of the stairway. Ninnuit was still in Goddess form and appeared the Goddess image of matronly beauty in the twilight of her years. Beautiful, powerful and graceful were mere words compared to all that emanated from her being to those who stood before her. She stood bravely before them emanating proudly woman's most valuable years, when the attractiveness of her body and youth matures to lead way for the loveliness of the mind to take command.

Her face, once pure and unblemished in the full height of her beauty was starting to wrinkle slightly, making her eyes seem smaller than the dark almond shaped eyes that she had for so long. Her eyes were of a lighter brown, almost heavenly, rather than dark and penetrating, as she had had for most of her youth. Her neck still tall and graceful held a still abundant head of hair. Her hair was sparkled with rays of the moon that emanated from her wizened temples outward from the blackest of the evening color of the hair of her youth. Her skin was not as pliant as it was in her youth, but still solid and tanned with the kiss of the Goddess of the sun.

Dimuzi was very young and had just entered the prime of his manhood before his service to the Goddess, and lay next to her in the splendor of virility that would never sire children on the Goddess in her evening years. He loved her and the human representative equally and it poured out to the new occupants and disturbers of their spent bliss on earth.

Innana spoke softly, commanding the first voice of this mighty and historical moment, "Ishut, you have come to destroy me?"

"Aye lady, I have. You and your women sicken me."

"Ishut, you have committed blasphemy and have escaped sentence, you know what you did."

Dimuzi sat silently lost in the trance of the moment in the power of the Goddess and the spell that she wove, as if new to the naked and beautiful form of his Goddess as her power controlled the chamber and the city below them. Dimuzi noticed how it seemed to grow quiet in the city below them. Even the cries of the dying had seemed to stop, held captive to this moment in time, lost to the voice of the Goddess as she spoke to them in her chamber above the world.

"Lady, she wanted it and she was no more a priestess than this whore that you have found to be your minion, this Ninnuit. Stop playing Goddess and let the world know who you really are Ninnuit!" Ishut beckoned.

"Nay boy... You took the body of a priestess against her will and tried even to take that of Ninnuit! You are no son of my house and mine. I saw what you did to that priestess; you had taken against her will, her secret blood from her that was for me alone to have in honor and consent. Yet, you were selfish and did not hear her cries or her begging for you to cease!"

"I have no fear of you Ninnuit!" Ishut pushed Dimuzi away from her. The sweat from love spent with his Goddess covered his body in tiny tears and glistened in the sun. He lay crumpled in a heap as tossed aside by Ishut. Still lost in the trance of his Goddess and depleted from giving her his last bit of strength and power to flow in her veins.

Ishut grabbed Innana in all of her nakedness and raped her. Her headdress toppled to the ground in a soft thump. Innana had an odd look on her face the whole time, a small smile of mockery and humor in this act of defilement that came upon the human form of Ninnuit.

Dimuzi stood up to the horror, silent in his rage. As he faced their height with his own, one of the warriors who stood there at the orders of Ishut, at the nod of his head swung out his sword at the head of Dimuzi and watched with a loud bellow of laughter as it was sent roaring out of the chamber to the streets of the temple below them. It took several swipes with their copper swords due to his long tresses that tangled in the flint-lined sword. The last stroke rang true and the head was severed and left the body out of the chamber to the streets below. It was gruesome and seemed to last a horrific eternity, yet it was done. The body of Dimuzi then crumpled to the floor as if finally surrendering. The soldiers then urinated on it, singing the most ribald of tavern songs on the dead consort. His young and beautiful blood flowed strong over that of the dainty feet of the priestess, as she stood motionless and dazed.

Innana took in the further defilements of the soldiers as they had their fill and she felt her body being taken downstairs for the rest of them who waited below to take into them the prize of the high priestess. Some urinated on her in those last moments as they did to Dimuzi. She then felt a swish as her head was released from her body. Her body was then dragged up to that most sacred of chambers and thrown down to the streets below as if only mere rubbish.

Ninnuit was no more. Yet, Innana was released from her earthly bonds and human form without another one to go into. She knew that if she did not find a consecrated Goddess born body to fall into, she would soon lose her power. In the small amount of time that she had left, it was not enough. The oldest girl-child of Ninnuit had not reached the time of her moon-blood. She had not been consecrated in ceremony to open her body to the reception of her power. The body that the Goddess was to find was to be near the temple itself and the earthly daughters of Ninnuit were no longer in this land. Her time was done on this earth and she knew it.

Yet, she had another hope of her daughter born of this bloody day and of the rape of one of her surviving priestesses. Since it was not born of ceremony and of delight, it was her only hope. She would make sure that their new God as his consort would choose this priestess, so that at least it will be born in the temple. This daughter conceived in the womb this day of her raped priestess, would be a much weaker version of her. Yet, she would be. At least she had that. She smiled weakly to the new world that her daughter would be born to and knew that her other daughters would be consecrated far away and will start their own pantheon in a foreign place. Inanna knew that they would have a better chance than this daughter would, newly conceived named Ishtar.

Only her earthly scribes could tell of her time in the magnificent city of Erech that would someday be removed of all traces of Goddess worship and be replaced with a new one of a selfish God who degraded women and kept them as property and breeders for their seed. Innana cried for that day and was glad that she would not be around to see it. She had seen its dawn and lamented it as the loss of her consort, the young and virile Dimuzi, whose body lay broken and in pieces down below.

Chapter 9

"Oh, my dear children! The end of your mother has come! Come to me for I will be your mother now."

Ua-Zit did not need to tell them of how she had arrived at this knowledge. She wondered if the children having been raised under the wing of the Goddess must have all shared the same dream of the death of their mother, the high priestess of Erech. Nevertheless, she felt deep inside her soul that they actually did.

Ua-Zit watched in mute horror from her paralyzed form the evening prior as the immortal moment played out for her. She knew why she was helpless, for she was only allowed this unceremonious vision as the one chosen by the Goddess to carry on her wishes for the next generation. It was knowledge that she required in her new role. She knew that she had to stay alive for her sister and her three children that would be coming to live with her.

She had to be strong for her cherished oldest sister Ninnuit. Ua-Zit was not only known by this name, it was the name that she took when she had come to serve the Goddess of this strange new land to the south of where she was born. Ua-Zit was the name of the Goddess whose form she took in honor of the land in the delta where she was sent to rule. Ua-Zit was the Goddess of the dangerous snake they called the cobra in Eshnunna and the iaret in Kemet.

The Iaret Goddess named Ua-Zit ruled the lower most part of the black land of Kemet of the Great River. In the part of the river that sprang upwards to the rest of the world towards the home of her birth in the shape of the sacred flower of this land called a lotus. The delta was the area where the Great River broke apart into many smaller rivers that flowed into the Great Sea. This same sea touched the banks of her daughter's land of Gubla and Retenu. The iaret ruled this part of her new land and thus she wore it on a crown always upon her head.

She was born the second daughter of Tefnut of her consort Simnt, the brother of Shu. Her birth name was Ishurti and her sister was born as Nemothi and was the daughter of Nucit, their cousin. All were in the line of this throne that she now ruled. All were born to the oldest houses of Kemet. Both of the birth names were lost as if only belonging to the little girls they once were, not to them as women and Goddess representatives. Nevertheless, it did bring to them a whisper of life under the wings of her mother, now long dead it seemed, joined recently by the soul of her oldest sister, Ninnuit. Ua-Zit had prayed for her older sister even though she knew her body would not receive the ritual funeral due to the violent nature of her death.

The fathers of her sisters were of the land that she now ruled over half. Her father's oldest sister was Ua-Zit and his youngest sister was Nekhebt, for all of the daughters born to rule were named thus. Which was why she had taken her aunt's name when she came to rule in the great power seat of Lower Kemet called Per-Uto.

Chapter 10

The dream of her sister came while she lay dozing along
the shores on the way to her home, after crossing the
great desert by caravan. They had then entered new
barges made of papyrus with canopies over their heads
to protect them from the harsh sun of the land. Tiny
Suti lay dozing in her arms while Au-Set and Neb-Het
were trying to catch a small yellow butterfly that had
arrived in the tent on their barge while they stopped for
more supplies and to rest.

They had been there for over an hour sitting in
the hottest sun of that day to rest from the frantic pace
they had set while rowing away from Erech. They had to
hug the shores in their flight from their homeland to the
land that she had ruled over since she was eleven when
she had received her first moon-blood.

She was jarred awake with the vision that the
Goddess had sent to her of the death of Innana. Most
important to her was the brave and tragic death of her
older sister, Ninnuit. She knew that the vision was made
stronger by her sister's soul touching hers to let her
know that she and their other remaining sister, now
Nekhebt were now the mothers of the "Innana born"
children in the barges now lazily lopping in the
treacherous sun. The little ones were supposed to be
taking a nap.

The form of Ua-Zit was startled when the vision of
Innana came to her in her sleep, distressing the toddler
Heru. He was wrestled from the peaceful play of her
curled up form with the sudden jarring movement that
she made in response to the fury projected before her
eyes in her dreams. The birds seem to stop their cries
while a slight breeze picked up around them sending the
butterfly away from the grasp of the two startled
princesses. All around them knew the meaning of the
sign and bowed their heads to the passing of a Goddess;
a mother, a sister, a daughter and a friend

Ua-Zit and the rest of the mourning family that
evening, lay on the mats of the barges while they
traveled by night reaching closer to her home in Per-Uto.

The colors were odd in the hours of the evening under the shade of the full moon as the bright stars above in a celestial canopy lit their path onward. The sounds of the insects droned on and seemed to chant a monotonous prayer that lazily accompanied them in their journey. The water from the sea seemed to smell stronger in the evening and the sounds only echoed louder in an eerie way.

Ua-Zit looked over to the slumbering mass of her sister's children all in a heap of exhaustion from the emotional trauma they had just experienced. Slumber came on mercifully fast as they were worn out from their muffled wailing and mourning in their escape from Eshnunna.

Chapter 11

Ua-Zit thought of her older sister with the honor of her passing. The memory of how Ninnuit was as an older sister to them, safe in the comfort under the wings of their mother; all of a sudden after years of blurriness became clear for her. She recalled how Ninnuit would always save her sweets that she had snuck from the kitchens and the watchful eyes of their mother, Tefnut, who was at the time the representative of the Goddess Innana.

She recalled fondly of how she and Nemothi would sneak into the older initiate priestess chambers to the bed of their sister on evenings of frightening thunderstorms. Ninnuit would never scold them as their own mother would and hold them close. She told them she had had never gotten over her own fear of thunderstorms to assure her little sisters of her love.

Nemothi and she knew that Ninnuit was like that; she was a great empath and drew others close to her in joining them in their pain and fears. She would draw it into her, almost as if she were taking it in to protect them. Ua-Zit recalled that she wanted the love most from her older sister Ninnuit, rather than her own mother who was too busy in her role as the Goddess representative. Their mother made every act her daughters did a preparation for their role as a Goddess, often forgetting that they were also little girls. Ninnuit, in her youth was not so separate from that and still had limitless amounts of love to dote on her younger sisters.

Ua-Zit knew that she had older brothers, though they were always sent away by their mother to learn the art of writing and magic cuneiform and had lived in fosterage of temples away from their sisters who were revered by their mother and by the Goddess for their future functions.

Ninnuit was the mischievous one who had whispered to her younger sisters of her first consort and of how she was falling in love with him. This simple man, whom all of them knew was doomed to die when he put the first signs of life in the womb of their oldest sister.

Yet, it was odd how Ninnuit did not conceive initially and had not, even until the time that Ishurti (as she was called so long ago in her youth) had received her first moon-blood and was consecrated in the ceremony of the Goddess.

Their mother saw a hint of the danger to come with what had been completed this day. Tefnut had sent her finest carpenters and stone builders south to the city of Per-Uto to build a palace and a temple for her second beloved daughter Ishurti, who had taken the name of the Goddess of the land named Ua-Zit. She left the childhood name of Ishurti in Erech and became Ua-Zit at her naming ceremony when she initially arrived in the city of Per-Uto for the first time.

Upon her arrival on the very first day, she delved right into her new identity to hide the pain that she experienced from leaving her mother and sisters in Erech. She knew her sister Innana had finally conceived four years later with Au-Set and Neb-Het.

Ua-Zit in that first ceremony after her moon-blood participated in the choosing of her first consort. She had never learned his name, not that it mattered much. She was then sent to Per-Uto to take up the Goddess representative role of Ua-Zit, soon after the conception of her daughter. The daughter that was born in the newly carved out temple in Per-Uto was named Astarte. She was a young mother of only twelve summers, at the time of her daughter's birth, for it seemed eons ago when all of this was new to her.

Her little twin nieces Au-Set and Neb-Het resembled her very much at their age, more so as if they came from her own womb, rather than that of Ninnuit. How odd does life shine from your own sibling in the possible guise of a past self.

Her Astarte was a prize from birth and was always eager to please and as a result, she was no trouble to raise. Astarte was always pliant, perhaps too pliant and eager, more like her younger sister Nemothi. They were not the traits of a leader. She had sons after

Astarte, four of them. All ruled over some district of this new land and served as consorts to women of the royal houses.

Chapter 12

Ua-Zit was greatly distracted over some of the customs of this land though. One of which she had been trying to curb or to cease completely. Nevertheless, she had found neither solid ground nor argument that would appease this motive to her people.

When a person died in this land, all who were close to that person participated in a bizarre ritual where those who loved them in a feast for this purpose in their honor consumed the deceased. The spouse would lovingly consume the heart of that person, while the children would eat the matter in the skull. The rest of the village would then ritually partake of different sections according to their import to that person and for their function in the village. They would literally take that person into them in this ancient ritual of honor to the dead.

Nekhebt and Ua-Zit found this tradition appalling and were not able to find a way to cease this macabre practice of their people. Every sanction they placed before the people had failed and the people continued this practice, to the dismay of their new ruler queens in secret. She was intensely thankful that they did not have to perform this on her oldest sister.

Ua-Zit and Nekhebt were sent to rule over this land since the leaders, who were sisters of their own fathers and the last of that line had died without issue. The thrones must be kept with the Goddess born in descent; however, there were no daughters of that line, only the sons of the two sisters who had passed on were left. The daughters of Erech had promised to union with the sons of the land of Kemet in order for them to rule to keep the blood of their family in the ruling house.

This land preserved the bloodline of their royal leaders. Thus, the marriages were only to those inside of the family to keep the blood of that line pure and unhampered with foreign blood. This was the first time in its known history that the family had to look outside of it, since no one worthy could be found in their own land to pass down the royal bloodline.

Recently an illness passed through Kemet, which had killed off most of the women and had left the surviving women of childbearing age sterile. Some believed that it was from the blight, which was found in the grain that had been tainted in the rare rains that swept through the villages along the Great River that year. Rain was sometimes not seen for years even, and it was rare that Kemet experienced non-stop rain for over eight days. This left the uncovered grain open to the elements, which brought in the disease. Some of the people went mad in the consumption of it, those that survived. The children born to the diseased pregnant women were malformed, grotesque, and slowed of wit. It was almost as if the Gods were punishing them, so great was the terror inflicted upon the people of Kemet after the rains.

Therefore, the people of Kemet had no choice but to look towards Eshnunna. They knew that daughters were born to the sons they sent away to the temple. They had sent delegates to Tefnut and appealed to her with the telling of their tragedy. The delegates pleaded with Tefnut and begged her to send her two young daughters to save Kemet. Tefnut assented, however insisted that it would occur after the moon-blood ceremony of each of them and only after, they had fulfilled their first duty to the Goddess. They agreed and thus, Kemet had two new queens for their land and their sons, which brought order back to Kemet, and hope for a future they thought lost.

Chapter 13

Ishurti who had arrived to take the cobra-iaret's secret name of Ua-Zit had no choice but to lay with the son of the prior Ua-Zit named Hetep. Hetep was mute from the illness and was a very solitary figure in all the time that she had known him. There was no other name for the women as each daughter chosen to serve Ua-Zit in her name was given that name to show their predestination and birth intention. Ua-Zit had to receive the name in a new ceremony created for the anomaly of the situation.

Her son and the new Ua-Zit's consort was named *Hetep* which meant that he was a "God who gave offerings" in their language. That he certainly did to the young princess once named Ishurti. He adoringly picked all of the wildflowers from the surrounding fields clean in admiration of her when they initially met years ago. He felt that she was beautifully alien to that land's grace with her fair skin and dark lustrous hair. Hetep bowed to each word that she uttered and welcomed her by teaching her with the help of a tutor, the language of her new home.

Hetep accepted her Astarte as his own, loved her, and doted on her until she was sent away.

Ua-Zit dreaded the day they came for the temple born daughter, Astarte and took her away from her wailing grasp. So unseemly in her duty and loss of composure, though she did not care and could not help it. She knew that daughter would not be hers to cherish since she had belonged to the temple from where she was conceived. This land had agreed to the terms of Erech before her marriage with Hetep.

Therefore, the princess Astarte was taken from her when she was only three summers old. Ua-Zit recalled vividly those three summers and burned them deeply into her memory. Soon after, she had conceived again, and the new land, which she had grown fond of, raptured in joy for a new daughter to be born to them.

They had a famine that year when the Great River left them empty. Thus, they cried when that daughter was born dead to add to all of the other dead princesses of that land. A land without daughters, they lamented and wondered what they had done to create this emptiness, the destruction of their own fertility when they had to accept the blood of strangers to bring them daughters. Nevertheless, even foreign daughters were not able to help much initially.

Thus, it continued, four more daughters were born to the house of Ua-Zit that were dead and the two sons grew strong. No one knew the cause of this great calamity. Her sons were healthy in appearance, but seemed rather odd to her, she could not quite figure out what it was. Something was off.

The same occurred with her sister in the upper part of this land, only each of her seven children was born dead.

Yet, the ritual cannibalism continued. Both Nekhebt and Ua-Zit were forced to consume ritually each of their own dead children in ceremony in ancient accordance to the dictates of their new land. What came from them went back into them literally.

With each bite of the flesh of her daughters, Ua-Zit tried desperately not to vomit for it would be a great insult to the people of Kemet. This ritual was ancient and had to be carried out for the people-if would be a grievous as she and her sister were so new in their rule to Kemet. It would be a grievous mistake to show such dishonor at the very beginning of their rule. Their customs dictated her doing this as each of the Goddess representatives and anyone else had at some point in their lives in Kemet. They held their breaths with each tiny bite that she took back into her, while her consort did the same.

The flesh was cooked and spiced to disguise the natural disgust to make it easier for their ritual duty. Ua-Zit knew that after her grief had abated somewhat, she would have to do something about this custom. She had tried in fact to end it earlier, though to no avail. She was too new in this land and in her reign to change something that had been sacred to them since the beginning of their history.

Nekhebt, her sister, kept wisps of hair from each of her lost babies, which she wore braided and attached to her garments close to her heart. All of the strands of each of her babies were now blended into one strand of her heart that had failed forever again to beat with feeling. The strands of her defeat, as she uttered one day in confidence to her sister Ua-Zit, who understood the loss of a child in her own soul.

Her two sons grew strong and with it her sorrow at the loss of her first-born and only surviving daughter and of her dead daughters which remained with her literally in body as well her heart. Her sons were named Hetep for their father and *Nebmaat,* which meant that he was a man of the law and language of her new land. Ua-Zit vowed that she would raise Nebmaat as the most moral and upright man in Kemet. She would make sure Nebmaat would uphold the new laws her family would soon implement in this land to bring about a more powerful order that it so desperately needed. Her other two sons no longer cared for her and wanted no part of the rule; they simply went on with their lives content as farmers. They were named Jedneth and Sut.

Chapter 14

After many evenings of travel, at last they reached their new destination of her city called Per-Uto. Per-Uto was the main and central city of the homeland of her people called the Iaret in honor of the serpent cobra that they worshipped.

This was the moment when the little ones would part from each other for the first time in their lives. Ua-Zit would let them all spend a week together in her palace before they were to be separated and Nekhebt was to take Suti, Heru and Neb-Het to her city in Nekhen in the upper part of Kemet. The other three would remain her own charges to raise as her own until they were old enough to rule Kemet on their own.

In the tradition of Kemet and for their family's future, the siblings would union to give the land new daughters, which seemed to birth only dead ones. The people of upper Kemet were called "the Shen People." The ruler Nekhebt would carry the sign of the shen, which was of a hawk for eternity.

Chapter 15

On a bright and sun dappled morning, Au-Set and her siblings first lay eyes on this new land which they would someday rule over to serve better the Goddess and her people.

Au-Set knew from her lessons that the Goddess was one and that she came to peoples of different lands under many names, but she was in essence the same form. Therefore, the Goddess was the same for the most part, whether she was called Innana, Ua-Zit, Nekhebt, or Astarte. The average person however was not as learned as the children were who were born in the temple and needed the symbolism to understand the vast complexities of the universe. They found it easier to relate to her power if the Goddesses were separate and localized for easier comprehension.

She was further told that the Goddess could separate in entity to serve her people and to become more than one over each part of the known world. This was all very complex although Au-Set and her siblings endured many years of tutoring to understand it all better.

Au-Set was amazed at how different these people looked from her own in Eshnunna. She and her siblings towered over most of the adults in this strange land and had skin of a much softer consistency. These people had shorter heads with large lustrous lips and had startlingly olive skin with thick hair of the most midnight of black in color, which made hers appear the darkest of browns, which resembled the color of a chestnut shell. She noticed that her family had longer heads than the people of Kemet did. She had their blood, but the blood of Eshnunna and of the Catal-Huyuk in her veins seemed to dominate theirs in her own appearance. She did inherit the large full lips the people native to Kemet. She, her siblings, and even her aunts had oval faces, while the people of the Iaret and Shen had square and broad faces, though beautiful and shining with an innocent hope for their future. Their limbs were shorter, broader and seemed to have much more strength than her family. She and her siblings had long graceful legs that made them tower over the people of this land, even in their youth.

The clothes of most of the people of the Iaret and Shen were made of a fine linen though plain and without adornment or color. The linen was woven with extreme care and allowed the sun and heat to breathe through acting as a sort of coolant to the wearer. The style seemed simple, yet she knew that it was probably untouched from the earliest days of one of the oldest of tribes in their known world.

Some attendants here had the blackest of skin in which their eyes appeared to glow. These people were taller than her family. She was told that these people were of the far southern tribes and were the most ancient of peoples. They were as black as ebony and tall and graceful. The women wore their hair very short like the men. They stood tall, proud, as these people were the most revered of warriors of the land, and hired themselves out to the people of Kemet. They wore kilts of which she had learned belonged to the leopard and lion, which were great and fearsome cats of this land. The cats teamed about in the wilderness and were larger than a grown man was. The royal family hunted them for sport and valor, though they were in reality protecting the people of Kemet from the monstrous cats that walked the land.

Au-Set sat beside her aunt Ua-Zit, with her brother to the left of her. Her beloved Tehuti sat to the right of their aunt. They were on a cart carried by donkeys as in Eshnunna. They at last entered the mud-brick walls that surrounded her new home and city of Per-Uto.

The sun beat down on them all in a passionate zeal. The attendants in the cart with them beat off the swarming insects that fought for hold upon the new royal siblings of their land. Au-Sar sat regally nodding at the people who crowded the streets before them. Tehuti sat transfixed upon their new home and mute from the emotions that passed through his young and impressionable mind.

All Au-Set could think of was returning home and soon. She wanted to be with her mother back in her normal life, back to when things were predictable and simple. She hated the fact that her other siblings would soon be leaving her and she would have to take on someday soon, the role of the Goddess. She felt like only a little girl who had lost her mother. She did not want the role of Goddess. Au-Set did not want the role that would be passed down to her if anything should happen to her aunt. Why could it not be normal and she could be in the temple to rule Erech beside her mother? Why did she have to be the one whose life would be jarred from the normality of all that her family had known from when time began and they arrived several generations before to Erech? Why did all of this have to occur in her generation? Deep inside of her, she knew that her life would never be normal again.

The princess and Goddess initiate from the house of Innana feared the momentous wheel of time and the inevitable vast change that would occur to all that she had known and thought was solid. The world was on the waters of a rough and torrential storm that would place them wherever it felt and at its own mercy.

She missed dreadfully her wonderful streets of Erech, its magnificent stone buildings, and many palaces with over flowing gardens that seemed to touch the heavens themselves. Colors were vivid and everywhere in her homeland; they fought in competition wherever one looked from painted buildings to the natural foliage.

The land before Au-Set appeared crude and ugly. All around her was dark and brown without any color as it surrounded her bleakly with each step she took further into this land. The people spoke in a language that she could not understand and it made her feel lonelier than she thought possible.

She would have to union her own half brother Au-Sar, that thought made her giggle with the very thought of it. Imagine, her own brother as consort! That would never have happened back home. Back home... she thought longingly.

She dreaded the day when she would be ripped apart from her other siblings and her beloved twin and shadow, Neb-Het. Au-Set knew that it would surely kill her! Maybe at night, she should gather all of them, sneak out of this dreadful city, and run back to the pleated skirts of their mother.

Were not she and her own sister, Neb-Het, all the more sacred since they were not only the first-born, but twins of her mother's very first moon-blood! Whatever did that mean? Surely, it meant new life, not the destruction of all that they had ever known or would ever know under the love of their mother. Why were they wrenched away from all they had ever known so suddenly?

She writhed in her seat trying hard to look at the woman that she will someday become and felt instead, only like a silly and sad little girl who had recently been ripped away from her mother. She looked at her aunt who truly loved her, her new land, and the people who paid homage to her and then to her little brother Au-Sar. That same Au-Sar, who was trying inconspicuously to pick his nose, right in front of them all as if he was not learned of any manners! In shock, she pinched him and he kicked her back. Tehuti giggled and their aunt stared strongly at all of them with a look that their own mother had often given them in ceremonies. This infamous glare would silently order them all to behave with every cell in their bodies.

This must be a look from the Goddess, and existed in every woman. She recalled that in the temple back in Erech, when she was at play with the other children, when the mother priestess would enter the room; that same look would appear on her face as that of her aunt at this moment. A look made the Goddess pass to the human forms of the mothers to make sure that her children would behave without saying one word of reproach. The look was definitely enough on its own since it was as primal as it was powerful! Au-Set missed that very look from her own mother. She missed sharing a bed with her mother when she was not in service of the Goddess. She and her siblings had shared her mother's bed since birth and had rarely left the side of their mother, except for now!

Oh, how those dreadful mud walls seemed to loom over her and to stop her thoughts of the past dead in its tracks. Foreboding softly whispered to her of the doom that she felt lay ahead of her. She had to grow up and face what lay ahead of her.

Her aunts informed her and her siblings that they had one week to spend with each other before they had to live the lives chosen for them by the Goddess and their mother.

They understood from birth the meaning of duty. All of the children of Ninnuit were the results of duty and duty was what kept them alive in this chaotic world. Duty kept the world and life from owning them. It made them a part of this world that was large and filled with wonder. One was born to a duty to fill them with the quality of life and to keep them from the endless void of just "living" life. Duty gave them a meaning and purpose. This sense of duty was breathed into her and whole family since the moment of their birth.

She was growing fond of her aunt Ua-Zit, for she was as full of wisdom as her mother was. Au-Set hated to think of her mother in the past pretext since the youth of her age and innocence of life would not allow it. She was rebellious against moving onto the next path of life and fought secretly inside herself against the thing that often pushed against her soul...the wretched words and life of duty! She loved it as much as fervently hated it and all it entailed. The duality of life baffled her sometimes.

Chapter 16

Neb-Het and she would wander around the palace grounds in search of something that they would call their own but everything they saw was so alien, they often pretended that it was all a dream so that they would perhaps protect themselves from the reality of what had so recently occurred to them. She and her twin both made a pact that they would never forget where they came from no matter what foreign duty they were called to perform for their Goddess in this strange new land. This land that was so devoid of color of any kind. It almost seemed as if the vast desert that surrounded them wanted to swallow them up completely.

The people of Kemet did not see this irony and just lived their simple lives devoid of color, like the walls made of dried mud and papyrus that surrounded them at every turn. Both of the princesses and Goddess born longed for some color and music and culture, anything from the land left behind. However, sometimes wondered to each other if that ever happened it might make their reality all too apparent, since none of this could be shared with their own mother and soon they must all part from each other in two separate groups.

The two princesses along with their brothers and brothers-betrothed were tutored in the new language that their mother's advisor Ma-At had created and learned. This was a new picture language and would later be called *"medu-necher,"* which consisted of beautiful symbols and colors. Ma-At and Tehuti labored over filling this stark new colorless land with beauty, color and vibrant life with the new language and writing created especially for Kemet. Ma-At told the children and their aunts that Innana and Ninnuit wanted to make sure that they understood their duty to the Goddess in her many names. They were all in this strange new place to give the people some common good to live for and to create new art and poetry for them to find further joy out of life. She assured the royal women and children that they were in the perfect position for this change to occur and to be accepted by the people of Kemet.

The landscape in this country was fresh and as blank as a newly dried clay tablet left open for their words that would give the people here a new hope for their very beings.

Chapter 17

When they arrived, Nekhebt and Ua-Zit began to see the land they ruled over as something new. They saw it as a stark new tablet of clay, perfectly wanting a new creation for the old ways of this land to press into, molding a new culture.

The people since the beginning had always been anglers who wove wondrous baskets from the tall papyrus that grew in numerous armies along the banks of this never-ending Great River. They lived along the shores and risked the attacks of the crocodile or hippopotamus who hunted along the banks as well.

They were afraid of the many forces of nature in its untamed danger and harsh beauty. They avoided the endless sands of the desert to bury their dead there. They called the endless surrounding miles of inhospitable desert the land of the dead while the living belonged on the banks where the river provided nourishment and cleanliness.

In the delta region of Per-Uto villages of huts teamed along the banks raised on stilts so as not to drown with each yearly inundation of the Great River. They had learned to predict the rising waters each year with the appearance of a star that never failed to shine brightly just prior to the river overflowing its banks in which would follow the black soil that their land was named.

Yet, the people of the land had not found the need for agriculture since the river in its natural abundance provided all that they required. The population was small and what they did not find along the shores in nourishment, they either caught in nets or hunted for.

They were happy and content with their lives and lived this way since the first people arrived on the banks of the Great River before time was remembered. They believed that they were truly created from the rich clay of the river by the Gods.

Yet, the daughters of their rulers could not gain a foothold on life long enough to provide them with the time-honored matriarchal rule from the Goddesses Ua-

Zit and Nekhebt. They knew that something had to change, but they had no idea how large that change had to be in order to ensure their own survival.

Chapter 18

In the generation before the arrival of Ishurti, who later became Ua-Zit, they had noticed that something must be done that was completely different from their traditions of endless generations prior. It was Hetep and his mother Ua-Zit, the sister of Tefnut's consort Shu. Another brother of Shu was the father of Ishurti. It was Ishurti's consort Hetep and his mother, Ua-Zit who had decided to leave the seclusion of their simple paradise and to break past the deltas at the bottom of their world to seek aid for their dilemma.

They silently elated on the completely new world that they found. They had crossed the great desert to their west in their upside down world based on the flow of the river. They ended up in the far-away land of Eshnunna.

Once they were in the land of Eshnunna, Hetep told the woman in rule that he and his mother had found a grand world in which they had realized that Kemet was so inconsequential. He further informed them that they wanted to be a grander part in all of this. They observed that Eshnunna was filled with wonders they had never seen before. The tall buildings made of stone and brick that seemed to touch the sky were beyond all of their dreams and the most amazing thing they had ever seen. Those same buildings seemed to glisten and sparkle to their further delight as the rays of the soft sun tickled them.

In their homeland of Kemet, there were many villages with houses made of papyrus matted and pasted with mud from the river. Never before had they seen bricks made of mud to create walls grander than they had ever seen.

To add to their illusion of such a heavenly place, were the many gardens that cascaded from all of the buildings that painted the city a stark riot of color grabbing at them as they walked by in wonder. The exotic fruits and flowers hung down lazily from the walls, buildings and temples and surrounding palaces assailing their senses.

They never in their lives had ever seen so many people living in one place. A vast conglomeration of diversity, each person fighting for individuality, appeared almost the same to the inexperienced eye. Homes were built on top of each other and were connected in a maze that assaulted the eyes in confusion. Ladders that reached the top of the dwellings from the pathways below only reached the living quarters of people. The complexities dazzled young Hetep and his mother. Each palace held populations larger than any village of their land that was filled with such a riot of loud and euphonious people. Yet each of these people spoke a common language that was understood by those around them. This urban life seemed foreign to the young man and his mother.

They also noticed in this strange land the unfamiliar concept of symbols that were drawn everywhere that seemed to convey something to the people. He noticed that the symbols were simple, a series of jagged lines that connected like a mad spider web. When they inquired of some inscriptions that were carved on the facades of the temples and even some of the houses, it was explained to them that it was called "writing" and the symbols were what words looked like when not spoken from the mouth. The average person was not able to decipher the words and that one had to be chosen by the Goddess for that ability and rained in the temple.

The temple had a sacred form of the writing that was more difficult to decipher than the common tongue of the people. Guides told them that the Goddess *Nidaba* was the founder of writing and the city of Erech contained the oldest writing of their land of Eshnunna. This ancient writing could be found and studied at the temple of Innana, the Queen of Heaven. A school for women scribes and the children of the royal family was founded there as well. Only the sons of a high priestess could learn this most sacred form of writing of the priestesses. Naturally, any woman could learn this too if they were training to be priestesses.

Ua-Zit soaked up the knowledge of the concept of writing and of how lucrative it was. That it would account for large concepts that could be repeated when read at any time, without missing one word. Large amounts can be recorded for future reference. The potential of this was astounding to Ua-Zit.

Their own people of Kemet had always relied on memory and the oral recitation of their past chronicles and history. So far, they had not required this to be used with trade, since it was in very small amounts and easily memorized. Yet, Ua-Zit hoped to open the future in a grand prospect for her people.

Ua-Zit and her son had plans for the future of their people and saw a grander vision. She had found the family of Innana and had questioned her at great length and stayed for two years along with her son to find a way to create a culture for her own people that was different, but incorporated the main elements such as writing, agriculture, education, and the building of large cities and temples. They had also hoped to reorganize the religion of the land to something uniform and not so complex and localized as it was currently.

Her sister Nekhebt closely guarded their land on this visit and eagerly yearned for her return and plans. They always worked together, as the other generations of Ua-Zits and Nekhebts since the beginning of memory.

The people of Kemet were similar to the earlier peoples of Eshnunna in that they all had separate deities and each city or village in her case lived under its own rules, until one day with the arrival of the family of the ancestors of Tefnut and of Innana to this land that they visited. Innana was a newer version of the local Goddess *Nina* for the city of Erech. The qualities of the two Goddesses were so similar that it was barely noticed, until gradually the Goddess Nina was forgotten. With the arrival of the *Tawannanas* of the Hatti peoples, the great unification of Eshnunna had begun. The main city of this new and unified land was called Erech with the sister city of Uruk nearby. Ua-Zit had found Tefnut in this city.

Tefnut, under the words of Innana, had told her the beginnings of the city of Erech, later to be called Ur in generations to come. The stories of Erech and Eshnunna had flowed out of her mouth and were absorbed willingly as if the nectar of the Gods by Hetep and his mother. They told of the great unification that had led to the land that it became as it was in that visit, that flourished under the prosperous and bountiful ways of the Goddess and her love for her people to live in culture and for them to be surrounded by beauty and art.

Ua-Zit had told her son that she wanted the same for her people when they returned and had even arranged for Tefnut to send her younger daughters as brides for her sons. The daughters of Tefnut had the blood of Kemet in their veins as strong as that of this land. Tefnut had agreed and had seen the advent of how her own land was dying by the anger of the new men to this land. She had secretly warned her daughter and heir Ninnuit of this. Mother, daughter found Ma-At, and Neferet to implement this in the most advantageous way for all of her daughters and granddaughters. Ninnuit had only hastened the actual implementation of the plans by necessity due to the increase in the number of attacks on Eshnunna and the ways of the Goddess.

Fate seemed to arrange for the transference of power from the daughters of the Great River to the daughters born in the land of Eshnunna in its apex of glory and before the final downfall with normal acts of nature. It came in the form of a disease that seemed to take away all of the daughters of the Great River which turned sour and stole with it all of the hopes of the future fruition of the land with old pure blood.

Tefnut and her daughter Ninnuit began to work diligently with Ua-Zit to create a new land that would welcome the Goddess. Hetep's future bride, Ishurti rose up to take over the lead of the prior Ua-Zit. Both had something, the other desperately needed as time wore on. Tefnut and Ninnuit needed a place for the children of their womb along with the Goddess-born and priestesses of the temple, to live and to be able to carry

on their line. It had been realized that their world was
being taken away piece by piece as the years wore on.
They were seeing that there was no possible hope for a
resurrection of the Goddess ways. A new dawn was
approaching for the people of Eshnunna and she wanted
to save as many as she could from this.

Ua-Zit and Hetep understood this and yearned for
trustful blood to carry on their own lineage and to
continue their rule over their land of Kemet. The rulers
debated the best way possible to ensure the rule of both
lands and decided that the most favorable place for this
would be in the faraway and obscure lands of Kemet.

Thus, the events occurred that had led to that
fateful day in Erech when the children of Innana and
Ninnuit had gathered under the palace in Per-Uto of
their aunt Ua-Zit to plan their future and that of Kemet.
One of the things they would start with would be the
unification of the Upper and Lower Kemet along with all
the smaller villages and deities.

Chapter 19

Both sisters, Au-Set and Neb-Het were learning this week under constant relentless waves of instruction of the new structure of Kemet and of their role in it. They both confided to each other in the darkest hours of the night while they slept on mats on top of the dour buildings made of mud and straw weave. How inconsequential they both felt in the great scheme of life. Both also knew that they would soon play a great and valuable part of the land new before them on which of their lives were swiftly being woven out in some dramatic act by the Goddess.

They whispered long into the evening hours while their siblings slumbered around them on their soft cushions in this land that feared the rain that hardly ever made an appearance.

"Sister...." whispered Neb-Het.

"Yes." Responded Au-Set who turned over to hear her younger sister and womb-mate.

"Will we ever see each other after this, when we have to leave?"

"Of course we will, I will make sure of it."

"I do not want to union with Suti! He stinks and he is still a baby!" At this, the sisters giggled in sibling bliss.

"He farts all of the time and is always red when he is mad!" Au-Set added.

"Why does he have red hair sister? He does not look like any of us at all."

"Does it really matter Neb-Het, he came from the same womb as each of us, for he is Goddess-born!"

"Aye that he is." Moreover, the matter was closed and finally both sisters gracefully succumbed to slumber from the long days of tutoring that they had endured thus far.

Chapter 20

The children were learning the ceremony created by Ma-At for this new land to awe the people in their awakening. They were creating the most spectacular ceremony ever seen in this land. The sacred unions of Au-Set to Au-Sar and of Neb-Het to Suti were to be splendid. They were the new life and hope of Kemet and a further strength in the unification. Siblings were always required in rule for both Upper and Lower Kemet to ensure peace. Sometimes it did not always work to their advantage, since sometimes the worst enemies could actually be siblings. Nevertheless, the last several generations of siblings were actually peaceful.

Au-Set and Neb-Het did not know the details of this ceremony, but soon after this sacred union, they were to take on two other husbands or consorts from this land to ensure the blood of Kemet were again linked to this land. One year and a day after the ceremony, linking the two newcomers to the land Hetep had planned for the princesses to be married to his own sons to solidify their blood link even further. Au-Set would marry his younger son Nebmaat and Neb-Het would marry his older son and namesake Hetep. He agreed with his queen that the children had too much trauma in their lives to endure another ceremony too soon after, so the time was set up for the girls to adjust to their life in Kemet. Hetep did not really care when they were told as long as his blood was carried on.

At the end of the week at the first ray of dawn, after a whole evening of ritualistic preparation the children of Ninnuit awaited their cue. The Nugig Ma-At carefully recorded this ceremony for future proceedings in the new form of writing with Tehuti in scribal training by her side.

Neferet prepared the princesses for their sacred union to their half brothers. Au-Set wore a gown made painstakingly of cobra or iaret skins that were kept in the temple for the deity of Lower Kemet. The shed skins of sacred snakes have always been carefully collected for ceremonial use over countless generations.

Elaborately made snakes homes were always kept under the Goddess temples for the snake had always been a sacred symbol. The homes of the snakes were most often made of clay with holes for them to crawl in and out. They resembled large cones and some could be quite intricate with several of them interconnected. Clay snakes were always carved on them resembling the live occupants. The iaret was especially sacred to the Goddess Ua-Zit.

On Au-Set's head was a crown or uraeus that resembled a golden cobra coiled around the top of her brow, with its hood spread in wisdom from the center of her brow. Under her floor length gown, she wore she softest linen found in her land. It was so delicate and soft that it matched the fragile river breeze that gathered around them and seemed to sing lullabies in the whispering melody. She could feel the powers of the Goddess of this land with each barefooted and dainty step that she took. The breeze that collected in the white linen seemed ethereal as it enfolded through her form. Maidens worked long into the evening before she was dressed in the otherworldly under-gown, her body was intricately tattooed in henna patterns of the new language they were incorporating in this new land. The temporary henna tattoos would be made permanent after the ceremony. Her over-gown was of the woven iaret skins that was carefully sewn with bone awls to produce a shorter version of the ethereal linen underneath and only went to her knees, causing the flowing undergarment to sway with the wind, while her figure in the snake skins stayed rigidly sublime and regal.

She had silver iarets running up her arms and her ankles were adorned with delicate silver anklets with whimsical bells that sang when she walked. In her nose, she had pierced a smaller version of the hooped iarets that were also in each ear. Silver had become the chosen metal of the Goddess Ua-Zit, since a mine of this was recently discovered and it had a limited supply. Ua-Zit had all of her jewelry made of this and would not allow it outside of her keeping, so rare a find it was. Au-Set felt honored that her aunt would allow her to have jewelry made from her most treasured mine.

On her fingers, she wore no rings, for it was becoming a symbol of restraint since the men of the northern tribes would capture the women of the Goddess. Those men would capture the women and cruelly pierce a rope through the women's ankles so that they would not escape. As the women became more docile, the rope was cut and a smaller reminder rope was placed on her finger of what would happen if they tried to escape.

Neb-Het was donned in golden robes in contrast to her sister. Nekhebt insisted on this, for this was her chosen metal. She would not switch to the new silver metal found, for she deeply honored tradition. She, also had the soft linen under garment, but had an over garment made to resemble the wings of a hawk on a heavier over-garment that was carefully painted in gold. This was the symbol of Upper Kemet and it was reflected in the golden jewelry that she wore. Her earrings were golden miniature wings. Her necklace was of outstretched wings that covered her shoulders. On her arms, she had coiled golden snakes in reverence of the Goddess climbing up her arms. Her ankles glittered in gold and sparkled in the unrelenting sun that climbed above them. She had a crown on her head made of real hawk wings that were sheeted in gold and enclosed around her brow. Her garment required the assistance of her other siblings as she walked to the ceremony.

This sacred ceremony was held outdoors on the roof of their palace for all of the population to witness. They had a large canopy stretched out over their heads to protect them from the dangerous rays of the sun.

Au-Set knew that her days as a child were ending and that she must learn to be a woman. The child in her wished and prayed fervently for the return of their mother and that this would all be deemed a play and nothing more.

Tehuti and Heru walked beside them and she and her sister were presented to their new consorts, Au-Sar and Suti with the bright red flaming hair.

Yet, the tiny feet of Au-Set trod gracefully towards her future and duty. Each step that she and her sister took further punctuated the solidly emanating form of their destiny.

At last, they reached the sides of Au-Sar and Suti. Au-Set was beside Au-Sar and Neb-Het beside Suti. Au-Sar and Suti were dressed in floor-length kilts made of the infamous purple color of Tyre to express their spirituality and their royal lineage. Their chests were bare to the elements. The light brown hair of Au-Sar was long and braided into tiny plaits that were adorned with tiny silver beads. The uraeus that he wore around his brow resembled that of Au-Set as the iaret of Lower Kemet. On his neck, he had an intricately carved silver snake that met at the center of his neck, under his chin. Long silver snakes coiled up his arms and his feet were bare.

Suti, in contrast to Au-Sar, had the golden snakes like Neb-Het's, coiled up his arm. He was dressed like Neb-Het since he was to be her consort and ruler over Upper Kemet. He had his golden crown of painted hawk wings over his brow and a robe of made similar to the over-garment worn by his sister of painted hawk wings. He and his brothers wore the long stiff linen kilts of the adult men of this land, which looked awkward, as they were only children.

The two couples of the sacred union looked glorious to the people who had never witnessed anything as glamorous as this ever before. They glowed like the Gods and all of the people bowed down in wonder of their beauty.

The siblings looked onto the crowd underneath the palace, when suddenly the music commenced. Slowly enfolding all of them were the dancing sounds of reed flutes, silver horns, pig skinned drums, bells and other such instruments. The music was soft at first and then picked up in a feverish pitch as the ceremony had reached the point of crescendo.

The people had seen Goddess ceremonies before, but always the men played minor roles. It was odd to the people that the male and female royal children were given equal stance in the eyes of their familiar Goddesses of their land. The people below were fixated on the holy priestess and Goddess representatives Ua-Zit and Nekhebt as they uttered in unison that the children would be their heirs *equally* under the eyes of the Goddess. This section was added in as a part of their plans in the temple of Eshur.

The queens had felt it wise that equal measure was given to the males in rule, so that they would not be so vulnerable to the power struggle that had taken away their birth-land of Eshnunna. The sisters had hoped that this would work in the new and pliable land of Kemet. They realized that it would cause a stir and it would be difficult to implement due to countless generations of women being in charge. All that the people of Kemet had ever known was about to change in order to protect the Goddess ways for the battle that would soon reach their humble land of Kemet. Little did they know back then that it would also pave the way for Kemet to cease the full worship of the ancient Goddess ways forever.

The ceremony was changed a bit to make Au-Sar the equal of Au-Set and Neb-Het the equal of Suti in power. Au-Set added on the name of Ua-Zit before hers and Neb-Het had Nekhebt preceding her own name.

They all knew their parts by heart for this great ceremony that was a lesser variation of the Great Rite ceremony of the Goddess Innana. However, in contrast to the traditions of Eshnunna, they were in the land of Kemet to rule. The consorts would live out their lives in equal power with their Goddess representative siblings. Au-Sar and Suti inaudibly breathed a silent sigh of relief in this as the words of their aunts solidified this in ceremony to the people around them that gasped in awe and pleasure of the meaning. Never had men in their family let alone in the entire world that they had known, held such power equal to that of a Goddess representative. It was unnatural in the order of things

and all that they were used to knowing. The two prince
consorts were proud but had not yet grasped the
complexity of their power due to their youth and recent
trauma.

With the beat of the drums native to the land, the
young sisters took the hands of their brothers as chosen
by their mother. Au-Set took the hand of Au-Sar,
brought it to her lips, and kissed it in joy. He turned to
her and kissed her forehead. Neb-Het and Suti only
looked at them and then each other quizzically. Suti was
still very young and considered a baby by all of them.
Neb-Het struggled to suppress a giggle at her union with
her baby brother who was barely tall enough to reach
her waist. He still had chubby baby legs. He sensed her
emotions and pinched her, at which Neb-Het had again
struggled to suppress and squeal in reaction. She knew
her duty and that her appearance had to be adult for
this ceremony.

Ua-Zit approached the dais as Au-Set, Au-Sar,
Neb-Het and Suti were led to their bedchambers. Since
this had occurred in her Per-Uto, she was the host of
the ceremony.

"People of this land, I offer for you your children
for the future fertility of this land. Ua-Zit Au-Set,
Nekhebt Neb-Het, Suti and Au-Sar are of this land as
well and share our blood. Their own grandfather was the
Great Deified Shu of this land. He was the brother of the
late Ua-Zit and Nekhebt, and the father of these
children's mother from the land of Eshnunna to the east
of the Great two Rivers. He brings this gift for us to
carry on our line and to give fruition and hope to us all.

"From this day on my sister and I will rule side by
side to further unify this land. We will meet together to
discuss the policy of this land in its reformations in
order to ensure our future. Per-Uto and Nekhen to the
north will be our home bases as have been established
in time before time.

"Together and for all of you we will create a new
land of prosperity and wealth. We will build tall cities,
learn new trades, and grow great crops for which we will
trade with other nations.

"These children are our future and they will give us hope and a reason to bring greatness to our land!"

The people around the palace exploded with applause and weeping for they so desperately wanted something new and saw their future in the young children's eyes.

After the ceremony and following celebration, the siblings were placed in their bedchambers. They had to get used to sleeping together for comfort and strength. They all knew that when they were old enough they would be expected to produce heirs to the land with the absolute purity of their unblemished blood. The act was no secret, since it was not hidden nor deemed wrong in any aspect, yet they were still children and they only curled up in each other's arms in comfort. Suti whimpered into the long hours of the night since he missed the warmth still of their mother and Neb-Het was too small to even resemble her. Suti was still only four years old and felt ripped away from their mother and deeply resentful of Neb-Het for this.

They all knew that they could not unite in body with their chosen union mates until they all reached maturity. The sacred union was there for the ceremony and message to the people of what was about to take place in the land of Kemet.

The great aunts looked with pride at how the ceremony commenced without flaw or mishap and of the reception of the people to the oddities placed in carefully. They dreamed that evening of the unification and saw Au-Sar and Au-Set as the ones to lead Kemet. They fervently hoped that Neb-Het and Suti would grow to love each other and to work together as a team, yet cringed at the odd chemistry between them. They hoped that time would erase this. The aunts still wondered why Neb-Het was not allowed to have a sacred union with Tehuti. They could not even begin to fathom the mind of their oldest sister, Ninnuit and her insistence of this. Even Heru would have been a better choice. Yet, in respect for her wisdom, they implemented her wishes for her children.

Chapter 21

On the day subsequent to the ceremony, Neb-Het and her consort Suti along with their brother Heru left with their great aunt Nekhebt to their new city of Nekhen. They traveled on long barges that flowed against the wind in unison with the current, so they made swift progress as they reached their destination. Neb-Het hugged desperately the siblings that she left behind. It was the first time in her life that she had been separated from them and she felt numb with pain. Suti cried in the evenings, as did Heru. Nekhebt tried in vain to console them and sat mute with her new charges buried next to her in blankets to keep the chill of the evening air from them while they drifted down the Great River to their city called Nekhen. This city was almost to the far reaches of their backwards and upside down land.

When they arrived at the docks, Neb-Het tried to hide her dismay since it appeared much smaller and more ancient in a decrepit and neglected way than Per-Uto. The old and crumbling walls seemed to yawn with pain and isolation. The huts made of the uniform woven mats covered in a mud plaster, seemed of a lesser quality than those of Per-Uto and were scattered about haphazardly in a chaotic pattern of disregard. The homes nestled inside the walls of the temple were ageless and bleached white from the ceaseless sun from generations of cloudless skies.

Neb-Het's eyes scanned for some hint of color and found none but the stars in the sky above them as they approached their new home. The colors of the listless dawn did nothing to neither condone nor forgive the many years of neglect.

The people waiting for them were covered with flowers that in the unrelenting sun wilted from their patient wait of the royal entourage. The royal children bowed down to the people of Nekhen in respect and received their blessing from the people who wept with joy filled with an innocent hope for a bright new future.

Anything was better than the bleakness that the simple people of this land had been born with.

Nekhebt tried to console her new charges but failed dismally for she had not the heart left after the loss of her own children years ago. She had soon after their arrival, left her new charges in the care of her personal attendants and of their tutor who came with them by the name of Neferet. She retired to her own peaceful chambers and to her state of numbness that was familiar and was left behind for her to deal with the events in Erech.

In the evenings, she would climb to the roof of her ancient mud-walled temple and in her sleeping robes, would cry out in vain to the Goddess whom she represented on earth.

"Why Goddess? Why have you given me this great test for which I am so unworthy? I could not even bring life from my own womb, yet you send these children for me to comfort and to inherit from me. Why were my own not worthy? I beg of you to give me wings for which to fly away from this colorless land and to be alone and weep!

"My consort Nebmaat no longer wants me, my womb is empty and yet your moon blood still flows within me! Please Goddess give me wings so that I may leave this earth."

Therefore, she sang her laments in wistful anger and desperation to her Goddess who was mute to her pleas for nothing had changed. Her niece and nephews were still below in the palace sleeping the slumber of innocents. While they learned from their tutor dutifully of her families plans for the birth of this new land, she felt lifeless and had no strength herself.

She performed in ceremony as was her duty, but it was not truly her for her life spark had long left. Her eyes could not see the pain of her new charges and she cared not for she avoided them whenever she could.

The Nugig of Eshnunna, Neferet, tried in vain as well to comfort Neb-Het and her younger brothers. She gave up completely on Suti for he had grown out of her control and would scream at all who would approach him, so deep was his pain and isolation. She saw how the only solace that Suti had found was in his finding a small pack of abandoned wild boars. Suti had taken in two of the piglets for him to care for and let no one approach them at all.

Chapter 22

Suit's new found love for the animals had distracted him from the pain that he felt and the anger not understood in one so young at the abandonment of his mother and of his favorite brother Au-Sar. He shouted in rage at anyone who mentioned her name, his red hair often appeared brighter in those rages much to the amazement of all who found themselves in his path. He threw rocks and sticks at his older sister whenever she tried to console him. He truly felt in his heart that their mother was still alive and could not comprehend the significance of her death. He blamed her for leaving them to this ugly land.

He was angry that Au-Sar did not stop him or follow him. He never saw his older brother's tears at their departure, for they were held at bay under his sleeve.

Chapter 23

Neferet noticed how Heru was often found sleeping by the side of his older sister, as if she was his own mother. Neferet sadly knew that he was not allowed in their aunt's chambers, as were any of the other children. Nekhebt barred the doors from even her own consort.

They all found the coldness and loneliness of Nekhebt disturbing, but could do nothing about it all, since she was the Goddess of this land and beyond all reproach from lesser people, even her own charges.

Nebmaat the elder, had appealed to Neferet one evening for warmth and together almost with the unseeing approval of the Goddess, they shared their evenings together. It appeared to all that Nekhebt did not care, she even came in on them one evening when they were in the throes of passion and sat beside the bed. She nodded slightly at them and then as silently as she entered, she left the room.

Neferet was young and beautiful and had many requests for consorts, though she denied them all. Nebmaat, the elder, had appealed to her because he was familiar to her and she loved the experience of an older man. She was too busy with the demands of the children that had been placed into her hands, to train a young man to her command. She felt contented with Nebmaat and of his confident embraces of her in the chill evening hours. Content because now that she had the permission of the Goddess, Nekhebt.

Neferet watched the children grow mostly under her own wings, since those of the Goddess were tired and chose to be alone and away from the company of her charges. It seemed to Neferet that the Goddess Nekhebt was letting the future have hold and was giving her free reign of her charges to take over that which she had no heart left. She even gave Neferet her own consort freely.

Suti was growing more handsome and maniacal with each passing year. He was always surrounded with his trained wild boars that would attack on command, so that many people grew to fear the approach of Suti, even his sister. He also grew more reclusive with each ensuing year. He let his bright dazzling hair grow long and flow free down his back in wild unconcern. He walked around with his bizarre entourage of wild pigs with his head held high like a confident king. He even fashioned kilts from the skins of those of his pets that had died as if to emulate them or to become one in spirit. He wanted to keep them closer to him in soul and in literal body. Suti's chest was bare and starting to show the first signs of manhood.

Heru, on the other hand, was docile and pliant and took well to the new land and his role as advisor to his aunt and sister. He loved to swim and seemed to have an instinct to avoid the natural dangers of the river. The young prince had no fear of the large and ornery hippopotami and the crocodile, nor any other creature that lurked in the depths. He learned his lessons well and showed great aptitude in writing and of speaking the new language that was being taught to all of the people along the banks of the river. The new language still kept many words of their own tongue and mixed with the language of Kemet.

Neb-Het was growing into a great beauty with long flowing mahogany hair and a keen intelligence. Her wisdom was swiftly gaining ground from the silent chambers of Nekhebt, who seemed in contrast to give up on life. Nekhebt let the world happen with no input at all or reaction in any form.

Neferet would often meet with Neb-Het and Suti, who had to be dragged to their official functions. They had to learn their official functions and co-ruler-ship over the land that was slowly being reunited under the skilled guardianship of the family of Ninnuit.

Great temples were being built of stone to replace the ancient ones of mud weaving and poles that were slowly becoming a part of the river in time. Palaces were sprouting out of the soil as if by magic, so rapidly were they being built. They were learning to make bricks out of mud and a mixture of grass, from their homeland of Eshnunna. When completed, they, on the idea of Tehuti, became great canvases to paint the stories of their new theology. They imported artists from their known world to create paradises of color on the new walls and buildings that were far greater in height than the ones replaced.

More and more land was being drained and irrigated for fields that were slowly dotting the ever-expanding greenery on the sides of the Great River. The people rejoiced at the new prosperity of the land, for many were growing wealthy enough to build palaces in attempts to rival the Gods and Goddesses of the land.

Chapter 24

In stark contrast to Upper Kemet, in Lower Kemet all were settling into a life, which grew to make them better in person. Ua-Zit was wise and had her sons beside her who grew strong. She knew that the time was coming to send down her son Hetep to Neb-Het as consort and for her other son Nebmaat for her own niece Au-Set.

Ua-Zit watched her own charges grow and was pleased with whom they were fast growing up to be. Au-Set and Au-Sar were growing fond of each other, which she knew would make the Great Rite easier for them to perform with the love they had for each other.

Tehuti was becoming more advanced in the new picture writing than its own creator Ma-At was. The writing of Eshnunna was simple and in the form of markings that were uniform and unimaginative as lines and grooves marked in clay. Tehuti was creating more elaborate symbols than her own simple ones, which made a lot of sense when applied. His writing skills soon surpassed all that she had known or created herself, it was obvious to all that he would be the one recognized for the "*Medu necher*" of Kemet. Ma-At stood aside for this, as was her duty. Tehuti even thought of setting up a school to teach the people of their land this new picture writing. Ma-At was greatly pleased with this and put all of her spare time in helping the prince to create his dream and to make it a reality.

Ua-Zit realized that her blood rang true in the princess Au-Set for her figure was growing tall and proud and her mind was very sharp. Her beauty would often overwhelm any room that she walked into. The young Goddess initiate, Au-Set had even grown fond of healing the sick of this new land. People had flowed to the temple for the miracle of her cures and her name was fast spreading up the delta to the Upper reaches of the land.

Because of this, Ua-Zit felt that it was time to bring her son as consort to the princess.

Au-Set woke up this morning and headed for her
favorite place, the temple sick house. Lately, many were
seeking out her cures in herbs and here she felt truly in
charge. She felt like an adult at the temple, unlike by
the doting side of her aunt. Only in the temple, did she
feel that she was not still under the control of her aunt,
whose name she had taken before her own in ceremony.
Yet, here in the sick house, she was truly in control. She
marveled at how her studying of the old ways of this
land and those she had brought with her from her birth-
land of Eshnunna, were being sought out by many.
When she added the ancient ways of her own land
together with the ways of Kemet and her own intuition,
she had healed many cases that they had doomed as
lost. It was almost as if her healing abilities were a direct
conduit from the powers of the Goddess herself.

　　　She brought new hope to mothers who were
thought on the threshold of death in difficult labors and
to infants who were also thought of as equally lost if not
more so. People marveled at her skills, and sought her
out everywhere and wrote down her advice on clay
tablets with the new writing that was being schooled
throughout the land by her brother Tehuti.

　　　She thought proudly of her brother Tehuti and all
that he had accomplished in the few short years of their
being in Kemet. He had created a new way of writing. All
writing prior had been done on awkward clay tablets
and were easily broken and difficult to transport. Large
storehouses had to be made for their storage. He had
looked in a direction never noticed before for this
dilemma. He usefully observed that all around them
were the tall grasses of the papyrus just sitting there
waving in the breeze. The only use thus far for them was
in the making of boats when bundled together and water
proofed.

　　　Tehuti discovered that when the nimble grass was
cut down and wet, they could be thinned out and woven
together to form a light pliant structure to write on after
they were beaten and flattened. This caused a sort of felt
from the beaten pulp, which meshed the single blades
together into one useful mass when dried. He gathered

many local villages to produce this in vast quantities for his experiments and from his diligence, almost perfected it.

Her brother also developed a shorter version of his writing that was not as elaborate as the sacred temple writing for normal temple functions and future trade. He created the shorter version to not only record symbolic meaning, but also phonetic as well for less repetition and smaller text. He wanted the special picture writing to be utilized for holy writing only initially, until his shorter version was perfected. He wanted his paint to last longer both on the temple walls and on the new papyrus. Therefore, he worked long hours into the night and often secluded himself in this task. He devoted almost every waking moment on perfecting his duty in bringing words to the people of Kemet for their viewing and beauty.

This creation of her brother's was soon being sought after from lands all around theirs, so uniform was it becoming in their own land after he deemed it suitable for teaching to others. Tehuti also fought valiantly to protect the secret of making this, to give his new land commerce and something to call their very own. This made them unique in this untamed world around them. Other lands started to take notice for the first time.

She was equally beaming over her other brother and consort Au-Sar. He had caught on to their duty in bringing agriculture to their land. He took her own idea and expanded on it as Tehuti did the ideas of Ma-At.

Au-Sar had revealed that he had incredible talents in agriculture and had absorbed all that she had taught him with relative ease and speed. From what she had learned from her mother, passed down from her family and that of her consort, Shu, Au-Sar absorbed it all and perfected it for their new land.

He had even devised a way to make clay waterproof pipes to bring water further into the desert, making more arable land in future inundation. He had inspired hundreds to collect the black soil deposited and to spread it further inland. He had also created a system of long poles that would move from the river to nearby to once arid fields with small buckets filled with water. The water could be scooped up and poured over to where and when it was needed. More farmland was appearing all around the Great River, giving them a much more bountiful harvest than ever dreamed of or seen before.

Artisans were arriving from other lands to find a new life in this raw and growing paradise. They brought with them talents in metallurgy and other cultural skills. The homes of the people of Kemet were filling with great works of art in silver, gold, and copper.

The palace in which they lived was soon filling with beautiful sculptures made of lapis lazuli, carnelian and malachite and other such stones. The precious stones even adorned the furniture upon which they dined and sat upon, as well as the walls that surrounded them. The stones were cut and inlayed on the walls in the beautiful mountain views of the many pastures of their homeland as well as some local harbor scenery. Every room opened new vistas of the artists' imaginations for those who lived there. The precious stones caught the sunlight that poured in through the carved archways of the chambers and glittered forth the surreal landscapes that would dance before them in the light of the oil lamps. The color was slowly birthed from the bland stark land of Kemet and danced around them in a cacophony of the tumultuous laughter of the new Gods who brought them to life.

With the talents and prosperity that was being brought to this land, they had more time for leisure and to perfect their trades until their land was being noticed for the first time by greedy kingdoms all around them. However, the people of Kemet were mostly unaware of this and lived in the solitude of their natural boundaries, oblivious to life beyond the Great River.

Prior to this, the people of Kemet were excluded from the rest of the world. All around them geography alone had prevented normal interaction from the rest of the world. Their boats were not strong enough to navigate beyond their Great River into the Sea beyond.

They were also surrounded by the fierce and endless deserts all around them.

Chapter 25

Au-Set reflected upon all of this as she left the sick house. Her love beamed out for her consort Au-Sar, who was busy this morning having risen with the sun. He left to instruct the men and women from a local village down the river who had sought him out specifically for his talents in irrigation. He was explaining to them some of her own ideas that he had modified, when she silently snuck up behind him. She had beamed in pride as she watched their admiration of her handsome consort.

She had noticed that though the ideas that he expressed were her own, he had added some interesting innovations that she had not heard of prior.

Au-Sar told the men before him, "So you see, the pipes must be carefully dried in the sun in halves and then coated inside with resin and pitch to make them waterproof when dried." The men nodded with the simplicity of this and wondered why something so evident had not been thought of before this instruction from one of their new leaders. They all secretly envied this bold young man before them with hair the color of the sun-captured sand. They rightfully admired him and patiently listened to all that they were taught.

There were four men rapt in the words of this prince before them. They were as old as his own father En was. Yet, they stood in avid attention, listening to the new ways in irrigation as taught to them by the fine young man who glistened in the sun, his bare feet planted naturally in the land that he grew to love. One would actually believe that he grew from the actual soil, so natural he appeared on lands of bounty.

Au-Sar was explaining to them his ideas on better irrigation.

The Great River rises from the time of the most dismal heat of the summer for another three moons until after the equinox. It was convenient for farmers since it covered the land with a very fertile silt of the black color, which gave the name to Kemet, or "the black lands." A farmer did not have to dig deep to plant life, for there was no fear of the seeds being washed away from rain.

Nevertheless, this left the farmers with a limited area since the Great River floods only covered a relatively small area on the banks of the river. Au-Sar implemented a system in which water was artificially brought out from the river to extend the area for their crops, which consisted of canals dug out or fabricated from the clay pipes.

In the delta where the people of the Iaret lived, the climate was mostly temperate all year round with very rare rainfall. However, over the rest of the Great River in the valley there were years before one ever saw so much as even one drop of rain.

The farmers had in the past generally only planted in the rich black mud as the water receded. Therefore, the people would only grow where the black soil actually reached. Au-Sar taught them how they could extend the area of crops by keeping the fields wet with a system of ditches, retaining ponds and *shadufs*, which was a counterweight pole arrangement for lifting pots full of water. The farmers who built levees between the areas of the fields controlled the shadufs. Floods were unpredictable and sometimes wiped out the smaller levees, so there was no point from building a big canal or levee systems. Natural flooding and simple systems were enough for the entire valley floor as irrigating outside the valley was impossible.

Au-Sar was even working on big canal systems for the area to expand it even more for farming. However, most of his attempts with the canals had failed to date since most of them had been washed away with each annual flooding. Au-Sar stood with the men trying to find a way to make a more permanent irrigation system that would not be washed away with the floods for the ones that he had created thus far were still rather new and flimsy.

Au-Set stood nearby and glowed with love and admiration for her consort. She had come to his side to tell him that it was time for them. She had recently completed the first year and a day after the commencement of her first moon-blood. When she had first-received it, she had performed the ceremony with her aunt that first night under the full moon and spread her first blood, carefully collected, over the kitchen gardens of their palace. This tradition was older than the Goddess was, she was told. This rite ensured the fertility of the land as women had in their wombs with the commencement of the moon-blood.

That morning, she had performed her duties with pride, knowing that her powers of healing were stronger than ever before, with her new connection to the Goddess. Her connection to the Goddess would grow even more powerful with the ceremony of the Great Rite that she knew must be done with Au-Sar and then the union would be sacred in body as well as name.

Au-Sar then noticed his Goddess wife standing beside him and looked over at her almost sensing her need of him. His body responded to hers. His speech rapidly ended the meeting when he looked over at her and they both walked off to the palace to tell their aunt Ua-Zit and Ma-At.

Chapter 26

When they reached the palace, all who glanced upon their young and eager faces could read their impatience. Their aunt was rapidly summoned and had to cut a meeting short to prepare her charges for the ancient ritual.

Ua-Zit saw the bright beaming faces of anticipation of her niece and nephew and brought them to a chamber prepared with incense and strewn with the blossoms of the white and blue lotus flowers among large pillows. A bowl of pomegranates and figs dipped in honey was there for them to dine on so that they would not be disturbed.

Ua-Zit had prepared them both for this ritual with the knowledge of each other's bodies, of the role and the meaning of the Great Rite, and of the value of any issue from this act. The two of them bowed down to her solemn words, but heard little of it in their anticipation.

Their bodies were carefully donned in the mystical scents of the Goddess and of fertility and they were each given a crown of brightly colored flowers from the palace gardens.

The first act must be witnessed, much to their dismay. There had to be proof of the maiden-blood leaving. This ceremony had to occur exactly one year and a day after the first moon-blood of the maiden to make it all the more sacred. It helped if her sacred union mate could participate, but if not another was brought in to act in his role until his maturity.

In every way, Au-Sar was mature enough in body for this rite. Until this moment, his seed was collected, prayed over and then added to the gardens so it would not be wasted. From this day forward when the Goddess deemed her ready, only she would have his seed within her to provide life for her womb and for their new land of Kemet.

As in the land of her birth, when Au-Set had the first stirrings in her womb Ua-Zit would step down in her role as Mother-Goddess to let Au-Set take over. She would then become the Crone-Goddess. Ua-Zit had felt the end of her moon-blood this past year anyways and she was tired of all of the duties that it entailed.

Ua-Zit sang the prayers for the ceremony and prepared the pillows for their comfort. She unclothed her Au-Set and Au-Sar in ceremony and led them to each other. She then silently left the chamber and joined the other witnesses to peer in through a woven screen as was required of her station. She was also there, if they had any questions.

Au-Set and Au-Sar stood naked before each other almost forgetting those behind the screen who watched in silence, so strong were their desire and curiosity. They had both been raised on great tales of love that hid nothing to the imagination, so open was this to their people and so necessary to ensure the continuation of their race.

Musicians blocked out the sounds from outside of the chamber and made the rest of the world new to the young lovers, and distant. They were lost to their own growing passion for each other.

As children, they had run around naked on the palace grounds as other children had. However, at the first sign of maturity, they had begun to adorn the clothes of adults, which sometimes concealed their growth. The sun was so fierce and constant that the clothes that were worn were light and airy. Most people were proud to show and to display what the Gods had given them, for there was no shame or disgust in the human body.

Ua-Zit whispered, as was her right, "Au-Sar remember to take it slow. Do not rush your seed. She is delicate and must be made to open freely to what you offer this land."

Au-Sar barely heard the words whispered for his instruction and continued to be lost in the form of the Goddess in the body of Au-Set. He had marveled at how she had grown even softer then what he recalled in youth, how her skin reacted with each breath that he took. She had grown into a woman and he had not even noticed it before. He had felt drawn to her with his whole body and soul and yearned to be inside of her, to become a part of her body. His breath quickened as did hers in response.

The music picked up in tempo in response to their bodies and the drums sounded almost primeval to them, yet they did not care. Slowly they fell into the bed of pillows after discovering the other's body in small kisses that grew larger with their rising hunger of each other. They became tangled in the blankets and in each other, when it finally happened. The Great Rite had been completed, but the two lovers did not care and continued in their youth and vigor to each other, filling the chamber with their cries of ecstasy that rang into the night in their newfound pleasure of each other. The others had long since left them for the new rapture of the lovers that they found in their blissful solitude.

Au-Set and Au-Sar never tired of each other's company. However, Au-Sar soon became enraptured in the effect that he had on the people who had traveled from faraway places to learn his secrets of irrigation and agriculture. He expanded on the ideas that he and Au-Set had. She nudged him in this direction initially in her grand ideas that she had for this untouched land.

They had to rely on some of what had been practiced in their birth-land and to develop upon it for this harsh land beyond where the black soil naturally touched the desert. Au-Set came up with many of the ideas herself and then went onto other things in Kemet that equally needed her attention and her fine skills in organization that he lacked. She was brilliant in handling many things at once and from several areas. She balanced the needs of the kingdom as if she were as wise and experienced as their aunt was. She was a natural.

However, Au-Sar had to focus on one thing in particular. When he did this, he would usually fall into it, noticing things that others could not. He saw the details and she was sublime with the whole picture. They were a perfect team. He could not understand how she could find the time to do so many things, excel at them all, and then still have the time to be wild into the wee hours of the evening. His mind was so focused in his tunnel vision that he was usually exhausted after much work on any dilemma that he had to face in his growing passion for agriculture.

He would often have to leave the familiar side of his Goddess-mate to travel to many of the villages of their land to check on their progress and to assist them with any questions or issues that they might have. In his passion for this, his trips became more and more often, leaving Au-Set feeling a little neglected from his absences.

Ua-Zit observed the somber face of her niece and knew the reason instinctively. They both knew that the work of Au-Sar was greatly enhancing the need of the people to their family with its great success. She knew that neither of them could complain, but she knew as a woman that Au-Set needed not only the body of her Au-Sar, but his attention as well. Sometimes men have a way of becoming obsessed with their projects, leaving a woman all alone. A woman in love craves the form and familiarity of her lover and feels complete when returned. If not, she feels neglected.

As much as a woman has the power for the most part, some things in nature were never explained. A wise man learns to pay attention to his mate and he will be rewarded with the most sincere devotion in return. A woman's heart is insecure and must be nurtured constantly in its fragility. She as well as most of her other woman confidants yearns for strength of heart such as men have. How men, for the most part could separate sex with love and duty. Women, even priestesses found that difficult and often hearts were tangled with duty. There are many tales of priestesses who grew attached to temple patrons and dreaded them leave. Such was the common tragedy, but this was more than understandable to Ua-Zit. She had learned long ago in her age and wisdom to numb her-self to perform the duty that she was born to and to open herself to her chosen consorts. Some, she had the luxury of choosing and others, in the beginning of her reign as a Goddess representative, that were chosen for her. Through this all, there was her palace mate Hetep always patient by her side.

She felt a hunger for the passions of the body and sought out young lovers to keep them satisfied. It was amazing how her body responded with its newfound freedom knowing that she could not have children anymore. It released her soul from obligation and duty.

Nevertheless, she felt that it was the prudent time to bring in her own son Nebmaat as consort to Au-Set. Especially now, since she felt the pining of Au-Set as it silently emanated from her soul. She also wanted her son to create life in Au Set, where Au-Sar had not been able to so far. She knew that heirs were desperately needed and she earnestly wanted a grandchild to dote on. Au-Sar had been gone for over a month, when finally Ua-Zit approached her niece.

"Dearest Au-Set, I have a matter of import to discuss with you."

"By all means aunt, have a seat."

"A- Set, it is now time for you to take another consort, for it is your duty to have life in your womb for the Goddess."

"But, aunt, I love Au-Sar, must he die as the consorts of my mother!" Her eyes began to fill with tears at the very thought of this.

"Hush now! Your thoughts are running away with your tears. We had all discussed that you would both be together until your natural deaths, for that is not the way in Kemet."

Au-Set wiped away her tears and fought to gain control," I promise I will have a talk with him, so that he will be around more often to perform his duties."

"You must curb your rash mind niece, I understand your dismay at this, but I have not finished." She paused and put her arms comfortingly around her young niece. "Let me bring your fears to rest. He does not have to be sacrificed. This is a new land. You can have more than one consort, my dear.

Better to insure your fertility. Perhaps it might even bring Au-Sar more often to your bed when he knows he has competition. You need someone to warm your bed when Au-Sar is out teaching."

"But aunt, I have no desire for anyone else but him! You must understand that I have no need for anyone else but him! Just the very thought of it makes me cry!"

"Hush dear! Do not be foolish. It is your duty to provide an heir for the Goddess Ua-Zit of whose names we both have. It is not only a privilege, but also an honor that comes with great responsibility. Many men find your beauty intense. For just to be in your presence delights them. Such power! Why abuse this power given to you by the Goddess? Use it to your advantage. There is no wrong and Au-Sar knows this. It is your right to take as many consorts as you need. Your duty is to be fruitful for the Goddess and for this land. You must have many children in your womb!" She let her words sink into the mind of her niece and then continued,

"My son, Nebmaat seeks your favor and blessings and I have approved this for you. You understand that it was one of the conditions for you all to come over to rule in Kemet. Do you? What say you to this? He is handsome, is he not?"

Au-Set nodded thinking of Nebmaat and his strong sinewy muscles that gleamed in the sun and of his dark and powerful skin and large hands. She was beginning to enjoy her secret thoughts of his hands wrapped around her waist in passion. Then she smiled at her aunt. It would certainly be blasphemous for her to have only one consort. She was beginning to like the idea.

There was no ceremony for women of rank to take her next consort, as it was often done and common. With that done, Ua-Zit sent her son in that evening to warm the bed of Au-Set. She had secret hopes that he would be placed in the fore over Au-Sar if he filled Au-Set with child first. She prayed for her son's seed to take hold in her niece and she welcomed the embrace of her own new consort with each ensuing evening thereafter.

Ua-Zit even laughed upon the return of Au-Sar and of his having to share the attentions of his Goddess-mate, for she was insatiable and they were both sent in to please her. All of them tumbled in a heap each evening. Oh, she thought playfully, the palace would never know of Au-Set's silence again! She then went to her own chambers for her mate and consorts. There were glistening youths from the finest houses of the land that fought to please her and to meet her every wish and desire. Oh, this palace is filled with the wills of the Goddess. All is right in the world. I hope that Au-Set will conceive the heir she prayed for longingly!

Chapter 27

In the city of Nekhen in Upper Kemet, Neb-Het had taken badly to her duty as the sacred union mate of Suti. His sad and untutored attempts to please her after the Great Rite were tiring her. Neither of them was schooled in this and was given a haphazard ceremony when Suti had finally reached his maturity. Neb-Het long since found a substitute consort upon the advice of Neferet. She was told that it was her duty to learn all that she could to ensure the fertility of the Goddess in her body. Her substitute consorts were rash, did not consider her feelings, and made the ordeal rough for Neb-Het. She dreaded even more Suti's lack of skill. She had welcomed all too eagerly the attentions of Ua-Zit's son Hetep who was sent down to be her second consort. She had soon learned to forget her duty to Suti, as did he.

Her feelings of repulsion on her duty with Suti as her main consort were further exacerbated by the great difference in age. She wanted children and he was still playing with his toys and smaller in height than she was.

Neb-Het had taken others in the past since her time of maturity and still felt unfulfilled. In desperation for a feeling that she longed to possess, she had passed through them like sweets to toss them aside when bored. Her new appetite for men grew ravenous and destructive as well. She was especially drawn to men that she could not have and began to tire of her regular consorts and of her official ones and sought out the men forbidden to her. She loved the men that belonged to other women, hoping they had learned something new that her other lovers had not.

Neb-Het with beauty comparable only to that of her own twin sister was not satisfied with what life had given her. She was a born princess and heir to the dynasty of Eshnunna, if it still existed, and the rightful heir of Upper Kemet and the Shen peoples of the Goddess Nekhebt. She was born to a power that she could not even begin to understand. Completely untutored in rule, she simply sat back and let life find her.

She was raised in a land of plenty as a princess, never knowing what it was like to want something. She never knew a day of thirst, nor of hunger. She could not even begin to understand this, since she was so young and inexperienced in life. She was only thirteen summers old.

Yet, she felt that she knew it all. In the beginning of her stay in Nekhen, she patiently waited for some word or piece of advice from her aunt-yet, none came. The tall doors of her bedchamber loomed ominously before her, always closed. Nekhebt was always in her chambers wishing not to be disturbed for any reason. She then tried to be a mother to herself and to her younger siblings Suti and Heru.

She was especially upset over her main consort Suti and had tried in vain to be a good mate, yet nothing grew in her womb. She sought him out constantly in the beginning, knowing it essential that she give birth to an heir. Yet, he was most often not to be found anywhere in the palace or temple grounds.

She felt lonely and desolate and wanted her own twin sister desperately for companionship. She knew that Au-Set was too busy in her own role as Goddess representative for Ua-Zit in Per-Uto so far away. She waited for the annual times discussed in the past when the two aunts would confer on their unified rule of the land at a meeting that seemed to be constantly delayed. She wondered if it would ever occur, and if she would ever see her other siblings again.

She was worried about her brother Suti, for he seemed to have unusual appetites when they were together that did not seem right to her and were often painful. She dreaded each meeting with him, though she knew that they had to occur in order for her to conceive. She had found out from her consort Hetep that the way in which Suti mated with her would not produce life in her womb. Therefore, she decided not to bother him anymore and sought out the attentions of others besides Hetep.

Neb=Het knew that she also needed to learn how to rule this land and of how to implement the new government that her mother created. Yet, she waited in vain for no tutor had arrived to take on that task with her. The palace life was growing dreadfully ominous to her in its silence and seeming lack of life.

Therefore, she sat day by day, usually in the gardens by the fish pool waiting for something to change and to give her some new meaning to her life. She had already counted all of the fish in the pond, which were fifty-eight in total. She had begun out of pure frustration to count the lotus blossoms and other flowers that surrounded her, until this too surpassed her efforts in futility.

As she sat there idly waiting for the day to end, Neferet entered her quietude and peace. "Your highness, I have recently received word from Per-Uto."

Every cell in her body jumped for joy at this, was it her sister? She looked up at Neferet expectantly.

"It is from Ua-Zit, she wishes to finally call a counsel for you and your aunt, and siblings to attend to discuss Kemet. I assume that she wants to see what has been done here." Neferet's eyes searched the dark hazel eyes of Neb-Het for some sort of reaction to the news and found none."

Neb-Het patted her hand to the soft dew drenched ground beside her at the foot of the pool and motioned for her tutor to sit. "Neferet, what have I done here? What exactly *is* my job here?"

"Well... I do know that it was the duty of your aunt to instruct you in the matters of rule. But I suspect that it had not been done at all?"

The princess nodded her assent to that and looked into the soft azure eyes of her tutor.

"I now see that you're learning and that of your brothers has been neglected while I have been busy in the temple?" In addition, Neb-Het nodded again, she continued, "I am sorry for that, but princess, do you not think that possibly you have the power to take the matter into your own hands? Could you not find someone to teach you all of this land?"

Neb-Het put her index finger into the still waters of the pool, as if looking for the small ripples she created to tell her the answer that she sought.

"I would not know where to begin. Everybody had always brought everything to me in the past. I am so bored…just waiting for something." Her hands subconsciously clutched the small silver necklace given to her as a child by her mother, a copy that she had given to each of her children that last meeting she had with them. Neb-Het's eyes wandered up to the small stone wall beside them to a flock of numerous ibis birds that had suddenly gathered to squabble over the fish in the pond. The fish were probably wondering which one of the ibis would be bold enough to prey on them with the two humans sitting there. Both the woman and girl giggled at this while watching the reactions of the birds, until a gloomy cloud passed overhead as if to remind them of matters that are more serious.

"Princess, all you have to do is find someone in the palace with whom you could trust to carry out all your wishes and to advise you on how to obtain things, such as the much needed tutor. Your aunt was supposed to take care of this, but I feel that she has been a bit melancholy and has lost her will and seemingly the loss of the desire that she once had to rule over this land. If I may speak frankly…"

Neb-Het nodded, the weight of endless boredom suddenly lifted from her shoulders.

"Well, it seemed that even upon our arrival this land had fallen into decay, while the land ruled over by her sister has prospered all the more. I am very concerned about this rate of neglect; you may not even have a land to rule over by the time that it is your turn." She lowered her eyes, waiting for some rebuke, observing none her confidence returned.

"If I were in your sandals…"

"If I were in your sandals…. I would slowly take control, since this land is sitting idle. Have you a relationship of any kind with either of your brothers?"

"Nay, they have their own interests."

"Well, it would be better if your family, if you were all united together in this. For you would all have great power working together while divided, well you know the old adage to that one..."

She continued since she noticed that the princess was lost in each word that she uttered. She noticed how desperately that Neb-Het needed the guidance that she offered on this day. She felt bad for her and continued, cautiously of course so as not to offend her.

"Your brothers are still quite young, let's see, you and Au-Set are sixteen and Tehuti is fifteen, Au-Sar is fourteen, Heru is twelve and Suti only eleven...."

The princess sat in rapt attention while she ponderously whisked away a stray fly that had wandered over to watch.

"It is only natural that Suti would know little in the ways of pleasing his princess. I would first set out to get him some sort of instruction in that area for the time when he is actually ready. There are always the temple women that we have brought along with us; I could send him there for a spell." Neb-Het nodded vigorously at that and let her mother's wise Nugig continue.

"I would then find some way to entertain your aunt from suspicion while you find out all you can about this land's affairs and what it requires to get it prospering once again. Then I would find a proper tutor for you and your brothers, while you can work on building a relationship for them. More than any family in the world, you need your brothers to be faithful and loving towards you. With the family meetings, I would tell your sister Au-Set about this and have her work with you on her end.

"To be an able and powerful ruler like your mother, you need two things, responsibility for your people and the ability to rule. Those do not come easy." She noticed that Neb-Het was starting to react to all that she had heard.

"The meetings have not been held for some years due to the adjustment that you children needed in your new homes and sacred unions. The aunts have been corresponding with each other, and I can only imagine what your aunt Nekhebt has been writing of the affairs of Upper Kemet. Something must have slipped for Ua-Zit to call a meeting with little notice and especially her request of a neutral ground for it to be held. She could have easily requested one right here. She could also be giving your aunt a chance to save face."

"You and your family are in the most lucrative position in the known world. You have a land new and waiting for you to tame it. It is pliable and lays waiting for some logical rule. They cry out desperately for the culture that we bring to them and for an end to the petty squabbling in the villages. They want strong leaders to rule them and to represent them in their needs. The threat of Eshnunna is far away from here. They probably think that Kemet is barbaric and not worthy of their attention. You know different. You see the potential, as did your mother, and even her mother before her. I advise you that by the time that they start to notice this land, you should build up a strong seat in rule so that they will not know the challenge that awaits them. Build up armies and educate these people. Teach them art and build them wonderful cities, better than anything you left behind and fill it with wondrous color. Yet, build it strong with a loyal family to back you and powerful and indestructible armies that will defend you. Be careful, for soon at the first step that we take in bringing Kemet out of the gloom and neglect and ignorance it lays in, the world will take notice and you and your family will have to protect it."

Neb-Het's eyes gleamed with all that she had started to see from the wisdom of this woman that her mother had wisely sent down with her and her brothers. She decided to use Neferet as her advisor in this scheme, since the woman saw so much that she had only begun to grasp. Her soul glittered with the possibility and she was not afraid, only eager to begin the first steps to make this plan effective.

Chapter 28

That next day, after a fresh and complete sleep, she wove her first plan and took that daring first step. She gathered her brothers and left her aunt, as usual alone in her chambers. She gained their vows of allegiance and together they all worked on ways to make this work. She had Neferet there as well.

The first thing that they decided to create was a new capitol and to call it *Abdjw*. Together they worked into the wee hours of the evening planning a scope for the new buildings that would tower higher than anything they could remember from the land of their birth. They had dreams of covering the walls in beautiful paintings of the new mythology of her family that they would set into motion.

"Whoa, my children, how could you create a mythology on your family when you are still children!"

"I take offence to that Neferet! For I am a man and married at that!" Suti had returned to the room, his face flushing red with anger.

"I am sorry my prince, For I had only meant to say is that none of you has done any deeds worth writing about since you are all still very young." She had bowed to the ground in supplication of her mistaken confidence that she had gained from the princess Neb-Het

"Hush, Suti.... We have much work to do. We have a lot to catch up on before the meeting. Much has not been done here at all while we bathed in the seat of luxury, waiting for it to be done for us! Meanwhile, the revenues of Upper Kemet have been draining without much to counter it! I am very worried."

"Heru, do you agree with our sister?"

"Yes, Suti." Suti was aghast; for his brother was so docile, he had always taken his side on all matters and palace adventures.

"Continue Neferet and Neb-Het, for our ears are ready to receive your great wisdom Suti, in the folly of his youth, aimed mockery to the room for no-one's benefit but his own.

"Brothers, I need you to be strong with me and at one with me in all matters. Our strength is our greatest power. For you know as well as I that for other royal families who have waged war against each other, nothing was gained at all and eventually in every case, the country was divided in the end and that family taken from power by a stronger family! We must pay attention to history and the lessons that it shall teach us. Our family grew powerful because we all worked together not against each other." She explained to her brothers the plan of how perfect this country was in its ability to be molded to improve.

"While our aunt Nekhebt sits in decay, we shall work hard to bring this neglected land back to power and greater than it has ever been. It is imperative that we all work together in this endeavor. We must meet at least three times a day and confer with each other about what we have done along with any new ideas that we may implement. Do you all agree?"

They all nodded. Neb-Het and Neferet noticed that in their youth, the brothers were starting to get noticeably bored and possibly were a little too eager to begin. She decided to end this meeting and assigned them tasks to complete for the next meeting.

"Brothers, we have only three months before we must meet up with the rule of Lower Kemet. This is only our first official meeting together on matters of import in the whole six years that we have been here. We must make sure that these meetings continue and urge for their frequency, if we have any chance of succeeding. Brothers pay attention to our tutor and advisor and work together to find a new architect for our new Abdjw. Neferet is available for any counsel that you may need until our next meeting and thereafter. I end this first meeting so that we may work on our dynasty!"

She laughed as her brothers and their newly appointed advisor joined her side. They knew what they were all capable of, though also looked out the window of their mud-walled palace and saw the town people in their huts making baskets of the tall papyrus that grew along the banks of this great river. They felt the people had much to learn indeed if they were going to forge any kind of majestic rule even in creating an illusion of one.

As her brother left the room, Neb-Het sat back in eager anticipation of their first meeting. Finally, for once in her life, she felt productive and was even feeling pride in what they would soon accomplish. She wondered how her sister fared in this endeavor and how prepared she was.

Chapter 29

Suti left the chamber and actually felt a building anticipation for the work ahead of them. He would try to be all that his older sister wanted and saw the logic of her plea. He felt that it might come to naught, since he was really a loner and did not care about how to make his sister a more effective ruler. He would love to have been born with her power. He would probably do a much better job indeed. He felt powerless in a land of women who had all of the power.

He then picked up his step, longing to see how his favorite sow was. She was expecting and was in great form. He waited eagerly for the piglets to be born and he needed to be there for her. When they were born, they were very small in comparison to their gigantic mother; he had to protect them from being crushed by her enormous weight.

Alas, when he returned he found out that his fear for her had been confirmed. When he arrived at his sleeping chamber, he found her on the once neat and fresh hay, deep in the throes of labor. Her screeches could be heard all down the long hallways. He had found that she had already crushed two of them that could not be revived, and then noticed a small one that could barely breathe. He picked up all of the surviving ones, placed them by her teats for their first meal, and then poured his attention over the smaller one in distress.

Instinct taking over, he cupped the tiny boar in his hands and began breathing with his own breath into the minute lungs of the smallest until he was strong enough for the nourishment of its own mother laying on her side from all of the exertion.

Slowly, the smallest started to find life again and Suti's heart leapt in joy, for his wild sow had meant the world to him. The only creatures who did not demand anything of him and who greeted him each time he entered the room with happiness displayed in wild grunts and squeals. He felt that the boar and the sow were truly his only family. He knew that they would never leave him alone.

He noticed sadistically, the attention his love for his boars brought him in the palace. The people of this land were naturally afraid of the wild boars, wanted nothing to do with them, and did not find boars suitable food as people did from the land of his birth. Only he knew that his boars would never be food for his table, for he would see to that with his life. People always gave him plenty of room whenever his sow and boar accompanied him. They felt fear from him as well, since no one in their own land had ever tamed a wild boar. He laughed at this and felt the additional power that it brought him.

He also thought sadly in retrospect, that he would never had had this power in his own land since he was not born female. He often wondered about the men from the north who had destroyed all that he ever knew. He had heard rumors that they had red hair like his own. Was he somehow connected to them? He liked how they instilled fear in all that he knew and had started this in his own way, perhaps to form some kind of connection to them. He felt very little kindness from those around him.

As he sat watching the three tiny piglets, for two more had been born and survived to feed from their mother; he felt the soft nuzzle of his own faithful companion and dog-named *Heh*. *Suaa* was the name that he chose for his sow, which meant "in adoration of" and *Suka*, the name of the boar, meant "remembrance for a bad dream or ruin and destruction." For his boar, he chose the first of the two meanings for he had Suka to remind him of the love that he gave freely to the boar that his own family had stopped giving to him. He would never stop the love to his own. The name of his dog meant in the language of Kemet, "God of hundreds and thousands of years." He chose the language of this land for the names of his companions, possibly because his life here would be different, and he wanted to make sure of that.

He let the people ponder of the name Suka, and let them wonder if he named the dog with the latter meaning in mind. He laughed at that one to himself. These animals had helped him to find some kind of love in this old and neglected land and they looked forward to his company, unlike his siblings it seemed.

"Heh, we have young ones to protect now!" Heh nuzzled contentedly against his master, almost growing larger. For Heh was large and gray, sleek with sharp features and alert ears. Slender and tall, he almost reached the height of the boy as he grew.

Suti had always confided in his entourage of animals, since he had felt as neglected as the walls around him. He missed his mother dreadfully and Au-Sar as well. At first, he could not even sleep, so used to sleeping by the side of his mother. Gradually he found solace in the baby animals that he had found, or rather that had found him. With them, he created a sort of motley family of his own. The animals all adored him in turn. He knew they would fight to their very deaths for him if he were threatened in any way.

He wondered if his real siblings felt that way. He silently doubted it. Heru was always following him, but it seemed that he did not really care for the wisdom of Suti. Heru only wanted to protect him and to keep him out of trouble. Suti also knew that Heru would get him anything that he wanted; all he had to do was ask.

Au-Sar was always running to protect him and was constantly taking his side in matters that seemed to involve him. Heru was different in a way from Au-Sar, for it seemed that Heru was always protecting everyone from him. Heru was the peacekeeper of all of the children of Ninnuit, rather than of just him like Au-Sar was. Suti felt truly abandoned over this.

Heru was always making a mess of his bright red hair and telling him that it gave him the power of fire and that he should always make sure to keep his temper under control. Suti knew that his older brother was referring to his temper that was already becoming legendary in the palace. He hated how his brother looked out for him as if he were still a young child.

Suti also wondered why his mother had chosen him to marry his half sister Neb-Het and not either of his two older more sedate brothers, Tehuti and Heru. Did she see something in himself that no one else had?

Heh whimpered almost as if sensing his master's dismay and ponderings and nuzzled closer to him. Why could not people be more like animals? People wore a mask for the world and rarely let others in to see the real reason behind it. None of this nonsense occurred with animals. They saw what there was and projected what they needed for necessity only. Animals never had to second-guess others to look for a motive. He felt that animals were very lucky indeed.

He also felt that women were the worst of all in humanity. They had all of the power and did not seem to yield it well. With his aunt, he noticed that she was always lying about alone in her chambers while the land rotted around her. He could not recall much of his own mother only that she was beautiful and powerful and seemed to control the very heavens. People bowed down to her and hung on her every word. In front of her, they marveled at his bright red hair and called it glorious and magical. Yet, when she was not around, they called it an abomination and an evil omen, as was his father.

No one told him that much about his father. Suti did not believe that his father was an official consort of his own mother only that people had referred to him as evil. Was he evil too? Was he going to be the downfall of his family? Yet, he still wondered why he was the one chosen to marry Neb-Het and not his other more valuable brothers who were older than he was?

He did not even like performing his official duty. His brother scolded him and told him that as he grew older he would enjoy it immensely and yearn for it.

Suti could not believe that could ever be true. His eyes would often wander towards other boys his age and not to little girls. He would picture them kissing him and holding him close. He secretly dreaded each evening with his mate. He would always find excuses. She even stopped seeking him out and had another consort to perform that wretched duty for her.

He also knew that his sister would often sneak out to find the attention of other men. It seemed to him as if she was playing some sort of game, for he had noticed the lines carved on her altar as if she were recording each conquest. Though he had to admit that he had not noticed this behavior from her lately, for she seemed bored to him and was spending almost entire days in the gardens watching the dumb fishpond thinking who knows what. She had seemed lately to him as if she had the life sucked right out of her soul, like their aunt. However, the life he knew that glowed in her seemed to have rushed back into her once again this very day.

He had to admit that he found her new zest pleasant and that it even made her a bit pretty. She sat there at the meeting with animated purpose. He found himself caught up in her plans and dreams and found logic in every word that she uttered. In that meeting, she might have found the color once lost to his boring life. Since its occurrence, he actually found that he was eagerly anticipating the next meeting. He desperately wanted to show his older siblings that he was not a baby anymore, and to show them that he could be very valuable to them.

Suti decided that he would start immediately in finding a stonemason and with him to discuss the shipment of granite and marble from their homeland and to find quarries here in this land to cut down on expenses. He also would look into finding materials for building in general, here in Kemet. He had already located a gold mine to the south of them in Kebet. His mind furiously whirled with new ideas and he ran into his sleeping chamber, grabbed a reed pen, and proceeded to throw down his ideas rampantly onto the papyrus that his older brother Tehuti had shipped down to them.

He loved the way his words looked on this crisp document and in how fast they dried. This was greatly unlike the clay tablets that he was used to writing things down on before. He recalled that in the land of his birth, the scribal priestesses would use a wooden pen with a flint piece dulled on the end to create the simple linear strokes that would make letters and then words. The writing that he was familiar with from his homeland of Eshnunna was really quite laborious and time intensive in waiting for each section to dry. The words produced were colorless, simple, and bland, unlike the multi-colored picture writing that was showing up around this land slowly. He hated when he found a mistake in his hard work on the clay tablets of large legal documents.

This papyrus was being made in vast amounts and could be worked over again or rubbed out. One would have to start a new one, once the words had dried on clay in the old fashion, for they were utterly non-removable once dried. He also loved how he could roll up his ideas once drawn out and transports them around with him all day to review at his leisure. He would not have to find a servant to retrieve the clay documents from the vault and wait for it. He was very proud of his older brother Tehuti for his ingenuity of this great stride in writing.

Chapter 30

Heru watched as his youngest sibling stormed out of the room after the meeting and set about himself to implement his own ideas that were swimming in his own head. He fervently hoped that Suti would see reason in all of this and had hoped that the boy was finally growing up.

Heru often worried about Suti and from their earliest days was always the one sent to look after him, as soon as it was discovered that Suti had a penchant for creating mischief. Suti was usually injured or created a huge mess in his constant endeavors. The boy never tired at all! Au-Sar on the other hand, felt sorry for Suti and tried to find reason in him. Heru saw everyone else's perspective and seriously was concerned that Suti would hurt himself, or others. Au-Sar could find no fault in Suti and refused to believe the reasoning's of Heru and the others around them. Suti soaked up the attention from Au-Sar, which fueled in his wrath. Heru, on the other hand, was the only one who could calm Suti's tyrannical behavior.

Heru wondered on the boy's constant infectious behavior and wondered how he never seemed to tire at all. It marveled him. People ran around desperately trying to keep things from breaking and the boy as well from being harmed with his ingenious inventions that were usually quite dangerous.

Heru also worried in the beginning of the boy's attentions to the wild boar and sow that he had found, and then to his added horror a wild dog was added to the dangerous menagerie of his! Heru was constantly in the boy's oblivious shadow, making sure that no harm came to him. He knew that the boy had a fierce determination in his independence and Heru did not want to stifle this, for it was unusual in one so young. Gradually he let the boy be in realizing that the animals truly loved their odd red-haired human master. He even began to feel comfort in their protection and shadow of the boy.

He laughed at all of the many adventures that Suti had been on, not knowing of the constant shadow of his older brother. Heru would peer from behind reeds as his brother would make little boats out of reeds and then crash them into each other. As the boats grew larger, Suti put bugs inside of them and then small animals. He almost screamed in terror as Suti bent down to pick up a scorpion, when Heh sounded out the alarm to his master, scaring it away. Heru breathed a tentative sigh away and squished it when it came close to his own foot. Heh must have grown used to his presence and let Heru tag along, probably thinking that it was some sort of game.

One day, to his horror, he watched as Suti laboriously made a boat for himself and for each one of his pets. They swam helplessly until Suti tied a rope to their small boats and then towed them behind his own. Heru thought it wonderfully humorous until he noticed one of the bushes rustle revealing the curiosity of a crocodile that had been jostled from its sleep to seek its morning brunch! Heru ran out after them all after grabbing his slingshot and sending a fatal shot at the snout of the predator. He brought the little army to rescue to the tears and anger of Suti, who wanted to be the hero! Suti seemed almost oblivious to any sort of danger and seemed to run towards it! Suti seemed to have no sense of safety for him and no concept at all for danger, while Heru had to pick all of the pieces of destruction in his wake of adventures.

Before, when he brought this to the attention of their mother, she had only laughed at Heru and of the little father that he made. Au-Sar seemed to encourage Suti and his adventures, finding them notoriously funny. She hugged Heru even more for his protection of the youngest sibling. She told him that it would always be his job for it was the fate of the Gods. Suti was always grasping at life and testing it. Heru, on the other hand, was born to the knowledge from even his cradle of the true dangers life held for them. Their mother had informed him that he was her one child that would forever be the most realistic of them. He recalled that she further told him that his logic was needed the most as the link that would keep them all together. Heru knew from her that he would be the one child that would eventually protect them all from their own troubles and that he was the only one strong enough to do it.

Heru was a great swimmer and had no fear only when in the water. He did it for a reason. It was almost as if he had to prove something to himself. From the time of his birth on, he was always thought of as the safe one, the one that would never rock the boat or tempt fate in any way. Part of him was jealous of little destructive Suti. Therefore, the only explanation that he had for his tempting fate in swimming was his way of balancing out his own personality. He had always felt that too much of his personality was boring and safe. He wanted to change that for himself, if not for anyone else.

From the wisdom of his mother, Heru learned to be grateful for his role in the family, as their guardian and protector from even themselves. They all seemed to find safety in his constant logic.

He knew that since he did not have his older siblings' fearlessness in life, he would always be the silent one in stories, possibly the brother most often forgotten in history. He also knew from his mother that they all would rule and live long lives because of him. Ninnuit had blessed him with the love of the Goddess and told him that he was the life-giver of the family and without him, they would never last. She had given him the confidence that he most desperately needed and felt love from her each time he rescued Suti.

He also felt great pride in the new light that was shining forth from his sister. He knew that he would be the one to make sure that her dreams faced solid ground and reality. Neb-Het had the tendency to dream a little too ahead of herself and then to get overwhelmed in everything that she had started. He knew that he would be the one to keep them all on track for the sake of their family. Heru was the thread that held them all together. That was what he remembered from their mother and of the last time that he saw her.

He felt excessively old for his age and knew that he grew up too fast in protecting his younger brother from his daring actions and in keeping his older sister from destroying herself with her reckless actions with the temple and palace men. How she treated them like sweets and discarded them often.

Chapter 31

The village of *Gerzah* was located at the base of the upside-down lotus. It was located also above the village called *Ineb-Hedj* or "white fortress" in its being a military base where an army for their land of Kemet was being trained. Neb-Het agreed to the suggestion for the long-awaited meeting to be held there. She felt that the journey that it would take them to arrive, would give her plenty of time to reflect on all of their plans and to put them in a logical format for presentation at the meeting.

In its location at the base of the delta, it made the merchants very accessible for the meeting. It was also considered the most able of villages to hold the large entourage of royal persons attending. It was more than just a village as it was gaining a fast reputation for its numerous markets that were sprawling all around the banks of the Great River. The local population was noted for its wonderful red and black pottery with extraordinary spirals that symbolized the eternal life of the people who made it. They also seemed to have a talent for the animals that they painted on the pottery that seemed almost to leap off in life. Both sides of the royal family were avid collectors of the pottery already and Au-Set especially was fervent on adding to her growing collection of these intricate pieces.

The old circular houses in the villages of ancient Kemet were being replaced with modern rectangular dwellings that had one door in the front and two windows in the rear of the dwelling. The round huts would only allow so many houses to be built in any given area. When the population grew, new round houses would leave to form a separate community. The rectangular houses allowed more buildings to be built side-by-side and even on top of one another, which solved the problem of housing the growing population of the popular market village. The ancient design of the round huts only allowed small sized villages. This new form led to a conglomeration of larger populations similar to what they had seen in Eshnunna.

The new rectangular buildings were only half-roofed, leaving the front open to the elements. The door that faced the street led to the roofed section where the family slept. In the open roofed section there were usually displayed wares made by the family to be sold. The family also cooked in that open section as well, while tending their children.

In the center of this new village was a well used by the men to wash the family clothes and a huge roof that covered the grain for the whole village in pits. The community collected this grain from the fields that surrounded the streets of the village. A large surplus was collected since all of them worked together. Whatever the village did not consume was sold in the market. Each person who lived in the village was responsible in some way for the grain collected in the communal roofed pits. This was their life source and it was what made them a community. Geese, goats, pigeons and a donkey or two roamed around fed by all who lived there.

This village was successful since it adapted to the growing population in the format of their dwellings and it kept the ancient ways that worked to keep a community close in working together to feed them. Each family specialized in some type of craft, whether it was beautiful pottery or flint tools. Merchants came from afar to set up a new life here and thus added to the growing diversity of the population. Gerzah was beginning to reach the size of a city and it flourished with life.

Most of the villages were fashioning themselves after this successful village, by building the rectangular houses to attract a population and by sharing responsibilities of feeding the village so they would have time to specialize in some sort of trade. This life was becoming very attractive and had been introduced by the family from Eshnunna, initially by Ishurti and Nemothi and expanded upon by the later generation.

Before the beginning of villages and small cities that were fast spreading throughout the land, much interspersed communities dotted the Great River Valley.

Most were isolated from one another and kept primarily their immediate family units, until this new attractive idea of larger populations working together to create merchant towns. People seemed to come out of the *Deshret* itself and from lands far away, so attracted to the idea of the open and communal village and city life.

The people of this village of Gerzah appeared ageless in that they all seemed as youthful as they were happy. Their joy in life kept age from their forms as if in mockery of time. They reveled in their new prosperity and time they now had in perfecting their intricate pottery and at the insatiable market for it.

The people were as decorated as their own pottery with spirals made of henna that swirled and danced all over their ageless bodies. Their hair was elaborately braided with beads smoothed down and made from the colorful rocks found along the riverbanks.

Au-Set, Au-Sar and Nebmaat walked with arms entwined through the winding and endless pathways of the market. Blankets woven of different colors and patterns separated each entrance courtyard-stall and created different worlds of delights to the shoppers and browsers. Several languages could be heard in various stages of bargaining. The scents of cooked delights assailed their nostrils and mixed in an almost amiable way with the not so pleasant smells of the market.

A rich pungent world met them and provided them with a never before seen view of the common people of the land. All their lives, they had been sheltered from all of the workers of the lands they lived in. With this was a gift with a new perspective, of which they were taking into to their souls with delight.

Ua-Zit wanted all of them to see a completely new way of looking at their world, to see creation of the new Kemet from its very rudimentary and smallest level. How could they create a completely new culture without seeing the way in which all of the details were created in their own land from one village?

"How wonderful to be able to create such beauty!" Au-Set exclaimed as she stooped low to pick up a piece of pottery in the form of a drinking vessel that had spirals that seemed to go nowhere.

"Do you know what the spirals represent dear sister?" Spoke up the normally quiet Nebmaat. She had learned that mates of this land were called sister and brother in greeting out of respect. This is because when one became consort, the closeness and protection one felt for them was similar to what one felt for a sister. Though Au-Set was one year older than Nebmaat, he felt a natural instinct to protect her and to teach her the ways of his people for she was an able learner and never forgot what he told her. Not that he felt that she needed protecting, since she was learning the skills of a warrior like her mother and his own, yet something deep inside told him that she could always use someone else looking out for her.

She nodded her head that she did not and seemed almost detached as if pondering over the answer herself.

"It is for the paths one must choose in one's life. For many times we walk over the same path and cross back and march on always looking for our specific meaning in life. On each of these vessels made by this particular artist, it may initially appear as if there is only one path, yet there are always nine separate paths, one for each part of yourself." The eager Nebmaat explained to Au-Set.

"I was only aware of two paths brother, the soul and the body that walked the earth. How can there be so many?"

"That is a very good question Au-Sar. Let me find the best way to explain this to you." The shopkeeper looked anxious to take back her work of art, wondering whether these three young people were going to purchase it. She paused at interceding when she noticed the faint glow around the inquisitive girl. It seemed as if it came from within and the taller boy beside her strengthened it. In the ways of her people, she bowed to what she could not explain, but inside herself, she felt that this was a good lesson that the two of them needed to learn from her prince. She sat back and listened to the young boy explaining who seemed wise for his years.

"We have our physical body called the *khat*. That is the vessel, like this vase that it is carved on to practically hold the water that we drink. Next is the *sahu* or spiritual body. It is a bit of our physical body that had retained some knowledge from the life it walked on this earthly plane of existence along with some glory and power meshed within. It has the power to communicate with the soul. When the physical body turns into the sahu body, it flies up to the heavens to dwell with the Gods and the righteous.

"The *ab* is the heart body which is considered the core part of your body and houses all abstract thoughts, personal characteristics, and motivations. This part of you contains good and evil thoughts. It moves freely within you but also has the power to dwell with the Gods above. You also have within your body the *ka* which is your double body or shadow."

"Like Neb-Het is to me? This is all very confusing brother... How do your people keep this all straight and memorized? It does sound wonderful and makes perfect sense though."

"We have wise ones to keep each of these paths in line for each person and village elders who tell the tales to the common people in words they most understand.

"As for Neb-Het and you....no, it is not the same as having a ka. For each of you have your own ka for you are separate individuals are you not?"

Au-Sar spoke up, "Sometimes we all wonder about that brother, for they always played tricks on us all pretending that they were each other and often that they were the same person." He looked at his older sister and they both giggled at the games that they played in their youth before this new life.

"Well the ka....." Continued Nebmaat as they both stopped for him to continue. They all sat with the small vase in Au-Set's hands looking down at it and trying to find each of the separate paths. It looked as if there was only one path that never touched the other parts of it.

The shopkeeper was equally into the story for it was one of her favorites. She had purposely painted each of the designs of the pottery that her husband created after this legend. No two designs were ever the same, like each person. She considered secretly her vases, her own little people, giving them each a personality and a life after this story and ancient philosophy.

"The ka is an exact copy of our physical body, yet is also the one with the meat and wine offerings for the dead as they are required to sustain the life of those buried in the desert."

"Wait, brother, for I am starting to get confused, I thought your people ate the dead to keep them within you. What is this mention of tombs as our people have?"

"Au-Set, you are always on top of things. Let me explain a little further. When a person dies in this land, we take in all that is wise and good of that person within ourselves. This way we are our ancestors and our children become us. We keep that knowledge of the ancients within us always and thus we are truly able to give it to the next generation.

"Yet, not all of a person is devoured within. We take into ourselves the deceased loved ones heart or literal *ab* to gain the most important part of that person's life meaning and decisions. We also take into us their leg muscles to support our life left behind, for they are our foundation. Their hands, for they were what created us within our thoughts and the life we lived around them. We take unto us their eyes, tongue, and ears for our lessons that were never taught in life by that person. With our own children we take into us each tender morsel of their flesh which came from us to create yet another valuable life."

"Most of the adults and our elders are left behind, which are buried in the part of the desert in the direction of the setting sun, where all paths lead to the end of our earthly existence.

"As the ka is our physical double and almost the same within matter, yet it is not. Nevertheless, it still needs sustenance after the physical body we see that dies. This dwells within the statue of the person that is carved in their form that they had in life. After that person dies and for those left behind, they could communicate with that person if they spoke to the statue where the ka of that person lives. They could also leave messages at the base of that same statue. The ka has the ability to understand words uttered to the statue and of the messages left. Sometimes people would paint on clay tablets the person's favorite food if there were a lack of real food and it would all be the same to the ka. No pain that was with the person in life is ever painted in a tomb, but rather a glorified life. We believe that what is painted on the tomb will become real for the deceased when they start to find their paths again.

"Then there is the *ba,* which is the equivalent of the soul for the people of Eshnunna. It means sublime or noble. It dwells within the ka and continues to possess substance and form after death. It has the power to visit the tomb, to enter the body of the deceased, to talk with it and to even, reanimate it, and to hold conversations with the physical body left behind. It has the power to take any desired shape and to travel to dwelling places of the Gods where it cohabitates with other perfect souls. Like the ka, the ba also needs sustenance and partakes of the funeral offerings. Most often, it takes the form of a body of a bird and the face of the person left behind in life.

"The next part of us is the *khaibit* or shadow. It is the shadow of the person left behind and it connects the ka with the ba as they ingest the funeral offerings and visit the physical form of the deceased person at their own wills. The khaibit does not possess the memories of the deceased and needs to always be by the person so fearful is it to separate from it. Even in life, the shadow is always near and is revealed to us in the rays of the sun, which is always present.

"Unlike the khaibit, the *khu* is shining and bright and translucent. It contains the intelligence of the person and their life. Human khus are surrounded by

the khus of the Gods at their death and assisted by
them to the sky where they dwell. Even though it
contains the intelligence of the Gods, it does not have
enough power alone.

"The *sekhem* is what your form body is called.
Even the simplest person could see one. At death, the
sekhem is called to dwell among the all of the other
paths of the person in life. All of the paths gather to the
sekhem in life and then separate from it after death. It is
within the collective power of each person to bring him
or her back to whole again so he or she could dwell
among the Gods.

"The most important part of oneself is the *ren*, for
it is your secret name body. It is the name that will put
together all of the paths and parts of that person that
separated after the physical death and it is what keeps
the person whole in life. It is not your earthly name, but
a name that is unique to each person that binds all of
us together. Only the Gods know this name. If the name
is taken away from that person after death, that person
will wander forever through eternity never to be
complete again and never sit by the Gods. We spend our
whole lives in curiosity trying to learn this name for
ourselves, for it gives us great power. Yet, once learned
must be kept from our enemies. They could use it to
destroy us. It could also be learned to save us if used in
love when ill for it could give one the power to never
leave the physical realm and to never age, and even to
stop an imminent physical death."

Au-Set and her first consort were even more
transfixed since one whom most people thought was
mute told the tale. Only the royal family knew how
rarely the sons of Ua-Zit ever spoke. Until recently, Ua-
Zit was concerned that the Gods touched them in a
simple way. However, as they grew older, when they
actually spoke, it was usually something profound and
much older than their actual age.

Au-Set and Au-Sar as well as the shopkeeper
were riveted in the words of the wise boy before them
deep in the intelligence of his words. Though the
shopkeeper had heard it during her youth from the

village elders, it seemed new and revived when told from this strong youth before her. All of the bitterness she had felt with the passing of many years and the loss of her beauty were brought back to her with such magic. She also saw that the two young pupils, who were told this tale, had a deep meaning for the future of this land, though she could not understand how she knew this. She felt the dancing of her sahu illuminating her with renewed vigor and inspiration to create new works of art. Over the last many years, she had been producing them in a monotonous fashion. Now, the meaning was brought back to her and it felt right.

"Please take this vase in remembrance of this beautiful tale so well told, young prince." Spoke the awakened merchant woman who looked at the prince and then nodded to Au-Set. The woman then gave the small vessel to Nebmaat for the beautiful knowledge that he gave her this day and Au-Sar nodded in agreement.

From the bustle of the crowd, their aunt Ua-Zit had emerged with servants behind her laden down with her most recent purchases. She appeared to them restless to return to their quarters to prepare for the meeting.

"I have been searching around for the three of you." She nodded at each of them in turn.

"Come let us return for they have at last arrived." She motioned for everyone to follow her as her graceful soft linen gown trailed behind her barefooted form.

Au-Set had at last been torn from her reverie at the knowledge she had just obtained from her second consort and was trying to identify each path and part of her as described. Au-Sar was doing the same thing, when her form had awoken to the present and to the sounds and smells of the market in an almost assaulting array. "Yes, let us part, thank you woman for your gift." She bowed down to the humble woman of the market stall they had been sitting at and then ran to catch up with the others who were leaving in the direction of the tents that were set up for their living quarters for the great meeting of the two lands.

Chapter 32

A large hall was given to them for the meeting from one
of the local nobles. He would profit greatly from this act
of kindness. The hall spanned almost the width of the
village of dwellings and was made of the usual mud
covered woven papyrus and palm frond walls of the new
rectangular design. The roof was exposed to the sky for
it seemed to hardly ever rain in this new land, years
would sometimes pass before even one drop of rain
would touch it.

It was still new to all of the young princes and
princesses from Eshnunna who were from a humid and
rainy land, which was always threatened by floods and
was known on more than one occasion to wash away
whole villages. Houses in Eshnunna were erected on top
of mounds resembling small mountains and hills to
keep the dwellings above the flood levels. Too many
times their country had to start over when all of the past
washed away from torrents of rain from the sky and
from the earth as the waters overflowed the banks.

Yet, this new land, some have never seen a drop
of rain. All their lives were lived with the annual flowing
of the river that led to eternity and had no source, so
large was the Great River that they lived on.

Most structures of Kemet were built of finely
woven mats of palm fronds, papyrus, or other river reeds
and pasted with mud until dried. They had little fear of
rain-washing away their dwellings, and if the flooding of
the river reached them, they were made quickly again.
Roofs were not required, except to protect them from the
sun and to provide shade. In public community
buildings, the roofs were open to the Gods for them to
be able to look down upon the people and their plans
inside to provide guidance or wisdom.

Meetings in the open public buildings were held
during the time of day when the sun was the least
harsh, such as early morning or late afternoon.
Au-Set ran over to her sister and embraced her joyfully,
almost desperately. She then ran over to her brothers
Heru and Suti. All of the siblings were united for the

first time in years. Their voices ringing in merriment and loudly filled the large hall with their joy and reunion. The two older sisters Ua-Zit and Nekhebt stood and watched the younger generation unite with all of their stories and exited tears. They smiled for they recalled similar reunions with each other in the past. Ma-At and Neferet joined the two queens and stood behind them. Nebmaat ran over to his mother Ua-Zit and brother Hetep and their smiles of reunion lit up the large room.

Ma-At noticed all of the delicacies that seemed to almost weigh over the long table that dominated the chamber open to the sky. The table was almost overwhelmed with all of the food that she wished to fill herself with, while she waited impatiently for the young ones to reunite. Neferet looked at her and smiled for she knew how much Ma-At loved to eat. Neferet was opposite and would often forget to eat, in her absorption of her studies.

Ma-At was more from the earthly plane, and mostly dwelled in words and in writing. Neferet was dreamier and was an expert at planning. She could see in her mind how each plan could possibly turn out. Ma-At was the reality that kept her well grounded as well as her charges on the south of this upside down land. Neferet could easily lose track of the hours of the day and evening, while Ma-At kept them all informed for she knew precisely within her the exact time of the sun hours. It was Ma-At who controlled the time in meetings and made sure that subjects were adhered to and the schedule kept at a reasonable time and pace.

The bell clanged delicately and each found a stool to sit on. No hierarchal order was kept for this was a strategic meeting and all would have equal say for the most part. The two queens would have the upper hand, but all were invited for an open discussion. The children were there to participate, but were there mostly to observe, for some day they would lead these meetings after the two queens were gone.

It was essential that food be served and present for any meetings such as this, since food was considered fuel for the mind and replenished intelligence and gave clarity of thought essential in a meeting of great import.

Ua-Zit sat at the south of the long table, while her sister sat to the north; all of the siblings were sitting on the sides. No organization, other than that which was adhered to in the seating arrangement was required. The Nugig and consorts were also present in this ensemble.

Ua-Zit decided that now was the time to bring the meeting to order.

"Welcome sister, nieces and nephews, sons, and wise women of Eshnunna. Let us begin."

"We all have knowledge to bring to this table and this now united land. Sister, would you like to start?"

Nekhebt looked startled as she was shaken from her reverie from the world deep inside of her. Yet, she was a master from habit of going through the motions of her station without missing a beat to others observing. "We have been busy in our land sister, with plans of building a new capitol city, for Nekhen is starting to reek from the decay of generations long past and is growing too small for our plans. It is present only in its beginning stages and it will not be ready for many years for habitation."

Neb-Het look surprised when her aunt swiped her own idea as if she were the one who created it. Nekhebt had not attended one meeting and Neb-Het was astounded by her knowledge of what had been done in her absence. Her aunt seemed to have had no interest until this very moment in her plans. Neb-Het just stared at the faces of her brothers and consort with a growing fury. Au-Set caught the reaction of her sister and wondered about it, yet listened as Nekhebt continued.

"I have found mines from our section in Kemet for which to quarry building stones to build our new city. There are architects willing to come all the way from Eshnunna, the lands of Canaan, and the Hatti lands to add their skills to this new land. Of the people here in Kemet, we have found them to be pliable and willing to learn from us."

"Excellent sister, for I would love to see those plans of yours. As for myself, we have strengthened the walls of Per-Uto and have added a new foundation for the palace and two more temples have been erected and a house of learning for scribes at *Khnum*."

"May we have use of those mines for our construction sister?"

"Most certainly, for we have need of some of your scribes to adorn our new temples and to beautify the stark walls that is much in need of adornment."

"Consider it done."

The siblings and advisors sat silently mute while the aunts were taking credit for all of their hard work and ideas and fumed.

Suti spoke out first, as he was not known for social grace nor did he care. His boar lay sleeping by the foot of his stool, until the sudden stirring of his master when he stood up in attention. "I have worked hard on this aunt, while you lazed in your chamber leaving us with this shell of a land that has to be worked on." The others were stupefied at his sudden audacity, yet glad for it.

"Yes, brother..." Au-Sar nodded to Suti recalling days when he protected his youngest brother. "I have been working hard as well in traveling to teach ways of irrigation and agriculture to the simple people of this land."

Nebmaat and Hetep were mortified at this insult to their people and both stood abruptly in deep offense, Nebmaat spoke with acid looking at each of them in turn. "I take offense at your careless attitude towards the people who have taken you in while your own land has died."

"Now children, we must cease this squabbling, for it will tear us apart. I am sure that Au-Sar meant nothing to offend, the ways here are vastly different from the land of his birth, for do not forget that I was from there as well and you are half of me!" Ua-Zit pointed at each of her sons to sit and then turned her attention to Suti who was turning red trying in vain to further quell his anger. She sensed this and spoke, "Beloved Suti, you are right in some things. For do not forget that I and my sister are the rulers of this land and not yourselves", she scanned the faces of each of her nieces and nephews.

"Your voices belong to us in this meeting; we speak them as if they are ours. All of you must agree at present, that the ideas brought forth belong to all of us and make our family strong. We must not break the string that binds us together in power by mere wording. The words are merely a formality. So, cease your anger and speak only wisdom in this chamber and do not focus on each word specifically, but on the whole of our plans."

Suti slumped down, while his boar had settled down at the changed and quelled anger of his master and focused his attention to a fly that had entered this chamber. The very same pernicious fly had landed on his nose!

The others in the room noticed this humorous change from the meeting that was beginning to take on the tones of wrath, yet wisely quelled by Ua-Zit. They all softened their mood to giggle at the boar and his feeble attempts to rid the fly from his nose.

Au-Set drank in the mood and discussions held in the room as slowly as she did her honeyed beer. Savoring each drop as she did the expressions of each person present to every topic as it was entered for discussion, she gathered it all to her mind. She noticed the wisdom of her aunt Ua-Zit and the calm acceptance of her other aunt. The offerings of the wise Ma-At and Neferet, who never seemed to age, were more apparent to Au-Set in this moment. She felt that the women Nugig looked her own age and yet, in this meeting seemed weighed down with the wisdom of crones older than her grandmother Tefnut did. The Nugig had aged, yet very few wrinkles were revealed on either of them. She wondered if perhaps both Nugig were born of the same priestess, though one was slender and the other not. The only difference was their size, yet both looked oddly the same to Au-Set for the first time.

Au-Set then cast her eyes around the room and saw her brother Suti being scolded by Heru for taking too much bread. She laughed silently at this and then found herself looking over at her sister and shadow. She noticed that whenever Neb-Het looked at either of her own consorts, she was either amused in a haughty way or repulsed whenever she especially glanced at Suti. Au-Set wondered on this. She observed her sister's eyes drift over to her Au-Sar to become secretly fixated there. She suddenly felt the lust within her sister as if it were her own. Neb-Het became aware of her sister's gaze, blushed, and quickly bent her head down to gather some oysters on her golden plate in the tiny silver pick used to collect each morsel to her mouth with vigor. Au-Set was startled by this feeling caught from her twin sister and did not know what to do with it. Tehuti, from next to her, nudged her from her wandering thoughts, "Sister, what think you of this apple from this land, the pomegranates. Odd how one eats the seeds from this fruit when we discard those from our homeland's similar fruit. Interesting..."

"Oh, Tehuti, you have saved me from my thoughts again." She whispered to him while the aunts were bent on a loud discussion about the new Gods of this land in the pantheon.

She whispered to Tehuti, "Have you noticed how Neb-Het stares at Au-Sar?"

"You have nothing to worry about sister, for Au-Sar cares nothing for anyone but you and the land that he plows." Finding the truth in this and the added humor in his unintended wording, they both giggled. Nebmaat from across the table reached over to send Au-Set a grape for her to eat from his fingers. Au-Set reached over to take the morsel offered and savored it on her tongue and then looked at her consort with promise of similar treatment from her own tongue to him after the meeting. He blushed. Au-Sar in his possessiveness reached over to his consort next to him, slid his arm around her waist, and held it firmly as if he owned it. Au-Set leaned towards him as well and made promises in turn. She directed his gaze towards the discussion at hand for it involved his own great love of the land and agriculture. His grip grew tantalizingly firmer as if the mere discussion of the land and its uses only made him all the more eager for her. She smiled.

Tehuti focused his attention on Ma-At and Neferet when the discussion turned to the new picture writing that he was creating and of his papyrus.

Chapter 33

Much was learned and discussed in this very first of many meetings that were to be held at the yearly inundation of the Great River. It had lasted into the wee hours of the evening when the brightest star had appeared and signaled the end. New meetings were added for the days ahead with a different topic for each day.

The younger siblings were always seen in each other's company at their leisure time along the banks of the river. They had found a spot where they would gather by the carcass of an ancient palm tree that bent over in a past flooding and used as a bench to exchange all that they had missed of each other. Tehuti and Heru would often exchange stories of the new land and of the lessons, they had learned. Suti was taking everything too personally though was calmed down by the patient Heru. Au-Sar had tried to find Suti several times to talk with him, but had found only silence and anger each time that he tried, so he soon gave up and sulked back to his corner not knowing what had changed this attitude in his youngest brother. Au-Set and Neb-Het sometimes would walk off alone to reconnect with each other.

During one of these walks when Au-Set and Neb-Het were alone meandering along steep banks of this part of the river on the outskirts of the settlement, Neb-Het spoke up to break their united silence, "Sister, am I your shadow, your khaibit?"

"Ah, you have learned as well about the ways of the people. No, you are your own person. Why ever would you feel that way?"

"I suppose that I just feel that no matter what I have to offer in this life, you will always get the credit. It has always been that way."

"Yes, even when it was something wrong, I was most often punished for what we both did together since it was my fault for leading you!" They giggled at this.

"Yes, I suppose that it has its good points as well. Again, it was you who thought of this."

Au-Set stopped and looked at her own reflection in the almost identical image of her twin sister. "Sister, we need each other. For you might be the reflection of us, but without even that we are only one dimension. You add the life to our family. You make us laugh and find wonder in everything. I find work and you find pleasure. I wish I had your ability in that aspect."

"I do the work too, but no one seems to care in the long run or they soon forget that it was ever my own idea in the first place."

"Does it really matter whose idea that it was, or should it really matter that the idea was eternal enough to stand the tests of time and that it was implemented at all to work? I mean, who will remember us long after our new cities fall prey to the desert? It will be our ideas collectively that will last long after our names and our bodies have been called to dwell with the Gods. Our names and memory really do not mean a thing in the grand scheme of things.

"Like a pebble thrown into a quiet pond. The pebble fills the silent pond with life and the new ideas ripple to the shores. That tiny little pebble that started it all is fast forgotten. But does it really matter when the idea has reached the shores and has changed it and hopefully for the better?"

"I love the way you see things Au-Set. You are true in that. I hope that I have your wisdom in this and can take it into practice."

"You do already, I have seen it in the meetings and know which ideas are really yours, and I feel them in my soul as they are a part of me as well."

Au-Set felt great love for her sister and felt it reciprocated. Still she did not like the way Neb-Het's eyes would always wander over to Au-Sar when he was present. She felt that Au-Sar was oblivious to Neb-Het's attentions and hoped for it as well.

Chapter 34

The meetings ended after eight days of debate and a lot of learning from each other, which was a full week in the calendar of Kemet. Au-Set felt the bonds of her family becoming strong in their alliance. Much was accomplished that would set the foundations of her family's rule in this land for years to come.

Au-Set reflected on this, oblivious of her surroundings as she made her way back to her tent after the last of the meetings. They were preparing for their return trip at first light. She was weary and trying to sort out all that she had learned, when she heard the first footstep behind her. She turned in curiosity to what had created it and found the silent form of her youngest brother, Suti. His eyes were glazed over from drink and seemed empty to her.

"Suti, what brings you out here, have you something more that you wish to discuss brother?" She held out her arms to embrace him and he pushed them away almost stumbling over in the process. She felt a sudden instinct to proceed wearily.

"Au-Set, I have listened to all that you have added to the meetings and I wonder do you see what I have done."

"Oh, course I have."

"You have always received all of the credit for all that we... what your younger siblings have done and I am tired of it." His eyes grew intense in his study of her and slowly roamed over her body draped in the moonlight through the dense palm fronds that dangled lazily and oblivious to their discussion.

"Brother, we all know what work was actually yours and you know that you have received great admiration from all of us. You speak with tired words brother, you need some sleep." She felt the air around her grow ominous and it seemed to close in on her. She felt invisible hands suddenly trapping her in place from the fear that grew within her at the look from his face.

Suti seemed to grow older than his thirteen years and taller than she did at the same time. She took a small step backwards and away from the eerie visage that he was creating. Au-Set wondered at his sudden hostility and was confused by it. She had noted that never before had his anger ever been directed at her... She wondered if perhaps she was misreading this situation and stood riveted.

It was then that she heard the growl that she knew was from her brother's shadow, from the beast that he always had guarding his side. She secretly detested this ugly creature and wondered what her brother saw in it.

Suti sensed her fear, it only seemed to give him more strength, and it filled his loins with the lust of power that he was feeling. He was tired of bowing down to her and of the power that she had as the oldest female sibling that would never be his. He felt that it was greatly unfair and wondered why she would forever reap the glory while he could only be the minion of his sisters and especially Au-Set. How he hated her and wanted to control her for once. He wanted to be the one with the power.

He reached out for Au-Set and grabbed her close to his body that was drenched in sweat with the mere notion that he thought of her in his control and power for once.

Au-Set was startled and wondered at his game, she could not believe the venom that sprung from his thoughts and now actions. In his grasp, she felt small and tried to break free. Yet, his grasp became tighter in response to her struggles and confusion. It became still tighter, almost smothering the life out of her.

Still, she was frozen in panic wondering if this were some sort of nightmare for the reality of the situation continued to delude her.

He tipped her chin up to look at his eyes. She tried desperately not to look into them as if pretending that this was someone else or an illusion. She hoped from deep within that it was in reality anyone besides her youngest brother, a daemon perhaps. Anything else would lessen the impact of what she was struggling to break free of.

His mouth found hers and brutally attacked it almost biting her. His intensity caused him to drool and finding power in her reaction, he stuck his tongue deep in her mouth trying to eat out her heart in essence. Au-Set was numb and found her body not reacting to her fear, she felt powerless to Suti's increasing physical demands.

Suti grabbed his hands violently on her buttocks molding them and then reaching under her gown between her legs. His hands firmly holding her and gaining strength from her struggles grew bolder by each passing moment. She tried to scream out, but his tongue was blocking her efforts and drowning within her, his hunger for her even more eminent with each movement that she made in fear.

He then threw her on the ground and brutally took her, claiming that she was now his and that she would always know it, for he would make sure that she would never forget this. Her lack of reaction only caused him to renew his strength even more and then took her again, while she lay mute and dazed. The adrenalin fueled his passions in the power that he had over her. She looked pathetic and stupid to him and he loved it. He loved how his power stole away all of her meaningless words. He knew who was in control and he felt stronger with each thought of it, for he knew that this would be the only way he could have a woman...to take her against her will. Though he did not particularly like them or find interest in them, he loved the way they were brought down to nothing when it was taken from them. He did not care that in the land of his birth, this was forbidden and he would have been given the worst death imaginable and forced to walk bodiless through eternity when his body would have been burned and lost, his ashes scattered to oblivion. He did not care. He truly did not care and had felt even more powerful because he knew that he would get away with this by the look in her eyes. He knew that she refused to see the reality in this from the stubborn determined look on her face. He looked at Au-Set and saw that as she was frantically trying to gather back her torn gown, she was desperately trying to block out this act, as if it would disappear with the rays of the moon and destroyed with the rising sun.

Au-Set in truth was doing just that, she felt the threat in Suti and of his faithful companion, whom she knew would only destroy her if she were ever to utter one word of this.

Chapter 35

Ever since Au-Set felt the first stirring in her womb and knew, it was from Suti and not from her consorts. Au-Sar was away so often and Nebmaat had been ill with the swamp sickness, only after several months had he recovered as if nothing had ever touched him at all.

The new palace was growing around her in splendor. With pride, she noticed the recently built walls of stone and mud-brick being painted with vivid scenes. Friezes from her homeland adorned the walls in border on a mother-of-pearl background of pastoral scenes that her brother Au-Sar had chosen.

Yet, inside her, she dreaded each movement of this new life created from such hatred of her. She felt strangely detached and tried to expel it on several occasions, yet this life continued to grow and thrive as a reminder of the loathing that she felt for her youngest half-brother.

Why was not the first life in her from her consorts? She wondered at the irony of this and why it had to be from Suti. Would this child be born with red hair like her brother, forever marking it as it did Suti's blood? She fervently prayed that it would not. Yet, she knew that his hatred of her only fueled the life within her and might have the power to dominate it as he did her body.

Her favorite lapis lazuli drinking vessel brought the sanity of the wine to her thoughts in the dark sky laden image of the natural stone. The first wave jilted her from her thoughts and her fight to clarify them and sent the vessel crashing in pieces as it struck the tiled floor.

The servants looked up and at attention; they brought her to the women's birthing chamber. This was the room where all of the women of the palace communed when the moon-blood came upon them. Women to bring forth life to the palace also used it. It was a sacred room of peace and solitude, when women could reflect during their cycles and with added magical strength, many spells were cast in this chamber. No men were allowed to enter at all. In this room Au-Set was led. The other women of the palace, especially those that were brought over from Eshnunna and her aunt had filled the beautiful chamber with their flurry of activity. More battles were fought in rooms such as this than anywhere outside.

The usual room for the Goddess Representative to give birth was in the highest chamber above the temple, but here in Kemet, they allotted a special chamber for all of the women to share in the center of the palace and in each village. It has been proven that when many women are around each other on a daily basis, their menstrual cycles merge together slowly over time, so it was normal for all of the women of the village or palace to be in the chamber during this cycle. Every village, city and temple had a chamber or room dedicated this and it was like this since the beginning of time.

The women would spend this time together away from their normal duties and there was even a room attached with sleeping cubicles for those who wanted to get away. Only women who were in cycle were allowed in the inner sanctum where all secrets were revealed. This was the one place in any settlement, where a woman could be herself and forget about all of her obligations, where they were equal with all of the other women despite their born positions.

After many hours of fighting the greatest battle of all, a princess was born finally to Au-Set. A tiny infant with the strongest lungs poured out her anger at her sudden release from the warm and damp womb of her mother. The other women delighted in this tiny addition to their chamber and passed her around breathing timeless wisdom into the new female to adorn their world.

"Her name will be Set for she is mine!" Au-Set screamed this with the last of her strength. "Set, Set, Set, Set", was uttered throughout the high vaulted chamber and drumbeats were added to each pronunciation of her name. The women snapped to her name and slowly started to beat their hennaed bare feet in unison to cry forth the new princess's name. Little Set was one of them now; more power was added to this sacred chamber with her femininity.

All whom danced in the chamber that evening knew that the tiny life that was held aloft by the daughters of the Goddess was still remembering her past life and was filled in that moment with ancient wisdom. All nodded in reverence as they passed the new princess in obedience to her knowledge.

All infants were born with the knowledge of their ancestors, though helpless to teach any of it. All infants could see the ancients who walked among them.

All of the women wept in their joy at the knowledge that the new infant would soon forget this great ancestral knowledge, as she would grow strong enough to talk and walk among them. Though wept again since that power would soon be found when they were brought back to the Great Mother in the sky. Life was a circle, and in this moment, the past met with the future, the connection of old life with this new life was made with the birth of each new child.

As the women danced around the chamber to the beat of the drums to the name of the princess, they reached out to the form of the new life and tried to grasp the power of her ancestors into them. This was the magic of the sacred women's chamber.

In this room, no woman was above the others as they normally were outside of the room. A queen was equal to the lowest slave in her femininity and all shared their knowledge with each other. No negativity that was normally outside of the women's chamber was ever allowed into this most sacred of holy spaces that every village or settlement possessed in all of the Goddess lands.

This tradition was so ancient and was embraced across the known world. No one knew the beginnings and no one could fathom the ends of this tradition of a women's sacred community. They all just marveled that the traditions were the same no matter what land they lived in and was older than the earth. This tradition wove women together and if this tradition were to end,

women would forever lose their most sacred feminine
traditions and connections to each other.

Chapter 36

Tehuti was enjoying his time spent in the *Temple of Words* where he taught the new picture writing language to all of the priestesses who came down with them from Eshnunna in their exodus. With his love for the written word and the creation of more and more elaborate pictures for the language and sounds, he always looked for more. For too long he had the knowledge of his birth land and had been silent to the rest on his feelings about it. No one here cared as they all soon settled into the daily demands of their life in Kemet and in the implementation of their plans. Their past seemed forgotten by his family, though not by him. He felt his past calling out to him each night, its grasp drawing him near, begging him to return and to find out more.

Word had recently reached him that with the new rule, the name of his beloved birth-city of Erech was changed to *Ur* and his land from Eshnunna to *Sumer*. It seemed as if they were trying to destroy all evidence of the past. He was practically dying of curiosity to find out the truth and to find the underlying cause of this heaviness he felt on the whole matter.

He had managed to convince his aunt Ua-Zit to allow them to return. Ua-Zit was gravely concerned for his welfare, fearing what he could find upon his return, yet she was as eager as he was to find out the fate of her sister and her temple. Therefore, she bid him good wishes on his journey and sent him with his brothers Heru and Suti along with the consorts.

They knew that they had to be invisible to the world in their identity, if they were to be truly safe in Eshnunna. They also assured their aunts that this would be a knowledge gaining expedition only.

In the silence of the evening, they had safely left the harbor of Per-Uto to sail down the river leading to the expanse of the great desert between the lands.

They would then travel under the evening stars until they reached the spot where the Tigris and Euphrates met at its most southern point by their direction and then on to the city itself, the new city called Ur in the new land of Sumer.

The stars guided them along with the knowledge of the Canaanites who seemed to have a great affinity to the open sea and knowledge that earned them a valuable reputation. They were still unblemished by the northern tribes and worshipped their own Queen of Heaven similar to that of Eshnunna. They normally kept to themselves and from the men of Eshnunna, spoke the language of the herdsmen of the deserts, and required the use of an interpreter for the young princes. They silently led them to the land of their birth and then to the city that they sought, in gestures made in the wee hours of the evening under the canopy of heavens under the protection of the Queen of Heaven.

When they had reached the shores of Ur in the dead of night, Tehuti, Suti and Heru along with the other men of Kemet led them to a quiet search in finding a place to pitch their tent during their stay.

They traveled under the guise of simple farmers and even obtained some vegetables to sell at the market. They knew the best place to obtain information was at the marketplace. The brothers and their entourage dressed in the simple homespun garb of modest farmers and they purported to be from afar so that they would not be known as familiar with the language of the new land called Sumer.

The three brothers blended perfectly into the markets of Ur and became a part of the lively stalls around them. As mates were sent out to purchase items at the market, they silently sold their wares as they listened to all of the gossip that surrounded them in a deafening roar in the marketplace. They had fun feigning ignorance of the language that they knew from birth.

They had learned that the temple was taken over by a priest and a new God was placed there by the name of Enlil. This new group of people from the northern tribes who had overrun and conquered their city deified the man who had raped and killed their mother. The men around them were now observed to be bold, not hiding under the weight of the Goddess of this land and of the prior reign. The men spoke venom of the old Goddess and of the power of the new God who had taken her and forced her to be his consort. The brothers tried to hide their pain for their mother when they heard this. It was difficult for them to pretend they did not understand the language around them. People were speaking as if they were not there, once their language barrier was discovered. They prayed in their fervent hopes that this was only the created propaganda for their God and cherished the secret hope that their mother was still alive. Her sons knew that she would have contacted them if she were still alive and that if she were allowed to survive the torments of rape, she would have taken her own life.

Chapter 37

After the noises of the daily market had dwindled down to their closing the stalls for the evening, they returned to their respective tents.

Tehuti had first spoken up, "Brothers, we must find out the truth of these rumors. If she is alive, she is probably being held as prisoner. However, she could no longer have children, since Suti was her last. We must find out though. And if she is still alive, we must save her, despite what the aunts made us promise!"

"Aye, you speak wisely brother. I agree," interjected the wise and thoughtful Heru.

Suti, who was always the one to stir trouble vehemently disagreed, "Brothers, I say we return and let her rot! Why you insisted on my presence in this quest, I will never know! She has abandoned us! I hope that it is not true, but in the market, it sounds all too likely that this is the way of things. I like it not and have nothing to say to her!"

Heru leaned towards his passionate younger brother and spoke soothingly in the tones he knew would quell his brother's anger, "Suti, you hardly remember her, how could you say such things. She loved us so and was a loving mother. She gave us a life in Kemet that never would have happened here had we stayed behind. She sacrificed herself so that we could live. We would have surely been killed by the soldiers for our birthright had we stayed there one moment longer!"

"Aye, Suti listen to Heru, he speaks wise words. Our mother likely died to save us; we just need to find out the truth. Are you with us? Or will you sit here and pout?" Tehuti ruffled the bright red hair of his youngest brother and playfully nudged him as Suti stewed in anger beside him. The mood in the tent changed as soon as a wrestling match broke out as the brothers became tangled in their blankets trying to pin the other down. They laughed as if to fight away any sadness they had in entering the tent that evening.

After listening to the men of the market for five days, they had finally learned that men had easy access to the temple as in the days of old. Men could enter a room and learn the meanings hidden within by the trained priestesses. They could easily petition the temple women as in the days of old to incredible delights that were essential to their humanity. Even in the new rule, each act performed by a priestess brought them closer to their Goddess.

However, the God Enlil reigned in the temple and made the high priestess his consort and first *wife*. A wife was a new word to the men born of Eshnunna as it meant the ownership of a woman, a new concept in their world. The word they used had more of the meaning of being cherished and loved. All of the other priestesses of the Nugig were made into his lesser wives and concubines. Their children born to them were still held in high regard but belonged to the God Enlil and not to the Goddess, for the God subdued her.

The brothers having learned of this had found a pleasure in this new power granted to men that they never had before. However, Heru and Tehuti felt hurt inside as if they were betraying the ways of the old in this feeling and especially their own mother. Yet, they had gained a renewed strength from this newfound knowledge.

Chapter 38

As supplicants, they made their way apprehensively towards the steep temple that they had left so long ago. With each step, they uttered the prayers appropriate in leading them towards the womb of their people that topped the great stairway leading towards the heavens above the city below them. The last rays of the sun of that day followed them as they reached the top. At the top, there were luxurious gardens that dripped down along the sides and led them to a great entrance under enormous columns with the ancient carved snakes of the Goddess coiling down to greet them. They suddenly felt small and in awe of the place of their own birth so long ago.

They felt their mother all around them, becoming them and seeping into their veins, stronger with each step they took towards the entrance. The doors were larger than the tallest palm tree of Kemet and towered above them. They were of wood that was inlaid with polished gold and gleamed with the fading remnants of days left long behind them. Intricate carvings on the doors told the story of their creation that was lost in meaning to the people of their own time. The temple was so old that no one could recall the time when it was actually created. They were from before his family came to Eshnunna and told the story of the creation of the city now called Ur. The ancient faces peered out in copper faded green to the brothers, perhaps knowing the secret of their actual identity, yet remained silent.

Two old men who appeared almost as ancient as the door they guarded opened the doors slowly to the new supplicants. Inside was an ominous passageway lit by oil lamps. Frankincense permeated the air and lulled them forward. The boys walked on as directed in curiosity, for never had they entered the temple before this way in their lives. They had recalled the priestesses and their family always used the secret passageways underneath the temple for entrance.

In the shadows, large and unrecognized statues beckoned menacingly to them. The statues appeared all the more horrific in the dim light of the narrow passageway. Suddenly, behind them appeared a priestess whose hair glowed in the diffuse light a brilliant gold. Unlike any, they had seen before, they all wondered if she were perhaps the Goddess herself. Behind them was only the entrance of which the doors had rapidly though silently closed behind. They knew not how she appeared behind them, as if from the very air itself.

"I am Ninlat, your guide." She nimbly stepped to the fore of the brothers. Her form was graceful and glowing in the oil lamp light from the lamps above them. She was naked before them, yet led the aura that she was draped in the finest linen garments of a queen, so fine were her tiny steps. Her golden hair cascaded around her and made her appear all the more otherworldly and unreal to them.

"Your wishes are my command. Do you seek audience with the God Enlil perhaps or delights from his priestesses?"

Suti was growing ravenous and wanted to grab this insolent woman to make her scream beneath him, his body reacted with the thought that was not hidden from the priestess. "We seek pleasure and power from the priestesses!" Suti whispered in a crackling voice.

Tehuti was slightly angered over his youngest brother's lack of control so he pinched him, which caused Suti to yelp.

"Great priestess and guide, we seek audience with the God Enlil for we have many questions that only he can answer." Spoke Tehuti to the patient priestess. Heru nodded in agreement with his oldest brother, while Suti wrenched from the grasp of Heru and uttered, "They seek answers while I seek women for I need replenishment from my travels!"

Ninlat rang a bell and out of nowhere behind them appeared another woman of equal beauty with hair of the brightest red that they had ever seen, made all the more glorious in the sacredness of the moment. "Delaag, bring this brother to the chambers of the priestesses."

Tehuti and Heru acknowledged their brother's desires since they knew that he would only be a hindrance in their mission with his uncontrollable will and temper, and he might even give away their secret identity. Tehuti addressed Suti, "Brother, meet us back in our tent in an hour." Heru let out a bellow of laughter, knowing that if he were in his brother's position, it would take longer than that. He looked at Tehuti and then they both snickered, "All right, we will see you there in the morning!"

As Suti was being led away to the chamber of the trained priestesses of the new God, the brothers followed the priestess down another passageway that led further up to the great heights of the temple to an area once familiar to them.

At last, the two remaining brothers were led to an inner chamber, which they recognized immediately as their mother's old greeting chamber. Murals of stars adorned the walls and ceiling of the chamber that was filled with tiles made of lapis lazuli. They recalled the stars were carved out of quartz crystal and glittered in the light from the large oil lamps that stood on silver bases raised from the ground. In the center of the large vaulted chamber was a raised platform that was lifted by eight columns. Curtains were bunched up around each column open for the supplicants to witness the God within. They had both recalled sitting on that very spot since their earliest memories on their mother's lap on official occasions. It was odd viewing this chamber from the view of the supplicant, instead of being inside of the platform.

The new *God* Enlil sat there on their mother's throne made of the darkest of onyx. He appeared ominously regal as he sat complacently on the usurped throne of their family, seemingly oblivious to the identity of his latest petitioners.

Priestesses with golden hair stood all around him waiting for his every command. They were garbed in clothing made of tiny golden beads that swayed with their every movement. Small diadems of gold encircled each head of the women surrounding this garrulous man before them. They gyrated around his form as if entertaining him in their seductions. He seemed unfazed by all of their attentions, almost as if the supplications of their attentions only enhanced his ability to think.

His robes were of the deepest purple imaginable, stealing the color of the Goddess for himself. The King was in his forties and had a luxurious head of red hair that hung down in curls that almost covered one of his priestesses as she rubbed against him mewing like a cat. He reached out, grabbed one of her breasts, and howled, "We have company, you dumb bitch!" With those words, he tossed her away. She fell in a heap and whimpered. The other tangle of women around him seemed unfazed by his anger and still fought for any attention from their king.

The two brothers watched them all and found themselves lost in the dramatic menagerie of pleasure and seduction that this man was experiencing. They envied how unfazed and regal he appeared to them when most men would not be able to concentrate with all of the external stimuli that this man seemed to experience on a daily basis. Their mouths dropped as they lost control of their bodies. They longed for a harem of their own.

"Come in further and join us, there is plenty to go around. They do whatever I want and more! I cannot have a day without this; I just need it for daily survival. If I lose my tower of strength and the seed stops, so will the power leave this land."

Some of the priestesses had slowly drifted over towards the two new faces that entered the room with the permission of their master. They proceeded to dance about them furiously noticing the power they had gained, tongues darting out tauntingly.

Through it all, the brothers were amazed at how the king would just talk and ramble on. They were lost and numb to all they were experiencing and forgot even their own names as their essence was licked and sucked out of them. They babbled as if fools trapped in sweet oblivion.

"I know who you two really are and I am not afraid. Your mother was delicious we all found her so. She is truly dead, for she lost the power to bring forth life from her womb and served no purpose to me. Come, now boys, did you not know this?"

Tehuti and Heru were being drawn into one act after another, each more intense and more impossible than the last. They had lost their words in the easy seductions of the women who filled the room and answered their bodies every need, even before they knew it themselves."

"You two boys are still young, and I could easily have you killed. Nevertheless, you humor me; you have much to learn about the ways of women! You should join me here, for see, how easily they bend to us. Here you may have many wives who will live for your every command. Here a man controls his house and the children are his alone!" He shuddered from the attentions of the priestesses talents on him. He pushed them off almost sending them crashing into the wall. He appeared to the brothers an oozing grotesque wall of primordial sex and were amazed at how the priestesses were undaunted by his appearance.

"Princes, you have need of this. It calls out for you. I can feel it!" The priestesses called out in the sudden desolation of their master.

"Feel the power of a man; see how they bow down to us! Feel the thrust of the God as he speaks from deep within you!"

Tehuti was lost and could not grasp the meaning of the words of this king, so weak was he in the power of the forces all around him that he did not feel it until it was too late. The king appeared by his side out of nowhere and took him in force to a place that no one had entered him before.

Tehuti screamed, "NOOOOOO, I will not!" His body was almost wishing for the attentions of the priestesses on him rather than this grotesque monster. Yet, his soul cried out in the sudden reality of the genuine predicament that he was in. He felt his humanity and pride leave his body in waves of ripping pain that seemed to engulf his senses.

The so-called king God spoke of a world of honey even as he was being psychologically stabbed. Yet, his words of power drew him almost into this older man's power. He could almost feel himself wanting to forsake all that he knew. He looked weakly over to Heru and saw that he was slightly wavering as well under the spell. Had the king not have been selfish in his lust for the princes, he might have actually convinced them never to return to Kemet.

His pride and dignity were taken away from him and his humanity had returned to him in one great swoop of consciousness. He felt the sticky remains of the king inside of him and watched in silent horror as the king went over to his younger brother Heru. Priestesses swarmed him then to prevent him from rushing to save his brother and had him then on the ground.

Tehuti felt her then as she straddled him forcing out any essence that he had left while another pushed figs into his open mouth to silence his screams and blocking out the visions of horror.

He tasted the madness of this king and his seed on the breath of the priestess nearest him. The figs were mixed with another taste, something foreign to his senses that seemed to blank out any more thoughts.

He realized that he had been drugged from something the priestesses had added to those delicate figs in order to subdue he and his brother. Alternatively, was it possibly given to save them?

The unreality of the evening prior seemed to haze in a fog that was smothering his wakefulness. His muscles were sluggish.

Tehuti had awoken in a sunlit chamber beside the naked form of his brother, who was just starting to wake himself. They were on a blanket that was covered in a weaving of the most brilliant and surrealistic flowers that he had ever seen. The windows were large and arched, into which the sun poured onto their sedated forms vigorously of renewal.

The priestess in the room was clothed now in a long white tunic that was tied at the back of her neck, for the garment was utilitarian in purpose. Her form lost in the garment. She spoke not a word and tended to them in silence. She was rubbing pungent smelling oil on their bodies that seemed to soothe their tired and aching muscles.

This priestess somehow looked familiar to the boys. She was tall, had long black hair like Heru and Tehuti, and had features that reminded them of their mother.

"Hush now, for it is I, Shedabbi, your cousin. He knows of you both! He wanted you both here to bend to his will and to serve him, even more power to him since you are princes of the true blood of the Goddess herself! I noticed how you saw though his act. It would have been your own death, for that is what he had planned. I was watching from the side, curious when I had recognized you both. I knew that he was planning to kill you with the poisoned figs and snuck a substitution in some other ones sent out to you by a friend of mine. He thinks that you are both dead."

She continued, noticing that they were both awake now, "He would have made you both his toys had you agreed with him! He then would have disposed of you both when he grew tired!"

It was then that the horrors of the evening before took physical form in their own bodies, for they had felt the pain at the humiliation caused by this new king in taking them against their will.

"Is it true that he killed our mother?" Tehuti whispered from a hoarse throat.

"Aye, it is true along with her last consort Dimuzi. Their valor is legendary and made them Gods not just representatives. They were killed in the holiest place of the temple. Innana was truly in your mother in the last moment for we all felt it. When she died, so did Innana."

She continued with a new strength, "Go back while you can and take your brother with you! This land has fallen into evil ways, the Goddess is dead here." With that, a small tear fell daintily down her porcelain cheek.

Heru looked up at his cousin, "Cousin, come with us, we have started a new land and the Goddess still lives strong there I assure you!"

Shedabbi looked lost, almost like the little girl they both remembered, "That I cannot do, for my place is here. My mother is Ninlil as he named her and serves as his first wife and *entu*, and I am a mere concubine, a *Sal-Me,* or a priestess of the second class. Due to this honor, my brothers were made *patesi* and serve as governors for two different cities here in Sumer.

"This is now the temple of the "Moon God" who is known to have raped and subdued Innana and who had killed her lover Dimuzi the God. This man has even created a new list of rulers birthing a new history for his Sumer as if he were even greater than the Mother Goddess was. He has thrown away our family and the reign of queens and Goddess-representatives as if they never existed. He placed the names of his ancestors under a paternal list of rule, wiping out any evidence of the Goddess's rule over Erech. Never call this city Erech you may be killed for that! Please, always call it Ur when any people are around. Never forget, deep in your heart our beloved Erech of Eshnunna! I never will! Yet, I am unfortunately lost in his power and the leash that my king and great husband hold me in. Such foreign names of never before kings, taste horrid on my tongue with each utterance or thought of them-yet, it would be by imminent death lest I forget!"

Tehuti and Heru just stared at their cousin and felt her shame mingle with their own at the wretched lusts of this so-called king. They both recalled that the honors of the priestesses were once sacred and revered as such and their touches were once whispers and gentle caresses, as in their own land of Kemet.

They shuddered at the maniacal lust that had permeated the great chamber the evening before that had stole away their senses that they fought desperately to forget and to erase from their memories. It sickened them how the women of Ur were being treated as objects and tossed around to the desires of the king. How they shivered in fear of him yet, bent to his will for his pleasure. They saw how the king grabbed and tore at the women not caring for them, but looking to his own pleasure in their cries and screams from each bit of pain that he caused to them.

Tehuti fought to block out what this twisted and wretched world that his homeland had become. He fought back the tears that he wanted to shed for the loss of all of their innocence from this selfish man who called himself a king and a God.

Neither liked what they had learned but also felt that it was all that they could take. They let their cousin lead the way to their brother and then out of the temple from the same long-forgotten passage they had escaped from in another life it seemed to them.

Chapter 39

The three brothers gathered their entourage and took flight. While resting one day in the desert a large dark man dressed in the elaborate clothes of a merchant of Ur entered their circle of tents and begged audience with the princes.

He knelt down low to the young princes his shadow covering a large span of ground around in him the light of the sun waning down above them. His equally large head gleamed in the sun and in the back; a single almost delicate braid hung down to his almost unnoticeable waist and was woven with tiny carnelian beads. His garment was of the softest and whitest of linens and was trimmed with leopard fur. When he rose, his chins were finely powdered to protect him from the sun. Such a sight he had made to the princes, they only stared. The silence was deafening while the large man trembled before them.

Tehuti spoke first in a pretended dialect of the new Ur, "Man, what bring you here and why you bow down, for we are only simple merchants."

He spoke cautiously as if weighing the very air around them to mark the validity of his identification of the young men dressed in simple merchant garb.

"I am sorry to bother you both, but I feel that I must. For you see, I am Qui...." He paused for it always caused quite a stir among men present since his name meant "little one" and that he was definitely not! He was used to this whenever he introduced himself, for when he was born, he was early and in fact rather small. Later on, it only became dreaming on the part of his mother who soon realized her attempts to get her young infant to gain weight and to catch up with all of the other children of the village, had proved more than successful.

They all stood transfixed for out of this large man came the most whimsical voice ever heard. It was loud in strength, yet sounded almost like a little girl in pitch.

"So sorry... speak Qui." Tehuti bravely tried to hide his reaction, but the larger and older man before him was undaunted.

"I was a loyal servant of your mother's, whose name was Ninnuit and Innana and have been in hiding for many years. I wish to serve and to protect your family.

"I have been searching for years for any word of your family and......it was believed that you were all dead as your mother, so well has your mother protected all of you."

"Why were you not sent down with us, loyal servant?" Heru could only utter out, as he was unbelieving of this strange man before them. He had forgotten the broken dialect they had all practiced in this moment of curiosity. He was especially nervous since they had taken such pains to hide their identity and now it seemed that at least this man here knew of them. He wondered if this man was a spy sent by the king Enlil, since the real Enlil was another man executed in the first invasion of the palace, which preempted the final attack that set this present nightmare into action. He looked over at his brother who knew what he was thinking and nodded.

"You see, that evening, your mother had sent me on a mission for a missing shipment of figs..."

The brothers winced at the reference to figs from their recent horrific experience. Qui had no idea why and continued in his unusual and undaunted manner, "And they were not found in the market that your mother had preferred, and on the way back to the palace....You see, she knew that an invasion was to occur, just not when. For each night, we went to sleep hearing the drums of the enemy outside of the palace walls, not knowing when the battle would start. It was almost as if they were teasing us." His head hung in shame almost stuttering on his words that he tried to keep inside him but knew that he could not, if he were to gain their trust.

"You see...I was distracted when I reached a stall in the markets that was selling my greatest weakness...."

Both princes were drawn to the words of this man who was large and almost grotesque, but in a seemingly innocent way. They nodded for him to continue.

"I stopped for a sample of some honeyed sweets and I lost track of time and had forgotten the errand. For I love them and I was a small boy at that time of twelve summers and whenever I smell honey I become lost in its smell." His head hung down low and he practically kissed the ground reaching out to kiss the toes in honor of the young princes and their station.

"I had failed your mother and you all miserably and have been living in punishment ever since. I have been hiding all of these years under the apprenticeship of a male accountant from Tyre who handles the accounts of this new king. For he will not allow a woman to handle his money as our priestesses used to, he believes that they are only good for one thing only and it is not in working with numbers, if you know what I mean." He rolled his eyes to the princes and they smothered a laugh at his drama in the seriousness of the present matter.

"Do not the priestesses, the Nugig, handle the temple accounts?" Heru inquired.

"Why no. No woman has any power since the throne of Innana crumbled." Wishing to change the subject, he cautiously continued for the princes, "I have many talents and have been trained and raised under the old master of eunuchs of the temple of the old days, for I was especially selected from my village in the land of Kemet for my beauty as a small child."

The princes smiled in good nature at this reference to his selected beauty.

"I might be large, but I am strong, a great singer, and am currently the master of accounts for that merchant of Tyre that I had mentioned, his name is Prosoneth. I am also a master of clothes and design and am sought out far and wide." He flicked his eyelashes appealingly to the young princes, who silently chuckled for this man who was fast becoming a welcome excursion to their expedition. They both looked at each other hoping for some answer to arrive.

Tehuti broke the tension that was building up for them to laugh at the predicament of this man in front of them who innocently presented his plight to them, and in politeness inquired, "Will not your skills in this land be missed?" He wondered if the priestesses would be willing to teach their skills in the new picture language to a man, even though he was a eunuch. However, their aunts would have to let him in, if he was talented in this respect, for it would only establish with the people of Kemet, their plan in equality. His mind pondered on this and of the added bonus, this man would be, if he were genuine. Yet, he remained wary.

"I do not care!" He stood up in his full height and towered over all of the men present with his large pendulous stomach swaying in his vehemence and determination. "I had almost given up finding you all and had to find some way to earn a living in this world turned upside down! Besides, I had to find some way to support my cravings for honey!" His face lit up and his dark complexion revealing to all present, large gleaming white teeth that were remarkably unblemished from his addiction to sweets. Dimples dotted his large cheeks.

Heru was amazed at the audacity of this strange man and yet at the same time found him wondrously humorous and untainted from the wretched new city of Ur. "Let us confer on this. He motioned to Tehuti to join him outside of the circle where the men had gathered in curiosity of the visitor.

Heru spoke first, "Brothers, he seems good and just and might add some life to our return trip. But, I wonder if he has any hidden motives."

"I agree, I will take him to Per-Uto and set him up as Au-Set's designer for her wardrobe, she could desperately use his personality to liven things up for her. She works way too much and needs to laugh more often!"

"Sounds like a feasible plan; do we have enough to support his honey and sweets habit?" Heru snorted in a fast snicker.

"I am sure we probably do and I will test him on the matter of his other claims and look into him since he will be close to our sister. I somehow feel that this is right and good and will benefit our sister greatly."

"What about Neb-Het, I am worried about her as well. She seems to have lost that light that she once had and her womb has been barren with some pain that she will not let us know about."

"We will find someone for her as well, possibly this Qui fellow has someone in mind. He must attract an interesting sort of people with his personality. He seems to beam with kind indifference to the cruelties around him, almost as if he was untouched by it all."

Heru wondered about this as well and added, "Do you really think that he has all of those talents that he had mentioned, for he seemed not to equate our coming from the land of his birth since his name is in the language of our homeland, and all we are speaking of is Eshnunna."

"That, brother, I cannot tell you. However, he seems harmless enough and curious about all of that as well. We can always dispose of him if he does turn out to be a spy; the river is large enough to hide even someone of his great size."

Heru smiled at his brother's great wisdom and agreed on the points mentioned. They both walked back to Qui.

"Qui, we have arrived at the decision to take you with us. However, we are also in need of someone wise such as yourself to look after our sister upon our return, would you know of anyone who could assist our other sister?" Spoke Tehuti.

Almost as if waiting for this, without pausing for a breath, Qui uttered in his large sonorous feminine voice that seemed to shake his belly and the world around him no matter how small. "Well, in fact I do know of someone. My brother Kekes is the one, who, like his name loves to dance and is very skilled in most dances of lands both near and far." He called out making those around him very concerned due to the volume of it. "Kekes, you may come out now!"

Tehuti had to cover his ears to keep them from exploding while all eyes traveled to the direction of Qui's bright beaming eyes. From out of the bushes at the edge of the camp jumped an equally dark man who was as thin as his brother was large, with bones protruding in almost every direction. The clothes that he wore seemed suspiciously feminine, though he was definitely a man due to his great height. Tehuti, Heru, and the rest of the men around both new men were mystified and drank in the contrasts of the two brothers as identified by Qui. The tall, thin one had the movements of a small bird who danced with each step. Unlike Qui, the identity fit his brother.

"How had he managed to escape and what did he do at the palace temple?" Questioned Tehuti of Qui, and then turned to the brother curious to hear his voice. He nodded for the question to be responded by Kekes.

Out of his mouth came the most feminine of voices. It seemed almost impossible after hearing the voice of his brother, from such a large and tall man it seemed oddly out of place, yet harmonious in a weird way. The voice was distinctly sensitive and teasing, uttered even on such a serious question, "I am the older brother of Qui and had come along with our family when our brother was made famous by his being chosen as a temple eunuch by your mother."

He continued, "Our family stayed in Erech supported by my brother until that awful night, ghastly, nasty." His face grimaced as if recalling the memory of it, largely enunciating the descriptions that played across his mind.

Qui chimed in, "They saved me and we all set up shop under that merchant from Tyre when it was safe and the city was settled, but we never gave up our search for your family. Our mother was a temple register and our father kept the house for us and was in charge of mother's wardrobe. We will travel wherever you lead us!"

"Wherever you lead us your gorgeous princes!" The voice of Kekes danced.

Tehuti and Heru smiled and found the brothers much fun. They both knew that the odd brothers would definitely brighten their sister's duties and possibly with any luck, be of value as well.

Tehuti noticed a squeaking at this point and had a look of confusion on his face when Qui noticed and added, "Oh, this is my pet, QuiQui!" Out of the large furls of fabric draped around him, he pulled out a tiny mouse that squeaked louder away from the warmth of his master. "He is no harm to anyone but himself, for he is always getting into trouble! He was almost served as a dinner on more than one occasion!"

"Qui, he keeps you out of trouble for he has more brains than you do!" His older brother bellowed. A laugh issued forth from Qui, which spread fast among those present, except for Suti who was silently stewing with his own issues.

However, Suti who was well content had enjoyed his visit so much that he wished fervently to stay and to join the king. He found much in common with him. Moreover, he felt his temper building at the control of his older brothers.

The priestesses told him secretly that he was the only true son of Enlil and therefore the only rightful heir to their present leader, the man who called himself the God Enlil. When conversing with the king, he realized that the older man knew of this and thus, offered to rule beside him and to inherit a place by the throne beside his oldest nephew in a joint ruler-ship. Though Suti was naturally suspicious of this, he could not help but to be curious at the same time. He liked the way things were here and felt that at least he was appreciated in Ur, unlike among the people of his mother in Kemet. They adored his red hair and told him that it was a mark of a king. While the people of his mother's side felt that, it was an abomination.

Of the two very odd men that appeared at their campsite, Tehuti and Heru sensed correctly that their younger brother was about to bolt the area. They had noticed his growing tension since they had all reunited. Tehuti reached out to hold his brother Suti.

"How dare you grab onto me like this! I am staying! I belong here and you know it!"

"Suti, you have a mate to care for and you are the main consort. We are your family! Come with us!" Tehuti was losing his patience and thought about leaving his youngest brother behind.

Heru had to plead with Tehuti on his brother's behalf. Part of him even wondered why but the voice of their mother who had found a way through had pleaded with his soul to save Suti.

"Brother, he must come with us, for you know it is the will of our mother. He knows not what he says in his youth for he was as drugged as we were." He pulled Tehuti aside to plead with him.

"Knock him out if you have to, bind him, and drag him back with us. When he wakes, he will have probably forgotten all about it for he still reeks of the drugs."

"Heru, you have great sense in this, as always when matters lead to Suti." Tehuti looked over at one of the guards and then at the size of Qui who stood miraculously silent beside his older brother, "Take care of him and bring him back though you might have to bind him or knock him out, if needs be."

Qui walked over to the stumbling brother who was raving incoherently about his wishes to become apprentice to the so-called king. "Why do you want to cause your brothers so much trouble?" He questioned Suti in such a soft voice that it was barely audible.

Suti stood there and responded, "I am not afraid of you, you big hippopotamus!"

Qui looked at Tehuti and then Heru and they both nodded in accord. Reading their thoughts with their granted permission and to prove his value, he quickly thonked Suti over the head with his massive arms, his golden bracelets glimmered in the sun in an almost feminine tune. Then just as quickly, Suti thumped to the ground in response in a very unrefined manner from the force of it.

The others were well impressed with the speed in which the very large man moved and with his agility.

They noticed that their young brother was unharmed and only stunned and very knocked out for the present moment. Qui with equal precision stepped over and caught the rope tossed to him by Tehuti and securely bound the rebellious youngest brother with such speed that the others stood transfixed.

Kekes danced up and down in the way of a little girl, squealing in delight at his brother's strength, "That' my brother, my big, bad brother! And don't you forget it!" The men around them rolled on the ground in a riotous reaction to the silly dance of Kekes.

Upon their return and after they relayed all of their new-found information at the yearly meeting with their aunts and other siblings, Tehuti settled back into the life of the new scribal school that he was setting up in Khnum. The horrific events suffered by he and Heru were forgotten with each step taken away from Sumer. They both vowed to seek vengeance on the new king to each other, though both knew that it would have to wait for the timing was not right.

They had to focus on working on making Kemet a stronger force to be reckoned with before such vengeance was to occur. They were bringing a new magic to the land, Tehuti with his words and picture language and Heru with his wisdom and grasping of the new legends and mythology that was springing forth making their family mythical and God-like to the people of this land.

Their pains suffered in the new land of Sumer bonded Heru and Tehuti. The new cities were slowly created around them and solidified in mud-dried bricks and stone as had never before been seen in their land. The people almost felt that the power of the reigning family was in each vein of the smoothly polished stones and they prayed to them as if it were true.

Chapter 40

While Suti, on the other hand, was even more impatient to return to the splendors that he felt waited for him in the land of Sumer. He acted out in anger and frequently beat his servants and slaves.

He knew that his treatment of the slaves was wrong since they were not completely lowly for the most part. Most were only serving time on a contract for the debts of their mothers as they were sold into slavery to pay out the terms. Some were even from the royal houses of Kemet and Sumer and some were even his cousins.

Yet, Suti felt the power that he had gained from his experience in Sumer. The women let him beat them, the temple priestesses had begged for more, or so he interpreted in his own twisted mind. Their screams woke him up in the wee hours of the evening, giving him such a hunger that he had to leave his chamber to seek out the same from the people of the settlement around Nekhen. He always brought along his dog Heh and the boar named Suka, his companions who kept vigil during his escapades in the village. Soon, all of the village boys, girls, and even the women shrank in terror at his form and tried to hide from his increasingly twisted demands on them. They knew that if they tried to alert his family of his nightly raids or if they screamed out during any acts that he demanded of them that his companions would tear them to shreds.

Neither Neb-Het nor Nekhebt were even aware in the slightest, of the drastic change in Suti. Only Heru suspected and tried in vain to hide the evil and dangerous exploits of his notorious brother. Sometimes, he would even resort to drugging his brother so that he would not wake in the evening to carry out his increasingly strange fetishes. He had heard the rumors of the people and he sensed the restlessness of his brother. He feared that the people would soon rebel against the new family due to the actions of Suti. The rumors seemed to override any good that he and his sister were doing. Despite all of this, it was still kept silent.

Nevertheless, Heru knew that the people were gaining far too much wealth from the new prosperity brought by opening up the land in trade. He knew, however, that the people would only remain silent for so long and he shuddered at the all too imminent thought of it.

He was tired of watching over his brother and felt his body grow weary from many sleepless evenings when he often wondered on new ways to prevent the wills of his brother in trying to keep one step ahead of him to protect the people. Heru knew his younger brother was becoming a master of torture and would often lure young girls and boys back to a chamber that he had hidden somewhere near the palace.

Yet, Heru had still not found this hidden place, though he heard the torments received there in trembled whispers that would cease at his presence. He felt almost as contaminated as Suti, in his not being able to find the place. Heru worried constantly about the mind of his brother and what had caused this. Suti was given everything he wanted. Heru shed silent tears at his brother's great anger and the fact that he did not know how to stop, control, or save Suti.

He recalled that his mother had great faith in his ability to bind the family together and that was why he was born. Unfortunately, he had failed with even the two that were sent here. He felt a dismal failure to their mother, wanted desperately to bring them all back together again, and to save them from the torments that Neb-Het, Suti and even his aunt seemed to inflict on themselves.

Heru also felt great sorrow for his sister Neb-Het for her womb remained empty of life as if Suti had sucked it all out of her. He saw how her early shine that he had witnessed some years ago had dissipated with the horrid treatment of her main-consort Suti. He suspected that Neb-Het covered bruises inflicted on her by Suti, but she never let him near to see them. Neb-Het became elusive and found excuses to dwell alone in her own chambers, which left the kingdom to Suti and himself to deal with on their own.

Neb-Het was becoming a shadow in reality and he sensed that she was dying inside, especially after Suti had taken a mistress. She was a lowly village woman who was dark and stooped over. Her face was pockmarked and she always had a horrid leer on her face almost as if she was laughing inside for all of the pain that she caused Neb-Het with her presence. Her name was Puanit.

Heru felt the pain of Upper Kemet and felt powerless to do anything about it. Each time that he pleaded with his brother to stop his demands on the people; it only seemed to make his brother more vivid in his anger.

Neb-Het would not even look at him in the face and avoided all of his attempts to gain her confidence. He noticed that the glow and independence that she had once shone with had dulled considerably and appeared almost lost on this earthly plane. Her thoughts were deep inside and locked tight from anyone. She was wan and thin and her once luxurious hair had now appeared dim and lusterless, like her world that she was building up around her in protection. She sometimes looked up at Heru and tried to let him into her pain but he knew that he could do nothing about it. He knew that Neb-Het desperately needed a child and a purpose in life and that, at present, she felt that she had none.

He had given up long ago on his aunt Nekhebt and could only find solace in the endless wisdom of Neferet and her never fading beauty. Yet their words and plans found no other ears than each other's and in the correspondence of his brother, Tehuti, whom he begged not to tell anyone. Heru was desperately trying to find a way to turn it all back and to take away the darkness that was absorbing them all.

Heru felt bad for their newly acquired Kekes who seemed to dance all of the time, oblivious to all of the pain around him, to music that had long ago ceased in the palace. He actually grew to like the strange and innocent man in whose size only made it more impossible not to grow fond. Kekes was always charming the children of the servants and slaves since Neb-Het and Nekhebt seemed impenetrable in their chosen solitude.

Heru in sympathy almost was tempted to send him down south in their land to Per-Uto where his talents for amusing others would be better appreciated. Yet, thought the better of it, for he desperately needed sunlight in this dismal land. Even though it was always bright outside the ominous walls, inside the sun seemed to die with all of the silence and unrequited dreams that had vanished long ago.

He discovered that Kekes was valuable in that he had great hidden intelligence. Most would think the man simple with his riotous and flamboyant appearance and garishly feminine attire. Yet, Heru had discovered that Kekes had a very keen mind that never forgot one detail and could travel unobserved which made him all the more important. Most would ignore a character such as him and find him too ridiculous to take seriously; therefore, much was spoken around Kekes that he repeated to Heru.

That was how Heru had discovered his brother Suti's dark secrets.

Chapter 41

Soon after the birth of Set in Per-Uto, there followed the birth of two more daughters from her consort Nebmaat, one after the other, both so much alike as to fool others that they were twins. So fast had the youngest grown to catch up with her sister. After Set came Renenutet and then Weret-Heka. Au-Set's womb had finally found that it loved life within and she responded to it with a newfound joy.

When her beloved Au-Sar had returned from his journeys to the Far East, he had added new life to her as well. However, this occurred after a sad event.

As she was growing large with her fourth pregnancy and reveling in the attentions from the entire palace, a messenger had arrived at the gate.

"Great Queen Ua-Zit and Princess Au-Set, I have dire news and I am deeply sorry for this to have to reach your ears."

Ua-Zit gently put down the older temple records on clay tablets that she was reviewing and nodded for him to continue.

"The mighty prince Heru is laying on his death bed as we speak and he begs to convey his wishes to his mighty sister and aunt." The words stumbled out of his mouth and he paused.

"Do continue you will suffer no ill." Spoke Au-Set in the softest barely audible whisper.

"Great Heru wished that you continue the family legacy and that he bids you all be weary of the....."

"Of the what, spit it out!" Ua-Zit exclaimed.

"The treachery of the prince named Suti." This had filled the room and Au-Set understood each word uttered by the messenger and the real fear that he felt, if it became known that this had reached Per-Uto and that he had delivered the fateful warning.

"The prince Heru sends his prayers to you great rulers of the north along with his workings and separate messages to each of you and for you to accept his servant and vizier, Kekes." He bowed to the floor in supplication as slaves were brought forward scrolls of papyrus and clay tablets that bore the family seal from Erech in the almost forgotten writing of the land. Kekes entered the room and its somber glow under the lamplight and with his own loss of a good friend and master.

The silence of the room was thick as the scroll from Heru was slowly opened by Au-Set, which was filled with the ominous stirrings of a new battle. The body of Au-Set trembled and almost shook the room around them.

Tehuti, who had been quiet up until this moment, chose this particular time to speak out to the room as he watched his sister's body grip in waves and the female servants running to her side to take her to the sacred women's room. "This child that you now carry will right all wrongs. I have seen it before my eyes just now...but at a great price!"

The silent Kekes let out a very feminine squeal at the immensity of the words uttered that echoed through the large chamber.

The women in the chamber then took up a great cry for wisdom spoken from the all-too silent brother and they trembled in his knowledge of the world of women that he was allowed a brief glimpse.

He continued as if speaking from another realm of existence and all in the room stopped, even the waves of life from Au-Set on the portal of delivering. "With this life enters the soul of our beloved brother. Our strength and wisdom... The very bond of this family! I feel our brother struggling to leave this world and trying to get into this child unborn! However, we must protect this child from the anger of Suti. Bring my sister to a small village far away from here to protect her! This child is not safe while it is in Per-Uto! Bring him back only when it is safe." He then ran over to Au-Set, placed his hand upon her sweaty brow, and kissed her nose as he had as a small child.

The women then caught up with time and rushed their charge out of the room to deliver yet another life to the palace. Au-Set and her women went not to the birth room of the palace, but to a secret place in the northeast of the delta in a hut built in the papyrus marshes. Au-Set named this place *Khemmis*.

Chapter 42

Au-Set was afraid that Suti would hear of this and try to take this child away from her. Suti somehow had found out that her first-born child was from him, her daughter Set. Due to the true paternity of Au-Set's first-born child and heir, he wanted Set to be the sole ruler of the next generation, not any child born of Au-Sar, such as this child was. The people favored her brother Au-Sar out of most of the family besides herself. Thus, her fright was rather justified.

As the soul of Heru left the earthly realm, all of the women present felt his essence enter the body of the infant as he was born and promptly named Heru, so that he could find his way back into this world.

Au-Set was nervous since her child was born with a larger than normal head and small legs. He seemed almost misshaped and hoped that they would soon grow into proportion to the rest of his body.

The women danced with their new prince and adored him as if he were the husband, father, and brother to them all. The only time a male was allowed in the hallowed chamber, even though this was a hut, was at his birth and entrance to the world.

The hut was decorated with all of the essential spells and charms to protect the mother and infant Heru. Spirals were painted on all those who entered the room to ensure the confusion of possible evil entities that might want to harm them.

For this special purpose and for further protection from the increasing threat to those in Per-Uto, Au-Set formed her own personal guard of women warriors. She called this group her *Scorpion Guard*. They were selected from the finest houses in this land of Kemet and trained in the only way of Eshnunna and of the Catal-Huyuk. There were seven of them.

Au-Set created their battle-gear to resemble that of a scorpion. Their helmets were fashioned in bronze, a new alloy of mixed gold and silver made all the more durable and strong. They were pointed up with horns resembling those of Innana out of tradition of the warriors past. The chest plates were made of bronze circles sewed on a padded leather shirt. Their breastplates were elaborate and spirals of the ancients were fashioned around them for added protection. The skirts were similar to those in the personal guard of her mother, for they were made of long plates of bronze sewed to the top. Underneath, they wore padded pants that tapered down to their knees. Their sandals were of hardened leather that wove around their strong ankles up to their knees. They had separated bronze arm plates over the top of their arms that were attached to the padded shirt; the same was over their legs in the front. Au- Set had deliberated long over how to make the tail of the scorpion into the battle gear and Qui had cleverly solved this for her. He suggested that they make their tails or their sting with the weapons that they trained in and carried. Her guard was not only armed with long bronze swords, but they also had a long hollow pole. The pole was used to deliver the most potent weapon of all. The warriors were trained to use the poles to send out blow darts that were filled with lethal venom from actual deadly scorpions. Au-Set loved this idea and felt that Qui, once again had proved his cleverness. She felt it wonderfully ideal in how her Scorpion Guard could protect her with the actual poison from scorpions.

Seven were chosen to be in her of her special elite guar. There were three women who would ensure that her path was clear, they were Petet, Tjetet, and Matet, there were Mesetet and Metsetef on each side. To protect her back were Tefen and Befen.

The Scorpion Guard of hers would be by her side at every minute of her life and those of her children that she had in her presence. She had another larger guard for her other children that she called her Iaret Guard.

In Khemmis with her newborn son and her special trained Scorpion Guard, she had decided to stay for a few months until the threat of Suti on Heru had died down a bit. Ua-Zit and her consorts Au-Sar and Nebmaat stayed behind under the protection of the Iaret Guard in the palace at Per-Uto. It seemed that the latest threats were solely on her newborn son Heru.

Au-Sar wanted to be by her side to protect her and their new son, but Au-Set would not hear of it. She pleaded with him that she needed him more at the palace to protect her other children, Set, Renenutet and Weret-Heka. Au-Sar reluctantly agreed and stepped down to Au-Set's powerful maternal instincts.

Tehuti and Kekes went back down to Nekhen to assist with the burial preparation for their brother Heru and to gather some information. Tehuti was hoping to speak with Suti about the dangers that he was causing for their sister in her newborn child. Kekes would do what he did best.

Au-Set felt confident that Tehuti and Kekes would ensure her way back to Per-Uto by minimizing the threat on her new son.

Meanwhile, Au-Set enjoyed Heru's new little baby body and reveled in counting his tiny fingers and toes repeatedly. She was always enthralled with the mystery of new life, the tiny perfection that came out of her. She felt a profound loss when each one of them had left her body, but cherished actually holding them and singing to them.

This little man in her arms was as miraculous as her daughters who were probably at this very moment, running about the palace on their chubby baby legs. She missed them dreadfully, but had all the confidence in Tehuti in smoothing the path back to Per-Uto. She hoped that this would not be for long.

Due to her hiding out in a hut in this small village, she had to keep her guard as well disguised as herself. She ordered them to wear over their battle-gear, the long robes of initiate priestesses. She dressed in the same robes herself. The people of the village knew her only to be a priestess who gave birth to a Goddess-born child, who was there while a new temple was being built. Au-Set happily observed that the practices of Innana and other ancient Goddesses were kept alive in this new land.

The men and women of the village had not experienced this in that they were a small fishing village and have never seen a temple before, nor heard much on the sacred practices of the priestesses. They bowed to them in passing out of respect and curiosity. The illusion was interesting on the effect that it had with the people of this simple village.

She advised her guard to use extreme caution in not giving away their identity. She had ordered them not to talk with anyone and to assume the vow of silence of the initiate priestesses.

This only made the curiosity of the villagers more intense. They were little informed on the mysteries of the priestesses and they appeared in their silence all the more powerful.

The village consisted mainly of people who lived off their profits from fishing. They would go out in the early hours of the morning in their boats made of papyrus and catch in their nets a bounty of fish that were later taken in and sold at the market.

Women were the owners of the small businesses and kept tallies of the fish caught and of the profit received, while the men labored and went out in the boats. Some women fished, while the men stayed home to tend to their children, for they also had the added duty of providing nourishment for their households as well.

The family men of this village were responsible for raising the children while their women went out fishing. The men also wove their clothes and prepared the food for consumption.

Au-Set and her Scorpion Guard were amazed at how established in this small village were the ways of the ancients. She smiled and taught her son of the wonders of this village.

This village consisted of round huts made of woven papyrus matted around poles. There was a large circle of huts in the center of the village with small pathways leading out of the main village with more circles of huts. In the backs of the huts belonging to the more prominent villagers, were rectangular rooms that were used to house the animals such as goats, geese, or chickens. There was usually only a door in the front of the round part of the building and two windows in the back in the rectangular section of the dwellings. The inside of the houses were usually below the ground and one would have to step down to enter the modest abodes of the people who lived in this village. This kept them cool in the sweltering heat of the delta summers.

She saw the contentment of all those who lived here in this great simplicity. Inside, she longed for the same with her incredibly complex life. How wonderful it would be to worry only about the fish that could be caught to sustain her own family. How sweet to think of the simplicity and peace of Au-Sar and Nebmaat at home preparing it and watching her children, while she went out and enjoyed the solitude and patience of the simple fisherwoman. To live the life of a modest fisherwoman and to provide, literally, the food for the table and an honest living seemed wonderful sometimes. She had to brush those thoughts away as of late, so frequent were they occurring.

Her life that she was born into at the palace was extremely complex and she worried not only about her own children, but for those all over Kemet as well. She prayed for a safe future for them and hoped that the threat of the northern tribes would not reach them here in this land. She feared every day for the safety of her family and of the people in this land that she helped rule over.

Chapter 43

The day started out like any other that she had spent in this small village of Khemmis, with the sun climbing high into the sky with ferocity and joy that never ceased to dazzle her little infant Heru. Her Scorpion Guard was resting under the shade of a canopy in the front of their hut in protection from the sun. They sat aware yet restless in their heavy battle-gear that they wore underneath the robes of the priestess. Au-Set motioned to them that she was bored and wanted to enter the village proper.

Therefore, she walked with Heru swaddled against her. In front of her, watching the path were Petet, Matet and Tjetet. On her left was Mesetet and on her right was Metsetef. Behind her to guard their backs were Tefen and Befen. In this order, they entered the mud and papyrus woven village proper.

She noticed how they were meticulously repaired and bleached in the sun. Small gardens overflowed from inside the courtyards into the street, as if to prove that life had no confines and was encouraged in its great profusion of color. The people of this village had also painted magical symbols on the neatly kept up facades of the houses. The roofs had colorfully woven blanket canopies for which the people slept on during the midday, when the sun was at its worst. In the evenings, they would remove the canopies and fall asleep on the roofs under the stars. She had done the same at her palace at Per-Uto amidst many pillows and missed the small bodies of her daughters as they had curled up next to hers in sleep each evening.

Her hut was built for modesty and thus appeared to the people of this village that they were under the vow of priestess poverty. Their robes were hand woven and humble, only their bodies revealed elaborate tattoos of the priestess, including Au-Set's own skin. As she became a mother, her body was richly adorned in the spirals of protection in elaborate and richly ornate tattoos for the protection of herself, so that she may be strong to protect the children of her womb. She also had sacred spells written down the inside of her thighs to make her more fertile. Spells were written on her feet, to make every step she took in ruling her people sure and steady.

The people of this village knew her power, since lesser priestesses always surrounded Au-Set. They observed the tattoos of a ruler on her bare feet when she took her walks. Yet, her humble garments eluded them even further into the mystery the great Au-Set projected during her extent in this village, as they were not schooled in the mysteries of Innana.

On this day after the midday nap spent under the canopy in the front of their hut, she and her disguised guard entered the village. Normally, she made this walk in the morning out of pure restlessness. Today, however, the reason was different. She needed a special ingredient for an unguent that she was preparing for little Heru. She was growing more concerned over his reaction to the sun and wanted to prepare something to cover his skin to heal the small rash that was forming under his arms and on his belly. She needed some more calendula flowers for their properties were great on skin, though not too harsh, in case his skin should break out further.

She reached the destination of the house of the village herbal woman. This position was the most highly esteemed in this village and others. The herbal woman held the health and comfort of all in the village with her vast magically collected herbs that were used in healing.

In this village, the herbal woman's name was Neten, and she was very young. Neten's mother had recently died while out fishing and had drowned. Thus, her oldest daughter inherited the position.

Neten was only fifteen summers old and was the young mother of a two year old boy. Her consort was out fishing, since Neten insisted that she stay to tend to their son and she was afraid to leave her position to her son or husband, since she had not had a daughter yet. She was raised in the ancient ways of matrilineal family rule. She held the great burden of her family and future in her own hands and felt heavy with the weight of the most important position in her village.

Every morning at daybreak, Neten would skillfully gather the special herbs for their booth. The most magical of herbs were gathered under the full moon, on solstices and equinoxes. The most powerful of herbs were gathered during an eclipse.

Neten had not much sleep in the past week and her patience was almost completely gone. She also noticed the young priestess walking through the village with her trail of initiates as if she was some kind of queen. She did not like this woman at all and wondered about the tiny child that was swaddled close to her body. Neten did not like the priestesses in that they felt that they were above the simple people of the village and felt entitled. They came into town and expected people to move out of their way in passing, as if the ground they walked upon was more holy than theirs was. Though they lived outside of the village proper, they had people from the village deliver food to them and living essentials. When they came into town, it was for leisure, it seemed. Everyone in this village worked hard for their bread and beer and did not like these strange mysterious women, Neten especially.

Neten was from a long line of village herbal women and was proud of her great ancestry. This woman seemed to command an even greater attention than did Neten, and she was new here with no background, only silence. She hated the silence from them more than anything did, as if the robed women were far above the simple village folk. Neten especially did not like the way the priestesses did not even utter one simple polite word in greeting, they only nodded.

So on this day, Neten was not too impressed when she found the strange woman herself at her very own door. The door had only a simple woven green and red blanket that hung down to protect her home from the street noises, but that was all she needed. Her village was very safe and had not been invaded for many generations before memory.

Neten looked at Au-Set as she gracefully moved the blanket aside to request entrance. Neten had just about enough of the silent and bold woman who rudely interrupted her only decent nap in a week. Neten stood up and confronted the woman who stood there in the rite of respect of those in this land and waited for Neten to invite her in. Au-Set was dressed in a rough woven robe with her infant swaddled underneath and close to her chest. Heru was silent as if he was waiting as well.

Neten looked Au-Set up and down and decided that she had to do something about this. She spoke firmly yet loud to her visitor who politely waiting to gain entrance, "You, humble priestess are not welcome in here! I have nothing for you. Please take your leave at once." She turned her back on Au-Set at the stirrings of her own son who was beckoning her at the tone of her voice. As she bent down to tend to her little boy, she felt something whiz by her neck. Her son responded with a startled cry that pierced the air in his insistence. She turned around and noticed that one of the women's attendants had just left the room.

Neten was confused, but tossed all worry about that matter aside as she tended to her own son who had just picked up his cry again.

Au-Set left upset over this encounter. She had no idea why this woman would react this way to her. She had used the utmost of caution in observing the practices of this land, especially upon gaining entry into the very abode of this woman. Au-Set had stood just outside the entryway, opened the blanket halfway, and peered in her head with a smile. Her guard was respectfully outside at a distance.

Unperturbed by this, she then moved on to the next house of the village and was stopped by a simple girl in rough garb like herself, though not long like the robes of a priestess. The girl was small and thin with fine wispy black hair trailing behind her on the river wind. Her feet were bare and unadorned. She looked up at Au-Set with huge dark brown eyes and said, "Lady, may I help you?"

Au-Set felt adoration emanating from this young girl, bent down to her eye level, and explained her dilemma in requiring the calendula flowers for the unguent that she wanted to make for her son.

The little girl stood there deep in thought, oblivious to the small entourage of robed women and their importance. "I know, on the banks of the small stream there lies a patch of it. I am sure of this great lady. Follow me!"

Therefore, Au-Set followed the simple and sweet little girl out of the village to the stream that she had mentioned. Sure enough, there was a small clump of it growing on the side of the stream. The flowers were large with bright yellow petals, which stretched out to the sun above them as it was starting to find its way to the western horizon. Au-Set smiled at the girl and then scooped up as many of the flowers and roots that she could for her son. She took one of the flower petals and tickled it to the tiny nose of her baby who was just wakening from his deep slumber as she was bending down. He giggled in delight at the sweet fragrance of the sun colored flowers.

Au-Set then reached down to a clump of violets nearby under the shade of a large tree and scooped them up. She made a small fairy chain to adorn the head of the little girl who brought her here. She placed it regally on the head of the little girl and told her, "Now, you are a queen. For your generosity on this day, I will never forget you. What is your name little one?"

"I am Edjo great lady. My mother is Mut of Ineb-Hedj, the fortress town up the river. I was sent to my aunt for fosterage. My aunt is Neten, the woman who was not so nice to you. I am sorry for that, but she chooses to stay with her son at all times and send her consort out to fish. She has not had much sleep for weeks, young Tatep is colicky, and my aunt works hard when he does sleep with the herbs. I am training under her so that when I go back to Ineb-Hedj, I will be a great herbal woman like my grandmother."

Au-Set pondered over this. "That makes a lot of sense and I am sorry if I misunderstood the intentions of your aunt. I could not understand why she refused my entry into her home. I only wanted some simple herbs."

"Sorry great lady, for she had little patience in her lack of sleep and is still upset over the death of my grandmother, for she cared for her as well. She also is very suspicious of strangers." She bowed her head down low.

"I understand. Maybe, I should send over one of my guards to tend to her so that she may get some more sleep. I truly understand the attraction of wanting to be by the side of the little ones, how odd that may be for women. Does her consort complain about having to work for the family?" She giggled at the thought of this.

"He certainly does lady." She giggled as well.

"Edjo, my name is Au-Set; never forget that, for some day I may be in the position to help you as well someday."

"Thank you Au-Set, I must return to help my aunt. Is there anything else you need?"

"No, run along Edjo, it was nice meeting you."

As the little girl departed, Befen, one of her rear guard approached her for audience. She looked up at Au-Set imploringly, "My Liege, may I have a word with you?"

"By all means Befen...? Proceed...."

"I think that I may have made a drastic mistake."

"You think you have, or did you?"

"I did." Befen looked down at her sandals that had trailed the mud of the small stream following her little queen on this quest.

She continued, knowing her guilt, "After you left the abode, I used my blowpipe and aimed it at the back of that arrogant and rude woman my lady." She stood there waiting for Au-Set to strike her. The silence was stifling, though she continued in admitting her intentions with the guilty thing she had just done.

"My lady, I know that type of woman and the world would be better off without them. I did not give her the poisoned dart, only the one that makes a person ill, to teach her a lesson. I am so very sorry."

Au-Set looked at Befen and saw the great worry on her oval face. It was a look of dread, especially after hearing about the story from her niece. The guilt was more of a punishment onto the matter than any one that Au-Set would have been able to give to the rash guard of hers. She saw that the guilt on Befen's face was consuming her. Well that it should thought Au-Set.

"Well, we will have to creatively remedy the situation. Befen, you will have to stay at the hut and fast to think clearer on the matter and hope that nothing has happened to this woman. We will have to use our disguise as priestesses when we approach her to heal her, for no one knows of these weapons.

"They are never to be used again in this matter! All of you! For if you cannot judge better for the use of a situation in which to yield this weapon, you will be asked to leave my guard!" All of the women bowed in respect for the little queen.

"Come, let us return to this home, and offer our healing skills. Befen, get my herbal bag and hang these flowers up. Petet, take the place of Befen until this matter is resolved!"

Neten was frantic for her son, Tatep's cries would not cease. She then noticed that he had developed a fever that grew steadily worse. She had to stop and sit on the side to stand away from being a mother for a moment and to be a healer. She had to use every cell in her body to think on what was wrong with her son. She wanted to rip out her hair in frustration initially, but then the answer suddenly dawned on her. His symptoms were similar to that of a scorpion sting.

As she ran over to his body to find, the stinger that could possibly still be inside her son, the blanket to her home was pushed aside frantically. She saw the figure of Au-Set.

At first, she was only angry, and then her instincts as a mother stepped in. She only stood there mute and helpless to the power of a priestess who probably had much greater healing powers than she did. She knew that priestesses were also skilled in the secret words of the Goddess that were much more powerful than just the herbs alone in healing. Desperate to save her son, she relented to the woman and nodded for her to enter.

Neten did not care how the priestess found out, for she knew that the Goddess must have told her. Why the same priestess that she had turned out of her home earlier that day would want to help her, she did not know. She did not care anymore. She only wanted her son to be safe.

Unbeknownst to Au-Set, Befen had stolen away behind them as they left. She desperately wanted to do something to make the world right in the terrible wrong that she had caused. Befen entered the abode and almost fainted in guilt when she had noticed that her dart must have passed the woman to hit the infant. Au-Set saw the reaction of Befen and motioned to her to take Heru from her and to hand him to Tefen, while she stood there ready for any order from Au-Set in making this grievous wrong a right. Befen was broken with remorse over her thoughtless actions and fought with her-self to be strong for this innocent child. She thought about how the amount of potion in the dart was only enough to make a grown woman sick, but could kill a child as young as the woman's son who seemed to be growing weaker by each endless minute.

Au-Set read the situation correctly and took command. "Lady, bring a basin of lukewarm water for his fever and a cloth made from the wool of the youngest lamb to wipe his brow."

Au-Set looked over at Befen, "Befen, hand me the bag." She ignored the tear that slid down the face of her guard. Au-Set knew that this was punishment enough for the young guard and took the bag from her, ignoring the fact that she had again disobeyed her orders. She reached inside for a small straw and bent over the child. Neten joined her and pointed out the place that the child was stung.

"Priestess, there is no stinger, only the hole. Here it is." Tears were welled up in the eyes of the young mother almost blinding her. Au-Set looked over at Befen and then to the ground to find the undiscovered dart underneath the table. She stepped on it and motioned to Befen to remove it when she had the chance.

Au-Set took the straw that was the narrowest that she had, bent down and proceeded to suck out the poison from the child. She found it bitter on her tongue and quickly spit it out as fast as possible. The less, she got in her system the better.

"Lady, you risk your life with this! I will take the poison in myself!" Au-Set only looked at the young mother and continued to drain out the rest of the poison in the child. When the last of it was sucked up, she stopped and looked over at Befen who was behind them, waiting her command.

"No worry young mother, the poison is gone. The rest went into his system. He must be cleaned out of the toxins. Befen, hand me that vial of vinegar and mix it with the water that was brought in."

Befen took the vial from Au-Set that she had taken out of her bag and mixed it in a large copper bowl with half a mixture of the lukewarm water that was brought in. She then smoothly put the mixture in a small clay-drinking vessel that she knew belonged to the little boy.

"Drink this little one. It will clear the rest of the poison out of your system." She looked over at the mother of the child and motioned for her to make sure that Tatep drank the potion. "Make sure that he has every last drop and the rest from this bowl. This will wash out his system of the toxins and it will come out in his urine. When his urine clears to the normal color, it will be right again."

Au-Set then stood over the mother giving her child the vinegar mixture and started to sing prayers with the other priestesses over the boy.

"Little one, hear the voice of the Goddess,
Little one, feel the love of the Goddess.
For Au-Set weeps for you
Ua-Zit sings for you!

> Little one, hear the prayers of her servants
> Little one, take in our love
> Little one, grow strong for us
> Ua-Zit weeps for you!
> Au-Set prays for you!
>
> Little one, cherish this night
> Little one, take this potion and heal
> Little one, feel our love for you
> Au-Set Ua-Zit shall heal you!"

This song was sung in the healing process to comfort those being healed and their concerned family members. A chant filled all of the hours of the evening. It became a background of hope, which assured that the boy would live. The devoted mother to her son slowly emptied the bowl of the contents, while the priestesses chanted over them.

The stars passed by overhead and eventually they went to sleep to make way for the birth of the sun for the new day. As soon as the first rays entered the comfortable dwelling of the herbal woman named Neten, the fever let go of its grip on the boy. The chanting then turned to elated cries of joy for the narrow escape of the mother at the possibility of losing her only child.

He looked up at his mother and weakly told her, "Mama, I need go tinkle! Why the pwetty music stopped?"

The mother held onto to her son ferociously in the fear that she almost lost him while tears of joy streamed down her thankful cheeks in gratitude. "Sure Tatep, be quick and don't mind the silly color, it is because of the medicine my love. You are better, that is for sure!"

The other priestesses joined in with the mother in a joyful laughter on the little boy and his precociousness. Au-Set reached over and ruffled the thick black hair of the boy as he ran out of the home on his chubby baby legs to tend to his toilette.

"Priestess, however can I repay you for saving my son? I can offer you whatever you would like in here, for it is all I own."

"No, lady... I only want a promise from you."

Neten was startled, "Of course my lady, what would you like?"

"Promise me that you will never turn away another who seeks your aid. The job of a healer is to heal, no matter what is going on in your personal life. Use your niece well, for she offers her assistance with you and your son. Show her a good example of what a healer should be. You know what that is like, for you are more like your mother than you think. You need to carry on her tradition with pride, show dear Edjo the legacy of your family."

"But great priestess, how do you know so much about me?"

"I make it my business to learn about all those I heal, and I notice as much as possible around me. Your niece shows great understandable concern for you. She knows that you are overtired and unused to this role in caring for your son. Get another consort to care for your son, for your position allows it. Stay by his side for your heart requires this. This, I personally understand, for I do the same myself. However, you also have the responsibility of your mother's line in healing the people of this village. With the help of another consort, you may do all of the things that you have to do and want to do."

"I will my lady; I just thought that I could do it all."

"As do all young mothers. Nevertheless, I have learned after a few children, that no one person can do it all. It takes a whole village to raise a child and not just one person. When you put too much on yourself, you will not have the time to be the good mother that you are capable of like your own mother."

The tears of Neten were freshened at the mention of her mother in her still strong grief; Au-Set walked over to her and wrapped her arms around Neten in comfort. "You will make a great mother, for your love has healed your own child, the Goddess weeps for you in joy, I feel it!"

Au-Set stayed in the village for five more months and befriended the young woman Neten and her vibrant niece, Edjo. The two women shared many cures and ideas strengthening their own supplies in herbs and knowledge. When Au-Set received the summons from Tehuti by way of Qui who had been sent out to her, she was almost reluctant to return. However, she missed her other children dreadfully and was eager to introduce them to their new brother who was slowly growing into the proper proportions.

Au-Set, in parting told Neten and Edjo the truth of her identity and told them to find her, should they need anything. She had all of the confidence in the world that Neten would heed her advice and had already found another consort to send out fishing, while her first consort was allowed to help with his son. Edjo, was a fast learner, wanted to become a priestess, and begged Au-Set to take her with them back to the palace in Per-Uto.

Au-Set responded to the pleas, "Little healer, you are needed elsewhere in life. For I see great plans ahead for you. You will be a mother one day and a ruler as well. You do not want to lock yourself in a temple, away from your future. Edjo, you, and I will definitely meet again in this life. I see it in my dreams. So have patience and learn as much as you can from your aunt Neten, for you will need this all someday."

After the tearful parting, and a safe distance close to the palace, all of the women gratefully shed their priestess robes and rode in the full splendor into Per-Uto as due their station. When placed in a wagon pulled by donkeys, Au-Set bent over to the walking form of her side guard named Mesetet and whispered, "I am glad that we had that journey sister, for I feel that I have truly learned a great lesson."

Mesetet smiled and responded, "Indeed little queen, I believe that we all have."

Chapter 44

Au-Set was sought by most women in the settlement of Per-Uto and from beyond. Her knowledge was so encompassing it was as if she had retained the knowledge from all of her past lives.

Her womb found great delight in receiving and bringing forth life in contrast to her twin sister. Soon after Heru, She gave birth to twins, a son and a daughter named Merul and Bast.

Au-Set grew even more beautiful with motherhood and her body grew well rounded in response. Her cheeks reflected the joy within her contented soul to all who were in her presence. She always had her children with her no matter how important the event. She even took them to the yearly meetings that had continued to be held in Gerzah and they filled the growing village with delight at the promise of the future generation.

When the younger ones grew tired and restless, she had the faithful services of Qui and Kekes to assist her in redirecting their attention. The children grew to love Kekes for his fun and innovative dances that he made up for the children for their entertainment. Qui would throw them high into the air while they squealed in joy; he would even pick up Au-Set who, even in her rounded mother-hood form, was still rather small for a woman from Eshnunna or Sumer as it was now called.

Her oldest daughter Set had fiery red hair like her own brother and an equal temper to match. Her moods were often unpredictable and most were cautious whenever approaching for fear of one of her tirades. She doted on her younger siblings and assisted her mother and the two servants in keeping them well behaved in public appearances.

The people in the south of Kemet were much enamored with their new fertile princess and sought her out constantly for advice. Ua-Zit was often by the side of Au-Set and was fast learning to appreciate and value of her niece in her sharp wit. Yet, sometimes Ua-Zit had to quell the bright eagerness of Au-Set as was expected by her youth. She noticed that Au-Set was very intelligent; the young queen initiate would often leap before she thought. She was not afraid to take chances, which was very good for a leader. Ua-Zit was just making sure that those leaps would have more consideration.

Renenutet and Weret-Heka were often inseparable and most often mistaken for another, since there was only a year between them. Their long, thick curly hair danced along with their dimpled smiles. They were often the ones creating the dances with Kekes and entertaining the others with their performances.

While Heru was fast becoming a handful, he was constantly trying to become a soldier and would often pick fights with boys equally eager for battle. He carried around a small golden sword that his father Au-Sar had made for him. While Renenutet and Weret-Heka were daughters of Nebmaat, the rest were from her most cherished consort, Au-Sar. She knew that Au-Sar desperately tried to interest his children, especially his first-born son Heru in following his interests in agriculture though it was in vain.

However, Bast was often seen following her father on such expeditions trailing behind her vivid father Au-Sar whom the people of the new land were growing to love, since he brought prosperity to their land with his brilliant innovations in irrigation. They were able to enlarge the land used for crops by a thousand-fold with his creation of clay water pipes which fed the land that had been dry for so long it eagerly soaked up the new water that now streamed into a wider territory.

Bast, when very small had discovered a tiny malnourished male lion cub that was abandoned by its mother for some unknown and mysterious reason of nature. She tamed the tiny cub which fast became large and overweighed all but the mighty form of Qui. Bast named her lion 'Herab', which meant "man of peaceful disposition." As Herab grew in size, he certainly lived up to his name and the family adored him. Bast would often ride him around and the people would marvel at this.

At first, Au-Set and the family were cautious about this practice of Bast, in riding her pet, though soon realized the value in her daughter's companion and of how Herab would obviously protect their daughter. Bast was always teaching Herab new tricks to perform and the humor of the two odd brothers was always a distraction.

Qui and Kekes were frequently in disagreement with each other and would threaten to throw the other to Herab for a meal. The children would roar in laughter, for Au-Set wondered if some if not most of the arguments between the brothers were staged for their benefit, since most of them were so outrageous.

Herab would roar in mention of his name when referenced to and would then pretend to lick his chops as if in anticipation of one of the brothers as a meal, the children would squeal in awe. One or the other would accidentally stumble over Herab and the lion would smother the poor soul in great slobbery licks.

Kekes and Qui were soon accepted members of the fast growing family and the children of Au-Set. Au-Set would giggle at even the thought of the brothers' antics and felt that the only harm that would come to either of them from Herab was in being licked silly.

Merul, on the other hand was constantly being worried over by his mother, Au-Set, since he was sickly from the time of his birth. While Heru grew into normal body proportions as he grew older, Merul seemed to grow out of his. Merul's head was larger than normal and his legs were squat and heavy with a wide torso. He could not run like the other children due to his unusual body proportions and thus, preferred his time spent in study. He wanted to be in charge of the family chronicles when he was old enough to learn the talent of picture writing taught to him by his uncle Tehuti. He was often ill with shortness of breath and a falling sickness. Au-Set believed it was sent from the Goddess, since he had also developed an uncanny talent in interpreting dreams. People would travel far to hear his meanings, and they were more than often visions of the future which seemed to come true almost all of the time.

While Merul was small and non-active, Heru was the opposite, for he was remarkably athletic, as if to make up for his lack of promise at birth. However, he was quick to temper and a little slow in thinking. He was aggressive and wanted to be a great and famous warrior when he grew up.

Merul was small for his size and was often caught up in his older brother Heru's experiments and most of the time was injured in them. Their mother knew that Heru meant no harm on his youngest sibling, but since Merul was a slow runner and gullible he made too easy a target. Au-Set was always sending the more nubile brother Kekes after Heru to protect Merul from accidental harm.

Chapter 45

It was never boring in Per-Uto, for other than her children and the flamboyant odd brothers, Au-Set had to deal with the constant competitions of her consorts Au-Sar and Nebmaat. She was most often with Nebmaat, who preferred to be by her side, though her love was more for Au-Sar. She loved Nebmaat as well for his calm temperament and sedate advice for he was a lot like his mother Ua-Zit with his patient teaching to her of this land. The only thing that ever seemed to have a reaction out of the calm Nebmaat was when Au-Sar instigated him. Au-Set hated when the two of them quarreled and competed with her for affection and sometimes even seemed to want some sort of possession over her. Yet, she knew that they would never harm each other for they had mostly grown up together here. It seemed to her a harmless brotherly competition. Nevertheless, it would sometimes annoy her. As if seeming to conjure up something new Nebmaat stomped into the room seeking her," Au-Set, he is at it again!" His countenance seemed shattered and his peace seemingly unstable now. Au-Set looked up from her clay tablet accountings that she was reviewing for Qui. Qui had soon after his arrival established his great talents in accounting and financial matters.

"Brother, your flawless eye makeup is ruined from the stress of Au-Sar." She tried to humor him, for it was true. Nebmaat was always in immaculate dress, no hair was ever out of place. While Au-Sar, in contrast, was always covered in his love for the fields and often smelled of earth as was the memories of her father, Geb.

"It is Au-Sar...." He looked at her beseechingly.

"What has he done now brother, for I shall have to take him over my knee..." She giggled, for it seemed to aggravate her Nebmaat.

"No, this is not like other times. This time he has gone too far! This time he has gotten hold of my beautifully and specially made malachite eye color and has used it for another experiment of his. It cannot be replaced for it is too rare!"

Au-Set understood the predicament of this situation and the validity of the argument as presented by her consort. Malachite was used around the eyes in a fine powder to reflect the intensity of the fierce sun of this land. It not only looked beautiful when applied, but it served a purpose as well. She knew how rare it was since it was newly introduced and she further realized that she had to approach Au-Sar on this matter in a more serious tone than in past matters. She also knew that Au-Sar never really did anything malicious to Nebmaat, but was often tempted to mischief since Nebmaat made such an easy target with the preciseness of his normal manner. Au-Sar cared nothing for such vanity. The sun often bit him harshly as he became lost in his agricultural projects.

"I will take care of this brother. For this is a dire predicament indeed. Though bear in mind that Au-Sar really means no harm!"

"You know as well as I, that he finds me an easy target!"

"I have to agree with you there, perhaps you should not let him know that it bothers you so, it might just make you safer in his future schemes."

"Mother told me the same thing."

Au-Set tried to appear genuinely concerned but sometimes she felt that Nebmaat was spoiled, as if he was the one who grew up in their luxurious homeland of Eshnunna and not them. She also more, often than not, felt like the mother of her consorts rather than their lover in matters such as this. She had almost forgotten how quiet he was when young and how the years seemed to create a different person.

As her consort left the room, in walked her brother Tehuti.

"Sister, may I have a word with you?"

"Yes, have a seat. I was just finishing accounts from Qui, excellent work, when Nebmaat walked in with another complaint about our darling brother!"

Tehuti let out an exasperating sigh, "again, what is the issue this time, was a hair of his highness Nebmaat taken out of place by Au-Sar?"

"Tehuti, that it not fair, Au-Sar had gotten into the malachite that Nebmaat had imported for his eyes....."

Tehuti let out a roar of laughter, "I can just imagine it!"

"Seriously, I understand the humor in the vanity issue, but malachite is also a rare and expensive stone and is found only in one place far to the south of here, or north for the people of Kemet. Do you think I will ever be able to think with the directions that they do here that are so upside-down from when we grew up?" She questioned, not expecting any response.

Gaining his composure after the expressed antics of his younger brother, he steadied himself for the discussion that he had initially planned for this meeting with his sister.

"First of all, Au-Set, Nebmaat is not our brother he is a whining brat." He saw the hurt look on his sister's face, "Sorry, he is just so exasperating sometimes!"

"I understand, apology accepted."

"Well, it has come to my attention after serious investigation that our youngest brother Suti is up to some further mischief and I am very concerned."

"Yes brother, I have been looking into the matter as well, though I have found no proof of the rumors whispered for the people in Upper Kemet seem to live in fear of him."

"As you know, I had sent down one of our flamboyant 'odd brothers', Kekes, for his unobtrusive talent in infiltrating the most interesting information." He used her favorite secret expression for the unusual brothers.

Tehuti continued, "And he turned up quite a bit of information in his usual inconspicuous and ingenious ways." Both of them smiled at this and knew that his talents were mysterious, yet all too true.

"Suti is up to something, though I am not sure exactly what. I am deeply concerned that it may be something to harm either you or Au-Sar. Suti makes his animosity towards you and Au-Sar well known to his people. I know that the fear had died down after the birth of Heru and it seems unlikely, this over concern. Yet....."

"Suti would never harm us." Her face struggled desperately in trying to hide her buried apprehension and to guard his horrific encounter at the first meeting, which led to the birth of her first child Set.

"You know damn well that Suti will stop at nothing to harm either you or Au-Sar. Though when he does, it will be so no one ever will know that it was he, so underground that he is." He looked at her and then continued, "Sister, why do you hide what he has done to you, even from yourself?"

After a great pause, she looked down at the intricately woven mats on the floor to avoid facing her brother on this. "The pain of what he did hurts me so much! I do not know why he reacted in such anger towards me. The reality of what he did is buried deep within my soul and that is enough punishment for one lifetime. I do not want anyone to hear of your suspicions. I prefer to not deal with it at all and that is *my* choice!"

Tehuti agreed fervently with her, though he knew that others secretly whispered about the flaming red hair of her first-born daughter. He let his sister hide in her denial and understood it as the way she protected herself. However, some reality had to be jarred within her to realize the imminent danger from Suti.

"We must call the yearly meeting at Nekhen instead of Gerzah. For to walk on his own grounds, might make it more obvious to you in his duplicity. He has kept up correspondences with us, along with Neb-Het and aunt Nekhebt. They have even kept normal appearances at the meetings, yet something is off about them. Do you not sense this sister? Like they are saying what we want to hear. They must be made accountable for their government and alleged actions and not just with their words and correspondences. I feel that little has been done in reality since that first meeting over ten years ago!"

Chapter 46

As the others were looking into the mystery of Nekhen, Au-Set had received a rather odd letter. The correspondence was from Re, the consort of her mother that had escaped the great sacrifice, years ago in Erech. She knew that Tehuti was his son and she wondered why he would write to her and not him. Not one word was heard from them since he left the palace and their mother so many years ago.

In the letter, Re had inquired about a marriage alliance for his daughter with her one of her sons. Au-Set was curious about this and made plans for the journey. She wanted Tehuti to go with her, but he was busy setting up his scribal schools. Then she had asked Au-Sar who told her that he was also busy with digging canals for the new clay pipes that he had built for a village up north in the river.

So she placed her children in the care of Qui and Kekes and went down to the white fortress of Ineb-Hedj to talk in person with Re about possible marriage negotiations.

Along the way, she thought about the distance that had recently sprung up between her and Au-Sar. With Nebmaat, she had a relationship that was certainly viewed more as a friendship. She adored Nebmaat, though was not attracted to him with his effeminate ways.

She loved Au-Sar and longed for each moment with him. She yearned for the sound of his voice and for the feel of his arms wrapped around her in the evenings. However, he had not been very attentive towards her lately and had been busy with his projects in new farming techniques. When he returned to her in the evenings, he was too tired for her. She understood and did not want to be rude in needing his attention. She felt selfish for even asking him. He would assure her, though she cried alone after he fell asleep.

She longed for his sensitive touches that he lavished on her when their love was new. She hungered for it, but slept alone beside him, when he returned to her. She was almost feverish for his embrace and sweet kisses. At night she closed her eyes and remembered how he held her and made love to her all night long. Her prayers were almost frantic at the time that she had to meet with Re, feeling alone and abandoned and wondering if his attentions were somewhere else. He almost treated her as if she was a burden to him. He made her feel guilty for wanting him to make love to her as much as her body and soul called out for him.

It was not the physical act that she craved; it was the closeness of their souls when they were together. She did love the physical act, but she craved for his closeness to her, his caress.

Her body and soul felt empty lately and thirsted for his attention to her. He made her feel like she was just a piece of furniture lately, a silly pestering ornament. She knew that it was mainly because he was tired, but it still hurt and drained her. She went though her obligations without vigor and played her role without soul. She needed him to need her, to want her, to make her feel like a woman that was loved and cherished.

At Ineb-Hedj, she was amazed at how built up that it had become. The main fortress was made out of mud-bricks bleached almost white in the sun. She knew that Re brought the skill down with him from Eshnunna and she marveled at how he had improved upon it. The mud-brick was made to resemble those buildings made of stone from Eshnunna or Sumer. There were tall arches and domes on the corner towers. The roof was made of large imported beams of cedar from Gubla. She was impressed as her entourage closed in the distance and made its way onto a ramp to cross the Great River into the actual fortress. The fortress gleamed in the sun so brightly it was often observed from miles away.

Inside the fortress, her wagons and leading donkeys were taken away to the stables and they were carried by a canopied litter into the palace compound that rose up from the center of the large white walls. The palace itself was made of quarried marble that was almost translucent in the rays of the sun and appeared magical.

She was greeted in the main room of the royal family of Ineb-Hedj. Re, who was tall and in his late thirties, walked out towards her with a charming elegance that caught her attention immediately. He introduced her to his parents, Mut and Khephra, His older brother Apep, his consort Het-Heru and their daughter Sekhmet, who appeared to be about ten years old, and his mother's younger consort, Ptah.

She was impressed at the beauty of this family. Re was tall with long dark-brown hair that was in a thick braid down his back, framed by dignified gray temples. His beard was regally touched with gray that appeared very handsome to her. He was tall and muscular and dressed in simple, yet elegant long robes of a brilliant dark green that was bordered in gold. On his head was a diadem of gold, which gleamed from the bright sunrays that streamed in from the tall arches of the chamber. His voice echoed under the vaulted ceiling of the ominous chamber and made his voice decorously powerful. His whole family was equally tall with dark brown hair elaborately braided with delicate hammered gold beads meticulously intertwined throughout.

His consort Het-Heru was tall and graceful with honey blonde hair that flowed down her waist in sumptuous curls. She knew that Het-Heru could not be from this land and wondered where she was from. Au-Set guessed that this woman was probably from the northern tribes due to the fairness of her complexion and in her seemingly submissive stance behind her husband. If she were correct in that assumption, it would explain why Re was making the introductions and not her, being the woman of the house. She had rarely witnessed such submissiveness in a woman before. However, she did notice that Het-Heru was happy and not forcefully submissive in any way. She thought it utterly curious.

Re's voice seemed to find a way into her lonely soul, for it reached her deeply. "This is my mother great queen, her name is Mut. She lost her voice, which is why I am making the introductions this day. Au-Set felt that the gown that this woman Mut was wearing, resembled wings of a hawk wrapped around her, and was impressed at the fine workmanship of the garment. The woman bowed down to her as was proper and rays of power that beamed forth from her elegant form almost stunned Au-Set. Au-Set noticed this woman was mute. She secretly wondered if the woman truly ruled over Ineb-Hedj rather than Re. She somehow felt a kinship with this older mother, especially after she had met her youngest daughter Edjo.

Apep stood there with an arrogant stance that seemed resentful that Re was the one who had called this meeting. She sensed great animosity between the two brothers.

Au-Set also, developed and instant dislike for Het-Heru in that she did not much care for weak women and felt that she could not relate to them at all. Her daughter on the other hand, seemed silly and frivolous in comparison to her parents and others in the room. Het-Heru was beautiful and commanded an air of grace and solitude. Sekhmet, in contrast seemed to radiate with a skillfully subdued exuberance that Au-Set knew was tactfully kept in check due to her visit. She guessed that this was probably due to the influence of her grandmother rather than her own mother, the silent and meek Het-Heru.

She knew that her assumption could easily be swayed for this was only her first visit to this fortress. Au-Set had only heard good things of this family and was curious to witness the family dynamics before seeing if her either of her sons would live with them in a union with Sekhmet.

Re seemed very proud of his daughter and Au-Set could see that they were close. He brought her close to him and told Au-Set, "Little Sekhmet has a small den of baby lion cubs that she is raising; she seems to almost be a lion herself! She wanted to bring them here for this meeting, but, I did not know how you would react to them."

Au-Set smiled and looked at the eager girl, "I have no problem with that idea and would love to see them. I certainly understand the attraction to wild animals. You see, my younger brother Suti has trained wild boars named Suaa and Suka and has a tall wild dog named Heh. My own daughter Bast has her own lion cub that she raised named Herab, who has practically become a member of the family!" The little girl seemed entranced and let out a sigh of amazement and then smiled at the regal woman who actually understood her.

Chapter 47

After Au-Set was shown to her sleeping chamber and settled in for the night, Apep and Re stood on the roof of the palace gazing out at the stars above them.

Apep, as always spoke first, "Brother, that woman is glorious!"

"Apep, she is a great queen, you must respect her always."

"But, just the thought of her, you had her mother did you not?"

"That was official, not to say that I did not enjoy it, but I was supposed to have been killed as her consort after she became pregnant with Tehuti, and then we would not be having this conversation, had things worked out as they should have."

"Well, I suppose not. Do you hate her for that? We don't do that here."

"Absolutely not, for I knew what my duty was in accepting the position as consort. Look what riches it has brought to our family. This fort, our palace... She still could easily have me killed as I stand here, though I do not believe that that is her motive since those days are past... Before all of that, we were living in a hut on the banks of the river, before Mother decided this. Besides, it could have been you, being the oldest and all. I still feel ashamed of the flight that I took from there in my youth, it has followed me ever since."

"I try to understand for you."

"That is no matter, I will spend the rest of my life making amends to that family, for they never came after me as they should. Also, look what events my actions had set into place. Do you regret that it was not you in my position as consort in seeing the beauty of her own daughter?"

"Absolutely not brother! I miss Nefrit and regret being back here. I feel that it was..."

"Your fault? You know that it was not. You had no idea that Sobek wanted Nefrit as a sacrifice. It was your duty to raise the children. It was her duty to work and to provide. Her family treated you well?"

"Yes, that was not it though. I felt that it was not supposed to happen that way. Nevertheless, that woman! To have her for even one night!"

"You cannot do that! You would be killed; she is a priestess and Goddess representative! She is sacred. It would bring our house down to ruin! I am surprised that they are even considering our family for mating with their own. I have done everything possible for this family and brought it fame, honor, and riches."

"Then I will win her affections, there is no harm in her taking a consort."

"No, brother I will find another home for you, you need a hearth to tend, you are restless that is all."

"What about your consort, shall you need another?" He smiled at his brother for he knew how much he cherished and protected Het-Heru.

Re was very protective and lavished attention on his quiet consort. He felt bad at the loss of her parents and of her having to live outside tradition with his own family. He wondered why he seemed to break every honor and tradition of his land and even those of Eshnunna and end up the better for it. He would like to think that it was due to the purity in his heart and genuine intentions for those other than himself.

His consort Het-Heru had a family that came down from the northern tribes and was used to females playing a submissive role. Still, Re was used to the ways of his own land and felt bad for her. Her father insisted that he pay the family of Re for her bridal price, as was tradition in their own land. His family was insulted since they had firmly expected to pay the price for Re. So Re and Het-Heru took matters into their own hands and built a hut for themselves until his mother relented and asked them into her home. A month before that Het-Heru's family was washed away and never seen again in the last inundation of the Great River.

His reflections were broken due to the notice of a star trail that raced across the sky, "Would that be a good portent for times ahead Re?"

"I hope it is for I want Sekhmet to take Au-Set's son as a consort. It would be a powerful move indeed for this family. We have come a long way from being mere potters."

"Grandmother's pottery was the most elaborate that this land has ever seen. She told us that she invented the potter's wheel and her figures of clay were sought throughout the land. We were never mere potters' brother and you know it. How else would we have even been allowed into the inner domains of the temple of Eshnunna or Sumer as it is now called?"

"I know that, I just feel that if it were not for that family, we would never have amounted to much more than that, we would have been lost in the sands of time."

"But that woman!"

"You are such a bull, could you not reign in your lust and let this visit from our future queen bring good portents from this family only. I need to have this union. You need a hearth of your own and I will talk to mother about finding something very soon for you. Just stay away from her while she is here. Please brother."

"Look, Re, I am the oldest and I will do as I please. I will find my own consort; maybe even ingratiate myself into being Au-Set's third! You will not decide my life for me!" He turned around and stomped off leaving a very upset Re standing there.

Re hoped that his older brother would control his lust and not ruin things for him and his daughter. He also knew that though his brother joked about Het-Heru, he did want her. Het-Heru was oblivious to this and Re felt very protective of her. He did not want her to be just another of his brother's conquests and his family to suffer for it. He knew that if Apep would dare make an advance, Het-Heru would not know how to respond due to her family's traditions, she might even fall victim and feel afraid to hurt his feelings or his advancements. He feared that she would even be put in that position.

Re did understand his brother's feelings for Au-Set though. She was beautiful and regal and seemed to have a powerful air about her. She was not the type of woman who would take no for an answer and always got her way. Re did secretly envy her consort Au-Sar for their legendary love that was known throughout all of Kemet.

He had never seen his son Tehuti and had fervently wished that he would have accompanied Au-Set on this visit and felt almost fallen when it was noted that he was not able to attend. Re inquired politely of Au-Set about his son and was proud of his great inventions and accomplishments. Re had noticed that she spoke of Tehuti with pride. However, there was something more in the tone of her voice. He noticed that whenever she referred to her first consort Au-Sar. It seemed to Re that she was lonely for Au-Sar when she spoke of him.

Chapter 48

Apep had requested the presence of Queen Au-Set one day and she had arrived promptly.

"Queen, I thank you for your presence and wish to speak to you on behalf of our mother Mut. She was unable to attend this meeting, since she has taken ill with a headache and apologizes profusely for that."

"I understand. Is this about the daughter of Re?"

"That it is."

"Then why does not Het-Heru speak for her?"

"Het-Heru does not feel comfortable in dealing with matters of import and has requested that I do this for her."

Au-Set understood this about Het-Heru since she seemed weak, but wondered why Re was not there since this involved his own daughter. She was silently suspicious of this meeting with just her and Apep.

He motioned for her to join him amongst the many large pillows that filled the room and to have some grapes with him. She sat down wearily for the journey there had troubled her with thoughts of Au-Sar on the way down and had taken a great emotional toll on her. She gratefully accepted the grapes and took each one in her mouth seductively thinking of Au-Sar and losing herself with thoughts of him from the room.

Apep did not know the reason for her lost seductions and misunderstood them to be for himself. He leaned closer to her. She seemed oblivious to him and the room around her.

"Great queen, may I speak boldly to you?"

"By all means."

"I find you beautiful and full of life, would you have need of another consort? For I guarantee you will never be lonely again."

Au-Set felt insulted at his invasion of her thoughts, though in the formality of their called meeting, she decided to change the subject. "I thought this meeting was about Sekhmet and your authority to decide her life?" Her tone was a bit abrasive and Apep immediately felt belittled.

"I assure you that I have full authority in dealing with issues concerning Sekhmet. As for myself, I promise you that you would not regret it."

"I thank you for your offer, Apep. However, I already have two consorts..."

"I understand your highness, but if they do not meet your needs, I assure you that I will."

Au-Set smiled uneasily and did not know where to go from this point; she completely did not expect this. She had the uneasy feeling that this was the only direction he had for this private meeting with her. She started to get up when Apep placed a hand on her shoulder for he knew that this meeting was not going where he had planned.

"Is that not the tradition of Sumer my lady? If your consort does not please you, you have the authority to dispose of him?" He smiled charmingly at her with hidden promises.

"I advise you Apep; do not forget your place." She looked sternly at him.

"I apologize profusely and meant no offence. But is that not correct?"

"That is none of your business Apep. No offence was taken. Also do not forget that this is not Eshnunna!" She looked forcefully at him, purposely not using the modern name for her land of birth.

"Please, forgive my brashness, but your beauty disables me. I merely meant to offer my services to your complete authority." He smiled at her and leaned closer to her.

She read his obvious thoughts and felt it not wise to offend him in that it might cause her future problems. Instead, she decided to end this situation as politically polite as possible. "Apep, would that I had met you years before. That is not the case. I have more than my share from my consorts. I feel that I would not be able to take on someone who deserves the amount of attention as you do. It would not be fair to you at all." She batted her eyelashes at him and gracefully got up and took her leave from the room departing the room with those last words.

She brushed the anger from her dress with her elegant hands and wiped her brow for a job well done as she completed rounding the corner. Her thoughts were elsewhere when she bumped into Re.

Under her breath, she muttered, "Not again!"

Re caught wind of this and guessed her dilemma. He was on his way to stop the meeting with the little queen and his brother. He had hoped to reach the room sooner and realized that he had arrived too late, though was impressed in that it seemed as if she handled the situation rather well.

With raised eyebrows and his incredible talent for composure, he read the situation and reacted. He felt the truth would be his only avenue with this woman.

"Your highness, I am sorry. I was on my way to prevent an awkward situation and I feel that I may have arrived too late?"

"No, certainly not! There was a situation and I handled it."

"I am sorry for my brother, your highness." He bowed his head down low in sincerity.

"Thank you, but it was not anything that I could not handle myself."

"Just beware, for he feels entitled, being the oldest and all." She was about the leave for her own chambers when she turned to face Re.

"I did sense that in him. I was under the comprehension that I would be dealing with the possible union matters of my sons and your daughter with you. He took me off guard with his assumption. I also want to add that it is rather odd dealing with you in the first place, since I had expected to deal in this matter with her mother, as is proper."

"Yes, your highness. I just do not think that Het-Heru wants to deal with that matter; she left it entirely in my hands. It is not the custom of her tribe. She would not know what to do about it anyways."

"I suppose that it is another oddity that I will have to accept." She laughed in order to lighten the situation. She suspected that Re was pure in this and seemed to have the best intentions.

"I am going to retire now to my own chamber. I feel that I have been through quite a bit this evening." She smiled and then turned around on her heels to go in the direction of her own chambers.

Re was left there in the hallway, feeling rather impressed with this monarch. She looked delicate on the outside, but was tough and knew what she wanted out of life. He was also impressed how she did not take any slack either. He smiled and watched her walk away with that magnificent confidence that she exuded with each step.

Au-Set left the presence of Re, she understood why Re was sent instead of Apep. With Apep, there was a sense of danger. With Re there was a charm in which one wanted more of it.

Chapter 49

On the next day she was invited to a formal discussion with Re in which the potential union negotiations were made. Au-Set had agreed that Merul would come to live here in the palace as was customary for their era. Merul would always be the top consort of Sekhmet and would have an equal say in all matters of their kingdom in the area of Ineb-Hedj. In turn, Sekhmet will be granted a seat in the meetings of Upper and Lower Kemet under the two reigning couples of Suti, Hetep and Neb-Het and she, Au-Sar and Heru.

She explained that currently, the table was based on no hierarchy for decision-making that everything was voted on according to the issue. However, Ua-Zit and Nekhebt spoke as the main voice pieces at the table for issues presented. She explained that they were in the process of adding a representative from each area of rule or mini kingdom of Kemet. Au-Set explained that she was in the process of creating districts in all of Upper and Lower Kemet that she wanted to call *Sepats*. She had arrived at forty areas thus far.

Re could not help but admire this woman and her grand ideas. He thought it impressive how hard she was working to give men an equal voice in the land. Up until this reign, the mother of the household decided all matters, with no input at all from the fathers. The women created life, ran businesses, fought wars, planned the futures of their own children, and made all-important decisions. Men had generally stayed home to raise the children, to prepare the food, and to shop at the market place, remaining dormant. Men accepted their lot in life, since they did not have the power to create life within them.

With the union of his wife, Re started to learn that he too had a voice, since Het-Heru was quiet and submissive. He had never witnessed this before. He had fought against it in the beginning and insisted that she rule beside his mother, as was her place and he would obey her decisions. However, Het-Heru was confused and sunk into a small depression. She never had any sort of power in her life according to the ways of her tribe and felt useless. No one had schooled her in any way what so-ever. Therefore, Re relented and learned from his mother how to take care of the family and run the business of importing their pottery. He found that he was quite successful at this as well. His mother smiled and grew proud of him.

He did know that when Edjo returned, she would be the one under his mother in the decision-making process and power of their family. Re missed his little sister and kept up their communication in monthly correspondences. He was impressed on how her writing was improving and how fast she was learning the new lecture language. She had even told him that she was being schooled in the ancient art of snake charming and that she had ten pet cobras that she had tamed to her command. Edjo gave them all names and wrote of them as if they were her own children. Re found this very amusing.

However, Re was growing increasingly concerned on how his brother was acting lately. Apep had always been given things in life, never wanting for nothing. Apep was never expected to make decisions and never had to. He just felt that he was very entitled and that he should get everything first due to this. It helped on how he was doted on by their mother as the first-born child. Re knew that after he was born and then many years later when Edjo was born, his brother's perfect world had crumbled. Upon the birth of Edjo, their mother had focused her attention completely on her only daughter, forgetting completely her sons, as if they had no worth at all.

Re accepted it and understood it, as it was the custom of the times for the daughter to have precedence and to be the heir. Nevertheless, he noticed his brother Apep boil at the attention he felt was taken away from him. Re grew very concerned on how Apep seemed to stew silently in anger and not say a word. It was made all the worse that Apep was coarse and crude of face and manner. He revealed no charm to anyone and felt that he did not have to.

Re observed how Apep would look at his consort Het-Heru, for her beauty was legendary and her charms were overwhelming to the average person. Yet, Apep looked at her as if he was the one who should have been chosen as her consort and not Re. This was very unreasonable since at the time Re was chosen, he was not attached to anyone and Apep was already a consort with a child on the way.

Re was concerned on Apep's way of reasoning with life situations as if life had to follow his rules, that everyone else was to blame for his actions, not himself. Re learned long ago to not leave Apep unattended.

Re brought up in the meeting with Au-Set the importance of finding a place as consort for his brother. She had mentioned that this was their mother's decision, but she would certainly value anything that he had to say about the matter of suggestions made. Re suggested her Nugig, Neferet from Eshnunna and Au-Set liked that idea and mentioned that she would bring it up with his mother.

Re loved the way that Au-Set valued his ideas and respected his knowledge in situations. He knew that he was falling for her and did not know what to do about this. He deeply respected Het-Heru, though was more attracted to strong women as she was not. Au-Set may not be as beautiful as Het-Heru. However, where Het-Heru was soft, fragile, and timid; Au-Set was dominant, powerful, and in control of any situation. This gave Au-Set a powerful grace which Het-Heru lacked.

Chapter 50

Re found that he was looking for any reason to be in the presence of this marvelous queen and enjoyed immensely her charisma and conversation. She seemed knowledgeable on all matters and was very educated. He could not help to compare her with Het-Heru. Where heads turned as Het-Heru entered the room, they were bored soon since she usually turned her eyes down and stood behind him. Au-Set would enter the room, was beautiful as well, but as soon as she opened her mouth, the passion she had in what she stood for and believed in was absolutely captivating and entranced each person within hearing. Au-Set radiated with power towards any situation as she entered each room she walked into. Het-Heru was beautiful in every classic way, but silent and chose to remain ignorant and uneducated.

This frustrated him tremendously. He gave up years ago in trying to teach Het-Heru strength and to educate her. His own mother hoped that in Het-Heru, there would have been a partner in rule. Nevertheless, his mother had to rely on his education, for Apep was never to be known as a scholar, as Re had become. Thus, the odd situation when he gained the right to rule under his own mother's house had evolved, passing over that of his wife.

He knew that his mother, Mut, prayed to the Goddess for Edjo to be like this fine young queen who had come to visit. Re knew that their mother would be proud when Edjo returned to their home after her fosterage.

Therefore, on this particular day he had found himself in their gardens, knowing that he would eventually find Au-Set. She was such a powerful woman that he found himself drawn to her as fish to bait. He laughed at the analogy silently to himself. He then sat by the pool of golden fish that his mother had stocked in the garden for their food. He soon found himself lost in their motions and lost in thought, not noticing how the shade of the trees grew longer and longer.

Suddenly, he looked up to find Au-Set behind him trying not to disturb him. She smiled in her magnetic way, which caught him in her power even further.

"Re, I hope I have not disturbed you."

"Not at all... I sometimes come out here to think, for it is so peaceful out here."

"Yes, I agree." She looked down at her feet. She found she too was being drawn to this older man. She was flattered that this man actually reveled in her company. She could not help but notice how he inconspicuously sought her out, as she did him this day.

Au-Set found that she was drawn to his voice and the easy way in which he broke precedent in their family by taking the command under his mother. Re performed unusual duties for a man with grace, almost as if it were natural to him. He ruled in a very natural way, with dignity and assurance. She felt drawn to him and found him very handsome with his slender form, dark hair, and graying temples. He looked very regal to her.

She was even more drawn to him as being strong enough to break precedent in escaping the ritual execution after her brother Tehuti was conceived. Her family never spoke much on that event, almost as if forgetting all about it. This was highly unusual in temple matters for an event such as that to be tossed aside, when he should have been killed. Yet here he was standing so dignified beside her, she was glad that he had survived and then secretly understood why he was never pursued. Her family must have fallen for his magnetic charm and the genuine goodness that seemed to reek from his very visage and presence. How no one could be caught in his spell, she wondered, then her mind returned to earth, and she quickly gained her usual regal composure.

"I must leave on the morrow, to return to the palace. I miss my children." She did not know why she added something so personal to him, but it just felt right and accepted.

"I look at you and still cannot see how you have given birth six times! I am sorry for so personal an observation." He bowed his head.

"Thank you; I do not know what to say to that. I do not feel like it though, for Au-Sar is always gone and Nebmaat more interested in clothing and jewels than in me."

Re looked at her and was amazed at this comment from her, for he felt her beautiful indeed and could not understand how a man could not want to be in her presence at all times. His mouth dropped in amazement and felt the urge to hold her close and to kiss her delicate lips that looked almost perfect in her little pout.

"Please, forgive how blunt that I am with you, but I am very impressed in how.... Well, in just about everything you do. I could not understand how any man could not practically beg to be in your presence. For you are a constant wonder to me. I feel very comfortable to be around you and ... It is almost as if our minds are on the same plane in matters."

She nodded her head, "Re, I feel very comfortable as well in your presence and look forward to meeting with you." She lowered her eyes feeling almost like a small schoolchild with a crush on her teacher.

Re could not help himself but moved closer to where she was sitting on the grass and cradled her in his arms. She did not move out of his grasp. In fact, she sunk right into it. For she felt tingling inside her almost as if their chemistry was reacting in a completely normal fashion. Time and place seemed to stand still in their great comfort. Nothing seemed improper, only just right.

Au-Set looked up at Re and their souls collided. Their embrace seemed natural and in perfect order in the universe. The stars peeked out of the clouds in the sky and the moon was sleeping, leaving the gardens in almost complete darkness. It was a moonless and quiet evening. The evening sounds blended with their love found. It was a desperate love, demanding, and hungry.

They did not care what others thought, or of any wrong was committed in this moment. It was selfish, yet complete.

After their bodies had received enough nourishment from each other, Au-Set fell asleep in Re's arms. They did not have to speak at all about everything that surrounded this event. They both knew what it was and did not expect anything to come of this. They knew that they had satisfied each other's hunger and that it was all that it was and would ever be. They both accepted this completely.

They got up, looked at each other in perfect understanding, and smiled for what they had briefly shared in each other's lives. They knew that this would be the end, yet bring them forever close as soul mates in understanding for the rest of their lives.

Chapter 51

Ua-Zit was concerned that Nekhebt requested a meeting at Per-Uto, rather than meeting at the usual market village of Gerzah of the famous pottery. It seemed to her in reading the correspondence of her sister that Nekhebt wanted them as far away as possible from Upper Kemet. All prior attempts to visit her sister had been politically thwarted in the past over the years and Ua-Zit was becoming impatient for she felt in her heart that something was dreadfully amiss.

Despite all of the flowery wordings of Nekhebt, there seemed something more in each tablet that she received, almost as if she were hiding behind something. Ua-Zit and her growing family desperately wanted to see if all that was put forth in the writings of the prior updates had come to fruition.

With all that was written and reported, one would almost expect a sprawling city almost larger than the one left behind in their homeland. It was reported that Abdjw was well underway and almost ready for habitation. Such comprehensive reports and descriptions were sent their way over the many years that it had been enough to withhold their visitations feeling that Nekhebt and Neb-Het had more than enough on their plates.

However, too many years had passed and Ua-Zit had wanted to see her younger sister in the flesh, words were just not enough anymore. Something called out to her that she needed to see her sister with her own eyes. Therefore, she made secret arrangements for them all to travel down there in two months time before a false meeting was planned for the usual Gerzah. She hoped this would distract them and to allay their thoughts of their family up in Nekhen. She wanted their guard to be down and finally put all pretensions to rest by bringing them to the foreground and out in the open.

She was also very curious about Neb-Het and in her not having any children from either consorts. This called out to Au-Set and her heart to be there in comfort of her sister, despite all of the assurances of Neb-Het that she had been too busy to start a family with her consorts. Therefore, the curiosity of Ua-Zit and Au-Set and the other siblings was seriously aroused and they wanted the truth. They wanted to see for themselves if something was truly amiss despite constant assurances that would come regularly from Upper Kemet.

Au-Set and Ua-Zit realized that after much correspondence and from secret sources, that this might be one of the last meetings with Nekhebt. Since her condition was waning and she would not be able to attend many more meetings. This information was all the more difficult, since Nekhebt kept this information from her family in Nekhen.

Over the years the two queens and twin heirs kept up a diligent correspondence, Nekhebt promoted an almost thorough and impenetrable mask of normalcy up until this point in time when the final truth of her malaise had at last reached the concerned Ua-Zit. Ua-Zit, in not being the only co-ruler of the whole land of Kemet, but a sister of Nekhebt as well was finally able to decipher her sister's ruse in being an able ruler. She had sent out spies that were even more thorough than Kekes, if possible. She understood why her sister kept this knowledge from her and from those around her. It would be easy to depose such an ill ruler and to have someone else take over her part in the rule of the land.

Due to the direness of the situation, Au-Set was forced to leave her six young children behind while they made a special trip to Upper Kemet to the city of Nekhen in all haste.

Chapter 52

Suti had received word from some of his spies that an entourage of his relatives were traveling down to meet them and would be there in a matter of weeks. When he realized the vast implications of this, he burst out in a fury that seemed to rock the very foundations of their very incomplete palace. He was irate at the nerve of them, especially of Au-Sar. How dare he presume that he was a more able ruler? Suti felt that Au-Sar was always jealous of him and all of the attention that he had received from their mother. Suti's thoughts had almost become a sickness to him that reeked in a growing hatred over the years of Au-Sar. Sure, his brother had not done anything to create this feeling in reality; on the contrary, Au-Sar had always chosen his side when they were little. Yet, it was there like a growth that reached the very precipice of his impenetrable soul deep inside of him and it was reaching out for blood.

Suti, could not understand this feeling, but since the first meeting that was held in Gerzah, over ten years ago, the face of Au-Set continued to taunt him. Since he had seduced Au-Set, he realized that he only wanted her because Au-Sar had her. Au-Set was the sister of theirs who would become the true ruler of this land, due to her personality and because she was the first-born daughter. Both of these reasons had cemented the hidden claim, for it was always there.

Despite all of the equality talk of both generations of sisters, he knew that the city that was truly the capitol of Kemet was in reality Per-Uto. This city of Nekhen was only a pacifier, so that both of the younger and supposedly equal heirs would be content.

Yet, he saw the truth. He wondered why Au-Sar was always the chosen one of their mother. Did their mother give the lesser sister to him to punish him for having the red hair of her destruction? He had finally found out the truth of his conception that had been kept from him for so long. He knew his father took the rights from his mother and was killed because of that. He knew that his father was a God, the God whom they called Enlil, that king who sat upon the throne was sitting in his rightful place, and he had been looking for a way to get it back. He had secretly formed a faithful guard of seventy-two men from this land that had sworn themselves to his service even after their natural deaths.

Suti had a plan that he told his faithful guard. He wanted the kingdom to encompass Ur as well as all of Kemet and all of the lands in between. He wanted Au-Set as his first wife, his property, since she was the one who had life in her womb and not the consort that he was assigned. Neb-Het had thwarted every attempt that he made on her, almost as if he repulsed her. Neb-Het barred the doors to her chambers and denied him entrance, which infuriated him even more.

His aunt Nekhebt had long ceased to exist in her silence and did nothing. She just existed in form alone. The only company she kept was her secret falcons whom she treated like her children; she gave them the names of all her natural-born children that she had lost long-ago. It was almost as if she believed that the very souls of her children were in her beloved birds. People felt very uncomfortable around her and walked the other way.

Suti felt that he was finally strong enough to put the first of his plans in motion. He had to get rid of Au-Sar. He had no interest and felt no threat from her other consort Nebmaat. He felt that the man was weak and easily pliable.

As soon as he learned of their journey to his part of the kingdom, he gathered all of his men and concocted a plan. It had to be brilliant and strong enough to lure Au-Sar into his net.

He knew that despite his brother's infatuation with the land, he had other weaknesses, which were his own vanity and the love of competition. He was a truly handsome man; one could not deny this fact. He felt how his own consort's eyes had traveled to him at the last meeting. He saw nothing but the repulsion in her eyes when they were directed at him. This further thought solidified his hatred of Au-Sar. He knew that his brother was well aware of the effect of women at his beauty and felt so confident about it that he did not attempt to gain their attention as did his consort brother, Nebmaat. Nebmaat wore the finest clothes obtainable and was always immaculate in appearance without one flaw ever in his garb.

It was disgusting how Au-Sar would return from the fields smelling of earth and women would fall even deeper into his spell. Suti knew that it was only a game to his brother. All he had to do was bat his long eyelashes and Au-Set, who would bow to no one, and she would come running at every request and practically swoon over him in adoration, as would his own consort, Neb-Het. It sickened him!

Therefore, he had decided to tempt his brother in his own game and weakness. He had a chest especially built with the finest materials available. Cedar was imported from the lands of Canaan, where his cousin Astarte ruled. It was finely interwoven with wood from the darkest jungles of Punt. Inlaid around in swirls that played with each other teasingly were many paths of precious gems such as carnelians, the rare malachite, quartz crystals, beryl, and other such rarities cleverly obtained in such short notice. Lining the great chest was the rarest metal of this land, silver. The handles were made of the pinkest of gold obtainable. This chest was made finer than any other in the land was and it had a remarkable attribute that would definitely arouse the curiosity of Au-Sar.

It was secretly fitted to the exact dimensions of his brother's body. His brother was legendary for his tall and thin form with broad shoulders and firm abdomen from many hours in the sun and fields. He knew that Au-Sar was always aware of the attention paid to him, even though the look he projected towards women was of pure innocence.

Suti wanted to present this at the closing banquet as a sort of contest. The competition was the additional lure to his brother. Therefore, the bait was made irresistible to his prey. The chest would be awarded to the one person who fit inside it. He felt that this would immediately be the final undoing of his pestering brother Au-Sar.

Yet, he wanted to make sure that it would be unknown to all others present. He wanted Au-Set to run to him for comfort. Though he would take her if something was to go amiss and he was forced to jump into action.

Therefore, he would don his mask for all to see and to adhere to his plans unknown to them. He sat there running his hands over the almost faience-like smoothness of the finely carved wood and admiring the way in which the stones caught the light that peered through the carved arches of his chamber.

Chapter 53

At dawn a week later, a ram's horn was sounded through the walls of the palace to notify them to the presence of the "unexpected" visitors. Neb-Het was startled from her midday sleep in escape from the brutal sun to hear the sounds emanating though the long dark halls. Who could possibly be coming here, to this ancient twisted no-woman's land? The decay all around her of the years of neglect and her solitude would be enough to keep any reasonable person away from here. She had not expected to leave for the Gerzah meeting at least for another week.

She had been up later the evening prior as in the past month trying to create false plans to appease the curiosity of her aunt and sister. She sometimes wondered at the results if she had actually created all that she had written about to those in Per-Uto. She had spent so much time creating shadows and dreams that she found herself frequently lost in them. They were not actually that bad, some of her ideas even surprised her in creating this great façade for them.

So many years ago, when her heart was fresh and the tears not dried from the loss of her mother and siblings, she actually believed that she had the power to create the reality of her dreams. She actually believed that the power of creation was in her and had felt even then, that she could build great cities and settlements like her aunt and twin sister in the delta.

Yet, she was too alone in all of this. Her aunt, Nekhebt, who had the true power, did nothing but hide in the shadows becoming a shadow herself, talking to her birds as if they were her lost children. Ignoring the ones left in her charges that were very alive, from her sister Ninnuit.

Neb-Het had long ago given up any hope for guidance and love from her neglectful aunt. Even the wise words of Neferet grew stale over the years. She had watched how the neglect of the woman's wisdom, caused Neferet to grow large as her sister over the years.

With each line that she drew in anticipation of the meeting, stale tears of anger would form in the reality that the lines of her plans were only a false façade and a dream that would never grow into fruition. It angered her and burned her hopes even further. She felt that she was truly a shadow with no substance. No one here wanted anything to happen. They just lived out their lives expecting it all to come to them. They forgot the early wisdom of Neferet that told them that they all had to reach out, grab their dreams, and together make them happen. Instead they all grew lazy and let the dreams and plans dissipate completely.

She truly missed her brother Heru, for he was the only supporting force behind her dreams, had he remained alive longer she just might have seen them become known to herself and to all of Kemet. Yet, with his illness and death years ago, all hope was truly lost with his body that was taken out to the darkest desert to his tomb in the new cemetery that she had started in her almost new city of Abdjw.

They, along with the help of her siblings and aunts, had all abolished the cannibal tradition with a more symbolic rite and the building of tombs for the revered bodies of the dead. They had convinced the people that the Gods had more use for the body parts consumed than the people themselves did. The parts most sacred would be now kept in sacred jars in offering to the Gods. The people along with the threat of execution to inspire them further accepted this. The priestesses made the consumption of the sacred body parts an abomination in the face of the Gods and began to spread a new tale. The people feared that they would suffer torments if they should ever revert to that practice.

Neb-Het felt it a true irony that the only thing completed in her new city was a cemetery. It almost spoke of her life's accomplishments all dead like the corpse of her brother which was the first to be buried within. The desert that surrounded him in his sleep smothered all of her dreams and plans back then, assuring her that they would never breathe life nor become reality.

The sounds of the horns jarred her from her thoughts, always thoughts, never a reality. She hastily got dressed to find out the cause of the commotion that she was beginning to hear throughout the cobwebbed covered palace.

Chapter 54

The startled Neb-Het stood there at the highest tower in a stupor when she realized that a party containing her aunt and siblings from Per-Uto caused the stir. She ran down to greet them after she had changed into the finest garments that she owned.

Neb-Het embraced her aunt and siblings with Suti on her left, the side of importance. Hetep was to her right. Suti then winked at her conspiratously as they were all going down to a banquet hall, to a banquet that she had no idea at all that was even prepared. She let herself be led by Suti as he brought them into the last edition of the palace that was never completed. For years, it sat empty with the hope of creation never reaching its blank and unadorned walls.

First, she noticed the wink from Suti, felt it odd, and then was further bedazzled with the long abandoned dining hall gleaming in freshly painted murals of the most rare and vibrant scenes she had ever seen before. The scents of the fresh paint assailed her nostrils under the heavy use of incense that she knew was primarily to disguise the actual age of it all. The fine and brilliant execution of the colors was truly spectacular and she reveled at the newly discovered genius of her youngest sibling. She was nudged by Suti to hide her amazement and wonder at the banquet hall.

Neb-Het was wondering how Suti knew of this change of plans and was a little upset that he had found it not necessary to inform her of this. She had no idea of this and yet, went into their act to perfection, out of pure obligation of the moment. How could he have known, when no one else here had any idea?

She was further amazed and tried to hide it when she saw the form of her aunt Nekhebt sit on a richly adorned and carved deep black throne of the darkest obsidian obtainable. She had never seen it before or her aunt in many years for that matter. Nekhebt appeared in the spark of health, any trace of insanity was hidden under her darkly made up eyes. Her hair was hidden under a veil woven in gold and the starkest of linen shrouded her body that seemed undaunted by the many years she had observed on the last occasion that she had seen her years before.

Neb-Het was amazed at the illusion presented and found her becoming equally lost in the game played out to Ua-Zit and her siblings. It was so well orchestrated that she found herself almost wanting to believe the illusion her brother seemed to have knowingly provided to appease them.

She noticed on her way out to the main dining hall that there were hundreds of villagers in the process of building an elaborate mud-brick wall around the city similar to those found throughout Eshnunna. She was amazed on how this was all going on without her knowledge. She beamed with pride as she almost stumbled to keep up with Suti and his entranced entourage.

Her arm was then entwined in that of her sister with their consorts all around them as well as the aunts and Tehuti. While they followed Ua-Zit who was being led on the arm of Suti, as if this was the normal routine for visitors. She had to fight bravely not to be amazed at this brilliant play that was being performed all around her, she truly felt that she was in a dream, so well did all appear to her. Suti left out not one detail in this farce.

The large columns slithered tall and taunting around them and made them feel as if they were mere ants walking among the legs of the Gods, so many were they. The columns were topped in the blossoms of the blue lotus sacred in their land and the feet at the bottom resembled genuine feet. They were all impressed with the hall and of the skill of the workers.

They walked down the center to the dais where her aunt sat in her magnificence. Next to Nekhebt, was an equally magnificent throne made of quartz for her sister Ua-Zit. Suti made sure that he was sitting next to Ua-Zit so that she could place her hand on his bright red hair as if he were her favorite child in adoration. She did and happily, his face beamed in response. They all joined in their places to hear the latest petitions from the nobles of Upper Kemet as was expected at the beginning of their meetings of joint rule.

Ua-Zit could not understand all that they had arrived to see. From the reports that she had received, she had expected a decaying mausoleum and nothing more. Now, before them was a grand palace which seemed in top condition with the finest artwork that she had ever seen. The city that she had entered was built up and thriving. She could see the workers on the nearby new city of Abdjw across the River to the side of the setting sun. She wondered how this could be. Her sister beside her seemed unfazed by it all as if life was normally in ceremony like this and everything was usual. Yet, she had sensed something more that she could not quite place her finger on that was reaching out to her.

She did notice the startled look from her niece Neb-Het upon entering the grand hall, and then was distracted by the look of Au-Set's face as well. Yet, the look on Neb-Het's face was so fleeting that she was doubting the validity of her thoughts on the matter, even now as she sat in this richly adorned and painted room receiving many faithful people of this Upper Kemet who seemed beaming in gratitude.

They were served the most exquisite and difficult to obtain food, as if anything were possible for this land so far from the reaches of the rest of the world. All of them engaged in delightful conversation on all that had occurred over the years since their last meeting.

Yet most of the words from those in Upper Kemet were making the fibers of the illusion stronger and alive to them to entertain the unknowing visitors. All was a glorious act played enticingly well by those who hosted this surprise visit. It seemed real, not the act that was played out by Suti.

Suti was pleased at the reactions of his great illusion and gloated to him-self. For as soon as he gained news of their all too imminent arrival, he ran into an almost maniacal pace of setting into motion the construction of

the elaborate chest and the rest of the façade. He had
found any man and woman that he could lure in to erect
the walls around their decaying village hiding it and
giving it the appearance of a built up city. They had even
worked under the light of oil lamps and each ray of the
sun at all hours to complete this miracle. Yet, inside all
but a few rooms, was nothing but the empty shell and
the ruins of the real city.

He was amazed at how lost his sister and aunt
were in their own worlds, that they had no idea. He had
informed his aunt first of their approach. He had artists
apply the finest makeup to hide the shadows under her
eyes and the white in her hair. He had her dressed in
the starkest linen added to her form to hide her thin and
emaciated body. To all Nekhebt appeared the vision of
health. He had to appease her with great promises to get
her to leave her comfortable and familiar chambers. He
told her that they would forever be left alone if she
would act for just this one time. She had long ago lost
her will to live and was just a shadow, that he knew her
greatest wish was to be only left alone with the souls of
her children in her falcons. It was enough for her.

So long did it take to persuade his aunt that he
did not have time to reach Neb-Het to warn her. He
could only wink at her upon their arrival. He actually
felt Neb-Het look at him, as she had not done in so
many years. It almost made him forget his plans so
almost charmed was he at her reaction.

After the welcoming banquet and the announcement of
their meeting, they had all been shown to their richly
adorned chambers in the newest section of the palace.
Neb-Het walked back to her own chambers as if in a
trance at the unreality that was presented to her. She
felt as if she was losing all traces of realism. She had
fallen asleep truly through all of this brilliant planning.
When she went to sleep the evening before, none of this
was realized. Then again, she kept mainly to her own
suite of rooms on the northern section of the palace far
away from this entire splendor and to her gardens
beside them, she could not have known about this.

However, she felt angry that Suti had done all of this without her knowledge. How could he have built this up over the years without her knowledge or consent? He had overstepped his position as consort and even went against the will of their aunt Nekhebt even though she was only a shell of the woman that she once was. Yet, even she appeared in the most vibrant of health. Did they leave her out completely and let her rot alone in her chambers while doing all of this? The many questions coursed through her mind giving a stale taste in contrast to all of the delicacies that they had consumed at the banquet.

For a moment, her thoughts swayed as she recalled her brother and sister's consort Au-Sar in all of his beauty. How he glowed in the torchlight. His eyes the deepest amber she had ever seen and his face perfect, he seemed like a God to her. He looked at her more than once at the banquet.

She sadly knew that he had always been fond of Suti, unknowing of that brother's true feelings towards him and hoped fervently that Au-Sar would not suffer for his illusions of his youngest brother. She saw that Au-Sar beamed at Suti and fought to gain his attention in genuine admiration of him. She worried about the innocence of Au-Sar and hoped that he would never find out exactly how cruel his little brother Suti really was.

She felt that the eyes of Au-Sar drifted over to her on quite a few occasions, yet at the same time seemed equally adoring of their sister Au-Set, as he fought for her attentions with Nebmaat on her other side to place tempting delicacies in her mouth.

Chapter 55

Au-Set sat beside her aunt and mentor Ua-Zit across the immense table in the banquet hall from Nekhebt and Neb-Het. Suti, Au-Sar, and Tehuti were sitting beside her while the consorts and sons of Ua-Zit were on the side of her aunt Nekhebt and twin. She kept trying to decipher the face of Suti for some underlying plan behind all of this and came up with nothing to sustain her assumptions. She was amazed at his control during the meeting. He was far different from the youth that he was at their last important meeting, so filled with anger then that she found herself almost believing his new strength.

Yet, she could not shake the memory of that violent meeting so many years ago. She would have thought it all a dream with how well he was playing this game, had it not been for her daughter Set. Au-Set was positive that he had no knowledge of her daughter Set and her likeness of him for she made sure of that. It was more for the feelings of her sister, and out of some fear of Suti. She knew that if Neb-Het were to guess the paternity of her oldest child, she would fall deeper into the shadow that she always called herself when alone with Au-Set. Neb-Het had no children of her own and she could almost feel the pain rip inside her at the mention of her children at each meeting. She felt her sister's pain through the smiles that she wielded like a sword in the room.

Au-Set sat and listened to the calm and assuring voice of Suti as he told them of the growth of Upper Kemet and its harvests. He also told them of the newly found riches in the mines recently discovered in the area. She found herself almost impressed with him. She knew that Ua-Zit was falling under his spell as well as the rest of them. Yet, she could not forget the darkness that she had seen in him years ago.

All she or the rest of them could see was the truth in her brother's words. She wondered on the validity of the spies that she had sent down and wondered what their motive was for them to send false reports. In contrast to what she had heard was what had greeted their eyes in actuality. It was this thriving land and seemingly nothing less as she had been informed.

"Abundant joys for you sister and your many children." Spoke Neb-Het to her, startling her reverie. She continued after catching her sister's glance, "I have hopes of seeing them soon, might we arrange something after this meeting on that?"

"Of course sister!" Her face beamed at her sister's sincere interest in her children.

Tehuti added, "Sister will you not be afraid that your own children would not be able to tell you apart from your own sister!" He laughed at this, as did the others in the room.

Au-Sar looked at both of the sisters that Tehuti was referring to and retorted," Why yes brother, you have a valid point there. I am sure no land surrounds us has such beautiful princesses as our very own sisters! So much alike as to fool any but us! Well, I assure you that if they would actually switch places, no one would ever know, not even your children Au-Set!"

"No, not quite exact, for Au-Set has the bloom of mother-hood and absolutely glows with it!" Beamed Suti in his usual way of speaking first before much thought on the feelings that some words could arise in those more sensitive like his sister and consort, Neb-Het. Au-Set noticed that her sister turned white at this and wondered if Suti had meant any offense at this remark. She decided that she would keep the latest news to herself, hoping no one of her Per-Uto crowd would announce anything.

As if on cue to break the sudden tension in the large chamber, the musicians broke out in a yielding ballad that rested upon the room like a soft blanket to lull them in splendor. Slowly they all got up to dance to form new bonds between them as if never broken by years and distance.

Au-Set in dance reached out to her mirror image and other half of her soul, Neb-Het, bringing her back to her. She felt the illusion beginning to break and some deep hidden pain in her sister called out at the innocent remarks made by their brother Suti.

After consuming much flavored beer and dancing through endless songs, they wandered back to their chambers one by one after a very productive meeting was echoing in their minds.

Au-Set was still weary, not forgetting the awful side of her brother Suti as presented to her many years ago. How could all of that anger suddenly have vanished to create the marvelously mature calm young man he presented to them all?

She saw her sister and mirror image smile and the room seemed to believe her, yet Au-Set saw through all of this and felt her deep lament inside. She needed to be there for her sister. She found her way across the other dancers to the side of Neb-Het, where she embraced her twin in dance and poured her soul out to her other half. She felt that she had reached her sister. She wanted to make sure that Neb-Het knew that she could always turn to her no matter what. Upon the comfort of her younger sister's received message, she left her embrace and walked over to where Tehuti sat on the side watching the family dance to the lingering sounds of the lutes.

She sat on the soft pillows beside him and tried to read his thoughts. He smiled when he noticed her. "Such a beautiful illusion, is it not sister?" She felt herself almost jumping at this very acute statement which she had wondered herself at. He smiled softly at her startled reaction.

"I cannot place my finger on it, it just does not seem right. Nothing does. Look how they dance around as if everything is normal. Moreover, it truly does look normal. That is the astounding part of it. Even aunt Nekhebt appears as she did so many years ago at the very first meeting. It was almost as if she had not aged even one week!

"I mean even our beloved Ua-Zit has aged a few years, though glows from all of the beauty that she has created in this strange land." They both softly chuckled over this, knowing how their aunt Ua-Zit would tremble if anyone saw any slight touch of age, so deftly an expert was she at hiding it all with her cosmetics.

"I felt something with Neb-Het when we embraced during the last dance. It was almost as if she was testing me to break this illusion for her, as if she needed me. Yet, it was not as she projected, her feet did not miss one step of the dance yet it was if time had stopped for the briefest of seconds so that she could send that message or thought to me." Her face contorted with her confusion and again she looked about the elaborately decorated walls around them and to the faces of merriment of all within the banquet hall.

"Do you not wonder why there was not a special room designated for the meetings sister? I know it seems small, but why are we always brought to this hall? I admit that it is truly a work of art but are there not other parts of this grand palace that they would want us to see?"

"And beloved brother, are my eyes playing tricks on me or is Neb-Het actually trying to seduce my Au-Sar?"

"Oh, no, it is part of the dance of the ancients of this land they just by chance found themselves in those steps. Would you question it if it was Neb-Het and myself or you for that matter?"

"No, I suppose not. My emotions seem to be playing tricks on me lately. I jump too fast with my heart." She silently thought of what she recalled her mother would often tell Neb-Het and her, that they should follow their deepest instincts, for it is very strong in women for how else would they be able to protect their own children?

"Be at rest with the knowledge that Au-Sar and Neb-Het truly love you. Besides, you are probably right about the illusion of all of this, for I have wondered the same thing, but have to find proof of this. Come, let us join them all for I feel we look like doleful old slaves musing about the past, we must become a part of this illusion if we are to crack it open!"

He made sure that he was behind her to hide his look of concern for the glances that he had witnessed from Neb-Het to Au-Sar. He did not find it appropriate to alarm Au-Set with all that she had to worry about in the normal course of just running the lower part of Kemet. He truly wanted her to have one less thing to worry about. He would take that last matter on his own to see the merit of it.

Chapter 56

Later on that evening when all had returned to their separate chambers, Neb-Het quietly found the way to the chambers of Au-Sar, in which she knew he was alone. After the banquet and dancing, she saw Au-Set and Tehuti leave deep in conversation towards the gardens bathed in the soft glow of the full moon. She briefly noticed the lavender hues of the many colors under the guise of the moonlight and felt that it looked oddly beautiful in a twisted way.

She saw the look of despair in Au-Sar's eyes at this and wondered if Au-Set and Tehuti were having their own tryst and realized that neither had it in their nature to do such a thing out of their life's plan. She felt Tehuti too dry of a person to entertain such thoughts, so deep was he buried in his clay tablets and papyrus scrolls. She laughed silently to herself at such thoughts and practically patted herself on her back at the opportunity that opened itself up to her with their conversation. She stole through the wee hours of dawn after the banquet to Au-Sar's chamber.

She entered his room and found him lying there peacefully in all of his glory. Her heart flooded with emotions and her body reacted in accordance. How beautiful he looked even in sleep. She found herself lying next to him drinking in each gleaming muscle. Slowly he roused from slumber and found her there.

She made sure that he had plenty to drink that evening so his thoughts would be dulled leaving him helpless to her desire that was growing with each glance from him the moment of his arrival to the very seconds that she lay next to him. Such crescendo was almost overwhelming to her that she happily drowned in his sleepy masculine smell of earth that was tantalizing to her nostrils. How different was he from Suti or Hetep, who were such a pliable puppets to her and bored her immensely. Besides, she desperately needed an heir from Upper Kemet; they had enough in Per-Uto!

With Au-Sar being such a dizzying array of mystery and beauty, it awoke senses within her that she did not know even existed. She had on her sister's sleeping attire and her favorite scent of Melilote oil to enhance this illusion.

His eyes slowly opened and he drowsily exclaimed. "Au-Set my love and heart!" His arms reached out to her and enfolded her in his strong grasp. Neb-Het did not care that he called her Au-Set. She did not care what he called her at this moment only that this moment was real and that it was not another one of her dreams. She felt herself slowly melting into him, becoming a part of his soul, and then of him entering her body. She held him there and took every ounce of his strength of him into her soul and future dreams.

Au-Sar did not realize until the very last drop was depleted from his strength that this was not Au-Set. Yet, it was so beautiful that he did not care. Au-Set had not loved him so deeply after her children were born. He had missed it dreadfully and constantly pined for remembrances of her lost kisses.

He felt he was dreaming and that his beloved Au-Set had returned to him. He understood why she had changed after the birth of her children, yet he missed it so. Tonight it was brought back to him and then he knew why. It was not her, but Neb-Het.

After she had left the room, he wondered if it was only a dream and was beginning to feel guilty of his betrayal to the only woman that he had ever loved or wanted. Then the rays of dawn seeped into his room he felt that it must have been a dream. No traces of it were present when he awoke and neither was Au-Set anywhere to be found.

He wondered about Au-Set and her avoidance of him ever since she had returned from her visit with Re. He knew there was something that happened; only he did not know what. He secretly suspected though. With this, he had secretly hoped that it was Neb-Het; if not a dream, it was better than nothing was at all.

As he got dressed for the day, he set about in search and found his sister where she always was, deep in conversation with Tehuti and Qui. Comforted by the normality of the scene that the last traces of the evening before had dissipated into the dream world where he had thought they had originated.

Chapter 57

After a week more of meetings and further illusions, Suti decided to hold a special banquet with contests for their amusement and in reward for the success, he felt with their surprise visit. The banquet was secretly to rather punctuate his achievement at fooling them all even Neb-Het, who constantly looked at him with venom as if she felt left out in the creation of all of this. Suti did not care, however, about Neb-Het.

Only Au-Set noticed the smile that flowered on her sister's features, as she would steal glances at Au-Sar. She wondered at them but put it away behind all that she was shown in the somber ceremony heard in memorial for their brother Heru. Au-Set poured out secretly in prayer all that she had missed with his presence and all that she had wished that he had lived to see. She missed her brother Heru and felt his absence very strong in this visit.

The banquet hall was especially decorated as if to surpass all of the other times spent in this chamber. Suti beamed at their reactions and took charge as usual in pleasing them all as the gracious host that he revealed himself their entire visit.

They all sat together enjoying each new delicacy presented to tease their refined palates even further and spoke to them all, his voice rose above the din of the musicians that assailed their senses yet further, "This evening I have planned a rather special event. For tonight will be a night of fun." He clapped his hands to commence the first of the contests.

Suti continued, "I have made up a list for each of us containing items and questions for each of us to complete. The first will be rewarded with one hundred plates of silver." At the mention of the prize, the servants filed into the hall laden with heavy silver plates that sparkled in the eyes of those present. They all knew how rare silver was to any land and how impossible it was to obtain, that only the smallest fraction of jewelry was made from it. Nothing too plentiful as what was presented to them this evening in the great amount of it, was ever seen by any in the room ever before in their lives. All mouths in the large chamber were agape with awe.

Tehuti always the wise one was equally dazzled in the sight of so much silver before him to be given away in a mere contest, he looked inquiringly at his youngest brother and questioned, "How have you found this great amount of silver, brother?"

He responded calmly, having expected this. In reality, he had it given to him from his secret alliance with Enlil. Yet, he had carefully planned his response for them," Why brother, had you not heard in the meetings that a great mine was discovered to the very wilds below us? It was in my reports?"

"I am sorry brother, for I must have missed that. I apologize for my ignorance." Tehuti cradled his doubts for a better time for Suti had masked the truth so wisely, that no one present saw through it.

Just then a wrong note pierced out from a lute player and in response the, up until now silent dog, Heh, responded with a powerful howl that made all of those present in the enormous vaulted chamber squirm in tension. The sound was eerie and had rattled each of them, especially the increasingly suspicious Tehuti who leaned over to his brother and spoke in an annoying tone, "Brother, must you always have those infernal and grotesque animals with you at all times?"

Suti looked deep into the eyes of his brother backing him down, "Brother, I know you meant no offense in that for you know how much I cherish the faithfulness of my beloved Heh, and my piggies Suka and Suaa." He nuzzled each of them in turn and took another bite of his favorite lettuce salad straight from his gardens. The others looked on numbly at this exchange. It made each of them more aware of their silent presence that had for the most part gone unnoticed until this evening. In reality, wild boars and dogs were dangerous creatures and were hunted in their birth-land for food on banquet tables.

Never before had anyone prior to Suti, been known to tame the wild animals. They had over the years, grown used to the eccentricities of Suti and his love for rather strange animals.

As soon as it was started, Heh settled eerily back into his slumber beside Suti as if nothing had ever happened. Suti felt that this was the perfect timing to reveal more, "So, each of you have your lists. Happy hunting, for everything can be found in this room." All of them in the spirit of the game got up and ran about the chamber forgetting their all too recent discomfort.

Suti sat back and watched them in their quest. The first to return was Au-Sar with his bundle and face beaming. Suti knew that Au-Sar loved competitions especially when he won over Nebmaat, who soon appeared fast on the heels of Au-Sar. Suti clapped his hands and drums were sounded to bring all of the others back to the table to announce the winner. Everyone reveled in the cleverness of Au-Sar, the shining one. Au-Set ran over to his side and playfully seduced the valiant consort to the stomping feet of the rest of them who were enjoying this event.

Suti then looked around the chamber and announced. "Now I have another contest." He waited for all of their excited chatter to die down before he continued, for he knew they were all amazed at the last contest and felt that it could not be topped in how clever that it was. They all waited eagerly.

"I now have for you a singing contest. You will all have one hour to create a song that will captivate us all. The song with the most applause wins." He noticed gleefully, the expressions of Nebmaat and Au-Sar. He recalled the exquisite voice of Nebmaat and knew that this would be very interesting indeed. He saw Au-Sar's face as well and knew that his brother would do almost anything to top his rival consort to please Au-Set.

Suti sat back and watched them all find spots to create their masterpieces. He enjoyed their reactions and amusement at this evening and felt glad that it was falling in place perfectly. So diligently had he prepared for this that he just sat back and watched them all, knowing each piece was fitting in perfectly and none of them knew it at all.

Suti sat back enraptured at the talent of his family as they all took their turns. First to sing was Ua-Zit and then Nekhebt, then Au-Set, Au-Sar, Tehuti, Neb-Het, and at last Hetep and Nebmaat. He made sure that Nebmaat's song was the last to be heard since he knew that it would be the most wondrous of all and wanted it that way.

Nebmaat stood before them in the room hushed for his talent was renowned to all. Before him was an even more elaborate prize, two hundred golden plates inlaid with the brightest gems in all of the lands, which sparkled in the great copper lamplights above them, suspended from the ceiling.

Nebmaat's voice rang out true and pure and caught each of them in the magic,

"My love for you is like a dream in form.
Yet, a whisper that calls forth in hesitation.
Yearning and purity of soul.

When will you see my heart?
You feel my soul in yours with each step.
With each step, I make towards your embrace.

The door remains open to your eyes,
Yet, your reception, not believed.
My voice quivers at your invitation.

Yet, feels no entrance to the truth.
May you see me for who I truly am?
And not who you want me to be?

Your soldier, I will fight for you.
I will save your tears and cradle you.
Upon your lips and whispers,
Am I truly divine?"

The room revered the words and the strength in which they rang forth from him. For all had believed he was truly happy, yet, something more reached out to them all in the room of his true feelings for Au-Set, for whom else could that song have been written for?

Even Suti was entranced and thankful that his spies had reported this talent truly to him. The whole room burst forth in riotous applause and stomped their feet and pounded the walls in pleasure at the true talent of the humble Nebmaat.

Au-Sar roared out in anger at Suti, "This contest is fixed brother! For everyone knows that Nebmaat's talent in voice is unsurpassed!"

Suti just sat back and watched the reactions the others had to Au-Sar's sudden burst of temper. He recalled when they had all reacted to him like that and loved the return. "Not true dear brother, for it has been many years since we have all last seen each other. Never had I heard his voice!" All heads nodded in agreement to the alleged truth of those words uttered by Suti.

"Brother, I know how you love competition; perhaps you could make up the draw in the next contest...." All waited eagerly in anticipation. It was obvious that they were all immensely enjoying this evening.

Into the room was brought the next and last prize of the evening. It involved, the elaborate chest that Suti had been working on since he initially heard of their unplanned visit. All heads turned towards it. He felt their hearts stopping in admiration at the fine beauty and workmanship of it that had surpassed anything ever seen before.

Suti's voice rang through the vaulted hall and tempted all those present, "For this prize is also the contest....." Whispers rang out, Suti toyed with them, and let them all rant about waiting for a lull to explain, for all were trying to figure out this last game.

"The person who can fit into this fine chest wins this very same chest as their very own! It has a unique size to it indeed. To prove this, I will have each one of my seventy-two guards try it. I guarantee you that not one of them will fit in at all to the specific proportions of it!"

They had all lined up and each, accordingly tried to fit in the gilded chest, yet none of them were the correct size. The curious clamor filled the room with their wonder at such a magical chest that was more beautiful than any they had ever seen before. They felt that this was a unique and curious contest indeed. It almost appeared to them that the chest would change its shape whenever anyone close to the size and dimensions of Au-Sar tried to fit inside. It became smaller and larger so slowly, that Suti gleefully noticed that no one had figured out the reality of this illusion.

Au-Sar was the last, he stopped beside it and exclaimed, "Alas, I will try, but I have seen others before me try to fit and none had. Are there no winners at all in this brother?" He looked playfully at his younger brother Suti, sitting there amused. He had noticed the careful movements of his skilled servants replacing the original form of the chest that he knew would fit his brother exactly.

"Why do you not try and find out for yourself Au-Sar, or have you given up the thrill of competition?" The challenge goaded any hesitation away from Au-Sar as he eagerly stepped inside.

"It fits around me like a glove brother! How magical! I am truly impressed!" Just then, the lid slammed down shut over Au-Sar startling the room into a frantic pace of worry. The practiced look on the face of Suti was revealed to all as a sudden look of surprise, which had concerned them further.

The muffled screams of Au-Sar were reaching them all from within the chest, they stood transfixed in panic for they knew that his air would probably soon run out and slowly dwindle with each moment wasted.

Suti ran over to the chest and looked as if he was doing everything possible to find some way to open the beautiful and now deadly chest. Au-Set and Neb-Het were weeping hysterically at this point as well as Ua-Zit, while Nekhebt was completely numb from the entire din around her. Nebmaat and Tehuti as well as their crying sisters joined in frantically looking for any lever or notch that would release their beloved brother. Suti began to pound the chest appearing lost in the desperation that was seizing the room.

Tehuti looked around the room for something that he could use to break it open and found nothing but the harmless items that adorned the banquet hall. Tears slid down his face as he saw his sisters taking golden pins out of their beautifully piled up hair, hoping to find something on the carefully and skillfully carved and seemingly flawless chest. The mark were it separated the top from the rest of the chest seemed lost in the artwork of it and had disappeared when it slammed shut.

Au-Set and Neb-Het's hair hung in disarray over their strained backs as they bent over the now becoming tomb of their beloved brother, Au-Sar. Tehuti stood transfixed and watched them all helplessly try to release his brother. He was angry that not one of the items in this hall could be used to pry open the chest just a little bit. Tehuti and Suti tried kicking it and then even resorted to striking it with anything they could find to hopefully break the chest open. Nothing worked.

The muffled cries within grew less and weaker by each moment that stood still in time against Au-Sar. They all cried out to Au-Sar pleading with him to find something inside to release him and keenly sensed that there was nothing inside of it but the softest pelt lining from a leopard. With each prior admired lack of any flaws at all, became the bitter detriment of the cherished Au-Sar who was trapped inside this grand chest of magic.

It was then that Au-Set straightened herself, stopping those in their tracks in desperation, and called out, "I want the chest brought to my own chambers for my prayers will bring him forth!"

Suti was riled, for he had not predicted his sister's emotions when factoring in his plans. All bowed down to her wishes and all around grabbed hold of the chest equally mystified for it seemed too light in all of its beauty and was completely unexpected.

Yet, they picked it up and brought it back to her chambers so that she may be all alone with her beloved.

The muffled sounds from within had stopped and all had assumed that he was lost to them. The wailing began of those who loved him and would miss his great beauty to the land.

Chapter 58

Au-Set sat alone beside the mysterious chest and looked carefully at it not missing one detail. She vigilantly scanned it and found it amazingly different without the clamor and confusion of the banquet hall. She started to notice things that no one before them had in their earlier desperation. Skillfully placed, underneath the gems she found levers and hooks which none had thought to notice in their panic. She touched them all cautiously, forgetting her loss and was mystified at the new clarity that overcame her now in the silence of her own chambers.

At last, touching a large carnelian and moving it aside she found a lever. After moving it, it opened the lid before her that revealed the very still form of her most cherished and beloved consort. So quiet was he that he appeared as if he were only asleep.

She bent down, cradled his face into her loving hands, and found him still warm. She then breathed her soul and love into his cherished lips, for instinct deep inside told her to offer her breath to him.

His form slowly took action and reached hungrily for her in response to her breath, which returned his life. He weakly wrapped his arms around her, "Nay, my love, out of this box of death first!" She whispered for she knew others were outside and she wanted to find the reason for this clever trick that she believed was truly meant to kill him. She helped him to climb out of the box and then over to the sleeping pallet, where they last made love. It was almost as if they were finding the most desperate way that their bodies could cling to life.

As his strength returned and she heard the last of them outside leave her door, after hearing nothing within the chamber, she turned to him, "Dearest Au-Sar, do you feel that there is something dreadfully wrong in all of this?"

"I could have died my love, to be forever without you....It is beyond unbearable to my soul!"

"I know, we all tried in vain to release you and Suti appeared the most shocked of all. I do not understand. However, something tells me that Suti wickedly planned this. You were supposed to die in this with no blame to him as all."

Au-Sar was shocked and still in denial about the truth of his youngest sibling. He was always innocently in dissent of anything negatively stated about Suti. He stated, "How could that be? For he has grown up so much, he is not at all that reckless child that we once knew years ago. He is a grown man who has done so much and is the beloved consort of our Neb-Het."

"Yes, but something tells me that there is much more to our dear brother than we see around us. In order to find out, we must let on like you are truly in here and dead."

"I am not getting back in there again sister!"

"No, I will weigh it down to appear as if you are truly in there. Come; let us find things from in here to weigh it down so that no one will suspect anything!" They both ran around the chamber frantically and quietly put in drinking vessels, clothing and anything else they could find to fill it. Au-Set then carefully put the lid down and they both searched for a hiding place for Au-Sar.

"Au-Sar, climb out of the window and return at once alone to our palace in Per-Uto!" He nodded and went out deftly to join the shadows of the night.

Chapter 59

When the morning arrived they found Au-Set prostrate over the chest asleep from the appeared exhaustion of mourning over her consort, they gently pulled her off.

Suti spoke for all in the chamber, "The funeral ceremony shall begin at last light for our beloved brother. We shall place his tomb next to that of Heru in our new family cemetery in Abdjw." He had his guard pick up the chest and move it to the hall for the arrangements to be made for this burial.

As this was being done Au-Set protested, "I want this chest brought to Per-Uto, so that I will always have him by my side brother, surely you will understand this?"

"I do, but what about Heru, shall he be alone until one of us is there to be by his side?"

"No, but... I need to be by his side." She lowered her head truly not knowing what to do. She secretly knew that Au-Sar was really on his way to safety as they spoke, but did not want to give it away. She hid her emotions from the rest of them with her delicate hands as they covered her concealed tears.

"Sister, do you not think that it best that Heru have the company of our other brother? Unlike our own mother, who rests alone, with no one to know where her earthy remains are, our brothers will have each other's company in the afterlife. Give them this sister, and let them know how much you love them both for this. What good will Au-Sar's body be alone from that of our brother to keep him company, if he is in your palace far away. Please sister, think of Heru as well, for he needs company!"

Trying to remain calm to the person, she knew who had tried to murder their own brother; Au-Set decided that she had to relent to this for it did make sense. She knew of no other alternative and she was still apprehensive about the safety of her consort alone in the desert running back to their home. She feared that when Suti went to have the body of Au-Sar preserved for the afterlife, he would discover the truth for it was inevitable. She hoped that by then, her consort would be safe.

She secretly thanked all of the Gods that she knew that she did not have to in reality deal with this issue. She forced herself to keep up the ruse for the safety of her Au-Sar and nodded her head in agreement to Suti and his reasoning's.

When all had returned to their own chambers for mourning, he motioned to his men to bring out the exact replica he had made secretly that was filled with small rocks to match the weight of his brother. He wanted to send his body out to sea unconsecrated to that he would wander eternity in the torment of being unblessed.

Little did he know that this action is what made Au-Sar's escape safer.

Chapter 60

Instead of going to her chambers directly from all that had just occurred, Ua-Zit went straight to the chambers of Nekhebt, her sister, for solace. She was disturbed that she had not been there in the morning when all of the rest of the family had gathered at the chambers of Au-Set.

When she arrived, she was deeply shocked at what she had found. Her sister lay still on the floor. Ua-Zit bent down and found the marks of the iaret on her neck. Even Nekhebt's birds were found lifeless in their cages as well.

Ua-Zit looked at the shell of her sister after finding no trace of the snake and was amazed. All of the makeup was washed off and it revealed her sister in her true age and state of neglect. The thinness of her bones were jarring out of her linen under-shift and had marked the true distress that her sister and the other's here in Nekhen had tried to hide from them all in Per-Uto.

In scanning the room, looking for the iaret, she found it eerily neglected like the rest of sections of the palace that she had been in when she went to look for her sister. The furniture was as old and worn as her younger sister was underneath all of that makeup.

Ua-Zit fell upon her lifeless sister and poured out all of her heart. She took all of the pain of her sister deep inside of her as if to make up for not seeing this before. She truly felt to blame for her sister's neglect, she could not even begin to fathom when the thread that bound them together as sisters had severed. She felt the arrow of distress wash over her in not being there for her sister and in not seeing through all of the lies presented over all of the years. She was unable to help Nekhebt at all.

Suddenly her tears stopped and an acute clarity overcame her senses when she slowly began to piece together all that she had missed in her visit. She had trembled at the time when Tehuti and Au-Set tried to bring her their own suspicions and of how she in turn, ignored them.

Her sister appeared normal to her. On the other hand, maybe, she was afraid to see the horrible reality beyond all of the glimmer created by Suti to fool them all.

Her rage began its first course through her when she called for Au-Set and Tehuti. At their arrival, she watched as they each entered the chamber and of their equally amazed expressions at the neglected state of their aunt, that death could not hide from them. They looked around the chamber and noticed what she had upon her own arrival here.

Au-Set was the first to speak, "Aunt, how terrible!" Moreover, she let forth a great wail as the others ran to find the cause of it. Neb-Het arrived at her side and joined in the wailing of her twin sister.

Ua-Zit in a calm manner spoke out as all had entered the chamber and gasped at what they had found. "All in here see this!" Her voice roared to all within, overpowering their wails of lament at two such deaths in so short an amount of time in their lives.

"I find something foul in all of this! Some evil is here and is now revealed to us all! You Suti come forward and wipe those false tears away from your brow immediately! This act of yours must end right now! This illusion you have so skillfully wrought has crumbled." All in the room were stupefied at the trembling and powerful words of their aunt. Tehuti ran over to the side of Au-Set and nudged her. Neb-Het just stared.

"Suti, you have betrayed us all and your consort Neb-Het." The room was startled by her accusations and they looked at each other for answers.

"Au-Set and Tehuti, you were right and now I see it all too clear before me. The lies of Suti and Neb-Het! I order them to be subdued at once and brought back to Per-Uto to be dealt with later. We will get to the bottom of this treachery at once!"

Chapter 61

The city of Nekhen was ancient and had been around since as long as anyone could remember and even before. The city itself was starting to increase in population with more and more people coming to live in the city from the countryside and along the Great River. People chose to live on the side of the river of the rising sun, the side of life. The village of the dead was on the side of the setting sun far away in the Deshret part of their land and across the river.

All of life was primarily along the river in the narrow river valley where plants could be cultivated to sustain the life of the inhabitants. Outside of the valley away from the Great River, was the desert "red lands" or the "Deshret" as those who lived near it called them. In the Deshret was the sister village of Nekhen, the home of those inhabitants who could no longer walk in the sunshine or the village of the dead.

It was whispered that, similar to Eshnunna, the living originally inhabited this village of the dead above those who had died. Until, like in Eshnunna, the dead overpopulated the living and those who walked in the sunlight had to seek a place closer to the life of the river.

No one knows why this village in the Deshret was inhabited in its location in the first place. No one cared, for long before memory, no one had lived here, and only the dust of their ancestors inhabited the pits that lined the dusty streets. The houses on top of them that were reportedly there long ago, had turned to dust before history was recorded. People of the living village of Nekhen called the tomb city, "the city of whispers." Over the years during the reign of the sisters and aunts of the new royal family, a new city began to grow out of the dust of the old.

This great family from Eshnunna had started to build the tombs, specifically for the dead. They were grand temples of illusion that never saw the breath of life, unlike the original purpose of this city. They did not like the pits that were there previously and wanted something that resembled their homes in Eshnunna.

This new family built their tombs of mud-brick over wooden beams.

The earliest of her family a few generations back even built large mounds on top of the pits, possibly to remind them of the mountains of their homeland far to the north that were almost non-existent here. Those older mound-tombs had the people placed in them curled up like infants in their mother's womb to enter the sacred spirit womb of the Great Mother. The dead were buried to face the rising sun and were covered in mats with a few clay vessels and jewelry made of natural formed copper and flint tools. These were things that all believed would help them in the after-life. In those older tombs, there was no resemblance at all of the legendary houses once belonging to the living, only dusty mounds.

The newer tombs were more elaborate and rectangular, built of the mud-brick mentioned. Inside were paintings on the walls of things that would comfort that person in their new home; their homes and fields they cultivated in life welcomed them in vividly painted murals.

When the family from Eshnunna initially came here, they brought with them larger paintings for the tombs and more elaborate pottery from their homeland and other places to the north of Kemet. The tomb of Heru was the most elaborate until these two recent additions. Heru's was a mud brick lined oval pit with the largest mound by far in this village of the dead. The paintings were done in a new style of very two-dimensional figures to display the highly symbolic meanings rather than reaching for realism. This family wanted to establish its new culture and influence and began to paint on every flat surface possible with their meaning.

The two latest tombs for Au-Sar and Nekhebt-Nemothi were the ideas of Neb-Het and Au-Set. They wanted something new in this village of the dead. They decided to send them into the womb of the Earth Mother in the form of mounds or mini mountains. The sisters wanted their brother and Aunt to live in a house in their afterlife with most of the comforts they were used to when they breathed the same air. They wanted the people to see that their family was eternal and lived even after their bodies could no longer walk the earth in material form. Neb-Het came up with the idea of creating houses for the dead of their family from now on.

Both tombs were made of mud-brick like that of their palaces with painted false windows that displayed scenery that they saw out of their sleeping chambers in life. Food and servants to serve them in the afterlife were painted on the walls. The dwelling of the dead had a doorway in the front facing the main street and in the back were the typical two windows of a country dwelling. There was no need of a palace in the after-life since they believed that all who died were on the same status until their day of judgment. Au-Set insisted that they had paintings on the walls of all that they were familiar with in life, so they would not be lonely during their wait for judgment.

Au-Set insisted that it resemble as much as possible the home that she adored in the village of Khemmis where her son Heru was born in the rectangular portion of the dwellings. She had skilled painters paint scenes of the inside of their chamber in the palace of Eshur from her memory. Those days of her very early youth, were the only times that she could recall in their life, when they were all together in the safety of their cocoon of love and simplicity, when their mother sang them to sleep.

Only she knew the reality of the empty funeral cedar coffin that was supposed to have contained the body of her brother. Only she knew. She wondered on this and struggled to hide that fact that her brother Suti had something more duplicitous in mind, or he would have found out by then in the preservation of the supposed remains. She wondered what it might be.

She had also suspected that there was more to the fraudulence of her brother Suti than she could possibly figure out. She feared he had other plans for Au-Sar than those brought to light. She was secretly thankful that her brother was safe down in Per-Uto. She knew that it was only a matter of time before Suti discovered that Au-Sar was not really in the chest that was about to be placed in the tomb.

All of the family was gathered for this event. From Lower Kemet, there was Ua-Zit, Au-Set and Nebmaat and their children and those from Au-Sar, as well as Tehuti. A person from each district as created by Au-Set was present for the People of the Iaret and Lower Kemet. The Shen Peoples were present and represented by the Sepat leaders in their full array of resplendent colors. Their rulers were there as well; Neb-Het, Suti, and his mistress Puanit slumped on his arm in blind adoration. Neb-Het stood there rolling her eyes.

Soon after the events that had transpired, Ua-Zit ordered Suti and the rest of the family to hold up appearances for the rest of Kemet. The family must create new traditions in this land with the building of the elaborate tombs where they all gathered.

Ua-Zit knew that after all of this, some matters had to be swiftly dealt with. During this ceremony, Suti and Neb-Het were shackled in chains underneath their long flowing robes to await their judgment in Per-Uto after all of this was done.

She also noticed the glow in Neb-Het's normally dull cheeks and wondered to the meaning of that. She hoped that finally she was with child from Suti for the continuation of rule in Upper Kemet. She needed to review all of the facts surrounding the events that led them to this tragic day.

She also noticed the same glow that she grew to recognize in Au-Set that shadowed her sister. She looked over at her son and then Au-Sar wondering which consort it was.

After this brief reflection on the dais where she stood, she raised her arms to the heavens to silence the murmurings below them of the crowd that had gathered to witness this new event.

"My people, we are here to witness a very mournful day for Kemet. We mourn the death of two rulers; the Queen Nekhebt of Upper Kemet and her nephew, the King Au-Sar." The crowd was quiet; the wind seemed to respond to make up for the lack of sound and sent whispers around them in silent fury.

"Look all around you and see the new glory of this land! Notice the tomb of prince Heru to the left of you that has placed new meaning on this once empty and neglected land. Prince Heru speaks of a new wonder, the wonder of preservation. Inside of that tomb, in reference to the ancient ways is the preserved form of Heru. Each piece of him is intact and ready to stand up for the Gods in judgment when his day is due. Not one piece of him is left out to stand trial. This is the way of the Gods. I feel Heru beside me lending me guidance for this ceremony. He whispers to me at night that his aunt and brother shall be preserved the same as he. He has found glory with the Gods, every piece of him. He wants the same for Au-Sar and Nekhebt, for them to have the full glory and to sit beside the Gods in the heavens as whole and complete beings." The people at first were silent, for they were used to the timeless tradition that allowed for ritual cannibalism and then the logic of the issue presented sunk in to them after a distant pause. Scatterings of foot stampings could be heard in agreement and then it rose to a crescendo of shouts, stomping and clapping at the brilliance of the idea. The approval of the Gods had only solidified the matter. The average person could not possibly comprehend a conversation with a God or Goddess, but had to rely on their earthly representatives to make sense out of their concerns. Ua-Zit had found a problem and solved it for the benefit of the people.

Ua-Zit was dressed in a simple stark white linen shift that was bordered in gold and purple. Her arms and legs were only adorned with silver bracelets that resembled the iaret symbol of her people that wove towards her heart. On her head was a simple silver diadem with the hooded iaret facing out above her third eye in the center of her forehead. Her ritual tattoos in the ancient cuneiform of Eshnunna, though faded, revealed her power as queen in the sacred writing of Eshnunna down her arms and legs and on the bottom of her feet. Her nieces had the same tattoos, but in the new picture writing of their land. The picture writing as elaborated by Tehuti was still in its infant form for the land of Kemet.

"I ask you to look at this beautiful construction that is the home of Heru. The stones were mined in this land and in turn were shaped in the primeval mound of creation. In this land was once a sea, the whole earth was covered with the sea of Nu and out of it raised the mound of creation from which life sprang forth. Now this mound reclaims the life it has given to walk the earth, to walk another plane.

"Notice to my right there are two more, one for Queen Nekhebt and one for her nephew and King Au-Sar. Look and bow down to their new home people." Everyone all around them including the royal family fell to the ground in religious supplication, bowing to a power, they could only begin to comprehend and felt so small next to.

"Queen Nekhebt ruled from her palace of Nekhen the whole of Upper Kemet. A wise and solid rule under this Queen you have had. She loved her people. She was the Hawk Goddess in human form, the ancient leader of the Shen Peoples in human form. She controls eternity and rises up to complete her task on the next plane. For each piece of her is intact for her judgment. Is she worthy to complete her earthly given task on the next plane? Only the Gods above know this. For every word that she uttered and every step, that she took will be reviewed from the time of her first breath onward. The Goddess felt it just to take back her daughter that day and all of you are called to witness the opening of her new home and the beginning of her next journey. Her mouth will be opened and inside the truth of her existence will be found by the Gods and Goddesses. The hawk Goddess spreads out her wings for her daughter, her earthly representative, to take her home." Ua-Zit motioned to the flutes and *sistrums* to begin their dirge and lamentation.

A sistrum is an instrument that resembles a rattle and is usually made of metal. Ua-Zit raised her hands to the heavens and swayed in the beat of the new music that was accompanied by the drums that were softly imitating the sound of a heartbeat. Her nieces rose up their hands and joined their aunts in this funeral dance. Ua-Zit looked at her nephews and the children of the next generation and motioned for them to join in this ancient dance. The people below them joined in as well.

They danced until tired out of respect for a lost queen. When done Ua-Zit faced them all and pulled over to her the form of her saddened niece, Neb-Het.

"Little queen Neb-Het; you are now Queen Nekhebt Neb-Het from this day forth, for your aunt will live on through you to carry on her rule. You will be the mouthpiece of Nekhebt from now on. Every Queen that has carried the name of Nekhebt will be inside of you from this day forth to lend their guidance!" The people cheered and filled the valley in hope for a new reign to take them out of the neglectful state.

The people could not see the shackles underneath and were blind to them. Ua-Zit hoped that this matter would reveal the innocence of her niece and nephew. She did not want the people to find out anything until the trial. She will continue for the moment with the traditions of descent and the reign ceremony at the funeral of her sister.

Neb-Het bowed to the people and then her aunt and held her arms up to silence the people so that she could speak, "I thank you and will do the best with this power to make Upper Kemet shine and to blend in beauty and unification with Queen Ua-Zit and Lower Kemet. I bow down to Kemet, for I truly serve her!" The people roared with approval of the small but eloquent speech of the new sovereign of Upper Kemet.

Neb-Het was elated and knew that this power would create a surge of energy in her. She vowed to herself that she would do everything in her new power to make all of her past dreams a reality. She also, knew that she had to face her aunt and family in judgment over what she knew that Suti had done. She hoped that the truth of the matter would shine forth and she fervently hoped that she would be vindicated and allowed to rule. She looked over at Suti with a secret loathing. She knew that she would also get rid of that wretched Puanit, she did not want that woman anywhere near her.

Nekhebt Neb-Het stood there enveloping the rush of adrenalin that surged through her veins. She knew that she had to conduct the second part of the funeral as the mouthpiece of the Hawk Goddess Nekhebt, the present holder of the Shen.

With arms proudly raised and her legs silently shacked underneath her gown, she motioned for the people to be silent for the final chapter of this funeral. She bowed to her aunt then addressed the people below her, "My brother, Au-Sar was one of the simple joys in my life in just his being my brother. Even when he was small, he protected us all. He always sided with Suti, seeing no fault in him." She looked over at Suti and noticed that he had struggled to keep the tears from his eyes at this. She knew that this at least, Suti had remembered about Au-Sar. It was the truth and she wanted Suti to remember Au-Sar for whom he truly was, not how Suti distorted him to be in his ruined mind.

She continued, "King Au-Sar never had a chance to be the main King beside his consort Au-Set, for his life was taken away from him at a very young age!" She felt the murmurings of the crowd rush through her, encouraging her to continue.

"He will never see his children grow up! Then again, maybe he will! For what was taken away, might just come back for the final judgment of this crime. His power grows stronger after his death. I feel it rise all around us! He wants to come back to judge those who wronged him!" She looked over at her aunt and knew that she did not approve of this. Before the ceremony, Neb-Het was told to adhere to the formal speech that was presented to her. She was instructed by her aunt not to mention the form of the death of Au-Sar, nor anything else personal. She saw her aunt boil, but she did not care. She wanted the world to know her love for him and that she desperately wanted him to obtain his day of justice. Her passion for the injustice of the matter controlled her speech and made her reckless.

Au-Set was amazed at the passion of Neb-Het and stepped over to join on the side of her twin sister in support. She looked her sister in the eyes to let her know that she would face the wrath of their aunt in this by her side in full support.

Holding her sister's hands, she gained confidence and whispered to her, "We will make sure that justice is done and that Au-Sar knows this. In the afterlife, he is sitting in judgment; I can feel it in my bones!"

Au-Set hugged her sister and knew that she would have to tell her family the truth soon about Au-Sar. Nevertheless, she also knew that for his safety, she would have to wait until the actual trial when Suti was brought forth to Per-Uto in chains. Then she would bring out Au-Sar and he would tell his story and her sister would be saved.

Au-Set hated keeping this secret from her sister, never before in her life had she actually kept anything from her.

They danced once more. This time they danced until they could dance no longer and fell where they stood in the rapture of the new entrants to the afterlife for their judgment.

The funeral was a celebration of death and of life and of death again. It was a recognition of the circle of life and death that all would face. They believed that each word uttered and each action made in life would be judged after their last breath. The life lived would determine if they could sit by the side of the Gods or to return to life again to learn the lessons that were meant to be learned in the life prior.

They believed that their paths would assist them in all of this or be their downfall. To ensure that all of their beliefs were met, their tombs were prepared to the best of that person's ability. Offerings would be left for the dead, so that they would not go hungry and food was painted on the walls as well, for the dead did not know the difference. Songs and prayers were painted on the walls, as well as their names in life to ensure that the name would live on to be found by that person when the paths were united after each life journey.

After learning all of the life's lessons, the secret name was found. Riddles were painted on the walls to assist the different parts of one's spiritual and physical being.

The royal family from Eshnunna not only embraced the nine paths of life from Kemet, they secretly believed that it made sense as well.

Chapter 62

On the journey back to Per-Uto, Nekhebt Neb-Het and
Suti were still in shackles and put in the last boat that
brought them down the river to the capitol of Lower
Kemet. Ua-Zit knew that the silent treatment was the
worst punishment they had to endure in their lives thus
far; she hoped that the importance of the situation was
being understood.

As the sun-kissed waters of the mighty Great
River lapped playfully at their boats traveling with the
current, Au-Set reached over, picked a lotus blossom
from the waters, and gave it to her sister Neb-Het. With
tears in her eyes, Neb-Het accepted this from her sister
and knew that it came with her love and belief in her
innocence.

Suti sat there with Puanit by his side in pure
indifference to the situation. He looked completely
stubborn and relentless to what could happen if his
guilt were established.

"It is not only Queen Nekhebt Neb-Het and King Suti
that are on trial this day, but the whole land of Kemet."
The people in the chamber murmured their curiosity at
this statement made by Queen Ua-Zit. They just saw
Queen Nekhebt Neb-Het and King Suti sitting there in
chains that were now revealed to the large vaulted
chamber. It was painted in the brilliant colors of the
picture writing that Tehuti was turning into an art that
was sought by all that dwelled along the Great River.

Her voice was amplified in power to those
hundreds of people assembled there. Of those present
on this day were the leaders of each of the forty districts
of the land in both Upper and Lower Kemet. Au-Set was
sitting on a smaller throne by the side of Ua-Zit. While
the equal throne adjacent to Ua-Zit that was meant for
her dead sister Nekhebt, sat empty. Nekhebt Neb-Het
was meant to sit in this large sister throne besides hers
after her judgment on this day. Tehuti in his scribal
regalia stood behind them, as did the consorts Hetep

and Nebmaat. Tehuti was the official recorder for their family and all of Kemet.

The Nugig Neferet and Ma-At where there to serve as judges along with the royal family for this grievous matter. Ma-At brought out a silver scale that she felt symbolically represented their reason this very day and in her hand she held up for all to see a large white feather. She placed the silver scale in front of the chained prisoners for all in the large chamber to see that this was a day of judgment for those who stood accused.

Ua-Zit nodded at the scale and of her Nugig holding the large feather and continued, "Yes, we are all in judgment. How can we protect a land when there is strife and discontent within? How can we set an example, if we cannot keep the peace in our own home? I ask of you all present on this day to help us decide, for you all are the voice of the People of the land of Kemet. This is only the earthly court. The truth, if not found here will be found when the guilty are dead.

"I speak now as the Goddess Ua-Zit and on behalf of my sister Goddess and earthly sister. I speak now for the son of my oldest sister, Ninnuit, the earthly representative of the Goddess Innana of Eshnunna.

"Look at the two of them. See the guilt or innocence inside each of their hearts and through their eyes. King Suti, you may speak first."

The guards pushed him forward so that he would be fully examined by the people. He graciously stepped around the silver scale that was in front of him. "I implore each of you here to see the truth in me! I know nothing of what happened on that visit. I simply loved my aunt and saw her last when she turned in for the evening. You people of the Iaret know that your totem animal is very sneaky and finds its way into the homes of even the most humble, why not the home of a queen?"

The people were astounded at this way of reasoning in that they were a very superstitious people. They could not imagine a cobra or iaret entering the home of a royal person or especially that of one chosen by the Hawk Goddess Nekhebt herself! The hawk or vulture was the only natural predator of the iaret in life.

Surely, this Goddess representative would have been able to defend herself against an iaret! The words of this king made sense to his family through their education of this land. Nevertheless, to the common people, it was blasphemy. Besides those people of Upper Kemet had already judged King Suti and it did not bode well for him. They were afraid of him and were long since weary of his injustices to his own people. Despite the actions of the Gods that were above the average person, they felt Suti was guilty by way of his actions towards them alone.

The symbolism alone of an iaret killing the Goddess representative of the Shen or Hawk peoples could actually be enough to provoke war and Suti knew this. It would take great eloquence and skill to divert this, Ua-Zit had the intelligence, and skill for this as well did Au-Set.

However, his own family would not have put it past him to commit this kind of treachery to place that iaret in her room that had not only killed her but her birds as well, helpless in their cages.

The crowd had begun to mumble. Ua-Zit seized the moment and spoke," People, you are his judge in this matter, what say you?" The crowd had already made this decision for the room reverberated with murmurings, so strong and mystified where their arguments.

Ua-Zit continued, "And of your brother, your defense on this?"

Suti knew that he had to talk fast for the crowd could turn against him at any moment," I only meant to honor the guests of Nekhen with a simple contest. It was a beautiful chest. There has been no other seen ever in this land or any other. The Gods must have decreed that Au-Sar's life be taken, for it was only a simple harmless box!"

"And what of its disappearance? It was not found after all had settled down?" Ua-Zit cried out. Au-Set sat there stunned and wondered what this new information meant. Was her plan discovered? She still knew nothing of any of this. Au-Set simply sat next to her aunt in silence.

This was true, for after all was said and done, the chest that really contained the confused Au-Sar was then filled with items from Au-Set's room had been sent down the Great River and out to sea by Suti in order for him to replace it with his own replica filled with stones. Suti and Au-Set sat there stunned since they both thought they knew where the true chest lay.

Suti thought that Au-Sar was still inside the one that he had secretly sent up the Great River or South in this land towards the delta. As far as his replicated chest that was filled with rocks, that too had somehow mysteriously vanished. This time it was by Au-Set who had thought that it was the first chest; she feared that Suti would discover the contents and panicked. She had it secretly loaded onto a boat and sent back to Per-Uto.

Ua-Zit had discovered this and looked into the matter. She had only begun to scratch the truth in her queries. She also found out that Suti had filled the replica with stones and had never intended to preserve the body of his own brother. She noticed Au-Set turn white with fear and knew that something was to be revealed this evening since Au-Set and Suti seemed to know something of the chests.

Only one of Au-Set's Scorpion guard knew of this. Therefore, at the funeral, there was only a painted chest to stand for a memory of the completely confused and twisted events. Au-Set replaced the original chest that had once contained the rocks with the items from Au-Set's room in their haste the evening of the fateful events. Suti and Au-Set had raised more questions of the whole event by working on their own agendas.

Suti had prepared an answer for this that he truly did not know would be his final undoing, "The Gods must have taken him and the chest to them, for how else this could be explained?" The people roared with approval at this for they saw this in their superstition. They truly believed that the unusual was natural in the ways of the Gods.

Au-Set struggled hard to keep herself from laughing at this and of the approval of the people. She would have loved to just sit there and take in the reaction of the crowd, but she knew that the time was right for the vindication of her sister in all of this and for the pure guilt to be established where it was deserved.

Au-Set stood up. "People, I know of only one person here who could tell you the truth on this matter. Come forward my brother, my *first* consort, Prince Au-Sar!" Everyone in that large hall gasped at the implication of her words and waited. Ua-Zit looked at her niece and did not know what this meant for she knew nothing of this. All she could do was wait in the building anticipation of the moment as presented by her niece.

All eyes in the large vaulted chamber were rooted to the doorway to where Au-Set pointed. Sure enough, it was the form of Au-Sar. However, he was green and his garments were black. He walked out somberly carrying the crook and flail of a ruler, the ruler of the ancients. This tradition had not been seen in life for it was so ancient. The last God to carry the crook and flail was the God *Andjety* of the delta who was a God of the underworld.

In his entire curious splendor, Au-Sar walked into the chamber to the astonished looks of all but Au-Set, whose idea this was. Upon his return, everybody assumed that he was dead and lost with the chest that she had yet to look for.

Au-Set suggested that they could mimic the ancient God Andjety of the delta's underworld. Au-Sar had his skin dyed green and his beautiful light-brown hair was dyed black. All of his linen royal regalia were dyed black and earthy brown with a border in gold. On his head were the combination of the hawk and iaret crown symbolizing that in the underworld, he represented both lands. Au-Set even added dead vines to trail around him to perfect this ghastly image. They hoped that this would prove their point and eventually he would return to normal.

Ua-Zit looked at Au-Set for an explanation. Suti was trembling and perspiring profusely in this unexpected turn of events, and his words turned against him. He truly believed that his brother had returned from the underworld to tell the truth, so affective was the strange garb and make-up on his brother.

Au-Set spoke as the crowd was waiting, "People see for your-selves Prince Au-Sar has come back for judgment! He was sent to the underworld and returned to us a ruler! He has come back to sit in judgment before you!" Everybody in the chamber including her aunt was lost in the illusory spell that was created before them all. Ua-Zit nodded and motioned for Au-Sar to sit beside her to preside over this trial on her sister's empty throne.

"What say you nephew, ruler of the underworld?"

Au-Sar sat down regally in his ghastly attire and looked over at Neb-Het," You sister had nothing to do in either plot and may sit by my side." He motioned to her and noticed that she was trembling. He winked at her so that only she could see when she was close to him. Her eyes questioned him but he looked out at the hall before him and spoke again, "And you brother are guilty of my death alone! Our aunt was truly taken by the Goddess Iaret as being her time to go. The time of the hawk has passed for the time being into the time of the iaret. However, in my own demise I saw that it was your idea and you made sure that it was carried out! My body is not in the tomb in Abdjw, but in a far away land from here!" Everyone in the room gasped at this, for they truly believed that he was buried beside his aunt and brother Heru in Abdjw.

He continued, "Guards take him away to be locked up. Only when my body is found, will he be set free to repent this evil deed that he did to his own brother!" He looked at Au-Set and then Neb-Het, "Sisters you have proven your devotion to me and I have only one request for you both...Please find my body and build a temple that towers over the tomb in Abdjw. Let it be large enough to stand the sands of time that destroy everything it its wake! Let my final resting place be grander than anything ever built before so that I may always have a home to sit in judgment over all injustices done to those who can no longer speak for themselves! And may Ma-At always wield her powerful silver scale of judgment for the truth to come to light!"

Ma-At walked up to the large silver scale that she had placed before them all and had positioned her large white feather on top of it. The feather tipped the side of the scale towards Suti revealing to all in sight the judgment of the Gods on this day. She then walked over to stand behind Au-Sar.

How wonderfully everything turned out for all, except Suti... All events played into each other forming a perfect stage for their family and all that it brought to Kemet.

The crowd roared in approval over his just words and of the judgment of the silver scale. Au-Set looked over at Nekhebt Neb-Het and with her eyes told her that she would find out all there was in this matter. She also placed a hand on her aunt's shoulder in reassurance. Ua-Zit smiled at approval over Au-Set taking matters into her own hands. She bent over and whispered to her, "I could not have planned it better myself. I cannot wait to hear both of you after this is all done!" She chuckled to herself in amusement at the precociousness of the situation. She also felt saddened inside of the sickness in Suti that was slowly being revealed for the world and she was glad that her sister Ninnuit was not here to see this dark side of her baby.

Chapter 63

Little Prince Heru was still very young though he was very perceptive. He took in all that was around him and processed it in his tiny toddler mind. He noticed the way his mother always looked for his father, who was usually outside covered in dirt. Heru believed that his father was actually made of the rich fertile soil, since he seemed to smell of it whenever he held him in his arms. He felt life and growth in the strong arms of his father.

His father would tell him that the growing plants would often talk to him about what they needed and wanted. He told Heru that if you listened to the sound they made in the wind, you could hear them. Heru strained very hard to understand what the plants wanted and still could not figure it out.

He did not remember much about his earliest years, but had heard bits and pieces of it throughout the palace. He knew that for some reason, his uncle Suti did not want him around. He knew that his mother risked her life hiding him until his uncle's anger was gone.

At the funeral, he sat on the lap of his oldest sister Set, who would be his mate when he grew up. He did not understand the meaning of that word, only that the Goddess Ua-Zit approved it.

At the funeral, he looked over at his uncle Suti and he seemed to look red. His face had a ruddy sun-touched look that made him appear very old to him. He thought that his uncle's hair was almost as beautiful as his big sister Set's glorious red hair. He just wanted to run his hands through it as he often did with Set. Set would drape her head over his while she kissed his tiny toes and giggle. He loved that. At the funeral, she just sat there and cried.

Heru could not understand many things in his life, it all seemed very confusing to him. For example, he was told that his aunt Ua-Zit was the Goddess of that same name on earth. He always believed that Goddesses were untouchable like the wind and the clouds above. Yet, his aunt was very real and would hold him close to her and touch her very real nose to his. She also seemed very old to him and very warm like the sun. He was confused on how she could actually he a Goddess and his aunt at the same time.

Heru also did not understand how his father loved a bunch of dirt so much. Sure, he had the power to make anything grow in land that was once believed useless. However, was he more fun than actual dirt? He always missed his father and longed for him to take him up in the air to kiss the clouds as he sometimes did.

He was told that his father was with the Gods now, but that did not seem right to him. He still felt his father around him.

He was even more confused at the trial that his aunt made him attend. He fidgeted and practically missed the whole thing. Then his mother motioned towards the door and everyone was looking. He almost fell out of Set's lap to see what the commotion was.

Then he saw what he believed was his father, but he looked like he rose from the dead. He was all green and black with dead plants on him. He did not understand what all of this was about. He cried out, "Papa!" However, as usual, he did not believe that his father had actually heard him, especially amongst all of the people in that room. Then again, his father barely ever had time for him, even before he turned green and black.

Chapter 64

Au-Set saw the reaction of her family to the plan that she had with her mate and consort. She understood their reactions, but did not know how to implement the plan any other way for it would have risked his being discovered before the time was right. She especially dreaded the look on the face of her oldest son Heru, how heartbroken and uncomprehending of the situation that he was. Bast and Merul were oblivious in their youth. She looked at her three oldest daughters Set, Weret-Heka, Renenutet, and saw that they looked as equally dazzled as the rest of the known world of Kemet and then she noticed flashes of anger from them at both she and Au-Sar. She expected this and prepared for it, but still it wounded her to see that look on her children's faces. Sometimes a person had to make sacrifices to save someone. She did not like it, but it did save his life.

After the trial, she explained the situation to all of them with Au-Sar by her side, as he was finally able to clean off all of the makeup and dye. Ua-Zit was present and had explained that from now on, out in public, Au-Sar would always have to dress like that due to the incredible reactions of the people. All of them saw the logic in this and reluctantly understood.

Au-Set also felt that the timing was right to tell her family about her pregnancy. "Now that that matter is settled and understood, I have one more matter to discuss with all of you."

Her children, brothers, consort and aunt looked up at her expectantly.

"There will be another addition to this wonderful family of ours, for in three months I will be having another baby!"

Ua-Zit went over, embraced her, and now understood everything perfectly. She had noticed that Au-Set chose to wear elaborate long gowns lately and seemed rather peeked a few months back. "Au-Set dear, may I have a word with you alone?"

As the others were ingesting the latest news, all in different ways, Au-Set walked out to the hallway to talk with her aunt.

"Au-Set, please tell me why you chose to hide this one? Surely you know all pregnancies are gifts from the Goddess?" She reached out, cradled her hands around her niece's hidden large tummy, and smiled.

"Aunt, I did not want to keep anything from you honestly. It is just that I was confused myself. I at first did not know whose it was. No, that is not true. I could never lie to you my beloved aunt." She looked down at the floor.

"Look at me in the eyes when you tell me something of such importance, for I feel that this is what it is."

"Yes, aunt... Before I went to speak with Re about Merul, I missed Au-Sar dreadfully. He never seemed attracted to me anymore. He wanted his plants more than I did. He loved the soil and was always too tired for me. And as for Nebmaat..."

Ua-Zit looked down at the ground realistically, "I know, Nebmaat prefers clothes and jewels more than anything. I am sorry. So Re, you both ended up together? Is this a permanent thing? Will he be your consort now?"

"No, aunt, he is a consort to a tribal princess from up north. She is a lot like Nebmaat in a way. Re and I just had a moment of need together. I truly believe that the Goddess approved of it. We both needed temporary love and it was provided for that brief and only moment."

"You know that there is nothing wrong in this. You may take as many lovers or consorts as you wish. I have quite a few my-self since Hetep is completely useless."

"No, it is not that. I know I did nothing wrong. Nevertheless, I feel that I have somehow betrayed Au-Sar or Nebmaat for that matter. They have done nothing wrong and I..."

"Oh, no, they made you feel lonely and unloved, that is a crime in itself to a devoted woman."

"Oh, Aunt, I love the way you look at life."

"When one reaches my age, you see things a bit differently. Things that used to upset me when I was a lot younger, no longer do anything for me. I had learned long ago to choose my own battles.

"You have done nothing wrong, yet a child resulted from this. Moreover, with six children already, there will be the jealousy you will have to deal with. In addition, with your consorts, if anything I think they will try harder to gain your attention. This just could be a blessing in disguise with Au-Sar and Nebmaat. As for your children, you would have had to deal with their emotions no matter who the father was. One word of advice though, stick to your position and defend your actions. Never lie about them but stand by them."

"I will."

"If you ever even have one thought of you doing something wrong, the others will latch on to that and will never let you live it down. Did you mean to hurt anyone? Were your intentions pure? Besides, it is your duty to create life and you have done it, gloriously in fact!"

"Thank you so much aunt!"

The time finally arrived when Au-Set gave birth. Instead of to one child, it was to twin girls whom she named Maat and Serqet. Everybody thought the twins were beautiful. Heru felt neglected when his latest sisters were born. With the arrival of his little sisters, his mother had been in bed recovering. He was mad at them because his mother was so sad all of the time. She was told that she could have no more children.

Papa was trying hard to be nice to her but, even little Heru sensed that something was wrong with him, for he made every excuse to be away from the palace. His father no longer made time with him to take him out to the large palace gardens. He was left alone in the nursery with the others, who seemed to whisper all of the time about his mother. He did not like the way his two youngest sisters took his parents away from him and did not want to understand it. He just sat there and stewed in loneliness.

Chapter 65

Au-Sar always felt in the shadow of his sister and mate, except when he was alone in his own garden. Whenever it involved irrigation or agriculture, he was sought out. At first, he made sure that the people knew which ideas were his and which ideas belonged to Au-Set. However, after a while, he seemed to understand his real calling in life. He more often than not, came up with even better ideas than she did and he was always trying to outdo what he did before. He would easily become lost in trying to work out his ideas to make them a reality.

He had heard about the consort that was his father, a merchant and farmer by the name of En. He had saved his family and his livestock when one of the greatest floods in the whole valley wiped out a good portion of the population in that area. His father was one of the greatest men in Erech, which was unusual in a woman's world. He guessed that he had inherited his father's miraculous powers of invention and innovation. His own just happened to be with irrigation and agriculture.

He cherished the time that he spent with his crops, because he found that he was starting to resent Au-Set and everything that she stood for. It seemed to him that she could do nothing wrong and always had a logical solution for everything. People sought her out on all matters, and of course their aunt as well. But not him... No one sought out his advice on anything besides agriculture. Therefore, he became that issue and lived for solutions.

When he was young, he accepted his natural position in life, for he knew nothing other than the ways of The Goddess Innana, his mother and grandmother. As he grew he felt sad, for he wanted to offer something else to this new land of Kemet and not just his birthright. That was when Au-Set found his talent in growing things. He prided himself in making something grow in the most inhospitable of climates. People were singing his praises as the improved agriculture of the land was giving them more food and jobs. People in the land of Kemet were becoming wealthy from all that he had created and the incredible surpluses of food that was now in trade.

Au-Sar knew that he was handsome due to the reactions of the female servants and most of the women that he met. Yet, he only had feelings for Au-Set. He felt that no woman in all of Kemet or Eshnunna for that matter could compare with her beauty and charisma. She seemed to charm even the bees to her waiting and patient hands.

Though as soon as she became a mother, she no longer had the time for him, especially since her duties were increasing under her aunt as she grew older. He knew that he always would have the opportunity to rule beside her as an equal, but he felt that he had nothing to offer. Au-Set or Ua-Zit was deservedly acquiring all of the attention and respect of their land.

Au-Sar knew he was born to a woman's world. It was a comfortable world full of love and females with great confidence. Not that men were inferior at all, that was just simply not the case. No. They were respected and taken care of. Nevertheless, he had learned from a very young age that women made all of the important decisions.

However in Kemet, things were going to be different, but he never gave them a chance. He did not feel comfortable making decisions and taking part in ruling Kemet, regardless as to how many times he was asked to and even ordered to do so.

With Au-Set, she always made him feel important and respected no matter how he felt. She could do no wrong in his eyes. He was deeply hurt when she took Nebmaat as consort, though understood, and accepted it. He had no choice, for she was the vessel of life. Then his fears of losing her were lessened when he noticed how Nebmaat cared more about clothes, jewelry, and makeup than anything else did. Au-Set even doted on this as well and provided him with only the finest attainable.

He was hoping that her first child would be from him, but it was not. Set was obviously not his, for she looked too much like Suti. Au-Set would vehemently deny her oldest child's paternity whenever questioned. What could Au-Sar do? If she was really Suti's child, it was accepted in Au-Set's being the Goddess representative on earth.

Then when the next two children that she had were from Nebmaat, he began to doubt his own ability in fathering children.

Finally, with the birth of Heru, Bast and Merul, any feelings of inadequacy were taken away from him. When Heru was first born he initially felt disgust at the odd shape of his head and body. However, it was not long after that he grew into his body normally and was even starting to show signs of looking handsome. He loved watching the little boy grow and looked forward to the time that he was finally old enough to take out for short outings in the garden where he could teach his son about growing things out of nothing.

Bast was tiny and fierce and had a pack of trained lion cubs that flocked around her from the time they were newly born. He felt that someday, she would be a fierce warrior indeed like the ancient women of his line.

In addition, there was Merul, how small and dainty he was; Au-Sar did not know how to react to him. However, he had the family features despite his having a rather large head and short legs. The boy was constantly at the books as soon as he learned some of the picture writing from his uncle Tehuti. He would look for the boy and he was always by the side of Tehuti in the scribal temple. Merul showed great talent.

Now with the latest addition to his growing family, he had observed features in the two little twins that did not resemble him or Nebmaat at all. He knew that Au-Set had the right to choose any consort that she wanted, but she would have let him know first. They were beautiful and showed great promise on being beauties like their older sisters and mother, but a feeling still nagged at him.

Au-Sar calculated the moon cycles and realized that the twins were not his, since he was in a town that he was building called *Busiris* overseeing a new temple. He was gone for three months. Moreover, he had serious doubts on Nebmaat showing any interest in anything other than his new wardrobe. Qui was constantly by his side enticing him with new imported fabrics.

Therefore, he wondered who the father of the twins could be. Au-Set offered him nothing, nor did she have to. Nevertheless, still he pondered over this and it tore at his soul. He realized that he did deserve this and it was probably due to her feeling neglected that she had to seek out the attentions of someone else. However, it still hurt him immensely, since he was getting used to her only seeking him out for amorous attentions. He had taken advantage of her love and pushed it aside for other things that he felt more valuable at the time. However, he realized seemingly too late, how much she really did mean to him.

He found himself often of late, walking out side in his gardens trying to find some sort of answer and way that he could get her back. He noticed that in response to his treatment of her, she had pulled away as well and spent all of her time with her children, when she was not busy at her official functions.

He had decided that he had to confront her on this, or they would forever be apart. Therefore, he stopped abruptly and turned around towards the palace.

By the time that he had finally reached the palace gates, his feelings were turned towards anger, resentment, and jealousy. He felt like a pot about to boil over and walked with purpose towards the chamber of Au-Set.

He opened the curtain to her chamber and found that she was sitting up on the sleeping pallet, with soft pillows in a cocoon all around her. As he walked in a nurse brushed him aside to take away the sleeping infant girls.

"Au-Sar, how are you?" She smiled up at him.

"I need to speak with you. May I have a moment?"

"Yes, of course, have a seat." She patted a soft red pillow beside her. Her smile faded when she sensed his tone.

"There is something that I have been meaning to ask you about but you have been understandingly distracted."

"Go ahead my love." She had a feeling about what he was going to ask her and sat back. She had waiting for this day, knowing that she should have approached him in the past, but she could not bring her-self to do that. She had dreaded this moment, but she recalled the words of advice from her aunt and was prepared to stand her ground.

"Please tell me who the father of Maat and Serqet is. I need to know, not that it matters. I just want to know for my own peace of mind."

"Their father is Re." Her eyes looked at him preparing for anything adversarial that he might say on this. She prepared for battle by sitting up straighter.

"Thank you. You have that right." He looked down. He wanted to shout at her but held his peace. An awkward silence seemed to drag on forever. He felt his temper rising, for he wanted to confront her on everything else. He finally decided to break the silence. He felt that he might not have another moment like this where he actually had the confidence that he felt coursing through his veins.

"There are other things I need to speak with you about." He looked at her felt her silence, and continued, "About Heru... is he?"

"Of course he is, and Bast and Merul. Why do you think you even have the right to question me about this? Does it really matter in the whole scheme of things? In the land of our mother, you would have only been around for one year and one day. Not only that but you would have had no say at all in things!" Au-Set felt her temper rising with these questions. However, they were not asked in anger or suspicion in any kind, but still deep inside she felt the need to defend her-self. She looked at him, sighed, and in a softer tone continued, "You are my only heart, my only love, but I felt that you had lost interest in me or worse, had gone to someone else!"

"Never, even if that were true, I would have been killed for that!"

"I know. But why all of these questions?"

"Perhaps there really is no actual reason. Not that I would treat the children any differently. You know how I love them all and certainly, I have room for the little ones. I just want to know. I just feel that you do not need me anymore!"

"That is how I feel about you. That is perhaps the reason why I went to Re. It was nothing you knew about at all. It was only one moment. We both understood that. I believe if anything, it only made me understand things a little better."

For some reason that was exactly what made him lose face. He felt all of his past anger well up. It was overwhelming but liberating as well.

"I understand that you have that option and that I can really do nothing about it at all. What about me? What about us? Does everything that we shared together mean nothing to you at all?" He looked at her with determination and knew that he would regret what he wanted to tell her. He wanted to tell her about Neb-Het. For some reason it felt like there was someone else telling his story. She could easily order his death for this and he knew it, but told her anyway.

"When we were in Nekhen, I felt that you no longer loved me. Then you came to me at night and it was like when we first celebrated the great rite. You smelled of Melilote, your favorite and it drew me into your spell and I was lost."

She looked at him quizzically for she did not remember this at all. Then it was easy to add one piece with another and knew that he was risking his life in telling her this.

"Please, I know what you are going to say to this. I did not realize that it was not you until it was too late. The wine went to my head and I did not think clearly. I genuinely thought that it was you, that you finally came to your senses. Wait, I did not mean it that way, but I was distraught. I was elated that it was you. When I realized that it was not you, it was too late. I was afraid to admit even to myself that it was not you. It took the longest time to realize that it was Neb-Het. Why would she do something like this? Anyways, it is not her fault. I was weak."

He continued with his eyes on the fine threading of the soft red pillow that he had buried himself into, "I offer myself for your authority on this matter and apologize for any presumption I may have had in misunderstanding you Au-Set. I can make this official and supplicate myself to your authority and judgment in the ways of Eshnunna, as I should." He put his head in her lap. He felt her hands slowly touch his temples and smooth away his hair. She had already made her judgment of him.

She spoke," My love, it is not your fault and it is not my fault and yet it is both of our faults. The only crime committed here is not communicating with each other. We let feelings get out of control, felt helpless because of it, and let ourselves fall apart from each other. I suppose by my having the twins from this act and possibly Neb-Het. I do not know about that. I will have to send down an inquiry on her health. I have heard nothing from her since she has been given leave to return to Nekhen. Perhaps, her unusual silence to me speaks a mountain in this matter...." She was quiet for a while deep in thought and then continued, "Perhaps the Goddess had her own reasoning for all of this to have occurred. Should we not try to find the lesson in all of this?"

She looked at him and with his questioning look at her said," For, if anything, I feel my love has grown stronger for you. I understand that you may not feel it that way. I am sensitive to your feelings on this matter, which is why I was afraid to tell you. I was not ashamed of what I did, not at all, but I did not want you to be hurt over this and to take it the wrong way."

"Yes, but technically, you have the right to end my life. Your indiscretion is accepted, mine is not."

"Yes, but you truly thought that it was I that evening?" She looked deep into his eyes and found that it was true.

"Then you did no wrong either. It would have been wrong to stop the mysterious work of the Goddess. Truly, she felt to disguise her intentions by your blindness. I have made my judgment; no one needs to know of this. From now on, we accept the will of the Goddess, live with what had occurred, and accept the consequences. We reap what we sow dear brother!"

"Indeed." He sank deeper into her lap in gratitude feeling his admiration and respect for this woman grow stronger and his love intensified like never before onto a completely new level.

Chapter 66

There he sat, day after day, until over a month had passed. Suti's life was spent entirely in a room made of colorless mud and plastered papyrus weave as in the days before them. It was ancient and lifeless. It must have been here prior to the days of his aunt's rule. He surmised that this room in its being far away from the rest of the decadent palace could easily be forgotten. He wondered if that was their actual plan. He truly felt that he was a failure to his family. He could not even father any children of his own. In the older regime, he would have been given only a year and one day, regardless.

Suti finally understood that in Kemet he was given a chance that he never would have had in Eshnunna. There he would only have been another useless noble and the consort of any royal brat. However, here, he was given the chance to rule. To rule what, he had no idea, because the shell that was left for he and his sister needed a lot of work.

His consort Neb-Het (now known as Nekhebt Neb-Het) was useless to him. She would have nothing to do with him and avoided him at every possible chance. Besides, he only liked to deal with people that he could control.

He had the fear driven into Au-Set and his proof was Set. He knew that she would never reveal that he was the actual father, for that alone she hated him. He loved that.

As for Puanit, she was ugly, but would do anything for him. While in captivity, he had managed to send her a message to gather his forces for his return. He knew that he could easily charm his way into his Aunt Ua-Zit's forgiveness. He just played innocent and with each of her visits, he felt that she was actually swaying, since he knew that she had great difficulty in seeing him for who he truly was.

While he worked on the sympathies of his aunt, he waited patiently for Puanit to give him some sign that his forces were ready. He also told her to inform the king in Eshnunna of his plight and to send down reinforcements. He was tired of all of this and felt that he had no real place in Kemet. It was obvious that Kemet was really for Au-Sar and Au-Set. He and Neb-Het were only figureheads to make their message seem more real.

Equality was mentioned. Nevertheless, who was really in charge? Au-Set was in charge. He hoped that someday Set would see the truth and come over to help him, because in her he saw the future of Kemet. With that future, she had his blood deep in her veins.

He saw nothing for himself here and waited for a sign from his God, Enlil. With no other God had he found more in common. Not only that but he was the true and only son of that God, this he had found out in the years since his visit from his own aunt Nekhebt before she died. He wanted no one to know of this just yet and made sure that she would remain silent on the matter.

It was after six whole months in captivity that he was finally released. He did not know what was said, or who had spoken on his behalf. He did not care. One day, the wooden door to his cell was opened and he just walked out. He wondered about this while he found himself in the city proper of Per-Uto in the process of finding a boat to sail up to Nekhen. He wondered if he was officially released or if someone had actually unlocked the door one evening hoping that he would discover this and walk out to his freedom.

He took that chance and he casually sauntered out of the palace onto the boat heading against current home. Not one person had questioned him nor stopped his progress. Not one person noticed him. He found this difficult to comprehend since his hair was a very bright red, almost never seen in these parts. His once decorative clothes were worn and tattered, having been the same ones that he was garbed in on the day that he was placed in the cell. They were practically attached to him. His hair was matted and unruly and he reeked of neglect. He was given a bucket of water to wash himself in once a week, but it hardly washed him in the way that he was used to or required in his normal toilette.

He walked through town as if he had a right to, but inside he trembled with the fear that someone would stop him. No one did.

In the cell, he had more than enough time to reflect on everything. He still thought that his plan with the chest was a brilliant masterstroke of genius. It was only a fluke of fate that Au-Set was able to save Au-Sar. That must have occurred while she was in the room apparently mourning over him. He wondered why she actually saved him, for she could have had the entire rule over Upper Kemet to herself. A woman's weakness was certainly her heart. He vowed that he would never let his feelings get in the way of what had to be done.

He loved how fate gave him the paternity of Au-Set's first daughter. That must have ruined Au-Sar. How he had to live with that, he would have no idea. He laughed over that one. Set was growing into quite a beauty, like none ever seen in the land of Kemet with her brilliant red curly hair and flawless white skin. Her bright eyes were azure and made her look truly like the Goddess that she would be someday. Suti made sure that she knew of him. He sent her gifts and made sure that she received his letters. She knew that he was proud of her and her studies. She was his one true joy in life. Set, his natural daughter was the only thing that he lived for. He also had the hope of someday ruling over the land of Sumer where he was born.

He could not wait to return to the new palace that he was creating in *Djedu* on the other side of the Great River, across from the tombs of his brother and aunt in the city of the dead called Abdjw. It was purposely set up on the side of the rising sun on the river. He wanted the city of the dead on the side of the setting sun. He felt that it truly spoke to the Gods this way.

In deep thought, he sat back and enjoyed the long trip back to his Djedu, for it was on his plans and layout. Every detail was his creation. He wondered how it would be when he returned, for plenty of time had elapsed for it to grow considerably. He hoped that Puanit carried out his plans that were left behind.

Back to Neb-Het again, he missed her, for she was catching the same loneliness and sadness that captured Nekhebt. He saw all of the signs, felt bad for her and then went on with his life. Never did his feeling of pity for his sister last that long, since he truly believed that each person had full control over their lives and they deserved what they got.

He understood his captivity and did not question it nor plead out of it. He had done wrong and had to be punished for it. Suti was more upset that his plan had failed. His defense had worked against him in favor of Au-Sar. For the superstitious attitude that Au-Sar raised in his trial only prepared the stage for this new game that he and Au-Set were playing.

Though it worked against him and was his final condemnation, he actually applauded their ingenuity in the whole thing. How brilliant! He wished that he had thought of it himself! *God of the underworld*! How brilliant! He sat back in laughter at the whole thing. It could actually have meant his own death, had his aunt and sister not been so sympathetic. It did not faze him one bit, for he was allowed a longer life to work towards what he really wanted. He would definitely not mess this chance up one bit!

Chapter 67

Nekhebt Neb-Het basked in the glory of her new power and the birth of her first child. She knew how rare a time this was for her in her life and relished it carefully with every cell in her body. She always had her little *Anpu* swaddled close to her at all times and slept with him every evening. He gurgled his pleasure at being by her side. Her heart beat for him for he gave her a completely new meaning in life. For him, Neb-Het had decided to take over the plans of Suti in his new city of Djedu and to make it her own. For she was the Goddess Nekhebt, it was truly her city. Suti would just have to deal with it.

She made sure that Puanit was put into a cell deep under the old palace at Nekhen and forgotten about. She did not care what had happened to this ugly and brazen woman. She knew that she was only the pathetic pawn of Suti and would do anything for him. Puanit did most if not all of the dirty work in her consort's schemes. Puanit probably built the chest that almost killed her favorite brother. She was definitely sure that she might have been the actual cause of the death of Heru with her knowledge of herbs. Nekhebt Neb-Het had no way to prove the duplicity of Puanit of course and did not have enough evidence to bring her to a trial, though she did not care. She made sure that Puanit would meet the fate that she had decided for her and would no longer be of use to Suti.

The months went by and she basked in the glory of mother-hood, oblivious that Suti had been set free. She had assumed that he met the same fate as his pitiful Puanit, forgotten. That would have been divine justice indeed for all the trouble he caused!

She shuddered to think if that clever plan of his might have actually killed her beloved Au-Sar, for he was the only brother left who actually cared about her wellbeing and now she carried his son in her arms.

She was afraid to tell her sister, because Au-Set could have him killed for this. It was her fault and she would plead for mercy, but she knew that she could lose her sister as well.

So she devoted all of her time with her son and making this city worthy of him. She relished changing all of Suti's plans for the city and purposely made them the polar opposite in location and layout. She grew more confident with each stone placed carefully into each new building of the palace and of the town around it.

Doing this kept her from focusing on any consequences that her actions may have caused. She lived in the fantasy of this city that she created as a cocoon from the world and its horrors and of her rash actions.

Only here was she truly meant to find her-self and to become who she really wanted to be; in this city that she was actually building on her own and in reality. This city was now real and no longer the one of illusion that Suti had made to fool people... Neb-Het alone had set into motion plans in which she kept up regular correspondence with her aunt and sister in Per-Uto. She attended many meetings with her son strapped close to her heart with her own people. She avoided those in Per-Uto and all mention of her child, Anpu. Upper Kemet was finally flourishing under her careful guidance.

Unfortunately, Neb-Het had no idea that all of what she had fervently wished for and had at last set into motion would soon cave in on her. She did not see the signs, nor chose to see them. She remained contentedly oblivious in her new role as a mother and queen of Upper Kemet.

Chapter 68

One day Neb-Het had little Anpu wrapped close to her as usual, feeling his heartbeat next to hers when she heard a great commotion outside of the palace gates. She stood up abruptly to see what the cause of it was. She regally stood up and with a slight but determined step, made her way to the loud raised voices that boomed up in the throne room.

It was Suti, in rags, looking very dirty from his captivity and travel here all the way from Per-Uto. "Well, *Nekhebt*! What brings you here to *my city*?"

She stood transfixed on the spot for it seemed surreal to her. Never had she expected this at all! She subconsciously rubbed her eyes.

"No sister, this is not a dream but another scroll in my wretched reality! What is this? No mourning, no crying over the loss of me! Moreover, what is this horrid thing that you call a city? You took my beautiful plans and turned it into this stupid and unorganized village that I see before me!" He looked at her with obvious mirth, of which she failed to see the cause.

She was silent and uncomprehending of the situation. She looked at Suti sitting on her throne as if she had walked in on his rule. She was afraid since she felt that he was truly crazy and did not want to provoke him. At the same time, she was livid in that he would dare to take over the beauty that she had worked hard to create from *his* stupid plans.

She worked up all of the strength that she could possibly muster for she knew that this confrontation would decide her fate now that he was back. She would not be weak to him. Never would she hide behind her fears or failings, like her aunt.

"How dare you come here as if this place is yours alone? Besides, I thought you were in prison. However did you escape, did that dog Puanit help you?"

"No, apparently the Goddess had other plans for me rather than to sit there and rot. One day the door was simply left unlocked, all the better for me... I walked right through town and no one cared. Besides, it was the perfect timing to see how creatively you took over the plans to my city and destroyed them. How confident you have become without me around... Would it have been better for you if I had died?"

"Of course not brother, for I have been so busy making sure this city was here for you in good order when you returned." She took the submissive stance hoping to not burn any bridges or to put him on the offence against her. She knew that this would bide her some time to think on what she must do about this whole situation. She had no idea and did not think that he would actually escape or even return. She was silently angry about her hopes being ripped away from her once again. However, with Anpu, she only felt her determination for survival grow inside of her.

"What happened here? I could barely find my way to this palace. The streets are completely different and the palace is backwards. Surely, you mock me in this travesty all around me! It seems to be obviously opposite of what I had created."

Making sure that her voice was calm, she spoke eloquently as if speaking to an older Anpu. "Brother, nothing of that sort was my intention at all! I had merely perfected your plans and made sure that they were carried out." She paused for effect and for the words to sink in, she also had to think of a fast reason why she had changed everything on his plans to suit her own needs and style.

She continued her reasoning, "The streets and palace are your idea, only different in the actual layout because a line of malachite was found." She was seriously digging and knew that this would appeal to him in his great love for the stone. Now she had to find a good amount to please him and to make this work. "It was a small vein and was emptied out. While that was going on, I wanted the city to be complete for your eventual return and worked around it. When it was completely mined, I had the small theatre built there. I did not think that you would object to this at all. Does this cause a problem with you? Do not forget that half of the decisions are mine to make and I had to compensate for yours while you were incarcerated." She held her ground and her son closer. Anpu cooed in response.

Suti's attention was immediately brought to the infant that she had swaddled to her inside of her long robes. "What is this? It is not mine?"

"He is from the Goddess. He is holy and Goddess-born"

He moved closer to her to peek at the tiny infant. "He must be out of here! This I will not put up with!"

"You have no choice! He is mine and where I am he will be!" She stood her ground, though felt the ground tremble underneath her. He stepped aggressively towards her closing in the distance and grabbed her by the hair at the base of her neck. Rage was written on his face. The infant Anpu sensed distress and whimpered at the change of atmosphere in the room. He released her almost throwing her in his strength across the chamber. She landed on her knees and the whimpering picked up in tempo to a wail.

"Remove him and yourself from my city woman! Guards!" Out of nowhere, an army appeared that was not hers. She reeled in fear looking all around her for some possible escape and found none.

"Guards, seize this child and expose him to the city of Deshret!"

"Deshret, there is no such city, for that is the desert! No brother, have a heart! Have some love for him! You can raise him as your own, no one will ever know! He is Goddess born!"

"There is no Goddess here, only me a God named Suti, king of Deshret and this city Djedu! Guards remove them at once! Puanit!"

Chapter 69

In what seemed like only a matter of seconds, Neb-Het's whole life and meaning was ripped apart from her from this astonishing anger of her brother Suti. She felt her child being ripped away from her as she was dragged out of the palace and placed in chains on a boat to Per-Uto. She cried until all sense of herself was drained out of her with each painful tear.

When she arrived in Per-Uto, she ran to the arms of Au-Set, her sunny half. She always felt like the stormy half. Where she was born, a rainstorm might be the cause of endless destruction and was feared and dreaded, as she felt now. However, in this land where it rarely occurred even in one lifetime, it would be a blessing. Neb-Het felt her life was meaningless and the dreaded rainstorm of her childhood while Au-Set was the sun always giving hope for all of them to live on. Neb-Het's despair was deep and seemingly bottomless. She hated to have to go to her sister once again, but she actually had no choice at all this time, for it was where she was taken in chains on a boat made swifter by the winds in sail against the slow and backwards current.

Neb-Het practically collided into the arms of her sister and blurted out the new horrors of their brother. She desperately pleaded for her little Anpu to be found. Au-Set looked at her sister, "I will find him for you and bring him back and when I return, we will deal with Suti!"

Au-Set set out at once and was gone for a whole month until little Anpu was brought safely back to the palace in Per-Uto. She did not tell one word of what happened on this journey, only that a bond had grown between her nephew and her. Neb-Het thanked her luck for this and felt comforted again by her sister's boundless love for her.

Chapter 70

A few years had passed and all was quiet and peaceful in Per-Uto, when they received a rather ominous letter from Astarte. She was concerned on the recent situation of her region of which the people of Kemet called *Retenu*. Astarte had explained to them in her correspondence, that for some time her land of the Retenu region had incurred damages from brief skirmishes of the northern tribes, which had almost full occupation of Eshnunna giving it the new name of Sumer.

Enlil wanted to establish his rule into the territory of Retenu as well his Sumer and was sending in forces. Astarte mentioned that she was also very concerned on the leadership of her son named Melanchor and his very submissive wife named Ria, who was a niece of Enlil from one of his queens.

Astarte had explained in the letter that she had not arranged for this marriage, as was her right. Her son abducted the poor girl, stole her away to their region, and made the sorry creature his wife. Not that the girl minded, she just sat docile in her own world and catered to her son. Astarte tried to instruct the young Queen Ria, but gave up in exasperation. She wanted Au-Set and Nekhebt Neb-Het to instruct the poor girl Queen. Astarte explained that she did not have a daughter, so her position and power would go to this weak girl. Astarte was frantic. She also requested assistance to subdue the threat and to help build up her army. She missed her cousins dearly and wanted to have a feast in their honor.

Therefore, Au-Set and Nekhebt Neb-Het traveled to visit with their cousin to offer their assistance. Au-Sar chose to stay with the children along with Tehuti, while the sisters were away.

The sisters traveled for weeks and slept in elaborate tents along the way. When they reached the gates of Gubla, they were impressed. The walls were well fortified and reached straight up to the sky. Spears were imbedded along the top of each city wall. The towers were tall, square, and unadorned. Imposing to any passing by for they explained deeply their purpose, to keep those away who did not belong. The streets were paved with flat round stones with common wells at certain uniform distances. A large and bustling village surrounded the walled city and fortress. The houses were so tall, that it was difficult to believe where the fortress ended and the city began. The village almost appeared to be just a large extension of the fortress.

Au-Set leaned close to her sister in the cart as they entered the city and whispered to her. "One thing for certain, if this city were to be properly defended the village buildings would have to be fortified as well or removed. I see far too many ways an army could breech these walls and not be discovered."

"I agree sister. At Djedu, I made sure that the village was lower than the walls of the fortress and a decent distance off, so that the villagers can come in for refuge and we would be able to see any approaching army. This worries me as well. How do we know that the northern tribes are not inside the city itself hiding and waiting?"

"We do not."

Chapter 71

"Welcome cousins! Please, know that your presence is deeply appreciated and honored in all of Retenu! First, we have a banquet for you and the usual introductions and then we celebrate this long awaited reunion with just the three of us!"

Au-Set and Neb-Het were impressed with their cousin who hardly looked older from the time they last saw her many years ago. Astarte was certainly very beautiful with sky blue eyes and dark chestnut colored hair that flowed down in ringlets. She wore a simple diadem around her brow and her gown was of the softest purple dyed linen that flowed about her with each graceful step. Her body contained none of the tattoos of Kemet and was bare and ivory colored. Her feet were also bare and adorned with tiny golden bells that danced with each step. She looked every inch a Goddess to her younger cousins.

Astarte led them into a large vaulted chamber that was simple and unadorned except for large oil lamps suspended from the ceiling. There were no windows. Large hand-woven carpets added color and artistic flair and were suspended from the walls. There were lush carpets along the floor and large billowy pillows to sit on. The diners rose to their feet at their entrance to the feast and bowed to the two queens of Kemet as they entered the hall.

Food of every possible kind and color was overflowing the large elaborately decorated pottery on the carpets. Amphorae were lined along the walls and vats of beer sweetened with honey were being warmed slightly on small coal pits in the corners of the huge chamber. Smoke holes were by each fire and slaves fanned the smoke out of room and up the smoke holes. Golden incense burners hung in each corner of the room adding a mystical quality to the chamber, as if the sumptuous smell of the exotic foods were not enough.

Astarte looked at the queens and addressed them in a voice that magnified with the acoustics of the chamber, "As tradition of this land, let me bathe your feet from the journey. Here sit on this bench, while I, as the hostess attend to you both in your honor." The sisters looked at her and smiled, for they had heard of this custom that Astarte herself had created as a beautiful ritual that showed her utter devotion to her guests.

They sat down and waited for the ritual.

"Nekhebt Neb-Het, Queen of Upper Kemet, we thank you for your visit." As she said those words, she took each of her cousin's feet and bathed them with warm rose-scented water of the dirt from her travels. "May you walk many more roads and always think of this one in Gubla and my love for you."

Nekhebt Neb-Het acknowledged her formal greeting, "I thank you dear cousin and hope to be of assistance to you in appreciation to your elaborate welcome this beautiful land." She bowed her head in reverence to her cousin and her city.

"Au-Set, Little Queen of Lower Kemet, and heir to Ua-Zit, we thank you for your visit. May you walk many more roads and always think of this road in Gubla and my love for you."

"I thank you dear cousin and I will respect the wonderful welcome of your hospitality." She bowed.

Astarte then led them to pillows that were vacant near her son Melanchor, his wife Ria and their sons, Maneros and Pelusias who were only six and eight years old at that time.

Au-Set and Nekhebt Neb-Het sat down on pillows indicated to them. There was a simple copper plate for their food and a small bowl between each of the diners. The bowls contained water that was scented with something that neither of them recognized yet added a mythical quality to their sanitary needs. The air around them exuded a mystery that was all encompassing down to the smallest detail.

When they sat down to join the others Astarte stood behind each of the diners, "This is my fist consort *Baal* of Mount Saphon, the Son of Dagon. Baal is also the father of my bull-headed son, King Melanchor." All around them laughed good-naturedly at that retort. He was around the same age as Astarte and was very regal yet seemed easygoing in nature with his genuine smile. "This is Rashef, my second consort." This man seemed much younger by ten years and seemed to be very high strung in contrast to Astarte and Melanchor in that his eyes darted shiftily around the room and he slightly shook as if in nervousness. The queens of Kemet bowed to him and he bowed to them in turn, first to Nekhebt Neb-Het and then to Au-Set according to their rank.

"And this is my stubborn headed son, Melanchor." She reached around him in a hug and cupped his cheeks as if he were a small boy. "Mom..." He then looked at the two queens and said, "It is such a pleasure to finally meet you two, for I have grown up on tales of your childhood and what you have done in Kemet as queens. I am honored to meet you." He bowed to them. The queens bowed in turn, though to Au-Set it seemed that his charm was a little too much and wondered at the validity of it.

Melanchor took the introductions from there, as was their custom for the most part. It would have gone to Queen Ria. "And this is my consort and union mate Queen Ria and our two wonderful and precocious sons, Maneros and Pelusias." Ria was fair with hair that was so blonde it almost appeared white. Her skin was ivory in color as to appear translucent. Her eyes were a soft gray. She was very beautiful though ethereal almost from another world, a ghost. The boys were fair like their mother with dark brown eyes that seemed to pop out of their heads of fine silver blonde hair.

Astarte broke in, "And now that you have met my family, next to little Pelusias is *Qedeshet*, who came all of the way from Kemet and my mother's palace. She was born in Eshnunna and was a young Nugig who was sent to be a nursemaid for me when I was conceived at the temple of Eshur for Innana.

"Qedeshet has been by my side from birth and then to this land and city of Gubla, my new chosen home. She was one of the finest warriors of Eshnunna and has trained myself and other women here in the ancient warrioress ways of the Catal-Huyuk." A small roar emanated at the sound of his mistresses name, "And that would be her pet, Dia." She laughed which the others soon joined. Au-Set knew this well, since her own daughter Bast had a special affinity for lion cubs herself. She reached over to pet Dia, to the startled amazement of the others.

Au-Set stated, "My daughter Bast has a few of these at home and we have all grown to love them. What an adorable kitty you are Dia! She nuzzled her face in the rich braided mane. He was male and let out a contented purr.

Qedeshet spoke up, "Queen Au-Set, I am impressed, everyone seems afraid of little Dia. See how amazed they all look!" Qedeshet was dressed in the warrior garb of long ago Eshnunna, in plaited copper skirt and bared tattooed breasts exposed to the elements as if in daring fear itself in her wildness. Her hair was braided and interspersed with white tresses along the rich black. She wore heavy copper bracelets that covered her arms and legs for protection.

Au-Set sat next to Qedeshet, leaned close to her during this exchange, and giggled along with her. In Qedeshet, Au-Set had found a kindred soul.

They sat cross-legged like the other diners and waited for the nod of Astarte. It was given and the diners began their meals while music sounded in the background. Dancers swayed to the exotic music behind them, mixed, and mingled with the diners.

Chapter 72

That evening the sisters followed their cousin to her own private chamber. "Now you have met my family, I would love to have a short while with you both alone. I cannot speak of some matters in front of my sheltered family. I promise that I will respect your need for rest after your long journey. It is just that I have missed you both so and longed for the chance to speak candidly."

"Oh cousin, have no fear, for the evening is young. Thank you for the feast, it was very elaborate and rich!" Spoke up Nekhebt Neb-Het.

"You family is beautiful and your grandsons, they are exotic!"

Astarte smiled at this. Her manner relaxed a bit and needed informality desperately. "Please tell me how your own family fares and my mother."

Au-Set looked at her and spoke, "Your mother is fine and never seems to age. I still have a lot to learn from her. Cousin, may I ask you a bold question?"

At the nod of Astarte, Au-Set continued, "Why did you give up your place in Kemet? You would have inherited it all. You are her only surviving daughter."

Astarte sighed and leaned back in repose, "I have my own family here and cannot bear to leave it in their hands to rule after me. You know that I was conceived in the temple in Eshur as Goddess born. Well, in order for my grandmother to agree to send my mother to Kemet to rule, they had to agree that should a child be born of that ritual, it would belong to Tefnut and not to Kemet. Well, Qedeshet was sent down to ensure that the bargain was kept and when I was born it was decided that I be sent to this temple here in Gubla, that has been in our family for centuries out of time and was almost lost to our family had I not been born. I was sent here when I was five years old, separated from my mother to learn the ways of this land. The other children of my mother went to Kemet, as you know.

"Besides, I spent practically my whole life here; it is a part of me and all I know. Au-Set you will do fine in Kemet, for your blood belongs there as well."

"Tell me of your children cousins, Neb-Het, you just had your first son..."

"Yes, his name is Anpu and he is wonderful. This is the first time that I have ever been separated from him and it pains me so."

The older mothers thought this endearing and Astarte spoke, "Soon you will cherish those rare moments alone! It is just that it is easy to forget yourself in the process and live solely for your children. Sometimes we have to make a distance and remember who we are, who we can be, and where we came from." At the somber note, all women lowered their heads at the wisdom in those words. "And you Au-Set? How are your wonderful many children, surely by now you have created an army for Kemet?" They all laughed.

"My girls are all strong willed and dominant as normal for our family and practically rule the palace. Set is fiery, and is learning to be a great warrior for she is already eleven years old! Renenutet and Weret-Heka are softer like Nebmaat and are always prettily adorned as their father, yet boisterous. Renenutet is nine and Weret-Heka is eight. Heru is training to be a fierce warrior along with Set and is seven. Bast has a pride of lions under her command and thinks that she is the main queen of the palace. She is only six. Merul is following in the footsteps of Tehuti as a scribe. At the age of five, he can already draw all of the characters in the new picture language created by Nugig Ma-At and Tehuti. And the little twins Maat and Serqet are beautiful with gorgeous black curls and giggle all of the time and adore being around their cousin Anpu."

"That is a mouthful dear cousin, the Goddesses rejoice in your fertility!" Both Neb-Het and Astarte bowed in reverence to Au-Set, but also in love and pride.

"I hope that this meeting between us does not infringe upon your deserved rest from your travels dear cousins? I just needed to speak with you. I wrote a letter to my mother, but she needed to stay in Kemet. She felt confident that you both could help me. I hate to make this wonderful reunion sad."

"Not at all Astarte!" Spoke up Au-Set, "Please, let us know what we can do for you. We are family. What has been going on here?"

"It is the whole mentality here, I fear. It is a contagious reaction to the rule of Enlil and his twisted ways of suppression. It has finally reached the borders of this region.

"At first, as in Eshnunna, there was the gradual meshing with the women here and then it escalated to small attacks. Lately the threats have been growing more powerful. Enlil wants my grandsons in fosterage to teach them the ways of their God Enlil! Ria is his niece and he has had no sons of his own. Ria has been raised in their ways and is useless in rule. I am nervous to leave this land over to her. She definitely would pass all matters of import to her uncle and then her sons would be brainwashed to his ways. I have seen the destruction of this land in my dreams as your mother once did. I feel helpless and ask that you work with her to teach her the ways of the Goddess. I have given up, for she is stupid in her submissive stubbornness."

She looked at the both of them and noticed that they were both affirmative on their position to help their cousin for they had guessed correctly the basic idea of this in the letter they received on the matter.

"Unfortunately my son Melanchor has fallen to the ways of the northern tribes and of Enlil in its attraction towards me. Thankfully, my consorts have not. For the life of the Goddess is all that they know and I have never treated them less than the men they are. Both of them help me in the decision process; never have they been treated as if they were inferior at all, like Enlil preaches to the young men in Retenu."

"Cousin, your consorts seem like wonderful men." Spoke up Neb-Het.

"That, they are. I have known Baal since I arrived here for his mother trained me for this position. Baal's mother was the older *Anat*. Anat is the name of the Goddess and her earthly representative here. When Anat died, I took over. Baal has been my best friend, lover and closest confidant. He is my breath and my soul, we are virtually inseparable."

"I definitely see that, and Rashef?" Au-Set understood this since that was how she felt about her Au-Sar.

"Oh, that was only a formality and done before Anat died on her suggestion. Anat felt it prudent that a queen and Goddess representative have more than one consort as she had done. Baal was her oldest son of eight consorts, all of whom gave her womb only sons. I was chosen to inherit this, since we are also of her blood. Her mother was a cousin of Tefnut.

"Rashef was sent as a gift to her from Upper Kemet; he is of the royal blood there as well and fancies himself a king removed from Kemet. He is so adorable, but more as decoration than of genuine use as Baal has been."

Neb-Het recalled that the garb that Rashef wore at the feast was more of Kemet than of this land. She had heard that he was a cousin of theirs through their grandfather Shu.

Au-Set spoke, "Astarte..."

"You must call me Anat in public for that is the position that I hold here."

"Of course. Is there anything else?"

"Not that I can think of, just be careful how you approach Ria and Melanchor, since I feel that Enlil has a lot more influence than I know of. Call it woman's instinct."

Chapter 73

The next day, Ria approached Au-Set. "Your highness, I love that fragrance that you wear, what is it? "

"Thank you, it is a flower in Kemet called the Melilote. Your sons are beautiful and look so much like you." The boys had just run into the room carrying handfuls of flowers for their mother, who giggled in delight as the boys showered her with the petals. They handed her flowers that had very short stems, as little children often do.

Au-Set thought this was adorable and recalled many such occasions when her children handed her such short stemmed flowers. She had hugged them and told them that they needed to have longer stems so that they could drink the water in the vases.

"Oh silly boys, how wonderful and full of love you both are. I am the luckiest Momma in the world. They are of the perfect size to put in my hair!" She placed her head down for the boys put them in her long silver hair, and all around them giggled at this.

"Now boys run along, you have lessons to learn!" She patted them on their little bottoms in play to send them on their way. Au-Set felt the love this woman had for her boys and felt a kindred spirit that all mothers feel at looking at this pure woman without one observable flaw. Her only fault was in her being meek and bowing to the ways of her husband. In her own land, the woman was faultless. How odd were perceptions. She felt admiration for this woman and in her completely all encompassing and devoted role of mother. This woman devoted every moment in being a mother and then a wife. Ria had nothing else to distract her, as she did. For a small moment, Au-Set found herself jealous of this woman. She sometimes wished that she could devote all of her time to her family, without all that she was born into and her responsibilities towards Kemet and her family for the Goddess.

It was brief, that feeling. All she knew was power and the deep responsibility that came with it. First, she was the representative in training for the Goddess Ua-Zit, then a mother and then a consort in that order. The Goddess chose her. She also felt a small anger at this woman, for she was Goddess chosen as well and chose to ignore it out of ignorance. How could anyone do such a thing? It was blasphemy to her.

Though her feelings for the woman conflicted, Au-Set felt that she was an adoring mother and sometimes found her-self resenting Ria for mostly that reason, in that she could not be such herself. Was this woman really stronger than she was in ignoring the principle and tradition of this land to be strictly just a mother? She appeared to her and Neb-Het to be weak and submissive. Nevertheless, Au-Set still wondered whether this woman was just acting like that to have total control over her sons and to be their sole provider. This woman never let anyone else care for her sons. She made all of their clothes and even prepared their food. She slept on a palate by their bed. She was completely devoted to them, not caring about responsibility or anything that would take her from her own sons. Her life WAS her sons.

"Au-Set why don't you come over to care for little Pelusias during his nap? I have never let anyone else do this before, but you are a much more experienced mother than I am. Besides, I need to concentrate on some plans that I have made for his blanket. It is the only time I have for this and he is a restless sleeper. I just want to focus enough to create this blanket that I have dreamed about for him."

"I would love to."

"Pelusias, Maneros, Come back for it is time for your nap." The boys ran over to where they were and ran in circles while the two women walked back to the palace.

They walked back to the fortress and to the living quarters with the two boys in tow running around them and giggling. The suite of this queen was beside that of her mother-in-law. It was large and consisted of a sumptuous eating and resting chamber adorned with wall hangings and carpets with pillows and suspended oil lamps. There was a fire pit in the center of the room with a hole in the ceiling for smoke to escape. This was the hearth of the home of Ria and all life of her family centered on it. This was the most sacred spot of the home. Smaller rooms were on all sides and had openings in the ceiling for the sunlight to stream through and for the release of the smoke from the hearth fires when in use. The walls were thick and made of mud brick, which left large ledges for placing plants and pottery on.

"I will be in this room, let me know if you need anything. Thank you very much from one mother to another."

Au-Set looked around the beautiful center chamber. What beautiful colors are in here! Where did you buy all of these wondrous tapestries and carpets?"

"Thank you! I made them all myself. All of my love for my family is in each stitch and color that I chose. Each one has a meaning in my life with theirs, for we are all connected with love and color." The boys rolled their eyes, but Au-Set felt that it was beautiful and she wished that she had such talent.

Ria went into a small chamber on the side, through the richly woven blanket in the doorway.

Au-Set settled down on the pillows. "Time for bed boys!" She then found a soft pillow that was almost as large as she was and then proceeded to lay down on it. She then pretended to be very tired and let out a loud and much exaggerated yawn.

Pelusias thought that this was very funny and started to giggle. Maneros looked at his little brother. "Pelusias, we must do as the lady wants, for she is a queen like mother. Besides mother would be upset if we did not rest. Why do you think that I am so tall?"

Pelusias giggled and Maneros went over to him, "SHHHHHHH, she's sleeping. Lie on this pillow, it is your favorite, Momma made it just for you!"

Therefore, Maneros lay down on the pillow next to his brother after looking at this strange new queen asleep near them. It was not long before he fell into a deep sleep.

However, Pelusias would not have anything to do with a nap; he was simply not ready for one and only wanted to play.

Au-Set saw through one eye she peeked open and did not want wake his older brother; she motioned for little Pelusias to be quiet and for him to come over to her lap. He did. She knew that she had to find some way to entertain this very active little boy. He reminded her of her own Heru and had to fight back a tear. She knew that she would return home soon, but her job was still not done and they were all in safe hands for the moment.

She knew that she had to find some way to keep little Pelusias happy without disturbing his mother in the next room of his older brother asleep beside him. She decided that the best way to do this was through magic.

"Have you ever heard the story about the magical fire-bird?"

"Ah-ah."

"Oh no? Well, do I have a wonderful story for you young man! Come over here on my lap and I will tell you this wonderful story." She sat cross-legged and he plopped on her lap with his head tucked under her chin looking up at her. She knew that he would not sleep at this time, so she had to keep him occupied. She smelled his soft baby-fine silver hair and marveled at the wonder of it. Never had she seen hair of this color. She softly brushed his hair back soothingly from his temples.

"A long time ago there was this bird. It was an ordinary bird. It was small and yellow. However, he looked like every other bird in the land. He would often be confused with his many brothers and even sisters! This little bird was called Kekes!" She thought that this was a funny addition for she missed her Kekes at home and thought that he should have been a bird.

"Kekes was a sad bird while all of the other birds were happy. They did not care that they all looked the same; they just wanted to play and sing all day and to dance around the sun.

"Would you not want to just play and sing all day little prince?"

"Yes, oh yes!"

"But you know that we cannot always have that... Some people or birds in this story are perfectly happy with that and they live a contended and full life. However, some birds want more out of life. They feel like they want something more than to sing and to play all day. For it is not enough for them.

"Sometimes this is a good thing, for inventions are created and good deeds are performed for this yearning. However, in a bird, it does not make much sense. Kekes wanted more out of life. His family told him that it was silly, for they had wings and a beautiful voice. They were made for singing and flying. Who would want more out of life than that?"

She noticed that Pelusias was deep into the story and even waved his arms like the wings of a bird.

"One day a big red fox came over to Kekes who was sitting on a low branch looking rather sad. Now the fox could easily have made a meal out of the little yellow bird, but he too was not like the other foxes. He felt that this little bird was different as well.

"Now this story takes place a long time ago, so the fox was not red like we know them to be but a dismal grey color. They only had dull gray foxes then and it was all they knew.

"The fox came over to the little bird and said, 'little bird, I could not help but notice how sad you are, could I help?' The little bird was so sad that he did not even care about the possible danger of being a meal for this fox, he responded, "Yes, I wish that there were something more for me in this life. I want more than to just fly and sing all day.' The fox sat back and pondered over this. 'I see what you mean. I feel the same way, there has to be something more...' He lowered his head and joined the little bird in great thought. The fox had approached the bird and wondered about something. He too was sad, he wanted something more out of life, and knew of a way. However, it was very risky and he was afraid to do it alone. He wanted someone else to go first.

When he saw the little bird and heard about his similar sadness, he realized that this little bird might be just the key to his problems.

"The fox was crafty, selfish, and lazy. Whenever he wanted something, he would find some other fox to get it. He was very clever, as he knew what to say. He told the little bird about this old woman who lived on the edge of the woods that had magic powers. What the fox did not tell the bird was that he wanted to visit this old woman himself, but knew that this woman demanded a gift for her magic. He did not know what to bring her and then he saw the little bird. He thought she would like the little bird to put in a cage to hear him sing or for a meal. Therefore, the fox convinced the bird to go with him to visit the old woman.

"The old woman lived in a cave and kept away from other people, except when they came to her and needed her cures or magic. Most of the people forgot about the old woman who chose to live away from them, but the animals did not. She loved animals and cared for any came to her door if they were hungry or injured or just needed her love.

"So Kekes and the wily fox arrived at her door. The old woman bent down and picked up little Kekes, 'How odd little one? That you have a fox for a friend?' She looked at the fox and wondered to his motives. Kekes felt the love and concern from the old woman and began to sing. 'What brings you here at my door you two?'

"The fox spoke first,' wise woman of the woods, this little bird wants to do more than sing and fly all day, he would like more out of life.' Kekes sighed and looked down. The old woman smiled, 'and you Mr. Fox, what would you like?' The fox stepped closer and bravely spoke to her, for she was much larger then they in her being human and told her,' you see, I would like the same thing. For I know that there is something important that I should do and I do not know what. I know I was meant for a lot more than just being a fox!' He proudly told her.

"I understand, but you do know that for me to use my magic for your own purposes, you need to bring me a gift.' That was when the fox looked at Kekes and then to the old woman and told her in turn,' I have brought you a gift."

"Now, the old woman could have performed her magic without the gift, but she wanted to know the motive that she sensed in the little gray fox and knew that she was right. He was selfish and did not care who was hurt so that he could get what he wanted. The little bird was another matter. She felt sad for him, but also, like the fox, she envied the free life of this pretty bird. To fly and to sing all day and to play in the sun! How could anyone want more? She turned to the fox and waved her wand,' you shall have something more out of life for from this day on you will be red!' Poof! The boring gray fox turned red right before their eyes. The fox danced around the room and then ran out the door, not caring what happened to the bird that he left behind as his gift.

"The little bird looked at the old woman in wonder, 'That fox is truly beautiful now!' He forgot about his sadness in the beauty of the transformed fox. He was truly impressed. The old woman saw this and the good heart of the little bird, who was only sad and lonely and spoke to him in a whisper,' little bird, Kekes! I have a better gift for you! I will turn you into a firebird. There will be no other than you, nor will there ever be. Every time you die, you will be reborn out of fire! You will be a magical bird! Be careful, for people will want to find you! However, you will be so powerful that no one can ever catch you! You also have the choice to hide out here and to be my friend. I will protect you. Not as a prisoner, but as a friend.' Kekes loved this idea, felt indeed that this kind of life would be wonderfully exciting, and accepted. Moreover, from that day on hundreds of years ago, Kekes made that decision and a friend. He now sang all of the time since he knew that his life finally had that special meaning that he craved. Kekes is still alive and still living with that old woman, for she is still alive as well to watch over him. You see, both are immortal and live with the Gods. "

Au-Set looked down at little Pelusias and noticed that he loved her story but was not quiet in the least. He looked up at her with his deep brown eyes and whispered in joy, "A bird made of fire that never dies!"

"Never dies love, never dies! When he does, it is only briefly and then he is born again more brilliant than before out of fire. The fire does not hurt him at all and only makes him sing more glorious than any bird ever born in history." She hugged this inquisitive boy and he giggled in wonderment at the whole idea of it.

"I wanna be a fire bird like Kekes!"

"Oh, no silly boy! Remember that there is only one magical fire bird!" He looked sad. "That does not mean that we cannot pretend to be one, now does it!" He almost squealed at this, she put her finger up to her mouth to silence him in front of his sleeping brother and busy mother.

"Watch, but be very quiet." She whispered. She stood up quietly and started to dance around the room, her robes were scarlet and billowed in her movements. "Here take my scarf so that you can be a little fire bird, but be quiet." She handed him her silken scarf that was of the color of blood and the two of them danced around the room around the sleeping form of Maneros.

They both had so much fun that they did not notice that Maneros was awake and Ria had entered the room. They both joined in.

Ria exclaimed, "Is this a new dance?"

"Yes, Momma, it is the fire-bird dance!"

Ria joined in the fun, looked at her little son and the great queen, and with their billowing red robes, felt that they did look like birds made of fire. She laughed and danced about the room with them. They danced all around and through each other's arms spinning about, until finally falling down in exhaustion. All the while little Pelusias sang his version and made up song of the story told of the firebird, Kekes to the others in the room.

Chapter 74

Over the next several weeks, Au-Set and Neb-Het looked for any excuse to visit with Ria. On one such occasion, Au-Set had found her combing wool from their flock.

"Your highness..." Au-Set had softly interrupted her.

"Your highness, please have a seat and join me. Do you know how to do this?" Au-Set patiently watched as Ria skillfully placed carefully measured out strands vertically across her lap and combed them out with a long pronged ivory comb. She deftly made sure the strands were in one neat direction before adding them in small hand-sized bundles to her beautifully woven basket that gathered all of them. Such skill was wonderful to watch and it easily enraptured Au-Set. She frowned in sadness that she had no such useful skill.

"I am sorry to say that I do not." She bowed her head in ashamed ignorance. She really was never taught this art since her servants and slaves attended to all of this work. "Why do you do this for you are a queen like me? Besides I always thought that this was a man's job."

Ria looked up at them and finished placing the last long tress of wool onto her lap to card or comb with the rest. She did this with long and graceful fingers, through slightly calloused from long years of this. The young queen would then take the combed wool and wound them up and tossed them into a basket with the other soft tussles of wool that would then be spindled to make yarn for scarves and carpets. It looked very relaxing to the young queen to be performing this simple task so happily.

"I understand your feelings on the matter, but my father always told me that there is nothing worse than an idle woman. The honest work of a woman should be in having children, caring for them, and clothing the family... We were taught from a young age to do this. It is considered very honorable for a woman to make the actual clothing for her family."

"But cannot you buy it? I am confused. It looks boring."

"No, it is actually quite relaxing and allows the mind to go to other places. I have my best thoughts when doing this; it is quite monotonous and allows for the mind to empty of things that could stress you."

"I understand, but why is it considered good for a woman to waste her time with making clothes when they have a household to run and important decisions to make and businesses to run for that matter?"

"Oh, I was born to serve, as all of the women in our tribe. The man rules over the family and owns the business and even our children."

Au-Set gasped at this, for it was unheard of. She thought the idea ridiculous and laughed at this. She saw the serious look of Ria's face and stopped. "You are serious, I am very sorry. It is just that I have never heard of such an idea. How could a man own a child, he does not give birth to it, a woman does. How can a man run a business, they have no training in this and are not too detail oriented. I feel that men would make poor business managers."

"On the contrary, for that is all I know. To tell you the truth, I feel very odd in this Goddess ruled land. I was always taught from birth to keep quiet and bow to the ways of my father and then to my husband. I know nothing else, nor do I want it. Anat is always trying to tell me that I should learn how to rule. I just do not understand why, for Melanchor is perfectly capable. Besides, soon my sons will be old enough to rule."

"What about daughters, will you not wait for them to be born? You can always take another consort besides Melanchor."

"No, I could not even think of it. I love him so and will obey his wishes."

"Are you not concerned about your sons, do you fear that your uncle will try to gain them for his throne in Eshnunna?"

"You mean Sumer? No, I do not worry about such things that are for the men to worry over. I care only for my husband and the boys." She continued to her work in smoothing out the rough wool. The pile was getting bigger by her feet of scrap and good wool to be worked together to eventually be felted, woven, or crocheted with her ivory awl.

Au-Set had been trying to reason with her on every possible matter that she could think of. She knew that Neb-Het was equally frustrated, though both persevered, hoping their youth and closeness of age to Ria would help them.

Chapter 75

While both of the sisters tried to work with Ria, they finally had to admit defeat at a meeting with Astarte. Astarte understood and told the sisters about the latest attack on the village outside.

Au-Set felt that this was the best time to tell her cousin what she had initially observed upon entering the city. Qedeshet was there as well with Dia dozing at her feet. "Astarte, I had noticed when we first arrived, how difficult this fortress would be to defend, if there were a large scale attack, which seems to be soon to occur."

"I agree Au-Set, what would you suggest?"

"That you lower the buildings of the village and block out any secret entrances that may have occurred over many generations. It would be easy to sneak an army inside."

"I agree with you and have tried to make a new village at a farther distance from here so that we could see every possible breach. However, the villagers would have nothing to do with this. This fortress and surrounding village is over five hundred years old and most if not all of the villagers have known no other life for their family. Each generation builds their home on top of the prior generation to create the chaos that you see. I will send Qedeshet out to account for every entrance though and to seal them up. That is the only compromise that I could make with them."

"Then we would have to entice the enemy to your fields below. The harvest was already done and they are useless for the moment. Plus, I feel any bloodshed would be viewed by the Goddess with pride in that it was shed for her."

"I agree, but what about my son and his dimwitted consort, what if they choose the side of Enlil? What of my grandsons? If I was killed, Ria will gain control, and then it would all would crumble out of her ignorance."

Qedeshet spoke up then, "The only thing that we can do is make sure that you do not lose. Maybe we can hide you?"

"Never, I will fight, for it is in my blood."

Neb-Het uttered, "But think of all that you have to lose, if you should die or become injured severely."

Astarte then spoke out of necessity and frustration, "Think of all we lose, if we do not fight and let them sneak in. I also would request for the sake of the family that you stay only until you feel that it is not safe, and to please take my grandsons with you, so that they would not be further corrupted by Enlil."

"But, what of Ria? Why take her children away from her? Should we take her as well?"

"She would never allow it. Besides, this is the only way. I do feel that you should probably take them away as soon as possible. Also, I have a little gift for you." Qedeshet smiled since she knew about this beforehand.

Astarte had pulled the cover off the table over which they spoke and it revealed the infamous chest that was thought to have been lost. Au-Set and Neb-Het gasped at this.

"Please take this chest and my grandsons with my blessings and good luck. I would advise this to be done this very evening, if you can. I will have the boys drugged and placed in your wagon along with their favorite belongings. As for Ria, I will distract her." Her face fell at what she was about to do, but found no other choice. She hated the idea of taking the boys away from her and from their own mother who loved them dearly. Nevertheless, her first duty was for her family. She continued, "Please tell me now if you have a better idea. It is all that I could think of. I have not slept for quite the while on this.

Neb-Het spoke up, "I understand and support you completely and will give my life for the protection of your grandsons. I hope that someday, you can send their mother to them."

All women in the room knew that they had no other choice and dreaded the steps they were about to set into motion from the moment they left the room.

Chapter 76

Neb-Het and Au-Set made quick pace to their rooms and bade their servants to pack for a hasty departure. It was well known that there would soon be a war and all were in accordance for their fast exit. Therefore, in the wee hours of the evening the sisters made haste to leave and found the sleeping forms of Pelusias and Maneros. Au-Set and Neb-Het wept for how the little princes would react when they woke.

She knew that they would cry out. Au-Set wanted desperately to find Ria and to take her along as well, but she knew that it would be useless. Au-Set feared that Ria was encouraging her uncle in his interest in the boys to rule after them. She also knew that all of them could not find a better idea to keep the Goddess traditions alive and had to make do with this one. Since they were all mothers, they grieved for what they were about to do and went with heavy steps to carry out their duty. They looked at each other with tears in their eyes for Ria and both vowed secretly that they would find a way for them to reunite after the threat of war was over.

Au-Set struggled with the rationale of her cousin, but still hated the idea of taking children away from their own mother, and one who obviously adored them. She knew that she would not sleep until she made sure that the boys would understand and see their mother again.

Chapter 77

Astarte watched the sisters leave. She had given the boys a mild sedative to make sure that they slept more sound in order for this to occur. She had hoped that her cousins would accept her idea; she prayed for her grandsons for many sleepless evenings and knew that her heart would not rest until she knew they were safe in Kemet. She also silently prayed that Ria would someday join them and perhaps lead her kingdom of Retenu well, though she knew that this last thought was as futile as her own future from Enlil. She made sure that Pelusias had his favorite pillow that his mother made for them as well as all of the beautifully woven blankets that she could grab.

Astarte could think of no other alternative and hoped that someone would offer her one. No other idea or option ever came, so she was forced to make this one happen. She knew that there would be desperate consequences and she knew that she would regret it. Nevertheless, she weighed it repeatedly in her head and still came up with no other option. Why was all of this left up to her, why does everything eventually end up with her? Sometimes she would fantasize that she would have been born a simple peasant girl with nothing to worry about but milking the goats in her time on earth.

Astarte did love being born into her station and made the best of it. She came from a long line of powerful women and men. She knew of nothing else, it was deeply imbedded in her veins.

So, before she approached her cousins, she made sure that this plan would work and she strengthened herself to make sure that it occurred. It was difficult in her being a mother as well. She dreaded that she had to take the boys away from their mother, it was killing her inside, but she knew of no other way. She strongly felt that their mother's family was poisoning the boys.

It was not the thought of another God that bothered her, but the wretched way in which the religion treated the women. She could not bear any daughters of her line to have to endure that treatment at all. She wanted the boys to learn the ways of their fathers as well as their mothers. The balance of the male and female was what she strove to bring her new land of Kemet. This Enlil taught that women were dirty and made good men fall. He bade them to believe that women were breeders and the chattel of the men that controlled them. Everything good would be lost with this philosophy.

Astarte knew that there would be devastating tears throughout all of what was to occur and knew that she would hate herself for this and the boys would hate her. However, she knew that the boys would be the only children of Ria; she had such a difficult labor with Pelusias that no more had been able to keep in her womb after his birth. Her son would not take another wife and if Ria took another consort? Regardless, the woman could not have any other children and it was up to the boys to carry on the ways of the Goddess and to find good women to rule beside them if this land could ever be saved.

Astarte knew that it was another fruitless impossibility, with the almost complete and total usurpation of the northern tribes. Those same tribes that have almost complete control of the whole region of Retenu now. She had tried almost her whole life to prevent the coming of the northern tribes and had exhausted every possible hope in futility. They were very skillful in gaining ground and had learned from the sloppy takeover of Eshnunna.

She also knew that a final battle against them was imminent and would occur soon. She heard the battle horn blow in the evening and the drums beating more erratically as if preparing for some crescendo that would happen very soon. She recalled the war drums as they breached Eshnunna years ago as told to her by her own cousins.

Astarte made sure that this would not occur at her actual city. Qedeshet, the commander of her army was sent the evening prior to negotiate with their commander by the name of Enlo. He was a man of honor, though on the enemy side. He followed the universal code in setting up a battleground, where they would all meet and fight this battle in nobility. They had agreed upon the fields of Mot, just outside the city three miles out. She had the armies of Lachish, Megiddo, and Ugarit. They gathered inside her fortress and trained by Qedeshet.

She knew that Enlo would keep his promise, for he was a man of honor in battle and would prefer a battle won under the light of day and full glory and view.

So that evening after her last meeting with her cousins, she snuck out and made sure that the boys were safely tucked in to their deep sleep inside the royal wagon snuggly buried in all of the homemade blankets woven by the love of their mother. The wagon that would lead them to safety and to a better future was safe and secure after her careful inspection. She kissed them on their foreheads and made sure that Ria was safely drugged as well. Neither of them knew of this and she knew that both of the boys would hate her for this. The only people that knew of her plan beside her cousins were her consort Baal and Qedeshet. Baal was the one who snuck in that evening and carried his sleeping grandsons into the wagon.

Qedeshet made sure that when all was set they were safely on their way out of the city and on their way back to Kemet. Astarte prayed to the Goddess Anat and even to Innana that she would be able to reunite her family again in safety.

Astarte as Anat also realistically knew that if the battle that were to occur on the morrow would be lost the boys would be the first to be killed as well as Ria and her son, and then herself. She feared for this and even thought of sending Ria along with her sons initially. However, Baal made her see that Ria was too brainwashed by her uncle, and would reveal the plans, not realizing that she was signing the death warrant of herself and sons.

Astarte knew that if the boys were to end up in the hands of Enlil and prepared to lead after him, it would be their mental and spiritual death as well as for everyone in this land. She saw the results of his leadership in Sumer and knew the women of this realm would rather be dead than to face the torments of the psychological death that awaited them as slaves to the men of Sumer. She feared for any daughters born to her line for what they had to face under that rule.

The next day dawned hesitantly and revealed the fields in their barren and desolate state. Two weeks ago had been the last harvest and the dead stalks stuck out as if knowing what was about to occur on them. Angry and menacing they waited for the battle to begin.

The mist encircled the hundreds of people gathered on this field that stretched for miles. Astarte and Qedeshet had gathered their army the evening before, where they faced the south, while the army of Enlo faced the north. This was traditional. The homeland would have the south facing fields and the approaching army would have the north facing fields. Out of etiquette, to have a battle of honor, no army was left to face the rising sun to blind them. The opposing army would have won out of cheating and disgrace.

The mist came in with the force of the lion and sprang into battle stance as if investigating all of the participants that waited eagerly for the sun to rise in the sky as commanded by honorable battles from the dawn of time. The ground was hardened by the dropping temperatures of the evening and would soon be turned soft with the rising temperature of the day expected. Astarte even wondered if there would be an early snow on this day, for the temperatures did not pick up as usual so soon after sunrise.

Astarte had prepared her army for this as well by making sure that small spikes of bronze were attached to the bottom of her army's sandals for traction. She knew that due to the season and the normal temperatures in this region, traction would be a requirement. She also prepared them all with padded undergarments and flexible bronze battle clothes. The shields of bronze were inlaid with her cow totem for her protection. She had four lines of foot soldiers on the front and in the rear. She even had four lines waiting out in her fortress for reserves. As for the mounted soldiers, she had them on donkeys.

Qedeshet was mounted on her pet lion Dia, whose roars would be heard as soon as the first rays of dawn touched the dew covered fields. She was dressed in the armor of the ancient *Tawawanna* warriors of the Catal-Huyuk. Her headdress was made of copper with a plume of lion hair attached and flowing in the crisp breeze. She looked regal and ancient as if she had walked straight out of an ancient wall painting of the land of their ancestors. She had violet flowers made in a garland around her neck and her large pet snake wrapped around her waist. Her weapon was a large spear tipped in copper. She looked impressive indeed.

Qedeshet had told Astarte that her spear was passed down matrilineal through countless generations. It was assumed that the spear was actually made by her ancestress from the actual Catal-Huyuk since it was of the naturally occurring copper and not created in a forge.

Astarte was on a strange animal that was found for her from the north called a horse. It was taller than their war donkeys and though sturdy, had longer legs that carried her much higher in the air. The pelt of the animal was a golden color and its mane was long and braided in its coarseness. She trained with this foreign animal and grew close to it in learning its ways. Astarte was naked on her horse, defiantly posed and appeared as if she feared nothing, not even death. She had violet tattoos painted on that made her appear as if she were a fearsome monster. Raised up to the winds was her famous battle-axe made of bronze and inlaid in silver that caught the rays of the sun and sprayed it all around her. Her hair was teased and matted to add to the full affect of fear that she radiantly emanated to all those opposing her. She engaged her enemy without fear, as she was a Goddess. This was how she appeared to all those who would fight alongside of her and face her in battle. She was a sight indeed to be reckoned with and to fear. She looked unpredictable and furious and saw no boundaries.

In truth, despite her battle gear, or lack of it, Astarte was in total control of the situation as it was all well planned out. She waited anxiously for the sound of her trumpets. She would give the command for the fighting to commence, as it was her ground that she was defending, according to the ancient war rules of etiquette and valor.

They all stood there waiting as the rays of sun danced with the mist that rolled about them. As the mist began to clear, she heard a sign that she was waiting for. She heard the chirping of a small bird on a tree above them all. With that sound, she gave the signal for the hollowed out ancient horns to sound for the battle to commence.

Astarte waved her left hand carrying her purple flag to signal the foot soldiers to advance; they did and met on the field in full combat. Blood was sacrificed on this field and many fell on both sides, a blood sacrifice to their Gods and the land they fought to keep.

She then gave the command for the middle left of her mounted soldiers to swing around to their right, while the opposite side went straight in the thick of it. Qedeshet was in the front of this contingent and met the enemy mounted soldiers.

Astarte and her people gasped in horror, for the mounted soldiers of Enlo were on taller horses than hers was and had spikes sticking out from their sides. The donkeys on the side of Astarte panicked and threw their riders, for they were not used to seeing such tall beasts in their land and felt incredible damage as the spikes on the sides ripped through them and their riders. It was pandemonium on the field for the side of Astarte. She watched in horror.

She looked at all of this deciding what to send in next and as she gave the signal for the slingshots loaded with small bronze balls with clay around them for size and lightness in flight. It was then that she noticed him. Across the field on a tall horse as black as the darkness of a moonless night, he sat. His battle gear was of another color than bronze and wondered if it was the rarest metal from the sky. Astarte noticed that the guard around him had the same metal and wielded it in the form of axes and tall swords with a double edge.

She felt her heart drop, though hid it. His mounted force met hers and controlled the field. She gave the signal for her archers on all sides and those hidden high up in the trees. Nothing came and she trembled and waved her signal more frantically. Still nothing happened. Enlo looked straight in her eyes and pointed to the left of the field that was blocked from view earlier in the rising sun. She looked over, saw all of her archers dead, and mounted on tall spikes in the field, their bows broken in piles underneath the clotted blood that was dripping down from them. She gasped and the anger built up inside of her, at the same time, she realized that she had met a very intelligent foe. While they prepared he had snuck in with his warriors and found all other archers, killed them silently and then dragged them out. In a large army, this would not have been noticed. She trembled at the thought of enemy soldiers in her midst, learning their plans.

Astarte knew from that horrific moment what it all meant. That she had no choice but to send all of her forces in for one last move. She wanted this to be won on merits, bravery, and strategy. However, he had played a very bold stroke, which crippled her tremendously. She admired his genius and wondered if someday she would ever meet this Enlo on safe grounds, for she was impressed. She watched Qedeshet fight bravely and fiercely, noticed Calvary on the left stealthily join in, and was led by her beloved Baal. He gave her the signal that she needed, for he sensed her plans and had agreed. She sounded her horn for the last charge and gave them the signal. All of her forces, even those in the fortress rushed in. She had noticed that all of his men were now in the field.

All of the forces of Astarte rushed out making fierce animal and nightmarish sounds in their mad dash for the center of the battleground. All was chaos as was her last plan, since all of the others had failed. Only now, she saw that she had nothing left to lose.

This was something that fell out of all of the ancient rules of Calvary that she had created as a failsafe. When all was lost, her army would rush in from every direction to the center screaming as loud as they could and in erratic fashion. This was to ensure mass confusion and put the enemy off guard. This was discussed in the beginning of their training and not brought up until now on the field. She was confident that this had not been spied on and she was right.

All of the planned order of the army of Enlo was now destroyed and lent askew. Astarte knew that if her army were to ever gain ground and to possibly keep it, that it would be now, and only at this moment.

Astarte rushed in and then noticed something totally out of place. Out of nowhere in the complete center of all of the chaos was the form of Ria. She was frazzled with grief and seemed completely oblivious to the battle that surrounded her on all sides. Her only thought was of reaching Astarte. Ria's eyes locked on her and held them.

Astarte made her way over to Ria to scoop her out of the chaos. She had thought that Ria was safely drugged in her chambers and away from all of this. Ria had no training at all in battle. However, Astarte knew that Ria made a more formidable foe than any one trained on this field, for she had a murderous look of her face. "Anat! Astarte! You stole my boys!"

How Astarte heard each word with such clarity among all that was going on around her was a miracle. She stopped dead in her tracks. She also felt the significance of the young queen using her birth name "I am sorry, but I did it for your own good, they are safe and I will bring them to you after all of this is done! Get out of this field and lock the door to your chamber; I will talk with you when all of this is over." She noticed a soldier heading her way and she slashed out and cut off his arm, clearing the path between her and Ria. "Get out of here!"

"Not without my boys! I know the whole thing! You sent them to Kemet! They are mine; you will poison them with your Goddess ways! They are meant to rule for Enlil, they are his heirs!"

"Never!" Astarte screamed viciously as she swung her axe at a soldier who was gaining on Ria from behind. Ria jumped out of the way at the movements of Astarte and she rode past her to kill the soldier. Ria did not care that Astarte had just saved her life; she only wanted to kill this obstinate woman for taking her sons away.

"Astarte! I hate you! You stole my boys, you mean to keep them, and I would rather die!" Moreover, with that Ria ran into the first sword that she found that was raised towards the soldier next to her. She pushed the soldier aside that was in the army of Enlo and ran into the sword of one of Astarte's own Nugig warriors that had escaped Eshnunna before the reign of Enlil. Ria ran purposely with all of her angered strength into the sword of the startled woman holding it, who was aiming for someone else. Ria had thrust herself through the whole sword to the hilt and screamed, "I hate you, and may Enlil have vengeance on your people!" The Nugig warrior realized the situation and then took her sword out of Ria and carried her body out of there off the field.

This moment occurred briefly in time, yet lasted an eternity, so unexpected that it was. Astarte refused to let it affect her now, since she had a battle to fight, mother-less grandsons to protect, and a land to give them.

She rushed in roaring like Dia and riding her mount in circles slashing with her axe, everything that came into her path. Blood spurted all over and painted her a deeper violet. Her eyes shone with the glazed look of the insane. Since, at this moment, she did not care, she felt the battle lust become a part of her; she fought desperately for it not to consume her and made meticulous strokes clearing a path for her toward Enlo, who was gaining ground towards her.

Just then she noticed her beloved Baal wielding his large sword and cutting while screaming at the top of his lungs walking towards Enlo, having spotting him. His instinct to protect his mate flooded him and blinded him in his fury. He did not see her coming up on his right side in full capability of defending herself. She had also noticed that a soldier mounted on a tall blood covered horse was nearing him from behind with a spear wielded towards his back.

"Baal!" She screamed at the top of her lungs, "Turn!" He did and slashed the oncoming horse, who in pain threw his rider. The rider almost fell on Baal who had quickly stepped out of the way. She breathed a sigh of relief.

"Baal this is my fight!" He ignored her and ran forward towards the waiting and patient Enlo. Enlo was waiting for this and had motioned to a guard on his side. The guard pointed up his sling and shot out a ball of that strange metal.

She saw this in slow motion as it tore through the right shoulder of Baal and made him bend over in pain. She watched in horror, since her distance was not gained enough to wield her axe. Her horror at this moment consumed her as she watched almost in slow motion outside of time as the spear held by Enlo swung high and was thrown right into Baal's exposed skull, for his helmet had fallen when he bent over in pain from the slingshot blow.

He went down and Astarte was riveted in place, trembled as he succumbed to his final death shakes, and then stopped. All around her seemed to grow dim, even though the sun was full in the sky. The cold cut through her in anger jarring her to her senses as she felt the first tiny snow flake fall on her shoulder.

It seemed as if in that moment when his last breath left his body that the sky released in fury a blinding snow of tiny flakes that fell all around them. The snowflakes responded angrily to rapidly cover the ground around them as she finally reached Enlo.

"Enlo, I challenge you! Dismount and face me!"

Both of them got off their horses to face each other. He jumped down, went to the body of Baal, and placed his foot on his chest so he could remove his spear. She grimaced at this as a fountain of blood rushed out of it covering the ground all around him. She kept up her maniacal posture.

All around them the fighting stopped to watch this most honorable of fights. This would determine the outcome, when two leaders faced each other in admirable combat.

Most of the soldiers on each side were trained and paid by the leaders and would literally walk off the field if their leader was killed and their pay stopped due to this. Some would even hire themselves to the opposing side, with no honor lost. They were paid to kill and it was all they lived for.

The other people that made up the army were another matter. Some were prisoners, who would flee at the first sight of their captors losing. Some were villagers who were fighting for their homes. Those last soldiers would fight on even after their leader died, since they were fighting for their own personal safety and that of their families.

Each person on that field knew the meaning of this honorable battle that was about to occur between their leaders. They dropped what they were doing in unison to wait patiently for the outcome.

The snow rushed about them violently; however, it also mercilessly covered the field of blood on which they stood. As the seconds wore on and the leaders faced each other, the flakes grew thicker and started to cover the people watching. They were too riveted in anticipation to shake it off.

Astarte did not feel the cold and the flakes that touched her skin that only enhanced her acute awareness of the moment. She roared as loud as she could and made erratic movements towards Enlo. Her hair was waving horrifically behind her and framing her in a violent fury. She raised her axe and poised it.

Enlo stood his ground and watched her. He felt that she looked like a ghost out of his nightmares. Astarte appeared the Goddess that she represented for these people in her wildly erratic demeanor that brightened in her full anger. She looked unpredictable and this made him more on guard. He could face a trained warrior, but this woman looked like she had no fear of death or of anything at all. She appeared as if she would do anything. She was small and painted dangerously to make her look like a daemon and it worked. She appeared ethereal and not of this world. She growled like a ferocious animal and made jumpy movements that were unpredictable. He felt that the only defense he had was to tire her out and let her make the first moves. He waited hiding all of the fear that he felt while she danced about like a person that had lost all sense.

Finally, she wielded her axe. He blocked it with his shield that was made from a metal mixture that he had recently discovered that he called iron. Her axe sustained blunting damage to the blade of it. She noticed this and stopped. This was all that he needed. In that moment, she was off guard at the power of the metal of his shield. Her sanity was revealed to her enemy in that one swift moment.

Enlo realized in that brief moment that her insanity was a ruse and out of spite and controlled anger, he jabbed his spear at her side. She moved out quickly, spun around, and lashed out with her axe again. He caught it with his shield and pulled from his sandal a small dagger. He jabbed her on her arm grazing her, forcing her to grab her arm while she ran at him in full force. He stepped to the side and she followed, his spear falling out of his grasp. She let her axe drop, reached for his dagger, and kicked his spear out of the way.

Now they were forced to wrestle without weapons. A battle of pure will and force can only be determined with strength and endurance as its outcome. She punched him and stepped to the side as he kicked at her. She grabbed his foot and held it there. He swerved around and got out of her hold. She ran into him with force and grabbed his long hair. He reached over and grabbed hers. They were locked in this grip and knocked over to the ground pulling with all of their strength, grunting out in anger and with each blow.

She bit him then on his cheek and he released his hold on her hair. She tugged even more on his hair and located her target, reached out and found her axe that was kicked over to reach her grasp. She placed her hands tightly around the handle, while he tried to staunch the blood pouring out of his cheek. She swung with deadly accuracy and gouged his throat. He went down and she followed swinging repeatedly in fury until his head was completely off his neck. She grabbed his head by his long blood matted hair and held it above her head in triumph.

"People the battle is over and Anat has fed on enough blood for today! There was much brilliance on both sides and this man has died in glory! Let us bow to how bravely he fought and honor him as a fellow warrior!" Men and women on both sides were all around them. They bowed in honor of a battle well fought and of the honor of this great woman leader who stood regally, though caked in matted blood and gore.

"Men of Enlo, I offer you service in my army. Let me know your pay and I will match it. There is much honor in your skill and I have need of you here. Will you fight for me?" The men of Enlo looked around the field and noticed that though Enlo was well prepared for this battle and had gained much ground, this woman had great strategic skill of her own and had defeated their leader in an honest battle. With shouts of 'Aye', they committed themselves to her service, for the moment or until the time that she lost. There is no dishonor for a professional in working for the opposing side after a loss. They earned their living in the way of battle; it was an art to them.

"Join with me then and let us burn our dead so that their life force meets the Gods of the sky for their bravery as fought today! The wounded may be brought to the tent inside the fortress. Come; let us gather the wounded so that we may properly honor the dead!" Shouts of approval rang out and those that were left standing and still able had gone about to gather all of those who could be saved. They were carried away to the tent.

Finally, all of the dead that were still left on the field were gathered for funeral preparations. Astarte had arrived to where Baal had fallen. There he lay on the field embraced grotesquely by the deadened stalks of the last harvest. He lay on his side; his face mercifully covered in matted blood, so she could not see his death grimace. His shoulder covered in crusted blood. His foot had been cut off after he had died.

It was difficult for Astarte in keeping her sanity behind her nightmarish face during her challenge to Enlo. Inside her, all she wanted to do was rip and tear at him. However, she knew that it would have been her death if she did not have a clear head. She wanted to avenge the only man that she had ever loved. However, she could not have done it recklessly since Baal had died in honor during battle. Murder did not take him away. The anger that Baal felt at her danger left his head murky and left him vulnerable.

Now she stood here looking at him after she gave orders for all to leave her alone in her grief. She bent over his form and with her spit; she wiped off the blood from his face to see his eyes once more. She shuddered at all of the wisdom lost to the world. Astarte trembled inside for all of those moments lost when he made her feel like a woman. Baal made her feel small and cherished in his strong embrace and she longed for it even more. She was blind to all of the blood and only saw the love that he always had for her. She knew that he died protecting her and vowed silently that she would never forget him and all that he meant to her. She would never take another consort again out of love as she had her cherished Baal. Rashef came over then and knowing the look on her face slinked away from her to tend to the rest of the death left on the field.

The snow had tapered down a bit and covered the blood even more on the field by now, almost purifying the field with the approval of the Goddess Anat. She brushed the tiny flakes of snow off Baal's eyelashes, face, and closed his eyes. She placed his hair over his skull to cover his deathblow wound. With the melted snow, she wiped off the rest of the blood from his face and sat back over him. He looked like he was sleeping. She would have been fooled had it not been for his body starting to grow cold and his face taking on a blue hue.

As her illusion shattered, she reached under him and lifted his body up over her shoulders. She braced her strong legs to support his weight and with love and honor for her mate, she slowly carried him off the field. All of the battle fatigue left her and a new rush of energy coursed through her veins as she thought of nothing more but finding a solitary place to burn her beloved out of honor. She placed him down by the side of a stream under a willow tree. The long branches hung over him sorrowfully, its leaves dripping as if crying at his loss as well.

On her way to this spot, she noticed that all of the warriors had gathered the dead and priestesses were chanting over the fallen warriors from both sides of the battle. The fallen warriors from each side of the battle were placed reverently together side by side, their unseeing eyes facing the skies of their own personal Gods. The remaining warriors gathered all of the branches and wood that they could find while the chanting of the priestesses droned on.

They day had left them as did the snow while first stars were appearing in the sky greeting them in mercy and pity.

Astarte heard the chanting in the background and was lost in her own world. She had gathered a large amount of wood in a pile over her love; she wanted him away from the others so that she could hide her tears. Her wounds finally caught up with her and she could not construct a proper bier on which to burn him properly.

Therefore, her main thought was to gather enough wood so that he may join the Gods. In a frantic rush of energy that was lost from her, she piled on the wood so that it completely covered her Baal's body. She found a piece of flint in her small battle pouch and struck it against her axe creating a spark that lit her love to oblivion and to the Gods. Thus, it caught as the last of the sun left the sky in a brilliant display of mauve and burgundy. Astarte sat there and was too stunned to cry for it all seemed surreal to her.

Suddenly someone softly tugged at her shoulder, "Come your highness, the funeral rites are about to begin, the priestesses await your command." Qedeshet had lowered her eyes in respect, bowing to the great love that Astarte had for Baal. She knew why the queen wanted to be alone and respected that, but now it was time to tend to her duties.

Chapter 78

That evening after Astarte bathed and entered her sleeping chambers, she called for a full tally of those lost and wounded, as well as those who had joined her side from that of Enlo's army.

Finally, after that was done she laid among all of her pillows feeling for the first time the entirety of which she was truly alone to face. She knew that there would be more armies and they would be stronger and more prepared. Nevertheless, she also had the assurance that her grandsons were safely out of their land and on the way to Kemet.

Astarte now had to pick up the pieces and face the decision that she had made. The horror of it all was finding her in flashes. The suicide plunge of Ria over the loss of her sons, as well as the loss of Baal and the battle with Enlo would not leave her mind. It all flashed before her as if pieces of a riddle that she was too afraid to comprehend.

She looked at each mark made on her body during battle and of her body washed of blood and dye that was caked all over her before. She looked into a piece of polished silver at what she now looked like. Though all that could be was washed completely from her, she still saw herself as if she was fresh from the battle. The gore was invisible, though not to her, of people who fought whether it was for money or for a cause that they truly believed in. She wondered that after all was done, if all of the lives lost were every really worth the pain that was always left behind in even the battles that were won.

She would often dream at night of a world where everyone would live in peace and where children would never go hungry. She knew from legends or so she was told. There was hope for this again, was there? She knew that it would never happen in her own lifetime and probably not for eons to come. She hoped that each life lost this day was not in vain, that it possibly paved even small steps to this dream of hers. She fervently prayed to the real Anat for this, especially this evening after all was done and so many lives were lost, even that of Ria, whom she felt responsible for.

She was numb for she did not recognize her own reflection. She wanted desperately to find the woman that she was before this battle and the decisions that she had to make and it was lost to her. She knew that she still had to face her son and then her grandsons eventually, if she lived long enough.

It happened sooner than she thought. Suddenly, the blanket to her chamber was violently pulled aside breaking the solitude of her sanctuary. Her reflection was now breached for in the doorway was her son.

"Mother! What have you done! I have nothing!" He ran over to her not knowing whether he should kill her and at the same time desperately wanting her to comfort him for his loss. He trembled before her locked in his tracks.

She stood up and walked over to him, "My boy! Please know that your sons are safe! I wanted to make sure that in case we lost, they would not end up in the hands of Enlil or to be killed by his soldiers!"

He finally lost his composure and fell into her arms like a boy. He forgot his size and she felt herself only with the child that she bore and raised. He wept in her arms and she wept too for all that she had decided and done.

"My son, you fought bravely this day! You will have songs written about you!"

"But, my sons and Ria! How did Ria end up on the battle field?"

Astarte lied and knew that it was for the better, since her son seemed to know nothing of her plans other than what he was told. She knew that in time she would be able to tell him the truth. "That I do not know my son!"

"Where are my sons, mother?"

"They are in safe hands away from all of this. I thought it wise until the threat of Enlil was gone from here."

"But they would have come to no harm regardless, for they are Enlil's heirs as well? He promised me!"

"You should know better than to trust your sons' lives into the hands of that monster! He killed my aunt in cold blood; and never forgets the destruction that he caused in Eshnunna!"

"I do not know what to believe now! My sons!"

"They are safe son! Let us now work on making our armies stronger, for they will return. We have the assurance that they are safe at least."

"Ria, oh Ria!" He collapsed into her arms as he did as a small child and she cried as well joining him in genuine grief at the lost of a mother who truly loved her sons.

Chapter 79

The journey out was silent for they raced to beat the moon high in the sky above them. Au-Set and the others raced to make good time to Kemet and to avoid any residual conflict from the battle. They went in various directions to avoid pursuit and made good time. Eventually they found that they had to cross the great river Phaedrus. Under the moonlight, it appeared fierce and determined. They hastily built barges on the side, while the boys slept in the carts unaware of all that they had endured. The moon was setting to make way for the sun. They tore apart at the carts to make the barges and borrowed wood from the surrounding trees. The boys were deep in their slumber due to the herbal supplements, oblivious to all that had occurred.

Nekhebt Neb-Het supervised the construction of the barges, while Au-Set sat watch over the boys. All was secure for the moment. When the barges were completed, they were all loaded on board and the donkeys on the last barge in the rear.

They set out on the river as the first flakes of snow fell from the sky onto the barges that were covered in dark tents, shading the occupants within from the cold autumn sunrise.

Despite the snow that began to fall heavily, weighing down the canopies, it was unforgiving and roused the sleeping boys within. First, to awake was Pelusias and then his older brother Maneros. Both looked at the two queens and then noticed that they were on boats in an unfamiliar place.

Au-Set had prepared for this moment and had not left their side to make sure that it went as smoothly as possible. "Little ones, you are awake!"

Pelusias spoke first rubbing his eyes looking about in confusion, "Where's Momma?"

Au-Set looked at him and smiled, "She will be along shortly; she will meet us in Kemet."

Then Maneros spoke, "Where's Poppa?"

"He needed to be home to look after Gubla with your grandmother."

They boys seemed to accept this for they had just woken up and cuddled next to Au-Set.

"Look, we have caught some fish for lunch! Are you boys hungry?"

They both nodded and for the moment forgot the confusion around them in their hunger. They were served fish rolled in lettuce and had a container of goats milk passed to them. They were given dried figs for desert. They both sat perched on the side watching their new surroundings as they made their way down the river.

A few hours later as the trees grew thicker; they entered the land of Sumer to reach the great desert. It was then that Maneros first started to wonder about the whole thing. He tugged at Queen Nekhebt's skirt as she sat there looking along the banks, dragging her fingers in the water.

"Aunt, please tell me why Poppa or Momma did not tell us about this? Momma tells us everything." He looked at her expectantly. He was hoping that her answer would solve all of his questions.

"I do not know little one." That certainly was not enough for him. Pelusias looked at his big brother and then started to cry, for he did not care anymore. He had never been away from her for this long at all. He had thought that this was some sort of adventure and his Momma would then meet them on the shores and tell them how brave they were. His uncertainly and the unfamiliar surroundings finally breached his pretended courage.

Pelusias looked up at his brother whom he felt knew everything and saw the questions in his eyes. He wanted this game to be over at once. "Can we go home now?"

Au-Set then moved over to them, put her arms around little Pelusias, and pulled Maneros closer to her, "Brave boys, you know that this is all one great, big adventure? Do you not? Your mother will be waiting for you, but first she had to take care of some important palace matters with your Poppa and Grandmother."

Maneros spoke up vehemently after he pushed out of her embrace, "Mother never lets us alone at all. This does not seem right. I demand to see my mother now!"

Pelusias wriggled out as well, stood over to the side of his big brother, and folded his arms across his chest mimicking Maneros. "I want my Momma now!"

Au-Set was exasperated and wanted to delay telling them the truth until they found out what happened with the battle that was probably being fought as they spoke. She desperately wanted the make sure that the boys were safely in Kemet so that the whole family could be reunited again. She also knew that it would be very hard keeping up appearances while they did not know what was happening.

She paused hoping for the right words to come to her," I swear to you that you are being taken to a place where your family knows of your own safety. We are your family."

Maneros was angry now, "That is not good enough!"

Pelusias looked at her and began to tremble in fright. "I want Momma!" Out of desperation and need, like a panicked doe he looked around anxiously and then jumped off the boat.

One of the handmaidens screamed and others jumped into quick action. Maneros then jumped in after his brother. Au-Set went after them and yelled up to her Scorpion Guard that had silently accompanied them, "Guards fan out and find them, and they do not know how to swim!" The waters were rough and very cold. Two little boys could easily be lost in the dark fast moving depths of the wide river.

Nekhebt stayed on board to wait for them and to arrange blankets and other items to warm them when found. She heard shouts and saw heads bobbing in and out of the water. Her eyes scanned the water and at one point thought, she saw the form of the older brother Maneros, but lost it as soon as it was noticed. She yelled to Au-Set and the others.

"I found something!" It was Tefen. She swam with something in her arms that was covered in her skirt. Her eyes were tear-streaked with pain. On the boat lay the form of Maneros who died trying to save his frantic little brother.

Au-Set clambered wearily onto the boat and cradled the small form in her arms. Frantically she cried out to the search party, "You must find his brother! The water is cold! How will they forgive us?" She cried fruitlessly over the form of Maneros in her pain and grief. She had never lost a child of her own and could not bear the reaction of Ria when she would find out about this.

The boys were left into her keeping. They were supposed to protect the boys! What could have possibly gone wrong? She knew that it was only the unpredictable pace of life was what happened. When there was a decision to be made of such a great magnitude of this, way too many potential things could occur. Too many things could alter the outcome, for way too much was valued here in this.

She knew that the drowning of Maneros was not her fault, but he was left in her care! She would never forgive herself over this. Neb-Het looked at her and then scanned the waves of the river and the searchers.

Neb-Het knew that her sister was taking the blame upon herself, as she was. She knew that their new quest would be the safe return of Pelusias to his mother, rather than the immediate return to Kemet as originally planned. She looked at Au-Set who was cradling the dead boy in her arms as if he were alive. Au-Set nodded at her and she took off her billowy skirt and jumped into the icy depths to join the others in their frantic search. She then decided in a minute moment of clarity from all that spun before her that it would be wise to stay with the original plan of going to Kemet. That was where they were all expected to be.

Chapter 80

Au-Set had seen the barges docked and a great fire was built up for all of those who searched. She cradled the dead boy in her arms and vowed to care for him until they reached Kemet where a tomb would be built for him beside that of her brother Heru in Abdjw, if they allowed her. His coldness seeped into her bones. She did not feel it as Neb-Het gently removed her wet clothes and replaced them with a large dry robe. Neb-Het started to remove the clothes of Maneros when Au-Set stopped her. "No, sister, I will do it." Au-Set then removed his clothes and fought to put the new ones on for his body was growing stiff with death. She placed him in the box that she had brought along that was the ornate chest, which was built by Suti to kill her brother. She placed the boy inside, memorizing the levers.

How ironic was this chest. It was supposed to have been a death trap for Au-Sar, yet in contrast made him more powerful to the people. Now all thought he was a God who had risen from the dead. She wished that the ornate chest had the magical powers that the people believed it did and the boy would wake up from only a sleep. She kept checking to no avail.

They had stayed at that spot for eight days when word finally arrived that the young boys' mother had run into a sword upon gaining knowledge of her sons being taken away. She knew now that Maneros would be with his mother safe in the underworld. Still Pelusias was never found.

Au-Set left behind some of her warriors that she brought along with them and with her sister, her scorpion guard, and the dead Maneros; they made their slow way back to Kemet.

She had initially wanted to return to Gubla, but decided that now was definitely not wise. Knowing that it was one less traumatic event for them to endure after the loss of Baal and Ria as reported to them. She wanted to give them time to heal from the battle and then let them know about Pelusias and Maneros.

Chapter 81

Astarte picked up the pieces of her kingdom and those of her tormented son. Word had finally reached them of the drowning of Maneros and the loss of Pelusias. Her once brave son was lost as was she.

With her family gone, she no longer had the will to fight against the northern tribes that had picked up a more frantic pace with their attacks. She lost her will to fight and so had her son and heir. Neither of them blamed Au-Set or Nekhebt Neb-Het since they knew that they were as lost as they were and perhaps more with guilt.

Her son was even more of a ghost and walked about the palace in a daze. He would not eat and slept all day. One day he walked out of the palace grounds and never returned.

Astarte was falling deeper into oblivion by the day. She began to look at her life. What was it all for? She wondered. She had no family to leave anything to anymore. There was no other word of Pelusias. He just disappeared like his own father. Her heart was numb.

Qedeshet finally decided to take action. "Astarte, let us go home!" Therefore, they went, giving up her palace and her name of Anat and all that she had built up her whole life. For she was still young in age, only twenty eight, but her soul felt like it was ancient and had seen too much.

On the journey to Kemet, she cried endlessly into the warm arms of Qedeshet. She could no longer remember what her mother looked like and did not know what to expect.

Chapter 82

Astarte was greeted with the usual hospitality due to another ruler with a lavish banquet. Due to the rather temperate day, it was held on the roof of their palace with oil lamps placed along the sides. It was truly sumptuous as was the style of Ua-Zit. She basked in the joy of seeing her daughter once again after so many years and saw how time and events had caught up with her. Her heart wept for her daughter. She saw how rigid Astarte sat as did the others since they had received word of the events.

After the banquet Ua-Zit summoned her daughter to her own sleeping chambers as she did when a little girl. They both curled up in each other's arms hoping for those simpler days long ago. Both mother and daughter desperately wanting time to have never arrived to this day.

The days wore on and Astarte was like a ghost, not caring to hear news of Gubla nor of anything else. She had found quarters of her own, locked her-self in there and had even reached the point of not accepting any food.

Ua-Zit desperate and determined saw how this resembled the actions of her own sister Nekhebt Nemothi. She would not let her own daughter succumb to the power of desolation and to become vulnerable as her sister had all alone. She refused to let that happen. She tried fruitlessly to entice her daughter out of her chambers on many occasions, never giving up hope. She felt that her daughter was truly wasting away and chose to let life pass her by. It seemed as if Astarte had given up and was patiently waiting for death, as she refused to participate in life.

Finally, one day, Ua-Zit broke the respected bounds of privacy and had the door broken in to the chamber of her daughter. When she entered the room, she had thought that her daughter was dead, as she was so still on the pallet.

Ua-Zit ran over to her daughter and covered her. Astarte was startled and her glazed look focused to that her of mother. Ua-Zit noticed that she looked starved. She scanned the room and found rotted plates of untouched food, some covered in cobwebs, and some in bugs. All of the chamber windows were covered in dark fabric as if her daughter wanted only to live in death, or, perhaps she was trying to re-create her own tomb. She had noticed that the only thing that was being consumed by her daughter was wine. Broken amphorae were scattered about the room and a drinking goblet lay by her pallet half-full.

Ua-Zit was desperate for her daughter to return to normal. She completely understood, but she refused to let her give up so easily. She angrily kicked the goblet off the table and watched it break. She then bent over her daughter and shook her. Calling out to her guards, she had her daughter brought back to her own sleeping chambers.

She sat with Astarte, every day for two days until she had recovered enough to reach her through the haze and withdrawal shakes. One day after her daughter was bathed; Ua-Zit decided that Astarte was ready to face her life again.

"Daughter, you know that I love you deeply, but you must get on with your life! This has gone on long enough."

"I am sorry mother, but I refuse to care again. I have lost everything. I have nothing left!"

"You can start again!"

"Oh can I? Moreover, what about all that I have lost? Huh? Shall I toss it away as if it never occurred? Shall I pretend that my son was never born? My grandsons? In addition, what about the order that I gave that killed Ria and her sons! My orders and plans!"

"Dear I understand how you must feel."

"Do you really? Have you ever raised a child and then lost them because of words or commands that you have given?"

"You know that it was not your fault."

"And how do I know this mother! I ordered my grandsons to be removed from their mother for their own safety! I had hoped to work on things and to return them to Ria and that everything would be alright!"

"But, you did what you thought was right. You made the order on your best instincts for their own welfare! You thought like a queen and the representative of Anat!" In a softer tone she added, "You did the right thing....hush now dear. Things have a way of working out in the end."

"It is the end for me. I have nothing. I do not want anything anymore. Everything that I have fought hard for is gone! My son, my grandsons, my Baal!"

"What about Rashef, he is here with you."

"No, he was never with me out of love, only duty. He is home and free to return. I have no longer need of his services."

"Daughter do not give up hope! You can still have children you are young. Your life awaits you."

"I do not want it anymore!"

"Look at all that you have in Gubla daughter, you need to return. Many people depend on you and wait for you."

"They do not. I left the city for Enlil!"

"I hope daughter that you have not! Our family has kept that land from time out of time, since the beginning of history! You would just throw it all away because your life turns out less than perfect? Have you lost your sense of duty?" Ua-Zit was beginning to lose her temper for she felt her heart beat faster as the words her daughter just told her. The idea of abandoning a born post was blasphemy to her.

Ua-Zit tried to be nice to her daughter and to have her see reason and realized that it was hopeless. "Astarte, you must get up and face your life. You were born into your life you have no choice! Your family was obviously not meant to be, that one at least. Anat has made her decision." She probed her daughter with her icy look of determination.

Astarte just sat there stubbornly and locked her gaze with that of her mother. "My family was obviously not meant to be?" She repeated for the horrid sound of it. "How could you say such a thing?"

"Daughter, I had faced the same thing long ago. I have lost children too and then you, my first born."

"Mother, why did you not run after me? Why did you not hide me? Was duty so important to you that you would just let me go?"

"You must understand I was born into this family, like you. I had no choice. I made a pact to rule in Kemet. I had no choice. You know this. Why return to the past. It is over! You must do the same and move on to find out what your next duty is. You must gain back Gubla, for that is what you were born to rule. You would be committing the most grievous of blasphemies if you turn your back on the Goddess. I will not let you to this."

Astarte turned her back on her mother and ignored her. Ua-Zit knew that she would not get any further and then stormed out of the room leaving Astarte there in her stubborn silence. Ua-Zit threw her hands up in the air in desperation.

The next morning they had found that Astarte had vanished without telling anyone. She just slipped out of the palace in the middle on the night. Ua-Zit wept and for some reason knew that it would be the last time that she would ever see her daughter again.

Chapter 83

Astarte just could not stay in the palace of her mother for one minute longer. Therefore, she packed up what little belongings she had. She walked straight out of the city of Per-Uto and followed the wind. She had neither idea where she was going or what she would do when she arrived. She was not even sure that she wanted to settle anywhere.

She knew that she had obligations and things that she just had to do. Nevertheless, she did not care. She knew that she was young enough to start over once again. However, she did not care.

Astarte knew that she had come a long way from when she was young and learning her reign in Gubla. Back then, she was very pliable and fell into whatever people wanted her to do. Was this her normal nature? To simply accept things? She hoped that it was not.

She recalled that she felt elated when she became a mother and that her whole agenda had changed. It brought her out of a gray existence and made her life full of meaning. When her darling Melanchor was born her life simply fell into place. She wanted to make sure that his life would be full and happy. She trained him to be the best ruler possible. She helped him to look for a proper mate.

It was amazing how life decided things for you and complicated every good intention. When she was young, it was simple. She was trained to rule and to be the Goddess representative of Anat. Everything was given to her, even before she knew she needed it. Her word was law for as long as she could remember.

She ruled the land and it loved her in return. The people gave and she gave to them. It was very black and white then. Until the day, she became a mother. After she had her first child that was a son, people then waited for a daughter from her. None came. No other children came from her womb at all.

That was when she decided that she would focus all of her love, plans, and attentions on her son. She told her council that he would take as consort a woman of good blood worthy to fill her role as Anat.

Yet, her son decided otherwise. He did not accept any of the women she had found for him. The good women that she and her council chose were from ancient blood and some were even beautiful and had a good sense of humor. What more could he want? She gave him everything that he could possibly want as a child he needed nothing. Nevertheless, he was never happy and felt that he was entitled to everything. Nothing ever satisfied him, even as a child.

Then one day he arrived with Ria. Ria was definitely beautiful and full of charm and turned out to be a good mother as well. In all good sense of the situation, she would have been the perfect mate for her son. Yet, she was not.

When Ria first arrived, Astarte had hoped that she could train the woman to take on her power. The woman appeared weak and pliable, yet stubborn. There was no reaching a woman who had been brainwashed from birth to be subservient to her mate. It sickened her that Ria had no backbone at all.

Ria was however, the perfect mate for her son, for everything Ria did was for her husband and sons. Ria did not know the meaning of the word, "selfish". She had a break since Ria entered her son's life, in that the young queen took on the overwhelming burden of pleasing Melanchor.

As she walked in this land and made shelter wherever she was too tired to walk anymore, she had plenty of time to reflect on matters.

Though Ria appeared docile and simple, Astarte could not help that the woman had a great hidden strength that was perhaps more intense than her own. Though the strength of Ria was hidden deep inside of her, her own was obvious and for all to see, still she wondered about it.

Even if they were born as simple peasants, Ria would have been the ideal mate for her husband. She was a loving and devoted mate and mother. Her hearth-place was immaculate and filled with things that she made for her family out of love and meaning. She made a safe and loving home for her family.

As Astarte walked aimlessly through the land of Kemet, she often found herself jealous of Ria and even wishing that she had the strength to stick to what she really wanted out of life, instead of following the rules set before her birth and just falling into the expected role.

It was sad how she refused to look at this side of her daughter-in-law until after her death. How it never occurred to her the weakness of Ria was really her strength. It was just not appropriate for her time and station in life. It would have been accepted and even admired in another land or time, thought Astarte.

As long as she could remember, she wanted nothing more than to be a mother. She would dream at night of having the freedom to love her family, without any worries of the land that she must rule over to distract her as it often did. Was she really the weaker one!

The more Astarte walked and thought to herself, she began to admire Ria and the life that she led. The more she started to hate herself for not knowing this woman and for doubting her. Ria was the ideal mother; she died for her sons when she realized that they were no more. Ria knew that no one could give her sons the love that she could. Maybe Ria felt herself useless, when she found that her sons were taken away from her. She would now never know the answer to that question.

Therefore, the fallen queen wandered until she cleared out all of the cobwebs from her tired soul. Her feet were bare and her clothes ragged. She looked as humble as she felt. She had stopped occasionally when weary, to weave herself a small hammock to sleep in. Her life was simple and this she needed.

In the evening, she would stop to hang up her hammock between some palm trees and then fall into the dream world where all she thought of during the day caught up with her and tormented her soul.

Finally, she found herself at a large fortress appeared magical. When she approached, she had gained from the villages that she had reached Ineb-Hedj, the home of Mut and Khephra and their family.

Astarte decided that this might be a good place to stop and to contact her family, since she knew that this was the home of her aunt's former concubine Re. She also knew that Re was the father of her cousin, Tehuti. She did not know that he was also the father of her Cousin Au-Set's twin daughters.

She found her self-welcomed by the family. They knew whom she was and took her in to stay for while.

Chapter 84

After a few weeks, Mut requested a private meal with Astarte to discuss her future. Astarte arrived in the chambers of this woman and noticed her lying down on soft pillows eating figs. Re was beside her as interpreter, for Mut had not spoken one word in many months. Mut referred to it as a "fast of words." Mut did this often for she believed that it cleansed her soul to do this. They had a language that she and her family had developed with their hands to communicate for her mind was clear and she was still the family matriarch.

Astarte sat down beside the cheerful woman, and knew that this discussion was important.

Re spoke first, "My mother wishes to know why you no longer listen to your own mother? She wishes to know many things, but we will start with that one. Is that fair to you?"

"Yes, very. You see, I love my mother dearly and it is not that I refuse to listen to her. It is just that it was hard to bow down to her when I have ruled alone for so long. I am or was a grandmother. I am no longer young and pliable."

"Understood. Mother respects this. However, do you not respect the sense of duty that you were born to?"

"I do, however, what is there that is left for me? All has been lost. I would have to start all over and I am not ready to part with all that I had. I do not know where either my son or my youngest grandson is. It was if they disappeared." Her eyes dropped and Mut reached over to embrace her and looked up at her son.

"Mut understands and sends her love, but also states that you must not give up on them, yet, you still are young enough to find a new mate and to take back Gubla. It is not lost you know. It could easily be returned to your family to rule again."

"It is too far gone under the dominion of Enlil. Besides, who would mate with me? I have only had one son and no more. I could possibly be barren."

Mut placed her hands gently on Astarte's womb and nodded her head vehemently.

Re looked at Astarte, "No, you are not barren. Life is waiting to be created within you. Perhaps the seed of Rashef is dead. Mut suggests that possibly you leave Rashef to this land and find another consort. She has been in correspondence with your mother, Nekhebt and Au-Set. Nekhebt Neb-Het left Suti for reasons, which she would not divulge and is now in Per-Uto. Suti needs a consort of royal lineage. However, she needs to be strong enough to tame him for he is wild and needs to be brought in line. They all wonder if you would be the one to be able to do this... Any child born from your womb and from Suti would be powerful indeed. Mut thinks perhaps there are daughters waiting to be born from you that would change the whole land of Kemet."

"I suppose that I have had enough time to just wander. My feet are tired and my soul yearns for a new challenge. I have heard that Suti has a powerful army that he is raising in the Deshret. Is there any truth to this?" Mut and Re nodded.

"Then perhaps I would be up to the challenge. Do you think that Suti would allow me to help lead his army so that I could take back Gubla?"

"You would have to make it worth his wile. He never gives anything to anyone. There is something he needs, though. He needs an heir." Re voiced in concern.

"We will make all of the arrangements and you think about what you can bargain with Suti, so that you both will win in the end."

Chapter 85

Astarte thought about this and composed a letter to Suti. In the letter, she requested a deal. She mentioned that she would offer herself in sacred union providing that he give her equal share in the control of his army. She offered to train the army to take back Gubla so she could reign there once again. In return, she would have her forces available for his defense and that of Kemet. She mentioned that she would keep her first-born daughter to be the heir of Gubla after her and that Suti would have the other children born to them. Another stipulation was that she and her first-born daughter would return to Gubla after the second child was born and the army was trained enough to gain back her throne.

Astarte hated the thought of giving up a child that she had not borne yet, but she knew of his reputation and did not want to be around him for longer than she had to. She also stipulated that Qedeshet and a council that she had trained would remain behind with the second child to make sure that her interests were met on behalf of the child and that the child would know her and remember her.

Suti agreed to her contract and accepted her as his consort. Astarte knew that by going down to rule beside Suti, she would also be secretly keeping an eye on him for the family, for they were very mistrustful of him due to past events.

Chapter 86

Astarte arrived at the city of Djedu and was impressed with what Suti had done to the city. She was not naïve at all anymore and saw right through the charming exterior. She knew that he must have some serious problems for Nekhebt Neb-Het to give up her seat of rule for the safety of Lower Kemet.

She took this on as the challenge that she greatly needed. She accepted the banquets and feast in her honor as there should be. She smiled back at the charming Suti, though refused to let her-self be fooled by him. Astarte waited like a silent cobra for his façade to drop. She in fact, eagerly anticipated this, for then the fun would begin. She knew that at this point, she had nothing to lose, and if she played this game right, had everything to win.

Thus, she sat back and enjoyed the entertainment while it lasted. She gave it four sunsets and was surprised just a little bit when it took eight for Suti's false façade to drop. Finally, he decided to let Puanit sit by his side.

This occurred one evening for the final meal of the day. He looked at her boldly. She smiled and quietly went over to the timid woman by his side and whispered in her ear.

"Puanit, here are the rules. I am in charge here and you are not. Simple as that! If I find you in his bed even for a brief moment, you will breathe your last!" This was stated softly, though loud enough for Suti to hear and to make her point clear. Puanit blushed and silently left the chamber.

Suti guffawed in laughter at the boldness of this woman. He clapped his hands, "One point for Astarte, this will be fun indeed."

"Indeed it will. You are younger than I am and obviously have much to learn. I forgive your neglectful upbringing, but it will stop right now. We have a bargain and I intend to see it through." She smiled up at him enjoying this immensely. He smiled back at her and actually admired her audacity.

Suti wondered how much she could take. He knew that she almost fell apart at the loss of her family in Gubla and hoped that he would be able to make her bend. He did want an heir and felt that his Set was too much under the wing of her mother.

He decided that he would have fun playing this game, for Astarte seemed for the moment a formidable opponent. As soon as the meal was completed he gave the order for her chambers to be locked from the outside, sealing her in. He laughed to himself and wondered if she would get out of this one.

Chapter 87

When Astarte woke the next morning, she was shocked to find that she was locked inside. At first she was angry and then she sat back to think. She was not a foolish woman and had prepared for this and made a chirping sound like a bird. This was a signal.

Since the time of her arrival, she had made sure to gain allies and had brought along her own contingent. Suti was obviously ignorant to this.

It did not take long for the doors to be opened. Then she sauntered through them to join Suti for the morning meal. She felt that this was too easy, though did not let her guard down for one moment.

She had even secretly befriended Puanit behind Suti's back. She had gained fast knowledge of the sad woman's torrid abuse from Set under the twisted guise of love. Astarte felt for this poor creature and had learned that he treated her no better than he treated a slave. It was easy for Puanit to fall over to her side. All Astarte gave her was love and the confidence that she never was allowed to have. She also warned Puanit to keep their friendship silent for her own protection. Astarte promised that she would save Puanit and take her back to Gubla. She was even teaching the woman to defend herself in the ways of the ancient Catal-Huyuk. She knew that Puanit would be a valuable ally in the years to come, providing that Puanit not let Suti know of her change. Puanit proved to be intelligent when allowed to thrive; she even began to enjoy playing her role.

With all of this arming and preparation, Astarte walked into the dining chamber with a large smile on her face as if nothing at all happened.

She had to keep from laughing when Suti noticed her and almost choked on his milk in surprise.

"My dear are you alright?" She went over to him and told him, "Breathe slowly, it is okay. How was your evening?"

Gaining his composure and wondering if his wishes were carried out, he managed to gasp out, "Fine, the milk tastes sour!"

She looked over to the servants to have his replaced with a fresh goblet. "And how is your favorite lettuce this morning? I picked it myself from the gardens and the bread was just removed from the ovens at day break." She smiled wickedly to let him know that the game was well underway.

"My word, you are impressive woman! You are like a cat!" Both of them laughed and ate their meal in obvious mirth, knowing that this would actually be quite fun indeed.

Suti was essentially beginning to find that he wanted this older woman around and that very evening sought her out to find out what made this woman so delicious to him. He was not disappointed; in fact, he had learned some things that he had not thought possible. He found that he actually wanted to be with her. He had never felt this way before. He had forgotten his usual tastes and actually searched her out. He had even found himself wanting to impress her. However, he did love the way she played with him and would not give up trying to put her off guard. The games were what attracted him to her, for she always saw through him and this only intrigued him.

He marveled at the wisdom that she had in governing Upper Kemet and how people seemed to cherish her presence, as did he. She was also a very skilled warrior and he loved the strange animal that she brought with her that she called a horse. She looked like a Goddess when she rode this animal.

Even the pets that everybody feared seemed to love her. She coddled to them as if they were her own children and he found himself falling deeper into her spell. Nobody had ever interested him before as she did. With her, he found that he had actually found his match.

Suti let her make some changes to his army that he called the Deshret after the Red Land of the desert from which he recruited most of them and where their training base was set up. Days were starting to make sense to him and thus went by with ease. He longed for the days when she was training his Deshret guard, for she looked powerful indeed!

One day she approached him and informed him that she was pregnant. He was elated and tried to treat her as if she were the most fragile thing in the world. She told him not to and smiled at him.

Astarte noticed the change in Suti and actually began to have hope for him, seeing that he had almost abandoned all of his bad habits and was trying to please her. She did not let down her guard though. She knew that as soon as he became bored, he could easily return to his old ways. She wondered if he was merely growing up, but would not let herself forget the vile deeds that he had done that so many people had reported to her.

He still played the occasional trick on her to test her, but she knew that he was losing ideas for them. She began to play tricks on him in good humor. He relished in them and anticipated them almost as if they were a drug that he craved. She learned that he would not ever be satisfied with the normal, that he needed challenges in order to survive. She also knew that it distracted him from tormenting the local villagers and kept him out of trouble.

One day after training the Deshret army, Suti and Astarte decided to rest under a tree in the shade. Suti uttered rather eloquently, "I was thinking of taking over the rule here in Djedu as Nekhebt."

Astarte thought this funny and started to laugh when she saw that he was serious. Not wanting to offend him, she decided to approach him politically and carefully on the matter, "Suti, do you honestly think the people will accept a man in a woman's role? Besides, Neb-Het was made Nekhebt and not you."

"Yes, but she is in Per-Uto, how can she rule this land when she is not even here."

"Good point. What are you planning? How do you think that this can work? Not that I do not doubt you, it is just that it eludes me. That is all."

"I am aghast, you the 'Mistress of all Answers', cannot you think of some way to make this work. I am sure that we can come up with something."

"Let us both think on this, for you have a good point. Neb-Het does not seem to want to return to the land that is ruled by Nekhebt the Goddess. In order to do that, she needs to be present."

Therefore, that evening they both sent a letter to Ua-Zit and told her of this dilemma.

Chapter 88

Neb-Het returned after much persuasion by Ua-Zit and Au-Set, for they needed her desperately to keep an eye on Astarte and Suti. Neb-Het agreed that she return only to rule in Nekhen and to leave the rule of Djedu to Astarte and Suti. Neb-Het wanted as much distance as possible from Suti.

He was still tormented on her wondrous son Anpu that was fathered by Au-Sar. Suti threatened to kill the child and to expose it to the wrath of the Deshret, should she leave him alone for one moment. This continued for almost a year until Neb-Het finally sent little Anpu up north under the protection of Au-Set and Au-Sar. She pleaded with Astarte to talk with Suti on this matter, which she knew was to no avail. She had learned from experience that no one would be able to reach Suti on any matter that he had set firm against and this was the most stubborn one yet. He wanted nothing to do with little Anpu.

The thing that made Neb-Het part with her son was the last time Suti tormented the child. On this particular day, little Anpu was out playing in the fields watching the longhaired bulls graze in the sweltering sun. Their long horns curved outward several feet and sparkled in the sun. Little Anpu had wandered out there as usual rooted in the spot in fascination of them in a youthful curious daze. All of a sudden, out of nowhere came a wild boar that ran into the field sending the cattle in a frenzied panic. Little Anpu was almost run over in the panic by the small herd. Little Anpu was found shaking in the empty field and had soiled his normally neat kilt in fear.

He stuttered what had happened and instantly the mother's instinct kicked in. Neb-Het knew from her first view of him that Suti had taken his threats to the next level so deep was his hatred for the boy. She knew that Suti was the cause of the stampede of the normally peaceful herd. To her further dismay and as usual for the nature of Suti, he was nowhere to be found nor was there any evidence of his duplicity and guilt in this.

Chapter 89

At the loss of her Anpu, Neb-Het focused her attentions elsewhere. She decided to complete the dream that was never accomplished for Nekhen. She started with the demolition of the old villages of round huts that were arranged in circles all over the place in confusion. It was such a maze that one had to have been born in this vast confusion to know where any place was. She decided that it all had to go. She then hired masons and bricklayers to build her city. She arranged streets that were sided by stone and mud-brick rectangular buildings that could be built up two and sometimes three stories in height instead of the normal one-story dwellings that had long occupied the area.

She wanted a real city like those she remembered back in Eshnunna, not the one story rectangular dwellings common to this land. She wanted something grand comparable to what she could recall of the city that her mother once ruled. She even had a large oval courtyard constructed out of stone pillars and cobblestones with the buildings of her main court jutting out like petals of a flower. Her palace was made of the tallest trees of cedar imported from Retenu. She had large pillars carved in wood with vines carved spiraling down them and painted to appear as living. She would finally make a reality out of all of the dreams of her youth in this city. This city was the city that she had to rule without her beloved son Anpu. She was too overcome with the grief at the loss of her son that she became naturally engrossed in creating Nekhen as the great city of her childhood dreams.

She had noticed that as soon as the streets were cleared away and the first of her new streets were laid out, people came in droves from out of nowhere to witness and to be a part of this new city. It was a sight that some of them had never seen the likes of before in their whole lives.

With first hundreds and then thousands of people arriving as the city grew around her, Neb-Het had to find some way to be able to support the new population and to house them. Therefore, she and Au-Set came up with the idea of requesting a certain amount of pottery and goods collected from each family to support the growing population and to grant them admittance to reside in her new city. In turn she promised them work on the actual city itself and even offered to pay them for their labor in a daily ration of bread and beer. She also promised them with their offerings to the city, to protect them.

Around the city, the wall initially built by Suti and then soon abandoned for his new city of Djedu, was not only added to but also enlarged and made taller as well. She even set in reasonable distances, towers made of wood to serve as lookouts. She had this wall expanded to encircle her growing city with large copper plated doors that would close to protect them from an invading army.

She was now in the process of building her temple to worship Innana made of huge slabs of stone from a local newly found quarry. It was erected and topped with a large wooden platform to emulate the mound where her mother once worshipped. On top of it would be built the temple itself out of stone. The wooden platform would contain hanging gardens, making it look more like a mountain from her ancestral homeland than ever when completed.

She looked out from the balcony of her palace and it made her proud, all that she created in her name on her own ideas. She looked down upon the open courtyards of her merchants in her growing city and saw them deep in their work of making pottery, mace-heads or tools of flint. She could see into their tiny worlds by looking down on the open part of their houses in the front attached to the streets. Under the roofs of each half-roofed dwelling, their lives were private. Sometimes on humid evenings, she could see the lucky ones in the highest dwellings sleep under canopies exposed to the open sky. She was on the highest part of the town and was able to look down upon them all; she felt like the Goddess and that the people believed that she was. Finally, she had come home and into her own being, as she never had before. She had accomplishments to be proud of and now, a legacy to leave her son.

Chapter 90

Nekhebt Neb-Het welcomed her sunlight and other half in rapture when Au-Set arrived with her growing son Anpu who was now five years old. Au-Set brought along with her some of her children, her oldest daughter Set, Weret-Heka, Renenutet, and the youngest twins that were raised with Anpu, who were Maat and Serqet. The three youngest children ran off to play together along with their older sisters out in the new gardens of the palace complex while the twin mothers reunited as if they had never parted over the past few years.

Both had talked long into the evening hours about how it had been for the years in which they were separated. Au-Set told Neb-Het that she and Au-Sar rekindled their relationship to a better point than it ever was. Neb-Het told her sister how she and Hetep were finally pregnant with their first child. Anpu's paternity was not brought up and had long since been forgiven. In turn, the paternity of Maat and Serqet was never questioned by anyone in the family. Not that the paternity of their children really mattered in the family hierarchy as long as they came from their maternal line, they just did not want to hurt anyone's feelings, as men could be quite sensitive about their virility.

Neb-Het had called for the assistance of her sister in her latest pregnancy from Hetep, whom they both hoped would be a girl. They had planned that if it were to be a girl, she would become united with Merul, who was back at the palace with Tehuti. Merul had displayed great promise of becoming a scribe with the famous picture writing that was fast spreading throughout all of Kemet as the latest rage. It was a 'must have' for all public and private buildings for the living and for the dead. Merul was talented in this and Au-Set was very proud of him. His works of art were fast filling the land of Kemet with wonder and they all knew that he might actually outdo Tehuti, the founder and creator of the *"medu necher"* or the *"words of the Gods."*

Neb-Het did not want to be alone in this pregnancy since she was already in her late twenties and felt that she was almost past her childbearing years. This pregnancy had come to her and Hetep as a wonderful surprise and blessing from the Goddess, the whole family was ecstatic over the very idea of it, while Neb-Het worried herself sleepless.

Thus, Au-Set made the great journey to the far north of their land to be at the side of her sister and to bring along to her for comfort her own son who was growing into quite a little wild man.

Anpu was always trying to tame the wild jackals of the town and had already found two baby cubs for his own to raise and had named them Aha and Mene. Au-Set had initially thought that they were wild dogs but was soon corrected after the boy had become deeply attached to them, much to her dismay. Well, it only made her smile at the reality of it and how her family seemed to prefer animals of the wild as pets than those more common.

The only person in her family who actually had a tame and easy pet was her own father Geb, who was always seen with his prized Goose. They heard stories as young children of how their mother called him lovingly, "the Great Cackler" due to his incredible ability to mimic the sound of it. Geese would come scampering from afar when he let out his infamous cackle to amuse her mother.

Other than that, her family members were legendary for their wild pets and becoming more so. Her brother Suti with his wild boars and the large grey dog, her daughter Bast with her lion pride that she had raised from cubs, her aunt Ua-Zit with her iarets whom she had charmed from their own poison. Even her other aunt Nekhebt had her hawks that she kept in cages and whispered and sang to them as if they were her lost daughters. Little Heru even kept a hawk of his own.

The list went on and on and growing larger with each new child. Serqet preferred scorpions, of which she removed their poison sacks; they ran to her as well when she called. Her own docile brother the scribe kept a flock of ibis. Renenutet and Weret-Heka had lately fond their own scorpions like their younger sister Serqet who had taught them how to remove their poison, so they would not be harmed. Even her own snakes such as those her mother kept and her Scorpion Guard named after some she had trained long ago as she had taught her own daughters.

How her family loved to dance with death and to display it for the amusement of the common people for which it appeared as if they had sacred powers over their ability to conquer the untamable. They simply had great patience and knew the arts of removing poison left over from their ancient matriarchal lines from long before history was ever written as passed down to their daughters. Therefore, her family walked beside death and laughed in its face.

Neb-Het looked at her sister who sat beside her with a sly grin on her face. "Sister, what are you thinking about?"

"Just how our family treads on the face of danger with even our pets..."

The look on Neb-Het's face was almost as comical as the thoughts of Au-Set. Au-Set continued to elaborate her thoughts to her sister, "Oh, it is just that I was thinking how it must look to someone who is outside of our family."

Since Neb-Het still looked confused, Au-Set added even further in depth, "With our pets, sister... To a family not from the priestly caste, our choice of pets must look quite frightening. You and I know that we would never risk our family and its power was really mocking death."

Neb-Het smiled, "I see what you mean. I had never really thought about how it must appear to someone looking in on our family. It must look quite frightening indeed! With all of the seemingly untamed and wild animals that find the way into our homes and especially to our children in finding them. How off that it must look!" They both burst out in giggles.

Neb-Het added, "I wonder what this child will find to frighten off the people of this land!"

Chapter 91

While the sisters were waiting for the child of Neb-Het's entrance into the world, they worked on building up the city of Nekhen. The women's house was prepared as well for the all too imminent arrival of the baby.

Au-Set worked on setting up a better taxation system for the building to the town and its wall that was almost completed. The people did not seem to mind since they were gaining their security and peace of mind. They always feared an attack, especially from Suti.

While they were building up the city of Nekhen, the city of Djedu was neglected. No matter how strong an influence that Astarte was to their brother, Suti would always be Suti. He was always preparing an army for conquering all of Kemet for his own, or so the reports stated that came back from Astarte.

Even Re was stirring up some trouble from down south in Ineb-Hedj. Re claimed that he deserved a fair share of the rule in Kemet. His claim was as being the consort of their mother Ninnuit and in being the father of Tehuti. He also whispered that he would reveal the paternity of Au-Set's children to her family if she did not give him more to rule.

Au-Set was flustered over this since Re had seemed quite content in the area that he had taken rule over. She had a few people check up on his progress and found Re quite happy. He was a more than able angler, despite the rivalry from his brother over the new prominence in business that he was establishing. He had even named his boat 'the boat of millions', which meant that this boat would stomp on and catch millions of fish. She smiled at Re and his entrepreneur talents.

Still Au-Set was surprised that with all of his success that he would want still more from her. Had she not given him enough? She knew that her family would not be angry with her over his paternity of the twins, still she had made great progress with Au-Sar, and they were happier than they had ever been and she did not want to hurt his feelings.

She also knew in her heart that what had actually prompted Re's latest feelings of discord was in her putting off the union of her Merul and his daughter Sekhmet. Sekhmet was nearing fifteen and was hoping for something soon. Au-Set just sighed for there was really nothing that she could do but make sure that the defenses were kept up in Nekhen and Per-Uto. She had also received a distressing note that Ua-Zit was ill and it had lasted for quite some time. Au-Sar, Tehuti, and Nebmaat feared for her. With all of this and no power to do anything but wait, she just placed her writing implements back in its case and waited for the birth of her latest niece or nephew. She was hoping for a girl that she would have for Merul rather than Re's daughter Sekhmet. She had promised her mother long ago as had her sister's that the unions must be kept as close as possible until their reign in Kemet was more secure.

Chapter 92

Finally, the day had arrived when Neb-Het felt the first stirring of life waiting to enter the earthly realm. They had all rushed her over to the women's house to wait and to comfort her until the harsh labor began.

Neb-Het was anxious and prayed to the Goddess that she would deliver a daughter, for she yearned desperately for one. Her son Anpu and the other men were nervous for they had noticed her waning health over the last three months and how her body seemed to thrive in the last stage of her pregnancy. She looked pale and weak. The other mother's in the women's house silently prayed for their queen, that she would survive this ordeal.

Neb-Het fought on like the bravest soldier that Au-Set had ever known and she was deeply proud of her sister. She knew that Neb-Het was fighting with strength that she did not believe that she even had.

As the greatest pain of the labor had begun, Au-Set gripped her sister frantically and willed her strength into her. It did seem to work, for after what seemed like an eternity, she had finally given birth to a tiny baby girl named *Meshkenet*.

After the women had all rejoiced while Neb-Het slept the sleep of the dead, after all that she had been through, the women brought up the tiny Meshkenet for her father to hold and for the whole city of Nekhen to rejoice over.

Neb-Het knew that now that she had her daughter and enough protection, she would be on her own with her two little wonders Anpu and Meshkenet. She would never let them out of her sight, ever, she had vowed to herself. Hetep knew this, understood, and silently returned to his own chamber, knowing that he had no choice. He had performed his duty; she had her miraculous daughter, which had given back her strength to rule, as she always should have. Now he knew that Neb-Het finally had her confidence back and that she would let nothing deter her from protecting her family and in bringing them great power. He just sat back and watched her glow with pride, a pride that he was never able to give her.

Chapter 93

After a while of a seemingly long peace, Au-Set had heard the first of another line of threats to her beloved Per-Uto from Re once again. Even Suti for once was quiet. She wondered if Suti was really waiting for the death of Ua-Zit. In lieu of this, she had strengthened the city walls to an even greater height and had set out regular patrols. Her Scorpion Guard never left her side, even when she was asleep.

She decided to approach Ua-Zit on her concerns. She had decided to meet with her aunt after their evening meal, while they both relaxed on top of the roof of the palace under the canopy of stars.

On clear evenings such as this one, Au Set loved to imagine that the stars were in reality her own mother who loved them so. She imagined from her earliest memories that her mother's body was arched over the earth covered in a thick rode of celestial stars in protection over her children so far away from the land of their birth. She painted this image on many of her new temples so deep was it etched in her mind. At each thought of it, she clenched the necklace given by her mother close to her beating heart in preservation of her honor and memory.

Both of them sat there seemingly content with all on the world, yet inside, both of them were about to collapse from the recent reports. The insects droned on and about the glory of the evening, waiting for the appearance of the moon to make its ascent in the sky.

"Aunt, I do not like silence. Rabble I can deal with but silence, it makes me nervous."

"I agree." Ua-Zit sat there wrapped in her robes even though the evening was almost sweltering. Au-Set ignored this, for she knew that it hurt her aunt's pride. Au-Set had regretfully noticed that Ua-Zit was getting ill and she might not recover. They had found a growth under her arm, which seemed to take over the body of her aunt. Her aunt was always a healthy and voluptuous woman, though lately, she seemed to be wasting away. Even her aunt's hair had lost its shine.

She was gaunt and appeared only a soft whisper of the physical woman that she always was.

Through it all, Ua-Zit kept up her air of decorum and the regality that she always had as a queen. She acted as though she were still in the prime of her strength. She extended her fragile and bony arm to her niece's shoulder for comfort and understanding.

Au-Set smiled and felt the warmth of her aunt's love for her, from her cold body. "I think that this is probably not a good sign from Suti. I know that Astarte is doing everything in her power to warn us.... I do not know, but something is up. For we have not heard from Astarte in over a whole moon cycle. And it is never good when Suti is silent."

"I agree dear, but what can we do about it?" Ua-Zit whispered as if afraid to break the silence of the sleeping Gods in their brightness above them.

Inside her, this upset Au-Set, for her aunt was never at a loss for a plan and this made her mortality even more real to her. She shivered when she compared it with the loss of her mother so many years ago, that she had never recovered from and knew that she never would. She needed her aunt and her wisdom. Her aunt gave her the strength to rule, for in the absence of her mother, she always had the comfort of her aunt being there and guiding her.

"I fear for my daughter. Is she safe with Suti? I never should have sent her down there. Do you think that he caught on?"

"I hope not, though I do not really think that it would matter, if he did. For he would risk so much, if he were to actually do something to her, for it would provoke much more than he is capable of dealing with."

Ua-Zit nodded her assent at this. "And what of Re? Is he the greater threat? You knew him intimately did you not dear?"

Au-Set looked over at her in astonishment, "However did you know?" Though they had discussed this years ago, Au-Set went along with things in fear of upsetting her aunt whom she loved with all her heart. Ua-Zit had forgotten their talk on the matter years ago.

"I may be ill, but I am not dead yet dear!" She smiled and continued, "For I remember that he had the charms that no woman could resist, even your mother. Good thing that he escaped when he did from Eshnunna, for had he stayed longer, your mother would never had let him be sacrificed and it would have set all of our families plans asunder. For all I now, your mother probably even helped Re in his escape. No one will ever know." She smiled at this.

"Aunt, did you find him handsome?"

"Aye that I did for I knew of his family in Kemet. His mother Mut was a beautiful woman and his father, the incredibly talented Khephra was equally beautiful. All of Kemet bowed down to their beauty."

She continued in her memory of the family of Re, "I find it rather odd that Re would even be any kind of threat at all, due to the ways of his parents. They were beautiful, but intelligent and loving as well. Something must be off with Mut, for I know that she would never allow her son to behave this way at all. Perhaps there is more to the matter than meets the eye. Do you think that my curiosity is reason enough for further investigation into the matter?"

"I certainly do! However, we need something to bring down to them from our family. What do we have to offer them?"

"We have Merul...Is he not finally ready to be in a union with Sekhmet? Moreover, what about Edjo? Should we not request that he have both of them as his consorts? We are the family in power and it would certainly bring his family into the lead here."

"Oh, Merul, he is still a baby. Besides, he loves the house of scribes and being with his uncle. I could not bear his pain at having to leave it. Tehuti told me just the other day, what talent that the boy has."

"You know as well as I that Merul is more than a baby and ready for a union. I do not know what to do dear, for my mind is so tired and not what it used to be. Do you have any ideas on this?"

After some pause and consideration on the issue, she finally spoke up, "How about requesting that they come here to Per-Uto? This way, we can find out the real reason for all of the reports coming up from Ineb-Hedj. I do have a sneaking suspicion that Apep is really behind all of this instigation. Re seemed to be a very calm person and not one to waste his time squabbling. Besides, he would have contacted me if he felt something was wrong in his treatment. In all of my correspondence with him, I had not sensed anything amiss. It is only from the reports that are arriving. I was also thinking that if my suspicions were correct in the innocence of Re, that we could definitely use him as an ally against our real threat, Suti."

"Certainly! Our family definitely has talents in diplomacy. Use your famous charms on Re if you have to, for I have faith in you."

Chapter 94

They all arrived during the waning moon in the first month of the inundation. There were feasts and temple rituals. Mut and Ua-Zit blended like little girls. Ua-Zit learned fast how to communicate with her old friend and felt protective of her. While Mut, spent every waking moment by Ua-Zit waiting on her despite the protestations.

After a few days of this renewal of old bonds Re finally found a moment alone with Au-Set. He had found her in her study looking over old clay tablets written in the language of her birth-land. "Where ever did you find these?"

"Oh Re, I had not heard you enter. These? Well, they were collected over the years from the temple that my mother ruled. I did not want them destroyed by the new *God* in residence. Many priestesses have risked their lives bringing them here to safety."

Re looked over at one that she was holding. "Can I see?" He traced his finger soothingly over the chisel marks that he knew were words.

"I am only familiar with some words that I have picked up on my own. Writing is still new here. I had admired your mother's study and she would sit with me for hours teaching the writing of your Goddess to me. Could you tell me what this piece means?"

"She smiled, for this was the Re that she recalled at her visit years ago. She felt once again comfortable in his presence and melted into his charms. She knew that her aunt would be disappointed in that she was supposed to be the one with the charm.

"This piece here is a lament. It is about a mother who loses her lover to the floods. It is really quite sad. It tells of her tears being greater than the rain that fell from the heavens."

"Rain, I remember that. The first time that I had seen it, I was still very young. Your mother marveled that I had never seen rain before. She laughed and laughed and we both ran and played in it until we both fell over in exhaustion." His eyes misted.

Au-Set knew that this man was not the one behind the threats, for he had excessively too much soul to be troubling her with small matters. "Would you like to hear it?" She began at his graceful nod of affirmation.

**"My love yearns for you and cries for you
The emptiness rips at my soul
For that one summer night
That took you away from me**

**I have protected you and you made me feel safe
So safe in your heart, it feels your loss
Rains take me away to be with you
Safe in the arms of Innana
Safe in the arms the arms of Innana**

**The rains never told me that they needed you
For I would have fought them had I known
I would have built our house higher to shield you
from the fate that took you**

**Safe in the arms of Innana and not in mine
Safe in the arms of Innana and not in mine"**

"That piece has never failed to move me."
"I can see why. I could never imagine how rain could possibly kill. That rain that I had witnessed seemed quite docile and refreshing."
"It can be, but it can also roar like a ferocious beast and throw its anger down on the people of the Twin Rivers with such force that it causes mud slides and mass mountains of water that rush in to crush everything in its path. I have heard of whole villages being swept away in a matter of minutes!"
He looked astonished at this, and she knew that he had not been in Eshnunna long enough to witness the spring flooding that was all too common in their land.
They had both witnessed the soft rising of the Great River in Kemet, but the Dog Star at its advent high in the sky predicted it. They had warning of it and

planned for it to give them life with the crops that grew from the black soil left behind. The black soil that was so important to the life force of the people of Kemet, they named their home for it.

She recalled the village houses built on tall poles in her birth land of Eshnunna way above the level of the floodwaters, and the mounds that the wealthy had built their homes on to protect them from the unforgiving power of the floods. They had all witnessed a story in each generation of how entire villages were swept away in oblivion while their helpless survivors stood by and watched in terror. The floods in her land were numerous and always unpredictable.

She knew that the danger of the floods had inspired great poems and stories of bravery and lost love. But then again, any kind of natural disaster seemed to cause this as well. "Is there not harsh nature enough here in Kemet to cause inspiration as well? What about the dangers of the beasts of the Great River itself? The ferocious crocodile?"

"Ah, yes, that is true and I do not know of any family that has not lost at least one family member to this ferocious beast. Though, perhaps there is a family that seems to not fear them."

"And who possibly could this be?"

"Why have you not heard of the mighty *Sobek* or as some call him *Sebek*, way up north in the wilds of *Ombo*?" He continued when she had nodded in the negative.

"Ah, Sebek is quite the anomaly in this land." He laughed, "And you thought your family was the only one to tame the wild beasts?" They both laughed at this.

"You see, Sebek is a loner or at least far away from any known village. He lives by himself way up in the farthest reaches of Kemet. He built himself a hut where he dwells alone. His only company being the crocodiles. He feeds them and has even been known to tame them for they eat out of his hands!"

"My Goddess! Does he truly live alone with his crocodiles?"

"I have heard that he lives with his life mate *Heqet* who feeds the frogs. One would hope not to the pets of Sebek!" They both laughed over this one almost toppling over.

"It seems that your family has caused quite the rage throughout Kemet!" added Re.

"I would certainly have to agree with you on that! Look at your own daughter. Does she not have her own pet lion?"

"That she does and my son *Shai* is constantly teasing her about this in that he tells her that she looks like a lioness with her long frizzy hair!"

"Oh, Re, your daughter does have beautiful hair. However, I understand the sibling thing there. My own do the same thing! About your son, why have I not heard about him before? I do have other daughters. There is Renenutet and Weret-Heka; they are old enough for union and for bearing children for the Goddess."

She looked up at him wondering why he had not brought his son up and felt hurt.

Re saw this and genuinely sought to comfort her, "Au-Set it is nothing like that. I have grown close to the boy. I knew that when he was chosen as a mate, he would have to live outside of my home. I cannot bear to part with him, he has been a great help with the business. Shai is almost seventeen now. I understand that you have the same feelings for your sons."

Turning to another point that he did not want to miss he told her, "There is something else, I have heard about the trouble that my brother Apep has been causing and I extend my deepest apologies on that. I assure you, from all that we have shared and how much you mean to me that it was never I. I want all the best for your family as I do my own. I beg of you to see the truth in this!"

"I do, though for only the briefest of moments have I ever truthfully wavered in my faith of you. I thank you for bringing this up to me in sincerity.

"How about we make this family bond stronger? How would you feel about giving Shai to Weret-Heka and

Renenutet? They could alternate between Per-Uto and Ineb-Hedj and we would all benefit from their young wisdom! What say you to that Re?"

"I say that it sounds more than fair. I accept this. And you have the aid of my family in any trouble that Suti is causing." He noticed her astonishment and continued, "Yes, even in my remote fort, I have made sure that you are safe. I have come across some reports from my own scouts that would only confirm your fears. I have also learned that Suti has been holding Astarte hostage!"

"That makes a lot of sense, since we have not heard from her in quite the while! Do you think she is harmed in any way?"

"No, from what I have heard, he keeps her in a state of incredible luxury, though without freedom."

"Sometimes Re, that is worse than physical harm. To lose one's freedom. I knew that I never should have intervened."

"Intervened? What do you mean?"

"It was long ago and it means nothing now, for we have more pressing worries. First we have a union to plan!"

Chapter 95

The union of Shai with his new consorts Weret-Heka and Renenutet was beautiful, as was the union of Heru and Set and Bast. The celebrations lasted for weeks with non-stop revelries and feasts.

When the parties of Re had left with her daughters, Au-Set went to the chambers of Set to see how she was doing after her own union with Heru. She had reached her daughter's door to find it wide open and nothing was inside. To her dismay, she reeled about to look for Heru to see if he knew about Set and where she could possibly be.

"Where is Set son?"

"She left."

"What do you mean, she left."

His eyes looked down at his feet and he repeated, "She left me for Re."

"Re?" Her eyes searched the room refusing to hear what she did from her son who looked devastated and lost. She reached over to take him into her arms as she did when he was a little boy who had just lost a race.

"Explain this to me son. How could something like this happen?"

"Every woman falls for *Re*, every woman. Set had been following him around like a lost puppy the whole time that they were here. Did you not notice this Mother?"

"No."

"Oh, I do not think that even Re knows of this, he seemed oblivious to this and had been nothing but polite to her. She took it as interest."

"Surely, you don't think?"

"No. I know that Re did nothing to lead her on and was only polite. But, she was insistent and blind in her devotions to him."

"Explain so that I can understand."

"I don't even understand her! He is old and gray. I am young and strong! Yet, she felt that he loved her back in her blindness. I begged her not to go, that she would have to face his consort Het-Heru. She only laughed at me!"

"Oh, this is not good! I will send out word and have my own Scorpion Guard return her."

"May the Goddess be with you on that one, for I feel that she is too lost in her blindness to see reason!"

"We shall see about that my son!" Au-Set stomped out of his room with determination and gathered her guard herself and made plans to delay the traveling party of the family of Re.

Chapter 96

When Re and his family arrived home to Ineb-Hedj and all had settled into their sleeping chambers while their baggage was being unloaded. Re had finally arrived at his own chambers. The stars were just settling in the evening sky for a beautiful and cloudless evening. Not that he was ever threatened by clouds; they were only there occasionally for their own amusement if nothing else.

Het-Heru was in her own chambers next to his preferring to sleep in solitude. Re respected that and enjoyed his own solitude. He lay on his palette looking up at the new painting on his ceiling when he felt something next to him. He wondered if this were only Sekhmet's lion cub confusing his bed for hers. Still the thought did not comfort him. When he looked under his beautifully woven covers, he was startled to find the naked form of the beautiful Set lying there looking up at him mischievously.

"Oh, no princess, this is not right! You must leave before anyone finds out!"

"Why? I thought you wanted me. I want someone mature and successful like you. I do have the right to chose you know!" She smiled up at him.

"I see, explain that one to your mother! You are also forgetting about Het-Heru, she will not like the idea of sharing me with anyone."

"I do not mind. My own sisters are sharing your son Shai. I can learn to share."

"Oh, I do not think so! I know enough about you to realize that that thought will never happen in that head of flaming red hair. You will come to your senses and want to be the only consort that I have. That will not do at all for you."

"I have made up my mind and I will stay. Just think, to be the consort of the first daughter of Kemet, you will be the most powerful king."

"Did your mother not have that in mind with Heru?"

"Heru is just a boy." Before she could say anything else, Re rushed out of his bed and ran over to find his robe to place over her.

"Do you not find me beautiful? No one has hair like me in the entire world! The color of fire, you said so yourself!"

"That is true and I do not want to get burned!" He tried to put the robe on her. "Now put this on, please until I figure out what to do."

Re was very upset about this and knew that Au-Set was on her way to retrieve her daughter. He had to find some way to keep Set here in his palace until her mother arrived. Re knew that Set was very sensitive and would run away to who knows where if he were to say anything that would shock her. He sent in Apep to keep her company, perhaps his boyish charm would keep her busy while he figured out what to do.

He called in Apep to lure her out of his room after telling him the situation.

"Do not worry brother; I will keep that beautiful treasure busy for you!"

"Keep her busy, but do not do anything to her that she does not want brother, it could start a war! And that is one thing that we cannot afford!"

"Yes, Re… I will keep that in mind!" He then turned to go into the chambers of Re to see the beautiful Set, while Re went to the chamber of his own consort.

"Het-Heru, we have a situation here." He hated to disturb her for she looked so beautiful with her golden hair shimmering in the moonlight. Her dainty arms folded under her beautifully arched cheekbones and her long lashes flickered in a deep slumber.

"Hmmmm, oh Re! Hold me darling for I was in the middle of a wonderful dream."

He climbed into bed with her welcoming the comfort, though hated to tell her the latest news. He stuttered, "We have a situation my love."

"Whatever can it be?" Her large bright eyes struggled to adjust to the dim light of the moon in the room.

"There was a secret visitor on our return trip."

"Oh was there?" Het-Heru hated how the women constantly fell at her love's feet, for this had happened before and he was always honest with her about it. She knew that Re loved her deeply and would never do anything to hurt her. He also knew that she could have him killed for betraying her, yet she never would. That was not the way of her people. She was used to the many wives of her father and her mother did not seem to care, as long as she was the first. She glorified in his only wanting her alone, which was extremely rare for most men that she had known in her life.

She then realized that never before had he ever woke her up to tell her this. This must be something important. She wondered who it might be. "Tell me love, who is it?

"It is none other but Set."

"Set! Did she not union with Heru? How could this be?"

"I have no idea how she managed this. Her family must be on their way over here. I am worried that it might lead to a war. Au-Set was determined to have Set union with Heru. She even gave us her two daughters for Shai. This will not go well with Per-Uto!"

"I thought that you and Au-Set were close enough to see through all of this. Have you no faith in her?" Het-Heru knew of her husband's indiscretion and forgave him for it. He sincerely felt as if he betrayed her. To his people he had, but she knew his heart and she understood the reason. Her people were not like the women of Kemet.

"I do, but this concerns her daughter! I know how an angry mother can be!"

"Yes, but Au-Set is reasonable. I know that she will see through all of this. Set is notorious for her determination. Moreover, on that note, we must keep her safe until her family arrives for her. Where is she now?"

"I had Apep lead her to her own chamber. Do not worry; I threatened him about touching her."

"Good. Now let me think about this." She raised her head to lean on her arm and looked at Re while she thought.

"I know. Listen closely. She is very sensitive and is in the middle of a crush. Due to her station, we cannot do anything to hurt her feelings. She could easily run somewhere and we do not want her to go to her own father that alone could be dangerous!"

"Do we have Apep distract her?"

"Most definitely not, for she will feel rejected and think that you passed him to her because you did not want to be bothered by her. That would only make her run faster and further away. We must keep her here until her family arrives.

"I know, she thinks that she is in love with you right?" He nodded affirmatively.

"Well, you shall take her in as a consort. She has chosen you right?" At his nod she continued. "Well, she is the first princess of this land and her choice is law, we cannot offend her."

"But...." He looked confused and hurt at this.

"Do not worry love, for our maturity makes us see beyond the lust of the moment. Remember that it does not last. I think that you shall drive her out of here, though not before her family arrives! We must be strategic about this and send notice of our plans to Au-Set and Au-Sar. Be honest about everything, as you have with me that is the way to a woman's heart my love!"

"You are brilliant my heart!"

"I might not be much help in ruling your lands, but I do know the heart of a woman! And with this plan, we shall have to tread with tremendous care!"

The next morning Re approached Set and welcomed her to his home. He even had a special chamber made especially for her. She delighted in all of the luxuries that he showered her with and danced about in her new room. The walls were tall and there were four large arched windows with a door in the center leading out to a balcony. The balcony was covered in the finest of translucent linens that blew in the breeze of the Great River to keep the insects out of her chamber.

The paintings on the walls were in the theme of the waters of the Nile. It almost looked as if her room was under water. Fish swam about her and hippopotami walked in a magical line darting around a happy crocodile that almost seemed to smile at her. It was so cleverly painted that she marveled at the effect of it for hours.

Re smiled and looked at Het-Heru, as the first step of their plan was successful. He had even sent away his brother Apep for a survey of their cattle. Re had the largest herd in the Great River Valley and it needed to be tallied anyways, since it was the calving season. He wanted to make sure that there was enough grassland for them, for he knew that grasslands were sparse. He wanted Apep to cull the herd so that they would not wear out their feeding grounds. He knew that this would keep him busy for while and Set would be safe from his charms.

Re and Het-Heru had another surprise. It was well known that his mother Mut had been sleeping alone, but they did not expect the latest news.

Mut had told them that she had given permission for her consort Ptah to take Sekhmet as his consort. She had liked the idea of keeping the family pure and she could no longer have children. She had initially offered this honor to Khephra, but he would not hear of this and loved the idea of having Mut all to himself. He pleaded that he was too old for this as well.

Ptah was only half of the age of Khephra and still quite handsome. Sekhmet accepted this union and settled quite nicely to it, much to the surprise of her parents. They recalled vividly that when they visited in Per-Uto, Sekhmet had politely refrained from being in a union with Heru. She stated that she simply did not like him. It was understood and explained to Au-Set, whom he knew was genuinely sorry that it would not work out.

Thus, she was able to arrange the union with her own daughters to Heru. Re marveled how time seemed to be the best gauge in making sure that everything turned out well, that seemed almost impossible in the past.

Chapter 97

Meanwhile Set was starting to come out of the blindness of her crush to Re. Even though he called her his first consort, she felt that it was not so in reality. Set felt more as if he was treating her, as she was his daughter.

Though she was still untouched and had not participated in the sacred union, she knew that there was much more between a man and a woman. When he held her, it seemed too sweet. He seemed to have an excuse for every time she went to his chambers and sometimes he was nowhere to be found.

Re was very kind and showered her with everything that she could ever want. He seemed to know what she wanted even before she did herself. She had no complaints of his treatment of her at all. Yet, there was something about him that she could not place her finger on.

This went on for what seemed like an endless amount of time and her curiosity of the sacred union ripped her apart at night. Did he not find her attractive? Was there something wrong with her?

Yet, each of those fears would melt away with the rising sun and his doting treatment of her.

She was almost on the verge of explosion of her natural curiosity, when she had heard the gossip of the palace slaves one morning. They had mentioned that the party of Au-Set was on their way to the palace.

Then all of it came together at once. To her growing anger, she realized that Re had not accepted her as his consort, but was playing with her to keep her here until her family arrived. As if, she was a disobedient child! The nerve of them all!

To think that she had almost fallen for it! She wondered if there was something wrong with her and pushed that away abruptly. She had also heard gossip that her two youngest sisters had really belonged to Re, that he was their father and not her mother's chosen consorts! She wondered on this and then pushed that away in anger as well. She felt the heat of her fury consuming her. Too many turns and possibilities raged inside her stormy thoughts.

She would show them! She had also heard that her father was not Au-Sar or Nebmaat, but Suti! She would go to her real father and join him against her mother and her consorts! That would show them! She was the first princess; she had a right to choose her own consort! What did they know?

She gathered up all of her belongings, grabbing all of the jewelry that was given to her by Re and left as soon as the sky grew dark enough.

Chapter 98

The days went by and melted into weeks until finally the party of Au-Set and her famous Scorpion Guard had arrived. Re and Het-Heru greeted them with the usual feasts and gracious hospitality.

Re took Au-Set aside and explained the situation to her and of their plans. She was grateful to Het-Heru and Re for their consideration of her daughter's feelings and her own. She also knew that there was something that Re and Het-Heru was not telling her. She saw them look back and forth to each other.

Re looked up at Au-Set, "We did everything that we could. She is gone."

They all knew where Set would have left to, especially with how things have been for her so far and feared for the worst.

Chapter 99

As Set neared the walled city of Djedu, she stumbled upon a rock and almost lost her balance. She ignored the possibly ominous sign of the destiny that possibly lay ahead of her, nevertheless, she held firm in her beliefs. She promised herself that she would not falter in her determination. Thus, she had left the palace of Re and his family, drawing an impenetrable wall around her failure. She held up her shoulders, fled with a new purpose, and renewed vigor for her next plan. Her whole childhood she had believed that she was the child of Au-Sar.

She always overheard palace gossip about her uncle Suti though never put much stock into what she had heard, until the day that she actually saw him. Then she wondered how the world could accept that her father was Au-Sar? Set had cried and anguished over this for months on end until one day; she just shrugged her shoulders and decided to use it to her benefit rather than her detriment. She just did not know how she would do this. Therefore, she just tucked away that valuable piece of knowledge and proceeded with the rest of her life. She suffered through the anguish of her misunderstandings with the beautiful Re and now, here she was on this road leading to the palace of her father deep in the Deshret.

She really did not know how she actually came upon being on this road and in this direction. When she left the palace of Re and the place of her humiliation she had no destination she just walked south, as far away in the opposite direction of home and Re that she could possibly be. She loved the freedom of the open trails along the banks of the Great River and lived only for the day. She felt small and humiliated and could not bear the thought of facing her family.

The days wore on while she followed the banks of the river. Set prayed to the mighty crocodiles to guide her way to her freedom and her new life. At night, she listened to the soft sounds of the Great River's evening bounty, a completely alien world to the daytime splendor. The sounds whispered ominously to her and assuaged her temperament and deep emotions to sleep.

She lived off the gifts of the river and ate them under the stars. She recalled the tales that her mother told her about her grandmother Ninnuit. Her mother would tell her that Ninnuit was the Goddess Innana in human form and that she held the stars in her eyes. Au-Set told her children that on the ceilings of the palace were painted stars in many forms and patterns of the glorious heavens that covered them by evening. Her mother even gave each of them a pendant representing the heavens that she so loved.

Set recalled her mother telling them each evening to look into the sky and to see the stars above them. She would smile and tell them that it was her mother, Ninnuit-Innana looking over them to protect them all. Au-Set would sing to them that her mother had become the sky above them to bless her grandchildren and to make sure that the world would be safe for them. Set recalled always finding comfort in the stars above. She smiled at the thought of her mother when she was young, actually looking for the form of her grandmother stretched out in the heavens over them all with stars painted on her body. That image was painted in her head whenever her mother would tell that story to them.

She actually woke this morning to witness a star from the sky drop down to greet the dawn and her amazed eyes. It was so surreal yet a welcome sight. She held firm that it was the conformation that she was doing the right thing in seeking her father. Only on the last few days had she realized where the whispering river was leading her and her destiny.

However, there was some sinking feeling in her gut that the Great River was truly whispering to her that she was betraying her mother in doing this. The falling star had relieved her somewhat in that her grandmother secretly approved of her notion. She wondered if her grandmother was actually trying to reach her to comfort her and to lead the way.

The colors of the sunrise were brilliant and seemed to vibrate with new meaning and confirmation in her quest. Set walked on systematically towards her father with the silent heartbeat of the desert sands at the end of the flora by the side of her guiding river.

Chapter 100

By the time the sun was highest in the sky and straight overhead, she spotted the great mud-brick walls of his fortifications. She had a brief moment of regret and almost wanted to turn around completely, then thought the better of it and walked on tall and proud, her bright red hair inherited from her father trailed out behind her following her path.

When she reached the gate, the guards nodded her admittance to the palace main and she walked further on. A tall balding man entwined his arm in hers and silently led her forward to an audience with her father. Her stomach suddenly felt nauseous and tangled with the power of her nerves. She almost faltered as they approached the throne room. She had actually stumbled, ever so gracefully of course as she approached the throne of her father.

He looked down at her and the two of them locked gazes. He had grown large and his complexion was ruddy and coarse, yet their hair was their crowning glory and it told multitudes of truth. He held out her arms to his only child and she ran, like a child into them.

Chapter 101

At Ineb-Hedj Au-Set faced Re along with Het-Heru and all formed an alliance due to all being parents. They knew where Set went and understood in the way that only parents could on the faults of their young. Yet Au-Set was also angry in the way of mothers in that her daughter did not know the whole truth of her paternity, nor of the reality of her father. She feared greatly for her daughter when she would actually find this out. Yet, in being the wise woman that she was, she knew that as she was at her age, her daughter would only learn lessons in life from her own experiences. She knew that her daughter needed to walk this path and thus she found her self-talking with Re on this matter one evening during her visit to his city.

"Re, do you think that our children were born to walk the paths that we failed to walk ourselves?"

"That sounds very mythical Au-Set. Sometimes, do you not wonder if there really is no plan at all and we all just haphazardly wonder where we will and our children as well?"

"Humph. So much is beyond us, I wonder if anyone will ever find the answers to those questions. I suppose only the Gods can know the facts."

"Come Au-Set follow me, I have something to show you."

Chapter 102

Her tiny soft footsteps matched his almost in the power of their strides. Au-Set followed Re's form under the light of the moon at its cradle in the sky. She wondered but silently followed him in trust. They walked out of the palace gardens and down a path that led them to the shores of the Great River. The River sounded docile under the kiss of the starlight almost lulled to silence; they both stood by it in wonder of the raw beauty of it.

"Look to your left and behold my own peace." She followed his gaze and found a wonderful papyrus boat tied to the shore. It was twice the size of the average boat and gleamed with his care. Though it was made of papyrus, noticeably it was carefully tended to make it almost glow. She noticed the magical colors that were painted upon it.

"This boat is my freedom and my peace. I take it out each evening and follow the path of the moon. It has been my consolation and the answers to my prayers. I call it my *'Boat of Millions,'* for it has held a million prayers close to my breast and to the waters that give us life. This boat has yielded food for our table for my family and has taught me mystery and pride." He looked at her with untold promise.

"You act as if this boat is the answer to any woe or problem"

"No, you know as well as I that it is not the boat, but the person guiding it. The stars will soothe your decisions and give you the answers that you seek. I have never let anyone on this boat, ever. Nevertheless, I lament with your decision and your torment over your daughter. I feel responsible for it and thus..."

Au-Set started to protest his guilt, but he held a gentle finger to silence her over her lips.

"I want you to take this boat and follow the moon with it to find out the next part of your plans, because I see that you are torn. You want to be a good mother and wonder whether you should run down there to save your daughter, or if you should let her learn her own lessons.

You know as well as I that only you can find the answer to that one."

"Re, you have helped me out wonderfully and have been a friend. You do not have to do this, for I know how valuable your boat is. It holds your personality. I am afraid to alter the power of it for you."

"No, something tells me that it is the will of the Gods, that it is somehow another step in your destiny that you search for your answers with my 'Boat of Millions'. It is written in the stars."

Reverently, Au-Set looked at Re and then the offering of the use of his prided boat. She knew that to refuse would have been a great insult to him. She daintily placed one slippered foot after the other into the smooth and brightly painted boat. She felt the boat tilt with her weight and she instantly balanced to support it.

Re smiled at her as if he had waited for this moment. She was amazed that there was no pain emanated at this parting of his favorite boat for her use, even if it was only for one evening. She saw only contentment and peace surrounding him with a supporting smile that he radiated out towards her with his approval. She nodded and started to lead the boat out in the direction of the path of the moon as he instructed to her.

Thus, she glided along the gentle waters in which were dancing with the stars of her mother's memory. She was reminded of her mother's all-reaching power in her favorite talisman of the stars around her regal neck as they led her in the wake of the moon. The moon only encouraged her further onward. Perhaps then, she would find her answers.

The young queen noticed that as her boat followed the progress of the moon, the soothing arms of her mother in the form of the stars were reaching out to guide her along. The water was smooth except for the small wake caused by the passage of her boat. It appeared almost as if her boat were floating across the sky, so dark and mirror-like was the water. Her emotions were reflected as well, for only in this moment was she almost as serene as the water that whispered around her. The blackness of the sky was like the mask of her soul as she protected herself. Now she had to face this monumental question on the fate of her daughter and on her emotional well-being.

She also smiled at the irony of the whole issue of her being on a boat on the water. How easy it would be to continue onwards to where she assumed that her daughter would be. She knew that she could easily guide the boat forward after the dawning of the sun directly to the far northern lands of Upper Kemet to the Deshret.

The waters of this river flowed from the north to the south, unlike others rivers in the world, making Kemet forever backwards from the land of her birth and all others. Au-Set followed the current in the wake of the moon and all she had to do in actuality was to turn it around and race with the current without the use of her oars, towards the land of her daughter. She knew that Re was perhaps wondering if this was her plan.

She would have answered yes when she initially stepped foot inside the boat. In fact, she had hoped for this. She knew that had they not stopped to visit Re, they would have gone north to Upper Kemet as their next stop. However, on this tranquil evening with so many possibilities before her, which were made more possible with this great gift of Re, she was given the gift of this rare moment of reflection. In this moment alone on this river, things appeared more lucid and real before her, almost as if she could see the path ahead of her in such clarity not normally seen during the light of day.

She saw her daughter in her soul walking towards the land of her father with many emotions playing in her mind, as completely understandable. Au-Set wondered if she should have revealed the paternity of her first-born daughter to the world and especially to her. Then she realized that regardless, she had to walk the path that she chose with the decisions already made.

She realized that there was only one true way to proceed from this moment on. She had to let her daughter go to discover the truth about her father and she had to trust that all of the love that she had taught her daughter would sustain and protect her. She had to have the faith to let her daughter solve her own problems and to walk alone. It was the most difficult task a mother had to do for her children, to let them go and walk on their own. She smiled and decided to return to the shore where Re was waiting with a renewed confidence in the ability of her daughter.

When she arrived, Re was skipping stones into the water and was smiling, for her answer was written on her face. He only said this to her in a whisper and she docked the boat, "See, they all have to go sometime. We hope that we arm them with enough knowledge and our families' love as a strong foundation, before this time arrives. When she returns, she will be a woman. Be proud for her."

Au-Set smiled, "I am."

Chapter 103

The months went by after Au-Set returned home to the palace to wait out her daughter's trials. Re and Het-Heru returned to their normal life at the palace.

Re had always been a handsome man, even in the evening years of his life and his age never seemed to touch him, for it seemed to be the last thing on his mind. His love for Het-Heru grew stronger with a more endurable foundation. Together, they had a history and endured much together. Their support in life was made stronger with the passing of the years. They learned to except their differences and to exalt in their similarities. They had long ago made the promise that when the last of their life came to be, they would die together so that they would be strong as a team in their afterlife. This promise made to each other sparkled in their eyes, others who knew them smiled and longed for the same themselves, for their love was rare. It had started out rough with their many differences, but the years made them softer and the reasons intense.

It was on this evening, when the two aged lovers were walking along the shore of the river, when their life forces met a hindrance. The moon was full and hung hungrily in the sky above them, almost seeming as if to swallow all of the stars surrounding it whole. They bathed in the warm glow that it covered them with and walked in the unspoken silence along the shore. Their hands entwined, their thoughts sacrificed to the stars and not each other, for there was no need. Het-Heru's hair seemed to glow like the brightest and rarest silver of the land in the moon light and her eyes appeared deeper to him than the heavens surrounding them. The abundant shore plants swayed in the fragrant breeze of jasmine that seemed to dull their senses and to pause time, if only for a moment.

It came out of nowhere, completely out of place in the tranquility surrounding them on this peaceful eve. A culprit of the dark nature that was always around them but mostly hidden during the day. It slithered out from a bush to attack the bare ankle of Het-Heru. The asp pounced, took his prey into its fierce jaws, and started the death grip to release its poisons. She let out a small cry that alerted Re to her demise. He shifted slowly, to view and comprehend the danger. He reached over to grab hold of the dark serpent, when the slick ground of the riverbank protested his form and slid him down. Re fell away from Het-Heru, while the time lent the poison deeper into her system. Her face contorted and her lips cried out to him in fervent silent prayer.

The mud under Re's feet remained stubborn and slick, preventing him from reaching Het-Heru in time to save her from the force and strength of the venom. She crumpled on the ground knowing that her breaths would soon cease and that she would be in the arms of her beloved and almost forgotten Gods of the land of her birth.

Re was frantic and stood up, his right side covered in the ooze of the Great River. In his haste to reach his beloved to hold her in his arms, his senses did not prepare him for his largest blunder. Time stood still while he had thought that he was finally able to stand upright and then the ground fell out from underneath him, created by the silent mockery of the slick mud beneath him. His body slid menacingly to the side and went down further away from Het-Heru, his head crashed into a large rock hidden under the foliage on the side. The rock had seemed harmless since they had passed it on their way to this dreadful spot, yet it reared its menace and claimed the senses of Re and took away his youth in the force of the impact of his skull against the rock.

Het-Heru watched Re and the fall helpless with the fast acting venom, that prevented her from assisting him. Paralyzed, she watched in horror as he fell. She knew that she was going to die and wanted to spend the last moment of her life in his arms that was wretchedly taken away from her.

In these last moments of hers, it mercifully passed slow enough for her to ponder the issues before her. She wondered if this death with her Re was granted in its separation due to her final abandonment of the

Gods of her birth for those of the new Gods. Was this her final test? She knew then that Re would also survive this, though he would never be the same. She cried that she would never see her daughter again or her son, Shai. She cried that she would not be able to keep her promise of dying with Re by his side.

She lie down and felt the poison dancing in her veins, bringing great pain with it coursing through her whole body. She looked over at Re with glassy eyes and blew a kiss to him with the last of her strength and whispered a soft goodbye. She fell and then joined the Gods of the land of her birth.

When Re awoke, he saw her form and cursed the snake for not taking him as well. Rage coursed through his body and pain from his own ordeal that brought him away from his heart when she was most in need. His head was in immense pain and he realized that he could not move his legs nor find the voice to cry out for help. He waited there in what seemed an eternity for some help while the world spun above him, rendering him sick and helpless in a heap beside the lifeless form of his beloved Het-Heru.

He knew that she was no longer in her body and that she had joined the Gods alone, without him. He wanted to join her but knew that it was too late. He was certainly not angry with her for this only at himself for leaving his beloved alone to walk the frightening paths of the halls of judgment on her own. He wanted to protect her since the Gods of Kemet were new to her. He was afraid that they would trick her if he were not by her side. The tears seemed endless and he prayed that he would form enough to drown him for his failure.

He somehow knew that with each tear that left his body, leaked out his youth and his reason. All that was left would be the helpless shell of the man that everyone knew who would babble and drool like an old fool. He did not care anymore and embraced the new path of his life. He realized that with this head injury all of his wrongs that seemed to catch up with him and his age would finally be realized. With the last of his reason, he thanked the Gods for giving him a full life and hoped that now his children would be able to find him and to take care of him.

The palace servants eventually found him, soon after they found the body of Het-Heru. She was given a burial as fit for a queen in Kemet. They all thanked the Gods that Re did not have enough senses left to feel the pain of her passing. He was found drooling and speaking incoherently.

The palace physician found out later that it was possibly caused by a head wound sustained from falling on the mud, possibly in trying to reach Het-Heru. The blood loss and location of the wound rendered him weak and helpless. Re was taken to his chamber in the palace and set up there to live out the last of his days. He had also lost the use of his legs.

The people who loved him could not understand why so mighty a man was struck feeble in the most productive years of his life. Even though he was old in their years, he was still handsome, his intelligence was renowned throughout the land and his wisdom sought out. Now, on the bed was a feeble man, almost emaciated from his current state that was only the wretched shell of what he once was.

Mut trembled in anger at the Gods for taking away her son and leaving her with this feeble monster in its place, she sent word of this to Au-Set, knowing of her legendary healing powers.

Chapter 104

Word of the illness of Re had finally reached the ears of Au-Set and she promptly set out once again for Ineb-Hedj. She was home barely one week when the summons arrived. Again, Au-Sar was left behind to watch over Ua-Zit and the children along with Nebmaat.

She had no idea what to expect when she arrived, but it certainly was not what she saw. Mut was the first to greet her at her arrival in the middle of the evening. Mut rushed Au-Set into her own private chambers and with her interpreter; she began to explain the events that had transpired since the incident occurred. Her interpreter was her first consort Khephra who stood beside her. Au-Set noticed for the first time an elderly man sitting beside her whom she had never seen before who nodded as she was received in the chambers of Mut. Sitting by her feet was her younger consort Ptah and his new consort Sekhmet the daughter of Re and Het-Heru. The confusion of a lady and her entourage was a normalcy in this land and Au-Set was well aware of her own. She bowed reverently to the aging Lady Mut and kneeled before her.

"My lady Mut welcomes you with great joy into her home, your highness Au-Set, and daughter of Innana of Eshnunna. Please be seated and rest after your journey."

Au-Set bowed again and sat gratefully on the large pillow behind her to face Mut and her faithful Khephra. "I thank you for your hospitality and inquire what I can do for you?"

"My lady Mut wishes that you may heal the afflictions of her son Re."

"I will do all that I can, could you tell me more about this."

All in the chamber mumbled at this and nodded their heads mournfully. Khephra's voice was loud and sounded throughout the chamber the wishes of his lady while all around her were in full support. Mut throughout would make signals with her hands and face

in expressions, which in turn would be interpreted by
her first consort.

He nodded and looked at Sekhmet to explain to
Au-Set. "My lady, my brother Re had last been strolling
along the banks of the river with his beloved Het-Heru
over eight evenings ago when this occurred. My brother
Apep, who is no longer here, had been the one who
found both of them. Het-Heru had suffered the bite of a
viper, while it appears that while Re was trying to save
her, he had fallen on the slick mud and sustained a
deep head wound. Apep summoned the palace and my
father Khephra and consort *Ptahtep* had carried them
back to be examined." Those in the room concurred to
the explanation of Sekhmet. She then turned to the
elderly man sitting beside her mother.

This ancient man looked so fragile that Au-Set
felt that a breeze entering the room could knock him
down. He was dressed in fine garments dyed in the rare
purple of Tyre with gold embroidered thread that swirled
in patterns around it. On any other man, this would
have looked resplendent, yet on this fragile man, it
almost looked silly. Similar in appearance to that of a
child dressed in clothes too big.

It almost seemed as if the room had cleared all
noise for this man to be heard. Au-Set had to strain to
hear him.

"I am *Tmu-Amun* or *Khephra*. I am the mate of
Mut and the father of the original Ua-Zit, Nekhebt, and
Shu through her. I am your relative as well young one."
He sat there regally in an elaborate headdress of two
large white plumes with the long horns of a ram on each
side. His gown of purple touched the floor. His beard
was braided and the softest white, which seemed to
reach the floor so great was the length. She smiled to
herself, because she wondered if the beard of Au-Sar
would ever reach this length in his old age.

Au-Set just sat there in amazement for she
certainly did not expect this. She sat there riveted to
each spider-webbed word out of his fragile lips.

"I came here years ago and thought that I was too
old for life and had sat in my bed chamber waiting for

death to take me. That did not happen. I sit here and wait for you. You are beautiful like your great-great grandmother and I feel her power in you as well. "It seemed as if his whole face formed one great wrinkle of a smile which burst through the room.

"I came here to be with Mut and her children, since they had a lesser place in this land now. My Ua-Zit, Shu, Nekhebt, and their-namesakes are long dead. Your line is a part of theirs and mine and has been the more powerful. We hope that the children of Shu and your mother in the forms of you and your siblings will lead this land to greatness, such as they have not. "

Au-Set sat there in astonishment in how this family was willing to step down for her and her siblings to control. She understood and felt them extremely brave and wise people in knowing the best thing to do for the land they loved. She felt that such self-sacrifice was very noble indeed.

Tmu-Amun continued, "We had hoped that our Re would lead us to lean beside you in this worthy cause..." His head was bent in sorrow, or was it a possible minute nap, for his breathing seemed deeper for a few breaths.

Suddenly his head was jarred to the present, "Since we had found Re, he has become a raving lunatic. He drools and runs around yelling obscene things and acts like one possessed by the moon at full, yet he does this every day! He yells to us all that we cannot know his secret name for it will be the death of him!" He looked over at Mut and then to Khephra who found his own voice.

In a deep sonorous voice, Khephra continued the story, "He is stark raving mad and we want our reasonable Re back, for he is the backbone of this kingdom and we are at a loss without him."

"I will do what I can, but I cannot make any promises!" It was then that her healing snake *Nefer* revealed itself from a cozy nap under her robes. The beautiful iaret reared its hood at all of the people in the room and then looked at its mistress. "Hush little one, these people mean no harm, we are here to help them.

Nefer, go back to sleep!" Her famous Scorpion Guard was around her as well and they let out small giggles because they always loved the reaction of those people when they first saw their mistress's new pet cobra. They knew that Nefer was trained from birth and was always by Au-Set's side.

Sekhmet's pet lion let out a roar when it glimpsed Nefer and his mistress tapped its nose to hush. "Sssssh star!" Edjo had just peeked out and giggled for she had her own pet iaret or cobra. The tensions in the chamber seemed to cease when the pets came out for viewing and admiration. The famous Scorpion Guard of Au-Set always around her and silent as trained were there in the shadows waiting for any danger to their mistress whom they protected.

Suddenly Re burst into the room looking as if he had just stepped out of a fog that only he could see. His hair was long and un-kept, with rabid snarls. His face bearded and untamed. His clothes were torn as if he battled something that only he could see. He looked into the room and shouted almost to the air, "There is danger about; I am here to warn you all. The clouds ate my dragon and the grass speaks to me of this!" Spit came out of his mouth with each syllable uttered.

Au-Set was amazed, as this was not the man she once admired. She wondered what daemon had possessed him. She looked around the room and spoke to Mut, since she knew that Mut could read her lips, "It will take some time, but I will try." Mut tried to hold back the tears at what her son had become. Au-Set sensed that the family was almost frightened of the new Re that seemed foreign to them all. They told her that sometimes he would walk and scamper around and other times he would stay in his bed for days on end.

Re then looked at a spider on the wall, scooped it up and tossed it into his mouth, jumped up and then scampered out of the chamber chasing something that no one saw but him.

Edjo spoke then, for she had been training to be a healer and was a great admirer of Au-Set, "You see that he has simply lost his reason."

Chapter 105

Au-Set had enlisted the skills of Edjo as her assistant in this new challenge of healing Re. She assigned all of the family to record their observations of Re along with the weather, time of day and everything that he ate. She wanted to see exactly what she was dealing with. Edjo had gathered up all of the herbs that she had learned the sacred properties of to assist Au-Set in this and silently waited for her next task.

Re seemed oblivious to all of the attention focused on him and continued to live for his bizarre world that only he knew the meaning. It seemed twisted and obscure to all of those around him and they prayed that Re's senses would soon be returned.

Finally, two days later, Au-Set came up with a plan. She cornered Edjo one day and whispered into her ear her idea. Edjo smiled and understood. "We cannot tell anyone about this, just in case it is not successful."

"I understand and I will do my part in this so that you will be proud." The eager Edjo whispered.

Au-Set smiled and proceeded to gather all that she needed. Au-Set read the observations of both families and reached the conclusion that there might actually be some hope. She felt that Re was truly in a land of his own imagination and fantasy. He refused to submit or to be a part of a world without Het-Heru. It seemed he almost blamed himself for her death and his failure in protecting her, so as punishment he decided to live out what he believed was a world that he deserved. This world was twisted and surreal, but made sense in that it was his punishment. He felt that he was not worthy of a world without Het-Heru and was afraid to face the consequences of his failure.

She felt that in order to reach him she had to breach the twisted and dark world that Re created. She needed to understand his pain in order to bring him back.

It was early in the evening when the moon first set about its evening path when Re, in his new and old life set out to work on his beloved 'Boat of Millions" and to set sail following the path of the moon to catch the best and largest fish of the Great River.

He had a path that he always traveled on that led him from the palace to his boat. A twisted path led a person who did not know the route to oblivion. Re loved his boat and feared that someone would steal it or destroy it, so he made a maze that only he knew of to reach his cherished boat.

The shadows were getting shorter while Re was skipping along the path with the energy of the very young pretending to catch little flying daemons that were blocking his path.

Au-Set was before him on his path carefully concealed behind the dense foliage, while Edjo was hidden even deeper. Au-Set tried desperately to stifle her giggles at the antics of Re as he hoped along to a beat that only he could hear. He shouted to bugs, "Stop and desist, you will not get my boat, you are evil little daemons and I will not let you win!" He grabbed a bug, stomped on it, and seemed to do a little dance crushing the poor creature into oblivion under his strange gaze.

It was then that Au-Set came out of the bushes in her costume. She and Edjo worked very hard creating it. It was a large costume of an iaret or cobra made of coarse linen with leaves stitched on as scales. It was beautiful and both women felt that it was very life-like.

"Re, you must cease your dance and listen to me!"

Re stood aghast and took in the costumed form of Au-Set trembling in place. His eyes appeared wider at the large snake before him.

"Who are you snake?"

"It is I, your judge and jury!"

Re then spit on the ground and turned his back on the large snake, "I have already decided my price, and I am living in my own judgment!"

"No Re, you have judged too harshly, I have seen all."

Au-Set reached out with her hand concealed under the costume and collected his spittle for her healing spell. Edjo who was behind her took it and ran back to place it into the potion that was brewing on the hearth in her private bedchamber back at the fortress.

"I am spit and I am excrement, Great Iaret!"

"You are not; you have done wonderful things in the life that you left behind. You are still needed and we need you!"

"I could not even save Het-Heru; I was too feeble to save her from your bite!"

"I had need of her beside me and your time was not up yet. She told me that she was worried about you and that you would not understand!"

"I do not! We were supposed to die together we made a promise! Yet, she died alone; I was not even man enough to join her! I have failed!"

"I was with her and she shed tears for you. It was not your fault that the mud played with you and took you first! Het-Heru had you by her side when she came to work for me. Your Sahu agreed and decided to stay behind, for it was the wisest decision."

"No, that is not true!"

"You dare to defy my word?"

"No, no, I do not. I humbly apologize!"

"You must return to the world of your family and know that Het-Heru is in good hands and is serving her Gods dutifully and with honor. You bring shame upon her by blaming yourself! You have no cause in this, for it was in the will of the Gods. What makes you feel so important as to be held responsible? This was not your decision to make. You must return to serve your people as you were born to do. Het-Heru has served her time on the earthly realm and now she must serve in the heavens by my side until all of her paths are joined and only then may she finally join oblivion. You must accept that Re!"

"I do not know! It is hard for me to take this all in. I just do not feel well at all! My soul yearns to join hers Great Iaret!"

"That you cannot do, it is not your time, and you will be needed in the years ahead. Your guidance is more than valuable for this land of Kemet!"

With those words, almost as if his body needed more strength to take all of this in, he suddenly fell to the ground in a faint. With this, Edjo came out of her hiding place and took the rest of the spittle from Re that Au-Set had collected for the completion of the cure. Au-Set then removed her costume and along with the assistance of Edjo, carried Re back to the palace for the rest of his treatment.

At the palace, she had explained that Re needed complete bed rest for one whole week, while his mind accepted the reality that it tried to deny. She had explained that Re refused to accept the death of Het-Heru and blamed himself. Thus, he made his own punishment in the horrific world that he created in his own mind.

She explained that Re just needed it to be told in a way that he could join the rest of them in this world and to abandon his dream world of punishment by gradually coming back. She told them all that his chamber needed to be filled with sunlight and the laughter of those he loved. He was also to take a draught of a potion that she had created with his own spittle along with some herbs that she had collected at the scene of the accident as described by those who found him. She felt it essential that those elements combined would lead to his complete recovery in blending the past with the present along with the psychological hope of a future where he was needed.

She sat there as the family had gathered by his bed and smiled for her work here was done and she was now able to return to her own home and family. She saw hope in the eyes of Re and the support of the family that he loved and loved him in return. She had given him his name back and thus his mortality was able to return to his body to join the living that he had, in desperation tried to give up. To comfort her further she looked into his eyes and she leaned over him after giving him his first draught of the healing elixir, he looked into her eyes and whispered, "My secret name is "Re of the Sun" for you have returned it to me and brought me back from a land of darkness! I will never forget this." This was only for her ears and she winked at him in her comprehension.

She then turned to the room and uttered to all, while she placed a hand over his, "Re has returned to us this noon of this day may we all rejoice for the further wisdom that he will bring to us and the land of Kemet!" The whole room resounded in joy. They were in need of him and could not wait for his recovery.

However, Apep, smiled outwardly only. Inside, he knew that this was an end to his own rule in the kingdom. He then decided to himself that he could perhaps join Suti in Upper Kemet, where he knew that he would be appreciated and not cast out as the lesser son. He knew that Edjo would be the one to assume his mother's role and then the wisdom of Sekhmet would be heeded after hers.

Re always had value to the whole family while he was only there to replace his brother while he was ill and until he recovered. He smiled to Re and inside he fought back his frustration at his lot in life and wondered how he could change things. He knew that he had a lot of offer and he had run things well during his brother's illness, yet, no one seemed to care or notice. He knew that when the sun set, his deeds would be forgotten as they always were.

Chapter 106

Au-Set was exhausted by the time that she arrived home and demanded that she was brought straight to her sleeping chambers for her rest. She had the Scorpion Guard tell everyone that she was not to be disturbed until she had rested in full. Everyone obeyed this order. It was well known in their family that the Goddess demanded the complete absorption of the healer in mind, body and soul, in order for a healing to occur. Au-Set had to submit fully to the Goddess in order to render a treatment that would work.

Nevertheless, upon her return to normal palace life and to the loving arms of her family and consort, she had found out that Ua-Zit was finally on her last journey. This was an accepted part of the wheel of life that they all were a part. She knew for a while that her aunt would not have much more time to be with them. She knew that Ua-Zit was performing her last dance to the Goddess in her dreams so that the Goddess Ua-Zit would accept her servant willingly and with love. The body of Ua-Zit was old and could not perform the dance in reality, so her servant performed it with the steps she had done every evening of her life, when she had the ability.

Au-Set went straight to the chamber of her aunt and lay beside her on her bed covered in cushions. The once beautiful and vibrant body of Ua-Zit who was born Ishurti of Eshnunna had only left a shell of the woman that she once was due to her age and the wrath of this new wasting illness. The fine lines of worry and love creased her brow as her niece looked in on her.

Ua-Zit looked up at her niece, "I am proud of you. I know Per-Uto will be in good hands with you to lead it."

"Hush aunt, do not talk that way, you are only a little ill that is all."

"Do not mock the power of the Goddess to take her servants."

"I never would, I just do not want you to leave, and there is still a lot that you can teach me."

"No, you are ready, the Goddess has decreed. However, you must watch your brothers. Suti is like a vulture in true, he waits for the power to be weak in order to strike. He will try to get you when you are down. Your strength lies in the union of you and your siblings. Neb-Het will be your greatest and most trusted ally. Au-Sar could be, however, his vanity is almost as great as Nebmaat's only not for clothes, but for the love of his people. Already he has taken that ruse of his being the ruler of the underworld to full force. He has taken the local legends of the God named Andjety and made himself the living son of that God. The people bow down to him, and truly believe that Au-Sar is *Andjety on earth*. He has forgotten our goals as he pleases them, lost in their worship of their God brought back to life." She smiled.

Au-Set let out a little giggle at the ruse of Au-Sar.

"Au-Set, you must rein him in and bring him back home, before things get out of control. I have left a scroll that has my burial wishes. Promise me that you will follow them? I also have called in Tehuti to record the dream that I had last night to be recalled to the people of the delta and Lower Kemet." Tehuti bowed his head in acknowledgement and showed Au-Set the dream words.

"Call in the others, my child." She looked over at Au-Set, who ran out of the chamber to retrieve the others as requested.

She found Nebmaat arguing over the price of cloth with Qui. Kekes was mimicking his brother in mockery. Upon her arrival, it looked as if Qui was winding up swatting his brother off like a fly.

"Qui, I really do not think that if the price was that low, it would be such the bargain that you were told."

"But, look at it!" He held it up.

"But, look at it!" Kekes mocked. The garment was orange and Au-Set thought it extremely garish. But then again Qui was quite ostentatious in everything that he wore and did. She felt it more suitable for Qui then

Nebmaat and was about to say so when she saw Qui winding up.

"Qui! How wonderful you look today!"

"Oh, my beautiful princesses, how you flatter, do not stop!" He ran over to smother Au-Set in his large hug.

"Qui, you are crushing me!"

"All the better to feel the love!"

"Qui, Nebmaat, and naughty Kekes. I bring you sad news."

"We don't want it, send it back!" Kekes shouted.

Nebmaat noticed the gloom that hung over his wife and motioned to the other two to be quiet.

"It is Ua-Zit, the time has come and she demands our presence while the dream of last evening is to be read to the people." They nodded and rose to help gather the others.

Ua-Zit was carried up to the top of the richly painted palace on the highest spot on the roof, where the announcements were made. Four slaves of the darkest ebony possible carried her up on her ivory throne. The contrast was amazing. Ua-Zit had become pale as she spent her time indoors in being too ill to leave her bed-quarters. Her hair was piled upon her head in ringlets of faded black. White had sparkled through to dominate it. Her eyes saddened and held the answers of a lifetime. Gathered around her was her daughter Astarte to her left in the place of honor, with Suti by her side. Neb-Het sat on the other side of Suti. To her right was her heir, Au-Set. Astarte had stepped down, after her mother's offer was renewed to her. She was done and not ready to take on anything new. She had too much that she had to heal from and she had fertile plans of soon returning to her Retenu.

Au-Sar and Nebmaat stood to the right of Au-Set. The children of the next generation were sitting in front of the gathered family. There was Set who refused to look at her mother and sat stubbornly by her true father Suti. Neb-Het's children were present, Anpu and the infant Meshkenet with her full head of dark curls.

Around Au-Set were her children, Bast, Heru, Merul, Renenutet, and Weret-Heka with their consort Shai, and the twins, Maat and Serqet on the lap of Bast. Tehuti stood over them in order that the people knew that he was the one to read aloud the secret words of the Goddess Ua-Zit.

Ua-Zit told them that they must create a spectacular show for the people and ordered them to dress up garishly. For the occasion, Qui and Kekes responded and came out with costumes made of woven gold.

For the Shen or Hawk Peoples ruling family of Suti, Astarte, Neb-Het, Anpu, and Meshkenet, they wore silver crowns of out spread wings. They had elaborately made collars of precious jewels that reached out to their shoulders in width of carnelian, pearl, malachite, obsidian, to name a few. The ruling family of the Iaret had the same garments, but wore crowns made to resemble a cobra wrapped around their brow and in attention looking out, with hood flared. Their eyes were heavily painted with Kohl to protect them from the harsh sun. It had soon become the latest in fashions, since it exaggerated their eyes. Malachite was ground and put over their eyes as well. Their lips were painted in a crimson paste, while a fine white powder made them appear almost translucent before the people. Their ethereal forms solidified them as a family and made them appear extremely God-like and powerful.

Tehuti read at the nod of Ua-Zit the following dream proclamation, "People of the River of the Shen Peoples and the People of the Iaret are united to hear this. I the Goddess Ua-Zit have sent to my earthly representation a dream as will be read by prince Tehuti.

"The river will be our uniting force and our destruction. Two people that stand here will be successful in uniting this land of the Upper and Lower Kemet. Divided, the land will be brought into darkness. You must see that through the people that are united a new culture will be brought to this land. We will last for several millennia. The way we dress, our new picture writing of the Gods, the color brought to enduring temples and our vitality, will last forever and mystify the world. In my dream I saw the natural enemies the hawk carry the iaret in love and support. They were united as this family is here today. However, we all must work together to make this a reality. I saw it so clear in the world of dreams, it will be so!" Tehuti looked over at Ua-Zit and saw a smile that erased many years and worry from her face. He bowed to her, as did all of the others. The people in the crowd below them prostrated themselves before their living deity, the Goddess Ua-Zit.

Two days later Ishurti as the living representative of the Goddess Ua-Zit left her earthly body to begin her journey of reuniting her nine paths in order to reside with the Gods. Being a representative of the Goddess and one of the Supreme rulers of Kemet, she was able to request her funeral wishes.

Au-Set made sure that Ua-Zit was buried according to her elaborate wishes. Ua-Zit wanted to start a new complex deep in the desert, near the delta on the side of the setting sun. She had a simple *mastaba* built to replicate the mound of creation where her people were created. Inside, there were complex traps set for future tomb raiders. A pit that was dug was lined with spears pointed up and covered in a weak false walkway.

Inside, the most elaborate paintings adorned the walls to occupy Ishurti Ua-Zit in the afterlife and on her quest. Paintings of offerings were on the walls along with paintings of her family in half animal likenesses. Au-Set was painted in human form and on her head was the throne, Au-Sar was green as Andjety, and the ruler of the underworld, Suti had the head of a jackal over his body, Thoth had the head of an Ibis over his human form, Bast had the head of a cat and so on.

Ua-Zit loved how they all had unique animals as pets and companions. The people of this land seemed to awe the royal family even more due to their power over animals previously thought untamable. Ua-Zit requested that this be incorporated into her tomb, the representations of her family as she saw them in her dream for the afterlife. She noticed in life that they each seemed to have some of the qualities of their pets. This is perhaps why she dreamed of her family mixed with their own pets to form one entity.

The dying queen left a note for Au-Set, Au-Sar, and Tehuti explaining her dream vision of them and of how it could work for them in ruling over the people in Kemet. She made Tehuti promise that for now on the family would always be represented in their half human-half animal or symbolic forms.

Au-Set had the throne, since she would be the one to inherit Lower Kemet and Ua-Zit believed that she was the one who would help unite it. This she saw in her dream and told no one but Au-Set of this. Instead, it was painted out on the walls of her tomb as her statement from the other world. On the walls were also painted scenes from Eshnunna and Kemet and on the ceilings were stars over a vivid blue sky in twilight.

Ua-Zit requested that she proclaim a law to the people, made even more powerful after her death and embrace of the Goddess. The law was that there was to be no more cannibalism, no more devouring of the family members by their descendants. She wished that her body should be perfectly preserved in its entirety so that the Gods of the underworld would recognize her. She wanted to be judged by them in her *full form.*

Thus, over her carefully wrapped and preserved body covered in silver charms was a simple wooden coffin that resembled the shape of her wrapped form. On the coffin, she had herself painted as she looked while in the prime of her beauty at the age of thirty. In this form, she would be judged by the Gods and find all of her nine paths to reside by them in eternity. This, she painted instructions for her family when they would meet with the after-life. Her suit of armor made of plated copper along with her copper weapons, stood sentry and was held by statues of herself in full warrior dress. Her favorite stone was the bright orange carnelian and it adorned most of her court jewelry that was buried with her. Offerings were placed inside her favorite pottery that was red with a black rim that was a specialty of the delta.

Au-Set was pleased with the result and knew that her aunt would be happy as well, since each of her charges secretly carried out her wishes. She smiled at the hard work that was put into it as the doors were sealed forever and the trap was completed. Throughout the whole process, the son of her sister, Anpu, assisted her. He had seemed to develop a flair for burials in his creativity.

Chapter 107

As with brilliance of any kind, sometime the beginnings of such were not very joyful in its creation. Thus, the dynasty of Au-Set and her siblings started out a little bit rough, once the kingdoms of Upper and Lower Kemet were completely in their hands.

Au-Set and Au-Sar had taken over the inherited rule of Ua-Zit. Au-Set became known as Au-Set Ua-Zit, Goddess of Lower Kemet and Au-Sar and Nebmaat as her official consorts. Neb-Het retained the name of Neb-Het Nekhebt, Goddess of Upper Kemet. Suti however made it known to all of them that he wanted sole control and had started his campaign to do so.

Suti told the people that sole rule over Kemet was his right in that he had the most holy birth of all of his siblings. He was conceived of two Gods, Enlil of Sumer, and Innana of Eshnunna. He told the people that his mother was also known as Nut, the Goddess of the evening stars above them. He stated that it was her form that covered them at night. He made himself the God of the Deshret or of the Red Lands. He was training an elite force to take over the rest of Kemet. He left Abdjw under the control of Astarte in his absence.

In Abdjw, there was not much of a resistance when Au-Set and Au-Sar came to claim the throne for themselves and their sister, Neb-Het Nekhebt and her son Anpu. In fact, Astarte welcomed them warmly.

Astarte told them at their arrival, "I am so glad that you are here, Suti and his daughter have gone completely out of control in their warfare games! I am sick and tired of it! It is almost as if he has gone mad and has taken Set along with his ravings, for she is a complete follower of his fanatical ideas!"

"Sister, we are here for you." Nebmaat proclaimed. The two of them embraced, for it had been quite the while since they were reunited.

Au-Set, in her usual "right to business tone" stated, "Well, where can we house the troops that we have brought? I am famished. After that, let's eat!" The rest nodded and went on with their setting up a new capitol in the best location. They wanted to quell the rebellion in the north before they could return to the south in the delta.

Au-Set and her entourage were in Nekhen for over a month while she and her sister developed plans for a fortified city made of six cubit deep mud brick walls. Inside was a planned out town with a palace overlooking the dwelling of the people who resided there who were mostly craftspeople and merchants.

While Au-Set and Au-Sar were busy assisting their sister and setting her up in her inherited reign, they left the city of Per-Uto vulnerable to attack. They had wrongfully believed that Suti was at his fortress in the Deshret with his sacred army, little did they know that he had watched them carefully while they were completely distracted in planning the new defenses of the city. He had then gathered up his forces and had sent them by desert route down south the Per-Uto.

Chapter 108

The city stood there gleaming in its ignorance, having no idea of what it would silently witness. Suti had gathered his forces on the outside of the city that his aunt and sister had built. He scanned it carefully to see if there were any guards on patrol at that time. He had sent in spies in order to determine the amount of warriors that were guarding the city as well as the time that they changed for the next patrol to guard. This latter occurred twice a day, half way between the day and evening. There was no formal ceremony, it just occurred in a jumble of movement. He laughed at how unorganized that all of this was.

He brought Set along with him and watched how eager that she was in learning the arts of warfare. She absorbed everything that she was taught and seemed to almost grow taller at the very thought of battle. He knew that she was angry over some girlish thing, though was thankful that it brought her over to his side. He was proud to be acknowledged in her paternity, as if anyone could deny it.

She had the same hair of fire that set him apart from his other siblings. Sometimes he felt that it was a beacon of hope for his well-trained forces to follow into battle, and other times he felt that it was a curse. He recalled all too well how people would talk about him and his hair when he was too young to understand it all. Suti never forgot the whispers behind his back, nor how it made him feel.

As an adult, he prided himself in his individuality and encouraged his daughter as well. Both of them wore their hair in long braids with carnelians and bloodstones woven throughout to enhance the redness. They choose to wear the skins of leopard recently killed in their first hunt together as father and daughter. She was even given one of the young piglets of her own to raise. She made her father proud when, as it grew to enormous size, she had trained it enough to ride it. She was very tiny which made this latest feat possible. They made quite the pair indeed, as they stood outside of the city analyzing the best way to attack.

Finally, after much debate, they decided that it would be more glamorous to strike the city at the highest hour of the sun to reiterate their point. Thus, unhindered by any planned or organized defenders, they were able to ride into the city to capture it with ease. They choose to set the inhabitants free while they torched the city, obliterating everything that stood to symbolize the city that Suti had grown to hate over the years.

Set obeyed the orders of her father and took out all of her bitterness and hatred over the confines of her mother's rule and in the restriction of her childhood. Along the side of her father, he encouraged her whims and celebrated every bad habit that she had. He seemed a complete anomaly and often wondered how he came to be this way.

She had asked him several times why he wanted to do this. The only thing that he told her was that it was to prove a point. He never told her which point this was. Then again, he never was one for talking that much and he certainly did not waste words. She knew that when she was ready, he would reveal his reasons for her. Silently she watched while the place of her birth went up in flames as it was fanned on by the desert winds that rose off of the Great River steadily and building as the day progressed. She watched as her father took great joy in hurling large rocks from great slingshots at the walls of the city and main palace.

As Set stood there transfixed, Suti caught her eye and winked at her. She just stood there embedded to the spot as if she was growing roots from her feet. She felt stagnant and in complete desolation as she watched the sun slowly set across the dying city. As the colors melted over what was once a whole and thriving city, it covered the last of the destruction with the merciful blanket of darkness. The stars bore silent witness to the tears that she fought hard to hold back, lest her father witness what he called 'careless emotions'.

Chapter 109

As expected, Au-Set could not believe the destruction of her beloved city. She felt that with each brick that was crushed, so was any memory of all that her aunt had painstakingly created. The tears flowed cleanly in deep respect for the loss of her aunt so completely and hurtfully that it made her head swim with vile thoughts. She found the people who were evacuated and knew why they were spared. Suti wanted it known that this was his idea and that it was done during the light of day in its full splendor was an added sore to her feelings. She had then realized how untrained and unorganized that her forces were.

She looked at Au-Sar and he bowed in return to her, "Sister, let me work on the forces that we have and gather more on the way. We need to return to our sister and save her, if that is where he plans to go next." She nodded solemnly and gathered her Scorpion Guard and her children around her to plan the next move. She never thought that she would have to defend herself against her brother!

Bast, Merul, Heru and the others brandished their spears with the honor of their family and at the loss of their home. "Mama, Herab is itching for war!"

Au-Set smiled at the enthusiasm of her daughter. She reached over to the reigns that her daughter made as she sat atop the ageing Herab, who was raised since it was a lion cub since she was old enough to train him. "Like a lion, kitten, you must wait for the proper time. Herab knows when the time will be ripe. Besides, Set is with him. She is your sister!"

Merul was just leaving the awkwardness of youth with his voice squeaking as he spoke up, "Papa promised that I would have a hawk like his and Heru's. I think that now would be the proper time for that since I need one to ride into battle."

Au-Sar looked at his son, ruffled his hair, winked at him, and then walked over to the side of Au-Set. "Do you think it wise that the children fight my love?"

Au-Set looked startled, "Why ever not? They are well trained. How better to learn the arts of defense and war tactics, if not in actual combat?"

Nebmaat looked disturbed and sauntered over to the side of his friend Qui and whispered to his large form, "Surely you do not think that she will make us fight? I would have nothing to wear!" Qui looked equally upset by this and looked pleadingly over to Au-Set.

Without one word, she knew the reason for the distress for her best dressed court members and smiled, "Do not worry Qui, Kekes, and Nebmaat, I will let you design our battle-gear! Make sure that it is not only beautiful, but practical as well. We want it to inspire fear, remember?"

Qui clasped his large meaty hands in anticipation and looked over to his two favorite assistants. "Come! We have much work to do!" Just as the two of them went off Kekes, looked disturbed. He trembled in his spot transfixed in horror.

"What is it Kekes!" Qui Screeched.

"Our workshop, there is nothing left! How can we work without anything to prepare it with?" Suddenly all three of them looked distressed.

Renenutet spoke up in deep sympathy for her childhood friends and on behalf of her own father, Nebmaat. "Papa, can you work on the boat instead?" She looked over at her mother.

"What a wonderful idea! Au-Sar gather your best farmers, since they are only sitting idle for the inundation and see if they can construct a fast fleet of papyrus boats to take us swiftly to Nekhen! I assume that Suti has taken the desert route. On the boat, you three can plan our gear and stop for supplies along the way. "Heru, send your hawk to warn your aunt Neb-Het of this! Anpu, gather the rest and help with the building of the boats!"

Anpu was the youngest of the lot and was sent to live in Per-Uto a few years back away from his mother in protection from Suti, who had threatened him from birth and banished them for the reason of his birth alone. Anpu was always by the side of his aunt, especially since she looked so completely like his mother that sometimes he fooled himself into believing that she were. "Auntie, are brothers helping too?"

Au-Set laughed, "And myself and your sisters as well. I think that we all will make one scary force to be reckoned with. I believe that Suti will think twice before he plans on separating our family like this again!"

She looked over at Au-Sar and whispered to him out of earshot of the children, "Brother, this is exactly what our mother raised us to prevent. What went wrong?"

The troubled look in his eyes spoke multitudes, "I think that no matter what ones intentions are in life and wishes, that sometimes, life and fate have something else in store for us."

He looked over at his family and the people of the destroyed city of Per-Uto, who had gathered, "Come, let us not waste any further time and build our way to solving this rift."

To the people who had gathered he spoke calmly, "Let this be a lesson of what could occur when unity is not achieved. When one does not prepare well and is unorganized... From now on, we will form a force that will be well trained and perfect. We will march on to Nekhen to establish a new capitol and rule together. If Suti wants to split this, let him try!" The people roared in approval and stomped their feet. They lifted Au-Sar and Au-Set into the air and passed them reverently around the crowd in adoration and pride.

With this fierce new pride of their rulers, the people of the Iaret made their swift river migration in Kemet's direction of north to Upper Kemet with the flow of the river. A new dawn had begun for the people who were willing to embrace unification for their own protection. Along the way, Au-Set and Au-Sar planned on how to approach the situation. Au-Sar wanted to go straight to Neb-Het to gain her help in this. Au-Set agreed, though mentioned that they should not upset her rule out of Nekhen, and rather work on setting up a sister city in Abdjw.

With that in mind and a place to set up their home base, they arrived in the darkest hour of the night and woke Neb-Het from her sleep. In her arms was her growing daughter Meshkenet whose raven curls were tangled on those of her mothers.

Au-Sar smiled since it reminded him of how Au-Set looked long ago with Bast. He felt that Meshkenet bore a striking resemblance to Bast that it almost made him think that he had walked into the past, especially since Neb-Het was the mirror of Au-Set. Such a wonderful way in which life wove its mysteries and sometimes mingling the past with the present to either remind one of days never to be recovered, or to tease them. It made one-recall things that they did not notice when it actually occurred in the past.

Neb-Het rubbed her sleep weary eyes and stared up at her sister and brother in surprise.

Au-Set sat down next to her and took her twin and mirror into her arms, "Sister, the time has come. Mother's worst nightmare has been realized! Our brother has finally waged war!"

"Wha..." her words failed her. Neb-Het felt that she had woken into some terrible nightmare and failed to see the realism in the whole scene that played about her. With the sudden embrace of her sister, she felt reality catch up with her as solid as a wall. "What do you mean?"

"Suti! Suti and his Deshret forces have attacked Per-Uto and leveled it to the ground!"

"That cannot be true sister! Set, where is Set? Is she not with our family?"

Heru spoke up now, "Aunt, in all due respect, Set is not a part of this family anymore! She has chosen to fight against us!"

Au-Sar looked over at his war hungry son and patted him on the shoulders and Heru brushed it aside and stood taller in front of his aunt and mother.

"Heru, Suti is our brother and your uncle. No matter what he has done, we made a promise long ago to our mother Ninnuit that we would all work together for this land. We are here to reason with him, not to kill him. Your sister is only misguided and very young. In her youth, she is not rationalizing properly the devastating moves that she is making by siding with our irrational brother!"

Au-Set moved closer to Au-Sar since he mimicked her true emotions that she was afraid to utter, so deep was her anger of their brother. "Yes, we made a promise."

Neb-Het clasped her sister's hand, "I remember."

Tehuti, who was on the side of them recording the events of the family, stopped writing and with a small tear in his eye in remembrance of the infant Suti that he held close in sleep, "Never forget our links and what made us. I honor that promise as should we all."

Heru was not pleased about this at all. He made no such promise and wanted the blood of his uncle in retribution for destroying his home. He wanted the blood of Set as well. He tried desperately to block out the memories of sitting on her lap when he was young. He felt more betrayed than the others did over Set, since she was his union mate and Goddess chosen. She had destroyed his pride in leaving him for an old man and then to betray her whole family by siding with their irrational uncle, it was too much for his anger to quell with simple words from his family.

Bast, who felt the same way as both of her brothers, looked over at him, giving him a look that warned him of silence. Merul knew that Bast had a plan. Renenutet and Weret-Heka as usual were oblivious of the three warrior children of Au-Set and Au-Sar. They went over to the side of their aunts and uncles and embraced her, to let them know that they would be on the older siblings' side as well.

Bast, Heru and Merul looked at each other and knew that they would be meeting soon to implement their own plans. None of them liked the idea of talking with their uncle Suti; they made no such promise to a long dead grandmother.

Chapter 110

It was a stormy evening when the rare clouds of a torrential rainstorm had gathered to stomp down on the weary townspeople of the settlement of Nekhen. They had not seen rain such as this in any lifetime to hit this area and it startled them into feeling that it was an omen of some sort. The meeting was planned to occur on the morrow at the first break of light.

Most people were startled as the rain woke their slumber on the rooftops and almost fell off in confusion. Rain was rare and sometimes not even one drop was seen for years, and when it did, the drops were usually small and pretty as was described in history annals. This rain was fierce and ravenous and seemed to be a nightmare spewed from the mouths of the Gods in anger. The clouds contorted with anger and bright colors rumbled out mighty and ferocious roars of fear that ripped through the startled hearts of the people born and raised in Kemet.

Au-Set and Neb-Het sat on the roof under the canopy recalling similar storms as very young girls in Eshnunna, looked down at the streets of the newly reconstructed city of Nekhen. Au-Set had noticed how some of the newer dwellings of mud brick construction started to give way. They had used the mud-brick due to the rarity of rain in this part of the world and she and her sister were undismayed by the storm in that it was something that did not even occur in a lifetime here. However, she knew that some of the newer buildings would have to be rebuilt and she did not shun for the future use of the same material.

Au-Set looked at the damage below and knew that it was only minor compared to what she and her united siblings had to face. She was proud of her sister and had told her so. "Sister, you have never been my shadow in deeds, only in heart."

She giggled, "Not to mention, your mirror. Only because you were born first! You would be my mirror, would you have been born second as I was." They both giggled and watched the clouds gather in strength. It seemed as if the skies wanted a battle and were telling them so. The canopy was rather flimsy and not meant in protecting them from rain, as it rarely occurred in the area that the desert constantly tried to capture. The canopies over the roofs were to protect them from the sun for an afternoon nap or in just resting.

"We won't have much protection, when it hits even harder as it appears to want to do!" Spoke up Au-Set wearily.

"No, we will not. What about tomorrow? Will we have protection then?"

"I hope that our blood protects us and guides us in this. We made a promise and we have to remind him of this. I hope that the message that he received relayed this adequately." She prayed for her daughter's sake, that Set would not be forced by her own father to fight against her mother and siblings.

It was then that the very first drops of rain fell triumphantly through the flimsy shelter and broke the barrier of their silence, that Qui entered their sanctuary on the roof. "Your warrior gear is ready!" His face beamed in the pride of his accomplishment.

Au-Set tried to hide her surprise, "Oh, Qui, I had forgotten about that! Could you by any chance change them to garments of a council instead, or perhaps official gear for our family?" She smiled weakly to him and felt bad.

"No worry, young queen. I shall change this and have it all ready for the morrow in time for your meeting of the minds!" His smile was wonderful and forgiving to Au-Set as she stood up and wrapped her arms around him as far as they could reach. She loved the wonderful friend of hers and definitely considered him a part of their odd family.

Chapter 111

Suti and Set walked side by side at the lead of their well-trained forces. Suti did not know why, but he actually felt that he should hear out what his brother and sisters had to say. He also recalled that promise made long ago. He felt that his life had changed things a bit and made things the way they currently were. He did not want to fight his siblings, but felt that he had no choice. However, he would hear them out and see what they had to offer in honor of their mother.

He looked over at the female version of himself looking regal and almost like the Goddess herself in her fierce fiery determination to appear grown up for her father. He smiled and spoke to her, "Set, watch closely, for a kingdom to be run properly, you must see all sides of reason. I am curious to hear what they have to say. Are you not little one?"

"Papa, I am far from little. I should be a mother now!"

"Oh, you will always be little to me, and I do not want to even think of you yet as a mother! Let us see the warrior in you first! But, stand by my side and do not speak one word!"

She nodded her head and continued to walk along the side of her father into the gates of Nekhen. Upon agreement, all weapons were to be left in a room at the gates of the city for this meeting to occur. Suti agreed and knew that there would be time enough to yield them. He also smiled in that he had his forces waiting outside under cover beyond the view of the city walls, with more weapons. All he had to do was give them a signal, in case things went against him.

They tossed their spears into the room with the guard and held up their arms to show that there were no more weapons on them. When approved, they were let inside and led to the chamber where the meeting was to occur.

Suti thought that he had his guard behind him as he and Set walked into the room and thought nothing of it until the large copper plated doors were closed behind their footsteps. The chamber that they walked into was completely engulfed in darkness, in fear and instinct, Suti grabbed his daughter's hand and yelled out to the darkness, "Is this any way to treat your brother!"

They stood there in a void of empty until a small light appeared as a wick was lit inside a large alabaster bowl. The small light of the fire grew to light up the area ahead of them. The glow was trying to fight through the veins of the transparent stone of the oil lamp.

Suti's sight slowly adjusted to the light and saw the focus of the soft illumination. He realized that it was the face of his brother Au-Sar. Au-Sar's face appeared eerie in the dimness of the alabaster glow. In the slight field of the light, his face seemed to float as if one the Gods. Au-Sar's face was painted in a green color to appear as if he were from the walking dead. Suti decided to see how this game played out. He knew that when his brother donned his makeup, it was mostly for the public and ceremony for the people. This fact calmed him somewhat as he was led forward with his daughter by his side.

"Yes, brother Suti, for in here we properly welcome you and Set. Please have a seat beside us as an equal as it was always meant to be." As he said the words that bounced throughout the room in its eerie acoustics, more lamps were lit and he saw that Au-Sar and Au-Set were in silver plated chairs. Au-Sar was to the right of Au-Set and an empty chair was between she had Neb-Het. He noticed that all were carved out of silver and were the same in every noticeable way.

Au-Set and Neb-Het spoke out at once, "Brother, have a seat, our meeting has begun." Suti, caught off guard by the theatrics, numbly walked over to his chair that was waiting for him while Set was led to the side by Bast, who appeared out of the darkness.

"What is the meaning of this?" Spoke up Suti.

Au-Set now spoke, "The people want an end to this petty sibling brawl. We felt that this would be the only way to get you to come to our meeting."

As she stated this, torches were lit along the walls of the chamber and Suti now realized how vast this chamber was, for it seemed as if hundreds of people lined the walls and crowded around the raised platform where their chairs were. Then he knew that his siblings had defeated him. Suti hated public appearances and in his fear, his plans were forgotten. He felt just a mere pawn to whatever the meaning to all of this was.

"Brother, we are all assembled to show to the people our family and the unity from which we rule. Do you agree?"

Caught off guard, he felt that he had no choice but to weakly agree. "Yes."

Neb-Het then spoke up, "We are here to implement new laws for the people and to establish a culture that will last forever. We are here to bring this to the people." She nodded to her sister.

Au-Set added, "We first, in honor of the law of Ua-Zit, implement and agree to the new funeral rites for the dead for all people that are to be practiced. That all people must be interred in properly dug mounds to return them to the primordial mound from hence they came. Their bodies will be intact and recognized in the afterlife."

The whole room knew of this, only now it was made official.

Au-Sar then added, "Next, we will request a small payment in produce and grain for the protection of our armies." Again, a law made official.

Tehuti then stopped his writing, for he was the official recorder of their family's history to utter, "Now and forever more this family is to be revered as Gods and Goddesses on earth and worshipped as such!" The people mumbled at this, for it was unprecedented. They had only heard of rulers being deified after their deaths, not while they were living.

An old woman spoke up from the crowd; she had the face of the people upon her brow and spoke with a village elder's authority to the now hushed room. "This is a vivid proclamation, though it has warrant for sure. We were small villages with nothing to do but pick offerings of the river, now we have crops. This was brought to us by Au-Sar. We also have the magic of the writing of the sacred words! We have an economy and can raise our heads tall with the rest of the world that we did not know was around us! I say, why not? They are not mere mortals to us, but the beginning of life and like the ancient Gods, they have created and molded us into something new!" The crowd roared with vigor and acceptance.

Suti was dizzy in his seat. This was something new, to be worshipped as a God by the common people! This was certainly worth listening to indeed!

Tehuti continued," From now on, the words I write will breathe life into a new culture and we will be the very first to live it! I will adorn the temples and palaces for generations not yet born, of our lives and what we have brought them!"

Suti clapped his hands almost forgetting himself, for he also noticed when the words had died down the costumes that they were all wearing. Au-Set was wearing their mother's headdress of a disc surrounded by long cow horns of the Goddess Innana. Au-Sar had a headdress that was plumed elaborately with the feathers of a hawk that seemed to embrace his head and in his hands, he held a wooden rod with wheat wrapped around it and a flail in the other hand to whisk away the flies of the room. He chuckled at this, for he knew that it would be recorded and made into his official gear. He noticed that Neb-Het had an elaborate headdress made of vulture feathers and the wings wove around her brow.

As the meaning of the words sunk into the crowd gathered, Suti looked up above him and noticed that the sky was slowly being revealed to them far above, through an elaborate system of hooks and weights. He smiled at the ingenuity of his siblings in this performance and thought that perhaps they just might have a chance. He knew that in order for his siblings and family to establish order and rule over the people, it would have to be done ceremoniously and with exaggerated ostentation. A mostly foreign family would normally find it difficult to establish itself as the reigning family, when there already was one.

However, his family did have a chance since they shared the blood of the royal family of Kemet itself and most of their own hereditary rulers had died out. He knew that it would not be easy at all and they would have to use considerable creativity to impress these people. Suti had to admit that he was impressed with this completely theatrical assembly and liked the way that when the sky was revealed, the sun's rays danced upon their costumes spraying it all around them with reflective tricks. Their costumes had tiny crystals woven to create this ingenious effect. Suti now understood why he was given a garment to wear before he sat down beside them. He guessed that this whole thing was probably the idea of Qui and Kekes, knowing them.

Au-Set winked at him when she noticed his reaction and leaned over towards him and whispered, "Do not worry it is almost over and then we will deal with the rest that must be talked about as was promised."

All he could do was shrug his shoulders in response. Suti hated to be the center of the crowd and this one was really starting to bother him. As the chamber filled with the rays of the sun and it slowly became a part of the outdoors, he got up to follow Au-Sar and then Au-Set and the others were behind him. They walked over to a spot by the rear of the raised platform and stopped. They seemed to be waiting for something. Then it happened, a huge puff of smoke appeared from the side and covered them. Au-Set nudged him to follow while their forms were covered from the crowd below them by the thick distracting smoke. She led him to a trap door that had been opened under a rug on the floor, which led to a secret passageway to another part of the palace that was lined with torches.

At last, when they reached the secret room of their destination, the costumes of his siblings were taken off gratefully, for they were very heavy and uncomfortable in their elaborate design.

As everyone had finally removed their garments of state and had reclined among the many soft pillows that lined the room a servant entered the chamber with large blue faience bowls that contained grapes. Goblets were produced as if from the air to be filled from tall amphorae made of clay. Suti sat back, not knowing what to expect next. He wondered what could possibly top what he had just unknowingly become a part of out there. He could still hear the cheers of the mystified crowds at their disappearance before their eyes.

"So, brother what do you think?" Au-Sar inquired.

"Well, that was quite something... I have to admit that the people now really do think that we are Gods, quite impressive." He leaned slowly winding up as a cobra does to strike and added, "Why involve me at all in this? You could easily have had me killed in front of all of those people, would it not have added to the magic of the performance?"

"Brother, you know that we all made a promise to our mother." Neb-Het whispered and was suddenly unsure of their plans.

Au-Set looked over at her sister and projected the confidence that she needed and told Suti, "Yes, and it is about time that we started to honor that promise, now that we are adults. This land would benefit with all of us in rule! We need to band together and to work as one. There is so much potential and need for what we can do for these people."

"Why honor a promise made when we were too little to understand all that it entailed?" Suti rolled his eyes in boredom.

"Because, we feel that it is necessary and we can also force you." Spoke Au-Sar, which added to the astonished and unbelieving face of his brother.

"We know of your hidden troops and of your plans, we have your mistress Puanit in captivity and she tells quite a story of your plans. Your brainwashed daughter is in awe of you still. However, when she learns the truth about you, I am sure that you will lose her too as you have lost the trust of so many others that have tried to help you in the past!"

"How dare you! I need no help from any of you! I have more troops besides the ones that you have captured..."

"Ummmm brother, you do not....we have those in the Deshret as well!" Spoke Neb-Het with a growing confidence, whose voice almost identically matched the powerful voice of her twin sister Au-Set.

"And all of your weapons and everything else, even your beloved pets..." Spoke up Tehuti, who up until then had remained quiet and in the background as usual.

"You cannot do that! That is so base and completely beneath you!"

"As base as destroying the city that your co-rulers reigned out of? How would mother see that act of destruction?" Tehuti mentioned, for he knew that it was a sore spot with Suti. He knew that no matter how much Suti insulted their mother and hated her for leaving them; he had always wanted to please her. He knew that this would hit Suti the hardest, as well as the taking of his pets.

Au-Sar looked Suti up and down judging and balancing his worth to the room and to the family. "Yes, we could easily have you killed and no one would suffer more for it. However, we did make a promise to our mother as well did you! There was great wisdom in her deciding that all of us work together in this. You know as well as I that when a ruling family separates, the land falls apart. The unity of our family will bring this land to the forefront of the known world!"

He let this sink into his brother and continued, "We have decided to place into effect Ua-Zit's wishes that she made of a tribunal. We will be the living Gods on earth, while under us will be chosen people to represent our land, which will be divided into sections or Sepats.

We saw how effective our love of strange animals was on the common people of this land and decided to use it to enhance our plans here. Each Sepat and ruler to them will be assigned a totem animal and symbol to represent them, if they have not chosen one already. In addition, from now on we will only appear to the people in our full theatrical gear as designed by Qui and Kekes. Yours still needs to be finished which is why you were given the cape in place. You can tell them what kind of headdress that you will wear and what symbol that you prefer."

"I see, this does have potential, is there more?"

"I thought that you would never ask brother," Spoke Au-Set, "This tribunal will consist of forty-two judges, one for each Sepat that I have divided this land into. They will serve as the administrators of the laws to the people as well as the judges for common disputes. When a matter needs our attention a main court will be called in our new base located here at Abdjw. Nugig Ma-At, Re, and Maat will be trained as the main judges of the land and we, the ruling family and siblings will have the only authority to overrule their decision. *Anmut* here has been chosen as the person to decide punishment or as we like to call her, *'The devourer!'* "The room burst into laughter at that one, for they knew how Anmut was in her punishments and felt that name was definitely fitting. This woman loved to dole out creative punishments and prided herself in being fair and inventive in having the punishment fit the crime to the best of her artistic nature.

Anmut just happened to be in the room with them as well as Re, their children, Mut and some others that he did not recognize. Anmut spoke up in her cackle of a voice that barely broke into the room, "I have prepared a pit of very hungry crocodiles for any especially rrrrancid people!" Her voice hissed out her pleasure in throwing people into her crocodile pit. She was renowned to be a very fair judge and those who were thrown in definitely deserved it!

Suti felt uneasy with the presence of Anmut.

Tehuti noticed this and leaned over to him, "Do not worry little brother, your time for the pit is not now. I would seriously consider cooperating with them, for you are here solely by their patience and I would say by your balls! I would guard them carefully and play their game, for you have to agree that it does have great merit"

Suti nodded, for Tehuti was right and would not have warned him unless for good reason. He knew that Tehuti was a very black and white person, with no in between. Tehuti always chose the winning side and wrote down what he saw of everything from a very standard perspective and point that was unblemished by any sentiment. The very practical Tehuti was certainly someone that Suti should listen to with respect and caution.

"You know little brother that you are very lucky that you are not the first to be placed in front of the tribunal this day to test it. We will let this act of aggression pass as the rash act of youth, especially since no lives were lost in Per-Uto." Then slowly Au-Sar leaned in for the further verbal kill. "We are watching you brother and you will be in our sight every waking moment of the life that you want to keep. Because I know that were mother alive and saw the acts that you have done on this family, thus far, you would not have lived this long at all! Only she had the power in this family to give us life and to take it away!" All of the others nodded in agreement to this and stomped their feet on the ground.

Au-Set decided to let this all sink in and felt that now it was time to close this first meeting. "We have a lot to think about, for we want this land to prosper and this tribunal should be very powerful and fair most of all in its dealings. We want the people to know that we care about them and also, that we will not tolerate any rash acts against us, ever again!" She looked over with piercing eyes at Suti.

Chapter 112

Thus began the golden era of a family that would bring monumental changes to the stark land of Kemet that would last unchanged for almost four thousand years.

Abdjw was reinforced yet again and made even grander when the mud-brick was painted in bright shades of the rising sun to symbolize a new dawn of the people of Kemet. The siblings ruled over the land from barges made of papyrus and from silver and quartz thrones that would amplify the suns powerful rays of the land, enveloping each of them in an aura of power to the common people. They would travel to the different family cities in splendor and ceremony shining their power and protection over the people of Kemet who basked in their glory, for due to this family their bellies full from prosperity.

The Sepats were assigned and temples were built where each of the chosen tribunal ruled from and administrated the wishes of the four rulers of the land. Au-Set and Au-Sar were given the power over the Lower part of the land and mainly in the delta, while Suti and Neb-Het reunited and were given the power once again of the Upper part of their land. Astarte stood by their side and waited for her heir to be born and for her return to Retenu. Neb-Het stood by the side of Suti in formality only and led her own life with her son and daughter.

Au-Sar took to wearing a tall white pointed headdress with elaborate plumes made of ostrich feathers that reached the sky. He chose to keep the colors of the underworld to let the people know that he would judge them in the afterlife as well. He was primarily painted in green or black to emanate the guise of death. He made a striking figure indeed with his elaborate headdress. He carried what he called his *backbone* or his *djed* pillar, which was merely a tall pole with wheat wrapped around it at the top to symbolize that he was the creator of agriculture and the God of the bounty. He always had his pet hawk tied to his wrist when sitting on the tribunal, which met once a month to decide cases or to make new laws for the land and to relate all that has occurred in the meantime.

Au-Set took to wearing a replica of her mother's crown of Eshnunna of golden cow horns surrounding a sun disc. She wore the crown that she inherited from her aunt, the ruler of the people of the iaret, the ancient and golden hooded cobra that looped around her brow to rear its hood in the center of her forehead. She would always have her trained cobras wrapped around her waist, one of the many that she had trained for the Goddess. She also had her infamous Scorpion Guard standing around each of them when banded together at the tribunal and around their mistress at all of her waking and sleeping moments. She bore the title, *"Lady of the throne"* for she had created their intricate and magical design. In paintings, Tehuti sometimes represented Au-Set with a throne on her head in full human form to show this deep meaning and inheritance from Eshnunna.

Suti had five of his Deshret Guard watch over him with the red body paint denoting the harshness of the desert and in further emphasizing his red hair. The rest of his full guard of seventy-two was always lurking around on his orders. He had grown quite stout in his older years due to his many excesses and his skin had taken on a ruddy appearance that always made him appear as if he was blushing. His hair still had the same vibrancy of youth. He was always eating lettuce and believed that it improved his virility. His temper was short as were his legs, under his chubby form. However, his character made people stop in their tracks when he was near, if nothing else but in fear. He chose to keep his dog Heh by his side, which he told some that the dog was part jackal. So narrow and sleek was this dog, that one would often wonder and give it great berth when nearing the notorious pair. His headdress was plumed like the rest of them but over a red headdress covered in bloodstones and his favorite carnelians, again to accentuate his hair and temperament.

Neb-Het wore the vulture feathers in her hair to emulate the wings wrapped around her head as worn by her inherited position from Nekhebt. She also wore a replica of their mother's crown of cow horns and a disc in the center and was usually by the side of her identical twin sister, almost inseparable had they become lately. She would have her pet hawk tied to her wrist as well. She bore the title, "*Lady of the Mansion*", for her many designs of the palaces, cities and temples. She was known as the great architect of the new Kemet and all of its cities since they were mostly her idea.

Tehuti chose the headdress of the feathered plumes like his siblings, though was always seen with a reed pen and papyrus, for he insisted on recording events of their family in rule to leave for future generations. He wove their lives out from his reed pen as if they flowed from the Great River itself, so wondrous was his rendition. It was laced with flowery poetry and fantasy. He would take real events and made them mystical almost as if real Gods performed them as they aimed to be and not just the ordinary mortals that they were in reality. He always had with him one of the many ibis' strutting to follow his footsteps wherever he went. Tehuti walked about; dropping to his ibis crumbs of bread from the pleats of his long stark white kilt that each of the brothers wore besides their other ceremonial gear, as he strode through the many halls inspecting his painters.

The brothers had muscular torsos as they were trained in war from birth along with their sisters. They wore only long stark white kilts and elaborate headdresses to challenge the heat. The sisters wore garments as equally white and transparent to show their beauty and to catch the kisses of the harsh sun of this land without burning their delicate skin in the process. They as well wore elaborate headdresses as the sign of their rank and power in every day mode so the people grew accustomed to them in their God and Goddess gear.

Each of the brothers wore their beards long and narrow, as was the fashion created by Kekes. The sisters thought it only silly, yet kept their counsel silent. However, they respectfully appreciated their brothers' new concern with their recent deification and its entrapments. Qui and Kekes worked long into the evening hours constructing further works of art for each of the rulers of the Sepats to wear in ceremony that was rapidly becoming high fashion and worn on common days as well, and accepted as norm for the people of Kemet.

A throne in the center was left open in memory of their brother Heru, on which a statue of a hawk was placed to represent his spirit form watching over them all. Heru loved to train hawks and taught it all to Au-Sar when very young. Au-Sar passed this love on to his son Heru, named after his uncle who had died on the day of his namesake's birth. Most felt that Heru was certainly the reincarnation of the unknown uncle that he was named in honor of. The siblings knew that young Heru displayed the more dominant traits of their brother's peacekeeping abilities in that the young Heru always called for action. The elder Heru normally called for council. Possibly this later form of Heru was the one in which their new world needed more and was the reason why the old one was called home to the Gods.

All of them when in state outfits wore along with their elaborate headdresses, simple linen tight fitting long gowns of the purest and whitest linen obtainable. This simplicity of the clothing they wore placed more power on their headdresses and what powers they wanted to reveal to the people that they ruled.

Chapter 113

On a typical day at the end of the month when the tribunal met, they were sitting in their usual places when Re suddenly appeared. He had been away on sabbatical, for Au-Set felt that he needed this in order that he may be more effective in his judgment.

Re returned to court in his usual splendor, for he loved the theatrics. He arrived riding on top of a brilliant bull. Everyone stopped to gawk at his bravery.

"Greetings all! I would like to offer you a gift of this glorious bull that I have found on my journeys." They all jumped up from their thrones and ran over to look at the strange creature that Re brought before them. "On my journey, he used to walk before me, almost taunting me that I could not ride him. People came to know that with this bull, I would soon arrive at their village. I give him to you my son!" He looked at Tehuti and handed the reigns over to him who looked up at Re in amazement. Never before had his father officially acknowledged him before and his smile lit up his face. Re patted his shoulder and held him close to embrace him.

In amazement, and in his usual steady way he responded to the gesture, "Father, I thank you from the bottom of my soul for your love, however, this gift would suit my brother Au-Sar even more, would that be all right with you father?"

"By all means, but know that I embrace you into my home and hearth as I should have done long ago." He nodded with a wink in his eye to his son Tehuti and opened his arms to Au-Sar who was standing mutely beside this transaction.

Au-Sar spoke up with his loud and onerous voice that could stop any crowd and bring it to his command, "I thank you honored Re and accept this from you and my beloved brother!" The others in the room stomped their feet at this gesture and in hope for the public acknowledgement of Re for his son Tehuti. Au-Set beamed in love for her younger brother Tehuti as he glowed from the attention given to him by his father. He almost seemed a young boy again.

The others had gathered around the anxious bull at this time and noticed its unusual markings. Re pointed out each of them, "See, he is all black as the starkest of nights in the deepest of the Deshret. However, notice the beautiful white perfect diamond on its forehead and the image in white of a vulture on its back perfectly in the center. He lifted up the great tongue of the beast and pointed further to them, "and this under his tongue, is the mark of the scarab-sacred in life creation to this land of Kemet. He is truly born from a lightning bolt in his entire splendor and I give this to you my lord!" He bowed to Au-Sar. The people in attendance on this great and miraculous day ripped wild in applause, while Tehuti wrote it all down, as usual, only this time with a very large smile etched on his face.

Chapter 114

Tehuti basked in the glow of the acknowledgement of his father, Re of Ineb-Hedj. He wanted to make his father proud of him so he went to work on perfecting his new papyrus and the process of creating it. He also sought to decorate every building their family made in all of Kemet. He wanted the colors to reach out to the very heavens of their family's glory.

Au-Sar, on the other hand was happy for his brother and sad for himself. He knew that in his heart he could never have the same. His own father, Gilgamesh, had died long ago in the ritual of the temple. To steady his heart, he went to work creating a powerful army and a fleet of ships for their protection. He based his operations out of Djedu of the delta region in Lower Kemet. He would also journey down to Upper Kemet with the flow of the river to look after Suti and Neb-Het in Nekhen.

Au-Sar still maintained the city of Abdjw as his city and took on the title of "*Wennefer*" which meant eternally good or eternally incorruptible to show the people that even after he was dead, he would never fade nor suffer the decay of death. Beside this and his title of "*God of the Bounty*" he also took on the name of "*Chief of the Westerners*" to symbolize the cities of the dead which the family had ruled that would be on the west bank of the Great River on the side of the setting sun. The cities of the living were moved to the eastern side of the Great River on the side of the rising sun.

The *Westerners* were considered those of the dead and underworld. It was also the name of the local God he supplanted in this region near Abdjw named *Khentimentiu*, who took over the characteristics of the delta God named Andjety. He felt that in order to preserve the properties of those ancient Gods almost forgotten by the people he would take on their characteristics as the leader of the underworld. He had also years ago taken on the characteristics of another borrowed God of this land called *Sokar*, in training his flock of hawks. Anpu, his son from Neb-Het, had taken on the canine characteristics of Abdjw's ancient God Khentimentiu and had actually trained a jackal as his mascot and totem.

Au-Sar took well to the administration of this land and thoroughly enjoyed the theatrics that went along with it. However, sometimes he just yearned to be a simple man. He wondered what his life would have been like had he been born a simple farmer or a brewer of beer. He had prided his own ability to brew the best beer in the land. He had watched over the preparation of the local brewers and had learned over the years to perfect this art to his own tastes. He took pride in his work so much that he made sure that he solely made most of the beer. However, Merul had taken to watching him silently while he worked.

Merul was amazed at how his father would shine when he was making his favorite beer. He watched how his father seemed to glow with the pride in his special 'henket' as the people of the land called it. His father would even bake the special cakes and hid his ingredients from everyone. He would cover them while he added the secret ingredients. After the cakes were done and pulled out of the oven, they were set out in the sun to cool off and then placed carefully over a screen made of carefully woven copper wire that covered a large deep vat made of red-fired clay with the infamous black lid as scorched from the bonfires over which it was fired.

Merul watched silently as his father then poured water taken from the secret well found in a small oasis that only his father knew the location. This water was slowly poured over the cakes on top of the screen until they dissolved into the vat.

Au-Sar would dance to the Gods unnamed to make sure that this brew would be tasty and then throw in spices from a pouch that he wore at his belt of large beads made of precious stones. This mixture was then left in a warm place that was locked until it fermented as was judged perfect by the prideful Au-Sar.

Merul was not normally interested in his father's pursuits of agriculture, though for some reason, his making of beer fascinated him. Everyone had to agree that the henket made by Au-Sar was certainly the best in Kemet if not all of the world to each known corner. It was not too alcoholic though it was heavy with nutrients. The local people yearned to have his recipe for its high nutritive content. Eventually Au-Sar relented and gave the people a lesser version, though a very good one of his infamous beer. This soon became the staple of everyday meals throughout all of the land along with their bread.

Chapter 115

Merul spent most of the time in the temple along the side of his uncle Tehuti and watched his older brother Heru from afar. He wanted badly to be a warrior like his older brother and would often dream about it. His family had chosen that he follow example of his uncle Tehuti, due to his unusual talent. Not that he did not love to learn and create new words of the sacred writing, it was just that he felt it awful boring sometimes and he wished to be out in the sun, rather than inside the shady deep dark endless halls of the temple school that his uncle created in his city called Khnum.

On his return trips, he would run over to see if his father were brewing henket, when his father would nod affirmative, he would race to keep up.

Au-Sar relished the enthusiasm of his younger son and cherished his visits so much that he decided to make it a game to keep his interest. This is why he playfully exaggerated all of the secrets. He would tell his son that no, he was not making any henket and would wink otherwise, very subtly. Merul always caught on and secretly followed his father. Au-Sar pretended not to see his son, though worked extra hard to perform the process.

On one such day, Au-Sar felt that it was time to let his son in on this, as he was getting older. He knew that the magic would not last much longer. It was on one such day that he looked directly into the eyes of his son, as he knew that he was always there and asked him, "Son, do you have any ideas for the ingredients of these cakes?" Merul jumped up and enthusiastically joined in making beer with his father. From that day on Merul was at his father's side whenever possible. However, at the ending of the inundation when the river was at its fullest his mother made sure that he was packed once again for his studies at the temple with his uncle in Khnum, which Merul also enjoyed.

Chapter 116

Au-Set was saddened by the disappointment of her son with her telling him of his duties in Khnum with his uncle. She felt bad for Merul, though knew that he was the one with the most talent for the sacred writing of the Gods. She knew that Merul cherished the time with his father, since before the henket there was never a connection between the two of them. Most of his early childhood had been spent in his older brother's shadow. At last, Merul had found a connection with his father and had almost become obsessed by it almost forgetting his true and more important calling in life as a scribe.

She watched as her son left in the caravan that led him away from her to study once again. His small form lost in the officials that guarded him and his slumped tiny shoulders. She had given him the largest hug that she could muster for him. Nevertheless, she knew that he was at the age when he started to look at his father. She was no longer the hero of her son; she had to stand on the side as her consort Au-Sar basked in this boys' adoration. She turned away to check on Puanit, who was under her watchful eyes this day in Abdjw. Astarte was sitting on a bench in the gardens as she approached and looked up at her, "Cousin, how are you this fair day?"

"Not well, for I will certainly miss Merul while he studies."

"That is the way of things, we raise them and then we watch them spread their wings and fly."

"Aye, cousin that it is. Would you care to join me? I am on my way to check on Puanit in her confinement."

Astarte's face beamed at the thought of her latest consort Suti's mistress in her just punishment. She was elated that this woman was finally bought low, as she deserved.

Au-Set However did not share those voracious feelings of her cousin. She felt nothing but pity for the wretched woman. How sad to have been brought down so low as to perform the whims and wishes of so cruel a master as she knew Suti to be.

She knew that her cousin had her same curiosity and pity for the woman in the beginning, however something had changed and now Astarte felt nothing but contempt for the vile woman. Au-Set wondered perhaps, if it had something to do with possible feelings for Suti and due to that, her curiosity shifted to jealousy.

The wind of the lush river valley seemed to talk to them as they walked side by side to the windowless enclosure where Puanit was held in complete isolation. Au-Set had her there so that she would not have to serve on her brother's commands and to save her. She also did not know what to do with this woman. She felt bad for her and hoped that she would use this time wisely to think on matters.

The building was small and desolate and shaded by ancient large leaved palm trees that loped down on the thatched roof. The door was wooden and barred in place with a plank that had to be removed in order to enter. Both of them ducked down low and they entered since it was built into the ground to make it cooler in the desert heat that seemed to surround them always.

Inside it was lit up with an oil lamp that filled the whole hut with a soft glow. This glow almost seemed to soften the sharp features of this woman. It was obvious that from birth the woman had led a rough life and had to work for every little scrap that she was allowed to have. Puanit was a servant from birth and only knew what it was like to serve. The woman looked older than her natural years from decades of toil for other people. Yet, somehow she seemed to glow as she was busy working over something on the ground. She sat cross-legged with a plate reverently placed on her lap. In fine lines, she was painting a design on this wide plate.

Astarte had felt pity for this woman once and had even tried to save her as well. She knew that Au-Set's attempts would be fruitless for this woman. However, she did manage a smile for the poor woman and was genuinely interested in the work of art that she was painting.

Astarte looked over at Au-Set ignoring the presence of Puanit and inquired about the beautiful wide vase that the knarled woman was miraculously creating.

"This is the sole creation of Puanit, did you not know? It is called *faience* or '*tjehenet*' or dazzling, since it surely mystifies the eyes in its uniqueness and beauty." Au-Set reached down and picked up the piece that was just about finished and offered it to Astarte to view in closer detail.

"It certainly is beautiful, how does she do this? I have seen the pieces before around the palaces but I never thought of where they came from."

"Puanit, why don't you explain this process?"

"Certainly '*Lady of the Throne*'" and she bowed. Her once sad and humble demeanor had suddenly taken on a prideful glow that almost seemed to make her age melt away as she animatedly explained how to make her treasures.

"The base is a ceramic material that I crush small pieces of quartz or granite in for its brilliance and plant ash. I add in a powder of a mixture of bright green glaze of a soda lime for the sheen of it when fired. It is shaped and formed sometimes free-hand such as this piece, or in a mold that I have made out of beeswax on the shelves over there." She pointed to the items on the shelves that almost weighed it down, in such abundance were they. She smiled and continued, "The glaze is a powder that makes the vessel shine when fired at the side of a large bonfire. This one was already fired in the pit that you passed outside and now I am painting a design on it in black kohl and ash paint as you see."

It was definably genius and Astarte suddenly had respect for this woman. How could only a simple person create such beauty as this, unless they have seen the beauty of the Gods in reward for her toil? There was definitely great genius inside this pitiful creature that amazed even her. She smiled and admired the beauty of the simple painted black designs over the brilliant bright blue and green backgrounds of the glaze.

Chapter 117

The children and grandchildren of Ninnuit were at their apex of their genius. They wanted to create a land that would last for many generations after they were gone. To bring the civilization of the rest of the world to terms that the people of Kemet would be proud of and in some cases would eventually eclipse those other civilizations that the new Kemet was being based on.

Heru was sent to start his own city that he called *Djeb*, where he was to establish another army to protect that of their new united Kemet. This one was secret and only known to Au-Sar and Au-Set, and it would be primarily to protect them in case Suti and his daughter Set had any more ideas of taking over rule again. They were kept close under guard and Set slowly came to realize the benefits of a united family as she was growing out of her teenage rebellion years and was actually waiting for a consort to be chosen for her. She knew also that she would eventually have to relent and take Heru as her main one.

She even went along with Bast to Djeb to help Heru out with the forces there. Her military skill was comparable to Heru and Bast's, especially with the mace head. Her father, Suti, had one especially made for her from the wood of cypress from the lands of the Retenu and the head was finely carved out of granite and pear shaped for better balance. This she wielded with expert precision. Her arms were well defined as a result.

Chapter 118

Au-Sar was perfecting the city of Abdjw with the completion of walls that surrounded the palace district. He had even created a courtyard complex that was reached after crossing a large field of reeds. He wanted it out there where he could watch over his fields for it was on a higher point than most of the town that lay below. He also loved the idea that in order for people to seek justice from his court they would have to walk through the labyrinth of the field of reeds that his court was built on the far side of. He could see them as they approached and they could not see him.

His courtyard was an open temple built out of mud-brick walls. The sky was the roof in that the Gods would be able to watch over the proceedings. Inside of the building, he had columns fashioned to resemble giant reeds such as the ones people had to cross. The walls were painted bright red in the color that he had chosen for the lands of the Upper Kemet and the red lands of the desert that the local people called the Deshret. There was a marvelous border of gold leafed triangles that symbolized the primordial mound from hence all life arose from. Inside was an altar for offerings and seats made of imported wood from cypress that was inlaid with tiny pieces of quartz crystal that pierced tiny rays of light whenever the sun hit it from above at so many angles, which in affect made the people who sat in them appear to glow.

Au-Set and his fellow judges always presided in this court in their full splendor of costume and headdress. This was considered the main court of the land whenever he sat upon it in his green painted form and brilliant sky-reaching headdress. By his sides were Anmut, who was now called by the local people "the Devourer" who doled out the punishments for the guilty parties. Maat was there holding her large silver feather that she told the people was her symbol for judgment. She would take that feather and symbolically weigh it against the story told to them in the court. Tehuti kept meticulous records of each proceeding, as he was the official record keeper of the land. Ma-At was there for guidance as she was the ageing Nugig from their homeland who had the most experience in these matters from their birth-land of Eshnunna. Sekhmet was also present for judgment riding into court on her pet lion Herab, which always sparked attention from the people who arrived at their court.

This court became well known to all of the people in the land, since they were considered to treat the people with the utmost in objectivity and fairness. Not one of their punishments was considered unjust, so famous had they all become. This court became known as the 'fields of Iaru".

Chapter 119

Au-Set worked with her sister in stabilizing Nekhen and even started their work on a new city that they had a more elaborate plan for that would be located at the mouth of the wadi *Hillal*, south of Ineb-Hedj and the fortress of Re and Mut. They decided to call the city *Nekhab*. Au-Set even promised Neb-Het that it could be solely her plan and that it would be the new capitol of the third Sepat of Upper Kemet. Neb-Het chose the site due to the feeling that it was once and ancient hunting site and felt the strong power of the ancients on this spot.

Maat would spend her time equally sitting in judgment at Abdjw by the side of her mother's consort Au-Sar and the other half in a new school that she created at the age of ten with the help of her uncle Tehuti. This was greatly encouraged by her mother Au-Set, as were the ideas of all of her children. All they had to do was tell her what they would like to build and Au-Set would see it done. The temple for her teachings was located near *IpetIsut*.

The young princess was unusually gifted, as were all of the children of the siblings from Eshnunna. When Maat was twelve, she created a code of ethics for the people of Kemet, which revealed her own talent to her family and anyone, who met this extraordinary girl.

She was a tiny girl and almost appeared younger than her age due to her small height. Her hair was long and the color of reddish black, she had mahogany curls and her eyes were very large and seemed to contain limitless empathy and fairness.

Her judgment in matters was soon becoming known as the '*divine order in the universe and most fair in judgment*'. People would make sure that she attended at the court in Abdjw due to her fast spreading fame. They knew when she attended by her symbol of the silver feather hanging at the entrance of the field of reeds that one had to cross to gain admittance to the new illustrious court. Au-Sar left his symbol of the hawk outside as well and Sekhmet would leave out her symbol of a small golden lion statue. This would let the people know who was sitting in judgment at what time.

Maat called her temple-school her main hall of judgment, which she lovingly called her "*Hall of Two Truths*". This was in secret jest because she had felt in her heart as was aptly revealed in her experience of sitting in the court, that there were always two sides or more to every story. She believed it her inane right that she knew them all. She firmly believed in a balance in all life and saw equality everywhere. In cases where someone was wronged, she felt that it was up to her to find out what could be done to restore the balance that was sent off kilter by the wrongdoing.

The people had come to love and value her judgment so much that they called her hall "*Maaty*" after her especially. For at her school or temple, she was famous for holding small sessions on her own for practice. Most cases were settled there and some of the rare larger ones were sent to the main court in Abdjw that Au-Sar presided over.

Au-Set encouraged her children to find their talents, which stirred truth in the meaning of each life on earth. Thus, a vast empire was forming around her with her busy children. Even Anpu was learning the arts of mummification to make sure that their bodies would be preserved in the afterlife so that their Ba would recognize them after their physical form was dead to begin the journey of relocating all nine paths of life and death. Anpu worked day and night at a feverish pitch with his many ideas and sent envoys to as far south as the dead sea to collect chemicals for his experiments. Neb-Het and she beamed with pride over the amazing accomplishments of Anpu. Anpu always had his trained jackal by his side that was most often sleeping in stark contrast to his maniacal paced master.

Even her daughter Bast was busy working on building a temple dedicated to her many cats of all kinds that she was fast attracting to her side. She seemed to attract every stray cat of any size into her home, that the number of them had outgrown room in the palace. Bast decided to go on a quest to find a place for a grand temple that she would build in honor of her many cats, lions, panthers, leopards, and even tigers that had found their way to her loving care and nourishment. Bast had even taken to wearing the skins of those cats of hers who had died of natural causes. Bast started to have them mummified as people were. She was afraid that they would not find peace in the afterlife and felt that their souls were perhaps those of people in past lives who had somehow become lost in their quests for the unification of the nine paths.

Au-Set was busy making sure that her empire was expanding and growing in size, which it was. Trade between her land and others of the known world was booming and people were even coming from faraway lands to settle in the cities in Upper and Lower Kemet. She had even sent out an expedition to the lands at the birth of the great river at its source called Yam to find out what they could trade. They had returned with reports of gold mines and silver and the vast bounty of crafts from the local tribes.

Chapter 120

Au-Set and her family had grown used to a peace that seemed to settle throughout the long winding sides of the Great River and had even started to bask in the glow of their accomplishments. Au-Set allowed this for she knew that it would not last forever and realistically she felt that there would always be something to disrupt any illusion of peace so painstakingly contrived. This she had learned from the days of her cradle that anything could happen.

Therefore, it did. However, in such tiny pieces of discord that it was almost completely indiscernible, if one was not looking for it. Au-Set was looking carefully and had found it though it almost escaped her brutal scrutiny.

At first, it was a small whisper, and then a distant mumbling. People were starting to wonder at the family's rule in Kemet. Suddenly, the voices were starting to reach her in the evening hours piercing her with a slowly forming anger. People were starting to ask for Suti and Set to rule Upper Kemet and to expel Neb-Het Nekhebt from her throne. They whispered and whined that she was not always in Nekhen, that she was at her new city of Nekhab instead.

Au-Set knew that none other than her precocious brother Suti certainly and most probably started this. She smiled because; she had wondered how long he would sit seemingly idle before he caused more mischief. Therefore, that very evening she summoned her favorite servants Qui and Kekes and gave them the task of bringing Suti back to her in Nekhen.

"My notorious odd brothers, you must make sure that Suti has no idea why he is summoned. This is why I chose you both, for you have creative minds that will definitely come up with something to lure him here."

"Oh, *Lady of the Throne*, Suti is a monster! Could it not be someone else, someone stronger perhaps, such as one of your sons, Heru or even Merul? What about Bast...."

"No Kekes, we need something more in this case than mere strength. I need your creativity! Only you two, I believe would be capable of luring him out. He feels you both are idiots and not worth heeding..."

"But..." stammered Qui whose voice suddenly boomed in protest at the idea.

"No, Qui and Kekes, you know that you are anything but that. You are worth mountains to me in your vast brilliance. However, Suti does not see as far and as complete as we do here and finds you both harmless." She smiled.

"We all know better than that. Besides, I am glad, because this will only work more for our plan. If the summons came from me, he would know that we were on to him and his mischief. His words must be stopped before they gain too much power!"

"But, lady....Could we have unlimited supplies for any props that we might need?"

She laughed; she knew that it would rest on good hands with the brothers for their theatrics were well admired and glamorous. She would expect nothing less but the most outrageous from the both of them. That is why she chose them to carry out her wishes.

In only one week, Au-Set was rewarded beyond her wildest hopes for their idea was brilliant and it worked. As she had Suti locked up underneath the palace she heard their story as told by the deep voice of Qui, "Lady, we knew that this plan should be something quite unique and not anything mundane would do? Therefore, we came up with this....

"We had snuck down to where he was training his forces in the Deshret along the side of your daughter Renenutet and son Heru and had followed him to see what his habits were. My, you would not want to know all of the details on that, would you?"

"Certainly not! Continue." Gasped Au-Set, for she had an idea from rumors that she had heard and from her own experience.

"We did find out that he loves his lettuce and has his very own garden for this which he works on when he first wakes up and before the last light of the day. Those lettuce plants are the finest plants that I have ever seen, such meticulous care does he dole out to them! Anyways, he also feeds his pets and talks to them two times a day as well, after he tends to his garden. Those habits never veered off course and were very predictable. We knew that we would never gain entry into his world through his nightmarish pets, so we avoided them.

"We noticed that he practically worshipped his lettuce and would bend low to almost hear them as if they were speaking to them such as he fancied his animals did. In every meal, he had lettuce of some form. He even made sure that his soldiers would eat plenty of this, since he felt that it had magical properties of strength.

"What better way than to put something on his precious lettuce! Which we did! We made a fine powder from the poppy seeds and sprinkled them all over his precious lettuce! My, can you imagine the results!

"The whole army after a ration was suddenly chasing rainbows, when there was no rain! It was hilarious! Someone..." He paused to smile, "put it in their minds that there were magic rainbows that could only be found under the wings of a butterfly! Of course, one knows that there needs to be moisture for this, but they did not know! Someone told them that if the rainbows were found they would find riches beyond imagination at the end of it! It was hilarious! They were running all around and bumping into each other!"

Au-Set interjected at this point, "But what about Suti?"

Kekes jumped in at this point, "We have saved the best for last! None of the people who ate the lettuce had any idea what was going on and became completely out of their minds! Suti became paranoid and jumped at every shadow! Therefore, naturally Qui and I hid behind many of them and encouraged his fear! He was so frightened of the tree that Qui hid behind that started talking to him that he jumped right into a cage that we had hidden in his garden. I came around and tied it tight! He had no idea what was happening to him, the tree or Qui told him that he was being punished for the rancid words that came out of his mouth! He should be punished for his trying to break a promise that he made to his mother! He trembled to this and we added to it by talking to him while he slept and repeating the same things until the effects of the drug wore off. And now here he is!"

"My, what an adventure you two have had! I think that now he should face the tribunal!"

"Do not forget your son Heru, my Lady! His strength brought him here for you! He led the boat that carried his cage and us to him and back!"

Au-Set turned to her son, "Thank you brave son, for you are a hero as well and should be rewarded in kind! She held him close and hugged him with a growing pride for her oldest son. He reminded her of all of her favorite qualities of his father Au-Sar in that moment of fierce pride. He beamed in her love and when he smiled, he did indeed resemble his father almost as to be his own twin in youth. All of the people had observed this at his smile as well at his own mother. Especially Neb-Het who stood to the left of her twin sister at the arrival of her consort again in captivity, she stood back and practically glowed with pride in her family.

Renenutet stood silently by, her part in this almost forgotten. She knew that her mother loved her and understood Heru's need for adoration. She was content with the love that she received from her family and did not thrive on it like her brother Heru.

Chapter 121

While all of this occurred, Neb-Het was growing bored and flitted between her new cities, Nekhen and Abdjw to watch over the court proceedings of Au-Sar. She had sat by his side on many occasions and would offer advice when needed. She desperately yearned for another night like the one that she had spent with him in what seemed a lifetime ago. She watched his form emanate a fierce power when he sat in judgment at his court. She saw his beauty shine even through the thick green makeup that made him appear as if newly raised from the dead. He basked in the glow of one who truly loves to perform. Neb-Het noticed how the people responded to his wisdom.

She yearned for his touch as that magical evening that was vivid and un-punctured by time inside her memory. She forgot that he honestly thought that she was Au-Set and had changed the memory to his knowing that it was she the whole time. That union gave her Anpu, her most beloved and only son. Anpu glowed in his father's adoration and Au-Set even grew to love him as her own. She had even raised him for a time while in Per-Uto until it was safe enough for him to return to the arms of his own mother.

Thus, she watched Au-Sar dole out his justice with her niece Maat by his side. Sekhmet sat glorious on her lion and seemed to stop time with her presence. Anmut in her ancient form sat smiling on the side waiting to dole out any punishments. She cackled that her pit of crocodiles was ready and waiting and her pets were hungry and wanted some vile and corrupt meat for their refined palates!" This taunting of Anmut never ceased to cause Neb-Het to giggle which in every case she had to muffle due to the seriousness of the court. However, occasionally she caught the humor in the eyes of her beloved Au-Sar.

On this day, it was after a rather disturbing case and Au-Sar was obviously worn out and in need of nurturing. He looked rather disturbed and almost stumbled out of his chair when it was time to close the doors for the evening. Neb-Het chose this as the moment to approach him.

"Brother, this case was well decided. How did you ever know about the family? They seemed so normal. In addition, the punishment that Maat decided was perfect! Tell me about the whole thing for I have only walked into it today."

He smiled even though clearly exhausted. Nevertheless, he loved to talk about his cases, especially right after their conclusion. "True." He looked at her as they walked through his field of reeds towards the walls of his palace that were colored in the rays of the tired sun. A bright orange seemed to paint itself onto Neb-Het and her hair seemed to glow. She appeared almost Goddess-like in that moment. He almost gasped and then recalled her question. "Let us sit here."

He pointed to a flat rock that was beside a tent in the market place that was used as a bench. It was well worn from countless rests of the weary. Neb-Het sat apprehensively, dangled her tiny feet to a rhythm in her mind, and sat to listen to his tale for the sake of hearing his melodious voice. His make-up washed just after leaving the court in the still sweltering sun he was now only Au-Sar and not some god. He was just a man and her brother in rule who sat beside her on a market bench, the theatrics of their family tossed aside when not in ceremony. The family found it easier to walk around the palace and in their towns without their makeup and not to be recognized. The people of the land saw them primarily now in ceremony garbed primarily in the formality of their costumes and were used to that.

"It had arrived to my attention that the old habit of the ritual eating of the dead in the time of our aunt Ua-Zit had been resurrected. You know the one that she abolished. We thought that the reason given of their bodies being intact gave the people much to ponder. It even seemed as if it had stopped completely, so well was the reason given by Ua-Zit herself years back.

"Anyways, some people were reporting that the old custom of eating the valued parts of their beloved deceased was being resurrected by this one family in particular. Some were doing this in private in the custom of their ancients. However, this family decided to be blatant about it and to hold it up to us in mockery. They made a large banquet in their village just to the south of Ineb-Hedj for the funeral of their family matriarch. The feast was well prepared and cost them almost all of their family earnings. In this feast, they mocked the new law that abolished this act and insulted our house and family! They carried out the tradition down to even to the smallest infant descendant of this woman! It was abominable! My heart tears for our aunts and what they endured when they were young!

"Nevertheless, the whole family was taken by the village and brought here for judgment. There were fourteen of them. The deceased woman has two daughters, their consorts and eight children between them. The youngest child being only two inundations old! This woman was named Thelina and the family told the court that it was her death wish. They stated that they hated the idea, since it had not been done in ten years and they had begun to cherish the new law of preserving their bodies for it made more sense to them. The oldest daughter spoke out for most of the proceedings and pleaded with the court on this matter. She fell to the ground in desperation and told us that she had no choice but to honor her mother. "

"Yes, that was when I walked in." Spoke up Neb-Het.

Au-Sar nodded and continued. "I was initially pondering the families release and had almost believed their pleading to be genuine. Even though the law forbade it, the law of the matriarch has always been absolute in this land and others. One would certainly have been torn indeed. I would have let them go if it were not for the voice of one of the children. I believe that the truth is certainly abundant in the children who are too young to understand it. This little girl was only about six years old and while her mother was pleading her innocence the little girl proclaimed, "Mama, you told me that this was the way it should be that the king and queen were stupid! You said..." The mother paled at this as did those old enough to understand their doom. She had tried to hush her child when I placed her on my lap.

"So, little one," I asked this tiny slip of a child, "What else did your mother say?" She responded and her cheeks glowed with pride for it was obvious that never was she paid so much attention to in her life before this moment and she was enamored with the plumes in my headdress. I pulled out a feather and offered it to her. "Tell me little one!"

"Mama and auntie said that this was the way of our people and that new people should not tell us how to live! That we must honor grandma and hope that the Great River swallows the kings and queens whole and their worthless laws!" This last bit she stated with a pride at having remembered such a long sentence by heart. I had no choice but to laugh at this and then looked at Maat and the others. We convened for an hour on this dilemma and Maat as usual saw through this and determined the most proper punishment for this utterance that could spark a rebellion.

"We had decided that the mothers should partake of the flesh of their own children while they were alive. How fitting a punishment. Maybe then, their souls would see how ridiculous and horrible that ancient custom was. Each time they refused this they would be struck on the head with a rock. I hope that the rock would knock some sense into the family. I hope that it would not go on long enough to cause the death of the children and just enough for it to sink into the minds of that family. Anmut is supervising this punishment as we speak and we will hear on the morrow how it went!"

"Very wise Au-Sar! It makes a lot of sense to stop that family before a larger rebellion was formed over their blatant insubordination and mockery of us! Could I tell you something?"

"Certainly Neb-Het!"

"I love you and would like to have you as my consort." She blushed and looked down, feeling her heart practically explode in anticipation.

Au-Sar leaned over and took her lovingly into his embrace, the embrace of a brother and not a lover. "You know that it would devastate Au-Set to have to share! Besides, I have grown to love her incredibly in all that she has done. I cannot do that to her. I know that you have the choice... I am sorry and I am deeply flattered by your approval." He kissed her on the forehead sweetly.

Nevertheless, Neb-Het was very distraught over this. She had not expected this at all and even fathomed that she had caught his attention. Her fantasies were all false, she felt foolish and even angry at Au-Sar. How dare he refuse such an honorable offer? She looked over at him sitting beside her so glorious in his honesty. She knew then at that moment that she felt his love for Au-Set truly honorable and his great heart should be praised and not thought negatively towards for any reason. She mournfully regretted his decision though accepted it and from that moment on, she decided that she would protect his honor and that of the woman that he loved, Au-Set. She would make sure that their love would not be tossed asunder and vowed to protect them for this life and the next.

In sadness, Neb-Het thought of that exchange between her and Au-Sar. She vowed that she would never consider those emotions again and thus, she arrived at Nekhen to sit by her sister's side as she received the news of Suti's captivity and the deeds of her son Heru. In Heru she noticed that aura of power that she felt only his father had. However, he was half her age she was certainly not old by any means and was still besides her sister considered one of the most beautiful women of Kemet.

That evening she stole into Heru's sleeping chambers and sat in a chair waiting for his return. She had fallen asleep since he must have gone to some brewery into the early hours of the morning in celebration. She had not counted on that and had therefore fallen asleep. She had woken up to the sounds of Heru stumbling in on the arm of a village woman.

The shadows slowly revealed her waking form and he let out a boisterous bellow, "Auntie, why are you here? You should be sleeping, like my mother. Women of your age would sure to end up in harm's way at this hour of the evening!"

Shocked but completely understanding her nephew, she smiled at him, "I am truly sorry, I thought that you might have had a particular scroll that I was looking for. Your pallet looked so inviting and I was so tired from being in court all day...." She stifled out a genuine yawn, which only added to her farce. She lied to cover the deep humiliation that she felt. However, could she have thought that Heru would warm up to her? Not only that, but she was the exact replica of his mother... She smiled meekly and backed out of his chamber to let the young enjoy each other. She practically kicked herself at her ridiculous assumption as she left out of earshot. She heard the laughter of the beautiful Heru bounce across the walls joined by the giggles of the maiden that he brought in there with him.

Chapter 122

Outside, Au-Set just happened to walk by. She had been in the chambers of her consort Nebmaat that evening going over the latest in costume designs that he had for their family to keep up with the years. She was constantly amazed at his creativity along with Qui and Kekes. She was also deeply proud of the latter and her son in bringing back Suti to her in yet, another very creative and ingenious way. She was on her way to thank her son again and turned when she noticed that he had brought someone with him. She was almost out of sight when she heard the voice of Neb-Het inside.

She could not help herself but to overhear. She was around the corner of the hall and could not see a thing that had transpired, but felt every emotion emanating from her sister in distress. She felt the true reason why her sister was there and felt her pain as well.

She had thought that Hetep was keeping her busy especially since he fathered Meshkenet. Apparently it was not so. She knew that Neb-Het was extremely loyal to the one that she set her heart upon and would never seek it from another unless certainly she felt neglected. She knew of Neb-Het's love for Au-Sar and trusted her in this as well after the whole situation with Anpu years ago. She saw her sister's eyes wandering over to Au-Sar but it was always very subtle and almost as if, she was resigning herself to the inevitable.

In Neb-Het's haste she did not see Au-Set in the hallway and had ran into her in her departure. "Oh, Oh, Oh! I am sorry!"

Au-Set truly felt for Neb-Het for her emotions were always on her face and only she as her twin could ever see into her sister's soul. She felt the pain of rejection and of feeling old that her sister radiated so gloomily. She grabbed Neb-Het into an embrace that was forgiving and full of love.

"Sister, let us talk about this? Follow me." Neb-Het with her tearstained face had nothing to do and numbly followed her sister. Neb-Het hoped that her sister would perhaps kill her so deep was the pain that she felt at that moment. Her tears were painful and she struggled to keep them under control.

They walked along the newly painted corridor towards her and her sister's favorite place, the garden enclosure. This was a very accurate reproduction of the garden that their mother once had in the temple of Eshnunna. Complete with carvings and vivid scenery in the false windows that portrayed the lush landscape of Erech. There were benches made of imported cedar from the lands of the Retenu with carvings of flowers and spirals on them. In the center was a small pool that looked like one of the many ponds of their homeland. It was even stocked with fish that were only from Eshnunna.

Au-Set sat down and Neb-Het joined her. They sat in silence for a while and listened to the fish jump out of the water trying to catch the flies that breached the serene surface of the tranquil pool. "Plip, plop, plip, plop!"

It seemed almost ominous and altogether too loud for the moment, yet it set a certain pace that was not recognized before this moment by either of them.

Au-Set looked into her mirror image with the bright hazel eyes and whispered, "Do you think that it is time that you found a new consort!"

Neb-Het laughed. That was always the difference, between the two of them. Au-Set was always to the point and she was too subtle and preferred to slide gently into announcements.

"My, you certainly do not waste any time. I am not going to ask how you know my heart. It always seems that when I really need you, you are here!"

Au-Set nodded and held her dear sister and mirror soul close to her.

"In answer to your question-yes... To sum it all out and to avoid all of the mess I feel inside my heart. I suppose that is all of it melted down in simplicity. Yes, I think that it is time for a new consort. Suti and Nebmaat have problems, shall we say of ....performing. No satisfaction whatsoever..."

"None?"

"None." Both of them sighed. "How about Tehuti?"

"I don't see why ever not at this point. Do you think that he would agree?"

"I don't see why not. Therefore, it is done. We might as well plan it along the union of Heru and Set?" Neb-Het nodded solemnly.

"It is done."

"None?"

"Nope, none." They sighed again.

Chapter 123

Bast knew that in order to please her parents she would have to be more than exceptional. She was only the fourth daughter after Set, Renenutet, and Weret-Heka, and after her older brother Heru, the fifth child of Au-Set. She sat on the sidelines for most of her childhood watching her older siblings and learned from them.

Bast felt herself to have the soul of a cat, which she tried to assimilate in personality. She would watch her many pet cats as well and learn from them. No matter what the size of cat or species they were hunters to be reckoned with. She watched how even those common cats used to kill the mice near the grain, would ponder their prey before going in silently for the kill. She found that there was much to learn from the cat and valued anything that they would let her learn from them.

Bast found from a very young age that all sizes of cats, would eventually find their way to her if they were left alone in the world. She became their mother and then as they grew older and their instincts as hunters kicked in, their pupil.

As far as her siblings were concerned, she watched them as well, silently. She saw how her oldest sister with the fiery temper to match her brilliant hair, mostly was tangled in her emotional passions. She did not want that and learned from Set's mistakes.

She saw how silent Renenutet and her almost twin Weret-Heka were and thought that they were more on point for the person that Bast would like to grow to become, yet too quiet. She wanted to be more like her mother who sat on the side and watched before she made an opinion. Sometimes, even her mother would become entangled in her emotional struggles and it would affect how she approached some issues but that was rare.

Bast decided that she wanted the best qualities that she could possibly muster for herself. Therefore, she learned from her pet lion Herab and her many kittens of all sizes. Soon she had cats in almost all the species that she knew about and even some new ones.

Her menagerie began to grow too large for the confines of the palace and her mother suggested that she build a sort of sanctuary for them. A place where they would have more room to roam free unencumbered from the walls of the palace.

She looked for almost the whole time it took for the Great River to swell with its full inundation and then it suddenly found her. She was walking around the delta region and Herab actually stumbled upon the area where her sanctuary would be built.

On that day, she had set Herab free so that he would catch their morning meal and he returned with a small statue of a small clay cat in its mouth. She took it from him as he dropped it on the ground. She looked at Herab and whispered in her usual voice, "Herab, what have you found? Let's see if we can find where this came from." Herab in all of his great size nuzzled up to his mistress knowing that he had pleased her and purred like a kitten.

She walked in the direction that he came from and had arrived at a foundation almost covered in the dense foliage. She started to brush away the thick growth that had tangled itself around the crumbling foundations and found it only one of a dozen chambers that had fallen into decay. It appeared as if this was once possibly a place of worship long before her time. The walls were made in the ancient way of woven reed walls with plaster covering them, for it was seen in several different spots where the plaster had fallen away to reveal the original structure underneath. She walked around the walls and noticed a wide platform and on it, covered in vines was a life-like statue of Herab! "How wonderful, Herab! It looks as if we have found your ancestor!"

For the rest of that day she worked hard in uncovering the structure so that it would be easily found when she returned with workers who would build her sanctuary here in this spot. She realized that this spot probably was already sacred to the cat and that it saw her intentions and chose her to bring it back to the world.

After clearing her area, she built a small makeshift lean-to out of the dead vines against the side of the wall and fell asleep nuzzled in the safety of Herab's large form. She dreamed of how it would look when done. She wanted to make sure that all stranded cats would find a home and that this would be brought back to the place of honor that it once was. She smiled in her sleep, for at last, she had found her meaning in life and she was content.

She had returned by boat to where her mother was in Nekhen to tell her the news. Both Au-Set and Au-Sar elated in the news from Bast and jumped to support her cause with great pride. Au-Sar made sure that she was sent one hundred workers and supplies that she needed for her new purpose.

However, that evening as she was preparing to go her mother had called her in to speak with her. Bast was shining with the glow of her new adventure that she was eager to embark on and wondered what her mother wanted of her before she left.

She walked down the many freshly painted corridors to where her mother's sitting room was and found her there looking out at the stars in the sky, as she always would do. Bast thought it beautiful how the moonlight would make her mother's hair glow to a brilliant blue next to the darkest black hair imaginable. Her curls cascaded down her mother's back. Her mother was wearing a simple linen shift, as she usually did in the privacy of her own family and outside of the public attention. All pretenses of the families' theatrics were dropped in the privacy of their own chambers.

Bast thought that her mother looked even more beautiful without the dark eye makeup surrounding her eyes and the pale powder that would take away the color of her skin. When in full makeup, her mother looked truly powerful and her eyes were enlarged and appeared almost dangerous. It was perfect for what her family needed to achieve. In full costume, her mother appeared every bit a Goddess and nothing less.

In contrast, she felt small and slight next to her powerful mother. Her voice could silence anything to her smallest command. Bast hoped that someday she would have that ability. However, she was more of the type to be in the shadows waiting for the proper moment to strike. She was small and prided herself in being able to sneak into any room without people knowing that she was there. Her family was constantly complaining of her always sneaking up on them and she loved it. She also was an expert in climbing and learned the art of acrobatic skills.

Her mother as usual did not hear her approach and she felt that it was not the time to sneak up on her mother in surprise so she coughed a little to announce the presence of her approach.

"Oh, Bast, how nimble like a cat you are! Come here had snuggle with your mother! You are not too old for that are you?"

Bast's face lit up at her mother's favorite compliment for her and she ran like a much younger child into her mother's arms. "Oh, Mamma, never!"

"Good! I see that you are growing into quite a capable young woman. You have recently attained your moon blood and are at the age that you should be serving the Goddess as all the women have in our family since the beginning of time."

Bast gulped for she knew what was coming. She was just not prepared for it and was hoping that she would never have to face it.

Au-Set noticed the look of almost horror in her young daughter's eyes. Comfortingly she whispered, "Now, now. It is not very bad. It will not have to be as strict as it was when I was a child and your aunts and uncles. "She looked at Bast and noticed that she was starting to calm down. " You know the purpose of this family and its ambitions. You are old enough for that, I know."

Bast grimaced with the truth of what her mother said, even though she tried her hardest to hide from it.

"Set chose Heru as consort not because she wanted to but because she knew that it was her duty for our family. The blood must be pure. You chose not to be with him, remember. You cannot be alone forever, my love. Renenutet and Weret-Heka chose Shai as their consort as a promise this family made to Mut and Re. You know that you must go to Merul as consort as your duty. You should also know that this is only for state and for the next generation only."

At the confusion of Bast, Au-Set explained, "It is only for the breeding of the next generation that the blood must be pure. You, as well as all Goddess chosen women can have any lover that you want. Their consorts as well may be their choice. However, you know that your first duty in this land is to your family and we must be kept together. It will be a union that will create the next generation for Kemet. You may have any lover that you want, just no children from them! I will teach you about your moon cycle so that you will know when you are most fertile and when you can play outside of your duty. Your consort can have the same freedom as well. However, they cannot father a child on anyone other than the one chosen in union for them. It would be instant death if that were disobeyed. That last rule was bent by this generation for in the old days in Eshnunna a man chosen in union for the Goddess born was not allowed to be with or touch any other woman than for the one that he was chosen for."

"I had heard about that Mama from Ma-At. She also told me that the consort of the Goddess representative was killed as soon as he impregnated the Goddess chosen, for it was their only duty. Was not grandfather Re a consort of Grandmother Ninnuit in Eshnunna? Why was he spared and what about her other consorts?"

"Fair enough question. Only the Goddess Innana knows the answer to that one but Re was lucky enough to escape. If he had not, we would not have the pleasure of knowing your two littlest sisters Maat and Serqet."

"Maat is not like a little girl at all she is too much like an old woman and it is spooky!"

"Hush, you must not speak of your family like that!"

"What about the other consort of Ninnuit, tell me the truth please Momma!"

"Well, you have certainly earned that and deserve no other. Will you be able to handle it? Sometimes fables are enough and the truth can be too difficult to bear."

Bast nodded her head, and looked up at Maat and Serqet as they entered the room. Obviously, they had been listening to part of the conversation and wanted to be included. "Come on in little sisters you might as well hear this as well, is that all right Mama?"

Au-Set looked apprehensive and then decided that if they truly wanted to know the truth as they looked at her in anticipation they had the right.

"Well, I suppose that you should hear the rest as well...

"Re was not the only consort who escaped, but he was one of the last. First, there was Tiamut who was the creator of the Eshnunna, as we knew it and her consort was Tmu-Amun. Tmu-Amun was very young and on the brink of manhood when he was chosen for this honor and did not want to be a king for a year and a day. He did his duty and fathered Tefnut who was the first star in the heavens. Tiamut had two other consorts before Tmu-Amun who were Simnt who was the father of the original Ua-Zit and Nekhebt. The same Ua-Zit and Nekhebt who fled to this land took over the old family, and established their rule in Upper and Lower Kemet. They built Per-Uto and Nekhen with their own two hands. Their fathers were killed, as was their duty before they were born. All of the consorts of Tiamut were from the land of Kemet and her children never forgot this and neither did Kemet. Tiamut gave birth to Tefnut who took as her consort Shu who was also from this land and fathered Ninnuit who was my mother and the mother of the sky above. *She who looks over us and from her lips the stars whisper to us in our dreams...* She gave her life for us or rather her human form so that she may better protect us as a Goddess.

"Ninnuit then became the Goddess representative and the "mother form of the Goddess," while her own mother Tefnut became "the Crone" form of the Goddess.

Ninnuit's first consort was Geb, *"The Great Cackler"*
From Eshnunna and the father of Neb-Het and me.
Ninnuit had fallen in love with Geb and almost broke
her vows to the Goddess had not her mother taken over
and performed her daughter's duties for her, so that the
next consort would take his place and tradition would
continue. The next consort of Ninnuit was Re, you know
him well from Ineb-Hedj. He escaped, as did one other
consort that I had mentioned by the name of Tmu-
Amun. In fact, Tmu-Amun, after he escaped from being
the consort of Tiamut came back to his homeland, met,
and fell in love with Mut. Mut gave him the daughters
Ua-Zit and Nekhebt whose thrones were taken over by
those of the same names that were born to Tefnut by
Simnt and Nucit. The names were actually quite
common and stood for ancient Goddesses of the land of
Kemet, as you well know. The Eshnunna Ua-Zit and
Nekhebt ruled for quite some time and would have
succeeded until their namesakes stole into the night
and killed them both in their sleep with asps that were
sent into their chamber. The Ua-Zit and Nekhebt from
Kemet took over their respective places though they as
well would meet with a tragic end.

"With Re, Ninnuit had Tehuti. Re escaped as did
Tmu-Amun, met Het-Heru, and had children with her.
Re was the son of Mut from her consort Khephra who
was a famous potter. She also had Apep from her
consort. With Het-Heru, Re was the father of Sekhmet
and Shai. Tmu-Amun's mother was Ptah, she was the
matriarch of this great family of Kemet, and that is
another story.

"What about the rest of your brothers?" Spoke up
an anxious Serqet.

"Husssh! Momma has not gotten to that part yet!"
Maat whispered. Then she looked at her mother, "Right
Momma?"

"Certainly... Well, Eshnunna boded the escape of
Re as a powerful negative omen which was very bad.
They also did not like the way in which Ninnuit had
failed to kill her consort Geb. The next consort was En-
Gilgamesh who was a very vain man though a skilled

merchant. He was a local hero in that land for how he saved a whole village in one of the greatest floods of many generations. He was the father of Au-Sar. En was also a talented farmer in the valley of the two great rivers of Eshnunna which is where Au-Sar receives his talents."

"But, I thought that Re was my grandfather not this En-Gilgamesh that I have never heard of."

"In this family we are all a part of one another. I found that it did not matter if you were corrected or not. What is a loyalty to a certain person in the family when all should be viewed as only a part of this great family that works as one." She smiled. "A long time ago way before my time and many generations back the children of the ancient tribes were raised by all. There was the birth mother and that was all that was needed to be known. All of the men served as fathers for all of the children born to them. It did not matter. They were close and almost indestructible in their family strength."

"All right, the rest Momma..." Spoke up Bast who was lost in rapt attention to this tale from her mother.

"Then there was Enkidu who was the father of Heru..."

The three of them looked confused at the mention of their brother's name in all of this.

"Another Heru or the first Heru of our family for whom your brother was named. He died at almost the same moment that your brother of that name was born and I still feel that first Heru lives still within the younger Heru to guide the rest of us as he did in life. Only the second Heru, your brother is the more active one in his passions of unification.

"Anyways, after that the palace was in uproar because Enkidu escaped as well and this looked even worse for Eshnunna and the people who worshipped Innana. Then there was a horrible attack on the temple palace by the men of the northern tribes and the leader of the group named Enlil forcefully fathered Suti from this event on my mother. This Enlil was later deified and that I will get to soon enough in this tale of our family.

"The Goddess Innana had decided that her time on earth was done and that her last Goddess representative must leave with her as well. This was Ninnuit. There was a great battle and the people of the Goddess gave way to the new raiders of the northern tribes who bore men who conquered women and enslaved them. Our mother Ninnuit saved us and sent us to live here in Kemet. Only we made a promise to her that we would stand as one. Thus, I made union with Au-Sar, Neb-Het with Suti and Heru and Tehuti were chosen to be our guides and advisors. Heru died young, and there were rumors on that. However, nothing was ever proven. Tehuti keeps a journal of all that our family is going through as we create a new land out of the desert and unites Kemet into one dynasty. Therefore, you see that you are all important parts in all of this as I am.

"Serqet and Maat will know soon enough their duty for it has yet to be determined. Bast, you must take Merul."

Bast nodded her head, as she knew her duty.

Chapter 124

Therefore, Bast took Merul as her consort. She did not think that Merul was that much to look as but he was very intelligent and was learning to be a scribe like Tehuti as well as a master brewer among other things. She tried to ignore the fact that his head was too big for his body that his torso over large and his arms and legs too small. He seemed greatly out of proportion. She knew that her father was quite upset by this and tried not to let them know. She had unfortunately overheard a conversation between her mother and father on the matter of Merul. It was a rare moments when she hated her silence. She wept for her brother Merul in that he did not have the love of their father and was therefore more able to take him in union for her family.

Thus, she hoped to be a mother and feared that it would not happen, so she went to Anmut for advice.

She found Anmut as she was feeding the crocodiles in her pit that she knew each by the names that she had given them. Bast blanched at the site of the hungry crocodiles.

"Oh Bast... No worry here, children of mine only feed when they are hungry. Besides, they only like the meat of rotten souls and evil. They protect us with their taste for bad people in ridding us of them and the dangers they provoke. "She saw the confusion in the girl's eyes and realized that she probably came here for advice about something that she could not share with her mother.

"What can I help you with Bast?"

"Well, I am not a mother yet!"

"Oh, you are still young yet. There is not rushing for that. Think of the liberation that you now have. That is not so with a babe on the breast. The babes take our soul and make you vulnerable."

"I know all about that, it is just that it is my duty and I do not want to fail Merul. I need a charm of some sort."

"Well, the old ones will not serve you in this; let us see if we cannot create our own. How many children do you want?"

"Many like a swarm."

"MMMM, what swarms?"

"Bees, locusts, flies...."

"Yes. Let's see Bees like honey and are for the Goddess are they not?"

"Yes, but that is an old charm, I would like something new."

"Locusts are too ugly...Yuck"

"Flies, flies.... They swarm and they attach themselves to you. I would want that loyalty from any children that I bear. Flies it is! I will contact the jeweler at once!" Off she ran leaving Anmut alone in the dust of her wake and youthful eagerness. She smiled. She could not wait to have charms made out in the form of flies for her fertility of her loyal tribe that she will bear from her womb. She decided to call them her 'atef charms.

Chapter 125

Not long after that exchange, Bast took to wearing her beautifully carved silver flies around her neck and in her ears. Her mother and the other women in her family followed suit since they felt that the charms did look beautiful in silver.

She had just finished trying on her mother's ceremonial garments while she was away. Bast felt that when she, herself dressed in the costume that her mother wore in public she eerily looked like her mother, especially when she carefully applied all of the makeup to complete the mirage. After being all dressed up, she decided to test her mother's likeness and walked out of the palace. She was alone for her mother had her famous Scorpion Guard with her and was touring the new guard towers that were recently completed. Each person that Bast passed bowed down to her as if she were Au-Set. Bast struggled to hold back the giggles. How could people not notice that she was alone and without the Scorpion Guard as this would never happen in reality? Yet, people saw what they wanted to see and believed that they were in the presence of Au-Set when it was really her own daughter. Bast tried to emulate her mother's graceful walk underneath the entire theatrical garb. Thus, she found herself again bored and walked towards the market. She had almost forgotten that she was dressed as her mother if it were not for the heaviness of it all and discomfort that it caused her.

Bast found herself sitting wearily on a bench near the busy market place. She was watching the people as they went about their errands and business. She loved the new atef pendant that was carved especially for her out of lapis lazuli and set in a brilliant gold pendant that made it look like the fly was covering the sun. She was twirling the cord that held it in place on her neck made out of carved lapis beads to match the stone of the fly symbol. She was twirling it and blurring her eyes to the people in the crowd when suddenly she spotted the form of Nebmaat walking towards her. Out of habit, she ran to hide in cover and set herself to following Nebmaat in her favorite childhood game. Like a cat, she prowled behind him as he joyfully sauntered through the maze of the market place.

Suddenly without warning Nebmaat turned around and grabbed Bast by the throat and held a dagger up to it. "What brings you here... little one?" She knew that he was probably seeing her like everyone else, until he was actually close to her enough to tell.

She was surprised in this unusual aggressive demeanor of Nebmaat whom she always thought as harmless and rather feminine in his taste for rare silks. She was stupefied in this change of personality in one that she thought that she had known her whole life.

"Father, please, I was only bored and thought that it would be fun to follow you!" All of the children of Au-Set called her consorts father for it was in the tradition of the old that was still in their veins.

"I have business here that should not be followed by a little girl. How much have you seen? What are you doing in your mother's clothes; surely you are too old for dress up?" He let out a twisted grimace as his humor.

"Truly nothing, I only came across you as you were walking down the lane of pottery."

"No, that is not right. I felt someone there before. It had to have been you."

Completely caught off guard by the strange behavior of Nebmaat, she stood there helpless. He seemed very unpredictable and she wondered if he was under the influence of something. Was he the master of some plan of which no one knows about? He looked extremely guilty and with the new strength neither that she nor anyone else had any idea that he even possessed, seemed to emanate as if he had this all along. Was this what he truly was? All of these questions ran through her mind.

He continued, "There is too much to lose with your knowledge in this. I need to do this." As he was building up his strength to kill her, Bast took this as the perfect opportunity to turn around and grab the knife. She then turned it back on him and pushed with all of her might. The vein that broke was powerful and flowed out aggressively covering her with blood. It seemed like an eternity until Nebmaat finally fell to the ground, even then he convulsed slightly as if fighting the grip of death.

She did not know that in the shadows was her older sister Set who ran promptly back to the palace to tell their mother.

Chapter 126

As Set ran to tell the palace of what she had witnessed, she stopped. She realized that she was given a valuable piece of knowledge that could possibly be used to her advantage. She did not like Bast in that she was too much her mother's puppet. She was finding that she hated her mother for all that was expected of her. Set hated being the first-born daughter with nothing to hope for but the duty as her family chose for her. She could not stand Heru and felt that he was awful childish. She escaped him whenever she could. This is how she ended up in the market place.

She was the one who had followed Nebmaat and had seen what he had done, not Bast. She noticed Bast sneak after him and was especially proud that she had out snuck the family sneak! Bast had no idea of her presence and neither did Nebmaat.

She saw how Nebmaat left the palace in his usual effeminate way. He did not see her as she was turning the corner, she had noticed that he stopped his effeminate walk and started to swagger in a very masculine way. It appeared to her as if the way he was to her family was all an act. He looked as if he had just dropped character! This had intrigued her and so she followed this strange new Nebmaat.

He walked out of the palace and to a small hut that was on the banks of the Great River. In here, he went inside as if he were swallowed completely. She worked on concealing herself even more to get closer to hear him.

Inside the voices were muffled but she could make out the main idea of it all. She heard Nebmaat speak in a very deep voice that she did not know that he even had at all.

"Enlil, your plan is almost done, shall we put into action the next phase?"

"My son, you have done your job well, no one would ever suspect your faith to the God in my name."

Set could not believe that she was hearing. The man that Nebmaat was speaking to had the same name as her uncle's father, Enlil or Enkidu. She was confused and strained to listen to the exchange.

"Set has been brought under the wing of her father and soon she will learn about her true heritage and legacy in Sumer!"

"Suti will be the next one after I die as is his birthright and Set after him!"

Set could not believe what she was overhearing and decided to keep this knowledge to herself until the time was right.

She was especially thankful that Bast did not hear this.

Chapter 127

Au-Set could not believe that this was happening. It felt as if the world had just turned upside down. She was in the garden one day looking at what Au-Sar had done for their own nourishment and basking in pride and then the next moment the palace guards had turned on her and whisked her away to the depths of the palace into the dungeons far below! She had no idea how long she had been there since there was no window for light so far below. All she heard was the dripping of the Great River wash from the latest inundation as it fought for space in all the crevices along the banks where their palace sat. The dripping seemed ominous and almost spoke to her of what could possibly have occurred to bring her here.

Many visions of plots and conspiracies ran through her tired mind. Could Suti have finally gathered enough strength to conquer all of Kemet? She felt that this was unlikely, since the land was still quivering from his abuse. She knew that the people were weary of him and would never accept his dominance unless decreed by the gods.

What of armies from other lands? Then again, she would expect the company of her family in this dark cell. Alternatively, possibly even their deaths. Still she sat in the cramped space with her legs drawn up underneath her for there was no room to stretch them. The cramps had set in long ago and she forced them aside out of pure survival mode.

She knew that Suti and others have been down here and suddenly felt a rush of sympathy and the cruelty of her own punishments for wrongdoers. Was this a final test of the Gods? That she personally had to endure her own judgment. She could only sit and wait for that answer that seemed to play with her mind in the endless dance of possibilities. Her body was too old for this and her mind was weary and saddened by the game that life presented her. She had made sure that she made the best of her life and the talents that she was born with. She was taught from her cradle that a truly doomed person was one who was born with gifts whether to rule or just plain talent of some sort and to have it wasted and unrealized.

Au-Set was born to rule and she made sure that she was the best ruler that she could possibly be. She made sure that she ruled in fairness and objectively. She was a mother and she made sure that she raised her children well. She gave them roots to be proud of and wings to soar over the world and to live long after she was gone from this land. She smiled at how wonderful each of her children was and knew that if she were to die on this day she would have at least done a good job as a mother.

The smile on her face was suddenly erased with the whisper that she recognized as Tehuti. "Sister? Are you well?"

"As well, as I possibly could be down here."

"I am sorry. It is just that you must face a trial."

"For what?" She searched her mind for any possible reason and found none that would release her from the torment of not knowing.

"It is Nebmaat."

"Nebmaat? What of him?"

Tehuti felt the honest question in his sister's voice even in the absolute darkness. He had always known in his heart that Au-Set had no part in this. However, all of the evidence had led to her. Still, he had to see for himself and was relieved at her honest questioning. One thing about his sister was even though the world might tremble at her power and bask in the mystery of her aura; she could not hide anything from her own siblings. Each emotion that she had was always plain on her face. She did not even bother to lie since she could not to her own family.

"Then you truly do not know?"

"Know what brother? Did he spend all of the money in the treasury at last on his vanity?"

"Shhhh Shhhh! You must not speak that way of the dead sister!"

"The dead? Whatever are you raving about brother? I demand an answer?"

"You are here sister, because the whole of Kemet thinks that you have murdered your consort Nebmaat in cold blood!"

Armed with this latest of news, Au-Set walked painfully to face the trial of a tribunal that she had helped organize. Her legs begged for mercy with each wretched step. The light assaulted her senses as it brought her from her imprisonment. She walked bravely on as led by her own Scorpion Guard who marched her on with ceremony. They, out of love, patiently walked slowly beside her as she found her legs to walk out of her own dungeon to the place of the official trials to the *"Field of Reeds"* or the infamous *"Fields of Iaru."*

Her left side guard, Metsetef, leaned inconspicuously over to her to whisper into her ear, "Lady, we are here by your side and believe in your innocence!" Au-Set looked Metsetef in her eye to acknowledge this without betraying her confidence with a smile. They walked on.

A crowd had gathered along their journey outside of the palace to see their queen brought down and to her own court for justice. The sun beat down upon them all as it was approaching the middle morning hour. The whispers of the people sounded almost like waves crashing against the shore in a land far away from her in this hour. As each wave in her mind crashed against the shore, a memory of her life as a child long ago fought for a hold in her mind to keep her inner balance of the moment at hand.

She saw her mother as if untouched by time and memory and felt the love flowing out of her and to her shadow and other half of her soul Neb-Het. She looked back in memory to see her and Neb-Het as they sat side by side on their mother's lap and were touching their fingers as if they were looking into a mirror. Their mother smiled in pride for the entire world but they knew how much alike the two princesses were.

Other memories pierced her heart as the sun invaded her long silence of many days in the dungeons of her mind and in the real life one in her own palace.

She saw her brothers being born in the palace ritual. Their mother gave birth to them all on top of the temple for the entire city to become a part. Her mother suffered for each one of their entrances to the world. Those came as flashes to her and then switched to the dark night when their mother held them all in her arms for the last time.

Flashes even to the more recent memories of her childhood in time to the endless evenings spent in fervent hope for their mother turning up in Per-Uto and for their family to be made complete again.

The flashes grew more powerful as she approached the field of reeds and the labyrinth created for all those on trial to walk through.

She saw the temple of judgment loom over the field. The pain no longer assaulted her as her own innocence freed her from each step. She held her head up high and smiled at the people that she had passed along the way. Her bare feet touched the unforgiving sand with her pride. Her sandals left in the cell that she had almost become. She knew that the sand was hurting the soles of her feet as she trod endlessly onward. Yet, she did not care. She was now anxious to hear the evidence.

They now approached the hall of judgment with tall stone columns that reached the sky that were painted to emulate the field of real reeds that they had just walked through. The sky looked down on them, for there was no pretense of a roof. The Gods were the witnesses beside the earthly chosen judges of the tribunal.

Au-Set was brought forward and beckoned mercifully to sit in front of the judges lined up on their thrones in their entire splendor. She saw Au-Sar with his tall plumes reaching almost to the heavens and sitting on his silver throne. She noticed that her throne beside him was vacant. She lovingly saw the faces of her siblings and cast no guilt upon them. She was confident they would be fair in her judgment. They grew up beside her and knew that she was not capable of a deed such as this.

She saw the other seats filled, as this was an important trial for Kemet. She saw Mut, Khephra, Tmu-Amun, and Ptahtep or Ptah, the younger (The original Ptah was a female and long dead), Re, Suti, Neb-Het, Tehuti, Apep, Sekhmet, and even her own children in their respective places on the tribunal. She lovingly noted that each Sepat was represented. She felt that her trial would be fair and hoped that her system of justice would work for her.

Au-Sar raised his green dyed arms to silence the gathered crowd. All were hushed except for the wind that made the reeds behind them dance as if oblivious of her trial and the possibility of her facing death if she were found guilty.

"People of this land, our queen Au-Set Ua-Zit has been accused of committing murder to her own consort to whom she had bore children. Nebmaat was the father of the princesses Renenutet and Weret-Heka. Children come forward to participate in this trial of your mother." Somberly in response, they walked forward as her two daughters and the beloved princesses of Kemet. Au-Set surged with pride at the proud way that her daughters carried themselves in front of the hungry crowd. She smiled at them both with her heart and they looked at her. She knew in her soul that they did not want to believe that she could do such a thing to Nebmaat. They appeared confused and tried hard to hide it from the crowd that struggled to hear each word uttered.

She looked ever and saw Tehuti and her beloved Merul taking down each word. She looked expectantly at Au-Sar and told him silently that she would obey his judgment and that he must do his job.

He looked at her and struggled not to take her away and to hide her from the wrath of the people. With her silent acceptance of his duty, he looked from her face to the crowd that had gathered below the dais upon which all of the seats of the tribunal faced out ominously. He looked up to the heavens praying for the mercy of the gods and for the truth to be revealed on this day.

"People, we are here today to determine the guilt or innocence of your queen in this accusation!" The crowd roared out and broke the silence of the reeds of sentinel behind them and around where they stood.

"Silence, The Nugig Ma-At and my daughter Maat will carry the symbolic feather of justice and bring it forward." Both the aged Nugig and young princess came forward carrying a large silver feather that was elaborately carved and from a sacred metal that had fallen from the sky. Thus, the silver feather was deemed all the more sacred as coming directly from the Goddess herself.

In the center of the stage was a large golden scale. On one side, the feather was placed and the other side remained empty. Au-Sar nodded to Ma-At and Maat at a job well done. He looked again to the people and then to Au-Set. "Sister, on this other side of the scale you must place your heart to be measured. In this it will be your side of the events as it transpired."

Au-Set nodded, and knew that this was part of the ritual they created for the judgment of their people.

"You will now hear the evidence as it was brought forward. Those who bring this accusation of your queen step forward to face her and her people!" He looked up to the heavens to make it known to the gods that he wanted them to sit in judgment as well.

Tentatively Set stepped forward, the sunlight capturing the fire of her brilliant curly tresses as they cascaded down her shoulders. Her hair surrounded the daughter of Au-Set as she walked to face her mother. Set looked defiantly at her mother.

Suti then walked to the side of his daughter and placed his arm around her shoulders. The crowd went wild at this in his public acknowledgement. They were told that Set was the daughter of Au-Set and Au-Sar. The truth was obvious before them with the flamingly accusatory hair of the pair.

Au-Set bent her head down in sorrow at this well-planned gesture of her brother. She knew that this would put doubt in the minds of the people at her lie being challenged in front of all of Kemet.

She saw with pride how Au-Sar looked over at this and went to the other side of Set to place his arm around her as well. This publically signified that he did not care and loved his daughter in a great show of his own support to the crowd before them. The crowd loved the spectacle and responded predictably, as they let out a bellow of approval at this act of their kings before them.

Au-Sar then went to the center of the dais and bellowed, "I also give those who protect the accused to step forward!" At this Bast walked out with a purpose and a strong step to the fore to bow low to the crowd. She winked at her consort who was writing this all down, Merul. She then stepped back and joined them.

"Now you will hear the events as proclaimed by those before you both princesses of the house of Au-Set. We all will sit in judgment at the words. If punishment is deemed required out of guilt, Anmut, *The Devourer of the Dead!*" will dole it out!" At this, the crowd roared at its anticipation of seeing blood.

Au-Set looked at her brother and bid him to continue with the trial. He acknowledged it and spoke, "Set, stand forth and tell your version!"

"I am a princess of the house of Au-Set and am the daughter of Suti! This I have only learned recently after being raised on lies! I will tell you of the true nature of my mother! She has always complained of her consort Nebmaat and of his reckless spending. She feared that he would run them all into poverty with his 'useless trinkets and silly garments' as she oft called them!"

Au-Set nodded for this was true, as she had often jokingly complained of her consort and of his naïve ways of believing each merchant that arrived at the palace gates. She could not counter this.

Set continued with a determination that almost made her form glow in venom. Au-Set almost shrank back for this was her own daughter that she had nursed from her own breasts, cradled, and protected. How could she hate her so! She wanted to crawl back into the cell where she was brought from at the pain of her daughter's hatred that wrecked her soul. She wondered why she had not seen any of this and wondered forlornly if she could have possibly prevented this.

"My mother has many secrets and is responsible for the death of Nebmaat. I saw it with my own two eyes! She followed Nebmaat to the market place dressed in the ceremonial garb passed down from her own mother! She worked sorcery to become the Goddess Innana and to kill and seek vengeance in her name! She preyed on Nebmaat and followed him. I could not hear what she said to him though it looked as if he tried to embrace her and she pushed him away and screamed something at him. Then out of nowhere, she produced a knife and stabbed him. The blood was everywhere! My mother looked around and saw that she was not followed and left. I came forward, found that Nebmaat was indeed dead, and brought him back to the palace. That is what happened. I saw the truth of my mother!"

The tears streamed from Au-Set's face as the shadows of the giant pillars hid it all from the crowd below her who stabbed at her with their accusing eyes. It seemed as if they had already made their judgment.

"Bast, now you must tell us all your version of this event as it transpired. For only the Gods know the truth and it will be made clear to us this day before all of Kemet."

She bowed and faced the people after looking at her mother and then scornfully at her older sister Set.

"I did a wrong and am here to correct it before you. I know that the clothes of the Goddess Innana can only be worn by her earthly representative and have been kept in reverence in the palace after they were retrieved a few years ago for my mother to keep. I know that no woman can wear her crown but my own mother on special occasions. For she was the first born of Ninnuit, the woman whom the Goddess chose. My mother would have inherited her place had Eshnunna not fallen to the red-headed tribes of the north!" She smiled at the crowd's reaction to this news. She knew this would attract their attention, as they were not told of the invasion of Eshnunna and of a possible threat to their very tranquil existence.

"Father and mother will verify this." She looked at them and they nodded affirmation to the people of Kemet.

Bast held in her breath to continue, "People, it is true that I donned the golden crown of my grandmother and that I had no right. I was afraid to tell anyone of this and was ignorant in my youth at the great distress that it would cause in the balance of things! I wore it and loved the feel of the weight of the gold upon my brow. I felt the power of the Goddess fill me and did not know how I ended up in the market place far from the safety and confines of the palace. It was the stupidity of my youth that led me outside. I bowed when I passed people and they thought that I was my mother! I felt glorious and proud for she is the most beautiful woman in all of Kemet and it felt wonderful to be mistaken for her!"

She bowed her head for a moment as if to catch her breath and then continued once again, "I did notice Nebmaat and out of curiosity followed him. I know that it was wrong in even leaving the palace and even in actually donning the whole outfit. Nevertheless, I was having fun. I was about to reveal who I was or actually to see if he could tell. I wondered if he could be tricked as well. But, instead of turning to see me behind him as he almost did he walked into an alley." She proceeded to tell all about how she encountered him and of his extreme change in character and of what he had told her. She knew that he wanted no one to know of the truth of his plans and had planned to kill her for having this knowledge.

"He grabbed me in his confession and I knew that he meant to kill me as he held a knife up to my throat. Yet in fear for my own life I took out the dagger from underneath the garment and stabbed him for my own preservation and to warn my mother of his treachery!"

"I ran back to the palace to only have been beaten by Set with her horrid version! I saw my own mother led away in chains for a crime that I had committed! I screamed inside and was afraid to tell anyone because I could easily have been put to death for disobeying the laws of the Goddess and wrongfully donning her clothes and crown! I feared for my life and hoped that all would see the truth of this! I did not stay to hear the story as told by Set because I noticed that I needed to prove the innocence of my mother and to let all know of the treachery of Nebmaat.

"I searched each city that our family built and had found out about a plot. Enlil, the God of the ancient land of Eshnunna that he calls Sumer has no son to send his rule down. The daughters he deems as unimportant and only uses for the breeding of council members. The only son that he can claim is Suti! The world knows that the Goddess Innana was raped by Enlil and produced Suti from this act of hatred! The guilt of his evil is in the color of his hair! Look at the fire of evil as it glows and that of Set!" Everyone went wild with this and the sky seemed to rip apart in confusion for all that the people had known to this moment was suddenly ripped asunder with a deviousness that they could only then begin to understand.

"I have found out that Enlil means to invade this land and was given inside information by Nebmaat with a promise of glory in the new land of Sumer! Furthermore, my mother would not admit even to herself the true paternity of my sister Set because it pained her so! She told no one of this but I had found out from the Goddess. My mother was raped by Suti and forced into submission out of pure anger for her. How that must have hurt her! That her own baby brother would have so much hatred for her! She wept and wept, as her tears became the rains of this land. So strong that she is in the burden of the pain that she has carried for so long. She would not even admit it even to herself."

Bast looked over at her mother who sat mutely there. She bent over to hold her mother. "I am sorry, but I know. I am sorry for wearing your mother's clothes and crown. I am sorry for being disobedient. I had to tell them all because it is time that you let the pain go and let us carry some of it along with you. You had done no wrong in any of this. You have done no wrong in anything. Your heart is pure and good and you love all around you!"

Au-Set's tears glimmered from the sun above them all and formed a solid path down her dusted cheeks of her confinement. She looked up at her daughter and told her with her eyes that she loved her and was proud. She even looked over at Set and let her know equally with her eyes of her love and forgiveness.

Bast looked at her father and then to the crowd. "It is me who should be sitting in that chair of judgment, not our queen!" She walked over again to her mother and carefully took her mother's dirt encrusted arms and led her away and over to her official throne beside her siblings. She then walked over, pride-fully, and sat in the simple unadorned chair of judgment. "Now judge me Gods and be fair!" She raised her arms to the heavens and heard the thumping approval of her family as they stomped their feet creating an ominous roar. She bowed her head to be judged by her father and Kemet.

It was then that Anmut stepped forward, "I the 'Devourer of the Dead" and the co-leader of the 'Hall of Two Truths" speak now on this day and the events that have unfolded before us all....

"The living and the dead are weighed against the feather of justice as protected by the Nugig Ma-At and the princess Maat. The scale is of the earth and of the heavens surrounding us. A problem is now bought forth. I have come across the solution. A grievous misunderstanding has arisen and an identity was mistaken. Truths are revealed before us in all of this and must be dealt with. I will confer with the others on what is to be done in this matter!" She raised her heavily tattooed arms to the sky and then to those sitting in judgment, "Come, let us find and decide what is to be done." They all rose to follow Anmut below the dais to confer.

Set, Suti, Bast, and Au-Set sat in silence waiting for what seemed an eternity. At last, as the shadows fell down upon them and as the day grew old they reappeared. Anmut came to the fore raised her arms and addressed the anxious crowd, "We have agreed upon the solution!" She then walked over to the scale, took out the large silver feather, and watched the scale balance once more with the air. "As you see the words of the gods are deemed fair by the scale and the answer is deemed good." She held the feather high and turned it to catch the rays of the fading sun. She shone the rays until they caught on the head of Au-Set who was still sitting on the chair that her daughter placed her.

"The rays shine your innocence in this matter, queen you are good and just. Your daughter has risked all even her life to make sure that the judgment be true. That all facts are revealed." She looked over at Bast.

"Princess, you have exposed facts that could end your life to save your mother and have been seen for this. Innana, believed dead to Eshnunna for the treachery of Enlil, has come down to tell us that you may live and that she chooses you to hail her memory instead of the prior rightful first-born Set. Set was born from the seed of the evil tribes of the north who seek our destruction. It is not her fault in this though Innana has deemed that you had chosen rightfully and from her whispers to don the garment that day. It was not revealed to you because this was her final test of your worthiness. You have revealed the truth to all despite what it could cost you and therefore, you have passed in the eyes of the Goddess!" Behind her, Anmut was handed something. "Come forward child and face your people."

Bast came over to where Anmut stood and faced the people in front of the old woman. Anmut produced the crown of Innana for all to see. The golden disc caught the brilliant reds of the sunset and showered the people. The horns of gold reached to protect the disc and gleamed in pride at it being worn in public again by yet another generation. She looked over at Au-Set and beckoned to her.

"Mother, place this crown on the worthy daughter!" Au-Set looked all around her through the roar of the people. She wanted to tear the crown apart and to give a piece to each of her daughters. She hated that she had to choose. She also knew the politics involved and yet, the conflicting line of ascendancy.

Her first-born daughter should receive the rights to don this in ceremony after her and yet, she was not born completely of the seed of her land but of a new race that was out to destroy the ways of the Goddess. She held judgment in her hands as she was initially brought here to receive. So much had revealed itself to her and to the people of Kemet. She knew that they shared in her pain and cried for the decision that she had to make. No mortal woman had to make this decision, and yet she must as her newly elected Goddess. She held the crown in her hands feeling the heaviness of its power. She knew that her actions now would forever determine the feelings of her daughters and of the people. Her instinct had always served her in the past and she chose then in what seemed like forever but was really the fraction of a moment- what she had to do.

She took the crown and felt the heat from the soft ancient gold that was beaten to form the symbol of the Goddess of Eshnunna in the sacred form of the fertile cow. She called out for all to hear, "Set, Renenutet, Weret-Heka, Bast, Maat and Serqet, come forward. As your mother, I order you here by my side to witness this." They all came forward willingly, as if commanded from their cradles. They all knew that voice that their mother rarely used and had not for many years to them as they were all older now. Yet, time reversed for her daughters and they were pulled forward by the summons of their mother.

Au-Set took the crown and told her daughters to grab onto it and to pull it with all of their might. They looked at her questioningly and obeyed her command. The crown was ancient and the disc, horned and the pieces of the crown base all fell apart easily in pieces of twisted metal. When done, it did not resemble the original structure at all. Yet, each of them held a piece of it in their hands. Au-Set smiled. "Now the will of Innana is in each of them. Each has earned a valuable piece that shall for now on be attached to their ceremonial gear and worn with pride as a symbol from the past generation. It will be a symbol that the bond of sisters shall never be broken!"

Au-Set had two pieces in her hands and looked over at her mirror and twin Neb-Het. "This sister is for you! Wear it with pride as you are my sister and my heart's completion!" Neb-Het came forward and reached out for the piece as handed her by her older twin. She placed it in her headdress to free her hands as Au-Set and the others had done and turned to look at the crowd and then at her sister. They both reached out to touch the fingers of the other as they did when they were young.

To the rest who witnessed this it looked as if there was a mirror on the dais, so startlingly similar did the two sisters and twins look despite their garments. One-half in splendor and the other half in rags and tatters. Both appeared every cubit, the Goddesses that they were. The crowd and their family rang out loudly in approval at the gesture and at the magic of the moment.

When it died down Anmut stepped forward. "A decision has also been reached. Bast, for risking your life to save that of your mother; you are absolved of your guilt and may walk in pride! Hold your head up, for your valor is worthy of your strong blood!" Anmut saw Bast fill with pride and saw the last of the little girl leave her at that moment, and mourned silently for it. Bast was now a woman. Au-Set had noticed this as well as the others of her family.

"Set, you, the first born; have chosen reckless paths that have led to your destruction. You have not chosen wisely those whom you should alliance yourself. However, we all do sympathize with your feelings of your newly revealed paternity. However, you have gone beyond the bounds of judgment and in what is your actual power to choose. We understand the loyalty to family and Suti is your father.

"You have forgotten the difference between nurture and blood. Your mother has raised you and saved you from your impatient decisions since you were old enough to make them. She took on your pain and kept some truth from you only out of love and protection! For this, Innana has passed over you! You know the actions of your mother this day are valid and are seen by the people but the Goddess knows more! You, Set are banished with your father from this land and from your birthright and are doomed to the Deshret that is the only thing besides your mother who may forgive you both!" At this, the lion of Sekhmet roared with approval of the judgment set forth.

Chapter 128

After the banishment of Set and Suti from the land of Kemet, Au-Set and Au-Sar worked on the fortification of their land and of the cities that they built from the sands of the Deshret. Au-Set was proud of how all of her family created wonder out of seemingly docile sand. The colors flowed over them in a vast array of accomplishment. The blandness of the mud brick was covered in the glowing writing of the Gods as created by Tehuti and Merul as well as Ma-At and Maat. They worked hard at creating a beautifully told story in delightful symbols that wove a tale out of the bleak and harsh climate of the vast Deshret that always seemed to surround them.

For years, nothing was heard of her daughter and brother. They almost seemed to disappear into the desert from where they built their home and started their hidden armies. She and her Scorpion Guard went out deep into the desert to see if that is eventually where they ended up.

Instead, all that greeted her was the silence of neglect and abandonment. The once tall walls tumbled down to join the desert from whence they had sprung. The wind whirled the dust in an eerie melody of emptiness that echoed only curiosity back to Au-Set. Au-Set knew they were still alive.

She did not know why but she had secretly hoped that she would find her daughter here and would be able to hold her in her arms. She had the forgiveness that only a mother could understand, when her children have erred. A single tear slid down her cheek, she turned to her guard and thus, they departed the desolate place and returned to the mighty kingdom of Kemet.

Chapter 129

At her return, Au-Set called for Tehuti. "Brother, I have a task for you. It is something that I believe you have already started in a way. I have noticed the glory of our family that you have painted on the many walls of our cities and have basked in the glow of pride." She smiled at her younger brother who had always seemed to her older in just the way of his character of silent carriage and pride of form. He smiled back.

"Could you perhaps make this into something grander? I was thinking of when we were young and new to this land, we were told of our purpose and duty." He eyes clouded over in the memory of her aunt's words as they echoed their mother's wishes. This occurred when they were still very new to Kemet and before they were separated from each other to perform their obligation.

"Remember that we were all told our duty and of what were expected of us. We were told of why our family was to remain in Kemet to forge a future. This land was raw to us and uncivilized. There were villages and many small kings and queens. There was chaos as there once was long ago in Eshnunna. Our family brought peace and reason to Eshnunna and civilized them. We brought together the many Gods and Goddesses under the love of Innana who was once Arinna of the Catal-Huyuk of our origins.

"How did they once bring order to chaos brother? Did not they tell the people of their myths and the religion they brought them? They told the people the stories of their Gods and Goddesses and gave them the reasons why. That, my brother is... what we shall do now! Could you perhaps, along with Merul, Ma-At and Maat go around to each Sepat and gather their stories as they want them told to the people of Kemet. They should then be painted in glory on our temples!"

"That is a marvelous idea, I shall begin at once!"

Au-Set smiled at how Tehuti had almost tripped in the elation of the new project that he was given. She sat there in the new silence of the glade of plum trees as it framed the full moon above her. She heard the bees end their gathering for the day and their progress as they prepared to head for their hives. She smiled at the ways of the Goddess, no matter what her name. She sat on a rock in her favorite spot and felt the air after her discussion with Tehuti as he left to embark on his new endeavor.

She felt the air around her tingle with a good decision and felt the universe fall into place as the peaceful vibes were spread even further. She was very proud of her family and thought of them as she watched the stars appear in the sky. She noticed the entrance of the Dog Star as it would signal the beginning of the yearly inundation of the Great River and knew that it was being recorded in the temple and that her brother Au-Sar was being alerted. Au-Sar was in charge of the agriculture and irrigation of their many cities. He would supervise any change in climate and the preparation of the crops and each phase.

In her busy thoughts of the ending day, she almost did not hear the footsteps of her sister as they approached.

"Sorry to disturb you Setti." She softly called out her childhood name, as it had not been uttered in decades. It brought the love of their childhood back to her and Au-Set almost wanted to reach out and grab the innocence of it all back to them for this moment of the approaching stars and knew that she could not. Instead, she looked up at her sister. She always knew when her sister was near, for she felt it. No matter how silent Neb-Het was, Au-Set could always sense her presence. Her heat would always jump at her sisters approach, so close was their bond.

"No worry, Nebby!" She smiled. She patted the flat rock next to her and moved over to allow room next to her for the form of her other half.

The two sisters sat side by side and watched the slow entrance of the stars in the sky and the colors of the day fade and disappear with the hunger of the evening.

Neb-Het spoke to the heavens as well as to her sister, "Does it not seem as if the moon swallows the colors of the day sister?"

"Yes, it does seem that way." They both sat there in silence enjoying the new comfort of the evening sky as it brought along a soft breeze that flew in from the Great River. The breeze that would bring in the black mud and soil that would fertilize the fields for the food of the people of Kemet.

Au-Set and her sister seemed to know deep in their heart when the Dog Star would appear since they were initially brought to this land, they would find the time in their busy lives to sit and greet it when it arrived. They did not know about this until they were older and reunited as adults by Ua-Zit when the talent that they both shared was discovered.

No matter where they were, they knew when the star would appear. No one until them had ever been able to predict it's occurrence though it had been noted since the beginning of time and relied on to give them life and food with the rich black soil that would later fill the sides of the Great River's banks.

Au-Set felt something else this time and glanced at her sister with the look that told her that it was safe to talk freely from her heart.

"Sister, as you and I know.....I am only the second consort of Tehuti and I feel that it should not be so. Now do not say a word and listen. Officially, I am his consort, but his heart belongs to another! I feel that he should live openly with her for our union has never been consummated."

"Ahhh, I had no idea. Tehuti had not mentioned another. I thought we were close."

"Oh you are, however, the one he chose is of low birth and you know Tehuti he is always a slave to duty and to our family. He has always put his needs after all of ours as our brother Heru had always done." Both of them took the others hand at the mention of their long dead brother Heru, whose memory they had sought to keep buried since it was too painful to face."

"Neb-Het, what is this woman's name?"

"*Nehmetaway.*"

"Than you are released! For once our brother shall have his heart's content. Send out for him and make it official will you sister!" Au-Set beamed to the mirror of her image in Neb-Het.

Chapter 130

Thus, the will of the land of Kemet was done and he could openly proclaim his love for his Nehmetaway with her fiery deep brown hair. He loved how soft it was and felt that it was a gift from the gods to be allowed to sit in her presence. He felt that she was not the simple daughter of a farmer but a Goddess made humble for the world to adore as he did. From that day forth on, his journeys he had by his side his loving consort as well as the aged Nugig from his Eshnunna and his niece Maat to complete their duty.

He was very proud at their vast accomplishments and the speed of their travels. They traveled by a boat made of papyrus to each Sepat of their kingdom and collected the stories of the leaders and their official totems. With all of this information, he and his assistants wove wondrous tales and created a new mythology for this land filled with color and intrigue.

They found that this was not hard since the people of this land had it in their very nature to create lives of vast color in stark comparison to the bleakness of the Deshret that surrounded them. The people of Kemet chose to favor the vibrancy of the Great River from which all life was derived to lead their lives on this material plane of existence.

Tehuti wrote of Re and his family of Ineb-Hedj and of their story in life. He told of the temple that Re dedicated to his consort Het-Heru and of how he ordered the priestesses within to celebrate the life of Het-Heru with laughter and joy and dancing in happy ceremony for a woman who loved life.

Tehuti especially loved the tale that Re created for the family of his own mother. It was well known that Re was the consort of Ninnuit who had escaped from Eshnunna. But Re enlightened him further by telling him of the love that he had for his mother and of how beautiful she looked and how her radiance in life was like that of the stars that somehow seemed to shine even brighter in Kemet than they ever did in Eshnunna.

With Tehuti, they came up with a myth to honor Ninnuit the Goddess representative of Innana.

In the myth she was still mentioned as the mother of Au-Set, Au-Sar, Tehuti, Heru, Suti and Neb-Het; however, in this particular legend Re is mentioned the foremost of her consorts.

Tehuti equally had fun with this and of how playfully Re took the results of the completed myth.

In the myth, Re was the consort of Ninnuit. Tehuti decided that the name Ninnuit was too foreign to the people of Kemet and changed it to Nut to mean star. Re was the sun and Nut was the very sky on which he rode across. Her body spread across the four corners of the earth to protect them from the coldness of the absence of the sun. Every morning she gave birth to the sun named Re and he would ride his '*Boat of Millions*" across the sky.

Tehuti and Re both laughed as how his favorite fishing boat was included in this myth, which would probably outlast even their bodies long after they turned to dust.

Tehuti gloatingly wrote a tale of how Re in a fit of anger forbids Nut to give birth on any of the days of the year. In the beginning of creation, there were only 360 days. Therefore, Tehuti intervened by creating four more days so that Nut could give birth to Au-Set, Au-Sar, Set, and Neb-Het.

Re looked over at Tehuti, "Will not the people question the inaccuracies of these tales?"

"Do people ever question the words of the Gods? Besides it is to teach them how to better honor the Gods and to live a just and honest life."

"I suppose you are right in this. We shall see. Tell me the other tales that you have created on this marvelous papyrus of yours."

"Would you like to know the story of you and your brother?"

"Oh, This I have to hear...." He sat back silently on the rocks by the side of the irrigation ditch to hear the tale created by his son.

Tehuti read the finished story from his cherished papyrus of how the two brothers deified were woven in this tale as the sun and his brother the serpent Apep. The sun battled each evening on the River *Duat* of oblivion a battle that had repeated itself from the beginning of eternity. Re would ride his trusted "Boat of Millions" and encounter Apep as a giant serpent each evening. Apep would swallow Re and his boat and then Nut would give birth to Re all over again to repeat the cycle that had started before time began.

Tehuti continued to explain to Re, "So, you see there is a creation story like that to each Sepat. That was where I ran into trouble. Each one of them wanted to be the creators of the universe and all life as we see it." He laughed.

"Such is the vanity of the people of Kemet!" Re added in equal mirth.

As the River unwound beside them, Tehuti told Re some of the other tales to the amusement and pride of his father.

He told of the story of his mother Mut and of her consort Khnum who was the famous potter. He told of how Khnum created people from the simple clay of the desert on his magic potter's wheel. He also told of how Khnum was also the master of the caverns of where the God *Hapi* lived.

"Hapi is a man who lives in the far northern regions of this land, near the source. He controls a mighty army of hippopotami that obey his every command. However, in reality he pays rent for his lands to Khnum even though he is the leader of his own Sepat.

"And your own mother Mut has her own story, she is known as the founder of your city Ineb-Hedj that she called *MenNefer*. It is odd of how her first consort was Tmu-Amun and through him; she had Shu, the old Ua-Zit, and Nekhebt from whom my aunts took over their rule. I wrote of how she found her voice in her journeys in the sky in her form as a hawk. Your mother had found out that the warrior *Amaunet* had stolen her voice and had ran away with it to gain the power of MenNefer. Amaunet wanted Tmu-Amun for herself as well as Khnum and the palace of white painted bricks along the Great River. Your mother sought her out and battled with her for eight days and finally won back her voice and her beloved city of MenNefer...."

"I never heard of Amaunet."

"I know, she almost did not tell me of her, for this happened long before you were born. Amaunet was her older sister and rightful heir of this land as inherited by the family matriarch Ptah the first potter of this land. Mut stole it from her and killed her consort the older brother of Tmu-Amun named *Amun*.

"Your mother was quite the warrioress and took what she wanted no matter what the cost! When she was very young, she banished Amaunet and her consort Amun to the most northerly lands of Kemet and took over the land of MenNefer. There she built her glorious city, which you live in and had improved as well with your own talent. However, with each wall that was built her voice became softer and softer until it disappeared altogether and she was left mute.

"That is why your mother Mut found out where Amaunet and her consort Amun set up camp and sought them out to engage them in a final battle. Her own mother Ptah told her that she would never have her voice returned until the day when she won this land fair and faced her sister in battle. Ptah reminded her younger daughter Mut that she had taken the land from her sister unfairly and had lost her voice as a result."

"Is any of this true son?"

"Only the Gods know for sure that is what she wanted written. And do not worry I have painted her in the full glory that we all know with her bright clothing of painted feathers and her crown of vulture feathers that she had stolen and then rightfully earned from the battle of her older sister Amaunet. I even added her cane of papyrus; however, I turned it into a scepter!"

"How clever, continue please as I find all of this very interesting and entertaining." He smiled at his son urging him to continue.

"Well, I made your mother Mut as the maternal influence to those who sit upon the throne of Kemet.

"I mentioned the name of the mother of her consort Tmu-Amun who was Nun. I wrote of how she traveled to this land of Kemet from a far northern place to escape the domination of the northern tribes. She came alone to Kemet to escape her land of chaos to live in peace with her son Tmu-Amun. Her consort *Naunet* followed her to beg her to return to their homeland. She refused and he stayed to watch over their son while she would provide food for their table. Naunet was a skilled weaver and wove wondrous garments for their son, some as soft as air and as gentle as butterfly wings. He found the beautiful Mut for his son and together they had Shu who was Ninnuit's father from her mother Tefnut.

I even included Mut's younger consort Ptah who was born Ptahtep and was originally her consort and was given to Sekhmet instead. I have Ptahtep as the master artisan that he is as learned from the family matriarch Ptah herself and his namesake. And I have Sekhmet as the continuation of her mother Het-Heru."

Re smiled at the thought of this and thought how similar that they actually were. Het-Heru was a much softer version of their daughter Sekhmet, though Sekhmet brought each quality of her mother out loudly and to the fore.

Chapter 131

With all of the magic occurring over all of Kemet, the people required further ceremony. They witnessed all around them the gleaming and tall cities rise out of the nothingness of the desert that surrounded their world. They saw a family that ruled in equality and together with a strong family bond. Never before had the people of Kemet witnessed this. In the past their land had been ruled by constantly warring factions until the final split eons ago of Upper Kemet and Lower Kemet. They knew that long ago before their time the land was together and whole as just plain Kemet. There were no upper and lower halves as there has been for the longest time imaginable. The people knew nothing else.

Au-Set and her siblings decided to create for the people a grand ceremony uniting officially the lands into one. They worked long into the evening hours creating a ceremony grander and richer than the people of Kemet had ever seen or themselves for that matter.

They had decided to call upon actors to perform the parts of Suti and Set. They knew that without Suti and Set the whole unification would be meaningless to the people. They wanted to see the magic of a unified and powerful family that held the power of their land.

It was extremely difficult to find hair of the color that they were famous for since it was rare in Kemet. A warrior party was sent out to capture people with that color hair and they had to travel far almost to the land of Sumer to find them. Their hair was shorn to create wigs that would adorn the heads of the actors in the full ceremonial garb of those two whom they portrayed.

On the day of the ceremony, the siblings gathered to be fitted into their ceremonial garb as created by Qui and Kekes. The effect was magical, especially as they walked up the steps leading on to the dais. They had decided to hold this ceremony in the exact center of their land to further its great significance.

Each one of them gleamed in the sunlight with the gems and precious metals sewn into their headdresses. Their garments were of the softest and starkest white of linens. Their simplicity added to the grandeur of the power they emanated as they walked to form a half moon on the large platform.

Au-Set and Au-Sar walked to the fore of the crowd and raised their arms to the Gods of the Sky and to the people. They wore their traditional elaborate headdresses and Au-Sar was dyed in the green of the underworld, which appeared even more garish next to the beauty of Au-Set.

They spoke in unison, their voices carrying far out to each person of the crowd that numbered in the hundreds of thousands. Each person of their land was requested for this ceremony and this monumental event.

"Today, we unite all of Kemet! No longer shall it be known as Upper and Lower Kemet, but Unified Kemet."

Neb-Het and the actor dressed as Set walked from where they were standing to their place beside Au-Set and Au-Sar. Neb-Het and the fake Set spoke in unison, "We unite our power this day with that of the Lower lands. The Shen People join in love with the People of the Iaret. I Neb-Het Nekhebt join to become one with my sister and twin Au-Set Ua-Zit. Together they walked to the front of the platform, took off their headdresses, and placed them on the ground. There was the white crown of Upper Kemet as donned by Au-Set and the red crown of Lower Kemet as donned by Neb-Het. They stepped back. Their brothers and consorts repeated the action. Set with his red crown and Au-Sar with his white crown. They stepped back as well and held hands with their respective consorts Neb-Het and Au-Set.

Tehuti along with Merul stepped out from his place and went over to retrieve the four crowns. It seemed magic to the people to whom they performed. Only those on the stage knew the truth of it all. Tehuti and Merul took the crowns and brought them over to an area on the platform that was blocked from the view of the people. They placed the four discarded crowns and took out four new crowns that contained the red and the white of the Upper and Lower Kemet to symbolize the unification in a display of magic that awed the people.

Tehuti and Merul with a grand flourish of drama placed the new crowns on the heads of Au-Set, Au-Sar, Suti and Neb-Het as the crowd roared with approval.

Tehuti then spoke up as the four newly crowned ones sat on their thrones of rare silver. "People, I now give to you the gift of writing!" He held up his papyrus with his beautiful words written on it for the people to see.

"I have created images that represent the sacred words of the Gods who speak to me and my family. Look behind you on this wall and witness the first whisper of the Gods to all of you!" Behind them, a large woolen blanket was lifted up to reveal the beautifully painted walls to the sunlight and to the enthralled people. For never before has the public witnessed the writing. It was only on the walls of the palace made of mud before this. The people had only seen paintings and murals on the temples never images that represented the words of their very own Gods.

"You people of the land of Kemet are blessed in that the Gods chose you all to see their tales before anyone else in this world!" The people roared in delight and waited expectantly for the next act to begin.

Unable to disappoint the people and pleased at the reaction that their ceremony was being received, the next act began.

This time the children of the four newly crowned ones appeared in the fore of the platform separated into groups of three. The actress dressed as Set was in the group with Renenutet and Merul, while Bast was placed with Heru, Weret-Heka and Anpu, the son of Au-Sar and Neb-Het. In the last group were the young and precious Maat and Serqet, Edjo, Sekhmet of Re and Shai. The first group was dressed in red linen beside the usual white linen. They all still had their elaborate headdresses. The second group was dressed in yellow dyed linen and the third group was dressed in blue dyed linen. They each went to a separate section of the stage.

Tehuti spoke out to all, "You will learn of the words of the Gods as written on these walls in front of you all. They tell the tale of three creations. It is meant for you to hear them all and to find out in the afterlife, which one is true. That is the lesson as taught by the Gods. They feel that we must decide which is the truth during our lives and it will be revealed to us upon our deaths and only if chosen by the Gods after their time of judgment. Children tell your stories;"

The first group in red as led by the fake Set sang in unison the first story of creation,

"This is the Yanu myth as told by the heavens...
Before the earth was here.
Before the leaves sang to us,
Before the great river ran
Was Yanu.

Yanu was an endless ocean,
A voice
A destiny
A beginning.

Yanu decided to give the people a name
A name that they could speak
A name that would not kill them
A name such as Nu."

"From the non-existence of the Nu rose a celestial firmament that was surrounded by the endless waters of the Nu. Atum was the firmament that rose out for it was the name given to this finality to the endless sea...

"Atum as the firmament and became the God of the sun as we see in the sky. Atum reigned from this firmament and named it Benben. The name of this God, Atum means "in the whisper of the Gods-totality." The people on this mound, this firmament called him the Sun God or their Monad, which means to them the forces of nature. For as Monad of the firmament of Atum he contains within himself the elements of creation."

"Atum was taken as consort by the nothingness from which he sprang by the female version of himself named Tmu. Together when they became one literally and they were known as Tmu-Atum.

"Through their love and union they created Shu and Tefnut. Shu means void or empty for he is the God of air. The medu-necher on this wall for Shu is called 'yshsh'. Tefnut means dew or moisture. The medu-necher for her name is 'tf'. Shu and Tefnut created Geb and Nut.

"Shu encompassed the concept of air through the rays of the sun. Tefnut is one with the atmosphere of the underworld. Geb is the earth, while Nut is the sky above.

"Nut spreads her body over the earth which is her consort named Geb. Shu, the sun God travels the firmament Geb and at the end of the twelve days that are allotted to him. Shu is swallowed up in a large gulp by Tefnut, queen of the sky. The sun God named Shu travels inside the body of Nut during the twelve hours of night and dawn. Tefnut then gives glorious birth to the sun God Shu renewed which is the full color of the dawn in all of its redness!

"Nut bore Geb four children; Au-Set, Au-Sar, Suti and Neb-Het. Set completes the legitimate line of the Goddess and God made whole as Kemet is once again united! This is one tale for you to learn and it is called the Yanu!"

The children in red went over to the great wall and pointed to the section on it that told the tale they revealed to the people of Kemet.

Tehuti then introduced the yellow clad children for their part. In unison, their voices rang loud and clear. All of them had rehearsed for weeks on end for this final celebration and their practice paid off well.

"This is a tale of the second creation and is found from the soil in Ineb-Hedj, once known as MenNefer and the

land conquered by Mut from her sister Amaunet. The matriarch of creation in this tale is Ptah the master creator and craftswoman of all time.

"This is the tale of creation as revealed by the God Tehuti in his dream of dreams...

"Ptah came from her home called 'TaTenen' which was the original primordial mound of life from nothing. It is similar to the mound as told by the Yanu.

"TaTenen rose from the Nu or primordial waters. Ptah gave life to all of the Gods including Atum of Yanu bemoans of her heart and tongue. She spoke to create life and gave the new Gods that sprang from her a voice and compassion. It is well known that the conception of the heart and the tongue determine action of every limb and thus the concept of the Gods sprang forth from Ptah. The 'Ennead of Ptah" is her teeth. By pronouncing the identity of everything, the authority of such an utterance was such that all known creation came to be. For we know that whatever the eyes see the ears hear and the nose breathes is delivered straight to the heart the core of being. Thus, the conclusion reached is that the tongue speaks the heart. This is how she commanded all of the Gods into existence and became the TaTenen, "from where all life emerged!"

Thus, the children in yellow spoke their tale. The yellow symbolized the nothingness from which the matriarch Ptah created life.

The children in blue dyed linen then approached the fore of the stage to reveal the third tale of creation.

"This is the 'Ogdoad'. From a place near the 'Temple of Men-Necher' as created by the God Tehuti, began creation. Tehuti saw the magic of this site and created the city called Khemnu. This is the home of the eight primary gods known as the Ogdoad.

"Out of nothing the air God named Shu created eight gods to protect his consort the Goddess of the sky named Nut. Nut had four children extracted from her being and from the four children; four more were created from them. The following...."

The children pointed to the third section of the wall which revealed the following chart and read it aloud to the people of Kemet,

"Gods (frogs) Concept	Goddesses (snakes)
Nu	Naunet
Primeval waters	
Heh	Hauhet
flood force	
Kek	Kauket
darkness	
Amun	Amunet
	concealed
	Dynamism

"Au-Set dreamed that this was the oldest tale the one created first by the Gods in the heavens as a part of our lesson on earth in this existence. As Tehuti became the lord at his city of Khemnu, he witnessed the explosive creation of the universe, as we know it before the creation of Shu and Nut. This is what he dreamed and told to Au-Set.

"It all began with a cosmic egg from which all life originated. The remains of this egg were found on the island of flame where Tehuti was born. Tehuti carried the primordial egg to the primeval mound at Khemnu for the birth of the Sun God. The Gods and Goddesses mentioned in the chart then came into being and gave birth to the sun that created Atum."

All of the children came together after the telling of the creation myths and bowed before the people whose applause of their perfect performance echoed through the valley of the Great River.

Au-Set had smiled at the reaction of Tehuti since that last part for her brother she had created. All of his tales mentioned the rest of them but not himself. She deemed him as important as the rest of them and wanted him to know this. He had taught the children a very different tale that made her the god born on the isle of flame and she secretly had the children practice her new version that honored Tehuti.

After the telling of this third tale of creation the children could not help their emotions for all of them loved their uncle Tehuti and giggled as they ran over to hug him almost knocking him to the ground in their joy. He laughed from under the heap of children and the crowd responded by stomping their feet in approval as was custom of this land. The drums added depth to the beat created by the multitudes gathered and was joined by the copper instrument that Au-Set created for this occasion was called a '*sistrum*". It rang and punctuated each beat. Together it sounded like the heartbeat of the universe. People became lost in the power of the beet and started to dance. The whole evening from that moment on was filled with dancing and celebrations. Au-Sar and Merul's famous Henket was passed around and the wine was plentiful.

Chapter 133

"My brother, my friend... Whatever would I do without you?" A tired Au-Set exclaimed. "The ceremony was a brilliant success and all due to you!"

"You must not forget to take credit where it is due that last creation epic was brilliantly changed by you. And I even noticed that you had the medu-necher painted to reflect this change." His smile was soft.

He continued, "Without me life would go on as it will when all of us are long gone. We will turn to dust and become a part of the desert that we ruled. People will forget that we even existed and breathed the same air as they. We might even become the myths created."

"Brother, I come in happiness; do not spoil it with talk so ominous! I came to watch how you made the papyrus! The people claim that you are a great magician and that it is 'poofed' into existence as you did the Gods and creation!"

"Now that is quite funny indeed!" His voice resonated with laughter and it spilled forth in torrents very unlikely for his normally calm demeanor.

"Follow me Au-Set." Together they walked over to where his workshop was in his city. After the ceremony, Au-Set decided to stay in each city as created by her family in turn and now she was at Khnum. His temple was created out of mud bricks that were painted with elaborate tales as told in the ceremony. His workshop was made of imported cedar from the land of their cousin Astarte, the land of Retenu. It was made of the logs that were notched and fastened together with dried sap mixed with straw. The building resembled their families' summer retreat from so many years ago that she almost stumbled when she saw it. She looked over at him.

"I know... something from a life far away from here. The people of this land think that this is a magical house for none other has ever been seen by them at all. To us, it is something familiar and from our childhood. Remember those warm summer days spent in the woods away from the temple life when mother took her rare vacations? I loved those days; they were filled with joy and innocence. I wanted to construct that aura in the house where I created things. I had each log imported and placed them together myself from memory. When inside the cabin my mind was free and open for conception. I have had this house for a long time and have perfected my vision of papyrus in this very room."

When they walked inside, they were almost transported back to their childhood in Eshnunna of the deep forests that dripped of rain. She recalled the dew-filled mornings when she tried to find fairies in the morning dewdrops that gleamed eagerly for their discovery on the flower-tops that filled the surrounding fields. She recalled that their mother told them that in the morning dew collected on a leaf would be the portal to the dream world and that of the Gods. When one looked into the leaf filled with the first morning dew one would be able to see whom one would end up with in union.

Au-Set looked around his small house and saw the workings of her brother's mind. She saw that every inch of space was filled with writing from rolled up papyrus to clay and stone tablets that looked ancient. She knew that he researched a lot on numerous matters and had many works from the earliest writing from their land of Eshnunna in the stark writing of her people on clay and stone. She marveled at his collection and admired it. Even the walls were covered in the complexities of his thoughts. Every inch of space was utilized with his ideas. For the first time she felt the incredible mind that her brother possessed and knew that the invention of their picture writing their men-necher could have only have been born of his mind alone.

He then saw her admiration, let it fill her mind and then beckoned her to follow him to a large workshop out back that was open to the sky for the rain hardly ever touched this place deep in the desert. Decades would pass before even a single drop of rain would ever touch the ground here. She looked up at the columns that seemed to touch the sky and then realized that they were the prototypes of those that were carved in the hall of reeds down in Abdjw. He smiled at her realization and was glad that she had noticed.

She looked around and noticed many people at work in different stages of making the famous papyrus. Au-Set was led to the first table that had four men working silently, choosing the best stalks of papyrus from large bundles that were brought in. They looked up and then down to continue their work.

The stalks deemed fit enough were gathered and placed on the next table. On this table was a woman and two more men who were engrossed in cutting the triangular stems of the papyri and then they in turn were placed on yet another table in which the stalks were then stripped after being cut. Five women were at this table and worked to a beat that they seemed to have created to make their work progress in a timely manner. Their work danced with the perfection that her brother demanded from every endeavor that he had ever been a part.

The next work area contained large shallow tubs of water in which the cut and stripped stalks were placed for a whole day. There were four tubs in different stages of soaking. In the tub with the stalks that were completely soaked, they were taken out by two men and placed on another table where many teenagers of girls and boys beat at them with small copper hammers to flatten the fibers in the soaked stalks for the next stage in this elaborate process. The flattened strips were then measured to the length of one cubit, which was the length of Tehuti's forearm. Only his was used in measurement for he demanded perfection and insisted that each sheet of papyrus be the same size.

In the next stage, the flattened and lengthened strips were laid on top of one another at right angles and beaten again in this position so that the mesh created was of a felted texture. It had the finished process of appearing 'woven'. Au-Set was astonished to learn that it was only an illusion created when the fibers were beaten. He assured her that the fibers naturally meshed together when beaten would dry together forming one sheet on totality of the perfect measurement that he had set forth.

"When I am not around, they have a stick that is cut to the exact measurement of my forearm for their measurement. Each one of these people has been here from the beginning and they have worked along my side having their own part in the perfection of this process." He looked at her and continued, "See how they are placed together when still wet to form the rolls that we write on? Observe how they are weighted down by large bronze weights while they dry. Thus, the completed papyrus that we are all now familiar with it the results of all you have learned about today. It is still a very tedious process and there are more demands than completed papyrus. I have orders from all over the known world backed up for three years from now. Each completed roll of papyri is accounted for and paid for. It is only awaiting delivery. In each day, more than five hundred scrolls are created and piled up. They are delivered on any one of the twenty reed boats that you see at the dock out back." He smiled and seemed almost to take it all in as if hearing it from someone else. He seemed also, as if lost to her and in his own world.

Au-Set looked at all that was going on around her and was thrilled to learn the secret of this process. She knew that this was valuable indeed for Tehuti had never let anyone else into this workshop besides Merul, so closely had he guarded his workshop and the creation of his famous papyrus. She knew that outside there were forty guards heavily armed to prevent any intruders. She felt much loved indeed to be allowed into his special sanctuary.

Tehuti noticed the look on his sister's face and knew as only siblings did the meaning. He wanted to elaborate on why he allowed her in here.

"Sister, you are the first person allowed into this secret world. You are the one whom I trust the most and I also want you to know how rare this knowledge is.

"Each person that you see lives here and is sworn to leave only when accompanied by an armed guard. They have each chosen to stay for the love they genuinely have for the creation of this magical and new papyrus. They are as obsessed as I am." A woman looked up at the queen in their presence who allowed the only glimpse of the outside world into their world filled with the perfection of papyrus. She walked over to them both and bowed down low, her brow touching the ground in front of Au-Set.

"Lady, I request your audience and consideration of this question."

"By all means go ahead! There is no need for formalities here this is a world unto itself." She smiled and silently bade the woman to continue.

Au-Set noticed that the woman was from the second table that she had passed and was short in stature with a thick build. Her frame looked strong and sure. This woman knew exactly what she wanted. She was curious to know her question.

"Lady, may I ask where you have found that beautiful wig that you wear? I mean no offence, I just find the hair stunning and have never seen curls such as that."

Au-Set was surprised at the question of simple vanity asked by this woman who initially appeared to have no concerns for such.

"Certainly! I realize that in this land with the heat many people shave their heads and body hair for comfort and to make sure that there is no place for insects to breed. However, this is my own hair; I wash it daily and sometimes twice a day. I find it refreshing in the heat to do so and have noticed that no insect has found its way in." She smiled. She looked at the woman and questioned, "Woman, why do you choose a life such as this? Do you have a family a loved one at home?"

"Nay, my lady, my home and family is here. I have all that I ever wanted right here in being witness to this wonderful creation of your brother's." She smiled and was lovingly embraced by Tehuti.

She knew that it was strange but Au-Set actually felt a little jealous at this secret part of her brother's life that no one until now had been allowed to enter even from his or her own family.

"Why now Tehuti, why have you finally broken your secrecy and why me of all people? Has your love Nehmetaway seen this?" She knew that he would nod in the negative at this deep in her heart.

"Because as with this finished papyrus on which you can only write on the side that we call the *recto*, it is the same with life... There is the rare person that you can trust in any lifetime to reveal your innermost and most precious secrets to and no harm would come of it. You are that person for all of Kemet. The people see this in you. I know that it is time to give some of the knowledge to someone who will carry it on after I am long gone. I know that you will treat this knowledge wisely and only share it with someone equally worthy. I have also brought Merul as you know into this but you are my sister and you will know everything." He looked at the beams of the roughened roof above them.

"Why do you speak as if life were to end soon for you brother?"

"Because it just might... No one truly knows when our time is up and we are called back to the Gods. I feel that my own time must be up since I have probably learned what I needed to know from my past life. I was born to create this and to make writing possible for each person. This process has speeded up the creation and increased production so much that it is starting to enter the homes of the common person. That is my dream and I can almost see it. What more do I have to live for?"

"Well, many reasons, your family, your lady love and so that I have someone to annoy with my dramatic life. Who else besides our brother Heru has the power to calm my erratic mind and to placate so beautifully my activities? You are the perspective in my life and have always been needed."

"You do know that life will go on for everyone, should any of us leave this realm." He beckoned her to follow him out of the workshop. She felt his deeply spiritual mood and followed him to the banks of the river to the end of one of the stone docks where his boats were lined up waiting for the next shipment.

They sat down and looked at the last of the day ready to end. They sat side by side in silence. She loved these moments in her life when she was let inside someone else's soul, if even for a moment. She thought in silence how often she had brought Tehuti into hers and never did he bother her about his troubles and tribulations. She had never before even wondered about it, so crafty was he in this, though she knew only out of good motives and for her own benefit. He had always placed her feelings before his own. He spent many hours by her side never before letting her worry even for one moment that he might have a life of his own.

Now she stood witness to the depth of his devotion to her and their family. By looking inside his secret world she had realized that her brother was a man who rarely saw sleep. He was devoted to the well-being of his family and to his obsession with the perfection of his papyrus.

"Brother, I thank you for letting me finally enter your world. In exchange, let me spend every moment by your side this week to truly witness your mind." She looked up at him in the deep innocence that only the young and pure of heart could ever possess. He saw that it was truly genuine and that it was the only way that she could possibly express her emotions and the guilt of not knowing all of this.

"Au-Set, I had not meant for you to be upset by this. I only wanted to let you know how much I value you. Even if you were not my older sister, I would have found you and supported you to my death. You owe me nothing."

"Brother, truly, will you let me be a part of your life and serve as your assistant. Please, please!" She smiled in her mischievous way.

"Fine, because I know that you will bug me until I allow this silly notion of yours. However, I do want privacy and to be left alone with Nehmetaway!" His grin was large and echoed with that of Au-Set. They both giggled like children.

She went to bed that evening and placed her weary head upon the rolled up soft linen pillow that her delicate neck rested upon. Her hair was fanned out behind her because she did not like the feel of it around her neck. She would usually have her female attendants braid it for her before retiring for each evening but she had left them behind in an earnest attempt to see her real brother for the first time.

She fell asleep to her thoughts on their conversation that day as it transpired, playing what she could have asked repeatedly in her mind lulling her to sleep.

She felt that he was reluctant to let her inside his world. He was raised from birth to protect her and to serve her and the others chosen by their mother. He accepted that role with love and adoration for she knew that he felt them worthy of his ceaseless devotion.

However, she felt there was something else that he did not want to admit, even to himself. She knew that if she did not enter his life now it would be too late. She was informed of this in the world of dreams, by the voice of their mother Ninnuit.

Chapter 134

In true form, Tehuti arrived and stood sentinel at the side of her sleeping pallet waiting for her to rise on her own accord. At first morning light, her eyes opened to greet the day. She was a light sleeper and always woke at the first ray of dawn.

She laughed as she saw the form of Tehuti waiting playfully by her side for her to wake. "Have you been up long brother?"

"Yes, though I waited for you, who are so very eager to play the role of my assistant." His smile reached from ear to ear at the game and that he had decided to accept her challenge. She knew that she would truly be in for it for he would make sure that she would regret that she even requested this.

Up with the rays of light was she as she ran over to where her linen shift lay on the trunk at the foot of her bed. It was pressed for the day. She saw the look of her brother as he smiled and turned for her privacy to dress in haste. She knew that he was purposefully setting a fast pace. She was determined to keep up with it and not to let him have the victory in this challenge.

She did not have time to put on her slippers, she ran barefooted to catch up with the brisk walk of her younger brother who seemed set in some duty of which she was about to find out.

She woke abruptly with each step on the dawn soaked grass of the riverbank and followed him to his cabin. There he sat upon a stool, while she stood sentinel behind him. She stood silently as a palace servant and in loving mockery of what she had observed of Tehuti in the many years by her side.

Au-Set watched as he spoke aloud of all that he was planning to do that day and truly marveled at his list. She knew that this was a typical day for him that she was allowed to witness. She ran to retrieve his every wish from his morning beer and onion to his noontime fig pie and flat bread. She tried desperately not to crack a smile and loved to be here for Tehuti for once. She knew that she would earn an even deeper respect than she had ever had for him in the past and in her whole life.

She knew that he was basking in this change of events in his life and exaggerated each routine for her to suffer in with the full joviality of being a sibling. They laughed at this together and she knew that it was all in fun.

Nevertheless, as the day wore on she had gotten used to his feverish pace. She followed him around and sometimes knew that he forgot that she was silently behind him, so deep into his obsession with the papyrus that he became a slave to it. She knew that when in this mode he was lost to the world around him. There could be an incredible earthquake or torrential rainstorm and he would not even budge from the purpose that he set for the day, so unwavering in his devotion was he. She basked in the wake of his pure genius and sometimes even forgot herself as she stood behind him engrossed in his fervor and devotion for his magical writing that he called the met-necher or the words of the Gods. He would paint the final scenes and words after scribes had drawn on the walls the rough forms.

She saw the school that he created for the scribes and painters of the words of the Gods and basked in the love that each student, no matter how young, had for her brother.

However, as the day progressed and the sun was long gone from the sky to sleep for the night, she noticed that he seemed "off" somehow.

As the days wore on she grew accustomed to his pace and was able to truly observe the concern on the faces of those that were in his secret world who lived in this city that he had created from a simple hill in the middle of the desert. The city had water piped in from the Great River in pipes made of clay to nourish the people who lived in this fertile oasis on the side of the delta.

She knew that each person that resided here on a normal basis loved him deeply and considered him a magician with his weird habits and the few hours that he required of sleep each day. Au-Set observed that he required only four hours and was fine. She knew that she needed at least seven hours for her to function as had most people.

Tehuti treated this all as a game, flourished attention on her and exaggerated his need of her assistance. She knew that he had servants for most of the tasks that he had her do. Tehuti knew Au-Set and was humored that she would be insistent in bugging him until he relented in the granting of her ridiculous request of being his assistant.

"You dear sister are the queen of persistence. For I know of no one who can be even half as ceaseless in your demands as you are. When you have something set in your mind the world will stop until your request is granted!" He stated this with his deep laughter and posed it as a joke, though they both knew that it was close to the truth of her personality. Perhaps that is the reason why she made a good leader. She had the power of persistence in getting things done. Thankfully, she used this talent for the good of her people and Kemet flourished as a result.

Chapter 135

In the moments each day, that he set aside especially for his consort Au-Set was granted the freedom to walk around. On the third day, she had really noticed the change in her brother and noticed that others had observed this as well. She silently went over to the side of that same bold woman that she had met on the very first day and inquired on the behavior of her brother.

"Yes my lady, even though he creates this game for you to ease your worry and to assuage your guilt, it is as you saw but a camouflage of the truth. He hopes that in distracting you and in creating your silly days together you will not observe the reality that he has been hiding from even himself. I had only noticed this in the past four months. He has been slowing and his mind is not as clear as it has always been. It is almost erratic at times and is something that never would have been allowed in his form ever in his normal demeanor." She breathed deeply almost afraid to continue.

Au-Set noticed the wrinkles of worry on this woman's wide brow and knew that Tehuti was deeply loved. "Please, feel freely to speak of him as if I were your sister and hold nothing back."

The woman then continued her voice becoming almost frantic in the desperation of her words finally being allowed to solidify in words that someone other than her own mind could ponder. She also blanched at how real the words made her concerns to both of them.

"I had wondered initially if he were actually ill or over-tired and needed a rest. Nehmetaway had observed his strange behavior as well and gently urged him to rest. Well, you and I both know how his personality reacted to that. It seemed as if he was trying to hide his weakness from everyone, even himself. He tried harder to keep a pace that never bothered him before. I know that his body not only grows old but also is struggling with something deep inside that is fighting to take control. He has lost weight and seems a shade lighter than his normal or former self seems. He uses makeup to hide the true color of his bland pallor from all of us and especially you. He would kill me if he knew that I caused you to worry even one thought over him. Please, I beg of you lady- never reveal to him what I have told you; use your best judgment to work with him yourself. For no one else would be allowed to breach his world, but you. He would let himself die before ever causing you to worry over him, so deeply does he take his service to you and your siblings."

At this, they both sat back to back almost afraid to look the other in the eyes. Maybe that would make their fears real, if the words were not allowed to fade and to be forgotten in the wind that had suddenly appeared out of nowhere to blow the petals off the jasmine bush behind them. The fragrance greeted their senses and warmed them both to happier times and they both sat in the silence of the comfort of the other's concern.

The days wore on and they both continued their game. She even felt that he was improving from whatever she and the others thought was plaguing him. Perhaps he was on his way to recovery. All around them seemed to let up a bit on their concerned vigil of him and went to bed the fifth evening to the sounds of his deep snoring as heard through the small cottages in his small village.

Au-Set smiled and fell into her own deep sleep.

Chapter 136

Au-Set awoke to the sound of a scream and of hurried footsteps in the direction of Tehuti's room. She gathered her sleeping gown and ran over to the direction that she found others in which led to the sleeping chamber of her younger brother.

She arrived and entered the doorway to find his form lying on the floor covered in blood. His consort was in obvious deep distress at his death and sobbing in an uncontrollable grief. Au-Set ran over to Nehmetaway to comfort her and looked around the room. A woman entered the room and relieved Au-Set of her comfort. Au-Set sat up and with the clearest of mind completely detached from the grief; she went right to the business of finding out why her brother was murdered in cold blood.

She would not let the reality of the event sink in to distract her from finding justice. Tehuti was cut down in the prime of his life. Au-Set felt deep sadness of a world that would never know the rest of the inventions in his mind, as they should have. She felt that he had many more in his mind waiting to come out besides his most famous of the legendary papyrus and his beautiful writing that was now being painted on all of the sacred temple walls of Kemet as well as in every day homes as was his most recent wish.

Au-Set gathered each person and took him or her each separately into the room to question them on everything they knew. Did he have any enemies or any one jealous enough to commit this vile deed? She questioned them long into the evening hours and into the next day until Neb-Het had arrived to find her sister in this state of disarray and erratic behavior. Neb-Het saw the obsession in the eyes of her twin sister and the guilt at not being able to protect him as he did them all.

Chapter 137

Neb-Het went over to her sister and gave her a juice made from peaches that had a small dose of belladonna to send her sister to sleep so that she would not fall apart out of sheer exhaustion.

Neb-Het took over where her sister left off in the investigation, while she slept. Neb-Het did not waver and reviewed each note taken by her sister and the many questions written down.

She spoke with the physician who had examined Tehuti and it was mentioned that the cause of his death was strangulation. It was discovered that he was stabbed in anger after he was dead as if to make sure that the deed was done. It seemed precise and methodic. It had to have been done by someone who watched him carefully to learn of his habits. For the only time that he would have truly been alone was when his consort went out in the evening to take care of her bodily functions in the latrines.

She had learned that Nehmetaway went to the wash closet at the same time each evening predictably like clockwork. Someone had to be close to know this habit and of the only time when he was vulnerable to assault.

Neb-Het also learned that it was also the time that the guard had changed to relieve the others. They had changed in ten-hour shifts.

After a whole day of needed sleep, Au-Set joined her sister and questioned her on the investigations that she knew were continued while she slept. Au-Set knew too much the heart of her sister and of her thought process.

"Well Setti, I have arrived at two possible conclusions; one that it could have been the work of our brother Suti." She saw the look of question on her sister's face and continued, "However, both you and I know that it is highly unlikely. He is not anywhere near and it would certainly have been reported to one of us, as he has many enemies. Besides, Suti is not the kind of person who would commit murder with his own hands.

He would have been more likely to hire someone for the commission of Tehuti's death." She blanched at her brother's name spoken aloud and in the same sentence of his mentioned death.

"As much as we know the horror of Suti's mind I do not feel in my soul that he would actually commit or even commission the murder of Tehuti. Out of all of us, even Heru... Tehuti was the one who acted as a father to us all as he was the glue and as Heru once was to keep us all together. However, Tehuti held Suti in his power for we know that Suti loved Tehuti like the father he never knew even though he hid it from even himself with his words towards us all.

"No, I do not believe that Suti would be a part to such a thing. However, in my investigation into this matter I have come across some startling information. You need to sit down for this Au-Set." In the formal tone of her name, Au-Set complied.

"After questioning each member of our family and those who knew Tehuti, I was brought back to an event that occurred many years ago. Do you remember when Tehuti, Au-Sar, and Heru went back to Eshnunna to find out the truth of what happened to our mother? Well, when the boys were in the temple, Suti was separated from them. Au-Sar had always wondered what happened to Suti for when they were reunited Suti had no more the face of a boy but the beginnings of a man with a purpose. Heru wrote of this in his memoirs that I have found in the archives of Per-Uto. Aunt Ua-Zit had retrieved this after his death to be kept safe. She had even feared something from Suti that she could not grasp.

"Well, even Qui and Kekes had noticed something about Suti when they were sent over years ago to investigate the death of Heru, which was never solved. We all suspected Suti of that and I still do, though there was never any proof. However, this is different. We had ransacked his abandoned chambers in his city deep in the Deshret and found a secret passageway that led to where he possibly escaped. On the floor was found a parchment that seemed to have the cuneiform official seal of Enlil." Au-Set inhaled deeply at this information and seemed almost to stop her breathing. She was proud of how hard her sister worked while she healed in sleep. She knew that Neb-Het possessed her mind only in a softer more reasonable degree. She was never being led into erratic behavior, as she was prone to do in her passions.

Neb-Het on the other hand was sure and steady in her mind and ideas. Issues in her mind worked themselves out to her in a methodic way not from inspiration, as she was prone to have in moments of restless sleep dwelling on matters.

"The other scenario that I see is that Tehuti was killed by someone from the guard of Enlil to bring our attention to them. Underneath the form of Tehuti was found a dagger that was last seen years ago in the armory room of our mother's in the temple confines.

"We all felt that it was too obvious and blocked it from our minds and replaced it with a more acceptable solution. We put it in our minds that it was brought over with us in the beginning and perhaps misplaced in the armory in Nekhen. This you and I both know realistically to not be the case. You know where you last saw this. How obvious can a clue be? It was almost as if the killer wrote it in the blood spilled by our brother. They want us to know that they are watching us and that our time in rule will end. This Enlil calls himself a God the '*Great Marduk*'. He must be brought down from his ego trip and placed on the earth. He thinks that we will tremble in fear of him."

"No Neb-Het we will not. We will strike in a way that he would not expect for I agree with you on your deductions and the conclusions reached in this investigation. Now may we bury our brother in the tomb that he carved in his favorite spot that he considered the most peaceful in all of Kemet near the other tombs in Abdjw?"

"We must not forget his favorite pet baboon *Hedj-Wer*, who refuses to eat after Tehuti's death. I have tried and I know that you have as well. I do not think that he will last long and will follow his master. Shall we bury him beside Tehuti if this continues?"

Au-Set only nodded her head. She had tried as well as Neb-Het to feed the poor creature. It only wailed this eerie sound into the wee hours of the evening. It plucked at its own fur and was in obvious distress at the death of Tehuti. Hedj-Wer had probably found him first or had been nearby when the whole thing occurred and was only found a few days ago, extremely emaciated and dehydrated. It seemed not long from death himself. It was almost as if the poor creature refused to be after Tehuti had died.

Chapter 138

Au-Set recalled the day that Tehuti first brought his strange pet home with him eight years ago. She was sitting at dinner when out of nowhere this strange white baboon appeared out of nowhere and jumped on their table and started to grab some of the clay bowls and throw them into the air to hear them crash. It was horrible the screeches it let out each time one crashed. Her youngest children were present and roared with laughter at the scene. Then Tehuti entered the dining chamber as casually as if it was a normal day, however he could not hide the large grin on his face.

He sat down on the large pillows that surrounded the table and leaned over dramatically to explain the presence of this strange baboon that had so radically entered their lives. Bast and Merul fought for a close seat next to their uncle and Tehuti reached out his arms to take the twins Serqet and Maat on his lap. They squealed in anticipation

"Well, you see, I was on a journey up to the darkest and most sacred regions of this Great River to the lands that no one had been to before. The farthest away from Eshnunna ever believed possible had I travelled. It was obvious that this part of our world had never seen a human before for the strange creatures seemed docile in a way as if they had nothing to fear. The land way up there was filled with the deepest of jungles and the river was hungry and roared with life. Rain came not only from the sky but seeped from the plants as well. There was so much moisture that it was everywhere.

"I had with me the bravest of the royal guard for a journey of this magnitude that was to this land of the unknown. My small flock of ibis, as you know did not want me to part with them, they never have. Therefore, I made special cages for them and brought them with me. Just as well, since their diet was very peculiar and I did not trust any servants with their care.

"Our small entourage had traveled in the unknown world for two weeks seeing wonders such as you could not possibly believe. The species of papyrus were numerous, however, none that I could utilize. None that surpassed what grows on the banks of our own Great River of this land.

"While I was there, as you know, I kept a careful log of the new animal species. One new animal had always been on the side of each place that we camped. They were a small group and very human-like in most ways. They communicated and reacted. They seemed hesitant, yet as curious of us as we were of them. They were of medium height and covered with hair with their eyes full of emotion. They were dark and blended in perfectly with the dense foliage. From tree to tree, they jumped as if one large game. It seemed as if they wanted to play with us. We started to leave out food for them and gradually they came closer. I even touched a few of them and they touched me with hands that looked so much like ours. Their feet had the power of their hands and could grasp things almost as well as their hands.

"However, beautiful they were there was one more that always hid from us that I needed to see. It was an albino of that odd species as is so rare in any species. Its eyes were red and the fur and skin was white. It was amazing how it survived there. It seemed to linger especially around the cages of the ibis.

"At first I thought it only wanted to eat them but as I studied this rare creature even more it seemed to compare the whiteness of his own fur to the white feathers of my ibis. It reached out to them and left food. Perhaps he felt a kin to those birds being of the same color."

Tehuti's eyes looked off as if to journey back to that time so etched on his mind was the event.

"Nevertheless, we packed up to leave the next day, since I realized that there was no better papyrus for my creation better than what we had already in numerous supply. We left with sad regret at having found a place in our hearts for those wondrous creatures, yet we needed to return home before the river went into inundation and made travel for us impassable.

"As we were well underway on our reed boats I was resting and watching the jungle thin out as we approached our homeland when I heard a rustle in my personal supplies. I checked the cage of my ibis and nothing was amiss each one of them was there. However, with them was a fresh handful of grass. This was perplexing, since I was the only one around to have fed them and was about to had I not noticed the strange noise.

"However, I was exhausted and preoccupied with getting my notes of observations organized when all of a sudden two hands appeared on my face and blocked my eyes as a child would. Startled I jumped up in the boat with such force that I almost capsized it. There was a loud screech in response and I looked behind me and found that the beautiful white baboon had bravely followed. Apparently, it wanted to be with the ibis and us. The look in his eyes was so endearing that I could not resist. I reached out my arms and he crawled right into them and fell asleep! That was how my Hedj-Wer came into my life. I found out that it was the name of a local God there called the *"Great White One"* which comes in the form of a white baboon. How appropriate for could not this little one here be also their God?"

The children roared with laughter at that one and Hedj-Wer joined in with his usual screech. Even Au-Set had seen the compassion in this strange animal's eyes and could not help but grow attached.

From that day on Tehuti was always with his pet baboon, which was never far behind, and sometimes in the arms of Hedj-Wer were the ibis that he had grown so attached to lay sleeping. Tehuti would joke that Hedj-Wer felt that the ibis were his babies due to their coloring.

Chapter 139

The funeral preparations and burial went on without incident as the new traditions were established. Tehuti went on to begin his journey to become one with the Gods. Au-Set knew that he would be the most likely that she knew to find the path to join all of his nine selves once more. She felt that though he was born after her that he was an old soul. She would miss his guidance and sound wisdom.

The days went on and Au-Set felt like her soul was going through a change with all of the different emotions she experienced due to the loss of Tehuti. At first, she was numb and could not accept the reality for she fought the truth of a life without Tehuti with every breath that she had. She ran from everything that reminded her of his absence. This did not work because as the days marched on to become weeks and then months and it was harder to keep those things away from her.

One day she woke up and she was filled with an overwhelming sense of anger. Everything that she had felt with the numbness became obsolete and meaningless for the anger consumed her. Au-Set snapped at everyone that she met in her daily duties because they were not her brother and advisor. She was angry with Tehuti for leaving her with everything to deal with alone. She loved Au-Sar and the rest of the family but none of them had the stability and soundness of looking at life and decisions that faced them as did Tehuti. He showed the most natural way of looking at all issues and how to find the most logical solution.

She did not realize that her family and those that cared for her began to give her a little space. They became cautious around her and let her have the time that she needed to heal.

One day the rage became so powerful that she jumped into her reed boat without telling anyone and sailed with the current to Abdjw to the tomb of Tehuti. She lost count of the days that it took her to reach her destination to the northern most reaches of their land

and Upper Kemet. She did not tell anyone and she could not even tell herself. She just sailed onward stopping only to eat food that she found on the banks of the river and in tying the reed boat along the shore to sleep. She sailed on in a fog of anger that propelled her onward.

Upon her arrival, all days leaked into one and she lost all concept of time. How could the days keep going with so many important people lost to her? Au-Set never knew her father though had heard a lot of him from her mother for he was her mother's favorite consort.

Her mother was the most difficult for with the loss of her all of the security and safety of the world that she was born into was lost. Her happiness seemed left behind with her mother and all of her cherished memories. She was afraid to experience anger at the loss of her innocence and happiness. Au-Set felt that any anger experienced on behalf of her mother and the loss of her birth land would be a betrayal to her. Therefore, life went on and they grew up. She and Tehuti held their family together with the help of their aunt Ua-Zit. She kept contact with Heru and with him kept the family together to the best of her ability so far away.

She felt that she finally had life under control once again when the news arrived of the death of Heru. He was the glue that held the family together. He was the one whom all of the siblings loved beyond all measure. Each one of them listened to his advice even more than that of Tehuti. Everyone knew that Tehuti favored Au-Set but Heru was on all of their sides. She even suspected that Heru also kept Suti under control from all of his vices before his death. Again, with his loss the family was ripped further asunder. Au-Set as usual took on the role of their mother and tried to keep their family together with the help of Tehuti. It was difficult at first and then slowly all began to fall together once again as life had a tendency to do after conflict. Issues became old and cycles turned around to make it easier to control.

It seemed that the loss of the others that followed in succession made the thread that bound their family together weaker. First with their aunt Nekhebt, their illusions of life in Upper Kemet were shattered and the reality left in her wake was bold and finally clear for them to deal with. She, Tehuti and her other aunt Ua-Zit banded together to bring them together once again.

Her children and the next generation for the family was slowly finding their niches into the family making further strength to work with even after the loss of those so essential to them.

As Au-Set grew older and more mature, her recognition of her responsibilities in life and with the land that she ruled no longer frightened her but were accepted and welcomed as new challenges. It was difficult but she even learned how to cope with out her aunt Ua-Zit as well.

As she sailed down the river, she looked at all of her life with a new insight. She knew that it was all for a reason, no matter how many years each one of them eluded her. With each loss, she learned a new strength and became more confident with the role she was born to perform. She found it in her sister as well.

However, she had always Tehuti by her side. He was the realistic one and she had a tendency to dream and to lose herself in visions. Tehuti brought her visions down to earth and helped her to make them a reality with his logic and magical words that trailed her doings on temples throughout the land in vivid color which were now marked forever to tell their stories and deeds for generations to come.

When she arrived in Upper Kemet she walked around numb with the new all consuming anger that powered each step that she took deeper into the Deshret and the land of the dead. She walked past the walled fortifications of the living city of Abdjw and then of her sister's city of the new Nekhen. She kept her head focused with each step and no one noticed that their queen walked by. She was dressed in rags and her makeup was long gone. She felt a phantom and a shadow and followed the path that seemed to unfold before her and to lead her to Tehuti and where his body lay to face his judgment.

Up ahead in the hazy heat of the day all rays of the sun seemed to lead her to the colorless gates of the Necropolis. She found it odd how in this new land her family chose to create a separate city for the living, unlike in her land of Eshnunna where the living built their homes above their ancestors. Eventually the living needed to create new space away from the dead that would always soon overwhelm and overpopulate the living. However, the living was always close by their ancestors. When a new village was planned, the first things that were built were the vaults underground that would house the dead beneath. They felt that the dead guided their descendants when they were honored with altars and offerings.

Au-Set wanted to keep this tradition though felt that the living should be on the other side of the river and on the side of the rising sun. She wanted the dead to have their own city on the side of the river of the setting sun. To make this balance out and to make it more feasible to accept for people from their land, Tehuti came up with the idea of making a room before the tombs that was a place that the family of the deceased could gather and have meals with them and to leave their offerings and prayers. There was a room with carved windows to let in the sun and the promise to the dead that the living would honor them. Tables and seats were carved into those rooms as well for the family to visit and to leave things on a statue that represented their ancestor in life in hopes of their guidance in dreams.

Au-Set walked by the silent tombs of Heru and then of her aunt Nekhebt. She went to each of them and spent a few moments in each tomb respectively. She had brought some bread, onions, and some of Merul's latest henket. She had morsels of the food in each of their tombs in the rooms left open especially for this and left them her prayers and an amulet that she had made for them by their statues. She noticed the new rooms added to the tombs of Heru and her aunt's, as Tehuti thought of them after the tombs initial completion.

She noticed with a smile that Tehuti secretly went to each of these new rooms himself and wrote his beautiful picture writing in songs of love and admiration on the tombs of Heru Nekhebt and even that of Ua-Zit.

She thought of them in life and then walked over to the new tomb of Tehuti. It seemed to her that the paint was still wet. She placed her finger upon it and found that it was not. She loved the new material used in the paints as to make them appear so fresh months later. Her smile filled her with love for Tehuti for he would have been proud at the tomb that was made for him.

She walked into the room that was open to the sun for her and the family. She found dried flowers that crumbled when she reached over to pick them up. She noticed a small piece of papyrus on which was a note written to him by his consort. Noting the privacy of the content, she rolled it back up and placed it in a corner away from notice out of respect for their love. Au-Set smiled and tears rolled down her face. She looked all around her and stood there as blank as the desert that surrounded her. She found herself mute and as blank as the empty walls that protected this city of the dead and sheltered them from the harsh winds of the Deshret.

Her tears only seemed to fire her anger for it created a spark from somewhere deep inside of her that found that it was building with power. She looked at everything around her, the beautiful picture writing, the newly carved benches, even the pillows that she knew that Neb-Het had skillfully made for their families comfort at their visits. Their vivid, bright, and whimsical colors seemed almost to mock her and to shout at her that Tehuti was gone and now she had to face life alone. She had Neb-Het and Au-Sar and her children; but with Tehuti, her logic was lost with the sands in the Deshret that surrounded her. The colors of the pillows seemed to call out to her. She saw the bright reds and noticed that the color seemed to dominate all others. Red. Red. Stark color, color of life, color of death, color of betrayal.

Red was the color of the hair of the people that killed her mother and all that she loved. Red was the color that made her grow up fast and to take on responsibilities in a land that she was not born to rule. Red was the color of blood that always seemed so easily shed in her family, even by their own hands. Red. Red was the color of Suti's hair. Red was also the color of her first-born daughter's hair. She looked at the pillows and then at the bright room around her and wanted to block out all of the red that seemed to torment her and it slowly began to fill her with a renewed anger. She was barefoot though it did not stop her anger. She kicked and punched the freshly made tomb and wanted to blot out all of the red that seemed to surround her.

Au-Set in that moment hated the color red and wanted to destroy all of the people with red hair. She knew that in that very moment she was filled with a new purpose in her rule.

Chapter 140

What happened after that was a blur. Au-Set knew that she had somehow gotten into her reed boat and sailed to the city of Nekhen and issued the orders that reached all corners of her land. It seemed as if over-night the people were filled with her rage and willingly complied with her order to round up all of the people with red hair and to bring them to Nekhen.

These were the dark days of her life where the clouds and shadows seemed to rule her every conscious thought. No one seemed to reach her or had the power to let in any light. She refused to neither see any other way nor want to travel down any other path. Her hatred seemed to consume her and it was aimed at the new race of the northern tribes. Au-Set felt that they were out to dominate her people in Kemet as they had in Eshnunna. Her steps grew dark yet were colored the red of purpose. She knew that the blood that would come of her orders would be red as well and hoped in her anger that it would be just and vastly preventative in saving her own.

"Love, this is getting out of hand. There have been too many deaths..." Au-Sar's voice seemed to trail into the darkness that surrounded Au-Set.

"This is necessary. If mother had done this in her day, all of this would be different. Eshnunna should be thriving instead of dusty streets and torn down monuments. The Gods in place of that land mock our family and us. The tribes that have come down into that land and now into this have spoken their final words. They will not be allowed to settle here or to breed their ways into the minds of the people of this land and our family! I will not have it!"

"But sister... the children, their cries have filled my nightmares and their lives are cut short for something that they cannot control... the color of their hair!" Neb-Het was frantic and could not understand this new attitude of her sister who was once her shadow and other half. This shell of her sister was filled with such anger that seemed to cloud all those in her presence. Au-Set's aura of vengeance touched all those around her. Her voice was charismatic and maniacal but created a mass amount of hysterical followers.

Neb-Het whispered to her sister in vain though knew that it would not be heard, "We would not have created the wonders all over this land if they had not invaded our home. We would not be who we are today if it were not for our experiences and even pain sister." Au-Set had already left the room as the words of Neb-Het trailed after her. She looked over at Au-Sar as their sister left.

"What has gotten into her, where she will not listen to reason?" Au-Sar inquired.

"Tehuti was the only one able to calm her when she had passions such as this. He had a way of bringing the reality of some of her ideas to her in a way that she could understand. You and I do not."

People were showing up to Nekhen at all hours of the day and night with whole families in tow, all sporting red hair that brilliantly lit up their fate. Neb-Het had no idea how many of the people of this tribe had found their way into Kemet and she was almost frightened at first at the amounts of them. Many people were brought to this city in bondage, enough to amount to a small army.

The women and children numbered in the hundreds and the men almost doubled that number. Neb-Het knew that the women in their tribe did not fight and were bound to duties of the hearth and care of children only, but, still, she knew that any woman whose children were threatened would find it in her to fight, ruthlessly in fact.

Chapter 141

On one particular day, Au-Set stood on the platform in all of her splendor, her charisma leading all in her power and zeal over the threat to their land. She was tall and her hair shone in the sun as it fell out from her golden crown with the raised hood of the iaret in full splendor. Her robes were white and flowed in the desert breeze. In her arms, she held a long pole with sharp flint gleaming from it. The flint sparkled in the sun as it rose to meet it and then mercilessly slam down upon the tender necks of those who awaited their death. They faced death because of the color of their hair! Each morning at the break of dawn, she raised the ceremonial axe for the first of the traitors that were lined up. Men and women of her guard finished those lined up for the day. Their bodies were taken to a large pit and then burned, their ashes gathered and spread to the winds of the Deshret.

On the third day, the killings stopped for there were no more people to be found in their land with red hair except Suti and her daughter. For some reason that fact had somehow alluded Au-Set and she refused to make the connection. Suti and Set were gathered with the rest of them as they were found hiding in the Deshret.

Au-Set looked at the bodies that were thrown in the pit and then at Suti and her daughter who were tied and the last ones in line.

Suti looked up at Au-Set and spit on her. He stood to face the people and shouted, "You would kill your own brother!"

Au-Set suddenly seemed to be herself all of a sudden and her shoulders stooped as she realized the full magnitude of what she had done and what should be done. She had made a law and it must be carried out, she should have thought of the full realm of her law in that it would reach her brother and daughter born with the red hair that she had created such a frenzy of horror. "Alas, brother, I cannot and neither you my daughter!" She looked over at Set. "Why have you left your family and those who love you? Why did you throw away my love daughter?" She wanted so hard to wrap her arms around her daughter, to clean her up and to take off the ropes that bound her.

"Mother, it was you who abandoned me long ago for look at my hair. I knew how you looked at me and then at my father. I could not understand truly how deep your hatred ran until this very moment." She bent down and placed her neck in front of her mother. "Mother, I understand your duty. I know my ancestors whose same hair I inherited have destroyed a mighty empire and found their way here to Kemet. However, do not forget that I also have the blood of the Catal-Huyuk in my veins. I was confused and have found my way mother. Do your duty and take my life as you gave it to me!" Tears trailed down her cheeks and soon a great wail went up from the mothers in the crowd.

Au-Set could not though she knew that she had to. She knew in that brief moment how her mother must have felt when she had to kill her consorts in ritual, especially Geb. She also knew that if Tehuti or Heru were here they would know the most feasible way to proceed. She did not have their logic only blank faces that waited for her command. The axe in her hands suddenly seemed heavy and the day melted into great sadness. She looked at her brother and daughter and whispered, "Forgive me!" She cut the rope that bound them and set them free.

People in the crowd stood there in amazement and then the fury of it hit. Angry shouts penetrated the air at her actions. Why their own families not spared and hers were! She might be a Goddess but it did not seem right that after all of the blood that it would not reach her own daughter and brother. The law of the land told them that a mother gave life to their children and they had the power to take it away. This right was magnified in their Goddess and queen.

Neb-Het saw her sister's anguish and ran to the Scorpion Guard that surrounded her sister and begged them to protect Suti and Set and to lead them and Au-Set to safety while the crowd died down.

Chapter 142

On the outside, to all observing quietly, was only a small woman named *Meretseger*. She had been born to a small village in Upper Kemet that had no name. She was the youngest in her family of ten children. Her mother had only one consort in her being a simple bread-maker. Her mother's consort named *Timt* was cruel when her mother was not around and tried to touch her in places that she knew was reserved for her own choice only and Timt certainly was not her choice.

So, one evening when the fish were jumping on the water and her mother had run out to gather her gear in the boat, Meretseger left her home and never returned. She wandered around for months aimlessly until she reached the home of a healing woman named Neten where she trained beside a princess named Edjo who was the daughter of Mut.

Edjo was a chatterbox and her sweet words soothed her as a soft lullaby would as her mother used to sing when she was small and had no worries in the world. It seemed now that her life with her mother and latest consort was a whole other life far away. She was known for her silence and in how she would diligently wait things out and then find the proper time for everything. She was learning the art of snake charming along the side of her new friend Edjo. Both of them had developed quite the aptitude in learning the art of the Goddess in snakes.

She and Edjo were given each an infant iaret from the egg. They watched them hatch, fed each meal to them, and made their homes out of ceramic clay pipes that swirled around their beds. The cobras grew and each evening would nestle close to them in their cots. Neten taught them the arts of this ancient craft as she learned it from her mother.

Meretseger stayed there for eight years and then found that it was time for her to find her way in the world. She left with the fondest wishes of her new family. Tears streamed down her shining face of the small face of her new sister named Edjo. They vowed that someday they would find each other. Meretseger knew they would, but first she had to find out what her purpose in life was.

Again, she found herself on the paths along the side of the Great River that brought all life. Her iaret named *Shesht* kept her safe while she slept in the reeds. She knew that Shesht would warn her of any danger.

She found herself in the market streets of Nekhen as the Goddess Au-Set had given mercy to her daughter and brother born of the dreaded red hair. She wept for the poor woman and knew that there was some lesson in this though she was not sure of what at that time. She decided that this was still not, where she was meant to be in her life. Forward she walked, basking in the bright sun of each day as it rolled across the Great River of her land. She decided long ago that she would follow the current to wherever it led her.

Meretseger wandered for many months when the days blended into each other. She searched for her meaning in life in the farthest northern regions of their land of Kemet. One day she found herself in a small village named *KomOmbo*. She appealed to the leader named Sebek. She was led to his hut and inside she met the great leader of this village and beside him was a familiar face. She had not expected a familiar face...

The face of Khons was the son of Mut whom she had met years ago when he came to visit his sister Edjo. Khons was fair and beautiful, though quiet and considered odd by his family due to his extremely silent demeanor. While people could not understand the boy, she found a companion soul and both of them had made an incredible connection so many years ago. He was in her life so briefly, yet affected it so greatly that her world just about exploded upon his vision in her life once again.

Years ago, they had expected never to see each other again and parted in tears even though their meeting was so brief. Yet, here he was, looking exactly the same as he did years ago; only his face was stronger and his chin had developed a handsome cleft that only made her sink into him all the more. She felt her heart slipping her away from the reality of seeing him once again.

Sebek noticed the strange look that passed between his assistant Khons and this beautiful young woman who appeared in his village. She appeared before them in all of her splendor as one trained in the arts of the ancient iaret, her charmed snake hidden in the folds of her cloak as she stood there blocking the sunlight from the doorway. Rays of the last of the evening sun seemed to form a soft whisper of a yellow aura around her form.

Sebek looked at the glances between the two youths and decided to leave the room for words did not need to be spoken in order for the world to understand the connection between souls that had found each other once again.

Chapter 143

Meretseger and Khons spent a lot of time together learning more about the other's lives. Khons had introduced Meretseger to his fellow students *Bes* and *Neith*. Bes was a small man with dark skin who was chubby and rather disfigured; however, he was kind and had impressive skills in assisting with the childbirths of the village. Neith was tall and lithe and was almost like a whisper in personality; however, she as well was as strong a healer as her male partners, Bes and Khons.

Meretseger accompanied the three of them in various healings under the tutelage of the patient and wise Sebek. Most often, people came to the mud-walled villa of Sebek, which was isolated on a small island and only accessible by a reed boat that people would whistle for when they needed simple healing or potions.

All four of them would venture out for the more serious cases and those women in labor. Meretseger felt that the skills of these people were incredible and found that she wanted to learn it all. She would sit quietly by the side and watch them dole out medicines to people who came to the island. She helped them with the daily chores of the mismatched family and watched them always silently. She learned that each of them such as herself were lost in the world and had no family. She knew they accepted her and that they made her feel welcome. She listened to Sebek as he instructed her on the chores necessary for their survival and in tending their small garden. Other than the daily instructions and common courtesies, not much was said and Meretseger was thankful for this.

On one such day, Neith happened to notice the quiet Meretseger in the shadow of the hut. Without saying a word, Neith went over to Sebek and inquired as to when Meretseger could begin her apprenticeship in the healing arts.

Sebek nodded his head and motioned for Neith to follow him and to summon the others as well as Meretseger. In his deep penetrating voice, he spoke to all of them while looking at the silent and petit Meretseger.

"You have probably been wondering why I have said little to you my foster child..."

Meretseger looked up as if startled by her reverie, such was the dreaminess of her demeanor, "No, lord, I have not actually. I understand the quiet."

Sebek grinned and looked at the others, first Neith then the small and ugly Bes and then the handsome Khons as each looked up at him expectantly. He paused taking all of it in as if weighing the words that he would choose to use. He spoke to all of those in the room as well as to Meretseger. "Well, as you know there is always a reason. I have been watching this young new addition to our home and know that she has no other home to her. I offer you officially a place to call home under my humble roof."

The small oval face of Meretseger glowed and bowed her head in gratitude.

Sebek continued, "I feel, however that your destiny is quite different from each of us in this room. You are the child of the iaret and sacred. I have seen how you cherish the one you keep hidden in your cloak." He winked at her.

Meretseger smiled and finally felt safe enough with the acknowledgement of her pet cobra that she had nestled in the fold of her cloak. The others in the room wanted to crowd around to glimpse at such a deadly creature that she held as if a kitten. They stood rooted to the spot waiting for the command that it was safe.

Meretseger looked at them and smiled, "She is silent like me. Her name is Shesht. However, she does get a little nervous with many people. In order to see her close you have to come up separately and not all at once."

First, to arrive at her side was Khons for he knew of this art from his family and admired greatly the skills that this girl possessed. He knew that only the most sacred women to the Goddess were chosen for this as was his own sister Edjo whom he had not seen in many years. He had to hide back the threatening tears at the thoughts of his family that had sent him here for his safety so long ago. He knew they loved him and only sent him here to keep him safe from the ignorant and angry villagers. His mother always told him that he was special in that he would never be able to thrive in a world full of loud people. He needed the silence of an isolated area to thrive and thus he was sent here. His family visited them as often as they could and brought with them the comforts of his home.

Chapter 144

Sebek let each of the youngsters visit with the snake of Meretseger and waited for them to settle down before continuing. "Meretseger, daughter of the Goddess' most sacred; you need to perfect those skills and to learn to use it to save people and to protect them. I have dreamed that when you are older you will be called upon to guard over sacred places of this land due to your talent. You will have many under your guardianship that will be trained.

Do not worry, I have sent word for your studies to continue under Hapi and his partner *Tuarif*. Tuarif is very patient and looks after my infant sister Heqet. I will take you there tomorrow for Tuarif was a pupil along the side of Mut and Neten's mother in Khemmis where they learned the ancient arts of snake charming for the oldest of the Goddess cults. You will be in good hands with them and they live on the edge of the river closest to this hut where it will be easy for you to visit for your studies or to live there if you so choose child."

Meretseger smiled in deep appreciation for this wonderful man who considered her welfare for he did not have to. He could easily turn her out of his home and leave her to the mercy of nature for in reality he owed her nothing. She felt for the first time in her life wanted and appreciated and it was a good feeling.

When all was said and done on the matter of the future of Meretseger, Neith stood up in her graceful and willowy way and in a windy voice uttered, 'I beg leave to depart to tend to my bee hive family." She looked at Sebek and he smiled. It always seemed to light up the room when the large man Sebek would smile which was more often than not.

"Would the honey be ready for the beer that is brewing dear Neith?"

"Almost, for I have experimented with sending them to a field of thyme this time. I want to know how you all like it when it is done."

They all could not wait for Neith was legendary in her skills of beekeeping. She had felt that they were a part of her very self and would often be seen whispering to them. She had many hives and surrounded each one with different types of herbs, which would lend flavor to the honey produced. She knew the mood of the hive was able to retrieve honey whenever she wanted. They all could not wait to taste the latest creation of Neith's bees.

Chapter 145

When the rooster had signaled the day to begin, the occupants of the dwelling of Sebek were roused awake by the noise of the small village on the mainland. A large fuss was being made as if someone important had arrived. Then they heard the whistle for the reed boat and Sebek's partner *Opet* jumped up and placed the reed boat into the water to retrieve the person requesting their healing on the shore.

They all waited in anticipation as to who the important personage would be and what was their request. They each waited until the form of the boat came into view with Opet standing leading the boat with her large elaborately carved guiding stick; for the river was quite shallow enough for a pole to reach the bottom as guidance for the reed boats. Next to her were the sitting forms of a large man who seemed as dark as the midnight sky and contrasted with the brilliant morning colors that painted the sky in all of the glory of the Gods. Next to the large man was a smaller figure with long flowing hair. As the boat approached, the female inside appeared royal to those who saw her even at a distance. As they neared the shores of their humble dwelling they reveled in the beauty of her dress and tattoos that covered her body, which revealed her identity with the symbolism of the royal family in their closeness to the Gods.

Opet brought the reed boat in and tied it to the large flat rock used as a dock and welcomed them to the island. She noticed that all were gathered and she introduced the new visitors as the princess Serqet, daughter of the Goddess Au-Set Ua-Zit and of Re, Lord of Ineb-Hedj and her servant Qui who was a large and pendulous man with glowing teeth and a voice that was magical. Next to the princess was another princess who huddled by the side of the older girl.

Qui spoke to them and acknowledged Opet, whom he rightfully took as the master of the home. "Fair lady Opet and lord Sebek; my master the Goddess Au-Set requests that you teach her daughter Serqet in the arts of the scorpion and of healing, such are your legendary talents. Her sister, the Goddess Neb-Het Nekhebt also sends her daughter Meshkenet for your teachings as well in the arts of the scorpion. She had sent notice and received your approval on the matter. Does it still stand?"

Opet looked at the frightened girls. The older one, which was the princess Serqet, was struggling hard to appear brave and proud, as a princess should. Huddled next to her was a smaller girl who appeared even more fragile than the older princess, who was the princess Meshkenet. "Dear child, I feel that this is the first time that you have left your home?" When Serqet nodded slowly, she reached over to take Serqet into her arms. "You have a twin, do you not?"

"Aye, my lady!" She faintly smiled "Her name is Maat and I miss her as I do Mama and Papa, though I know that this is my duty and bow to your skills in the arts of the ancient Goddess for my mother tells me that you all are famous for it!"

Opet glanced over at the smaller girl and finally caught her attention, "Little one, you have nothing to fear here." Her smile was so magical that it was contagious to all who witnessed it.

"Yes girls, let me wipe your tears away and understand that I will take good care of you as I would my own children had I been blessed with one." The others had gathered around and were excited at the two new girls in their home and wondered on how the strange and pretty princesses would be able to adjust to their humble home."

Sebek looked at the frightened girls and in an attempt to lighten the mood and to relax the two new visitors; he smiled and bellowed, "Well, it looks as if we now have the makings of a school here! I hope we live up to what you have heard about us here fair princesses and know that you are welcome in this home!"

Khons spoke up at this point, "Now there are way too many girls!" They all giggled at that and the day unfolded around them in colors of gold and raw umber.

Chapter 146

Au-Set and Neb-Het watched the last of the redheaded foreigners bodies placed into the large pits dug for them in the city of *Nubt*. She chose that spot due to its location to where the executions occurred as she was in the area to check on the village, which was in charge of the gold mine that was recently found. She felt that the fierce people that seemed to live in this village would keep the souls of the people in line. The people of Nubt were known especially for their aggression and violent attitude. Visiting the village could only be done with an armed guard beside her usual Scorpion Guard.

Au-Set felt that only here would the villagers be fierce enough as to not be frightened by the threat that this new tribe could have been to Kemet. Each other town that she appealed to for them to contain the bodies of those executed refused them due to it being a possible bad omen. However, the people of Nubt had no such fears and actually assisted in the digging of the mass graves for the pottery vessels that contained the remains. After the first few hundred were burned, she had lost her anger and the people felt pity even for the remains of the enemies and worked on wrapping the bodies to be carried away from the site of the executions.

The two sisters sat side by side numb to the burial process almost looking at it as a business procedure for the people of Nubt who were very methodical and had soon worked out a system to speed up their duty.

After a while, they stopped burning the dead and wrapped them in accordance with their own traditions. The bodies were pale and stiff as some had been dead longer as their lifeless arms frozen as they silently screamed unheard pleas to the gods that were not there to save them. The red-hair in various shades of glory was dulled as if when the life was taken from them, so was the vibrancy lost from their red hair.

The body of a little boy was on the top of the pit closest to them and Neb-Het looked at Au-Set, knowing that she had noticed as well. "Why the little ones sister? Could they not have been saved and possibly raised by us?"

"I had thought of that, however, they would grow up and look into this and find great anger at the executions of their families and parents and would end up our enemies once again. Besides, it is easier to recognize them in their hair and wretched dots that cover their pale skin." The venom of the people from Au-Set was apparent and for the most part shared by Neb-Het due to the repeated nightmares of their birth land of Eshnunna.

"But Setti, the children could have grown up harmless if raised with love and nurture; I even think that they might be sometimes considered beautiful due to the oddness of their coloring. Do you not think that of your own daughter?"

"Set, is one of the most beautiful women of this land, her hair is intoxicating, but I never considered her to be of the same kind as they who have only sought to destroy us. I would pray to the Goddess for her mercy in what I have done. Nevertheless, we cannot take that chance for the destruction from their kind is too well known and I will make sure that it will never be forgotten!"

Au-Set looked at her sister and spoke to herself as well as to her twin, "Well," She stood up and brushed the sand from her soft dress, "Time to take back Kemet from Bast and Heru, don't you think? I trust that you and Anpu had guided them well, since I have not heard of anything amiss while we were busy with this mess. Now that it is cleaned up we can return to our rule."

Neb-Het stood up as well and in a mirror-like motion that went unnoticed by her sister, did the same, and joined Au-Set. They turned from the pits of the dead people who were no longer a threat to the sun beginning to set in the deepest Deshret that surrounded them.

Chapter 147

Au-Set and Neb-Het wanted to put their latest threat behind them now that it was all suppressed and quiet. No more was heard of the strangers that had tried to take over Kemet as they had Eshnunna. They were finally able to relax a bit.

Au-Sar and Au-Set were sitting on the roof of their palace in Nekhen and catching the warm breeze in their hair that hung free. Au-Sar's beard had grown worn in the latest style that he started. His beard was cut round and hung straight down from his chin. Small braids were intertwined around it to make it appear solid and fierce. His hair was long and curly and hung down past his shoulders. His tattoos appeared to Au-Set almost as if they were fading. This evening they sat in very casual dress and not in the garish costumes that the people normally observed lately.

They looked at the peaceful rooftops of the city that was growing around them. It seemed almost as if it appeared larger with each day. They were both proud of all they had done and were now sitting peacefully waiting for the appearance of the famous Dog Star that signaled the beginning of the inundation that was the life of their land.

This star was officially recognized and noted by the Nugig named *Sopdet* who was the official palace astronomer. Sopdet had a deep knowledge of the heavens of Eshnunna and was now in the process of recording the skies and their progress in the land of Kemet. She had heard from the people of this famous star, verified it for the royal family, and had even started a celebration around this star. As soon as it was noted, bonfires in all of the temples in the area were lit one by one and eventually all would be lit in unison in recognition of the life force of the star and the significance of its appearance. The light from the numerous temple and village fires lit the night sky a deep crimson shade almost appearing as the life force of the sacred womb blood as shed at the beginning of life. This only added to the sacredness of this newly found tradition. The symbolic fires that were lit all across the land for this event would signify the beginning of the inundation that would bring new life and food for the people of Kemet. As soon as this star appeared, it would signify the beginning of the black soil that was fertile and ripe that would come with the flooding of the river. This was the life force of the people of this land.

Au-Set and Au-Sar sat there peacefully contemplating all that had passed in their lives. "What would momma think if she saw all that we have done in her name? Would she be proud or angry at us?"

"Setti, I think she would certainly be proud for you have stopped the threat of those people from taking over this land as well. I know how this has torn you apart. Mother would have continued the executions to all of the surrounding lands. You know that they will come back..."

"Yes, I know. Look, there is the first bonfire at the temple that Sopdet is in!" They watched it sparkle and then it was followed by others that seemed to glow like stars in the halls of the Gods above them. "It is glorious, to see so much peace in this land for once."

"You know it will not last almost like the calm before the storm. I feel that it will be a long time before you see such peace again my sister."

"Did you have one of your dreams my brother?" She knew that he often dreamed of his worst fears and felt pain for his emotions that he tried hard to conceal.

"No, it was Merul who told me." His eyes seemed to lose focus.

Au-Set thought this strange in that Au-Sar was not close to his youngest son Merul and she noticed that her brother would avoid the son of his. The only time that Au-Sar spent with the boy was when they made the legendary Henket that was becoming a favorite of the people. Au-Sar felt that it was somehow the fault of Au-Set that Merul was born deformed. His head was large in comparison to his thick small neck, short trunk, and chubby stump-like legs. His arms appeared too small for his odd frame and hung to his sides.

However, Merul was the most valued of any of the children of Au-Set in that he had the gift of prophesy. His dreams were fast becoming legend. For the boy to have sought out and spoken to his father was out of his rather meek character. Merul seemed to grow even shorter in the presence of his powerful father.

Au-Set shivered at the ominous omen brought to her on this quiet evening that signified life for their land. Yet the words seemed to rip at her and leave their mark for her not to forget no matter how peaceful it seemed to be.

She looked dreamily and spoke almost to the air, "I thought when we were children all was wonderful with the world. Remember? Our mother and the palace were all that we knew. We thought the world ended and began on the steps of the temple. We thought the whole world was our view from her sleeping chamber at the very top." Her eyes shaded over when the memory of hearing that it was in that very room that their mother was killed along with the Goddess Innana. The women of the Goddess who were left behind and suppressed under the new rule told their stories that were reaching people in Kemet of that event and were swiftly becoming a legend.

She had heard the story told as how the powerful God Marduk swept over the weak and timid Goddess Innana and killed first her lover Dimuzi in her arms and then chopped off her head and fed it to the stars.

Au-Sar knew his sister consort so well that he could tell what she was thinking and recalled the legend himself, which always made him grimace with pain. He had always remembered his mother as powerful and strong and knew that she was a skilled warrior as well. He looked at his sister's Scorpion Guard with pride in that they were trained in the warrior arts that his mother had taught them that was from the ancient lands of the Catal-Huyuk and then to Eshnunna and now in Kemet.

It was in that secluded moment that Au-Set first heard the crunch of stone as belonging to a silent footstep on the roof. She thought that they were alone.

At first, she thought that it was one of her children for only they could breach her guard that always protected her even in sleep. They were in the room below them and guarded the only access which was a wooden ladder fastened with ropes in the old way.

Their backs were facing the opening when she slowly turned in time to see the face of her brother Suti as he smiled and then all went black. This was the dream of Merul that Au-Sar had relayed to her on the roof that very evening. It seemed to her frightening and surreal, yet not a reality when her brother initially told it to her. However, she knew that source was to be valued and it was.

Chapter 148

Au-Set awoke in a dark pit that seemed damp and murky with a wretched smell that reminded her of death. She could not see anything though knew that the room she was in was small by the shallowness of her breath.

She had never felt so alone nor angry in her life. She called out, "Brother! What is the meaning of this?"

She heard laughing that seemed far above her and knew that it could only belong to Suti. She was tired and sore from being carried in haste to this spot. Her head swam with pain and many questions.

"Oh, great Queen!" He mocked her. "How nice to see you in a place that suits you rather well!"

"That is not funny Suti. All right, you win. What lands do you want?" She knew that she would probably have to buy her way out of here and wondered where the rest of her family was. She longed for the daughter that he stole, Set and then realized that she was silent by her father. Au-Set felt the presence of her daughter and knew her scent of preference, the small lilies of the river.

"Set."

She heard nothing in response though she knew that her daughter was there, as only a mother would know. "Please daughter, let me know what Suti wants. Surely he must have told you?"

"You mean my father?"

"Certainly Set. Your father... tell me what he wants." Her face shrugged at the reality of her first born-daughter's paternity.

"You know what I want sister." The notorious deep voice of her brother maniacally cackled.

"I thought you both were far from here, where were you?"

"I know that you are trying to change the subject but I will bite on that. I went to Sumer to speak with my father Enlil."

"You know that he is not the real Enlil but a man in his pla...."

"Enough, sister I am not daft. However, this man has no heirs and he has offered me rule in his kingdom if I were to hand over Kemet to him."

Au-Set gasped at this silently though had training in hiding her emotions as the ruler of Kemet. She struggled though the chamber was dark and fought to quell her emotions at hearing this.

"I plan, dear sister to tell him that he can have Kemet but naturally not really hand it over to him. I would like you as my main wife and for us to have sole rule over all of Kemet along with Set and she will be our heir."

"She is already my heir being my first born daughter."

"I realize that but I also want you to bear me a son."

"Papa!"

Au-Set felt Suti losing hold of his daughter over that and could almost see the reaction on his daughter's face. She sensed this through the pitch-black chamber where she lay in pain from her bruises. Bruises well earned as she moved around trying to learn the dimensions of the chamber and the height without arousing the suspicions of Suti. This was all done while talking with him.

"Think it over sister, for I have Au-Sar and your children in another pit. Do not bother yelling for they cannot hear you. They all know that their life rests in your hands."

She heard above her his footsteps leaving the room that he called down to her from and a door slamming behind him as it was locked secure.

She gradually got used to the darkness of the room in what seemed like an eternity though knew it was perhaps only minutes, dreadfully long ones at that! Au-Set could see faint shapes and the outline of the pit's opening above her. There must be a small window in that chamber and it must be night due to the grayish glow that emanated above the pit. She reached around and found that the dimensions were not that wide; she could barely stretch out her legs and could only unbend them when she stood up. She knew that she was also quite far down and it would be impossible to jump up. She felt the sides of the pit and found that it was of a chalky substance and that gratefully, she could possibly carve some steps with her nails. Her clothes were in rags that felt damp around her form and she heard the squeaking of small rodents in the chamber above as she fervently prayed that they would not fall into her pit. She assumed that this might have been used for storage of food or amphorae prior to it being used for a prison for her.

Slowly, she began to carve into the wall with her fingernails. She carved a deep enough indent to fit in her toes and wondered how many of them it would take to reach the top and if she would be granted enough time before, it was discovered.

Surely, they knew of this and there might be something above her to thwart her progress to safety. However, she blocked that from her mind and knew that she would deal with that when and if the time arrived.

Au-Set also knew that Suti would not put anything deadly up there because he wanted to have more children with her and valued her as a breeder. The thought of that left a bitter and contemptuous taste in her mouth, almost as sour as the dust that came from her gentle carving in the sides of her prison pit.

It seemed as if many hours had slowly passed as she was clawing her way to freedom. She felt her stomach tying in knots as the hunger tore at her insides screaming for nourishment. The thirst was even more dreadful and thus she felt her tongue sticking to the roof of her mouth in protest. Nevertheless, she knew that she had to persist in this without taking a break for it meant her life and that of the others whom depended on her. She had carved seventy-eight toeholds with herself lifted with each precarious step upwards until she finally felt the top.

The thirst was powering her onwards and she thought only of her children and her beloved Au-Sar and sister, Neb-Het. First one hand and then the other and then with much effort that she did not think that she had left, she hauled herself over the edge into the chamber above her from which she heard the voices earlier of her daughter and Suti. The air was different and felt almost "wider" if that could be possible.

She was completely on the side of the pit, slumped down in a heap in exasperated relief and sheer exhaustion, and waited until her eyes adjusted to the early morning light that was streaming into the chamber in which she now lay.

"I was waiting for you mother." It was Set. "I had almost gone down there to get you myself but when I heard what you were doing I decided that it would give me time to think. I am sorry."

Au-Set looked around, suspecting a trick and looked at her daughter with a burst of love and emotion.

The red hair of Set glared out at her like an angry scream of how her daughter and brother were left alive and had she done her total duty, they would be dead as well as the other foreigners of the tribe with red hair. She would not be in this position looking at her daughter's eyes in astonishment. Au-Set had noticed that her daughter had turned into a woman and had filled out gracefully and had become quite beautiful indeed, almost a rival to her own mother's legendary beauty that was still sung about in the new land called Sumer.

"Mother, I thought a lot about both you and father and have come to beg your forgiveness. I know that you should have had us killed and it would have been just." Au-Set started to speak.

"No, mother, let me finish. After being with the both of you long enough to get to know how you both work, I have decided that you are the one who truly loves me most."

"Daughter, it does not matter who loves you most. I love you more than life and my heart has been empty with pain at your long absence."

"Could you ever forgive all that I have done mother? I have caused you much grief with my stupid actions and do not know where to begin in trying to have you love me again. You should have killed me that day Momma!"

Au-Set ran over to her daughter with a renewed vigor and strength that only a mother would have for a child in need and took Set into her arms as if she were an infant. She twirled her long red tresses in her fingers as she had when Set was only an infant with a head full of ringlets. Only now, the hair was long, thick and curly, spiraling around them and mixing with her ebony hair.

"Never daughter! You are my life and only a small part of you is descended from the tribes. Your father has not always been thus. He once was a little boy who was afraid, missed his mother, and hated to be separated from any of us. Do you know that he once worshipped your uncle Au-Sar?"

"But, Father hates him! He is always planning to take everything away from Uncle! It scared me when he spoke of it and I tried to hide my feelings from him. For uncle Au-Sar has always been good and just to me and silly too!" Her eyes filled with emotion in the dark room though felt by both of them in their equal sadness.

"Well, once Suti was always in the care of Au-Sar and I believe it all started when we were separated. Suti was very young and was barely walking when this all happened. He clung to the legs of my aunt Ua-Zit and begged to stay with Au-Sar. However, the aunts made a promise to my mother and she divided us. Suti was to go with Neb-Het and Heru to Upper Kemet in Nekhen with our aunt Nekhebt. Au-Sar, your uncle Tehuti and I, were sent to Lower Kemet and our aunt Ua-Zit. I always felt that it was my fault; I should have checked on them down in Nekhen, I should have begged Aunt Ua-Zit to visit more often.

"For when we finally did see them for the first time since the separation they had changed though it was not quite noticeable then to us, for they had become great actors in hiding the neglect that they lived with. Aunt Nekhebt ignored them and they knew no love from her, so deep was the pain at losing her own children that she could not care for her sister's three children that were thrown into her control. She simply ignored them and the others hid it from us and pretended that everything was all right. I know that Suti blames Au-Sar for not having known this. I do not know why but he blames Au-Sar for all of this. He also hates that the inheritance of our family is passed down to the women and that is why he hates me. He hates Neb-Het because she could not bear him children, though bore Au-Sar her son Anpu and through her consort Hetep, she bore Meshkenet. He has so much hate. I wish I could take him into my arms and make everything better for him."

"He will not let anyone near him, not even the ugly Puanit! He pretends to love me. However, I have felt that I am more of a pawn to lure you and Au-Sar over to where he can control you both. I was never sure of that fact that he only wanted a son until he spoke to you last night."

"Where are the others?"

"Au-Sar escaped and ran into the night as a distraction and to send out for reinforcements to get the rest of you and father left me here to guard over you while he searched for Au-Sar. Mother, I think that this time he plans to kill him!"

"Then we cannot waste time! Let us get the others and find some boats. He is probably going to Abdjw?" Set nodded.

Chapter 149

They ran through the musty corridors while Set told her that they were deep in the desert and that they would have to walk well into the day to reach the banks of the great river. They both shivered in dismay despite the torrid heat that was already starting to attack their bodies despite their being deep underground.

Set first ran into the stock room and grabbed water pouches and copper axes and spears tipped with flint. She also grabbed some bread loaves and a sack of onions. "Follow me"

She ran down the dark halls only lit by torches along the way. She felt that it was probably underground to keep them from the heat of the Deshret and they were near a water source used to maintain the fort.

It was then that she heard it. A trickle could only mean a running source of water. Set noticed that her mother had brought attention to this.

"I had almost forgotten that it is the well and there is a secret underground river that it is connected to."

"That will be our escape!" They finally reached the locked chamber where the guards were. Au-Set was an expert at sneaking up in quiet stealth; she brutally brought down her mighty copper axe with force and cleaved a neat gash into the guards face. When he slumped, the joined in swift succession and covered the body of his fallen friend, now collaborates in death.

Set opened the chamber and found Bast, Merul, Heru, Weret-Heka, and Maat inside all huddled together for security. The room was also dark and she woke them, "Quick, we must hurry! They will notice our absence very soon."

"Yes, hurry!"

Weret-Heka let out a gasp at the recognition of Set's voice.

"Yes, children, it is Set and she has come to help you. I do not want to hear another word unless it is in kindness to her! She missed you and admitted her wrong judgment! We must forgive her for she is your sister! It is important that our family stick together!"

They had no time to argue the matter and swiftly followed their older sister Set whom they had not seen in quite a few years as their family's adversary. In their youth, the past was easily forgotten. Their legs were sleep weary but adjusted fast in the fear for their very lives.

"I will take us where you suggested mother. This is the route that only the slaves use and due to that it is virtually untraveled at this time of day."

Set led them to a narrow passageway that seemed to lead them deeper into the ground than thought possible. Au-Set felt as if she were walking into the very tombs of the Gods themselves and shuddered at the thought of what could possibly lurk this far below ground.

The walls were soon slick with moisture and seemed almost lit up with large deposits of quartz that caught the light from the torches that many of them carried. It was eerie and seemed a suitable place for the dead to walk.

They arrived in a huge cave through which flowed a large subterranean waterfall and a huge lake. Au-Set could not even see the shores on the other side.

"How are we ever going to cross this? I see no boats!"

"We swim!"

Au-Set tried to keep them calm and add humor and lightly mimicked her daughter, "We swim, she says! Well, we do not have time to dawdle, just lead the way out of here my beloved daughter!" They all could feel the proud mother's smile.

Set looked at her siblings with trepidation and knew that the only way she could ever gain their trust was to lead them to safety, which she desperately wanted to do. She decided to take them to a place of which she had known of for a while. Set had discovered it by accident while she was bored and followed the slaves. She wanted to know where they were getting the water from since they were so far from any sign of water and many days from the Great River that she was amazed. She knew they were deep in the Deshret and thus had no idea about water source where they all were at present. She felt the value of this in her soul and could not wait to gain it for their family once again.

Set found this place and did not want anyone to know of it since it bore witness to her solitude. It was in this place where she decided to go to her mother to save them. She told Au-Sar of this she thought of him as her real father, as it was he who raised her. She cried as she told him of this and he knew her well enough to believe her despite all that she had done in the recent years.

Set knew there was a cave underneath the waterfall that would lead out of here in an underground river deep under the Deshret. She knew that it was many cubits below ground level, as no one knew of this except the slaves of the fort who brought water to her. This spot was chosen specifically for its location in being near the underground river.

However, in fear she had never followed the underground river behind the waterfall; she only went a short way but saw that it stretched on forever. She prayed to the Goddess that it would eventually lead them to the Great River and to safety. She did not let them know this. Then she noticed a sign that her father Au-Sar had left her. Carved on the rock by their feet was a hawk symbol. She pointed this out to the others who smiled which affirmed her lead.

She looked briefly at the indentation in the sand where she had sat up all night and dove into the grand lake. She waved at them to follow her. Each of them followed Set to the spot behind the waterfall.

"How incredible! And cold!" Bast gasped in between strokes in the dank colorless water. She referred to the waterfall of course. It sounded as if it reached high above them from the sheer power of the sound. When they jumped in they had to raise their torches and knew that they were about to lose them when they reached the waterfall. The mist blocked out sound as well. It was quite eerie and seemed to envelop them into an underworld quite literally.

"However, did you know about this sister?" Spoke the tireless Heru who was fast gaining the lead behind Set.

"I needed a place where I could think about everything. That is why I am here! We must hurry because my father Suti is searching for our father Au-Sar and I fear for him when he is found! In addition, I know that the guards are probably searching the fort for you all by now!

"Now grab onto the person in front of you as soon as you let go of the torch in this fall! It will be dark. Just float with the current!"

Her last words were lost in the roar of the fast flowing water above then from the falls. It was not heard when each torch was doused from the spray as they neared it. They put their faith in Set and felt the wet fabric of the person in front of them.

When they reached the other side of the falls, Au-Set wanted to make sure that all made it and called each of their names. Each answered to her relief.

They gradually let the water lead them as they clung to the fabric of the person in front of them. The underground river led them into vast chambers that echoed as they entered and then into close confines that turned and almost threatened to break them apart in the absolute darkness. However, their family was made of strong stuff so they instinctively persevered and eventually they found themselves at the end for the glow of the sun almost blinded them after being so long in the dark underground river.

As each of them reached the end of the tunnel, they were torn apart from the others and thrown up into the air and down a smaller fall into a lake that was a known tributary located near Nekhen. Au-Set recognized it as one that she actually built to connect the fields outside of the city from this area to the Great River. She practically cried with relief for here at this spot she decided right then that she would gather an army.

They all slumped on the pure white sand of the bank of the cut tributary that connected the Great River to this lake. The sand covered their waterlogged and cold bodies making them almost appear as if they were all the same animal.

They all found Set and ran over to embrace her. They ended up in a heap as if they were small children and rolled over in sheer exhaustion and happiness that their lives were saved. Set knew that she was forgiven, but it would be a long road ahead of her to gain their complete trust. This was only one small step. Regardless, she relished it all the same, so much had she missed all of their embraces. She looked over at her consort Heru and ran over to him, "Will you ever forgive me?"

He could not resist the charm of his older sister, and uttered, "Perhaps someday!" He smiled and she took it as a cue to jump on him to tackle him as they did when little.

Au-Set beamed with the joy at seeing her children together for it had not happened in such a long time. "I am sorry to cut the reunion short children but we need to find father!"

"And fast! I fear that his life depends on it!" With that, they swiftly ran to the walled city of Nekhen to summon Neb-Het and the army that they had there.

Chapter 150

It was actually beside the small village of *Gahesty* in the district of *Nedyet* that Suti had finally caught up with Au-Sar. The sun was relentless above them and fought to take them into its power with the constant mirages that surrounded them in the dense heat of the day.

The sun had reached its highest point in the sky and the most deadly. The two brothers glared at each other as Au-Sar was sitting on the bank of the river enjoying the refreshing water and waiting for his younger brother Suti to catch up with him. He was tired of running. He wanted to save the others, but before he felt that, he had to settle things finally between him and Suti.

"I think, brother that we finally need to settle matters now for good!"

"I agree." Suti looked at Au-Sar and observed that Au-Sar had aged a bit over the years with slight wrinkles beside the eyes and above his brow. Perhaps the wrinkles were from the worry of his power, Suti gloated inside. He smiled.

Au-Sar took it to mean that they would now talk to resolve things between them.

"I feel that first we must refresh ourselves in that we have traveled far to reach this spot. If we do not resolve matters and it comes to a physical confrontation we can face each other in a fair fight."

Suti thought about it and actually considered ending the talk of his brother right then with the flint knife that he had tied to his ankle, which Au-Sar obviously did not notice, in exhaustion.

His brother had definitely shown the results of an active life. His skin was dark from the sun and many hours spent outdoors with his precious crops and irrigation inventions and his hands were deeply calloused to show his only life's exertion. He knew from his spies that Au-Sar had preferred the company of his crops and of other farmers to the men of battle and his armies. He knew that the armies were led by his sister Au-Set and recently by Neb-Het.

Suti knew that he could easily kill his older brother with his bare hands. Instead, for some unknown reason he went over to sit beside his brother and looked into the flowing water as if to hide his intense emotions in this moment.

Au-Sar knew that he would have to begin the dialogue and did, "Why brother do you hate me so?" With the emotions dragged up from deep inside after being repressed for so many years a small tear fought to break free from his bright green eyes. He looked at his brother Suti and instead of seeing him as the grown man that he had become, red and blotchy from an over indulgent life; he saw him as a little boy crying so many years ago for him to stay.

"You know why... I can see the memory of it in your eyes. I needed you and instead you left me with that dried up old bitch Nekhebt. She was so weak that she was like a ghost even when she was alive. She never shed one tiny smile or word of love to any of us! It was almost as if we were not even there. In addition, to make it worse we had to pretend other- wise to the three of you when all I wanted to do was shout. Honor and pride! The most wretched words of this torrential family of ours! Duty, my ass!"

"Suti, you know that I had no choice! It was our duty for we promised mother. She was wise enough to know how best to carry on after her in this strange land."

"But think of it truly, did she really choose wisely? Neb-Het bore no children for me only Au-Set" He basked in the horror that it caused when brought up to Au-Sar and continued undaunted. "And Heru, what good was he to us all far away in Upper Kemet, especially when he died so young and then Nekhebt... We got the rotten end of the bargain, face it brother. Mother was wrong."

"Well, she might have been and possibly not for our lives are still being lived and we will not truly know the result of her wisdom until the actual moment of our deaths brother. I wanted to go to you but aunt kept us busy with all of the tutors and court education so that time went by fast and before we knew it, it was time to visit with all of you!"

"You promised me that you would always take care of me. I loved you and trusted you! I waited for you to rescue us for you were always the golden child, the hero of this family!"

"That is not true! You know that I would have rescued you all but I had no idea until it was too late!"

"No, it was too late from the moment that you abandoned us all to our predetermined fate. Do you know what happened brother while you were safe in Per-Uto in your city of gold? I thought not. I received the brunt of it. The guards had taken a particular liking to me and called me an abomination while they raped me repeatedly and passed me around! I was their toy! It killed me deep inside and I vowed to get my revenge on them someday. I did, do you not worry about that? That is yet another story."

"But what about Aunt Nekhebt?"

"She certainly did not care for it kept her guards busy and occupied; she probably even cheered them on. As for Neb-Het, she was oblivious and retreated into her own little dream world. As she grew, she started to treat those same soldiers as her game board and lured them into her pretty heart and then stomped on them and ate them alive. I watched them fight to please my sister and admired that sometimes she could experience as many as ten men in one evening!"

"Stop! This is sickening! There is no way any of this happened, what about Heru?"

"Heru? Heru was oblivious to it all and kept busy on errands around the kingdom while this occurred. He never suspected a thing and never even commented on the pain in my eyes that I prayed that he would notice!"

"Suti, I cannot..."

"You really have no choice in whether to believe this or not since it happened! It was true history and made us what we are now. I did take my revenge but always thought of how Heru and you abandoned us! How could you not know?"

Au-Sar sat there on the bank of the river staring into the truth that shone in Suti's eyes and broke down in sobs over how he had wronged his brother and sister. He should have known!

Suti looked at him and for some reason felt an uncontrollable rage build inside of him. Colors never looked as bleak around him as they did now. In slow motion, his body took on the will of his deepest emotion and he felt his hand grasp his flint knife as if he were watching it occur somewhere else. He felt as if he was standing apart from the whole scene instead of possessing the hand that held the flint knife above the head of the oblivious Au-Sar deep in the grief of the past brought forward to him.

He did not see the knife come down to cut his brother clean across his neck until Au-Sar's eyes finally focused on him at the realization of the moment. It seemed as if Suti were watching a play, so far was he removed from any emotion but his own anger even the numbing. It seemed to take forever for the blood to spurt from the clean wound in Au-Sar's handsome neck.

"A little too late are we? I should have done this years ago!"

Suti watched the color drain from his older brother's face and the blood taking on a will of its own as it started to spurt out in a gush. He wondered how someone could possibly have so much blood inside of him. Au-Sar was dead before he had even slumped onto the ground. Suti stood there staring at the empty spot where his brother's face once was.

As the last of the life left his brother, it was almost if the anger had suddenly dissolved. In its place was something else, deeper and more pronounced. Suti felt as if he was born new inside of his old body and that all of his past pain and hurt was resolved. He felt safe and in a cocoon that was peaceful.

Again, as if he were watching a play he saw himself take the flint knife and very methodically bend over and proceed to cut Au-Sar into sections. He cut off the head and placed it carefully on the side with eyes staring in the sheer horror as he realized what Suti had done. Then he separated the legs and arms from the once handsome trunk with his still muscular abdomen and wide shoulders. Suti sliced into his manhood that cut it clear and threw it to the side. He would deal with that later. He then separated the hands and feet from the arms and legs and cut a large incision down the length of his trunk from his neck to his missing parts. He had placed each now separate piece side by side and examined them.

Au-Sar who was once a whole and vibrant human being was now cut into ten pieces as if he were a slab of meat. He took out the heart and imagined that it was still beating and placed it in a clump beside the pieces in order. Then he ripped out his backbone because he did not feel that Au-Sar should have one after how he treated his siblings in Nekhen! Then he took out the intestines as he tried to unravel them and gave up after several attempts. Last, he took out his brother's once vivid green eyes and held them up in front of him carefully so they would not fall apart and tried to look through them as if to see that he saw or even more important what his brother had missed and had not seen so long ago.

Suti sat back and admired his handiwork as he was completely removed from reality; it was almost as if he had just cut up the carcass of a long-horned steer! He realized that he was meant to do something else. He went over to where he tied his own reed boat and noticed his brother's own *Neshmet* boat tied behind some bushes.

He tipped over the boat and had half of it on the shore. He felt that when the others would reach this area it would look as if Au-Sar had merely drowned. It was not that he was not proud of what he did... Suti needed to buy some time for the next part of his plan. He wanted to find places to put each of the parts he had skillfully cut so Au-Sar could never join his nine paths in the afterlife. He did not want the Ba of his brother to recognize his physical form so deep was his hatred over his abandonment that occurred so long ago. He even took a piece of his brother's cloak with his broach carved in the head of the hawk that was his favorite symbol. He knew that there would be no doubt as to who allegedly drowned at this spot. He felt confident that it would buy him some time to find burial spots for each of the body parts.

He then carefully wrapped each piece in the tall papyrus that grew dense on the banks of this river and placed them carefully in his reed boat. He left the scene to the Gods as he departed with the remains of his brother beside him in his boat.

End of Book One

Smd
8-30-05
Revised 10-31-2011
Revised 11-02-2012**
Smg (Sharon Goding)

**Note to readers: please let me know what you think. I am always open to feed back and would love to hear from you. As you can see, my novels are constantly being revised as I listen to you and all you have to offer ☺ You can contact me at the official author site at www.sharondnovels.com
On Facebook: Sharondnovels.com or Sharon Desruisseaux
On Twitter: smbrooksi
Or on Amazon amazon.com/author/sharondnovels

"Preview into Book Two; Au Set the Goddess"

In the next book of "Au-Set the Goddess," the two sisters, Au-Set and Neb-Het will investigate the disappearance of their brother. You will witness a tale a devotion of two sisters to their brother Au-Sar. They search for resolution and for an end to the rivalry of Suti. A battle wages between the siblings and the next generation that will end all of this and bring about the Egypt that we know of in history today.

A tale of how the royal family made the land into the magical and mysterious land of myth and promise that we know of from thousands of years of the preservation of what they created.

The family of Au-Set and Neb-Het fought to protect their land against a northern tribe that sought to destroy the ways of the Goddess and was the early formation of the religions that we are familiar with today.

In the second book, you will witness the glimmer of the first dynasty of Egypt and of how it came to be.

This is a tale of the mythology of Egypt and of how it started. Sometimes, no matter how fantastical the tale or legend, deep down inside; if one looks hard enough there is the truth and reality of it all. For inside of each story there is some glimmer of what really happened.

-Sharon Desruisseaux

"Authors Note"

I wrote this story of Au-Set due to my love of ancient Egypt. I had become fascinated with all of it, the history, and the mythology at a very early age. It only intensified, as I grew older.

When I was 28, I was finally able to visit Egypt and to view in person all that I have studied and dreamed about since I was in the second grade. I stood in front of the pyramids of Giza and Saqqara. I saw the paintings in the tombs and was able to touch them, knowing that they were painted thousands of years before my visit.

I could stand in person to witness the actual devotion that lasted thousands of years for their Gods and Goddesses. So much passion was expressed in the way a culture was created and formed over the wondrous mythology, that I was lost in its spell.

Over the years, I had collected as many versions as I could on the ancient mythology of the Pantheon of Ancient Egypt. I was especially fascinated by the story of Isis, Osiris, Thoth, and Set, whom I have written about in this novel.

I wanted to make it as authentic as possible in giving them an actual life and meaning behind the legends, as if they were real people at some point in time.

In reading so much history and theology on religions modern and ancient I realized that in the earliest days of religion when it was first recorded that royalty and heroes were deified after their death. Real people were made into Gods. This was apparent in the ancient King lists of Sumer (later known as Babylon and now as modern day Iraq). In Ancient Egypt, the Pharaoh was considered by the people the actual God Horus himself and as the direct descendant of Isis.

So I took the information gained from Sumer in its being the first actual language written about and added it to what I found out about Predynastic Egypt. There has also been evidence of writing in a Predynastic necropolis of writing as early as that found, if not earlier in Sumer.

We only know history from what is discovered in archaeological digs. It is normal to find that history has been written for the benefit of the King or person in power to please them and was even used as early propaganda for their reign.

Therefore, when researching history you need to have an open mind and to obtain every possibly record of each event. For with everything that occurs in history and the present time there are several different versions as is proven in a court of law in the present time.

I looked at the history of the world and compared it to that in Egypt. I wanted to know that if the people in the mythology of Egypt were to exist when would have been the most feasible time for their existence.

It was obvious that the land of Egypt was transformed and based their whole culture on the mythology. This infamous pantheon lasted for approximately three thousand five hundred years in a relative unchanged state in building construction, mythology, culture and even in the way they dressed.

I have also read about the archaeological finds of Predynastic Egypt and related them to characters in this story and to real people that existed in the period of this story to the best of my ability.

I grabbed as much as I could from history at that point in time from the names of villages and cities as they were called in the Gerzean II phase (again to the best of my knowledge); of the names of the deities to new ideas and concepts that initially appeared then. I gave the characters names as they were known then not the ones that are popular to us now as given to us by the Greeks who tried to translate the early mythology that was ancient by the time their own culture arrived.

The people depended on this black soil and inundation so much that they named their land after it to *Kemet*, or the *"Black Lands."* The *"Red Lands"* or *Deshret* was the great desert that encompassed most of the actual geography of Egypt. Most of the population was around the River itself and in small oases in the desert. Early agriculture was known to have begun and made vast improvements with irrigation and crops. People had also started to keep larger herds of long-horned steers and sheep.

The Nile flows backwards so the people of the land based their direction on that. Therefore, Upper Egypt is in our south and Lower Egypt is in our north on the maps of Egypt in comparison to the rest of the world. The Lower part of Egypt contains large tributaries that open to the Mediterranean Sea and is called the delta region. Most of the archaeological evidence from the delta is sparse due to the rate of decay of the moist climate in the soil's high moisture content.

In Upper Egypt most of the evidence has remained intact for discovery due to the desert climate. Early mummification consisted initially of people being preserved intact, wrapped up, and placed in the desert, which they had learned preserved bodies better.

However, with all of this information and keeping in mind the great transformation in the Gerzean II phase in ancient Egypt, I put in my own theories as to their meshing in my novel. I found it the perfect time in history for Egypt to be born and for legends to exist.

How could such wonderful mythology ever be created without some real people actually behind it all?

As an endnote to all of this, I am neither an archaeologist nor Egyptologist only a single mother with dreams. I have always loved history and research. I have always wanted to be both though life would not allow that for me. Therefore, in pursuit of my dreams I made it my life's hobby to research and wonder. In all of my spare time, which really is not that much at all, I have researched with every means available to find any answers that I could in order to write this novel for you. I bought and borrowed every book available that gave me the answers that only led to more questions and then eventually to the creation of this novel.

So please understand that if I have any historical information wrong in this book, please let me know for I am always searching for the truth and I can only do what I can with the resources available. This is not meant to be an accurate portrayal of events in that era only my theory as to what may have happened had there been a real Isis and her family. In addition, remember, this is only part one for there is much more to her life and legend.

How could I encourage my daughters to reach for their dreams if I never tried to myself? I have infinite fun in creating, researching, and writing this novel and others that I have written, and do not plan to stop.

"Cities in novel"

1. _Abdjw_= New capitol in Upper Kemet to replace old one named Nekhen, known as modern "Abydos" in Egypt.

2. _Bubastis_= Temple site dedicated to the Goddess Bast found in the delta region. The city was built over an older site that worshipped lions. The Goddess Bast in its most ancient form was that of a lion and then later became that of a domestic cat.

3. _Busiris_= Cult center of the _djed_, burial place of Osiris' backbone. Now known as Hermopolis Magna in Egypt.

4. _Dilmun_ =City of Sumer. Sumer later became known as Babylon and is now known as Iraq.

5. _Dja_ =Temple for cobra Goddess Renenutet, known as Medinet Maadi in Egypt.

6. _Djeb_= City founded by Heru, modern day Edfu. Hawk symbols carved there at a fortress uncovered found there.

7. _Djedu_= New capitol city of Upper Kemet. Commissioned by Set (Suti) and built by Nepthys (Nekhebt Neb-Het) in the novel. It was located across the River from Abdjw.

8. _Edfu_= City in Upper Kemet that records in archaeological findings a different tale of Suti and Heru.

9. _Erech_ = Ancient name for Ur in Babylon, town where Abraham of the Old Testament was from.

10. _Eridu_ = Cultural center of Sumer.

11. _Eshnunna_= Later known as Sumer, then Babylon, now modern day Iraq.

12. _Gahesty_= A small village in the district of Nedyet near the banks of a tributary of the Nile located in Upper Kemet. This is the legendary spot where Set (Suti) killed Osiris (Horus).

13. _Gerzah_ = A Predynastic town in Egypt famous for its red-based pottery and as a market town.

14. _Gubla_= A city in Retenu, later known as Byblos of Ancient Canaan. Now located in modern day Israel.

15. _Ianet or Iunet_= Located in Kemet. The Predynastic city and home of historical Mesta and Sata. It is now known as Dendera in Egypt. A Cult was established there for Hathor (Het-Heru) where mummified cows were found.

16. _MenNefer_ = Means "established and beautiful," a new capitol when founded by Menes, or *_**Ineb-Hedj**_* (means "white fortress, easy to patrol") was founded by Isis (Au-Set) and Osiris (Au-Sar) in the novel when they united Kemet. It is now known as Thebes. In dynastic times, it was a capitol of Egypt called Memphis.

17. _IpetIsut_= City in novel where Maat establishes a school for teaching her skills in judgment. Now the modern day Karnak in Egypt where one of the few temples to this Goddess was found. Maat was mostly portrayed in the temples of other Gods.

18. _IPOs_ =Temples of the fertility God Min in Egypt.

19. _Iunu_= Modern day Heliopolis. Site of the first known sun temple dedicated to Ra (Re). Cemetery for the chief priests of the temple found here as well.

20. _Kebet_= Gold town in Predynastic Egypt.

21. _Khemmis_= Place in the papyrus marshes in the northeast delta where in legend and in novel Horus (Heru) was born from Isis (Au-Set).

22. _Khnum_ = Cult center of Thoth (Tehuti), later known as Djedu in Dynastic Egypt. In the novel, Thoth (Tehuti) established his first school for scribes here. Also known as Hermopolis Magma in modern day Egypt.

23. _Lebann_= Later known as the modern day country of Lebanon.

24. _Lagash_ =City of Ancient Sumer, now located in modern day Iraq.

25. _Nekhab_= Located at the mouth of the wadi Hillal in Upper Egypt. In the novel it was created by Isis (Au-Set) and Nepthys (Neb-Het), built over an ancient hunting site in Neolithic times.

26. _Nebt_ = Nebt was also known as Nubt in Ancient Egypt. One of the largest Predynastic sites of Egypt later known as *Nagada* in modern Egypt. This was located across the river from the Predynastic city of Nekhen.

27. _Nedyet_= City in mythology where Osiris (Au-Sar) was killed by Set (Suti). It is located by the wadi Hillal in the Ancient District of Nedyet near the River of the same name.

28. _Nefrit Ombos_ =Home city of Hapi and Tuarif. Later known as Kom Ombos in Egypt. Located in Upper Egypt.

29. _Nekhab_= City founded in legend by Nepthys (Neb-Het), where she established a temple that was located south of Luxor. Now it is known as modern day Elkab in Egypt.

30. _Nekhen_ =Old capitol of Ancient Upper Egypt, replaced in novel by city built by Nepthys (Neb-Het) later named Djedu. Home of the Shed peoples of Ancient Upper Egypt. This city is now known as Hierakonopolis and the oldest painted tomb was found there as well as the Narmer palette and the Scorpion mace head.

31. *Nubt (Nebt)* = Ancient Predynastic gold town, now called in modern Egypt, Naqada. A Large amount of foreigners were found buried there and were incorporated this in the novel. In addition, contained brick built graves of the elite in the Gerzean II phase. (When this novel occurred). This town was called gold town and was able to benefit from its location near Koptos for the minerals located there in mines.

32. *Per Bastis* =Bast's city where the temple of the Goddess Bast is located, later known as Bubastis or Tell Basta in Egypt.

33. *Per Uto* =Later it was called Buto in Egypt. Capitol of Ancient Lower Egypt. Home of the people of the Iaret. Later known as Tell El Fara in modern Egypt.

34. *Retenu* = Region of Gubla as called by people of Ancient Egypt, now known as modern day Israel.

35. *Sa-el-Hagar* = Later known as Sais in modern Egypt. This is probably an ancient Moslem name since no earlier name had been found for this city; this name is used in the novel.

36. *Sippar* and *Opis* =Cities of pre-Sumer that were occupied by the Martu peoples north of the Euphrates River. Now located in modern day Iraq.

37. *Uruk* =It was a sister city of (Erech)Ur in Ancient Sumer that was located near the gulf.- It was the home of the temple of the Goddess Innana at some point it then moved to Erech.

38. *Waset* =Cult center in Ancient Egypt located near modern day Thebes.

39. Yam= Modern day Ethiopia, where the source of the Nile is located. There was evidence of journeys made during Predynastic Egypt, possible trade missions.

40. *Yanu*= Ruins of this Predynastic settlement found under modern day Cairo. It was a cult center in ancient times.

"Au Set"
List of main characters

Note=
Legendary and mythical characters
Historical people
Italics= People made up for novel, fictional.
1. **Astarte**= (Sumerian) Goddess of the region of ancient Canaan (Israel). She was a fertility Goddess.
2. **Anpu**= (Egyptian) Known to the Greeks as Anubis.
3. **Au-Sar**= (Egyptian) Known as Osiris to the Greeks.
4. **Au-Set**= (Egyptian) Known as Isis in to the Greeks.
5. **Heru**= (Egyptian) Known as Horus to the Greeks.
6. **Het-Heru**= (Egyptian) Goddess of love. Known to the Greeks as Hathor.
7. **Innana**= (Sumerian). Sumerian Goddess in the cities of Erech and Uruk.
8. **Neb-Het**= (Egyptian) Known as Nepthys to the Greeks and twin sister of Isis.
9. **Nekhebt**= (Egyptian) Ancient Predynastic Vulture Goddess of Upper Egypt.
10. **Ninnuit**= (Egyptian) Goddess of night and stars. Known as Nut to the Greeks. She was the mother of Isis, Osiris, Thoth, Horus, and Set.
11. **Shu**= (Egyptian) Consort to the Goddess Tefnut and father to the God Geb and the Goddess Nut.
12. **Suti**= (Egyptian) Known as Set to the Greeks.

13. **Tefnut**= (Egyptian) Mother of the Goddess Nut and the God Shu.
14. **Tehuti**= (Egyptian) Known as Thoth to the Greeks. The God of the scribes and the mythical founder of writing.
15. **Ua-Zit**= (Egyptian) Cobra Goddess of Lower Kemet.

Chronology of Characters

Tmu (Amun)   m.   Tiamut
(Creator Goddess of Babylon

/

Tefnut   m.   Shu (From Egypt, brother of Nekhebt
(Hetep's mother)

                                  Simnt
              Nucit
/   /
         /
Ninnuit   -Re   Ua-Zit
      Nekhebt
        -Geb
        -Gilgamesh
        -Enlil
        -Enkidu

Children of Ninnuit with consorts
Children of Au Set with consorts

From Geb: From
Suti:

    Au-Set   Set
    Neb-Het   from
Nebmaat:
From Re:
    Renenutet
    Tehuti   Weret-
Heka
From Gilgamesh: From Au-
Sar:
    Au-Sar
    Heru
From Enkidu:
    Bast
    Heru
    Merul
From Enlil: From Re:
    Suti
    Maat

    Serqet

"Characters"

Children of Ninnuit (Nut);

1. ***Au-Sar (m.)=** Osiris. Egyptian God of the underworld and of judgment after death. Consort and brother of Au-Set (Isis). God of Agriculture before death. Father of Anpu (Anubis) with Neb-Het (Nepthys), his half sister. Son of Ninnuit (Nut) and the novel of Gilgamesh a Sumerian. In Egyptian mythology, his father was Geb. He was the father of Heru (Horus) from his consort Au-Set (Isis) in mythology. He became known as God of Bounty and Chief of Bounty. He also took on the name of Khentimentiu, to supplant the ancient local God of Abydos in Upper Egypt that he took over. In Lower Egypt, he took on the characteristics of the delta God named Andjety who was a god of the dead and dressed himself to emulate death as he ruled over the underworld and rose from the dead. His love for hawks and the training of them was from an ancient God of the land called Sokar that he also gained the characteristics.

2. ***Au-Set (f.)** = Isis. Egyptian Goddess of All. She was the Mother Goddess and Healer. Daughter of Ninnuit (Nut) and Geb, and twin sister of Neb-Het (Nepthys). Goddesses of the throne were the pharaohs sit, guardian. Also known as a warrior Goddess. The cobra was her symbol and the throne. She helped to unite both Upper and Lower Egypt with her consort, Au-Sar (Osiris). In mythology, she had a guard that she called the Seven Scorpions. ***The Seven Scorpions*** were; front Petet, Tjet, and Matet. Sides: Mesetet, Metsetef. Rear: Tefen and Befen. She married Au-Sar (Osiris) and gave birth to Heru (Horus). The later people of dynastic Egypt believed that the Goddess Au-Set (Isis) was the throne that they sat on to rule. They believed that the pharaohs were descendants of Isis and the reincarnation of her son Heru (Horus). She had a throne on her

head to symbolize her as the seat of power in Egypt.

3. ***Heru (m.)**= Horus. Also known as Hor or Her. Guardian of the siblings and son of Ninnuit (Nut) and Geb. He was the mediator of all disputes between them. Brother of Au-Sar (Osiris), Au-Set (Isis), Neb-Het (Nepthys), Tehuti (Thoth), and Suti (Set). He was the Egyptian Sky God. Confused often with his nephew Heru (Horus), who was born right after he died and was named after him. He had the head of a hawk.

4. ***Neb-Het (f.)**= Nepthys. Twin sister of Au-Set (Isis) and daughter of Ninnuit (Nut) and Geb and sister to Au-Sar (Osiris), Suti (Set), Tehuti (Thoth), and Heru (Horus). She was the Egyptian Goddess of Protection and devotion. Her symbol was the disc and cow horns. Mother of Anpu (Anubis) from Au-Sar (Osiris) and consort of Set. She was noted in the mythology for her devotion to her sister and brother. After the death of Au-Sar (Osiris), she followed Au-Set around Egypt to find the missing pieces of Osiris after Suti (Set) killed him.

5. ***Suti (m.)**= Set. God of the Red lands and of Lower Egypt. Brother of Au-Set (Isis) and the rest of them by Ninnuit (Nut) and Geb. In mythology, he had red hair and a dangerous temperament, loves pigs, dogs, and his favorite food is lettuce. He helped to defeat enemies of Re (Ra), but later murdered his brother, Au-Sar (Osiris). He helped restore the wounded eye of Horus. Is symbol was the dog and was noted for his insatiable lusts. He had a personal guard of seventy-two men of whom he used to try to defeat his brother Au-Sar (Osiris). He is a main character in the mythology of Egypt as being the consort of Neb-Het (Nepthys) and of lusting after his other sister Au-Set. He constantly battles with Au-Sar and then later his son Heru (Horus) for rule over Egypt. In the earliest myths was portrayed as being good and then later was changed into a darker

character and full of evil and destruction. He also helps the God Re (Ra) in defeating his enemies. He had the head of a canine in paintings of him.

6. ***Tehuti (m.) =** Thoth. Egyptian God of the secret art of writing. He was the son of Ninnuit (Nut) and of Geb. God of divine intelligence, writing and speaking, calculating time, right, and truth. He was the messenger of the Gods and had the head of an Ibis. In paintings, he holds reed pen in his left hand and papyrus scroll in his right hand. He was considered the inventor of hieroglyphs and was a master scribe and magician. He was the brother of Au-Set (Isis), Neb-Het (Nepthys), Au-Sar (Osiris), Suti (Set), and Heru (Horus). Also depicted as a baboon, in this form he was closely associated with a god called Hedj-Wer (the great white one). He was worshipped along with a little known consort named Nehmetaway, at his city of Khnum (Hermopolis Magma). He was closely associated with the moon and was shown with a headdress consisting of a disc and crescent symbolizing the lunar phases. He is depicted as weighing the results of the heart in the book of deeds after death in later mythology. He was considered guardian of the deceased in the netherworld.

Au Set's Children;

1. **Set (f.) =** Female version of Suti (Set). I changed this for the novel. In the novel, she was the daughter of Au-Set from her rape by Suti.
2. **Renenutet (f.) =** The Goddess of fate and the wife of Shai. Goddess of fertility, harvest, fate, fortune and plenty. The cobra was her symbol. She married Shai, who was the son of Re (Ra) and Het-Heru (Horus). (In the novel, she was the daughter of Au-Set and Au-Sar)
3. **Weret-Heka (f.) =** The Goddess of magic. The cobra was her symbol. She was also the wife of

Shai who was the son of Re (Ra) and Het-Heru (Hathor).

4. **Heru (m.)** = Horus. Son if Au-Sar and Au Set. He was often confused with the less mentioned sibling of his mother and father, the older Heru (Horus). He was the left eye and the right eye was Re (Ra) that was used in powerful magic symbols of power and healing in hieroglyphs. He avenged father's death by fighting his uncle Suti (Set). He also was depicted with the head of a hawk. In mythology, he was considered rash and hot headed.

5. **Bast (f.)** =She was the Goddess who personifies sistrum. The cat Goddess. In older mythology, she was depicted as a lioness warrior and then later as the domestic cat. In legend, she creates the capitol city of Bubastis in the delta.

6. **Merul (m.)** = He was rarely mentioned in mythology, though as the deformed son of Au-Sar (Osiris) and Au-Set (Isis). He had a large head, short neck, arms, and legs. Au-Sar in mythology did not like him due to his deformities.

7. **Maat (f.)** = Maat. She was the creator of justice in Egypt. Her symbol was the feather for it balanced truth against lies. She created a school of justice called "The Hall of Two Truths." The people of Egypt called it the hall Maaty after her.

8. **Serqet (f.)** = Serqet. Goddess of the Scorpions. She guarded tombs from harm in legend. She was represented as a scorpion.

Note: **For purposes of this novel, the characters are listed by the countries originally came from.**

Eshnunna (Later known as Sumer, then as Babylon, and now as Iraq)

1. ***Dimuzi (m.)** = Last consort of Innana. The God who was her most famous of lovers and who died with her in legend.
2. ****En (m.)** = Consort of Ninnuit in the novel. He was from the city of Erech (Ur) in Sumer (Babylon). His father was known as Lugal Banda in Sumerian legends. He later was called Gilgamesh and was the legendary hero who saved the people of Sumer from death by the flood that covered the world. He built and ark and saved his family and animals in pairs. He was later called Noah in the Old Testament of the Bible.
3. ****Enkidu (m.)** = In the novel, he was the consort of Ninnuit (Nut) and the father of Heru (Horus). In Sumer, he was listed on the Kings lists as a God who was formerly a mortal king.
4. ***Enkil (m.)** = God of Sumer and later Babylon. A God that probably originated from the northern tribes that conquered the Goddess religions in Mesopotamia. He is depicted as raping Astarte and of killing her lover and consort, the God Dimuzi in legends. Astarte in legends of ancient Sumer was worshipped along the side of Innana and was similar in characteristics of the Goddess as well. In the novel, I separated them.
5. ***Enlil (m.)** =The Main God of Babylon, who later became Marduk. Enlil suppressed and raped the Goddess Innana. In the novel, the man Enlil was the leader of the northern tribes and the father of Suti. He could have also been the more warrior-like qualities of the ancient Hebraic God called El-Shadai, for he also ruled from the mountains. People built Ziggurats and temples to resemble mountains.

6. **Eshnunna**= Ancient name for Sumer, later called Babylon and now modern day Iraq.

7. **Etnu**= First wife of the king of Sumer and Babylon. Taken from Sumerian literature.

8. *Geb (m.) = Consort of Nut and child of Shu and Tefnut. Egyptian God of earth. His symbol was the Goose and he was called "The Great Cackler." His parents were the Gods of Air and moisture. He was also the God who laid the primordial egg that hatched humankind in some creation legends of Egypt. He was the father of Au-Set (Isis), Au-Sar (Osiris), Neb-Het (Nepthys), Suti (Set), Tehuti (Thoth) and Heru (Horus).

9. *Ishtar (f.) =Goddess of Babylon and consort and lesser Goddess to the God Marduk. She was dominated over by Marduk. Priestesses served in her honor at the temple. Her lover, Tammuz, in a jealous rage, killed her.

10. *Marduk (m.) =Main God of Babylon, after Sumer was gone. He became a powerful God who ruled over all others.

11. **MesAnniPadda (m.) = He was the consort of ShubAd and King of Sumer. His tomb was found in an archaeological dig. I could not find his name on the King list.

12. **Naditu (f.) =the women of the ruling class of Sumer who worked for the Goddess Representative in temples.

13. *Nammu (f.) =The Goddess of Sumer who gave birth to the earth and the heavens.

14. *Nannar (m.) =the Moon God of Sumer. He was one of the earliest recorded Gods of Sumer.

15. *Nanshe (f.) =She was the patron Goddess of the city of Lagash of Sumer. Known as the mother who loves orphans and the sick and she who seeks justice for the poor and shelter for the weak.

16. *Nidaba (f.) =She was the patron Goddess of Erech.

17. *Nikkal (f.) =the great Mother of Sumer. She was one of the earliest recorded Goddesses of Sumer.

She was the wife of Nannar, the Moon God. Arinna was added to the name of Nikkal in later generations.

17. *Ninnuit (f.) = Nut. Egyptian Goddess of the night and stars. In paintings, she carried the evening sky on her back that was depicted as being arched over the four corners of the earth. In Egypt, her symbol was the sky and a cow. Thunder was considered the laughter of Ninnuit.

18. *Ninsikil (f.) = Patron Goddess of the city of Dilmun of Sumer.

19. *Shu (m.) = Egyptian air God. Consort of Tefnut, the daughter of Tmu and Tiamut. He was the father of Nut and Geb from Tefnut of mythology. The ostrich plume is the hieroglyph for his name.

20. **Shub-Ad (f.) = Queen of Sumer whose tomb was unearthed in a recent archaeological dig. Her last consort was MesAnniPadda.

21. *Tammuz (m.) =Lover of the Sumerian Goddess Ishtar who had killed her in a jealous rage.

22. *Tefnut (f.) = Egyptian Goddess and consort of Shu. Egyptian Goddess. Daughter of Tiamut and Tmu. She was the mother of Nut and Geb from her consort Shu.

23. *Tiamut (f.) = in the novel she was the consort of Amun or Tmu and father of Ninnuit (Nut), Ua-Zit and Nekhebt. She was also the Creator Goddess of Babylon and Sumer in mythology.

24. *Tmu (m.) = the consort of Tiamut for the novel. Egyptian God of air. Symbol was the goose and ram.

Peoples of Anatolia (later known as Turkey)

1. *Arinna (f.) = Sun Goddess of the Hatti peoples of the Catal-Huyuk. In the novel, she was the human ancestor of Au-Set. This Goddess took on a consort who would rule as the thunder God of the later Hittite lands.

Kemet (Later known as Egypt)

1. **Amaunet (f.)** = Goddess who was in the leading role of the triad of Thebes and was usurped by the Goddess Mut.

2. **Anmut (f.)** - Goddess of the Crocodile. She was known as a Goddess of Judgment and called "The Devourer." It was believed that during the opening of the mouth ceremony she had the head of a crocodile and would eat those with an evil heart.

3. ***Anpu (m.)** = Anubis. Son of Au-Sar and Neb-Het from affair in novel and mythology. He was painted with the head of a dog or jackal. He was the Guide of the *Tuat* and protector in the magical universe

4. ***Anqet (f.)** = Scorpion Goddess of Egypt. She is listed in mythology as marrying Tuamutef.

5. ***Apep (m.)** =Apothis. God of Egypt and the son of The God Khephra and the Goddess Mut in mythology. He was the natural enemy and brother to Re. He was a serpent God. In paintings, he takes form of crocodile or dragon.

6. **Bes (m)** = A dwarf God of Egypt depicted wearing a lion skin as a cape. He is associated with protecting birth-houses and in banning snakes from the family homes. His assistant was Taweret.

7. ***Edjo (f.)** = She was an ancient cobra Goddess of the earliest recorded history of Egypt. She mainly ruled over Lower Egypt.

8. ***Hapi (m.)** = God of Ancient Egypt. He was almost androgynous in paintings, though seemingly male. He was the God of the Nile River and was seen in the form of Hippopotami. He married Tuarif. His home was at Kom Ombo. He was a Hermaphrodite and was a pot-bellied bearded man with pendulous breasts and a headdress that was formed of aquatic plants. He dwelled in

the caverns along the Nile among the rocks of the first cataract.

9. ***Heqet (f.)** =She was a frog Goddess and sister of Sebek. She married Quebhsenuf. She was also proficient in assisting in childbirth.

10. ***Hetep* (m.)** = **Son** of Ua-Zit and Hetep in novel. Consort of Neb-Het. Had a daughter with Neb-Het named Meshkenet.

11. ***Hetep* (m.)** =Consort of Ua-Zit (Ishurti). Means the God who gives offerings.

12. ***Het-Heru (f.)** =Hathor. Consort of Re. Mother of Sekhmet and Shai with Re. Signified as a woman with the ears of a cow, as a cow, or as wearing a headdress consisting of a wig, horns, and sun disc.

13. ***Jedneth* (m.)** = Son of Ua-Zit and Hetep.

14. ***Kekes* (m.)** = Tall man with a small delicate voice. He was a talented dancer despite his large size. He served Neb-Het. Older brother of Qui. His mother was a register of Eshnunna.

15. ***Khephra (m.)** = He was an Egyptian God and consort of Mut and father of Re, Apep and Edjo with Mut. He was considered in mythology to be the creative consciousness. His symbol was the scarab.

16. **Khnum (m.)** = He was the ram-God at Aswan, associated with Satet or Seta. Considered a creator God. Rams were sacrificed to this god while sheep were considered unclean.

17. **Khons (m.)** = He was the moon God whose name means 'wanderer'; he was occasionally depicted as hawk-headed or as a baboon. He was originally associated with childbirth and an assistant to Bes and Neith in mythology. He was the son of Mut and Amun or Tmu.

18. ***Ma-At (f.)** = in the novel, she was a Nugig of Sumer who was sent to Per-Uto with Au-Sar, Au-Set, and Tehuti.

19. ***Maat (f.)** = She was the Goddess of Egypt and the personification of the divine order of things,

truth and justice. She was the first judge. The ostrich feather was her symbol. The Goddess Maat created the first code of ethics for the people of Egypt in legend. She was also present in the judgment of the dead when her feather was weighed against the heart of the deceased. The place of judgment was called 'the hall of two truths'.

20. **Menes (m.)** = He was a king near the end of the invasion by the northern tribes. He is sometimes noted as the first king of the Old Kingdom of Egypt and reined around 3500 B.C.E. He founded the city of Ineb-Hedj as his capitol where he established the fertility God Min as patron deity. He is listed in the Kings list and sometimes is called Aha.

21. **Meretseger (m.)** = Goddess of Egypt who protects the cemetery. She was a Snake Goddess. In addition, a cobra Goddess, her name means 'she who loves silence'. She would punish those workers for crimes committed by inflicting them with blindness made of her venom.

22. **Meshkenet (f.)** = She is Goddess of Egypt and is known as the Goddess of fate. In the novel, she is the daughter of Neb-Het with her consort Hetep. She becomes the wife of the God Shai.

23. **Mesta (m.)** = Listed as an historical person of ancient Egypt, he married Sata who became the Goddess of Dendera (Ianet).

24. **Mut (f.)** =Mother Goddess of Egypt and consort of Khephra. Wife of Amun or Tmu-Amun who was much older than she was. Maternal love and protection. Original deity of Thebes (Waset). She was the mother of Shu, original Ua-Zit, and Nekhebt with Khephra. She had Re, Apep and Edjo. Vulture symbol. Married to Tmu and her consort was Khephra.

25. **Narmer (m.)** = in history, he is sometimes known as Menes or Aha. Some believe him to be the son of Menes. He is also known as the first

King of Old Kingdom and founder of Memphis or MenNefer. He is buried at Saqqara. He is sometimes painted with the head of bull. Inside his tomb was found the legendary and exaggerated in size, "Palette of Narmer" on which he was depicted as "smiting" his enemies with a pear-shaped mace-head.

26. ***Neith (f.) =** She was the Egyptian Bee Goddess. In legend, she was Au-Set's official Beekeeper. She was also known to be a healer and a midwife in early mythology.

27. ***Nekhebt (f.) =** Goddess of Upper Egypt in Predynastic times. City she ruled from is Nekhen. Her symbol is vulture or hawk. She was the ruler of the Shen Peoples of Upper Kemet.

28. ***Nebmaat (m.) =*** in the novel, he became one of the first judges of Kemet. He was the son of Ua-Zit, Hetep, and consort of Au-Set. The meaning of his name was "man of the law."

29. ***Nebmaat (m.) =*** in the novel, he was the consort of Nekhebt (Nemothi).

30. ***Neferet (f.) =*** She was a Nugig (Highest caste of priestess under the main high priestess of Innana) of Sumer and was sent to watch over Neb-Het, Suti and Heru to Nekhen in the novel.

31. ***Nehmetaway (f.) =*** Low birth mistress of Tehuti. She was known as his true love in the Egyptian mythology.

32. **Nun (f) =** God of Egypt in legends, for this novel a Goddess. She was personified as the original formless ocean of chaos from which Atum rose. She was the mother of Atum and came from a land far away. Her consort's name was Naunet (changed to male for this novel). In this Goddess, everything outside the order of the universe was contained in her in mythology.

33. **Opet (f.) =** She was a consort of the God Sebek who was a teacher and resided on an island at the very far reaches of Upper Kemet in Kom Ombo.

34. ***Ptah (f.)** =Creator God of Ancient Egypt. His temple was located at Memphis (Ineb-Hedj). In this novel, Ptah is a female and the grandmother of Re, the matriarch of his line. She was the one who created humanity from her potter's wheel out of the clay of the Nile as depicted in mythology.

35. ***Ptahtep (m.)*** = in the novel, he was the younger and second consort of Mut. Ptahtep took on the name of the family patriarch named Ptah. He is described in this novel as the God Ptah in mythology and was known to wear a skullcap and had a long beard as was fashionable for the times, however his beard was usually was curled at the end and touched the ground. Creator of the opening of the mouth ceremony. He was known as the leader of artisans like the family matriarch and namesake was.

36. ***Puanit (f.)** = Suti's mistress in mythology and in this novel.

37. ***Quebhsenuf (m.)** =in the novel, he was the son of Menes and Weret-Heka. He was the third son born to them and married Heqet. He was listed in mythology and being one of the four sons of Horus.

38. ***Qui (m.)*** = Large dark man from Kemet with a small voice. Good singer. Chosen by Ninnuit for the eunuch school. Schooled in accounts by a male merchant from Tyre in the new regime. Has a pet mouse by the name of QuiQui. His brother is Kekes. He served Au-Set.

39. ***Re (m.)** =Ra. He was the Sun God of Egypt. He was the son of Mut and Khephra, who was Mut's second consort. He was also the brother to Apep (Apothis) and Edjo. He married Het-Heru (Hathor) and had a daughter named Sekhmet and a son named Shai with her. In mythology, he also had an affair with Au-Set and she had twin daughters named Maat and Serqet from this. In legend, he rides through the heavens on a sun chariot and had the head of a hawk. His daughter Sekhmet

cared for him in his old age. His enemy was his brother Apep. Au-Set stole his secret name in one story. He rode a boat named the "Boat of Millions" across the western horizon in other stories before the chariot came to Egypt. Note: Chariots first were seen in Egypt with the invasion of the *Hyksos* during the New Kingdom and later dynasties. They were so revered that it was later added to the legend of Re. Re usually wore the hawk-headed headdress that Au-Sar and then Heru adopted with a sun disc headdress.

40. **Renenutet (f.)** = She was the cobra Goddess and protector of the king. In the novel, she was the daughter of Au-Set and her consort Nebmaat. She was sometimes represented as a woman with the head of a cobra. Her name may be translated as 'nourishing snake'. It was considered that she as an important guardian of the king and when reunited with the Wadjyt (Ua-Zit). She would become a fire-breathing cobra to protect the kings and later pharaohs in the underworld. She was also the protectress of the linen garment worn by the king, which was thought to instill in his enemies with fear in the afterlife. She was sometimes connected with the provision of mummy bandages. She was known as 'the lady of the fertile fields' and 'lady of the granaries', she was responsible for securing and protecting the harvests.

41. ***Sata (f.)** =Serpent Goddess of Ianet and married to Mesta. Goddess of lower cataract of Nile near Aswan, great-granddaughter of Re in the novel. She was also called Satet and was associated with the ram-god named Khnum. Sata was depicted as a woman wearing a white crown with antelope horns on either side of it. She was sometimes regarded as the wife of Khnum. She was also considered the mother of *Anuket*, the huntress. Sata was mentioned as a Goddess concerned with purifying the dead. Her temple was located on the Elephantine Island and was

situated at the point at which the first waters of the inundation would be heard from before the flood itself became visible. Her function was as the Protectress of this border in which she was said to repel invaders with arrows.

42. ***Sebek (m.)** =Crocodile God. Brother of Heqet, the Frog Goddess. He was often depicted wearing a headdress consisting of the horned sun disc and upright feathers.

43. ***Sekhmet (f.)** = in the novel, she was the daughter of Re with his consort Weret-Heka. She was the sister of Shai. She was the lion-headed Goddess of war and strife. She was depicted as the darker side of her mother. She was also mostly known for healing and had doctors and healers as priests. In mythology, she married Ptah. Sekhmet established the rite of holding a sekhem scepter for positions of power in her right hand while holding a mace in the left hand, which meant power. She was given the title of 'she who guards the beautiful house'. She was talented in having spells to heal a person from the venomous bites of scorpions.

44. ***Serqet (f.)** =Scorpion Goddess who assisted with birth of Gods and Pharaohs. In the novel she was the twin sister of Maat from an affair with Re and Au-Set.

45. **Seshat (f.)** = She was the Goddess of writing and measurement. Represented as a woman clad in a long panther skin dress and wearing a headdress consisting of a band surmounted by a seven-pointed star and a bow. She was regarded as assisting the king in the foundation ritual of the 'stretching of the cord'. She is also shown as recording the loot and captives taken in war. She founded the measurement of time and recorded the passing of it on a notched palm rib. Her male equivalent was Tehuti (Thoth).

46. ***Shai (m,)** = He was the personification of lifespan and destiny. He had two wives, who were

considered the Goddesses of fate (Renenutet and Meshkenet).

47. **Sopdet (f.)** = Goddess of the Dog Star Siris that signified the beginning of the inundation of the Nile. In the novel, she was the astronomer of the palace and the star was named after her after she officially recognized it and noted it to Neb-Het when they created the calendar together. She was a Nugig from Eshnunna in the novel.

48. *Sut (m.)* =in the novel, he was the son of Ua-Zit and Hetep.

49. *Taweret (f.) (Opet)*= The Goddess usually associated with Bes. In the novel, she was his assistant. She was the household deity in the form of a hippopotamus. She was associated with women and childbirth. She was usually portrayed with the arms and legs of a lion and the back and tail of a crocodile, or even with a complete crocodile perched on her back. In paintings, her heavy breasts and full belly indicate pregnancy. She had a headdress with two low plumes and carried a *SA* amulet for protection and an ankh symbol. Opet was her name during the old kingdom.

50. **Tchar (m.)** =another name for the Scorpion King. In some legends, he is mentioned as being the son of Mesta and Sata. His tomb was found at Busiris (Abdjw in novel and early history) and was noted as first king by some historians. He used the lapwing birds to symbolize those who were captives and under his control, the wings of the *rekhyt* bird. He established this as a symbol for subjugated peoples. The rekhyt bird is depicted as a small bird with its wings behind its back and human arms raised in prayer outwards.

51. **Tmu or Amun (m.)** = A Creator God of ancient Egypt. He was the husband to Mut and was very ancient in the novel; he was the father with Mut of the original Ua-Zit and Nekhebt as well as Shu.

He wore a headdress of double plumes with ram's horns on each side.

52. ***Tuamutef (m.)** = in the novel, he was the fourth son of Menes and Weret-Heka. He married Anqet. In Egyptian mythology, he was one of the four sons of Horus.

53. ***Tuarif (f.)** = She was the hippopotamus Goddess of Nile. She married Hapi in mythology. She established the capitol at Nefrit Ombos.

54. ***Ua-Zit (f.)** = Wadjyt. She was the Goddess of Lower Egypt by the delta region. City she ruled from is called Per-Uto. Symbol is the cobra. Ua-Zit was born as Ishurti of Sumer and was the daughter of Shu and Tefnut and the sister of Ninnuit and Nekhebt. Married Hetep of the first Ua-Zit and had three children, Astarte (from a consort in Sumer), Hetep, and Nebmaat. She was the ruler of the people of the iaret. Her surviving sons were Hetep (consort of Neb-Het), Nebmaat (consort of Au-Set), Jedneth, and Sut.

55. **Weret-Heka (f.)** = The Goddess called 'The Great Enchantress". In the novel, she was the daughter of Au-Set and her consort Nebmaat, the full sibling of Renenutet and half siblings of Heru, Set, Bast, Merul, Serqet, and Maat. In the novel, she later became the concubine of Menes and bore him five sons.

Gubla (Later known as Byblos of Canaan)

1. ***Anat (f.)** =the ancient earth Goddess of the lands of Canaan. Gubla and later called Byblos was where her main temple was located.

2. ***Astarte (f.)** = The Goddess from Sumer, who was sometimes confused with Anat in the lands of Byblos. Her consort was Baal. She was also added to Egyptian mythology as being the consort of Set.

3. ***Baal (m.)** =The God of the lands of Canaan. His consort and Queen was The Goddess Astarte.

4. *Enlo* **(m.)** = Leader of the northern tribes that invaded Gubla.

4. **Qedeshet (f.)** = Goddess of Syria depicted naked on a lion with flowers and snakes in her hands. In the novel, Qedeshet was a Nugig warrior from the temple of Eshur in Eshnunna and was sent to protect Ua-Zit with her Goddess-born child when she went to rule in Lower Kemet and then followed Astarte to Gubla.

5. **Rashef (m.)** = Consort of Astarte.

6. **Queen Ria (f.)** = Wife of King Melanchor, from northern tribes. Not sure is she is legend or real. She is written in legends as being a real person though no tomb has been found of her to date.

7. **King Melanchor (m.)** = Son of Astarte in the novel.

8. **Maneros (m.)** = Older son of Melanchor. Mentioned in the legend of Astarte and Isis, when she returns to Gubla to find the chest of Osiris and takes the children of Maneros home with her. In the myth, Isis becomes enraged at the boy in the boat and in anger drowns him while his younger brother escaped and founded the land of the Philistines.

9. **Pelusias (m.)** = Younger son of Melanchor. He is the boy who escaped from the wrath of Isis in the legend of Isis and Astarte.

"The Nine Paths of Life"

1. **KHAT**=Physical body or vessel.

2. **SAHU**= Spiritual body. A bit of the physical body that had retained the physical knowledge from the life walked on earth. It has the power to communicate with the soul. When the physical body dies, it turns into the sahu, flies up to the sky to dwell in the heavens with the Gods, and is righteous.

always near and is revealed to us in the rays of the sun, which is always present.

7. **KHU=** Unlike the khaibit, the *khu* is shining and bright and translucent. It contains the intelligence of the person and their life. Human khus are surrounded by the khus of the Gods at their death and assisted by them to the sky where they dwell. Though it contains the intelligence of the Gods, it does not have enough power on its own.

8. **SEKHEM=** the *sekhem* is what your form body is called. Even the simplest person could see one. At death, the sekhem is called to dwell among the all of the other paths of the person in life. All of the paths gather to the sekhem in life and are separated from it after death. It is within the collective power of each person to bring him or her back to whole again so that he or she could dwell among the Gods.

9. **REN=** The most important part of oneself is the *ren*, for it is your secret name body. It is the name that will put together all of the paths and parts of that person that separated after the physical death and it is what keeps the person whole in life. It is not your earthly name but a name that is unique to each person that binds all of us together. Only the Gods know this name. If the name is taken away from that person after death that person will wander forever through eternity. They will never be complete again or sit by the Gods. We spend our whole lives in curiosity trying to learn this name for ourselves for it gives us great power. Yet, once learned must be kept from our enemies. An enemy could use it to destroy a person. It could also be learned to save us if used in love when ill. It could give one the power never to leave the physical realm and to never age, and even to stop an imminent physical death.

Words and notes on era of novel:

1. **Atef charms**=Fertility charms or amulets made in the form of flies. This form was found on jewelry in many ancient Predynastic sites of Egypt.

2. ****Catal-Huyuk**=Peoples who possibly founded the ways of the Goddess from the lands north of Mesopotamia in the mountains. They created wheeled vehicles and great architecture, such as arches and columns. They also brought to the valley metalworking and works of art and beauty. This civilization was believed to have started in Anatolia. The Hatti peoples ruled this culture in later times.

3. **Clothing and style in Kemet**= The men wore long and narrow beards. Their torsos were bare and they wore long kilts of fine linen. The women wore long kilts as well made of linen sometimes their breasts were bare and sometimes the kilts were tied up over them. In paintings, both sexes wore elaborate headdresses in the royal families as depicted in tomb paintings and glamorous hairstyles. They wore kohl around their eyes to protect them from the sun as well as powdered malachite. It became a fashion statement as well. They wore semi-precious stones as amulets in jewelry and in their hair as ornaments. Rings were worn as well as necklaces and earrings. Some people wore tattoos as a religious statement. Most people wore makeup. The makeup palettes became symbolic and were exaggerated in size and buried with them in tombs to express the importance of their vanity. The famous palette of Narmer was one such example.

4. **Creation stories as told by Tehuti**=In the creations stories of Yanu, the creator is Atum; in the "TaTeten" creation story for the city of MenNefer or Ineb-Hedj the creator is Ptah; and the Ogdoad, where the creator is Tehuti.

5. **Fields of Iaru**= The main court of Au-Sar (Osiris) that sat in a field of reeds in which people had to walk through to seek justice. It was the main court and power of judgment of all Kemet. In mythology, it was located near Abdjw (Abydos).

6. **Gerzean II Phase**= This was a phase in archaeology of Ancient Egypt that occurred during the Predynastic era. This era occurred long ago around 3500 B.C.E. The novel takes place in this time. Most of what we see of Egypt today was started during this point in history. It was when the land started its unification of Upper and Lower Egypt and had a large increase of population. Trade was to a wider area of the world where items from Mesopotamia had been uncovered in tombs such as codex's and seals. The rectangular houses of Kemet mimicked those from Mesopotamia as well. Therefore, there was a definite influence of this culture on Egypt as found in archaeological digs to date. The first writing has been found in Kemet. However, this is currently disputed. Egypt seemed to develop its own traditions and culture during this time and became prosperous. Many radical changes occurred during this time in which most held well for over four thousand years for Egypt. Red-rimmed pottery was found throughout the land mostly from the Nekhen area. The towns mentioned in this novel were in existence during then and most had the names that they were known for originally. This was still the copper age and most weapons were made of it. Bronze was only just being discovered and used very rarely since few were skilled enough to make it. However, iron made from meteors were possible though not of the welded kind that we know of today.

7. **Henket:** Beer of Kemet made famous by Au-Sar and then Merul.

8. **Houses of Kemet**= Before this archeological phase the houses of Kemet were round and made

of straw matting and placed in circles. As the population grew with the advent of the Gerzean II phase, the houses began to resemble those of the Mesopotamian region in being made of mud brick and rectangular. The houses were also made halfway into the ground; where one would have to walk down to enter the dwellings. The roof covered half of the dwelling where the unroofed section became a sort of courtyard where trades were mostly done and wares sold as merchants became more prosperous. The new rectangular format allowed villages to grow in size and population and was easier to wall around them for protection as invaders became more frequent.

9. **Iaret Peoples=** the people of Lower Kemet, the main city was Per-Uto. Ua-Zit ruled over them with the symbol of the cobra or iaret.

10. **Kner-heb= Master=** Adept of Kemet. Known as a reader priest. They established a connection with the *Neter and Khert* (magical universe). Tehuti (Thoth) was the first.

11. *Medu necher*= "words of the Gods" or later called hieroglyphics in the land of Kemet. It was probably named thus initially due to the possible fact that hieroglyphs were used strictly for religious and magical writing. After the knowledge was passed, it became more commonplace and for mundane writings throughout their historical phase to be seen regular. A more common way of their writing later became known as Coptic which in Coptic Christianity in modern day Egypt is still spoken today. Most people thought the language was lost, though it was noted that it exists for that modern church in a later version of it.

12. *mummification and tombs*= The tombs were originally mounds and then during this phase became the early mastabas which eventually were placed on top of another to become the infamous pyramids that we know of today. There is record in some obscure sources to the cannibalism of the dead of the ancient

Predynastic Egyptians. This era seems to have the first examples of mummification. However, the early mummies were preserved intact, as there were no canopic jars. The early mummification process was relatively new to them and they were still experimenting. Few examples remain today are to be found due to the raw techniques they used.

13.   **Nugig=** Highest priestesses of the temples of Sumer or before that Eshnunna. Advisors of the high priestess and the royal families. In this novel, Ma-At and Neferet were Nugig to Innana and her children.

14.   **Patesi=** Governors of cities in Sumer.

15.   **Sal-Me=**Priestess of the second class of the new land of Sumer and city of Ur.

16.   **Sem priests=** High priests of Kemet, originally semi-priests.

17.   **Shen peoples=** the people of Upper Kemet, the main city in the rule of Nekhebt (Nemothi) was in Nekhen. Nekhebt ruled over them with the symbol of the vulture. She would hold the symbol for eternity or the shen symbol.

18.   **Sunu=**Lay physicians of Ancient Egypt.

19.   **Tawawannas=** High priestesses of the Catal-Huyuk of later Anatolia and now present day Turkey

20.   'Tjehenet'= Faience, or "dazzling." It was an artistic form of pottery that was glazed and appeared glasslike. It first appeared in the Gerzean II phase when this novel takes place and was perfected then. It was traded widely throughout the Nile area and beyond. The base of the items are pottery on which is rubbed ash and crushed quartz that is mixed with a glaze of soda-ash or lime, this creates the green glaze glass-like appearance when fired. Designs were painted over it on black kohl to stand out on the glazed and glass-like surface.

21.   **Wabu=**Priest physicians of Ancient Egypt.

22. ___Weapons___= They used spears made of copper and flint and swords. They wielded axes made of flint and copper as well. They used mace-heads in battle and appeared often in tomb paintings. The pear-shaped mace-head was initially found during this phase, which supplanted the old style.

Smd
2-6-06
Edited October 31 2011 by Sharon Goding
Edited and revised November 4, 2012

*Note from author. Please excuse any inaccuracies in my definitions and glossary of terms and characters for I did the best I could on my own.

*Formatting revised November 30, 2012

www.ingramcontent.com/pod-product-compliance
Lightning Source LLC
Chambersburg PA
CBHW070500040726
47505CB00021BA/1927

3. **AB**= The heart body, considered the core part of the body and houses all abstract thoughts, personal characteristics and motivations. The part of a person that contains their good and bad thoughts. Moves freely within the person, but also has the power to dwell in the heavens with the Gods.

4. **KA**= The part of person that is the called the double body or shadow. It is an exact copy of the physical body. When the physical form of the person dies, the ka needs food and meat to sustain its life. Offerings are given to the ka of people when they die in tombs. The ka dwells inside of the statue that is carved in the tomb in the form that the person had in life.

5. **BA**= The ba is the part of the person that is the equivalent of the soul. It means sublime or noble. It dwells within the ka and continues to possess substance or matter after death. It has the power to enter the tomb and to enter the body to talk with it and in some cases can reanimate it and to hold physical conversations with the physical body left behind. It has the power to take any desired shape and to travel to the dwelling places of the Gods where it cohabitates with other perfect souls. Like the ka, the ba also needs sustenance and partakes of the funeral offerings. Most often, it takes the form of a bird with the face of the person in its life.

6. **KHAIBIT**= is the *khaibit* or shadow. It is the shadow of the person left behind and it connects the ka with the ba as they ingest the funeral offerings and visit the physical form of the deceased person at their own wills. The khaibit does not possess the memories of the deceased and needs to always be by the person so fearful is it to separate from it. Even in life, the shadow is